YEAR'S BEST SF 18

YEAR'S BEST SF 18

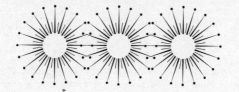

Edited by

David G. Hartwell

TOR®

A Tom Doherty Associates Book
New York

YEAR'S BEST SF 18

Copyright © 2013 by David G. Hartwell

A Tor Book
Published by Tom Doherty Associates, LLC
175 Fifth Avenue
New York, NY 10010

www.tor-forge.com

Tor® is a registered trademark of Tom Doherty Associates, LLC.

The Library of Congress Cataloging-in-Publication Data is available upon request.

ISBN 978-0-7653-3815-0 (hardcover)
ISBN 978-0-7653-3820-4 (trade paperback)
ISBN 978-1-4668-3818-5 (e-book)

Tor books may be purchased for educational, business, or promotional use. For information on bulk purchases, please contact Macmillan Corporate and Premium Sales Department at 1-800-221-7945, extension 5442, or write specialmarkets@macmillan.com.

First Edition: December 2013

Printed in the United States of America

0 9 8 7 6 5 4 3 2 1

COPYRIGHT ACKNOWLEDGMENTS

CONTENTS

10 | **Contents**

YEAR'S BEST SF 18

INTRODUCTION

THIS IS A book about what's going on now in science fiction. We are moving through decades of change, and as SF—often called the literature of change—represents that, we have to change in our daily lives as well, and that is not always comfortable. But science fiction remains vigorous and challenging and eminently worth reading.

This is a book full of science fiction—every story in the book is clearly that and not something else. It is my opinion that it is a good thing to have genre boundaries. After all, as I said in the first volumes of this series, without them, ambitious writers would have nothing to transgress. I try in each volume of this series to represent the varieties of tones, and voices, and attitudes that keep the genre entertaining, surprising, and responsive to the changing realities out of which it emerges, in science and daily life. It is supposed to be fun to read, a special kind of fun you cannot find elsewhere.

This volume is intended to represent the variety of fine stories published in the year of focus. But bear with me for a few paragraphs as I first give some characterization of the year in SF. The year 2012 was one of recovery for the publishing industry, and of adjustments to new publishing realities. Growth of e-book sales slowed, but still they grew. Tor Books became the first of the major publishers to go DRM free on its books, and found, as they had hoped, that it did not increase piracy or lower sales in any measurable way. Others are still hesitant to follow, though many of the smaller publishers—Baen Books, for instance, in SF—do not have DRM. The sky did not fall, and the world economy continued its fragile recovery.

As I observed last year, physical books are still where the money is. For seventeen years, this annual has appeared as a mass market paperback, a publication format that is less and less viable as a publishing medium nowadays, with diminished expectations. And so it was time to try to move the series to hardcover and trade paperback, and continue it in e-book formats as well. I hope readers will approve. In the e-book industry, the real profit is in the sale of devices, which are replaced by newer devices, rather than in the sale of books.

And it appears that e-book readers are giving way to multipurpose devices that are also readers: tablets and phones.

Certainly SF continued to appear in *Analog Science Fiction and Fact* and *Asimov's,* in *Fantasy & Science Fiction* and in *Interzone,* and in a lot of original anthologies. The longest tenured magazine editor in the modern history of SF, Stan Schmidt of *Analog,* retired, but the magazine continues in fine form under the editorship of Trevor Quachri. *Analog* is the last bastion of the science-based fiction that used to characterize the whole genre, and it will be very interesting to see how it evolves with a new editor.

Straightforward genre stories continued to be a bit scarcer. A lot more fiction graded off into fantasy or mixed genres (and away from science), while fantasy fiction (not in any way Science Fiction) quite obviously proliferated. One entertaining feature of 2012 was the resurgence of Heroic Fantasy, the old Sword & Sorcery subgenre founded by Robert E. Howard's Conan stories, and repopularized by the success of George R. R Martin's Game of Thrones series.

Short fiction venues remained about the same in 2012, and a pale shadow of what they were a decade or more ago. But that they remain in any form is a kind of triumph for the field. Science fiction magazines once again lost some circulation. Online venues, which might pay contributors but make little money, grew or failed again this year. Nonprofit sites such as Strange Horizons and Tor.com appeared the most stable of the online bunch. *Clarkesworld* and *Lightspeed* did distinguished work again. Small publishers of anthologies, especially the Bay Area cluster of Night Shade and Tachyon and Michigan-based Subterranean, were vigorous—it was a kind of final fireworks display, a blaze of glory for Night Shade, which has now been sold to another publisher.

And as usual, a large amount of the best short fiction originated in the year's new crop of anthologies. Among the best of these were: *Solaris 1.5,* edited by Ian Whates; Eclipse Online, edited by Jonathan Strahan; *Edge of Infinity,* edited by Jonathan Strahan; and *The Future Is Japanese,* edited by Nick Mamatas and Masumi Washington.

What struck me most this year was the unremitting pressure of new writers seeking a place in the field. In spite of everything, a really talented new crop of writers has emerged online and in fringe markets in recent years, as well as in the major magazines and unusual venues such as *Nature.* Some of them are in this book.

And so to the book: The stories that follow show, and the story notes point out, the strengths of the evolving genre in the year 2012. I make a lot of additional comments about the writers and the stories, and what's happening in SF, in the individual introductions accompanying the stories in this book. Welcome to *Year's Best SF 18.*

David G. Hartwell
Pleasantville and Westport, NY

OLD PAINT

Megan Lindholm

Megan Lindholm was born in 1952 in California, raised in Alaska, and currently resides in Tacoma, Washington. She began selling short stories for children when she was eighteen, but quickly moved on to attempting to write fantasy and science fiction. *Harpy's Flight* was her first fantasy novel, which she sold in 1982. She wrote a number of novels as Megan Lindholm, of which the best known is *Wizard of the Pigeons*. She continues to write short stories as Megan Lindholm, and is a Hugo and Nebula finalist under that name. Her most recent Lindholm stories include "Blue Boots" and "Neighbors." She also writes as Robin Hobb. Her first published work as Robin Hobb was the Farseer Trilogy (*Assassin's Apprentice, Royal Assassin,* and *Assassin's Quest*) and the most recent Hobb novels are the Rain Wilds Chronicles (*Dragon Keeper, Dragon Haven, City of Dragons,* and *Blood of Dragons*).

"Old Paint" was published in *Asimov's*. The future setting is subtle and convincing, and the family dynamics portrayed are evoked and displayed with masterful precision and emotional impact. It reminds me of the work of Connie Willis at her best. I chose this story to begin this collection because I think it will be read, and enjoyed, and admired long into the future.

I WAS ONLY nine when it happened, so I may not have the details absolutely right. But I know the heart of my story, and the heart is always what matters in a tale like mine.

My family didn't have much when I was growing up. A lot of lean years happened in that first half of the century. I don't say I had it as tough as my mom did, but the 2030's weren't a piece of cake for anyone. My brother, my mom, and I lived in subsidized housing in the part of T-town they call New Tacoma. It sure wasn't new when I was a kid. Tacoma's always been a tough town, and my mom said that her grandpa kept her on a short leash and she survived it, and so her kids would, too. Everyone knew we had the strictest mom in our apartments and pitied us for it.

We weren't like a lot of folks in the subsidized housing. Mom was ashamed to be there. It was the only thing she took from the government, and I think if she had been alone, she would have lived on the streets. We got by on what she made working at an old folks' home, so we budgeted hard. She cooked our meals from scratch and we carried our lunches to school in the same battered lunch boxes and stained backpacks, year after year. She mended our clothes and we shopped at the Goodwill. Our cellphones were clunky and we all shared one computer. And we didn't have a car.

Then my great grandpa died. Mom had hardly seen him in years, and we kids didn't know him at all, but she was in his will. She got what was left in his checking account, which wasn't much, and the old furniture in his apartment, which was mostly particle board crap. The old rocking chair was good, and the ceramic canisters shaped like mushrooms were cool. Mom said they were really old and she remembered them from when she was little. But the one big thing he did have was a car, parked in his parking slot where it had been gathering dust for the last twelve years since they'd taken his license away.

The car was vintage, and not in a good way. Back in the 2020's, there was this rage for making new energy-efficient cars that looked sort of like the old classic gas guzzlers. People wanted rumble and roomy to go with their solar and alternative fuels. I guess my great grandpa had been a surfer back in the day, because what he chose was something that was supposed to look like a station wagon. The first time we went down to the parking garage and looked at it, Ben, my older brother, groaned and asked, "What is that crap on the sides? Is it supposed to look like wood or something?"

"Or something," my mom said absently. She pushed the button on the key, but the battery for it was long dead. So she opened the car the old-fashioned way, putting the key in a hole in the door handle. I was fascinated and proud of my mom for knowing you could do that.

The outside of the car was covered in fine dust, but inside it was immaculate. She sat in the seat for a little while with her hands on the wheel, acting like she could see out the windshield. She was smiling a little bit. Then she said, "The smart thing to do is sell him. If the interior is this good, I bet he kept the engine cherry, too." She reached down and pulled a little handle, and Ben and I jumped when the hood of the car popped up.

"Mom, I think you broke it," Ben said. "Maybe we shouldn't touch anything until we can have a mechanic look at it." Ben was fourteen then, and for some reason, he now believed that if he didn't know something, Mom didn't know it either. She just snorted and got out of the car and went around to open the hood the rest of the way.

"My goodness," she said softly. "You did take care of him, Pops."

I didn't know what she was talking about, but I do remember that the inside of that engine compartment was spotless. She shut the hood, unplugged the car from the supplemental charger, and retracted the coil. She had a license and knew how to drive, because that was part of her job at the old people's home. I was still surprised when she slid in behind the wheel and put the key in a slot-thing and turned it. The vehicle had an anti-theft box on the steering column. She hesitated, and then put her forefinger on the sensor. "Hello, Suzanne," the car said in a rich, brown voice. "How are you today?"

"Just fine," she said quietly. "Just fine."

Ben was freaked. Mom noticed that and grinned. She patted the steering column. "My grandpa's voice. A little customization he did on the systems." She tossed her head at the back seat. Ben opened the door and we both got in. There were shoulder strap seat belts.

"No airbags?" Ben asked in disbelief.

"They're there. But when he was new, cars had both. It's safe. I wouldn't put you in a car if I thought it wasn't safe." She closed her eyes for a minute and tightened up her mouth as if she'd suddenly wanted to cry. Then she opened her eyes and shifted her grip on the wheel. "Let's blast," she said loud and clear, and the engine started. It was a lot louder than any other car I'd ever heard. Mom had to raise her voice to talk over it. "And when he was new, cars were electric and internal combustion. And much noisier than they are now."

Ben was horrified. "This car is running on gasoline, right now?"

Mom shook her head. "Sound effects. And loudest inside the car. My grandpa had a sense of humor." She stroked the car's dash. "All those years, and he never took me off the security system."

"How smart is this car?" Ben demanded.

"Smart enough," she said. "He can take himself to a fueling station. Knows when his tires are low on air, and can schedule his own oil change. He used to talk to the dealership; I wonder if it's even in business still. He's second generation simulated intelligence. Sure fooled me, most of the time. He has a lot of personality customization in his software. My grandpa put in a bunch of educational stuff, too. He can speak French. He used to drill me on my vocabulary on the way to school. And he knew all my favorite radio stations." She shook her head. "Back then, people wanted their cars to be their friends. He sure was mine."

"That's wack," Ben said solemnly.

"No, it was great. I loved it. I loved him."

"Love you too, Suzanne," the car said. His voice was a rich baritone.

"You should sell this thing, Mom," Ben advised her wisely.

"Maybe I should," Mom said, but the way she said it, I knew that we had a car now.

Ben had begun to think he was the man of the house, so he tried to start an argument with Mom about selling the car and using that money and her inheritance money to buy a real car. She just looked at him and said, "Seems to me it's my inheritance, not yours. And I'm keeping him."

And so that was that.

She opened a little panel on his dash and punched in our address. She moved a handle on the steering column, and the car began to ease backward. I held my breath, thinking we were going to hit something, but we didn't. She stopped the car, moved the handle again, and we slid forward, smooth as a slide, up and out of the parking garage and into the daylight.

On the way home, she kept pushing buttons and chatting with the car. It didn't have instant-net, but it had a screen that folded down from the ceiling. "What good is that? You have to sit in the back seat to see it," Ben complained. Mom reached under the seat and opened a drawer. Inside was a bunch of old style DVD's in flat plastic cases.

"They're movies," she said. "Supposed to entertain the kids in the back seat. The screen is back there so the driver won't be distracted." She picked up the stack and began to sort through them. She had a wistful half-smile on her face. "I remember all of these," she said quietly. "Some were my favorites."

"So the driver's supposed to just sit up front by himself and be bored?" Ben demanded.

She set the movies down with a sigh and turned to him. "The driver is sup-posed to drive." She turned back and put her hands on the wheel and looked out over the hood. "When this fellow was built, cars were only allowed to go a short distance without a licensed driver in the driver's seat. Less than a mile, I think it was. The auto-brains were really limited back then. Legally limited more than technically limited. People didn't really trust cars to drive them-selves. They had emergency services locators, of course, so they could take you to the hospital if you passed out, and sensors to help you park, but when he was built, drivers still did most of the driving."

"Why do you keep calling the car 'he' and 'him'?" Ben demanded.

"Old habit," my mom said, but she said it in a way that ended the conversa-tion.

We had a parking spot at our building that we'd never used before. The first time we pulled up in the car, every kid hanging around outside came to see what the noise was. They watched as the car plugged in to charge. Our car was about twice as long as any other car in the lot.

"Look at the size of those solars," one boy whispered, and Ben's ears went red.

"Old piece of junk," said another knowingly. "Surprised it still runs at all."

Mom did the one thing that Ben hated the most. I didn't much like it either. All the other moms in the building would have just ignored the wanna-be gangers hanging around the parking lot. Mom always looked straight at them and talked to them as if they were smart, even when they were so drugged out they could barely stand.

"He's old, but he runs like a clock. He'll probably outlast most of the Tupper-ware crates here. They still used a lot of steel when this guy was built." Mom set the alarm, and the tattle-tale light began to circle the car.

"Wha's that stuff onna size spozed to be?" Leno asked. He was smiling. Leno was always smiling, and I'd never seen him with his eyes more than half open. He looked delighted to see the car, but I'd seen him look just as enthusiastically at a lamp post.

"It's wood. Well, pseudo-wood. My grandpa was so proud of it. It was one of the first nano-products used on any car. It was the latest thing, back then. Guaranteed not to peel or fade or scratch, and to feel like wood grain. Most minor dents, it could repair, too." She sighed, smiled, and shook her head, remembering something. Then, "Come on, kids. Dinner to cook and homework to do."

"Homework," one of the boys sneered, and two girls laughed low. We ignored her and followed Mom into the house.

Ben was mad at her. "How come you know so much about that car? I thought you didn't have anything to do with your grandpa. I thought he, like, disowned you when you were a kid or something."

Mom gave him a look. She never talked much about her family. As far as I remembered, it had always been just her, Ben, and me. Someone must have been our father, but I'd never met him. And if Ben remembered him, he didn't say much. Mom firmed her mouth for a minute and then said brusquely, "My grandpa and I really loved each other. I made some choices in my life that he didn't agree with. So he was really angry with me for a long time, and I was angry with him. But we always knew we still loved one another. We just never got around to making up in time to say it."

"What decisions?" I asked.

"Getting knocked up with me," Ben said, low. Either Mom didn't hear him say it or she didn't want to discuss it.

So, after that, we had a car. Not that we drove it much. But Mom polished it with special wax, cleaned his solars, vacuumed out the inside, and hung up an old-fashioned pine tree scent thing from the mirror. Once we came home from school on the bus, and found her asleep in the driver's seat, her hands on the wheel. She was smiling in her sleep. Every once in a while, on the weekend, she might take us out for a ride in the station wagon. Ben always said he didn't want to go, but then went.

She didn't upgrade the car, but she made it ours. She put us both on the car's security system, and updated the old GPS settings with our home, schools, the hospital, and the police station, so in an emergency either of us could get help. The car greeted us by name. Ben pretty much ignored its personality program, but I talked to it. It knew a lot of corny old jokes and had a strange program called "Road Trip Games" about license plates and "Animal, Vegetable, or Mineral." I tried out every seat in the car. I watched some of the old movies on the little screen, but they were really long and the people talked too much. My favorite seat was the one in the back that faced backward. I liked watching the faces of the people as they came up behind our car. Lots of them looked surprised. Some of them smiled and waved, and some turned their heads to look at the car as they passed us. The only time I didn't like it was at night when the headlights of the cars behind us would hit me right in the eyes.

The car was a sometime thing, and mostly it didn't change anything about our life. Sometimes, when it was pouring rain and we had to walk to the bus stop and then walk home again, Ben would grumble. Other parents sent their cars to pick up their kids from school. Ben whined about this a lot. "Why can't the wagon pick us up from school when it's pouring rain?" he'd demand of her.

"Your grandfather was a 'drive it yourself' guy. Like me. I doubt he ever had the block removed."

"Then it's just a software thing? You could take it off?"

"Don't get any ideas, Benny-boy!" Mom warned him.

And for a while, he didn't. But then he turned fifteen. And Mom decided to teach him to drive.

Ben wasn't that interested at first. Most kids didn't bother with a personal license anymore. As long as a car met the legal standards, anyone could get in it and go. I knew little kindergarteners who were dropped off by their cars each day and then picked up again. Mom said it was stupid that it took three thousand pounds of car to transport a forty-pound kid to school, but lots of people did it. Ben and I both knew that Mom could have had the car's brain upgraded or unblocked or whatever, and we could have had wheels any time we wanted them. But she chose not to. She told Ben the only way he was going to get to use the car was if he knew how to physically drive it. Once he passed his test, she told him that we might even have it updated so that he could just kick back and tell the car where he wanted to go.

So that was the big attraction for Ben. I got to ride along on his driving lessons. At first Mom took us way out of town in the evenings and made him practice in parking lots outside vacant strip malls. But Ben actually learned to drive pretty well. He said it wasn't that different from a lot of his video games. Then Mom reminded him that he couldn't kill himself or someone else with a video game. She was so serious about it, and Ben got so cranky. It was a thing they went through for about a year, I think. Any conversation about the car always turned into an argument. He hated the "dorky" paint and wood on it; she said it was "vintage" and "classic." He said we should get a cheaper car; she said that all the metal in the body made it safer for him to drive, and that he should be happy we had a car at all. Their conversations were always the same. I think Ben said, "I know, I know!" more than a million times that year. And Mom was always saying, "Shut up and listen to what I'm saying."

Ben was absolutely set on getting the car upgraded so he could ride around with his friends. Most of his friends' parents had said "no way" to them riding if Ben was actually driving the car, even after he got his license. He kept telling

Mom how the car would be safer if it could drive itself and how we could get better mileage because it would self-adjust routes to avoid traffic or to take short cuts, and that statistics showed that car-brains actually reacted faster than human brains in dangerous situations.

"Maybe so, but they can only react one way, and human brains can think of a dozen ways to react in a tough situation. So the answer is still no. Not yet. Maybe never."

Mom scored big points on him the next week when there were dozens of accidents on I-5 that involved driverless cars. Mom didn't care that it was because of a virus that someone had uploaded to the traffic beam. No one knew who did it. Some people said it was an environmental group that wanted to discourage private cars. Other people thought it was just a new generation of hackers making their mark on the world. "It wasn't the cars' fault, Mom!" Ben argued. "The beacon gave them bad information."

"But if a human had been holding the steering wheel, none of those accidents would have happened," Mom said. And that was the end of it, for a couple of months.

Then in June, Ben and Mom got into it big time. He came home from school one day and took the car without asking. He brought it home painted black, with a rippling hint of darker tiger stripes. I stood and stared at it when he pulled into the apartment building parking lot. "Cool, huh?" he asked me. "The stripes move. The faster you drive, the faster the nanos ripple."

"Where'd you get the money to do it?" I asked him, and when he said, "None of your business," I knew it was really going to blow up.

And it did, but even worse than I'd expected. By the time Mom came home from work, the vintage nanos in the "wood" paneling were at war with the tiger stripe nanos. The car looked, as Mom put it, "Like a pile of crawling crap! What were you thinking?"

And they were off, with him saying that the black made the car look better and that the new nanos would win over the old ones and the color would even out. When it came out that he'd raided his college money for the paint job, she was furious.

"It was too good of a deal to pass up! It was less than half what it would cost in a standard paint shop!"

So that was how she found out he'd had it done in one of those car-painting tents that had been popping up near malls and swap meets. They were mobile services that fixed dings in windshields or replaced them entirely. They could install seat covers, and add flames or pin stripes. The shady ones could override parental controls for music or video or navigation systems, erase GPS tracking, and alter mileage used. Or, in the one Ben had gone to, do an entire nano-paint job in less than an hour. With the new nanos, they didn't even use sprayers anymore. They dumped the stuff on and the nanos spread out to cover any previously painted surfaces. The men operating the paint tent had promised Ben that their nanos were state of the art and could subdue any previous nanos in the car's paint.

Mom was so furious that she made us get in the car and we drove back to where Ben had had it done. By law, they should have looked at the owner registration before they nanoed it. Mom wanted Ben's money back and was hoping they had call-back nanos that would remove the black. But no such luck. When we got to where the tent had been, there was nothing but a heap of empty nano jars and some frustrated paint crawling around on the ground trying to cover crumpled pop cans. My mom called the cops, because it's illegal to abandon nanos, and they said they'd send out a containment team. She didn't wait for them. We just went home. When we got there, Ben jumped out of the car and stormed into the house. Mom got out more slowly and stood looking at our car with the saddest expression I'd ever seen on her face.

"I'm so sorry, Old Paint," she told the car. And that was how the car got his name, and also when I realized how much her grandpa's car had meant to her. Ben had done a lot worse thing than just paint a car without her permission. I thought that when he calmed down, I might try to explain that to him. Then I thought that maybe the best thing for me to do was to stay out of it.

The paint on the car just got worse and worse. Those old nanos were tough. The wood paneling took to migrating around on the car's body, trying to escape the attacks of the new paint. It looked scabby, as if the car were rotting. Ben didn't want to be seen in the car anymore, but Mom was merciless. "This was your decision, and you are going to have to live with it just like the rest of us," she told him. And she would send him on the errands, to get groceries or to return the library books, so he would have to drive Old Paint.

A couple of months later, my mom stayed home with stomach flu. She woke up feeling better in the afternoon, and went to the window to look out at the day. That was when she discovered Old Paint was gone. My brother and I were on the bus when we got her furious call. "You probably think you are smart, Benny-Boy, but what you are in is big trouble. Very big trouble." He was trying to figure out why she was so angry when the bus went crazy. Ben dropped his phone, bracing himself and me on the slippery seat. Mom told us later that the Teamsters contract with the city had always insisted that every city-owned mass transit unit had to have a nominal driver. So when the bus started honking its horn and flashing its lights and veering back and forth over three lanes, the old man in the driver's seat reached up and threw the manual override switch. He grabbed the wheel and wrestled us over to the curb and turned off the engine.

The driver apologized to everyone and asked us all to sit tight until the maintenance people could come. He called in for a replacement bus, but everyone on the bus heard the dispatcher's hysterical response. Twelve bus breakdowns in the last ten minutes, three involving bad accidents, and there were no more replacement buses to send. In the background, someone shouted that an out of control ambulance had just rear-ended a bus. Dispatch put the driver on hold.

We were only three blocks short of our stop, so we asked to get off and walk. Ben grabbed his phone off the floor, but Mom had hung up and he didn't really want to find out just what she had discovered that had made her so mad. Ben had a lot of secrets in those days, from rolling papers in his gym bag to a follow-up appointment at the STD clinic Not that I was supposed to know about any of them.

We'd gone half a block when we heard the bus start up. We looked back and saw it take off. I'd never known a city bus could accelerate like that. We were staring after it, wondering what had happened, when a VW Cherub jumped the curb and nearly hit us. It high-centered for just a second, wheels spinning and smoking, and two kids jumped out of the back seat, screaming. A moment later, it reversed out into the street and raced off, still going backward. The teenage girl who had jumped out was crying and holding onto her little brother. "The car just went crazy! The car just went crazy!"

A man from a corner bar-and-grill opened the door and shouted, "You kids get inside now!"

We all hesitated, but then he pointed up the street and yelled, "OMG, now, kids!" and we bolted in as the Hot Pizza delivery van came right down the sidewalk. It clipped the awning supports as it went by and the green-and-white striped canvas came rippling down behind us as we jumped inside.

The place was a sports bar, and a couple of times we'd had pizza there with Mom when her favorite team was in the playoffs. Usually every screen in the place was on a different sports feed, but that day they all showed the same rattled newsman. He was telling everyone to stay inside if they could, to avoid vehicles of all kinds and to stay tuned for updates to the mad vehicle crisis.

Ben finally called Mom and told her where we were, because the tavern owner refused to let us leave by ourselves. When Mom got there, she thanked him, and then took us home by a route that went down narrow alleys and through people's backyards. Every few minutes, we'd hear a car go roaring past on the streets, or horns blaring, or crashes in the distance.

Not every vehicle in the city had gone wild, but a lot of them had, including Old Paint. Mom had been mad because she thought Ben had upgraded Old Paint's self-driving capability by removing the block on his software. She looked a bit skeptical when he denied it, but by late evening the news people had convinced her. The virus was called the "7734, upside down and backward" by the hacker group that took credit for it. Because if you wrote 7734 on a piece of paper and looked at it upside down and backward, it looked a little bit like the word "hell." They said they did it to prove they could. No one knew how they spread it, but our neighbor said that zombie nanos delivered it right to the cars' driving computers. He said that the nanos were planted in a lot of car stuff, from wiper fluid to coolant and even paint. So Ben said there was no proof he'd infected the car when he got it painted, but that was what Mom always believed.

By evening, the internet news said the crisis would solve itself pretty fast. For a lot of cars, it did. They wrecked themselves. Cops and vigilantes took out some of the obvious rogues, shooting out their tires. It made the owners pretty angry and the insurance companies were arguing about whether they had to pay out. The government had people working on a nano anti-virus that they could spray on rogues, but nothing they tried seemed to work. Some people wanted all the auto-recharging places shut down, but people with un-infected cars objected. Finally they decided to leave the auto charge stations open because some of the rogue cars got aggressive about recharging them-selves when they encountered closed stations.

Mom tried to explain it to me. Cars had different levels of smartness, and people could set priority levels on what they wanted the cars to do for them-selves. A lot of people had set their "recharge importance" level high because they wanted the car kept charged to maximum capacity. Others had set their cars to always travel as fast as they were allowed, and turned the courtesy level down to low or even off. There was a pedestrian awareness level that was not supposed to be tampered with, but some people did it. Pizza delivery vans and ambulances were some of the most dangerous rogues.

At first, the virus paralyzed the nation. It didn't infect every car, but the ones that had it caused traffic accidents and made the streets dangerous. No one wanted to go out. Schools shifted to snow-day internet mode. The stores got low on groceries and the only delivery trucks were vintage semis, with no brains at all and old guys driving them.

By the third week, the infection rate was down, and most of the really dan-gerous rogues had been disabled. But that left a lot of cars still running wild. Some seemed to follow their normal routines, but speeded up or took alternate routes. Kids were warned not to get into infected cars, even if it was the family van waiting outside the school at the usual time, because sometimes those cars behaved reliably, and sometimes they abruptly went nuts. A new little business started up, with bounty hunters tracking down people's expensive vehicles by GPS and then capturing them and disabling them until the virus could be cured. But some owners couldn't afford that service, or the car wasn't worth what the bounty hunters charged.

So Old Paint was left running wild. At first, we'd see him in the neighbor-hood at odd times. He always drove himself very safely, and he just seemed to be randomly wandering. Twice we caught him in our parking spot, recharg-ing himself, but each time he took off before we could get near him, let alone open his doors. Mom said to leave him alone, and she'd worry about it when the government came up with an anti-virus. Then we stopped seeing him at all.

One night, when Ben was really bummed about not having a car for some school dance that was coming up, he checked Old Paint's GPS. "That crazy bastard went to California!" he shouted, half impressed by it.

"Let me see that," Mom said, and then she started laughing. "I took him there one spring break when I told Grandpa I was only going to Ocean Shores. I wiped all the data off his GPS before I came home. I guess the virus must have brought it back into his memory."

"You did things like that? You'd kill me if I did something like that!"

"I was young," Mom said. She smiled in an odd way. "Sometimes, I think being a teenager is like a virus. You do things that go against every bit of pro-gramming your parents ever put into you." She made a "huh" noise as if she were pushing something away. She looked over at Ben. "Becoming a parent is the anti-virus. Cured me of all sorts of things."

"So how come you don't let me just be a teenager like you were?" Ben demanded.

Mom just looked at him. "Because I learned, the hard way, just how dan-gerous that can be to a kid. Running wild is a great thing. For the kids that survive it." She turned off the monitor then, and told us both to go to bed.

In the weeks that followed, Old Paint went all sorts of strange places. Once he went off to some place in the Olympic National Forest where Mom had once gone to a rave. And he spent two days crawling around on an old logging trail near Chrystal Mountain. Mom looked worried when he went off on that jaunt, and the night she discovered that he was now headed for Lake Chelan, she was so relieved she laughed. In a way, it was really cool that Old Paint did all that traveling. Mom would look at his location at night, and tell us stories about when she was a teenager and living with her grandpa and making him crazy. She'd tell us about close calls and stupid ideas and how close she had come to getting killed or arrested. Ben and I both started to see her differently, like someone who really had been a kid once. She didn't cut us any more slack than she ever had, but we began to understand why.

We kept expecting Old Paint to run out of charge, but he didn't. He'd go sedately through the auto-charge places, I guess, looking like some family's old car. Ben asked Mom why she didn't block him from using the credit card, and she just shrugged. I think she enjoyed reliving all her wild adventures. And he wasn't that expensive. A lot of cars had back-up solar systems, and Old Paint had a really extensive one. Sometimes he'd stay in one place for three or four days, and Mom figured he was just soaking up the rays before moving on. "And if I cut him off, then he may never come home to us." She gave an odd smile, one that wasn't happy and added, "Tough love isn't all it's cracked up to be. Sometimes, when you lock a door, the other person never knocks on it again."

So, as the weeks passed, we watched Old Paint move up and down Old 99. Ben and I went back to walking. All the city buses and delivery vans had been set back to full manual, and all sorts of old guys were chortling about being suddenly employed again. My mom said it was a huge victory for the Teamsters, and some people insinuated they had backed the hackers.

The government people came up with three different anti-viruses, and everyone was required to install them in their vehicles. The trick, of course, was getting the scrubber nanos and anti-virus program to the infected vehicles. Everyone with an infected vehicle was required to report it, and Mom had filled out the forms. A package came in the mail with the scrubber nanos in a spray can and a booklet on how to disinfect the car and then install the anti-virus. Mom set it on the kitchen window sill and it gathered dust.

By the end of summer, most of the infected vehicles were off the road. They'd either destroyed themselves or, in the case of the really aggressive ones, been hunted down and disabled. There were still incidents almost every day. Three fire trucks in San Francisco were scrambled for a five alarm fire, and instead they went on a wild rampage through the city. Someone deliberately infected fifteen Harley-Davidsons parked outside a bar with a variant of the virus, and ten of the Hells Angels who mounted them and rode away died a mile later. A fuel delivery business in Anchorage faced huge fines when it was determined that they had neglected to use the proper anti-virus. The fines for the environmental clean-up were even bigger.

In late September, during a heavy rainstorm, I spotted Old Paint near the school. He was idling at the curb, and I ran toward him, but Ben grabbed me by the shoulder. "He's infected. You can't trust him," he warned me in a harsh whisper. He looked over his shoulder, fearful that someone else might have overhead. By then, they were disabling even non-aggressive vehicles because they thought they might be able to infect other vehicles. As we walked toward the bus stop, Old Paint slowly edged down the street after us.

"Why is he here? He never did auto-pick-up for us."

"It's in his programming. He knows what school we go to, and what time we get out. Mom put it in just in case she wanted to use it someday. Probably just glitching."

When we got on the bus, Old Paint revved his engine, honked twice, and passed us. When Mom got home from work, we told her and she smiled. That night, really late, I heard her get out of bed and I followed her to the living room. We peeked out the rain-streaked window and Old Paint was charging himself at our parking slot.

"Doesn't look so bad for being on the road so long," Mom said. She smiled. "I bet I'll find a car wash and oil change on my credit card bill this month."

I went to the kitchen and came back with the scrubber and anti-virus. "Shall we try to catch him?" I asked.

She pursed her lips and shook her head. "Not in the rain. Let him get used to coming at night to charge. On a dry night, I'll go down and spray him."

And we went back to bed.

September became October. I saw Old Paint in the streets sometimes and

I suspect he came and charged up at our place more than once. But the weather stayed wet and that was Mom's excuse for not trying to catch him. Ben was playing football for his school and seemed so different it was like aliens had re-programmed my brother. Most days, I had to ride the bus alone. I noticed that Old Paint would show up at the school on the really stormy days and shadow me until I was on the bus. Once he was at my bus stop and followed me home. I knew I wasn't supposed to get inside him, but no one had said I couldn't talk to him. So I edged toward him as he followed the sidewalk and ran my fingers along his fender. "I miss you, Old Paint," I told him. The locks bit down, he revved his engine and leaped away from the curb. He tore off through the afternoon traffic with other cars honking at him. It really hurt my feelings. I didn't tell Mom or Ben. I was afraid she might report him as borderline aggressive and give his GPS code to the police.

January brought really nasty weather. Snow fell, melted into black ice, and more snow fell. For a solid week, the cycle repeated. The worst part was that all the busses were running on the "snow routes" that avoided hills. So our usual three block walk to the bus stop became six blocks to a main street. Each day, Old Paint was outside our apartments, edging along behind us as we walked to the bus stop. Ben ignored him, except to cuss that he could be inside a warm car instead of wading through snow and ice.

Our bus stop was right in front of a charging station. There was a line for the quick charge, and while we were waiting for the bus, a black van pulled up, blocking a car in. The lettering on the sign said Road Dog Recoveries. "Bounty hunters!" Ben said. "Cool. Watch this."

They fanned out around the car they wanted. A man in a car at the end of the line shouted, "Don't shoot those so close to the station!" Because they had their special tire piercing guns out and were taking aim at the red Beamer they had blocked in.

But that wasn't the car they should have been watching. Two cars back in line, a black sedan with big wheels suddenly cranked its wheels and cut right through the median and the bushes and right at us. It hit one of the men as it did so and he went flying. The other men all fired at it. And missed. Then the red car freaked out, backed into the car behind it to gain a bit of space, and it shot over the curb into the median and high centered.

Ben grabbed me and jerked me to one side, but it wasn't quite enough. I hadn't even seen the black sedan coming toward us. It clipped me and the impact snatched me out of Ben's grip. I went flying and rolling out into the street. When I hit the ground, I slid on the black ice and I thought I was never going to stop. Ben was yelling, cars were honking, and when I finally stopped the whole world was spinning. But I was okay. I got up. Ben was running toward me.

Then my arm started really hurting and I realized I couldn't move it. I screamed.

And Ben shouted, "Run! Run, Sadie, get out of there!"

The black sedan had slewed around and was coming back at me. Later, I found out that it had belonged to a security service and had an attack mode if anyone tried to harm the VIP inside. It had interpreted the bounty hunters as assassins. No one could say why it came after me. But as it came at me and I turned to run, I saw something even scarier. Old Paint was roaring at me, full speed in reverse. I was going to be crushed between the two cars. I screamed, the black sedan hit me, and I was airborne.

But Old Paint's rear door had opened upward and as I flew toward him, he shifted into first, burned rubber, and faded away from me like a catcher back-pedaling for a fly ball. I landed in the rear-facing back seat as air bags blossomed. It wasn't exactly a soft landing, but his actions meant that it was the softest possible landing. I collapsed there as the hatch was closing, and then I fainted as his air bags puffed up all around me.

I woke up on the way to the emergency room. I couldn't see anything because I was surrounded by air bags. I heard Ben shouting my name and then he was pushing the bags back. He was in the middle seat, leaning over the back, trying to reach me. "Who's driving?" I asked, but he only shouted, "Are you okay? Are you okay?"

Old Paint ignored traffic signals and one way signs all the way to the hospital. Horns blaring and recorded voice shouting, "Emergency! Emergency! Out of the way, please! Emergency!," he beat out an ambulance and was opening the back hatch as he backed up to the emergency room loading dock. Ben jumped out, screaming for someone to help his sister. The air bags around me deflated and people in white lifted me out. I had one glimpse of Old Paint as he roared away from the ramp. His rear bumper was pushed in and his back window was crazed.

"What happened to Old Paint?" I cried. They had me on a gurney and were rolling me in. Ben trotted beside me, his cell phone to his ear.

"Compared to that black sedan? Nothing. He worked that car over until it couldn't even turn a wheel. Slammed into it over and over. I thought you were going to be creamed in there. Mom?" Ben talked into his phone. "Mom, yeah, we're at Mary Bridge Children's hospital. Sadie got hit by a car, but Old Paint saved her. Come fast, they want our insurance number and I don't know it."

I wasn't hurt that bad. My arm was broken and I was bruised all over. They kept me six hours for observation, but my concussion was mild. Mom stayed by my bed. Two cops came to ask what happened. Ben said a crazy car had hit me. Mom said she had no idea what good Samaritan had picked me up and gotten me to the hospital, but she thanked them. The policewoman said that the other witnesses had said the car had behaved in an extraordinary manner to save me. Ben looked at Mom and said, "Some old dude was driving it. After he busted up that black car, he opened the door and yelled at me to jump in. He said he drove in stock car races, demolition derbies when he was a kid. Then he brought us here. He left because he didn't want to get in trouble."

The cops asked him some more questions, but Ben just kept saying, "I don't remember" or "I didn't see, I was worried about my sister." After they finally left, my mom said very quietly, "I hope the charging station didn't catch the plates on camera."

Ben just looked at her. "Yeah. Me, too," he said. "But I couldn't let them go out and disable him after he saved Sadie's life."

Mom took a deep breath. "Ben. Sadie. We both know it's probably going to come down to that, eventually. He can't run wild forever. And we all know that Old Paint is just following the directives of his programming. He's not really . . . alive. He seems that way because we think of him that way. But it's all just programming."

"Saving Sadie's life? Catching her in the back seat like that, cushioning her with air bags while he pounded that sedan into scrap?" Ben laughed and shook his head. "You won't convince me of that, Mom."

The hospital let me go home that evening. We all went to bed right away. But about midnight, I heard my mom get up, so I did, too. She was looking out through the blinds at our parking stall.

"Is he there? Is he okay?"

"No, baby, he's not here. Go back to bed."

Ben and I overslept the next morning and didn't go to school. Mom hadn't bothered waking us. We had a good six inches of snow outside, and school was cancelled for the day. When we came out to the living room, Mom was sitting at the computer watching a dot on a map. It wasn't moving. There was a backpack at her feet and a heap of winter clothes beside her.

"You kids get your homework off Moodle," she said. "I'm going to be gone for a while." She sounded funny.

"No," Ben said. "We're going with you."

We hiked through the snow to a bus stop and took a bus to a City Car rental lot and checked out a tiny car. Riding in it after riding in Old Paint was like crowding into a shower stall together. Mom sat in the single front seat and Ben and I had the back seat. There was barely room for us with our coats on. Mom plugged in the co-ordinates, and the car demanded that she scan her credit card again. It had a prissy girl's voice. "Macintosh Lake is outside of Zones 1 through 12. Additional fees will apply," the car told her.

She thumbed for them. The car didn't move. "Hazardous conditions are reported. Cancellation recommended. You will not be charged if you terminate this transaction now."

Mom sighed. "Just go," she said, and we went. It wasn't too bad. The main roads had been plowed and salted, and once we got on I-5, the plows and the other traffic had cleared most of the mess down to almost pavement. It felt really odd not to have Old Paint's bulk around me, and I leaned against Ben.

We didn't talk much as the car hummed along. Ben had tossed a bunch of stuff in his backpack, including my pain medicine and a water bottle. I took a pill and slept most of the way. I woke up to Ben saying, "But there's a chain across the access road."

"So we'll get out here," Mom said.

I sat up. We were out in the country, and the only tracks on the snowy road behind us were ours. It was a very strange feeling. All I could see was wind-smoothed white snow and snow-laden trees on either side of the narrow road. We had pulled off the road into a driveway and stopped. There were two big yellow posts in front of us, with a heavy chain hung between them. A hunter-orange sign said, "CLOSED." The road in front of us was mostly smooth snow and it wound out of sight into the woods.

Mom told the car to wait and it obediently shut down. We struggled back into our coats. None of us had real snow boots. Mom grabbed her pack and Ben brought his as we stepped out into smooth snow. The skies had cleared and it was cold. This snow wouldn't melt any time soon. Ben followed Mom and she followed the ghost tire tracks that left the road and went around the access gate to the lake. Snow had almost filled them and the wind was polishing them away. I came last, stepping in their footprints. Mom pulled her coat tighter as we walked and said, "There were some great raves out here when I was in high school. But in summer."

"What would you do to me if I went to a rave out in the woods?" Ben asked.

Mom just looked at him. We both knew he'd been to raves out in the woods. Ben shut up.

Mom saw Old Paint before we did, and she broke into a run. Old Paint was shut down, back under the trees. Snow was mounded over him; only the funky paint job on his sides showed. Twigs and leaves had fallen on his snowy roof during the night. His windows were thick with frost. He looked to me like he'd been there for years. As we got closer, his engine ticked twice and then went silent. Mom halted and flung out her arms. "Stay back, kids," she warned us. Then she went forward alone.

She talked to him in a low voice as she walked slowly around the car. She kept shaking her head. Ben and I ignored what she'd said and walked slowly forward. Old Paint was still. Both his front and back bumpers were pushed in and he had a long crease down his passenger side. One of his headlights was cracked. His rear license plate hung by a single screw. "He's dead," I said, and I felt my eyes start to sting.

"Not quite," my mom said grimly. "He doesn't have enough of a charge to move. His nanos have been trying to pop his dents out and fix his glass, but that will take time." She went around to the driver door and unlocked it with a key. She leaned in and popped the hood, and then tossed the keys to Ben. "Look in the back. There's a hatch in the floor. Open it. Get out the stuff in there. Looks like we're going to need Grandpa's emergency kit."

She dropped her pack on the ground in the snow and then wrestled a

Charge-In-A-Box out of it. Ben and I were staring at her. "Hurry up!" she snapped.

We walked to the back of the car. Mom already had the cables out and she plugged Old Paint in. His horn tooted faintly. "Easy, big fella," my brother said as he slid the key into the lock. He saw me looking at him and said, "Just shut up."

We pushed the deflated air bags out of the way. We found the floor hatch and opened it. "Look at all this stuff!" my brother exclaimed. My mom walked back and looked in. She had a grim smile as she said, "My grandpa was always trying to keep me safe. He tried to think of everything to protect me. 'Plan for the worst and hope for the best,' he always said." She took a deep breath and then sighed it out. "So. Let's get to work."

Ben and I more watched than worked. It was weird to watch her fix Old Paint. She was so calm. She pulled his dipstick, wiped it on her jeans, studied it, and then added something out of a can. Then she pulled another dipstick, checked it, and nodded. She checked wires and some she tightened. She replaced two fuses. She looked inside his radiator and then felt around under it. "No leaks!" she said. "That's a miracle." She stepped back and shut the hood.

Old Paint woke up. His engine turned over and then quit. Turned over again, ran a bit rough and then smoothed out. He sounded hoarse to me as he said, "Right front tire is flat. Do not attempt to move the vehicle."

"There's Fix A Flat in there," Ben said, and Mom said, "Get it."

He came back with it and his backpack. I stood next to him, stroking Old Paint's fender and saying, "It's going to be okay, Old Paint. It's going to be okay." Neither one of them made fun of me. While I was standing there, his front bumper suddenly popped out into position. You can't really see nanos working to take out a dent, but he already looked less battered than he had. Ben handed Mom the can and she reinflated the tire.

"Tire pressure is corrected," Old Paint announced.

Then Ben took the scrubber spray and anti-virus box out of the pack and handed it to her without a word.

Mom took it and stood up slowly. She walked slowly to the back of the car and I followed her. She put away the leftover emergency supplies. She gently shut the door. The glass nanos were at work on the rear window. It was almost clear again. She walked around the car and Ben and I both followed her. She got to the driver's door, opened it and climbed in.

"Mom?" Ben asked her anxiously and she waved a hand at him. "I just want to check something," she said.

She opened a little panel on his dash and a small screen lit up. She touched it lightly, scrolling down it. Then she stopped and leaned her forehead on the steering wheel for a minute. When she spoke, her voice was choked and muffled by her arms.

"My grandpa considered himself something of a hacker, in an old school way. He made some modifications to Old Paint. That's Grandpa's voice you hear, when Old Paint speaks. And you know how I told you some people remove the safety constraints from the car's programming, the 'do no harm to people' or bypass the speed constraints? Not my grandpa." She sat up and pointed at the screen. "See all those red 'override' indicators? You're not supposed to be able to do that. But Grandpa did. He gave Old Paint one ultimate command: 'Protect logged users of vehicle.'"

She flipped the little panel closed over the screen and spoke quietly. "I should have known. I was a wild kid. Drinking. Doping. So he broke into the software and over-rode everything to make 'protect the child' the car's highest priority. Hm." She made a husky noise in her throat. "Got me out of a corner more times than I like to think about. I passed out more than once behind the wheel, but somehow I always got home safe." She dashed tears from her eyes and then looked at us with a crooked smile. "Just programming, kids. That's all. Just his programming. Despite all his tough talk, it was just his programming to protect, as best he could. No matter what."

Ben was as puzzled as I was. "The car? Or Grandpa?"

She sniffed again but didn't answer. She reopened the panel on his dash and accessed his GPS. She was talking softly. "You remember that one spring break, my senior year? Arizona. And that boy named Mark. Sun, sun, and more sun. We hardly ever had to stop at a charging station. That's where you should go, old friend. And drive safely."

"Don't we always?" he asked her.

She laughed out loud.

She got out and shut the door. He revved his engine a few times, and then began to pull forward. We stepped back out of his way, and he moved slowly past us, the deep snow squeaking under his tires. Mom stepped forward, brushing snow, twigs, and leaves off the solars on his roof. He stopped and let her clear them. Then, "All done. Run free," she told him, and patted his rear view mirror.

When she stepped back, he revved his engine, tooted his horn twice, and peeled out in a shower of snow. We stood there and watched him go. Mom didn't move until we couldn't hear him anymore. Then she pitched the packet of anti-virus as far as she could into the woods. "There are some things that just don't need curing," she said.

We went back to the City Rents car and climbed in. My sneakers were soaked, my feet were numb, and my jeans were wet halfway to my knees. We ate some peanut butter sandwiches that Ben had packed, Mom gave me another pain pill, and I slept all the way home.

Three nights later, I got out of bed and padded toward the living room in my pajamas. I peeked around the corner. My mom's chair was rocked back as far as it would go and her toes were up on the edge of the desk. The bluish monitor light was the only light in the room. She was watching a moving dot on a map, and smiling. She had headphones on and was nodding her head to music we could barely hear. Oldies. I jumped when Ben put his hand on my shoulder and gently pulled me back into the hallway. He shook his head at me and I nodded. We both went back to bed.

I never saw Old Paint again. He stayed in Arizona, mostly charging off the sun and not moving around much once he was there. Once in a while, I'd get home from school and turn on the computer and check on him. He was just a red dot moving on thin lines in a faraway place, or, much more often, a black dot on an empty spot on the map. After a while, I stopped thinking about him.

Ben did two years of community college and then got a "Potential" scholarship to a college in Utah. It was hard to say goodbye to him, but by then I was in high school and had a life of my own. It was my turn to have spats with Mom.

One April day, I came home to find that Mom had left the computer running. There had been an email from Ben, with an attachment, and she had left it as a screen saver. He'd gone to Arizona for spring break. "This was as close as I could get to him," Ben had written. The scene had been shot under a bright blue sky, with red cliffs in the distance. There was nothing there, only scrub brush and a dirt road. And in the distance, a station wagon moved steadily away, a long plume of dust hanging in the still air behind him.

THE GHOSTS OF CHRISTMAS

Paul Cornell

Paul Cornell lives in Faringdon, Oxfordshire, England. He is a writer of SF and fantasy in prose, television, and comics, and has been Hugo Award–nominated for all three. He's the winner of a BSFA Award, an Eagle Award, and a Writer's Guild Award. He's written three episodes (two of them Hugo finalists) of the modern *Doctor Who,* and many titles for Marvel Comics, including *Captain Britain* and *MI-13,* and is the creator of *Doctor Who* character Bernice Summerfield. His first novels were *Something More* (2001) and *British Summertime* (2002). His first urban fantasy novel, *London Falling,* was published in 2012, and the sequel, *The Severed Streets,* will be out in the United States in early 2014. He has published more than a dozen short stories.

"The Ghosts of Christmas" was published at Tor.com. What if you could see your own future but not change it? or your own past?

IT WAS BECAUSE of a row. The row was about nothing. So it all came from nothing. Or, perhaps it's more accurate to say it came from the interaction between two people. I remember how Ben's voice suddenly became gentle and he said, as if decanting the whole unconscious reason for the row:

"Why don't we try for a baby?"

This was mid-March. My memory of that moment is of hearing birds outside. I always loved that time of year, that sense of nature becoming stronger all around. But I always owned the decisions I made, I didn't blame them on what was around me, or on my hormones. I am what's around me, I am my hormones, that's what I always said to myself. I don't know if Ben ever felt the same way. That's how I think of him now: always excusing himself. I don't know how that squares with how the world is now. Perhaps it suits him down to the ground. I'm sure I spent years looking out for him excusing himself. I'm sure me doing that was why, in the end, he did.

I listened to the birds. "Yes," I said.

* * *

WE GOT LUCKY almost immediately. I called my mother and told her the news.

"Oh no," she said.

WHEN THE FIRST trimester had passed, and everything was still fine, I told my boss and then my colleagues at the Project, and arranged for maternity leave. "I know you lot are going to go over the threshold the day after I leave," I told my team. "You're going to call me up at home and you'll be all, 'Oh, hey, Lindsey is currently inhabiting her own brain at age three! She's about to try to warn the authorities about some terrorist outrage or other. But pregnancy must be *such* a joy.'"

"Again with this," said Alfred. "We have no reason to believe the subjects would be able to do anything other than listen in to what's going on in the heads of their younger selves—"

"Except," said Lindsey, stepping back into this old argument like I hadn't even mentioned *hello, baby*, "the maths rules out even the possibility—"

"Free will—"

"No. It's becoming clearer with every advance we make back into what was: what's written is written."

Our due date was Christmas Day.

People who were shown around the Project were always surprised at how small the communication unit was. It had to be; most of the time it was attached to the skull of a sedated rhesus monkey. "It's just a string of lights," someone once said. And we all looked appalled, to the point where Ramsay quickly led the guest away.

They were like Christmas lights, each link changing colour to show how a different area of the monkey's brain was responding to the data coming back from the other mind, probably its own mind, that it was connected to, somewhen in the past. Or, we thought only in our wildest imaginings then, in the future.

Christmas lights. Coincidence and association thread through this, so much, when such things can only be illusions. Or artifice. Cartoons in the margin.

How can one have coincidence, when everything is written?

I ALWAYS THOUGHT my father was too old to be a dad. It often seemed to me that Mum was somehow too old to have me too, but that wasn't the case, biologically. It was just that she came from another time, a different world, of austerity, of shying away from rock and roll. She got even older after Dad died. Ironically, I became pregnant at the same age she had been.

WE WENT TO see her: me, Ben, and the bump. She didn't refer to it. For the first hour. She kept talking about her new porch. Ben started looking between us, as if waiting to see who would crack first. Until he had to say it, over tea. "So, the baby! You must be looking forward to being a grandmother!"

Mum looked wryly at him. "Not at my age."

"Sorry?"

"That's all right. You two can do what you want. I'll be gone soon."

WE STAYED FOR an hour or two more, talking about other things, about that bloody porch, and then we waved goodbye and drove off and I parked the car as soon as we were out of sight of the house. "Let's kill her," I said.

"Absolutely."

"I shouldn't say that. I so shouldn't say that. She *will* be gone soon. It's selfish of me to want to talk about the baby—"

"When we could be talking about that really very lovely porch. You could have led with how your potentially Nobel Prize–winning discovery of time travel is going."

"She didn't mention that either."

"She *is* proud of you, I'm sure. Did something—? I mean, did anything ever . . . happen, between you, back then?"

I shook my head. There was not one particular moment. I was not an abused child. This isn't a story about abuse.

I closed my eyes. I listened to the endless rhythm of the cars going past.

THE PROJECT WAS created to investigate something that I'd found in the case histories of schizophrenics. Sufferers often describe a tremendous sensation of *now*, the terrifying hugeness of the current moment. They often find voices talking to them, other people inside their own heads seemingly communicating with them. I started using the new brain-mapping technology to look into the relationship between the schizoid mind and time. Theory often follows technology, and in this case it was a detailed image of particle trails within the mind of David, a schizophrenic, that handed the whole theory to me in a single moment. It was written that I saw that image and made those decisions. Now when I look back to that moment, it's almost like I didn't do anything. Except that what happened in my head in that moment has meant so much to me.

I saw many knotted trails in that image, characteristic of asymmetric entanglement. I saw that, unlike in the healthy minds we'd seen, where there are only a couple of those trails at any given moment (and who knows what those are, even today?), this mind was connected, utterly, to . . . other things that were very similar to itself. I realised instantly what I was looking at: What could those other things that were influencing all those particle trails be but other minds? And where were those other minds very like this one—?

And then I had a vision of the trails in my own mind, like Christmas lights, and that led me to the next moment when I knew consciously what I had actually understood an instant before, as if I had divined it from the interaction of all things—

The trails led to other versions of this person's own mind, elsewhen in time.

I REMEMBER THAT David was eager to cooperate. He wanted to understand his condition. He'd been a journalist before admitting himself to the psychiatric hospital.

"I need to tear, hair, fear, ear, see . . . yes, see, what's in here!" he shouted, tapping the front of his head with his middle fingers. "Hah, funny, the rhymes, crimes, alibis, keep trying to break out of those, and it works, that works, works. Hello!" He sat suddenly and firmly down and took a very steady-handed sip from his plastic cup of water. "You asked me to stay off the drugs," he said, "so it's difficult. And I would like to go back on them. I would very much like to. After."

I had started, ironically, to see him as a slice across a lot of different versions of himself, separated by time. I saw him as all his minds, in different phases, interfering with each other. Turn that polarised view the other way, and you'd have a series of healthy people. That's what I thought. And I wrote that down offhandedly somewhere, in some report. His other selves weren't the "voices in his head." That's a common fallacy about the history of our work. Those voices were the protective action that distances a schizophrenic from those other selves. They were characters formed around the incursion, a little bit of interior fiction. We're now told that a "schizophrenic" is someone who has to deal with such random interference for long stretches of time.

"Absolutely, as soon as we've finished our interviews today. We don't want to do anything to set back your treatment."

"How do you experience time?" is a baffling question to ask anyone. The obvious answer would be "like you do, probably." So we'd narrowed it down to:

How do you feel when you remember an event from your childhood?

How do you feel about your last birthday?

How do you feel about the Norman Conquest?

"Not the same," David insisted. "Not the same."

I FOUND MYSELF not sleeping. Expectant mothers do. But while not sleeping, I stared and listened for birds, and thought the same thought, over and over.

It's been proven that certain traits formed by a child's environment do get passed down to its own children. It is genuinely harder for the child of someone who was denied books to learn to read.

I'm going to be a terrible parent.

"WILL YOU PLAY with me?" I remember how much that sound in my voice seemed to hurt. Not that I was feeling anything bad at the time; it was like I was just hearing something bad. I said it too much. I said it too much in exactly the same way.

"Later," said Dad, sitting in his chair that smelled of him, watching the football. "You start, and I'll join in later."

I'D LEFT MY bedroom and gone back into the lounge. I could hear them talking in the kitchen, getting ready for bed, and in a moment they'd be bound to notice me, but I'd seen it in the paper and it sounded incredible: *The Outer Limits*. The outer limits of what? Right at the end of the television programmes for the day. So after that I'd see television stop. And now I was seeing it and it was terrible, because there was a monster, and this was too old for me. I was crying. But they'd be bound to hear, and in a moment they would come and yell at me and switch the set off and carry me off to bed, and it'd be safe for me to turn round.

But they went to bed without looking in the lounge. I listened to them close the door and talk for a while, and then switch the light off, and then silence, and so it was just me sitting there, watching the greys flicker.

With the monster.

I WAS STANDING in a lay-by, watching the cars go past, wondering if Mummy and Daddy were going to come back for me this time. They'd said that if I didn't stop going on about the ice cream I'd dropped on the beach, they'd make me get out and walk. And then Dad had said "right!" and he'd stopped the car and yanked open the door and grabbed me out of my seat and left me there and driven off.

I was looking down the road, waiting to see the car come back.

I had no way of even starting to think about another life. I was six years old.

THOSE ARE JUST memories. They're not from Christmas Day. They're kept like that in the connections between neurons within my brain. I have a sense of telling them to myself. Every cell of my body has been replaced many times since I was that age. I am an oral tradition. But it's been proved that a butterfly remembers what a caterpillar has learned, despite its entire neurological structure being literally liquidised in between. So perhaps there's a component of memory that lies outside of ourselves as well, somewhere in those loose threads of particle trails. I have some hope that that is true. Because that would put a different background behind all of my experiences.

I draw a line now between such memories and the other memories I now have of my childhood. But that line will grow fainter in time.

I DON'T WANT to neglect it.

I'm going to neglect it.

I don't want to hurt it.

I'm going to hurt it.

They made me this way. I'm going to blame them for what I do. I'm going to end up being worse.

I grew numb with fear as autumn turned to winter. I grew huge. I didn't talk to Ben or anyone about how I felt. I didn't want to hear myself say the words.

In mid-December, a couple of weeks before the due date, I got an email from Lindsey. It was marked "confidential":

Just thought I should tell you, that, well, you predicted it, didn't you? The monkey trials have been a complete success, the subjects seem fine, mentally and physically. We're now in a position to actually connect minds across time. So we're going to get into the business of finding human volunteer test subjects. Ramsay wants "some expendable student" to be the first, but, you know, over our dead bodies! This isn't like lab rats, this is first astronaut stuff. Anyway, the Project is closing down on bloody Christmas Eve, so we're going to be forced to go and ponder that at home. Enclosed are the latest revisions of the tech specs, so that you can get excited too. But of course, you'll be utterly blasé about this, because it is nothing compared to the miracle of birth, about which you must be so excited, etc.

I looked at the specs and felt proud.

And then a terrible thought came to me. Or crystallised in me. Formed out of all the things I was. Was already written in me.

I found myself staggered by it. And hopeful about it. And fearful that I was hopeful. I felt I could save myself. That's ironic too.

My fingers fumbling, I wrote Lindsey a congratulatory email and then re-wrote it three times before I sent it so that it was a model of everything at my end being normal.

I knew what I was going to be doing on Christmas Day.

DUE DATES ARE not an exact science. We'd had a couple of false alarms, but when Christmas Eve arrived, everything was stable. "I think it's going to be a few more days," I told Ben.

I woke without needing an alarm the next morning, to the strange quiet of Christmas Day. I left Ben sleeping, showered and dressed in the clothes I'd left ready the night before. Creeping about amongst the silence made me think of Father Christmas. I looked back in on Ben and felt fondly about him. That would have been the last time for that.

I drove through streets that were Christmas empty. My security card worked fine on a door that didn't know what day it was.

And then I was into the absolute silence of these familiar spaces, walking swiftly down the corridors, like a ghost.

The lab had been tidied away for the holidays. I had to unlock a few storage areas, to remember a few combinations. I reached into the main safe and drew out the crown of lights.

I PAUSED AS I sat in Lindsay's chair, the crown connected to a power source, the control systems linked up to a keyboard and screen in my lap. I considered for a moment, or pretended to, before putting it on my head.

Could what I was about to do to my brain harm the foetus?

Not according to what had happened with the monkeys. They were all fine, physically. I could only harm myself. We'd theorised that too long a connection between minds, more than a few minutes, would result in an extreme form of what the schizophrenics dealt with, perhaps a complete brain shutdown. Death. I would have to feel that coming and get out, or would have to unconsciously see it approaching on the screen, or just count the seconds.

Or I would fail my child completely.

I nearly put it all away again, locked up, walked out.

Nearly.

I put the crown on my head, I connected the power source, I took the keyboard in my hands and I watched the particle trails in my own mind begin to resolve on the screen, and I concentrated on them, in the way we'd always talked about, and I started typing before I could think again. I hit *activate*.

THE MINDS OF the monkeys seemed to select their own targets. The imaging for those experiments showed two sets of trails reacting to each other, symmetrical, beautiful. That seemed to suggest not the chaotic accident of schizophrenia, but something more tranquil, perhaps something like a religious experience, we'd said. But of course we had nothing objective to go on. I had theorised that since it turns out we evolved with every moment of ourselves just a stray particle away, the human trait of seeing patterns in chaos, of always assuming there is a hidden supernatural world, was actually selected for us. We'd devised a feedback monitor that would allow a human subject to watch, and, with a bit of training, hence alter the particle tracks in one's own head via the keyboard and screen. I had hypothesised that, because the schizophrenic state can be diagnosed, that is, it isn't just interference like white noise but a pattern of interference, there must be some rule limiting which past states were being accessed, something that let in only a finite number. It had been Lindsay who'd said that perhaps this was only about time and not about space, that perhaps one had to be relatively near the minds doing the interfering, and thus, perhaps, the range was limited by where the earth was in its orbit.

That is to say, you only heard from your previous states of mind on the same calendar date.

Which turns out to have been what you might call a saving grace.

* * *

IT WAS LIKE being knocked out.

I'd never been knocked out. Not then.

I woke . . . and . . . Well, I must have been about three months old.

MY VISION IS the wrong shape. It's like being in an enormous cinema with an oddly shaped screen. Everything in the background is a blur. I hear what I'm sure are words, but . . . I haven't brought my understanding with me. It's like that part of me can't fit in a baby's mind. This is terrifying, to hear the shapes of words but not know what they mean. I start yelling.

The baby that I'm part of starts yelling in exactly the same way!

And then . . . and then . . .

The big comfort shape moves into view. Such joy comes with it. *Hello, big comfort shape! It's me! It's me! Here I am!*

Big comfort shape puts its arms around me, and it's the greatest feeling of my life. An addict's feeling. I cry out again, me, I did that, to make it happen again, more! Even while it's happening to me I want more. I yell and yell for more. And it gives me more.

Up to a point.

I PULLED THE crown off my head.

I rubbed the tears from my face.

If I'd stayed a moment longer, I might have wanted to stay forever, and thus harmed the mind I was in, all because I wasn't used to asking for and getting such divine attention.

Up to a point.

What was that point? Why had I felt that? I didn't know if I had, really. How was it possible to feel such a sense of love and presence, but also that miniscule seed of the opposite, that feeling of it not being enough or entire? Hadn't I added that, hadn't I dreamt it?

I quickly put the crown back on my head. I had a fix now, I could see where particular patterns took me, I could get to—

OH. MUCH CLEARER now. I must be about two years old. I'm walking around an empty room, marching, raising my knees and then lowering them, as if that's important.

Oh, I can think that. There's room for that thought in my head. I'm able to internally comment on my own condition. As an adult. As a toddler.

Can I control . . . ? I lower my foot. I stand there, inhabiting my toddler body, aware of it, the smallness of everything. But my fingers feel huge. And awkward. It's like wearing oven gloves. I don't want to touch anything. I know I'd break it.

And that would be terrible.

I turn my head. I put my foot forward. It's not like learning to drive, I already know how all this is done, it's just slightly different, like driving in America. I can hear . . .

Words I understand. "Merry Christmas!" From through the door. Oh, the door. The vase with a crack in it. The picture of a Spanish lady that Dad cut off the side of a crate of oranges and put in a frame. The smell of the carpet, close up. Oh, reactions to the smell, lots of memories, associations, piling in.

No! No! I can't take that! I can't understand that! I haven't built those memories yet!

Is this why I've always felt such enormous meaningless meaning about those objects and smells? I put it all out of my mind, and try to just be. And it's okay. It's okay.

The Christmas tree is enormous. With opened presents at the bottom, and I'm not too interested in those presents, which is weird, they've been left there, amongst the wrapping. The wrapping is better. This mind doesn't have signifiers for wrapping and tree yet, this is just a lot of weird stuff that happens, like all the other weird stuff that happens.

I head through the doorway. Step, step, step.

Into the hall. All sorts of differences from now, all sorts of objects with associations, but no, never mind the fondness and horror around you.

I step carefully into the kitchen.

And I'm looking up at the enormous figure of my mother, who is talking to . . . who is that? A woman in a headscarf. Auntie someone . . . oh, she died. I know she died! And I forgot her completely! Because she died!

I can't stop this little body from starting to shake. I'm going to cry. But I mustn't!

"Oh, there she goes again," says Mum, a sigh in her voice. "It's Christmas, you mustn't cry at Christmas."

"She wants to know where her daddy is," says the dead auntie. "He's down the pub."

"Don't tell her that!" That sudden fear in her voice. And the wryness that always went along with that fear. As if she was mocking herself for her weakness.

"She can't understand yet. Oh, look at that. Is she meant to be walking like that?" And oh no, Mum's looking scared at me too. Am I walking like I don't know how, or like an adult?

Mummy grabs me up into her arms and looks and looks at me, and I try to be a child in response to the fear in her face . . . but I have a terrible feeling that I look right into those eyes as me. I'm scaring her, like a child possessed!

I TOOK THE crown off more slowly that time. And then immediately put it on again. And now I knew I was picking at a scab. Now I knew and I didn't care. I wanted to know what everything in my mother's face at that moment meant.

*   *   *

I'M SEVEN AND I'm staring at nothing under the tree. I'm up early and I'm waiting. Something must soon appear under the tree. There was nothing in the stocking at the end of my bed, but they/Father Christmas/they/Father Christmas/they might not have known I'd put out a stocking.

I hear the door to my parents' bedroom opening. I tense up. So much that it hurts. My dad enters the room and sighs to see me there. I bounce on my heels expectantly. I do a little dance that the connections between my muscles and my memory tell me now was programmed into me by a children's TV show.

He looks at me like I'm some terrible demand. "You're too old for this now," he says. And I remember. I remember this from my own memory. I'd forgotten this. I hadn't forgotten. "I'm off down the shops to get you some presents. If I can find any shops that are open. If you'd stayed asleep until you were supposed to, they'd have been waiting for you. Don't look at me like that. You knew there wasn't any such thing as Father Christmas."

He takes his car keys from the table and goes outside in his dressing gown, and drives off in the car, in his dressing gown.

I'M EIGHT, AND I'm staring at a huge pile of presents under the tree, things I wanted but have been carefully not saying anything about, things that are far too expensive. Mum and Dad are standing there, and as I walk into the room, eight-year-old walk, trying, no idea how, looking at my mum's face, which is again scared, just turned scared in the second she saw me . . . but Dad starts clapping, actually applauding, and then Mum does too.

"I told you I'd make it up to you," says Dad. I don't remember him telling me. "I told you." This is too much. This is too much. I don't know how I'm supposed to react. I don't know how in this mind or outside of it.

I sit down beside the presents. I lower my head to the ground. And I stay there, to the point where I'm urging this body to get up, to show some bloody gratitude! But it stays there. I'm just a doll, and I stay there. And I can't make younger me move and look. I don't want to.

I'm nine, and I'm sitting at the dinner table, with Christmas dinner in front of me. Mum is saying grace, which is scary, because she only does it at Christmas, and it's a whole weird thing, and oh, I'm thinking, I'm feeling weird again, I'm feeling weird like I always feel on Christmas Day. Is this because of her doing that?

I don't think I'm going to be able to leave any knowledge about what's actually going on in the mind I'm visiting. The transmission of information is only one way. I'm a voice that can suggest muscle movement, but I'm a very quiet one.

I'M FIFTEEN. OH. This is the Christmas after Dad died. And I'm . . . drunk. No, I wasn't. I'm not. It just feels like I am. What's inside my head is . . . huge. I *hate* having it in here with me. Right now. I feel like I'm . . . possessed. And

I think it was like that in here before I arrived to join in. The shape of what I'm in is different. It feels . . . wounded. Oh God, did I hurt it already? No. I'm still me here and now. I wouldn't be if I'd hurt my young brain back then. No, I, I sort of remember. This is just what it was like being fifteen. My mind feels . . . like it's shaped awkwardly, not like it's wounded. All this . . . fury. I can *feel* the weight of the world limiting me. I can feel a terrible force towards action. Do something, now! Why aren't all these idiots around me doing something, when I know so well what they should do?! And God, God, I am horny even during this, which is, which is . . . terrible.

I'm bellowing at Mum, who's trying to raise her voice to shout over me at the door of my room. "Don't look at me like that!" I'm shouting. "We never have a good Christmas because of you! Dad would always try to make it a good Christmas, but he had to deal with you! Stop being afraid!"

I know as I yell this that it isn't true. I know now and I know then.

She slams the door of my room against the wall and marches in, raising a shaking finger—

I grab her. I grab her and I feel the frailness of her as I grab her, and I use all my strength, and it's lots, and I shove her reeling out of the door, and she crashes into the far wall and I run at her and I slam her into it again, so the back of her head hits the wall and I meant to do it and I don't, I so terribly don't. I'm beating up an old woman!

I manage to stop myself from doing that. Just. My new self and old self manage at the same time. I let go.

She bursts out crying. So do I.

"Stop doing that to me!" I yell.

"I worry about you," she manages to sob. "It's because I worry about you."

Is it just at Christmas she worries? I think hard about saying it, and this body says it. My voice sounds odd saying it. "Is it just at Christmas?"

She's silent, looking scared at how I sounded. Or, oh God, is she afraid of me now?

This is what did it, I realise. I make this mind go weird at Christmas, and they always noticed. It's great they noticed. What I grew up with, how I was brought up, is them reacting to that, expecting that, for the rest of the year. This makes sense, I've solved it! I've solved who I am! Who I am is my own fault! I'm a self-fulfilling prophecy!

Well, that's pretty obvious, isn't it? Should have known that. Everybody should realise that about themselves. Simple!

I find that I'm smiling suddenly and Mum bursts into tears again. To her, it must seem like she's looking at a complete psycho.

I TORE OFF the crown. I remembered doing that to her. Then I let myself forget it. But I never did. And that wasn't the only time. Lots of grabbing her. On the verge of hitting her. Is that a thing, being abused by one's child? It got lost in the layers of who she and I were, and there I was, in it, and suddenly it was the most important thing. And now it was again.

Because of Dad dying, I thought, because of that teenage brain, and then I thought no, that's letting myself off the hook.

Guilty.

But beyond that, my teenage-influenced self had been right: I'd found what I'd gone looking for. I'd messed up my own childhood by what I was doing here. That was a neat end to the story, wasn't it? Yes, my parents had been terribly lacking on occasion. But they'd had something beyond the norm to deal with. And I'd been . . . terrifying, horrible, beyond that poor frail woman's ability to deal with.

But that only let them off the hook . . . up to a point.

Hadn't that bit with there being no presents, that bit with the car, weren't those beyond normal? Had me being in that mind on just one day of the year really been such a big factor?

Would I end up doing anything like that? Would I be a good parent?

Perhaps I should have left it there.

But there was a way to *know*.

IN *A CHRISTMAS CAROL,* we hear from charity collectors visiting Scrooge's shop that when his partner Marley was alive, they both always gave generously. And you think therefore that Scrooge was a happy, open person then. But Scrooge doesn't confirm that memory of theirs. When we meet Marley's ghost, he's weighed down by chains "he forged in life." He's warning Scrooge not to be like he was. So were the charity collectors lying or being too generous with their memory of Christmas past? Or is it just that they sometimes caught Scrooge and Marley on a good day? The latter doesn't seem the sort of thing that happens to characters in stories. I've been told that story isn't a good model for what happened to me. But perhaps, because of what's written in the margins there, it is.

I SAT THERE thinking, the crown in my hands. I'd been my own ghost of Christmas future. But I could be a ghost of Christmas past too.

Was I going to be a good parent?

I could find out.

I set the display to track the other side of the scale. To take me into the future, as we'd only speculated that some day might be possible. And I put the crown back on before I could think twice.

OH. OH THERE she is. My baby is a she! I'm holding her in my arms. I love her more than I thought it was possible to love anything. The same way the big comfort thing loved me. And I didn't understand that until I put those moments side by side. This mind I'm in now has changed so much. It's hugely focussed on the little girl who's asleep right here. It's a warm feeling, but it's . . . it's hard too. Where did that come from? That worries me. She's so little. This can't be that far in the future. But I've changed so much. There's a feeling of . . . this mind I'm in wanting to prove something. She wants to tell me it's all going to be okay. That I have nothing but love inside me in this one year in the future. And I do . . . up to a point.

Oh, there's a piece of paper with the year written on it sitting on the arm of the chair right in front of me. It's just next year. That's my handwriting.

The baby's name is Alice, the writing continues. *You don't need to go any further to hear that. Please make this your last trip.*

Alice. That's what we were planning to call her. Thank God. If it was something different, I'd now be wondering where that idea came from.

Oh, I can feel it now. This mind has made room for me. It knew I'd be coming. Of course it did. She remembers what she did with the crown last year. But what does this mean? Why does future me want me to stop doing this? I try to reach across the distance between her and me, but I can only feel what she's feeling, not hear her thoughts. And she had a year to prepare, that note must be all she wants to tell me. She wants me to feel that it's all going to be okay . . . but she's telling me it won't be.

Ben comes in. He doesn't look very different. Unshaven. He's smiling all over his face. He sits on the arm of the chair and looks down at his daughter, proud and utterly in love with her. The room is decorated. There are tiny presents under the tree, joint birthday and Christmas presents the little one is too small to understand. So, oh, she was born very near Christmas Day. We must make such a perfect image sitting together like this. I don't think I can have told Ben about what I know will be happening to me at this moment on Christmas Day. I wouldn't do that. I'd want to spare him.

But . . . what's this? I can feel my body move slightly away from him. It took me a second to realise it, because it's so brilliant, and a little scary, to be suddenly in a body that's not weighed down by the pregnancy, but . . . I'm bristling. I can feel a deep chemical anger. The teenager is in here again. But I look up at him and smile, and this mind lets me. And he's so clearly still my Ben, absolutely the same, the Dad I knew he'd be when he asked and I said yes. It's not like he's started to beat me, I can't feel that in this body, she's not flinching, it's like when I'm angry but I don't feel allowed to express it.

Is this, what, post-natal depression? Or the first sign of me doing unto others what was done to me? A pushed-down anger that might come spilling out?

I don't care what my one-year-older self wants me to do. She can't know that much more than me. I need to know what this is.

ALICE IS ASLEEP in her cradle. She's so much bigger, so quickly, two years old! Again, that bursting of love into my head. That's reassuring. Another year on, I'm still feeling that.

But the room . . . the room feels very different. Empty. There's a tree, but it's a little one. I make this body walk quickly through the rest of the house. The bathroom is a bit different, the bedroom is a bit different. Baby stuff everywhere, of course, but what's missing? There's . . . there's nothing on that side of the room. I go back to the bathroom. There are no razors. No second toothbrush.

Where's Ben?

I start looking in drawers, checking my email . . . but the password's been changed. I can't find anything about what's happened. I search every inch of the house, desperate now, certain I'm going to find a funeral card or something. She knew this was going to happen to me, so wouldn't the bitch have left one out in plain sight? Why doesn't she want me to know? Oh please don't be dead, Ben, please—!

I end up meaninglessly, uselessly, looking in the last place, under the bed.

And there's a note, in my own handwriting.

I hate you.

She's deliberately stopping me from finding out. I can't let her.

Alice is looking straight at me this time. "Presents," she says to me. "I have presents. And you have presents." And I can see behind her that that's true.

That rush of love again. That's constant. I try to feel what's natural and not be stiff and scary about it, and give her a big hug. "Does Daddy have presents?"

She looks aside, squirms; she doesn't know how to deal with that. Have I warned her about me? I don't want to press her for answers. I don't want to distress her.

I need to keep going and find out.

I'M FACING IN the same direction, so it's like the decor and contents of the room suddenly shift, just a little. Alice, in front of me, four now, is running in rings on the floor, obviously in the middle of, rather than anticipating something, so that's good.

Ben comes in. He's alive! Oh thank God.

I stand up at the sight of him. Has she told him about me? No, I never would. He looks so different. He's clean shaven, smartly dressed. Did he go on a long journey somewhere? He hoists Alice into his arms and Alice laughs as he jumbles up her hair. "Happy Christmas birthday!"

Alice sings it back to him, like it's a thing they do together. So . . . everything's all right? Why didn't she want me to—?

A young woman I don't know comes in from the other room. She goes to Ben and puts a hand on his arm. Alice smiles at her.

"We have to be gee oh aye en gee soon," he says to me.

"Thanks for lunch," says the girl. "It was lovely."

The fury this time is my own. But it chimes with what's inside this mind.

She's been holding it down. I take a step forward. And the young woman sees something in my eyes and takes a step back. And that little movement—

No, it isn't the movement, it isn't what she does, this is all me—

I march towards her. I'm taking in every feature of her. Every beautiful feature of that slightly aristocratic, kind-looking, caring face. I'm making a sound I've never heard before in the back of my throat. "Get away from him. Get your hands off him."

She's trying to put up her hands and move away. She's astonished. "I'm sorry—!"

"What the hell?!" Ben is staring at us. Alice has started yelling. Fearful monkey warning shouts.

Something gives inside me. I rush at her. She runs.

I CATCH HER before she gets to the door. I grab her by both arms and throw her at the wall. I'm angry at her and at the mind I'm in too. Did she set me up for this?! Did she invite them here to punish me?! So she could let her anger out and not be responsible?!

She hits the wall and bounces off it. She falls, grabbing her nose. She looks so capable and organised I know she could hit me hard, I know she could defend herself, but she just drops to the ground and puts her hands to her face. I will not make her fight. She can control herself and I can't.

Ben rushes in and grabs me. I don't want him to touch me. I struggle.

"What are you doing?!" He's shouting at me.

I can feel this mind burning up. If I stay much longer, I'll start damaging it. I half want to.

I RIPPED THE crown from my head and threw it onto the ground. I burst into tears. I put my hands on my belly to comfort myself. But I found no comfort there.

But my pain wasn't important. It wasn't! The mistakes I'd made were what was important. What happened to Alice, *that* was what was important.

I got up and walked around the room. If I stopped now, I was thinking, the rest of my life would be a tragedy, I would be forever anticipating what was written, or trying . . . hopelessly, yes, there was nothing in the research then that said I had any hope . . . to change it. I would be living without hope. I could do that. But the important thing was what that burden would do to Alice . . . If I was going to be allowed to keep Alice, after what I'd seen.

I could go to the airport now. I could leave Ben asleep, while he was still my Ben, and have the baby in France, and break history . . . No I couldn't. Something would get me back to what I'd seen. Maybe something cosmic and violent that wouldn't respect the human mind's need for narrative. That was what the maths said. Alice shouldn't have that in her life. Alice shouldn't have me in her life.

But the me who wrote the first note wanted me not to try to visit the future again. When she knew I had. Did she think that was possible? Did I learn something in the next year that hinted that it might be? Why didn't I address that in future notes?

Because of anger? Because of fatalism? Because of a desire to hurt myself?

But . . . if there was even a chance it might be possible . . .

I slowly squatted and picked up the crown.

I'VE MOVED. I'M in a different house. Smaller. I walk quickly through the rooms, searching. I have to support myself against the wall in relief when I see Alice. There she is, in her own room, making a wall out of cardboard wrapping-paper rolls. Still the love in me. I don't think that's ever going to go. It feels like . . . a condition. A good disease this mind lives with. But what's she doing alone in here? Did I make her flee here, exile her here?

She looks up at me and smiles. No. No, I didn't.

I find the note this time on the kitchen table. It's quite long, it's apologetic. It tells me straight away that Ben and . . . Jessica, the young woman's name is Jessica . . . understood quite quickly after I left her mind and she started apologising. She apologises too for not doing anything to stop what happened. But she says she really wasn't setting me up for it. She says she's still working at the Project. She says she's still looking for a way to change time, but hasn't much hope of finding one.

I put down the letter feeling . . . hatred. For her. For her weakness. For her acceptance. That whole letter feels like . . . acting. Like she's saying something because she thinks she should.

From the other room comes the sound of Alice starting to cry. She's hurt herself somehow. I feel the urge from this mind to go immediately to her. But I . . . I actually hesitate. For the first time there is a distance. I'm a stranger from years ago. This isn't really my child. This is *her* child.

THE NEXT FEW visits were like an exhibition of time-lapse photography about the disintegration of a mother and child's relationship. Except calling it that suggests a distance, and I was amongst it, complicit in it.

"YOU GET SO weird!" she's shouting at me. "It's like you get frightened every Christmas that I'll go away with Dad and Jessica and never come back! I want to! I want to go away!"

BUT THE NEXT Christmas she's still there.

"WILL YOU JUST listen to me? You look at me sometimes like I'm not real, like I'm not human!" The mind of the future learned that from her memory of my experiences, I guess, learned that from her own experience of being a teenager with added context. Alice has had to fight for her mother to see her as an actual human being. I did that. I mean, I did that *to* her. I try now to reach out, but she sees how artificial it looks and shies away.

"Do I . . . neglect you?" I ask her.

She swears at me, and says yes. But then she would, wouldn't she?

AND THEN THE next year she's not there.

A note says the bitch arranged for her to stay with Ben and Jessica, and it all got too much in terms of anticipation, and she's sure she'll be back next time. She's certain of that. She's sorry, and she . . . hopes *I* am too?!

I go to the wall in the hall. I've always used bloody walls to do my fighting. I stand close to it. And as hard as I can I butt my head against it. I love the roaring of the mind I'm in as the pain hits us both. Feel *that*, you bitch, do something about *that*! I do it again. And then my head starts to swim and I don't think I can do it again, and I get out just as the darkness hits.

THAT WAS WHY she "hoped I was sorry too," because she knew that was coming.

I wonder how much I injured myself? She couldn't have known when she wrote the note. She was so bloody weak she didn't even try to ask me not to do it.

I am such a bully.

But I'm only doing it to myself.

THERE'S NO SIGN of Alice for the next two Christmases. When the bitch was *certain* she'd be back next time. The liar. There are just some very needy letters. Which show no sign of brain damage, thank God.

THEN THERE'S ALICE, sitting opposite me. She wears fashions designed to shock. "Christmas Day," she says, "time for you to go insane and hurt yourself, only today I'm trapped with you. What joy."

I discover that Ben and Jessica are on holiday abroad with their own . . . children . . . this year. And that the bitch has done . . . some sort of harm to herself on each of these days Alice wasn't here, obviously after I left. Is that just self-harm, am I actually capable of . . . ? Well, I suppose I know I am. Or is she trying to offer some explanation for that one time, or to use it to try to hurt Alice emotionally?

"No insanity this year," I say, trying to make my voice sound calm. And it sounds weird. It sounds old. It sounds like I've put inverted commas around "insanity." Like I'm trying to put distance between my own actions, being wry about my own weakness . . . like Mum always is.

I try to have fun with Alice in the ten minutes I've got. She shuts herself in her room when I get too cloying. I try to enter. She slams herself against the door. I get angry, though the weak woman I'm in really doesn't want to, and try to muscle in. But she grabs me, she's stronger than me.

She slams me against the wall. And I burst into tears. And she steps back, shaking her head in mocking disbelief at . . . all I've done to her.

I SLIPPED THE crown from my head.

I was staring into space. And then my phone rang. The display said it was Mum. And I thought now of all the times, and then I thought no, I have a cover to maintain here, I don't want her calling Ben . . . I didn't want to go home to Ben . . .

I took a deep breath, and answered.

"Is there . . . news?" she asked. I heard that wry, anxious tone in her voice again. Did I ever think of that sound as anxious before? "You are due today, aren't you?"

I told her that I was, but it didn't feel like it was going to be today, and that I'd call her immediately when anything started to happen. I stopped then, re- alising that actually, I did know it was going to be today; Ben said "Happy Christmas birthday" to Alice. But I couldn't tell her that I knew that and I didn't want to tell her I felt something I didn't feel. "Merry Christmas," I said, remembering the pleasantries, which she hadn't.

She repeated that, an edge in her voice again. "I was hoping that I might see you today, but I suppose that's impossible, even though the baby isn't coming. You've got much more important things to do." And the words hurt as much as they always did, but they weren't a dull ache now, but a bright pain. Because I heard them not as barbs to make me guilty, but as being exactly like the tone of the letters the bitch had left for me. Pained, pleading . . . weak. That was why I'd slammed her against the wall, all those years ago, because she was weak, because I could.

"I'm sorry," I said.

"Oh. I'm always sorry to hear you say that," she said.

I said I'd call her as soon as anything happened.

Once as she was off the phone, I picked up the crown and held it in my hands like I was in a Shakespeare play. I was so poetically contemplating it. I felt like laughing at my own presumption at having opened up my womb and taken a good look at where Jacob Marley had come from.

I had hurt my own mother. I had never made that up to her. I never could. But I hadn't tried. I had hated her for what I had done. And I could not stop. And in the future, the reflection was as bad as the shadow. I had become my mother. And I had created a daughter who felt exactly the same way about me. And I had created a yearly hell for my future self, making sure she never for- got the lesson I had learned on this day.

I would release myself from it. That's what I decided.

I put the crown on for the last time.

* * *

I'M STANDING THERE with my daughter. She looks to be in her late twenties. Tidy now. A worried look on her face. She's back for a family Christmas, but she knows there'll be trouble as always. She's been waiting for it. She looks kinder. She looks guilty. The room is bare of decoration. Like the bitch . . . like my victim . . . has decided not to make the effort anymore.

"Get away from me," I tell Alice, immediately, "get out of this house." Because I know what I'm going to do. I'm going to stay inside this mind. I'm going to break it. I'm going to give myself the release of knowing I'm going to go mad, at the age of . . . I look around and find a conveniently placed calendar. Which was unbelievably accommodating of her, to know what I'm about to do and still do that. I will go mad at the age of fifty-six. I have a finish line. It's a relief. Perhaps she wants this too.

"Mum," says Alice, "Mum, please—!" And she sounds desperate and worried for herself as well as for me, and still not understanding what all this is about.

But then her expression . . . changes. It suddenly becomes determined and calm. "Mum, please don't do this. I know we only have minutes—"

"What? Did I tell you about—?"

"No, this is an older Alice. I'm working on the same technology now. I've come back to talk to you."

It takes me a moment to take that in. "You mean, you've found a way to change time?"

"No. What's written is written. Immediately after we have this conversation, and we've both left these bodies, you tell me everything about what you've been doing."

"Why . . . do I do that?" I can feel the sound of my mother's weakness in my voice.

"Because after you leave here, you go forward five years and see me again." She takes my hands in hers and looks into my eyes. I can't see the hurt there. The hurt I put there. And I can see a reflection too.

Can I believe her?

She sees me hesitate. And she grows determined. "I'll stay as long as you will," she says. "You might do this to yourself, but I know you'd never let your child suffer."

I think about it. I do myself the courtesy of that. I toy with the horror of doing that. And then I look again into her face, and I know I'm powerless in the face of love.

I'M LOOKING INTO the face of someone I don't expect to see. It's David. Our experimental subject. The schizophrenic. Only now he's a lot older, and . . . oh, his face . . . he's lost such tension about his jaw. Beside him stands Alice, five years older.

He reaches out a hand and touches my cheek.

I shy away from him. What?!

"I'm sorry," he says. "I shouldn't have done that. We're . . . a couple, okay? We've been together for several years now. Hello you from the past. Thank you for the last four years of excellent family Christmases." He gestures to decorations and cards all around.

"Hello, Mum," says Alice. She reaches down and . . . oh, there's a crib there. She's picked up a baby. "This is my daughter, Cyala."

I walk slowly over. It feels as odd and as huge as walking as a child did. I look into the face of my granddaughter.

David, taking care not to touch me, joins me beside them. "It's so interesting," he says, "seeing you from this new angle. Seeing a cross section of you. You *look* younger!"

"Quickly," says Alice.

"Okay, okay." He looks back to me. And I can't help but examine his face, try to find the attraction I must later feel. And yes, it's there. I just never saw him in this way before. "Listen, this is what you told me to say to you, and I'm glad that, from what Alice has discovered, it seems I can't mess up my lines. It's true that you and Alice here fought, fought physically, like you say you and your mum did. Though I once saw her deny that to your face, by the way. She sounded like you were accusing *her* of something, and she kept on insisting it hadn't happened until you got angry and then finally she agreed like she was just going along with it. Oh God, this is so weird—" He picked up some sort of thin screen where I recognised something quite like my handwriting. "I was sure I added to what I was supposed to say there, but now it turns out it's written down here, and I'm not sure that it was . . . before. I guess your memory didn't quite get every detail of this correct. Or perhaps there's a certain . . . kindness, a mercy to time? Anyway!" He put down the screen again, certain he wouldn't need it. "But the important thing is, you only see one day. You don't see all the good stuff. There were long stretches of good stuff. You didn't create a monster, any more than your mum created a monster in you. You both just made people." He dares to actually touch me, and now I let him. "What you did led to a cure for people like me. And it changed how people see themselves and the world, and that's been good and bad, it isn't a utopia outside these walls and it isn't a wasteland, she wanted me to emphasise that, it's just people doing stuff as usual. And these are all your words, not mine, but I agree with them . . . you are not Ebenezer Scrooge, to be changed from one thing into another. Neither was your mother. Even knowing all of this is fixed, even knowing everything that happened, even if you only know the bad, you'd do it all anyway."

And he kisses me. Which makes me feel guilty and hopeful at the same time.

And I let go.

*   *   *

I SLOWLY PUT down the crown.

I stood up. I'd been there less than an hour. I went back to my car.

I remember the drive home through those still empty streets. I remember how it all settled into my mind, how a different me was born in those moments. I knew what certain aspects of my life to come would be like. I had memories of the future. That weight would always be with me. I regretted having looked. I still do. Despite everything it led to, for me and science and the world. I tell people they don't want to look into their future selves. But they usually go ahead and do it. And then they have to come to the same sort of accommodation that a lot of people have, that human life will go on, and that it's bigger than them, and that they can only do what they can do. To some, that fatalism has proven to be a relief. But it's driven some to suicide. It has, I think, on average, started to make the world a less extreme place. There is only so much we can do. And we don't see the rest of the year. So we might as well be kind to one another.

There are those who say they've glimpsed a pattern in it all. That the whole thing, as seen from many different angles, is indeed like writing. That, I suppose, is the revelation, that we're not the writers, we're what's being written.

I write now from the perspective of the day after my younger self stopped visiting. I'm relieved to be free of that bitch. Though, of course, I knew everything she was going to do. The rest of my life now seems like a blessed release. I wrote every note as I remembered them, and sometimes that squared with how I was feeling at the time, and sometimes I was playing a part . . . for whose benefit, I don't know.

I REMEMBER WALKING back into my house and finding Ben just waking up. And he looked at me, at the doubtless strange expression on my face, and in that moment I recall thinking I saw his expression change too. By some infinitesimal amount. I have come to think that was when he started, somewhere deep inside, the chain reaction of particle trails that took him from potentially caring dad to letting himself off the hook.

But that might equally just be the story I tell myself about that moment.

What each of us is is but a line in a story that resonates with every other line. Who we are is distributed. In all sorts of ways. And we can't know them all.

And then I felt something give. There was actually a small sound in the quiet. Liquid splashed down my legs. And as I knew I was going to, I went into labour on Christmas Day.

Ben leaped out of bed and ran to me, and we headed out to the car. Outside, the birds were singing. Of course they were.

"You're going to be fine," he said. "You're going to be a great mother."

"Up to a point," I said.

PRAYER

Robert Reed

Robert Reed lives in Lincoln, Nebraska, with his wife and daughter and is by himself enough to put the state on the map in the SF world. He has had stories appear in *at least* one of the annual Year's Best anthologies in every year since 1992. He is perhaps most famous for his Marrow universe, and the novels and stories that take place in that huge, ancient spacefaring environment. In 2012, a new Marrow book, *Eater of Bone,* collecting four novellas, came out, and another Marrow novella, "Katabasis," appeared in *F&SF,* a terrific original work.

"Prayer" was published online in *Clarkesworld.* In a future war, climate change has built into a global crisis. The United States now occupies Canada in the name of its AI, Almighty. And somehow the story projects the disturbing feeling that this dystopian future is already here.

FASHION MATTERS. IN my soul of souls, I know that the dead things you carry on your body are real, real important. Grandma likes to call me a clotheshorse, which sounds like a good thing. For example, I've always known that a quality sweater means the world. I prefer soft organic wools woven around Class-C nanofibers—a nice high collar with sleeves riding a little big but with enough stopping power to absorb back-to-back kinetic charges. I want pants that won't slice when the shrapnel is thick, and since I won't live past nineteen, probably, I let the world see that this body's young and fit. (Morbid maybe, but that's why I think about death only in little doses.) I adore elegant black boots that ignore rain and wandering electrical currents, and everything under my boots and sweater and pants has to feel silky-good against the most important skin in my world. But essential beyond all else is what I wear on my face, which is more makeup than Grandma likes, and tattooed scripture on the forehead, and sparkle-eyes that look nothing but ordinary. In other words, I want people to see an average Christian girl instead of what I am, which is part of the insurgency's heart inside Occupied Toronto.

To me, guns are just another layer of clothes, and the best day ever lived was the day I got my hands on a barely used, cognitively damaged Mormon rail-gun. They don't make that model anymore, what with its willingness to change sides. And I doubt that there's ever been a more dangerous gun made by the human species. Shit, the boy grows his own ammo, and he can kill anything for hundreds of miles, and left alone he will invent ways to hide and charge himself on the sly, and all that time he waits waits waits for his master to come back around and hold him again.

I am his master now.

I am Ophelia Hanna Hanks, except within my local cell, where I wear the randomly generated, perfectly suitable name:

Ridiculous.

The gun's name is Prophet, and until ten seconds ago, he looked like scrap conduit and junk wiring. And while he might be cognitively impaired, Prophet is wickedly loyal to me. Ten days might pass without the two of us being in each other's reach, but that's the beauty of our dynamic: I can live normal and look normal, and while the enemy is busy watching everything else, a solitary fourteen-year-old girl slips into an alleyway that's already been swept fifty times today.

"Good day, Ridiculous."

"Good day to you, Prophet."

"And who are we going to drop into Hell today?"

"All of America," I say, which is what I always say.

Reliable as can be, he warns me, "That's a rather substantial target, my dear. Perhaps we should reduce our parameters."

"Okay. New Fucking York."

Our attack has a timetable, and I have eleven minutes to get into position.

"And the specific target?" he asks.

I have coordinates that are updated every half-second. I could feed one or two important faces into his menu, but I never kill faces. These are the enemy, but if I don't define things too closely, then I won't miss any sleep tonight.

Prophet eats the numbers, saying, "As you wish, my dear."

I'm carrying him, walking fast towards a fire door that will stay unlocked for the next ten seconds. Alarmed by my presence, a skinny rat jumps out of one dumpster, little legs running before it hits the oily bricks.

"Do you know it?" I ask.

The enemy likes to use rats as spies.

Prophet says, "I recognize her, yes. She has a nest and pups inside the wall."

"Okay," I say, feeling nervous and good.

The fire door opens when I tug and locks forever once I step into the darkness.

"You made it," says my gun.

"I was praying," I report.

He laughs, and I laugh too. But I keep my voice down, stairs needing to be climbed and only one of us doing the work.

SHE FOUND ME after a battle. She believes that I am a little bit stupid. I was damaged in the fight and she imprinted my devotions to her, and then using proxy tools and stolen wetware, she gave me the cognitive functions to be a loyal agent to the insurgency.

I am an astonishing instrument of mayhem, and naturally her superiors thought about claiming me for themselves.

But they didn't.

If I had the freedom to speak, I would mention this oddity to my Ridiculous. "Why would they leave such a prize with little you?"

"Because I found you first," she would say.

"War isn't a schoolyard game," I'd remind her.

"But I made you mine," she might reply. "And my bosses know that I'm a good soldier, and you like me, and stop being a turd."

No, we have one another because her bosses are adults. They are grown souls who have survived seven years of occupation, and that kind of achievement doesn't bless the dumb or the lucky. Looking at me, they see too much of a blessing, and nobody else dares to trust me well enough to hold me.

I know all of this, which seems curious.

I might say all of this, except I never do.

And even though my mind was supposedly mangled, I still remember being crafted and calibrated in Utah, hence my surname. But I am no Mormon. Indeed, I'm a rather agnostic soul when it comes to my interpretations of Jesus and His influence in the New World. And while there are all-Mormon units in the US military, I began my service with Protestants—Baptists and Missouri Synods mostly. They were bright clean happy believers who had recently arrived at Fort Joshua out on Lake Ontario. Half of that unit had already served a tour in Alberta, guarding the tar pits from little acts of sabotage. Keeping the Keystones safe is a critical but relatively simple duty. There aren't many people to watch, just robots and one another. The prairie was depopulated ten years ago, which wasn't an easy or cheap process; American farmers still haven't brought the ground back to full production, and that's one reason why the Toronto rations are staying small.

But patrolling the corn was easy work compared to sitting inside Fort Joshua, millions of displaced and hungry people staring at your walls.

Americans call this Missionary Work.

Inside their own quarters, alone except for their weapons and the Almighty, soldiers try to convince one another that the natives are beginning to love them. Despite a thousand lessons to the contrary, Canada is still that baby brother to the north, big and foolish but congenial in his heart, or at least capable of learning manners after the loving sibling delivers enough beat-downs.

What I know today—what every one of my memories tells me—is that the American soldiers were grossly unprepared. Compared to other units and other duties, I would even go so far as to propose that the distant generals were aware of their limitations yet sent the troops across the lake regardless, full of religion and love for each other and the fervent conviction that the United States was the empire that the world had always deserved.

Canada is luckier than most. That can't be debated without being deeply, madly stupid. Heat waves are killing the tropics. Acid has tortured the seas. The wealth of the previous centuries has been erased by disasters of weather and war and other inevitable surprises. But the worst of these sorrows haven't occurred in the Greater United States, and if they had half a mind, Canadians would be thrilled with the mild winters and long brilliant summers and the supportive grip of their big wise master.

My soldiers' first recon duty was simple: Walk past the shops along Queen.

Like scared warriors everywhere, they put on every piece of armor and every sensor and wired back-ups that would pierce the insurgent's jamming. And that should have been good enough. But by plan or by accident, some native let loose a few molecules of VX gas—just enough to trigger one of the biohazard alarms. Then one of my brother-guns was leveled at a crowd of innocents, two dozen dead before the bloody rain stopped flying.

That's when the firefight really began.

Kinetic guns and homemade bombs struck the missionaries from every side. I was held tight by my owner—a sergeant with commendations for his successful defense of a leaky pipeline—but he didn't fire me once. His time was spent yelling for an orderly retreat, pleading with his youngsters to find sure targets before they hit the buildings with hypersonic rounds. But despite those good smart words, the patrol got itself trapped. There was a genuine chance that one of them might die, and that's what those devout men encased in body armor and faith decided to pray: Clasping hands, they opened channels to the Almighty, begging for thunder to be sent down on the infidels.

The Almighty is what used to be called the Internet—an American child reclaimed totally back in 2027.

A long stretch of shops and old buildings was struck from the sky.

That's what American soldiers do when the situation gets dicey. They pray, and the locals die by the hundreds, and the biggest oddity of that peculiar day was how the usual precise orbital weaponry lost its way, and half of my young men were wounded or killed in the onslaught while a tiny shaped charge tossed me a hundred meters down the road.

There I was discovered in the rubble by a young girl.

As deeply unlikely as that seems.

* * *

I DON'T WANT the roof. I don't need my eyes to shoot. An abandoned apartment on the top floor is waiting for me, and in particular, its dirty old bathroom. As a rule, I like bathrooms. They're the strongest part of any building, what with pipes running through the walls and floor. Two weeks ago, somebody I'll never know sealed the tube's drain and cracked the faucet just enough for a slow drip, and now the water sits near the brim. Water is essential for long shots. With four minutes to spare, I deploy Prophet's long legs, tipping him just enough toward the southeast, and then I sink him halfway into the bath, asking, "How's that feel?"

"Cold," he jokes.

We have three and a half minutes to talk.

I tell him, "Thank you."

His barrel stretches to full length, its tip just short of the moldy plaster ceiling. "Thank you for what?" he says.

"I don't know," I say.

Then I laugh, and he sort of laughs.

I say, "I'm not religious. At least, I don't want to be."

"What are you telling me, Ridiculous?"

"I guess . . . I don't know. Forget it."

And he says, "I will do my very best."

Under the water, down where the breech sits, ammunition is moving. Scrap metal and scrap nano-fibers have been woven into four bullets. Street fights require hundreds and thousands of tiny bullets, but each of these rounds is bigger than most carrots and shaped the same general way. Each one carries a brain and microrockets and eyes. Prophet is programming them with the latest coordinates while running every last-second test. Any little problem with a bullet can mean an ugly shot, or even worse, an explosion that rips away the top couple floors of this building.

At two minutes, I ask, "Are we set?"

"You're standing too close," he says.

"If I don't move, will you fire anyway?"

"Of course."

"Good," I say.

At ninety-five seconds, ten assaults are launched across southern Ontario. The biggest and nearest is fixated on Fort Joshua—homemade cruise missiles and lesser railguns aimed at that artificial island squatting in our beautiful lake. The assaults are meant to be loud and unexpected, and because every soldier thinks his story is important, plenty of voices suddenly beg with the Almighty, wanting His godly hand.

The nearby battle sounds like a sudden spring wind.

"I'm backing out of here," I say.

"Please do," he says.

At sixty-one seconds, most of the available American resources are glancing at each of these distractions, and a brigade of AIs is studying past tendencies and elaborate models of insurgency capabilities, coming to the conclusion that these events have no credible value toward the war's successful execution.

Something else is looming, plainly.

"God's will," says the nonbeliever.

"What isn't?" says the Mormon gun.

At seventeen seconds, two kilometers of the Keystone John pipeline erupt in a line of smoky flame, microbombs inside the heated tar doing their best to stop the flow of poisons to the south.

The Almighty doesn't need prayer to guide His mighty hand. This must be the main attack, and every resource is pulled to the west, making ready to deal with even greater hazards.

I shut the bathroom door and run for the hallway.

Prophet empties his breech, the first carrot already moving many times faster than the speed of sound as it blasts through the roof. Its three buddies are directly behind it, and the enormous release of stored energy turns the bathwater to steam, and with the first shot the iron tub is yanked free of the floor while the second and third shots kick the tub and the last of its water down into the bathroom directly downstairs. The final shot is going into the wrong part of the sky, but that's also part of the plan. I'm not supposed to be amazed by how many factors can be juggled at once, but they are juggled and I am amazed, running down the stairs to recover my good friend.

THE SCHEDULE IS meant to be secret and followed precisely. The Secretary of Carbon rides her private subway car to the UN, but instead of remaining indoors and safe, she has to come into the sunshine, standing with ministers and potentates who have gathered for this very important conference. Reporters are sitting in rows and cameras will be watching from every vantage point, and both groups are full of those who don't particularly like the Secretary. Part of her job is being despised, and fuck them. That's what she thinks whenever she attends these big public dances. Journalists are livestock, and this is a show put on for the meat. Yet even as the scorn builds, she shows a smile that looks warm and caring, and she carries a strong speech that will last for three minutes, provided she gives it. Her words are meant to reassure the world that full recovery is at hand. She will tell everyone that the hands of her government are wise and what the United States wants is happiness for every living breathing wonderful life on this great world—a world that with God's help will live for another five billion years.

For the camera, for the world, the Secretary of Carbon and her various associates invest a few moments in handshakes and important nods of the head.

Watching from a distance, without knowing anything, it would be easy to recognize that the smiling woman in brown was the one in charge.

The UN president shakes her hand last and then steps up to the podium. He was installed last year after an exhaustive search. Handsome and personable, and half as bright as he is ambitious, the President greets the press and then breaks from the script, shouting a bland "Hello" to the protestors standing outside the blast screens.

Five thousand people are standing in the public plaza, holding up signs and generated holos that have one clear message:

"END THE WARS NOW."

The Secretary knows the time and the schedule, and she feels a rare ache of nervousness, of doubt.

When they hear themselves mentioned, the self-absorbed protestors join together in one rehearsed shout that carries across the screens. A few reporters look at the throng behind them. The cameras and the real professionals focus on the human subjects. This is routine work. Reflexes are numb, minds lethargic. The Secretary picks out a few familiar faces, and then her assistant pipes a warning into her sparkle-eyes. One of the Keystones has been set on fire.

In reflex, the woman takes one step backward, her hands starting to lift to cover her head.

A mistake.

But she recovers soon enough, turning to her counterpart from Russia, telling him, "And congratulations on that new daughter of yours."

He is flustered and flattered. With a giddy nod, he says, "Girls are so much better than boys these days. Don't you think?"

The Secretary has no chance to respond.

A hypersonic round slams through the atmosphere, heated to a point where any impact will make it explode. Then it drops into an environment full of clutter and one valid target that must be acquired and reached before the fabulous energies shake loose from their bridle.

There is no warning sound.

The explosion lifts bodies and pieces of bodies, and while the debris rises, three more rounds plunge into the panicked crowd.

Every person in the area drops flat, hands over their heads.

Cameras turn, recording the violence and loss—more than three hundred dead and maimed in a horrific attack.

The Secretary and new father lie together on the temporary stage.

Is it her imagination, or is the man trying to cop a feel?

She rolls away from him, but she doesn't stand yet. The attack is finished, but she shouldn't know that. It's best to remain down and act scared, looking at the plaza, the air filled with smoke and pulverized concrete while the stubborn holos continue to beg for some impossible gift called Peace.

MY GRANDMOTHER IS sharp. She is. Look at her once in the wrong way, and she knows something is wrong. Do it twice and she'll probably piece together what makes a girl turn quiet and strange.

But not today, she doesn't.

"What happened at school?" she asks.

I don't answer.

"What are you watching, Ophelia?"

Nothing. My eyes have been blank for half a minute now.

"Something went wrong at school, didn't it?"

Nothing is ever a hundred percent right at school, which is why it's easy to harvest a story that might be believed. Most people would believe it, at least. But after listening to my noise about snippy friends and broken trusts, she says, "I don't know what's wrong with you, honey. But that isn't it."

I nod, letting my voice die away.

She leaves my little room without closing the door. I sit and do nothing for about three seconds, and then the sparkle eyes take me back to the mess outside the UN. I can't count the times I've watched the impacts, the carnage. Hundreds of cameras were working, government cameras and media cameras and those carried by the protesters. Following at the digitals' heels are people talking about the tragedy and death tolls and who is responsible and how the war has moved to a new awful level.

"Where did the insurgents get a top-drawer railgun?" faces ask.

But I've carried Prophet for a couple years and fired him plenty of times. Just not into a public target like this, and with so many casualties, and all of the dead on my side of the fight.

That's the difference here: The world suddenly knows about me.

In the middle of the slaughter, one robot camera stays focused on my real targets, including the Secretary of Fuel and Bullshit. It's halfway nice, watching her hunker down in terror. Except she should have been in pieces, and there shouldn't be a face staring in my direction, and how Prophet missed our target by more than fifty meters is one big awful mystery that needs solving.

I assume a malfunction.

I'm wondering where I can take him to get his guidance systems recalibrated and ready for retribution.

Unless of course the enemy has figured out how to make railgun rounds fall just a little wide of their goals, maybe even killing some troublemakers in the process.

Whatever is wrong here, at least I know that it isn't my fault.

Then some little thing taps at my window.

From the next room, my grandmother asks, "What are you doing, Ophelia?"

I'm looking at the bird on my window sill. The enemy uses rats, and we use robins and house sparrows. But this is a red-headed woodpecker, which implies rank and special circumstances.

The bird gives a squawk, which is a coded message that my eyes have to play with for a little while. Then the messenger flies away.

"Ophelia?"

"I'm just thinking about a friend," I shout.

She comes back into my room, watching my expression all over again.

"A friend, you say?"

"He's in trouble," I say.

"Is that what's wrong?" she asks.

"Isn't that enough?"

TWO RATS IN this alley don't convince me. I'm watching them from my new haven, measuring the dangers and possible responses. Then someone approaches the three of us, and in the best tradition of ratdom, my companions scurry into the darkness under a pile of rotting boards.

I am a plastic sack filled with broken machine parts.

I am motionless and harmless, but in my secret reaches, inside my very busy mind, I'm astonished to see my Ridiculous back again so soon, walking toward the rat-rich wood pile.

Five meters behind her walks an unfamiliar man.

To him, I take an immediate dislike.

He looks prosperous, and he looks exceptionally angry, wearing a fine suit made stiff with nano-armor and good leather shoes and a platoon of jamming equipment as well as two guns riding in his pockets, one that shoots poisoned ice as well as the gun that he trusts—a kinetic beast riding close to his dominate hand.

Ridiculous stops at the rot pile.

The man asks, "Is it there?"

"I don't know," she says, eyes down.

My girl has blue sparkle eyes, much like her original eyes—the ones left behind in the doctor's garbage bin.

"It looks like boards now?" he asks.

"He did," she lies.

"Not he," the man says, sounding like a google-head. "The machine is an It."

"Right," she says, kicking at the planks, pretending to look hard. "It's just a big gun. I keep forgetting."

The man is good at being angry. He has a tall frightful face and neck muscles that can't stop being busy. His right hand thinks about the gun in his pocket. The fingers keep flexing, wanting to grab it.

His gun is an It.

I am not.

"I put it here," she says.

She put me where I am now, which tells me even more.

"Something scared it," she says. "And now it's moved to another hiding place."

The man says, "Shit."

Slowly, carefully, he turns in a circle, looking at the rubble and the trash and the occasional normal object that might still work or might be me. Then with a tight slow voice, he says, "Call for it."

"Prophet," she says.

I say nothing.

"How far could it move?" he asks.

"Not very," she says. "The firing drained it down to nothing, nearly. And it hasn't had time to feed itself, even if it's found food."

"Bullshit," he says, coming my way.

Ridiculous watches me and him, the tattooed Scripture above her blue eyes dripping with sweat. Then the man kneels beside me, and she says, "I put the right guidance codes into him."

"You said that already." Then he looks back at her, saying, "You're not in trouble here. I told you that already."

His voice says a lot.

I have no power. But when his hands reach into my sack, what resembles an old capacitor cuts two of his fingers, which is worth some cursing and some secret celebration.

Ridiculous's face is twisted with worry, up until he looks back at her again. Then her expression turns innocent, pure and pretty and easy to believe.

Good girl, I think.

The man rises and pulls out the kinetic gun and shoots Ridiculous in the chest. If not for the wood piled up behind her, she would fly for a long distance. But instead of flying, she crashes and pulls down the wood around her, and one of those very untrustworthy rats comes out running, squeaking as it flees.

Ridiculous sobs and rolls and tries saying something.

He shoots her in the back, twice, and then says, "We never should have left it with you. All that luck dropping into our hands, which was crazy. Why should we have trusted the gun for a minute?"

She isn't dead, but her ribs are broken. And by the sound of it, the girl is fighting to get one good breath.

"Sure, it killed some bad guys," he says. "That's what a good spy does. He sacrifices a few on his side to make him look golden in the enemy's eyes."

I have no strength.

"You can't have gone far," he tells the alley. "We'll drop ordinance in here, take you out with the rats."

I cannot fight.

"Or you can show yourself to me," he says, the angry face smiling now. "Reveal yourself and we can talk."

Ridiculous sobs.

What is very easy is remembering the moment when she picked me up out of the bricks and dust and bloodied bits of human meat.

He gives my sack another good kick, seeing something.

And for the first time in my life, I pray. Just like that, as easy as anything, the right words come out of me, and the man bending over me hears nothing coming and senses nothing, his hands playing with my pieces when a fleck of laser light falls out of the sky and turns the angriest parts of his brain into vapor, into a sharp little pop.

I'M STILL NOT breathing normally. I'm still a long way from being able to think straight about anything. Gasping and stupid, I'm kneeling in a basement fifty meters from where I nearly died, and Prophet is suckling on an unsecured outlet, endangering both of us. But he needs power and ammunition, and I like the damp dark in here, waiting for my body to come back to me.

"You are blameless," he says.

I don't know what that means.

He says, "You fed the proper codes into me. But there were other factors, other hands, and that's where the blame lies."

"So you are a trap," I say.

"Somebody's trap," he says.

"The enemy wanted those civilians killed," I say, and then I break into the worst-hurting set of coughs that I have ever known.

He waits.

"I trusted you," I say.

"But Ridiculous," he says.

"Shut up," I say.

"Ophelia," he says.

I hold my sides, sipping my breaths.

"You assume that this war has two sides," he says. "But there could be a third player at large, don't you see?"

"What should I see?"

"Giving a gun to their enemies is a huge risk. If the Americans wanted to kill their political enemies, it would be ten times easier to pull something out of their armory and set it up in the insurgency's heart."

"Somebody else planned all of this, you're saying."

"I seem to be proposing that, yes."

"But that man who came with me today, the one you killed . . . he said the Secretary showed us a lot with her body language. She knew the attack was coming. She knew when it would happen. Which meant that she was part of the planning, which was a hundred percent American."

"Except whom does the enemy rely on to make their plans?"

"Tell me," I say.

Talking quietly, making the words even more important, he says, "The Almighty."

"What are we talking about?" I ask.

He says nothing, starting to change his shape again.

"The Internet?" I ask. "What, you mean it's conscious now? And it's working its own side in this war?"

"The possibility is there for the taking," he says.

But all I can think about are the dead people and those that are hurt and those that right now are sitting at their dinner table, thinking that some fucking Canadian bitch has made their lives miserable for no goddamn reason.

"You want honesty," Prophet says.

"When don't I?"

He says, "This story about a third side . . . it could be a contingency buried inside my tainted software. Or it is the absolute truth, and the Almighty is working with both of us, aiming toward some grand, glorious plan."

I am sort of listening, and sort of not.

Prophet is turning shiny, which happens when his body is in the middle of changing shapes. I can see little bits of myself reflected in the liquid metals and the diamonds floating on top. I see a thousand little-girl faces staring at me, and what occurs to me now—what matters more than anything else today—is the idea that there can be more than two sides in any war.

I don't know why, but that's the biggest revelation of all.

When there are more than two sides, that means that there can be too many sides to count, and one of those sides, standing alone, just happens to be a girl named Ophelia Hanna Hanks.

THE BATTLE OF CANDLE ARC

Yoon Ha Lee

Yoon Ha Lee lives in Baton Rouge, Louisiana, and "has not yet been eaten by gators." She has been publishing her carefully crafted stories in the genre for about ten years. Her fiction has appeared in *F&SF, Lady Churchill's Rosebud Wristlet, Lightspeed,* Tor.com, and other venues. *Conservation of Shadows,* her first short story collection, came out in 2013.

"The Battle of Candle Arc" was published in *Lightspeed,* the fine ezine edited by John Joseph Adams. Critic Lois Tilton characterizes this story as follows: "Yoon Ha Lee does mannerist military SF, as stylized as a chess match. I'm reminded of the legendary duels between swordmasters who stare their opponents into defeat before a single blow is struck. Except that Lee doesn't forget that fatal blows in the end are struck and real people die . . . the essence of the piece is strategy."

GENERAL SHUOS JEDAO was spending his least favorite remembrance day with Captain-magistrate Rahal Korais. There was nothing wrong with Korais except that he was the fangmoth's Doctrine officer, and even then he was reasonable for a Rahal. Nevertheless, Doctrine observed remembrances with the ranking officer, which meant that Jedao had to make sure he didn't fall over.

Next time, Jedao thought, wishing the painkillers worked better, *I have to get myself assassinated on a planet where they do the job right.*

The assassin had been a Lanterner, and she had used a shattergun. She had caught him at a conference, of all places. The shattergun had almost sharded Jedao into a hundred hundred pieces of ghostwrack. Now, when Jedao looked at the icelight that served as a meditation focus, he saw anywhere from three to eight of them. The effect would have been charming if it hadn't been accompanied by stabbing pains in his head.

Korais was speaking to him.

"Say again?" Jedao said. He kept from looking at his wristwatch.

"I'll recite the next verses for you, sir, if that doesn't offend you," Korais said.

Korais was being diplomatic. Jedao couldn't remember where in the litany they were. Under better circumstances he would have claimed that he was distracted by the fact that his force of eleven fangmoths was being pursued by the Lanterners who had mauled the rest of the swarm, but it came down to the injuries.

"I'd be much obliged, Captain," Jedao said.

This remembrance was called the Feast of Drownings. The Rahal heptarch, whose faction maintained the high calendar and who set Doctrine, had declared it three years back, in response to a heresy in one of the heptarchate's larger marches. Jedao would have called the heresy a benign one. People who wanted the freedom to build shrines to their ancestors, for pity's sake. But the Rahal had claimed that this would upset the high calendar's master equations, and so the heretics had had to be put down.

There were worse ways to die than by having your lungs slowly filled with caustic fluid. That still didn't make it a good way to die.

Korais had begun his recital. Jedao looked at the icelight on the table in front of them. It had translucent lobes and bronchi and alveoli, and light trickled downward through them like fluid, pale and blue and inexorable.

The heptarchate's exotic technologies depended on the high calendar's configurations: the numerical concordances, the feasts and remembrances, the associated system of belief. The mothdrive that permitted fast travel between star systems was an exotic technology. Few people advocated a switch in calendars. Too much would have to be given up, and invariant technologies, which worked under any calendar, never seemed to keep up. Besides, any new calendar would be subject to the same problem of lock-in; any new calendar would be regulated by the Rahal, or by people like the Rahal, as rigorously as the current one.

It was a facile argument, and one that Jedao had always disliked.

"Sir," Korais said, breaking off at the end of a phrase, "you should sit."

"I'm supposed to be standing for this," Jedao said dryly.

"I don't think your meditations during the next nineteen minutes are going to help if you fall unconscious."

He must look awful if Doctrine was telling him how long until the ordeal was over. Not that he was going to rest afterward. He had to figure out what to do about the Lanterners.

It wasn't that Jedao minded being recalled from medical leave to fight a battle. It wasn't even that he minded being handed this sad force of eleven fangmoths, whose morale was shredded after General Kel Najhera had gotten herself killed. It was that the heptarchate had kept the Lanterners as clients for as long as he remembered. Now the Lanterners were demanding regional representation, and they were at war with the heptarchate.

The Lanterner assassin had targeted Jedao during the Feast of Falcon's Eye.

If she had succeeded, the event would have spiked the high calendar in the Lanterners' favor. Then they would have declared a remembrance in their own, competing calendar. The irony was that Jedao wasn't sure he disagreed with the Lanterners' grievances against the heptarchate, which they had broadcast everywhere after their victory over Najhera.

Korais was still looking at him. Jedao went to sit down, which was difficult because walking in a straight line took all of his concentration. Sitting down also took concentration. It wasn't worth pretending that he heard the last remembrance verses.

"It's over, sir," Korais said. "I'll leave you to your duties." He saluted and let himself out.

Jedao looked at his watch after the door hissed shut. Everything on it was too tiny to read the way his vision was. He made his computer enlarge its time display. Korais had left at least seven minutes early, an astonishing concession considering his job.

Jedao waited until the latest wave of pain receded, then brought up a visual of Candle Arc, a battledrift site nine days out from their present position and eleven days out from the Lanterners' last reported position. The battle had taken place 177 years ago, between two powers that had since been conquered. The heptarchate called the battle Candle Arc because of the bridge of lights that wheeled through the scatter-hell of what had once been a fortress built from desiccated suns, and the remnants of warmoths. The two powers probably had called their battle something else, and their moths wouldn't have been called moths either, and their calendars were dead except in records held locked by the Rahal.

Some genius had done up the image in shades of Kel gold, even though a notation gave the spectrum shift for anyone who cared. Jedao was fond of the Kel, who were the heptarchate's military faction. For nearly twenty years he had been seconded to their service, and they had many virtues, but their taste in ornamentation was gaudy. Their faction emblem was the ashhawk, the bird that burned in its own glory, all fire and ferocity. The Shuos emblem was the ninefox, shapeshifter and trickster. The Kel called him the fox general, but they weren't always being complimentary.

The bridgelights swam in and out of focus. Damnation. This was going to take forever. After pulling up maps of the calendrical terrain, he got the computer algebra system to tell him what the estimated shifts looked like in pictures. Then he sent a summons to the moth commander.

He knew how long it took to get from the moth's command center to his quarters. The door chimed at him with commendable promptness.

"Come in," Jedao said.

The door opened. "You wished to see me, sir," said Kel Menowen, commander of the *Fortune Travels in Fours*. She was a stocky woman with swan-black hair and unsmiling eyes. Like all Kel, she wore black gloves; Jedao himself wore fingerless gloves. Her salute was so correct that he wanted to find an imperfection in her fist, or the angle of her arm.

Jedao had chosen the *Fortune* as his command moth not because it was the least damaged after Najhera's death, which it wasn't, but because Menowen had a grudge against the Shuos. She was going to be the hardest commander to win over, so he wanted to do it in person.

The tired joke about the Kel was that they were strong, loyal, and stupid, although they weren't any more prone to stupidity than the other factions.

The tired joke about the Shuos, who specialized in information operations, was that they had backstabbing quotas. Most of the other factions had reasonable succession policies for their heptarchs. The Rahal heptarch appointed a successor from one of the senior magistrates. With the Kel, it was rank and seniority. The Shuos policy was that if you could keep the heptarch's seat, it was yours. The other tired joke was that the infighting was the only reason the Shuos weren't running the heptarchate.

One of Menowen's aunts had died in a Shuos scheme, an assassin getting careless with secondary casualties. Jedao had already been in Kel service at the time, but it was in his public record that he had once been Shuos infantry, where "Shuos infantry" was a euphemism for "probably an assassin." In his case, he had been a very good assassin.

Menowen was still standing there. Jedao approximated a return salute. "At ease," he said. "I'd stand, but 'up' and 'down' are difficult concepts, which is distressing when you have to think in three dimensions."

Menowen's version of at ease looked stiff. "What do you require, sir?"

They had exchanged few words since he boarded her moth because he had barely been functional. She wasn't stupid. She knew he was on her moth to make sure she behaved, and he had no doubt her behavior would be exemplary. She also probably wanted to know what the plan was.

"What do you think I require?" Jedao asked. Sometimes it helped to be direct.

Menowen's posture became more stiff. "It hasn't escaped my notice that you only gave move orders as far as the Haussen system," she said. "But that won't take us near any useful support, and I thought our orders were to retreat." She was overenunciating on top of telling him things he knew, which meant that at some point she was going to tell him he wasn't fit for duty. Some Kel knew how to do subtlety. Menowen had an excellent service record, but she didn't strike him as a subtle Kel.

"You're reading the sane, sensible thing into our orders," Jedao said. "Kel Command was explicit. They didn't use the word 'retreat' anywhere." An interesting oversight on their part. The orders had directed him to ensure that the border shell guarding the Glover Marches was secured by any means possible.

"Retreat is the only logical response," Menowen said. "Catch repairs if possible, link up with Twin Axes." The Twin Axes swarm was on patrol along the Taurag border, and was the nearest Kel force of any size. "Then we'd have a chance against the heretics."

"You're discounting some alternatives," Jedao said.

Menowen lifted her chin and glared at him, or possibly at his insignia, or at the ink painting over his shoulder. "Sir," she said, "if you're contemplating fighting them with our present resources—" She stopped, tried again. The second try was blunter. "Your injuries have impaired your judgment and you ought to—"

"—let the senior moth commander make the sane, sensible decision to run for help?" Jedao flexed his hands. He had a clear memory of an earlier conversation with Commander Kel Chau, specifically the pinched look around Chau's eyes. Chau probably thought running was an excellent idea. "I had considered it. But it's not necessary. I've looked at the calendrical terrain. We can win this."

Menowen was having a Kel moment. She wanted to tell him off, but it wasn't just that he outranked her, it was that Kel Command had pulled him off medical leave to put him in charge, instead of evacuating him from the front. "Sir," she said, "I was *there*. The Lanterners have a swarm of at least sixty moths. They will have reinforcements. I shouldn't have to tell you any of this."

"How conscientious of you," Jedao said. Her eyes narrowed, but she didn't take the bait. "Did you think I had some notion of slugging it out toe-to-toe? That would be stupid. But I have been reviewing the records, and I understand the Lanterner general's temperament. Which is how we're going to defeat the enemy, unless you defeat yourself before they have a chance to."

Menowen's mouth pressed thin. "I understand you have never lost a battle," she said.

"This isn't the—"

"If it's about your fucking reputation—"

"Fox and hound, not this whole thing again," Jedao snapped. Which was unfair of him because it was her first time bringing it up, even if everyone else did. "Sooner or later everyone loses. I get it. If it made more sense to stop the Lanterners in the Glovers, I'd be doing it." This would also mean ceding vast swathes of territory to them, not anyone's first choice; from her grim expression, she understood that. "If I could stop the Lanterners by calling them up for a game of cards, I'd do that too. Or by, I don't know, offering them my right arm. But I'm telling you, this can be done, and I am not quitting if there's a chance. Am I going to have to fight you to prove it?"

This wasn't an idle threat. It wouldn't be the first time he had dueled a Kel, although it would be frivolous to force a moth commander into a duel, however non-lethal, at a time like this.

Menowen looked pained. "Sir, you're *wounded*."

He could think of any number of ways to kill her before she realized she was being attacked, even in his present condition, but most of them depended on her trust that her commanding officer wouldn't pull such a stunt.

"We can do this," Jedao said. He was going to have to give this speech to the other ten moth commanders, who were jumpy right now. Might as well get in practice now. "All the way to the Haussen system, it looks like we're doing the reasonable thing. But we're going to pay a call on the Rahal outpost at Smoke-watch 33-67." That wasn't going to be a fun conversation, but most Rahal were responsive to arguments that involved preserving their beloved calendar. And right now, he was the only one in position to stop the Lanterners from arrowing right up to the Glover Marches. The perfect battle record that people liked to bludgeon him over the head with might even come in handy for persuasion.

"I'm listening," Menowen said in an unpromising voice.

It was good, if inconvenient, when a Kel thought for herself. Unlike a number of the officers on this moth, Menowen didn't react to Jedao like a cadet fledge.

"Two things," Jedao said. "First, I know remembering the defeat is painful, but if I'm reading the records correctly, the first eight Kel moths to go down, practically simultaneously, included two scoutmoths."

"Yes, that's right," Menowen said. She wasn't overenunciating anymore. "The Lanterners' mothdrive formants were distorted just enough to throw our scan sweep, so they saw us first."

"Why would they waste time killing scoutmoths when they could blow up fangmoths or arrowmoths instead? If you look at their positions and ours, they had better available targets." He had to be careful about criticizing a dead general, but there was no avoiding it. Najhera had depended too much on exotics and hadn't made adequate use of invariant defenses. The Kel also hadn't had time to channel any useful formation effects, their specialty. "The scoutmoths weren't out far enough to give advance notice, and surprise was blown once the Lanterners fried those eight moths. What I'm getting at is that our scan may not be able to tell the difference between mothdrives on big scary things and mothdrives on mediocre insignificant things, but their scan can't either, or they would have picked better targets."

Menowen was starting to look persuaded. "What are you going to do, sir? Commandeer civilian moths and set them to blow?" She wasn't able to hide her distaste for the idea.

"I'd prefer to avoid involving civilians," Jedao said coolly. Her unsmiling eyes became a little less unsmiling when he said that. "The Rahal run the show, they can damn well spare me some engines glued to tin cans."

The pain hit him like a spike to the eyes. When he could see again, Menowen was frowning. "Sir," she said, "one thing and I'll let you continue your deliberations in private." This was Kel for *please get some fucking rest before you embarrass us by falling over.* "You had some specific plan for punching holes into the Lanterners?"

"Modulo the fact that something always goes wrong after you wave hello at the enemy? Yes."

"That will do it for me, sir," Menowen said. "Not that I have a choice in the matter."

"You always have a choice," Jedao said. "It's just that most of them are bad."

She didn't look as though she understood, but he hadn't expected her to.

JEDAO WOULD HAVE authorized more time for repairs if he could, but they kept receiving reports on the Lanterners' movements and time was one of the things they had little of. He addressed his moth commanders on the subject to reassure them that he understood their misgivings. Thankfully, Kel discipline held.

For that matter, Jedao didn't like detouring to Smokewatch 33-67 afterward, but he needed a lure, and this was the best place to get it. The conversation with the Rahal magistrate in charge almost wasn't a conversation. Jedao felt as though he was navigating through a menu of options rather than interacting with a human being. Some of the Rahal liked to cultivate that effect. At least Rahal Korais wasn't one of them.

"This is an unusual request for critical Rahal resources, General," the magistrate was saying.

This wasn't a no, so Jedao was already ahead. "The calendrical lenses are the best tool available," he said. "I will need seventy-three of them."

Calendrical lenses were Doctrine instruments mounted on mothdrives. Their sole purpose was to focus the high calendar in contested areas. It was a better idea in theory than practice, since radical heresies rapidly knocked them out of alignment, but the Rahal bureaucracy was attached to them. Typical Rahal, trusting an idea over cold hard experience. At least there were plenty of the things, and the mothdrives ought to be powerful enough to pass on scan from a distance.

Seventy-three was crucial because there were seventy-three moths in the Kel's Twin Axes swarm. The swarm was the key to the lure, just not in the way that Commander Menowen would have liked. It was barely possible, if Twin Axes set out from the Taurag border within a couple days' word of Najhera's defeat, for it to reach Candle Arc when Jedao planned on being there. It would also be inadvisable for Twin Axes to do so, because their purpose was to prevent the Taurags from contesting that border. Twin Axes wouldn't leave such a gap in heptarchate defenses without direct orders from Kel Command.

However, no one had expected the Lanterners to go heretical so suddenly. Kel Command had been known to panic, especially under Rahal pressure. And Rahal pressure was going to be strong after Najhera's defeat.

"Do you expect the lens vessels to be combat-capable?" the magistrate asked without any trace of sarcasm.

"I need them to sit there and look pretty in imitation of a Kel formation," Jedao said. "They'll get the heretics' attention, and if they can shift some of the calendrical terrain in our favor, even better." Unlikely, he'd had the Kel run the numbers for him, but it sounded nice. "Are volunteers available?"

Also unlikely. The advantage of going to the Rahal rather than some other faction, besides their susceptibility to the plea, was that the Rahal were disciplined. Even if they weren't going to be volunteers. If he gave instructions, the instructions would be rigorously carried out.

The magistrate raised an eyebrow. "That's not necessary," he said. "I'm aware of your skill at tactics, General. I assume you will spare the lenses' crews from unnecessary harm."

Touching. "I am grateful for your assistance, Magistrate," Jedao said.

"Serve well, General. The lenses will join your force at—" He named a time, which was probably going to be adhered to, then ended the communication.

The lenses joined within eight minutes and nineteen seconds of the given time. Jedao wished there were some way to minimize their scan shadow, but Kel moths did that with formations, and the Rahal couldn't generate Kel formation effects.

Jedao joined Menowen at the command center even though he should have rested. Menowen's mouth had a disapproving set. The rest of the Kel looked grim. "Sir," Menowen said. "Move orders?"

He took his chair and pulled up the orders on the computer. "False formation for the Rahal as shown. Follow the given movement plan," he said. "Communications, please convey the orders to all Rahal vessels." It was going to take extra time for the Rahal to sort themselves out, since they weren't accustomed to traveling in a fake formation, but he wasn't going to insult them by saying so.

Menowen opened her mouth. Jedao stared at her. She closed her mouth, looking pensive.

"Communications," Jedao said, "address to all units. Exclude the Rahal."

It wasn't the first speech he'd given on the journey, but the time had come to tell his commanders what they were up to and brace them for the action to come.

The Communications officer said, "It's open, sir."

"This is General Shuos Jedao to all moths," he said. "It's not a secret that we're being pursued by a Lanterner swarm. We're going to engage them at Candle Arc. Due to the Lanterners' recent victory, cascading effects have shifted the calendrical terrain there. The Lanterners are going to be smart and take one of the channels with a friendly gradient to their tech most of the way in. Ordinarily, a force this small wouldn't be worth their time. But because of the way the numbers have rolled, Candle Arc is a calendrical choke: we're arriving on the Day of Broken Feet. Whoever wins there will shift the calendar in their favor. When we offer battle, they'll take us up on it."

He consoled himself that, if the Lanterners lost, their soldiers would fall to fire and metal, honest deaths in battle, and not as calendrical foci, by having filaments needled into their feet to wind their way up into the brain.

"You are Kel," Jedao went on. "You have been hurt. I promise you we will hurt them back. But my orders will be exact, and I expect them to be followed exactly. Our chances of victory depend on this. I am not unaware of the numbers. But battle isn't just about numbers. It's about will. And you are Kel; in this matter you will prevail."

The panel lit up with each moth commander's acknowledgment. Kel gold against Kel black.

They didn't believe him, not yet. But they would follow orders, and that was all he needed.

COMMANDER MENOWEN ASKED to see him in private afterward, as Jedao had thought she might. Her mouth was expressive. Around him she was usually expressing discontent. But it was discontent for the right reasons.

"Sir," Menowen said. "Permission to discuss the battle plan."

"You can discuss it all you like," Jedao said. "I'll say something if I have something to say."

"Perhaps you had some difficulties with the computer algebra system," she said. "I've run the numbers. We're arriving 4.2 hours before the terrain flips in our favor."

"I'm aware of that," Jedao said.

The near side of the choke locus was obstructed by a null region where no exotic technologies would function. But other regions around the null shifted according to a schedule. The far side of the choke periodically favored the high calendar. With Najhera's defeat, the far side would also shift sometimes toward the Lanterners' calendar.

"I don't understand what you're trying to achieve," Menowen said.

"If you don't see it," Jedao said, pleased, "the Lanterners won't see it either."

To her credit, she didn't ask if this was based on an injury-induced delusion, although she clearly wanted to. "I expect Kel Command thinks you'll pull off a miracle," she said.

Jedao's mouth twisted. "No, Kel Command thinks a miracle would be very nice, but they're not holding their breath, and as a Shuos I'm kind of expendable. The trouble is that I keep refusing to die."

It was like the advice for learning the game of pattern-stones: the best way to get good was to play difficult opponents, over and over. The trouble with war was that practicing required people to die.

"You've done well for your armies, sir. But the enemy general is also good at using calendrical terrain, and they've demonstrated their ruthlessness. I don't see why you would pass up a terrain advantage."

Jedao cocked an eyebrow at her. "We're not. Everyone gets hypnotized by the high fucking calendar. Just because it enables our exotics doesn't mean that the corresponding terrain is the most favorable to our purpose. I've been reading the intel on Lanterner engineering. Our invariant drives are better than theirs by a good margin. Anyway, why the hell would they be so stupid as to engage us in terrain that favors us? I picked the timing for a reason. You keep trying to beat the numbers, Commander, when the point is to beat the *people*."

Menowen considered that. "You are being very patient with my objections," she said.

"I need you not to freeze up in the middle of the battle," Jedao said. "Although I would prefer for you to achieve that without my having to explain basics to you."

The insult had the desired effect. "I understand my duty," she said. "Do you understand yours?"

He wondered if he could keep her. Moth commanders who were willing to question him were becoming harder to find. His usual commanders would have had no doubts about his plan no matter how much he refused to explain in advance.

"As I see it," Jedao said, "my duty is to carry out the orders. See? We're not so different after all. If that's it, Commander, you should get back to work."

Menowen saluted him and headed for the door, then swung around. "Sir," she said, "why did you choose to serve with the Kel? I assume it was a choice." The Shuos were ordinarily seconded to the Kel as intelligence officers.

"Maybe," Jedao said, "it was because I wanted to know what honor looked like when it wasn't a triumphal statue."

Her eyes went cold. "That's not funny," she said.

"I wasn't being funny," he said quietly. "I will never be a Kel. I don't think like one of you. But sometimes that's an advantage."

She drew in a breath. "Sir," she said, "I just want to know that this isn't some Shuos game to you." That he wasn't being clever for the sake of being clever; that he wouldn't throw his soldiers' lives away because he was overeager to fight.

Jedao's smile was not meant to reassure her. "Oh, it's to your advantage if it's a game," he said. "I am very good at winning games."

He wasn't going to earn her loyalty by hiding his nature, so he wasn't going to try.

It was even easier to win games if you designed the game yourself, instead of playing someone else's, but that was a Shuos sort of discussion and he didn't think she wanted to hear it yet.

* * *

THE ELEVEN FANGMOTHS and seventy-three calendrical lenses approached Candle Arc only 1.3 hours behind schedule. Jedao was recovering the ability to read his watch, but the command center had a display that someone had enlarged for his benefit, so he didn't look at it. Especially since he had the sneaking feeling that his watch was off by a fraction of a second. If he drew attention to it, Captain-magistrate Korais was going to recalibrate it to the high calendar when they all had more important things to deal with.

The crews on the lenses had figured out how to simulate formations. No one would mistake them for Kel from close range, but Jedao wasn't going to let the Lanterners get that close.

"Word from the listening posts is that the Lanterners are still in pursuit," Communications informed them.

"How accommodating of them," Jedao said. "All right. Orders for the Rahal: The lenses are to maintain formation and head through the indicated channel"——he passed over the waypoint coordinates from his computer station——"to the choke locus. You are to *pass* the locus, then circle back toward it. Don't call us under any circumstances, we'll call you. And stick to the given formation and don't try any fancy modulations."

It was unlikely that the Rahal would try, but it was worth saying. The Rahal were going to be most convincing as a fake Kel swarm if they stayed in one formation because there wasn't time to teach them to get the modulation to look right. The formation that Jedao had chosen for them was Senner's Lash, partly because its visible effects were very short-range. When the Rahal failed to produce the force-lash, it wouldn't look suspicious because the Lanterners wouldn't expect to see anything from a distance.

"Also," Jedao said, still addressing the Rahal. "The instant you see something, anything on scan, you're to banner the Deuce of Gears."

The Deuce was his personal emblem, and it connoted "cog in the machine." Everyone had expected him to register some form of fox when he made brigadier general, but he had preferred a show of humility. The Deuce would let the Lanterners know who they were facing. It might not be entirely sporting for the Rahal to transmit it, but since they were under his command, he didn't feel too bad about it.

"The Rahal acknowledge," Communications said. Jedao's subdisplay showed them moving off. They would soon pass through the calendrical null, and at that point they would become harder to find on scan.

Commander Menowen was drumming her fingers on the arm of her chair, her first sign of nervousness. "They have no defenses," she said, almost to herself.

It mattered that this mattered to her. "We won't let the Lanterners reach them," Jedao said. "If only because I would prefer to spend my career not having the Rahal mad at me."

Her sideways glance was only slightly irritated. "Where are we going, sir?"

"Cut the mothdrives," Jedao said. He sent the coordinates to Menowen, Communications, and Navigation. "We're heading *there* by invariant drive only." This would probably prevent long-range scan from seeing them. "Transmit orders to all moths. I want acknowledgments from the moth commanders."

"There" referred to some battledrift, all sharp edges and ash-scarred fragments and wrecked silverglass shards, near the mouth of what Jedao had designated the Yellow Passage. He expected the Lanterners to take it toward the choke. Its calendrical gradient started in the Lanterners' favor, then zeroed out as it neared the null.

Depending on the Lanterners' invariant drives, it would take them two to three hours (high calendar) to cross the null region and reach the choke. This was, due to the periodic shifts, still faster than going around the null, because the detours would be through space hostile to their exotics for the next six hours.

Reports had put the Lanterners at anywhere from sixty to one hundred twenty combat moths. The key was going to be splitting them up to fight a few at a time.

Jedao's moth commanders acknowledged less quickly than he would have liked, gold lights coming on one by one.

"Formation?" Menowen prompted him.

There weren't a lot of choices when you had eleven moths. Jedao brought up a formation, which was putting it kindly because it didn't belong to Lexicon Primary for tactical groups, or even Lexicon Secondary, which contained all the obsolete formations and parade effects. He wanted the moths in a concave configuration so they could focus lateral fire on the first hostiles to emerge from the Yellow Passage.

"That's the idea," Jedao said, "but we're using the battledrift as cover. Some big chunks of dead stuff floating out there, we might as well blend in and snipe the hell out of the Lanterners with the invariant weapons." At least they had a good supply of missiles and ammunition, as Najhera had attempted to fight solely with exotic effects.

The Kel didn't like the word "snipe," but they were just going to have to deal. "Transmit orders," Jedao said.

The acknowledgments lit up again, about as fast as they had earlier.

The *Fortune Comes in Fours* switched into invariant mode as they crossed into the null. The lights became less white-gold and more rust-gold, giving everything a corroded appearance. The hum of the moth's systems changed to a deeper, grittier whisper. The moth's acceleration became noticeable, mostly in the form of pain. Jedao wished he had thought to take an extra dose of painkillers, but he couldn't risk getting muddled.

Menowen picked out a chunk of coruscating metals that had probably once been some inexplicable engine component on that long-ago space fortress and parked the *Fortune* behind it. She glanced at him to see if he would have any objections. He nodded at her. No sense in getting in the way when she was doing her job fine.

Time passed. Jedao avoided checking his watch every minute thanks to long practice, although he met Captain-magistrate Korais's eyes once and saw a wry acknowledgment of shared impatience.

They had an excellent view of the bridgelights even on passive sensors. The lights were red and violet, like absurd petals, and their flickering would, under other circumstances, have been restful.

"We won't see hostiles until they're on top of us," Menowen said.

More nerves. "It'll be mutual," Jedao said, loudly enough so the command center's crew could hear him. "They'll see us when they get that close, but they'll be paying *attention* to the decoy swarm."

She wasn't going to question his certainty in front of everyone, so he rewarded her by telling her. "I am sure of this," he said, looking at her, "because of how the Lanterner general destroyed Najhera. They were extremely aggressive in exploiting calendrical terrain and, I'm sorry to say, they made a spectacle of the whole thing. I don't imagine the Lanterners had time to swap out generals for the hell of it, especially one who had already performed well, so I'm assuming we're dealing with the same individual. So if the Lanterner wants calendrical terrain and a big shiny target, fine. There it is."

More time passed. There was something wrong about the high calendar when it ticked off seconds cleanly and precisely and didn't account for the way time crawled when you were waiting for battle. Among the many things wrong with the high calendar, but that one he could own to without getting called out as a heretic.

"The far terrain is going to shift in our favor in five hours, sir," Korais said.

"Thank you, good to know," Jedao said.

To distract himself from the pain, he was thinking about the bridgelights and their resemblance to falling petals when Scan alerted him that the Lanterners had shown up. "Thirty-some moths in the van," the officer said in a commendably steady voice. "Readings suggest more are behind them. They're moving rapidly, vector suggests they're headed down the Yellow Passage toward the choke locus, and they're using a blast wave to clear mines."

As if he'd had the time to plant mines down a hostile corridor. Good of them to think of it, though.

Menowen's breath hissed between her teeth. "Our *banner*—"

His emblem. The Kel transmitted their general's emblem before battle. "No," Jedao said. "We're not bannering. The Lanterners are going to be receiving the Deuce of Gears from *over there*," where the Rahal were.

"But the protocol, sir. The Rahal aren't part of your force," Menowen said, "they don't *fight*—"

That got his attention. "*Fledge*," Jedao said sharply, which brought her up short, "what the hell do you mean they're not fighting? Just because they're not sitting on a mass of things that go boom? *They're fighting what's in the enemy's head.*"

He studied the enemy dispositions. The Yellow Passage narrowed as it approached the null, and the first group consisted of eight hellmoths, smaller than fangmoths, but well-armed if they were in terrain friendly to their own calendar, which was not going to be the case at the passage's mouth. The rest of the groups would probably consist of eight to twelve hellmoths each. Taken piecemeal, entirely doable.

"They fell for it," Menowen breathed, then wisely shut up.

"General Shuos Jedao to all moths," Jedao said. "Coordinated strike on incoming units with missiles and railguns." Hellmoths didn't have good side weapons, so he wasn't as concerned about return fire. "After the first hits, move into the Yellow Passage to engage. Repeat, move into the Yellow Passage."

The fangmoths' backs would be to that damned null, no good way to retreat, but that would only motivate them to fight harder.

If the Lanterners wanted a chance at the choke, they'd have to choose between shooting their way through when the geometry didn't permit them to bring their numbers to bear in the passage, or else leaving the passage and taking their chances with terrain that shaded toward the high calendar. If they chose the latter, they risked being hit by Kel formation effects, anything from force lances to scatterbursts, on top of the fangmoths' exotic weapons.

The display was soon a mess of red lights and gold, damage reports. The computer kept making the dry, metallic click that indicated hits made by the Kel. Say what you liked about the Kel, they did fine with weapons.

Two hellmoths tried to break through the Kel fangmoths, presumably under the impression that the Rahal were the real enemy. One hellmoth took a direct engine hit from a spinal railgun, while the other shuddered apart under a barrage of missiles that overwhelmed the anti-missile defenses.

"You poor fools," Jedao said, perusing the summaries despite the horrible throbbing in his left eye. "You found a general who was incandescently talented at calendrical warfare, so you spent all your money on the exotic toys and ran out of funding for the boring invariant stuff."

Menowen paused in coordinating damage control—they'd taken a burst from an exploding scout, of all things—and remarked, "I should think you'd be grateful, sir."

"It's war, Commander, and someone always dies," Jedao said, aware of Korais listening in; aware that even this might be revealing too much. "That doesn't mean I'm eager to dance on their ashes."

"Of course," Menowen said, but her voice revealed nothing of her feelings.

The fangmoths curved into a concave bowl as they advanced up the Yellow Passage. The wrecked Lanterner hellmoths in the van were getting in the way of the Lanterners' attempts to bring fire to bear. Jedao had planned for a slaughter, but he hadn't expected it to work this well. They seemed to think his force was a detachment to delay them from reaching the false Kel swarm while the far terrain was hostile to the high calendar, and that if they could get past him before the terrain changed, they would prevail. It wasn't until the fourth group of Lanterners had been written into rubble and smoke that their swarm discipline wavered. Some of the hellmoths and their auxiliaries started peeling out of the passage just to have somewhere else to go. Others turned around, exposing their sides to further punishment, so they could accelerate back up the passage where the Kel wouldn't be able to catch them.

One of Jedao's fangmoths had taken engine damage serious enough that he had ordered it to pull back, but that left him ten to work with. "Formation Sparrow's Spear," he said, and gave the first set of targets.

The fangmoths narrowed into formation as they plunged out of the Yellow Passage and toward five hellmoths and a transport moving with the speed and grace of a flipped turtle. As they entered friendlier terrain, white-gold fire blazed up from the formation's primary pivot and raked through two hellmoths, the transport, and a piece of crystalline battledrift.

They swung around for a second strike, shifting into a shield formation to slough off the incoming fire.

This is too easy, Jedao thought coldly, and then.

"Incoming message from Lanterner hellmoth 5," Communications said. Scan had tagged it as the probable command moth. "Hellmoth 5 has disengaged." It wasn't the only one. The list showed up on Jedao's display.

"Hold fire on anything that isn't shooting at us," Jedao said. "They want to talk? I'll talk."

There was still a core of fourteen hellmoths whose morale hadn't broken. A few of the stragglers were taking potshots at the Kel, but the fourteen had stopped firing.

"This is Lieutenant Colonel Akkion Dhaved," said a man's voice. "I assume I'm addressing a Kel general."

"In a manner of speaking," Jedao said. "This is General Shuos Jedao. Are you the ranking officer?" Damn. He would have liked to know the Lanterner general's name.

"Sir," Menowen mouthed, "it's a trick, stop talking to them."

He wasn't sure he disagreed, but he wasn't going to get more information by closing the channel.

"That's complicated, General." Dhaved's voice was sardonic. "I have an offer to make you."

"I'm sorry," Jedao said, "but are you the ranking officer? Are you authorized to have this conversation?" He wasn't the only one who didn't like the direction of the conversation. The weight of collective Kel disapproval was almost crushing.

"I'm offering you a trade, General. You've been facing General Bremis kae Meghuet of the Lantern."

The name sounded familiar—

"She's the cousin of Bremis kae Erisphon, one of our leaders. Hostage value, if you care. You're welcome to her if you let the rest of us go. She's intact. Whether you want to leave her that way is your affair."

Jedao didn't realize how chilly his voice was until he saw Menowen straighten in approval. "Are you telling me you mutinied against your commanding officer?"

"She lost the battle," Dhaved said, "and it's either death or capture. We all know what the heptarchate does to heretics, don't we?"

Korais spoke with quiet urgency. "General. Find out if Bremis kae Meghuet really is alive."

Jedao met the man's eyes. It took him a moment to understand the expression in them: regret.

"There's a nine-hour window," Korais said. "The Day of Broken Feet isn't over."

Jedao gestured for Communications to mute the channel, which he should have done earlier. "The battle's basically won and we'll see the cascade effects soon," he said. "What do you have in mind?"

"It's not ideal," Korais said, "but a heretic general is a sufficient symbol." Just as Jedao himself might have been, if the assassin had succeeded. "If we torture kae Meghuet ourselves, it would cement the victory in the calendar."

Jedao hauled himself to his feet to glare at Korais, which was a mistake. He almost lost his balance when the pain drove through his head like nails.

Still, Jedao had to give Korais credit for avoiding the usual euphemism, *processed*.

Filaments in the feet. It was said that that particular group of heretics had taken weeks to die.

Fuck dignity. Jedao hung on to the arm of the chair and said, as distinctly as he could, "It's a trick. I'm not dealing with Dhaved. Tell the Lanterners we'll resume the engagement in seven minutes." His vision was going white around the edges, but he had to say this. Seven minutes wouldn't give the Lanterners enough time to run or evade, but it mattered. It mattered. "Annihilate anything that can't run fast enough."

Best not to leave Doctrine any prisoners to torture.

Jedao was falling over sideways. Someone caught his arm. Commander Menowen. "You ought to let us take care of the mopping up, sir," she said. "You're not well."

She could relieve him of duty. Reverse his orders. Given that the world was one vast blur, he couldn't argue that he was in any fit shape to assess the situation. He tried to speak again, but the pain hit again, and he couldn't remember how to form words.

"I don't like to press at a time like this," Korais was saying to Menowen, "but the Lanterner general—"

"General Jedao has spoken," Menowen said crisply. "Find another way, Captain." She called for a junior officer to escort Jedao out of the command center.

Words were said around him, a lot of them. They didn't take him to his quarters. They took him to the medical center. All the while he thought about lights and shrapnel and petals falling endlessly in the dark.

COMMANDER MENOWEN CAME to talk to him after he was returned to his quarters. The mopping up was still going on. Menowen was carrying a small wooden box. He hoped it didn't contain more medications.

"Sir," Menowen said, "I used to think heretics were just heretics, and death was just death. Why does it matter to you how they die?"

Menowen had backed him against Doctrine, and she hadn't had to. That meant a lot.

She hadn't said that she didn't have her own reasons. She had asked for his. Fair enough.

Jedao had served with Kel who would have understood why he had balked. A few of them would have shot him if he had turned over an enemy officer, even a heretic, for torture. But as he advanced in rank, he found fewer and fewer such Kel. One of the consequences of living in a police state.

"Because war is about people," Jedao said. "Even when you're killing them."

"I don't imagine that makes you popular with Doctrine," Menowen said.

"The Rahal can't get rid of me because the Kel like me. I just have to make sure it stays that way."

She looked at him steadily. "Then you have one more Kel ally, sir. We have the final tally. We engaged ninety-one hellmoths and destroyed forty-nine of them. Captain-magistrate Korais is obliged to report your actions, but given the numbers, you are going to get a lot of leniency."

There would have been around 400 crew on each of the hellmoths. He had already seen the casualty figures for his own fangmoths and the three Rahal vessels that had gotten involved, fourteen dead and fifty-one injured.

"Leniency wasn't what I was looking for," Jedao said.

Menowen nodded slowly.

"Is there anything exciting about our journey to Twin Axes, or can I go back to being an invalid?"

"One thing," she said. "Doctrine has provisionally declared a remembrance of your victory to replace the Day of Broken Feet. He says it is likely to be approved by the high magistrates. Since we didn't provide a heretic focus for torture, we're burning effigy candles." She hesitated. "He said he thought you might prefer this alternative remembrance. You don't want to be caught shirking this." She put the box down on the nearest table.

"I will observe the remembrance," Jedao said, "although it's ridiculous to remember something that just happened."

Menowen's mouth quirked. "One less day for publicly torturing criminals," she said, and he couldn't argue. "That's all, sir."

After she had gone, Jedao opened the box. It contained red candles in the shape of hellmoths, except the wax was additionally carved with writhing bullet-ridden figures.

Jedao set the candles out and lit them with the provided lighter, then stared at the melting figures. *I don't think you understand what I'm taking away from these remembrance days,* he thought. The next time he won some remarkable victory, it wasn't going to be against some unfortunate heretics. It was going to be against the high calendar itself. Every observance would be a reminder of what he had to do next—and while everyone lost a battle eventually, he had one more Kel officer in his corner, and he didn't plan on losing now.

DORMANNA

Gene Wolfe

Gene Wolfe lives in Barrington, Illinois. He is one of the genre's most widely respected writers. Adding to his many other awards, he was named a Grand Master by the Science Fiction Writers of America in 2013, was the first winner of the Chicago Literary Hall of Fame award in 2012, and was inducted into the Science Fiction Hall of Fame in 2009. Much of his finest shorter fiction was collected in *The Best of Gene Wolfe* (2009). *Shadows of the New Sun,* a tribute anthology edited by Bill Fawcett and J. E. Mooney, was published in 2013, and featured two new Wolfe stories. His last novel was *Home Fires,* and his forthcoming novel is *The Land Across.*

"Dormanna" was published at Tor.com as part of the Palencar Project and is based on a painting by John Jude Palencar. It is an interesting contrast to two of the other stories from this project reprinted here, by Michael Swanwick and Gregory Benford.

AT FIRST IT was a small voice, a tiny tingly voice that came by night. Ellie was almost asleep—no, she *was* asleep—when it arrived. It woke her.

"Hello," chirped the small voice. "Greetings, arrive Dutch, good-bye, and happy birthday. Is this the way you speak?"

Ellie, who had been dreaming about milking, was quite surprised to hear Florabelle talk.

"I am a friend, very small, from very far away. When others speak of you, horizontal one, what is it they say?"

She tried to think, at last settling on, "Isn't she a caution?"

"I see. Are you in fact a warning to others, Isn't She A Caution?"

Ellie murmured, "They don't pay me no mind, most times."

"That is sad, yet it may be well. Will you take me with you?"

She was almost awake now. "Where are we going?"

"You are to decide that, Isn't She A Caution. You may go anywhere. I ask to accompany you. Can you see me?"

Ellie turned her head to look at the pillow beside her. "Not yet."

"If you go to the heat spectrum?"

"I don't think so."

"Later then, when your star rises."

Her door opened. "Time to get up," Ellie's mother told her. "Get up and get dressed, honey. Pancakes 'n' bacon this mornin'."

"I have to go to school," Ellie told the small voice.

"And I, with you," it replied.

Ellie giggled. "You'll be gone when I get there."

"Not hope I."

The small voice said nothing while Ellie dressed. When she was cutting up her pancakes, she told her mother, "I had an imaginary friend this morning."

"Really? You haven't had one of those for quite a time."

"Well, I had one this morning. She came in a dream, only after I woke up—sort of woke up, anyway—she was still there. I've been trying to think of a name for an imaginary friend that comes when you're asleep. Can you think of one?"

"Hmmm," said her mother.

"I thought of Sleepy and Dreamy, but they sound like those little men that found Snow White."

"Sleepy *is* one of the Seven Dwarfs," Ellie's mother said.

"So I don't like those very much. You think of one."

"Dorma," Ellie's mother said after a sip of coffee.

"That's not Anna enough." Anna was Ellie's favorite doll.

"Dormanna then. Do you like that?"

Ellie rolled the name around in her mouth, tasting it. "Yes. I do. She's Dormanna, if she ever comes back."

A tiny voice chirped, "I am ungone, Isn't She A Caution. I watch, I taste, I listen."

"That's good," Ellie said.

Her mother smiled. "I'm glad you like it so much, Ellie."

"Ellie's my real name." Ellie felt she ought to straighten that out. "Not Isn't She A Caution. That's more of a nickname."

"I know, Ellie," her mother said. "I guess I use nicknames too much, but that's only because I love you."

"I love you, too, Mom." Ellie paused, struck by a sudden thought. "I guess that's a nickname, too. I ought to call you Elizabeth."

"Elizabeth is a fine name," Ellie's mother said, "but Mom and Momma are the finest, most honorable, names in the whole world. I'm hugely proud of them."

There was a knock at the kitchen door, a knock Ellie recognized. "Mr. Broadwick's here."

Ellie's mother nodded. There was something in her eyes that Ellie could not have put a name to. "Let him in, please."

He was tall and lean, and there was something in his face that made Ellie think of Lincoln's picture—not the one on the penny, but the one on the wall in Mrs. Smith's schoolroom. "I brought over some scrapple," he told Ellie's mother.

He cleared his throat. "I made it last night, only by the time I got done I figured you 'n' Ellie'd be asleep." He held out an old enameled pan with a lid and a handle.

"Why thank you, Don. I'm afraid it comes too late for Ellie and me this morning, but I'd be proud to cook some up for you and Betsy."

Ellie collected her lunch and her books, and slipped quietly out the door; neither her mother nor Mr. Broadwick appeared to notice.

"If you want to see me, put your finger in your ear," Dormanna told Ellie as she was walking down Windhill Road to the place where it crossed Ledbetter and the school bus stopped.

Ellie did.

"Now pull it out."

Ellie did that, too.

"Do you see me now?"

Ellie looked, squinting in the sunlight. "There's this little white blob on the end of my finger." She squinted again. "Sort of hairy."

"It is I, Ellie. You see me now. Did I pronounce your name correctly?"

"Sure. You ought to comb it."

"Those are my arms. With them I walk and swim and fly and do many other things. Now I hold on to your finger. Would you wish to see me fly?"

"Sure," Ellie said again. She herself had stopped walking and was standing in the dust at the edge of the road, staring at the tiny blob.

The tiny blob rose and seemed to float in the air an inch above the end of her finger. "Gosh!" Ellie exclaimed.

"Indeed, white is an impressive color. Do you like it?"

"I like it a lot," Ellie confessed. "White and pink and rose. Rose is my number-one favorite."

Dormanna promptly blushed rose. After that Ellie tried to return her to her ear, but got her into her hair instead. Dormanna said that was perfectly fine, and she would explore Ellie's hair and have an adventure.

On the bus Ellie decided that an adventure in hair would be an interesting thing to have, but she herself needed to be at her desk before the bell rang. As soon as she got off the bus, she put her lunch in her locker and opened her backpack to put her civics book on her desk. Class always started with civics this year.

"Today I'm going to begin with two hard questions," Mrs. Smith told the class. "They are questions I won't answer for you. You must answer them for yourselves. I know what my answers would be. Your answers don't have to be the same as mine to be right, and I want to emphasize that. They must be yours, however. You must believe them and be prepared to defend them."

Ellie could feel the tension in the room. She felt tense herself.

"Here's my first question. From the assignment you read last night, you know that nations are formed when tribes—whether they are called tribes or not—come together to form a larger political unit. You know that mutual defense is often given as the reason for this coming together. My question is, what reason *ought* to be given?"

In front of Ellie, Doug Hopkins squirmed in his seat.

"And here's my second question. Why are some nations so much richer than others? Raise your hand if you think you have a good answer to either question."

Mrs. Smith waited expectantly. "Come on, class! I'm sure all of you read the assignment, and many of you must have thought about it. Maybe all of you did. I certainly hope so."

Somewhere behind Ellie a hand went up. Ellie knew one had because Mrs. Smith smiled. "Yes, Richard. What's your answer?"

Dick Hickman said, "They should come together so that everybody will be happier. That's what I think."

Betsy Broadwick said, "Sometimes a lot of work takes more people."

Ellie whispered, "What is it, Dormanna?"

Mrs. Smith smiled again. "I can see you're thinking, Ellie. Tell the rest of us, please. Stand up."

Ellie stood. "I think the best reason for people coming together like that is so they won't fight each other. Only sometimes they come together but they fight anyway. That's the worst kind of fighting, because when anybody fights like that she's really fighting herself."

Softly, Mrs. Smith's hands met over and over again, applauding a dozen times or more. "Wonderful, Ellie. That's a perfectly wonderful answer. Don't sit down yet."

Ellie had begun to.

"Do you have an answer for our other question, too? I'd love to hear it."

Ellie hesitated, gnawing her lip. "I guess sometimes it's oil wells or gold mines or something. Only lots of rich countries don't have any of those. Then it's mostly the people, good people who work really hard." She paused, listening and longing to sit. "It's freedom, too. People who are free can do the kind of work they want to, mostly, like if they want to farm they can do it if they can get some land. It's people who want to farm who make the best farmers. So freedom and good laws." She sat.

She remained seated that afternoon, when school was over. When the last of her classmates had trooped out, Mrs. Smith said, "I believe you want to talk to me. Am I right, Ellie? What do you want to talk about?"

"I cheated, Mrs. Smith." It was said very softly. At Mrs. Smith's gesture, Ellie rose and came to stand beside Mrs. Smith's desk. "Those answers you liked so much? I—I . . . Well, I've got this imaginary playmate today and she told me."

Mrs. Smith smiled. "You have an imaginary playmate?"

"Yes, ma'am. I dreamed about her, only when I woke up she was still there. Still here, I mean. She wanted to go to school with me. I think she's still with me right now."

"I see. You don't know?"

Miserably, Ellie shook her head.

"Can I see her?" Mrs. Smith was still smiling.

"I don't think so." Ellie sounded doubtful and felt the same way. "She's real little and rose-colored, and she's in my hair. Her name's Dormanna."

"You don't have head lice, do you, Ellie? Are you telling me you have head lice?"

Ellie shook her head. "No, ma'am."

Mrs. Smith got a comb from her purse and parted Ellie's hair several times anyway.

"Did you find Dormanna?" Ellie wanted to know.

"No. No, I didn't. I didn't find any head lice, either. I'm glad of that. Now listen to me, Ellie. Are you listening?"

"Yes, ma'am."

"You didn't cheat. Answers you get from an imaginary playmate count as yours. You said we needed good laws."

Tentatively, Ellie nodded.

"That's one of them. Suppose I were to say that Paris is a beautiful city with wonderful churches and museums, and someone were to say, 'You cheated, Mrs. Smith. You've never been to Paris. You got that out of a book.'"

"That's not cheating," Ellie protested. "We learn things from books. That's what books are for."

"Exactly." Mrs. Smith nodded. "Learning from an imaginary playmate isn't cheating either. What you learn is coming from a hidden part of your mind. So it's yours, just as a fact I learn from a book becomes mine."

Betsy Broadwick had been picking wildflowers outside while she waited. "You're smiling," she said.

"It's okay," Ellie told her. Ellie's smile became a grin. "Everything's all right."

"We missed the bus."

"We can walk home," Ellie said. "The snow's gone, and everything's beautiful."

A tiny voice in Ellie's ear chirped, "Try to remember this, Ellie. Even when you are grown-up like your mother and Mrs. Smith, you will want to remember this."

"I won't forget," Ellie said.

Betsy stopped picking to look around at her. "Remember what?"

"To pick flowers for Mom," Ellie said hurriedly. "You're picking those for your dad, aren't you?"

Betsy nodded.

"Well, I think my mom would like some, too."

Betsy gestured at the patch of wildflowers.

"You found those," Ellie said, "and you were picking them. I didn't want to make you mad."

"You can pick too. I won't be mad."

Ellie picked. They were blue cornflowers and white-and-yellow daisies for the most part. When she got home, she put them in a mason jar with plenty of water before she presented them to her mother.

When supper was over and the washing-up was done, Ellie went upstairs to do her homework at the little table in front of her window.

That was when Dormanna, who had been quiet for a long, long while, spoke again. "Will you do me a favor, Ellie? It will only take you a brief time, but it will be a very big favor for someone as small as I am. Please? Isn't that what you say?"

"When we want a favor?" Ellie nodded vigorously. "Sure, Dormanna. Anything you want."

"Open the window? Please?"

"I'm supposed to keep it closed at night," Ellie said as she opened it, "but it's not night yet. Pretty soon it will be."

"I will be gone long before your star sets." For a moment, Dormanna was silent. "Will you remember this day, Ellie? The flowers and the sunshine, and me riding in your ear?"

"Forever and ever," Ellie promised.

"And I will remember you, Isn't She A Caution. Is it all right if I call you that again? Here, at the end? Already it has made me feel better."

Ellie nodded. There was something the matter in her throat. "There won't be any more imaginary friends, will there? You're the last, and when you're gone that will be over."

"I must rejoin all the other parts that make up our whole. Each of us returns with new data, Ellie, and the data I bear will be good for all your kind."

Ellie was not entirely sure she understood, but she nodded anyway.

"You spoke to Mrs. Smith of people coming together, many tribes uniting to create a great and powerful nation. We do that, too. We come together to make a great and powerful us. It is because we do it that I was able to tell you what I did. Look to the sky and you may see us, all of us as one."

Quite suddenly, there was a rose-colored Dormanna with many tiny limbs hanging in the air before Ellie's eyes. It said something more then, but though Ellie had good ears, she could not quite make out the words.

Very swiftly, Dormanna sailed out the window. Ellie had just time enough to wave before Dormanna vanished into the twilight. Ellie was still looking for her when she saw her mother. Her mother had come out of the house carrying a flower, and it was one of the daisies Ellie had picked, not one of the wild roses Mr. Broadwick had brought that evening.

While Ellie watched, she pulled off a petal and let it fall. Then another; and it seemed to Ellie that her lips were moving, though Ellie could hear no words.

Another petal . . . Then she froze, staring up into the darkling sky.

Ellie looked, too, and saw a thing impossibly huge with a thousand writhing arms, a thing darker than the clouds that for half a breath blushed rose as if dyed by the setting sun.

Ellie's mother never forgot the vast sky-thing as long as she lived. Neither has Ellie, who for some reason recalls it each time she kisses one of her granddaughters.

HOLMES SHERLOCK:
A HWARHATH MYSTERY

Eleanor Arnason

Eleanor Arnason lives in St. Paul, Minnesota. "I fell in love with science fiction in the 1950s, while living in Design House #2 behind the Walker Art Center in Minneapolis." Growing up in a cutting-edge house-of-the-future may have influenced her. The early TV show *Captain Video* certainly did. Since 1973, when she published her first story, she has published six novels, two chapbooks, and more than thirty short stories. Her fourth novel, *A Woman of the Iron People,* won the James Tiptree, Jr. Award and the Mythopoeic Society Award. Her fifth novel, *Ring of Swords,* won a Minnesota Book Award. Her short story "Dapple" won the Spectrum Award. Other short stories have been finalists for the Hugo, Nebula, Sturgeon, Sidewise, and World Fantasy awards. "Holmes Sherlock" is one of a group of stories which pretend to be fiction written by the *hwarhath,* an alien species first portrayed in *Ring of Swords,* after they encounter humanity. Another *hwarhath* story, "The Woman Who Fooled Death Five Times," also came out in 2012. A collection of non-hwarhath short stories, *Big Mama Stories,* came out in 2013, and another of Icelandic fantasy stories, *The Hidden Folk,* is forthcoming.

"Holmes Sherlock: A Hwarhath Mystery" was published on the excellent, short-lived Eclipse Online, another project of editor Jonathan Strahan. The droll, mature, deadpan voice of the *hwarhath* fits the Holmes template to a T. This is a story with wit and real Holmesian charm.

THERE WAS A woman who fell in love with the stories about a human male named Holmes Sherlock. Her name was Amadi Kla, and she came from a town on the northeast coast of the Great Northern Continent. It became obvious, when she was a child, that she was gifted at learning. Her family sent her to a boarding school and then to college in the capital city. There she learned several languages, including English, and became a translator, working for a government department in the capital.

She did not translate military information, since that was done by *hwarhath* men in space. Nor did she translate technical information, since she lacked the requisite technical knowledge. Instead, she translated human fiction. "There is much to be learned from the stories people tell," the foremost woman in her department said. "If we are going to understand humans, and we must understand them since they are our enemies, then we need to study their stories."

The fiction came out of computers in captured human warships. At first the Department of Translation picked stories out of the human computers randomly. Most were as bad as the novels read by *hwarhath* young men and women. But it turned out that the humans made lists of important stories, so their young people would know the stories they ought to read. Once these lists were found, the Department began to pick out famous and well-considered works for translating.

The foremost woman said, "It may be possible to learn about a culture by reading trivial fiction. There are people who will argue that. But humans are not a trivial species. They are clearly dangerous, and we should not underestimate them. If we study their least important work, we will decide they are silly. No one who can blow apart a *hwarhath* warship is silly."

After nine years in the capital, Kla began to long for the steep mountains, fjords and fogs of her homeland. She requested permission to work from home.

"This is possible," the foremost woman said. "Though you will have to fly here several times a year for meetings."

Kla agreed, though she did not like to fly, and went home by coastal freighter.

Her hometown was named Amadi-Hewil. It stood at the end of a fjord, with mountains rising above it. Most of the people belonged to one of two lineages, Amadi or Hewil, though there were some members of neighboring lineages; the government kept a weather station on a cliff above the fjord. The two men who cared for the station were soldiers from another continent. Of course they were lovers, since there were no other men of their age in the town. Almost all young males went into space.

Most of the people in the town—women, girls, boys, old men and old women—lived off fishing. The cold ocean outside their fjord was full of great schools of silver and copper-colored fish, insulated with fat. There was a packing plant at the edge of the town, that froze the fish or put it in cans; smaller operations made specialty foods: dried seaweed and smoked or pickled marine animals.

The town had rental apartments and rooms for fishers whose family homes were farther in the mountains. Kla decided to take one of these, rather than move back into one of the Amadi houses. She had gotten used to living on her own.

Her room was furnished with a bed, a table and two chairs. There was a bathroom down the hall. She had a window that looked out on a narrow street that went steeply down toward the harbor. There were plenty of electrical inlets, which was always good. She could dock her computer and her two new lamps on any wall. A shelf along one side of the room gave her a place for books and recordings. She settled in and began to translate.

It was in this period that she discovered Holmes Sherlock. There was little crime in her town, mostly petty theft and drunken arguments. But there was plenty of fog, rain and freezing rain. The street lamps outside her window glowed through grayness; she could hear the clink and rattle of carts pulled by *tsina*, coming in from the country with loads of produce.

The human stories seemed to fit with her new life, which was also her child-hood life. Much human fiction was disturbing, since it dealt with heterosexual love, a topic the *hwarhath* knew nothing about. Holmes Sherlock lived decently with a male friend, who might or might not be his lover. While the male friend, a doctor named Watson John, eventually took up with a woman, as humans were expected to, Holmes Sherlock remained indifferent to female humans.

The stories were puzzles, which Holmes Sherlock solved by reason. This appealed to Kla, who was not a romantic and who had to puzzle out the meaning of human stories, often so mysterious!

After a while, she went to a local craftsman and had a pipe made. It had a bent stem and a large bowl, like the pipe that Holmes Sherlock smoked in illustrations. She put a local herb into it, which produced an aromatic smoke that was calming when taken into the mouth.

Holmes Sherlock wore a famous hat. She did not have a copy of this made, since it looked silly, but she did take an illustration that showed his cape to a tailor. The tailor did not have the material called 'tweed,' but was able to make a fine cape for her out of a local wool that kept out rain and cold. Like Holmes Sherlock, Kla was tall and thin. Wearing her cape, she imagined she looked a bit like the famous human investigator.

For the rest, she continued to wear the local costume: pants, waterproof boots and a tunic with embroidery across the shoulders. This was worn by both women and men, though the embroidery patterns differed.

Twice a year she flew to the capital city and got new assignments. "You are translating too many of these stories about Holmes Sherlock," the foremost woman said. "Do it on your own time, if you must do it. I want stories that explain humanity. Therefore, I am giving you *Madame Bovary* and *The Journey to the West*."

Kla took these home, reading *Madame Bovary* on the long flight over winter plains and mountains. It was an unpleasant story about a woman trapped in a life she did not like. The woman—Bovary Emma—had a long-term mating contract with a male who was a dullard and incompetent doctor. This was something humans did. Rather than produce children decently through artificial insemination or, lacking that, through decent short-term mating contracts, they entered into heterosexual alliances that were supposed to last a lifetime.

These were often unhappy, as might be expected. Men and women were not that much alike, and most alliances—even those of women with women and men with men—did not last a lifetime. The *hwarhath* knew this and expected love to last as long as it did.

Bored by her "husband," a word that meant the owner of a house, Bovary Emma tried to make herself happy through sexual liaisons with other human males and by spending money. This did not work. The men were unsatisfactory. The spending led to debt. In the end, Bovary Emma killed herself, using a nasty poison. Her "husband" lived a while longer and—being a fool with no ability to remake his life—was miserable.

A ridiculous novel! Everyone in it seemed to be a liar or a fool or both. How could humans enjoy something like this? Yes, there was suffering in life. Yes, there were people who behaved stupidly. But surely a story this long ought to remind the reader—somewhere, at least a bit—of good behavior, of people who met their obligations, were loyal to their kin and knew how to be happy.

Maybe the book could be seen as an argument against heterosexual love.

When Kla was most of the way home, she changed onto a seaplane, which landed in her native fjord and taxied to dock. The fishing fleet was out. She pulled her bag out of the plane and looked around at the fjord, lined by steep mountains and lit by slanting rays of sunlight. The air was cold and smelled of salt water and the fish plant.

Hah! It was fine to be back!

She translated *Madame Bovary* and sent it to the foremost woman via the planet's information net. Then she went on to *Journey*, an adventure story about a badly behaved stone monkey. But the monkey's crimes were not sexual, and it was obvious that he was a trickster, more good than bad, especially after he finished his journey. Unlike Bovary Emma, he had learned from experience. Kla enjoyed this translation, though the book was very long.

While she was still working on the monkey's story, she met a woman who lived on another floor of her rooming house. The woman was short and stocky with pale gray fur and almost colorless gray eyes. She was a member of the Hewil lineage, employed by the fishing fleet as a doctor. She didn't go out with the boats. Instead, sick and injured fishers came to her, and the fleet paid her fees. Like Kla, she preferred to live alone, rather than in one of her family's houses. She walked with a limp, due to a childhood injury, and she enjoyed reading.

They began to meet to discuss books. The doctor, whose name was Hewil Mel, had read some of Kla's translations.

"Though I don't much enjoy human stories. They are too strange, and I can't tell what the moral is."

"I'm not sure there is one," Kla said and described *Madame Bovary*.

"I will be certain to avoid that one," Doctor Mel said firmly. "Do you think your translation will be published?"

"No. It's too disturbing. Our scientists will read it and make up theories about human behavior. Let me tell you about the story I am translating now."

They were walking along the docks on a fine, clear afternoon. The fleet was in, creaking and jingling as the boats rocked amid small waves. Kla told the story of the monkey.

"What is a monkey?" asked Doctor Mel.

"An animal that is somehow related to humans, though it has fur—as humans do not—and lives in trees."

When she finished with the story, leaving out a lot, because the book really was very long, Doctor Mel said, "I hope that one is published in our language."

"I think it will be, though it will have to be shortened, and there are some parts that will have to be removed. For the most part, it is decent. Still, it seems that humans can never be one hundred percent decent. They are a strange species."

"They are all we have," Doctor Mel said.

This was true. No other intelligent species had been found. Why had the Goddess given the *hwarhath* only one companion species in the vast darkness and cold of interstellar space? Especially since humans were more like the *hwarhath* than anyone had ever expected and also unpleasantly different. Surely if two similar species were possible, then many unlike species ought to be possible, but these had not been found; and why was a species so like the *hwarhath* so disturbing? Kla had no answer. The Goddess was famous for her sense of humor.

In the end, Kla and the doctor became lovers and moved to a larger apartment in a building with a view of the fjord. When she had free time, Kla continued to translate stories about Holmes Sherlock and handed them around to relatives, with the permission of the foremost woman. Some stories were too dangerous to spread around, but these were mostly safe.

"People need to get used to human behavior," the foremost woman said. "But not all at once. Eh Matsehar has done a fine job of turning the plays of Shakespeare William into work that we can understand. Now we will give them a little more truth about humans, though only in your northern town. Be sure you get your copies back, after people have read them, and be sure to ask the people what they think. Are they interested or horrified? Do they want to meet humans or avoid them forever?"

When Kla and the doctor had been together almost a year, something disturbing happened in the town; and it happened to one of Kla's remote cousins. The girl had taken a rowboat out into the fjord late one afternoon. She did not come back. In the morning, people went looking for her. They found the rowboat floating in the fjord water, which was still and green and so clear that it was possible to look down and see schools of fish turning and darting. The rowboat was empty, its oars gone. People kept searching on that day and days following. But the girl's body did not turn up, though the oars did, floating in the water only a short distance away.

The girl was a good swimmer, but the fjord was cold. She could have gotten hypothermia and drowned. But why had she gone out so late in the afternoon? And how had a child from a town full of skilled sailors managed to fall out of a boat and been unable to get back in? Where was her body? It was possible that the ebbing tide had pulled it out into the ocean, but this was not likely. She ought to be in the fjord, and she ought to float to the surface.

All of this together was a mystery.

After twenty days or thereabouts, Kla's grandmother sent for her. Of course she went, climbing the steep street that led to the largest of the Amadi houses, which was on a hill above the town. The house went down in layers from the hilltop, connected by covered stairways. Kla climbed these to the topmost building. Her grandmother was there, on a terrace overlooking the town and fjord. The day was mild. Nonetheless, the old lady was wrapped in a heavy jacket and had a blanket over her knees. A table with a pot of tea stood next to her.

"Sit down," the grandmother said. "Pour tea for both of us."

Kla did.

"You still wear that absurd cape," the grandmother said.

"Yes."

"I have read some of your stories about the human investigator."

"Yes?" Kla said. "Did you like them?"

"They seemed alien." The grandmother sipped her tea, then said, "We have a mystery in our house."

Kla waited.

"The girl who vanished," her grandmother said after a moment. "People are saying she must have weighted herself down and jumped into the water deliberately. Otherwise, her body would have appeared by now. This is possible, I think. But we don't know why. She had no obvious reason. Her mother is grieving, but refuses to believe the girl is gone. I would like you to investigate this mystery."

"I am a translator, not an investigator."

"You have translated many stories about investigation. Surely you have learned something. We have no one else, unless we send to the regional government or the capital. I would like to keep whatever has happened private, in case it turns out to be shameful."

Kla considered, looking down at the green fjord, edged with mountains. Rays of sunlight shone down through broken clouds, making the water shine in spots. "I will have to talk to people in this house and look at the girl's computer."

"The girl erased all her files and overwrote them. We have not been able to recover anything. That is a reason to think she killed herself."

"Then she must have had a secret," Kla said.

"But what?" the grandmother said. "It's hard to keep secrets in a family or a small town."

Kla could not refuse. Her grandmother was asking, and the woman was an important matriarch. In addition, she wanted to see if she could solve a mystery. She tilted her head in agreement and finished her tea. "Tell the people in the house I will be asking questions."

"I will do that," the grandmother said. "The girl was only eighteen, not yet full grown, but she was clever and might have become an imposing woman. I want to know what happened."

Two days later, Kla went back to the house and questioned the women who had known the girl, whose name was—or had been—Nam.

A quiet girl, they told her. She had no close friends in the family or elsewhere. When she wasn't busy at household tasks or studying, she liked to walk in the mountains around the town. She always carried a camera and did fine landscape photography.

One aunt said, "I expected her to go to an art school in the capital. She had enough talent."

"Can I see her work?" Kla asked.

"Most is gone. It was on her computer. You know she erased it?"

"Yes."

"But some of us have photographs she gave us. I'll show you."

Kla followed the woman around the Amadi house. The photographs hung on walls in public and private rooms. They were indeed fine: long vistas of mountain valleys and the town's fjord, close-ups of rocks and low vegetation. The girl had potential. It was a pity she was gone.

Kla went home to her apartment and filled her pipe with herb, then smoked, looking out at the docks and the water beyond. When Doctor Mel came home from looking at a fisher with a bad fracture, Kla described her day.

"What will you do next?" Mel asked.

"Find out where the girl went on her walks. Do you want to come with me?"

"With my leg? I'm not going to limp through the countryside."

"Let's rent *tsina* and ride," Kla said.

They went the next day, which was mild though overcast. Now and then, they felt fine drops of rain. The *tsina* were docile animals, used to poor riders, which was good, since neither Kla nor the doctor was a practiced traveler-by-*tsina*.

They visited the town's outlying houses. Most were too far away to be reached by walking. Nonetheless, they contained relatives, Amadi or Hewil, though most of these were not fishers. Instead, they spent their days herding or tending gardens that lay in sheltered places, protected by stone walls. Some of these people remembered the girl. They had seen her walking along farm roads and climbing the hillsides. A shy lass, who barely spoke. She always carried a camera and took pictures of everything.

Some had photographs she had given them, fastened to the walls of herding huts: favorite livestock, the mountains, the huts themselves. The girl did have an eye. Everything she photographed looked true and honest, as sharp as a good knife and balanced like a good boat that could ride out any storm.

"This is a loss," Doctor Mel said.

"Yes," Kla replied.

After several days of exploring the nearby country, they returned their *tsina* to the town stable and went home to their apartment. A fog rolled in at evening, hiding the fjord and the neighboring houses. Streetlights shone dimly. Sounds were muffled. Kla smoked her pipe.

"What next?" the doctor asked.

"There are paths going up the mountains above the fjord. No one lives up there, except the two soldiers at the weather station. We'll ask them about the girl."

"It's too steep for me," Doctor Mel said.

Kla tilted her head in agreement. "I'll go by myself."

The next day she did. The fog had lifted, but low clouds hid the mountain peaks. The fjord's water was as gray as steel. Kla took a staff and leaned on it as she climbed the narrow path that led to the station. Hah! It seemed perilous! Drop offs went abruptly down toward the gray water. Cliffs hung overhead, seeming ready to fall. She was a townswoman, a bit afraid of heights, though she came of mountain ancestry. Her gift was language and a curious mind.

The station was a prefab metal building, set against the cliff wall. Beyond it was a promontory overlooking the fjord. Equipment stood there, far more complicated than an ordinary weather station. Well, it was maintained by the military. Who could say what they were watching, even here on the safe home planet? No doubt important women knew what was going on here.

A soldier came out of the prefab building, a slim male with dark grey fur. He wore shorts and sandals and an open jacket.

Casual, thought Kla.

"Can I help you?" he asked.

She explained that she was looking for people who had met Amadi Nam, a shy girl who loved to photograph.

"No such person has been here," the soldier replied.

"Hah!" said Kla and looked at the magnificent view of the fjord beyond the equipment.

Now the second soldier appeared. He was the same height as the first male, but much broader with thick, white fur that was lightly spotted. He also wore shorts, but no jacket. His fur must be enough, even on this cool, damp day.

He agreed with the first man. The girl had never been to the station.

Kla thanked them and went back down the mountain. She arrived home at twilight. Lamps shone in the apartment windows. The electric heater in the main room was on. Doctor Mel had bought dinner, fish stew from a shop in town.

They ate, then Kla smoked, settled in a low chair close to the heater. Doctor Mel turned on her computer and watched a play on the world information net, her injured leg lifted up on a stool. Kla could hear music and cries of anger or joy. But the dialogue was a mumble, too soft to understand.

The play ended, and Doctor Mel turned the computer off. "Well?"

"I have a clue," answered Kla.

"You do?"

Kla knocked the dottle out of her pipe. "It is similar to the dog that made noise in the night time."

"What is a dog?"

"A domestic animal similar to a *sul*, though smaller and less ferocious. The humans use them to herd and guard, as we use *sulin*. In this case, in a story you have apparently not read, the dog did not make any noise."

"Kla, you are being irritating. What are you trying to say?"

"The dog did not do what was expected, and this was the clue that enabled Holmes Sherlock to solve the problem."

"You met a *sul* on the mountain?"

"I met two young men who said they never met my cousin, though she climbed every slope in the area and loved to photograph splendid vistas."

"They are lying?"

"Almost certainly."

"Why?"

"I have no idea."

Doctor Mel looked confused. "They belong to far-off lineages and have no relatives in town. Why would they become involved in something here? If Amadi Nam had been a boy, one might suspect a romance. But she was a girl, and the soldiers are lovers, as everyone knows."

"This is true," Kla replied. "But I am certain the soldiers are lying. I need to confront them."

Doctor Mel rose and went to pour two cups of *halin*. She gave one to Kla and settled back in her chair. "If they are telling the truth, they will think you are crazy and may tell people in town. You will have to endure joking. More important, if they are lying, then they are crazy and may be dangerous. I'd go with you, except for the climb."

"I'll go to my grandmother tomorrow and explain the situation. She will know what to do."

"Good," said Doctor Mel.

The next day was clear and cold. Ice rimmed puddles in the streets and made the street paving stones slippery. Kla could see her breath.

Her grandmother was inside, next to an old-fashioned brazier full of glow-ing coals.

"Help yourself to tea and pour a cup for me," the old lady said. "Then tell me what you have found."

Kla did as she was told. When she had finished her story, the matriarch said, "The soldiers must be confronted."

"My lover has suggested that they may be dangerous."

"Hardly likely. But this story is disturbing. Something unpleasant has hap-pened." Her grandmother drank more tea. "I want to keep this in the family. I'll pick two of your cousins, large and solid fisher-women. They'll go with you up the mountain. Even if the soldiers are crazy, they will hardly do harm to three women, all larger than they are, though you are thin. The fishers will not be."

A day later, Kla went back up the weather station. It was another clear, cold day. The fjord sparkled like silver.

The two fisher-women were named Serit and Doda. Both were second cous-ins to Kla, and both were tall and broad, with big knives in their tunic belts. Serit carried a harpoon gun, and Doda had a club.

"Is that necessary?" Kla asked.

"Always be provided," Serit replied in a deep, calm voice.

"The soldiers have been trained for war," Doda added. "But the war they were trained to fight is fought by ships in space. How can that help them here? We, by contrast, have struggled with many large and dangerous fish, while the fish thrashed on the decks of our boats. If the soldiers threaten us, though that does not seem likely, we will know what to do."

When they reached the station, both men came out.

"How can we help?" the dark soldier asked.

"We are certain Amadi Nam came here," Kla said. "Since you lied about this, we are going to search your building."

What did she hope to find? Some evidence that Nam had been there—a picture that had been printed out or her camera, full of pictures. People did not easily throw away Amadi Nam's work.

The dark soldier frowned. "This is a military installation. You can't exam-ine our equipment or building until you get permission from the officers in front of us."

Serit lifted the harpoon gun. "This is not space, where your senior officers make decisions. This is our town, our country and our planet. Our senior women are in charge, and you are here on this mountain with their—and our—permission. If we want to know what you do in your building, we have the right."

"We will go in," Kla said.

"Women do not fight and kill," the dark soldier said, as if trying to reassure himself.

"What nonsense," Serit replied. "Doda and I fight large and dangerous fish and other sea animals."

"But not people," the dark soldier said.

"Of course not. We are fishers, and we are still young. But who decides which newborn children will live? Who gives death to those who have nothing left but suffering?"

"The old women," said the spotted soldier in a resigned tone.

"So," Serit continued in a tone of satisfaction. "Women can fight, and we are able to kill. We will go into this building."

Kla felt uneasy. As a rule, men and women did not interfere with each other's activities. If it had been up to her, she would have waited for the soldiers to consult their senior officers, though she suspected they were stalling. What did they have hidden which could be better hidden, if they had time?

But her grandmother had picked Serit and Doda. She must have known how aggressive they were.

The spotted soldier exhaled. "I will not fight women, Perin, even for you."

The dark soldier made the gesture that meant be quiet!

So, thought Kla, there was a secret. "I will go in and search. The two of you watch the soldiers."

Doda made the gesture of assent, and Serit tilted her head in agreement.

Kla entered the building. It was messy, as was to be expected, with two young men living alone, no senior officers near them. Unwashed dishes stood on tables. The beds were unmade. Kla saw no sign of the girl, even in the closets and under the beds. But there were pieces of paper tucked between one bed and the wall. She pulled them out, surprised that she had noticed them. Printouts of photographs. They showed the green fjord, the black and white surrounding mountains, and the dark soldier, Perin.

She took the printouts into sunlight. "What are these?"

"I took them," the spotted man said quickly.

This was almost certainly a lie. Kla knew Nam's work when she saw it. She gave the printouts to Doda and went back in the building, going through it a second time. An uncomfortable experience! She was a translator, not someone who poked around in other people's homes.

This time she found the girl, wedged into a low cabinet and folded over like the kind of scissors that bend back on themselves, the blade points touching the handles.

"Come out," said Kla.

"No," said the girl, her voice muffled.

"Don't be ridiculous," Kla replied. "I might not be able to get you out, but I have two large, strong fisher-women with me. They can easily pull you from that hole."

After a moment or two, the girl squeezed herself out, groaning as she did so. Once she was upright, Kla could see her clearly. A plump young woman with badly rumpled clothing and fur. She looked miserable and angry.

Kla gestured, and the girl followed her outside.

"Now," Kla said to the girl and the soldiers. "What is this about?"

The girl looked sullen. The soldiers looked more unhappy than before. No one spoke.

"Very well," Kla said. "We will all go to see my grandmother. If the girl has a jacket, get it."

The spotted soldier did.

"Put it on and pull the hood up," Kla said to the girl. "I don't want people to know you are alive, until Grandmother has made a decision."

The girl obeyed, and they all went down the mountain, Serit last, holding the harpoon gun ready.

Once again her grandmother sat by an old-fashioned brazier, though it was difficult to see the glow of the coals this time. The room was full of sunlight, coming in through east-facing windows. The red floor tiles shone, and it was easy to see the paintings on the walls: flowers and flying bugs.

Doda pushed the girl in front of the old woman, then pulled back her hood.

"Well," the old lady said. "You've had all of us worried, Nam." Then she glanced around at everyone. "Pull up chairs. I will hurt my neck, if I look up at you."

The men brought chairs from the walls and arranged them in front of the old woman.

"Sit!" Kla's grandmother said. "You found Nam at the weather station. That much is evident. But why was she there? Why was the boat left floating empty? And why was her computer erased?"

"I think the soldier with spots might tell us," Kla answered. "He seems to be the most reasonable of the three."

The man clasped his hands tightly together. "I know I am dead. May I tell this the way it happened?"

"Yes," said the grandmother. "But try to be brief. And tell me your name."

"I am Sharim Wirn."

"Go on."

"My lover always took walks. I did more of the work than he did, but willingly, out of love. Recently, he has taken longer walks, and I began to notice food was disappearing. I do the accounting. I knew how much food we bought and how much we usually ate." The man paused, glancing briefly at his comrade. "I thought he might have a new lover. But where had he found the man? And why would he feed him? It made no sense. So I followed Perin. He went to a cave in the mountains. I went inside after him, expecting to find Perin with another man. Instead, I found him with the girl, sitting by a little fire and sharing food. Not eating with her, that would be indecent, but giving her food from our supplies.

"I asked what this was about. At first he refused to speak. At last, he told me the story. He had met the girl during his walks. They both liked the mountains, and they were both solitary. The girl had no one to love, apparently, and Perin had only me. I was not enough." The soldier's voice was bitter. "They began by talking and ended by having sex."

The two fishers drew breath in sharply. Kla's grandmother hissed. Kla was too shocked to make a noise. Men and women had mated in the past, before artificial insemination, but only after their families had agreed to a breeding contract, and only to make children. Of course there had been perverts. But they were not common, and she had never expected to meet any. She certainly had not expected to have one in her family.

"Go on," the grandmother said, sounding angry.

"The girl became pregnant and came to Perin, insisting on his help," the spotted soldier went on. "He knew he would be told to kill himself, if this story became known. So he hid the girl, until I found them. I insisted on bringing her to our building. The cave was cold and damp. She would become sick. I was not willing to be responsible for the death of a woman, even one as foolish and selfish as this girl."

He lifted his head, glancing briefly at the old lady. "I know that I should have told my senior officers, but I loved Perin. I knew he would die for what he did, and it would be my fault for telling. I could not bear the idea of him dying."

"How could you love him after he had sex with a woman?" Serit asked.

The man looked down at his clasped hands. "I don't know. But it became obvious to me, after spending time with her, that the girl has the stronger will. I believe she seduced him; and then she entangled him with her plan."

This did not seem likely. Nam was only eighteen, two years away from adulthood.

Kla looked at the girl and saw her grim, determined, angry face.

"What plan?" asked the grandmother.

"She emptied her computer, so no one would know where she had been and what she photographed; and then she left evidence of her death—the boat, floating in the fjord, empty. Then she went to Perin and insisted on his help. He had no choice. If she told her family—you—what had happened, he would die. Or if not that—his family has influence—he would get a really bad assignment.

"She could not stay here in this town, because her family would discover what she'd done. And she could not travel while pregnant. A woman alone in that condition would arouse too much interest and concern. People would stop her and offer help or ask about her family. Where were they? Why was she alone?"

"You say that you love this man Perin, but now you tell this terrible story," Kla's grandmother said.

"There is no good ending," the spotted soldier replied. "If the girl gave birth, she would do it alone, with no one to help except Perin and me. Hah! That was frightening! If the child lived, what would happen to it? Children don't appear out of nowhere. They are the result of breeding contracts. They have families. No mother with a child is ever alone."

"This is true," Kla's grandmother said.

"It became apparent to me that the child would die, even if it was healthy. How else could Perin and the girl hide what they had done?" He paused and took a deep breath. "The girl said she would travel to the capital after the child was born. There are people there who live in the shadows and make a living in irregular ways. She planned to become one of those. She never spoke of the child.

"All the time, while this was happening, my love for Perin was wearing away. How could he be so stupid? It was obvious to me that the girl had the stronger will. He was acting the way he did out of weakness and fear of discovery. I would have told your family or my senior officers, except by this time I had gotten myself entangled. I was at fault. I would be told to kill myself, once this was known."

"True," said Kla's grandmother. She looked at Nam. "Well, child, why did you do this?"

"I love him," Nam said stubbornly, though Kla was not sure the girl meant it. How could love endure this mess?

"How can you?" the old lady asked. "He is male."

"I cannot change what I feel."

"Certainly you can."

"No," the girl replied.

"Tell them all to kill themselves," Serit put in. "They are disgusting."

The old woman looked at Kla. "You have studied human crimes. What is your advice?"

"Two suicides close together would cause talk," Kla replied. "Though we might say it was some kind of lovers' quarrel. But why would both commit suicide? No one was stopping their love. It would be a mystery. There would be talk and wondering and possibly an investigation by military. We don't want that.

"As for the girl, everyone thinks she is dead. But we would have to hide her body, if she killed herself. Otherwise, people would wonder where she had been before her death. And she is pregnant. That's another problem. If Sharim Wirn is right, the girl planned to kill the child or let it die. We have no reason to believe the child is defective. I am not comfortable doing what the mother planned to do."

"Yes." The grandmother leaned back in her chair and closed her eyes. "Be quiet, all of you. I need to think."

They sat, as sunlight moved across the floor and out of the room. Kla needed to pee and would have liked a cup of tea or *halin*. But she kept still.

At last, the grandmother opened her eyes. "The important thing to keep this story secret. One solution would be for all three of you to die. But as Kla says, that might cause talk and wondering; and there is the problem of the child. So—" She gestured at the two soldiers. "You will volunteer for service in space, far out in the war zone, where you will not meet women. My family has relatives who are important in the military. They will make sure you get the assignments you desire.

"As for you, Nam, you will stay in this house until your child is born. You have a cousin who is pregnant now. We will say that she had twins. I am not comfortable with this, since I will be deceiving the lineage that provided semen for your cousin. But we do what we have to do; and I hope you are ashamed at the lies you are forcing your relatives to tell."

Kla looked at the girl. She did not show any evidence of shame.

"After the child is born—" the grandmother said. "I will give you two choices. Either you can stay here and study art on the world information net, or you can leave and go into the shadows. If you stay here, we will watch you for further signs of misbehavior. We cannot trust you, Nam. You have initiative, a strong will, no self-control and no sense of family obligation. This is a dangerous combination."

"I will go," Nam said.

The grandmother exhaled. "If you want to live in the shadows in the capital, fine! But don't tell anyone your family name."

"I won't," the girl said. "I despise all of you and this town."

"Why?" asked Kla, surprised.

"Look at you," the girl said. "In your silly cape, pretending to be a human."

"What harm does it do?" Kla asked.

"And you," the girl stared at Kla's grandmother. "Pretending that none of this happened, because you are afraid of gossip."

"Gossip can cause great harm," the old lady said.

"The world is changing," Nam said. "There are aliens in the sky! But your lives remain the same, full of fear and pretense."

"There are no aliens in the sky," Kla's grandmother said firmly. "The humans remain a long distance from our home system." She paused for a moment. "I hope your child has your gift for art, without your difficult personality. This has been an unpleasant conversation. I'm tired now. I want to take a nap. Everyone go."

"You stay in the house," Serit said to Nam. "We don't want anyone outside the family to know you are alive."

The girl made the gesture of assent, though she looked sullen.

Kla left the house with the soldiers. "Thank you," the spotted soldier said before they parted. "You said that our suicides would cause talk. For this reason, Perin and I will remain alive."

"Behave better in the future," Kla said.

The man showed his teeth in a brief smile. "We will have no chance to behave badly in a war zone." He glanced around at the mountains. "I will miss this country. But space may be safer."

The two men took off, walking rapidly. They kept well apart, as people do who have quarreled.

Kla went back to her apartment. It was late afternoon by now, and the sun was behind the mountains, though the light still touched the high peaks, streaked with a little snow. The fjord was still and gray.

Doctor Mel was in the main room, drinking tea. Kla sat down and told the story. Even though Mel belonged to another lineage, she was a doctor and knew how to keep secrets.

At the end, Mel said, "You have solved your mystery."

"It's an ugly story," Kla said. "I wish I still believed the girl had drowned."

"That is wrong," Mel said firmly. "Her life may be hard, but she still has a future. The dead have nothing." She refilled her cup and poured tea for Kla. "Most likely, she will give up her unnatural interest in men. If she does not— well, there are people in the shadows who know about contraceptives."

"There are?" Kla asked.

Mel grinned briefly. "You know more about crime in the ancient human city of London than you know about bad behavior here. Of course there are *hwarhath* who behave in ways we do not find acceptable; and of course these folk learn to deal with the consequences of their behavior. Doctors know this, though we rarely talk about it."

"In the stories I have translated, the solution to the puzzle is satisfying. The ending seems neat and finished, though—of course—I don't understand everything. Humans are alien, after all. I can translate their words, but not their minds. This ending does not satisfy," Kla said.

"How could it? Most likely the young men will be fine, once they are in a military unit with officers to watch them; and most likely the child will be fine, born in your grandmother's house and raised by members of your family. But the girl is an unsolved problem. Maybe she will decide to stay here and study photography. Her work is full of possibility."

"I don't believe she'll stay. She is angry, though I don't know why. Maybe it is shame. She said our lives are full of fear and pretense."

"We live with rules and obligations," Doctor Mel said. "Most of us fear what will happen if we break the rules; and we may—as in this case—pretend that a rule has not been broken, rather than deal with the idea of broken rules. Is this wrong? I don't think so. I would not like to live in chaos, without the net of kinship that holds us all, and without front-and-back relations. The girl may want more honesty. However, most of us want a comfortable life."

Mel paused, obviously thinking. "The girl is right about one thing. Our universe is changing in ways that people could not have imagined a century ago. Look at your job, translating human literature. It did not exist in the past.

Now, through your work, we learn about Holmes Sherlock and the shadows of London, also that irritating woman who lived in her own shadow."

"Bovary Emma. That translation will never be released. It is too disturbing."

Mel smiled briefly. "See how we protect ourselves!"

"Rightly!"

Mel gave Kla a look of affectionate amusement, then continued her line of thought, like a *sul* following a scent. "There have always been people who feel constrained by our rules. Most stay in their families and are unhappy. Others leave, going into the shadows. Some are criminals. Others are outcasts or eccentrics. Doctors know about them, because we must watch everyone—even people who are difficult—for signs of illness. Public health requires that we treat everyone, even those we don't approve of.

"Is it possible to be happy in shadows? I think so. Holmes Sherlock was happy, though he lived outside a family and made his own rules, and so was Watson John, who was odd enough to enjoy living with Holmes Sherlock. The irritating woman—remind me of her name."

"Bovary Emma."

Doctor Mel tilted her head in thanks. "Was unhappy, but she does not sound—from your description—like a person able to live a difficult life. Or even an ordinary life."

"These are humans, and they are imaginary!"

"We can still learn from them. We can always learn from other people."

"Are you saying the girl might be happy, even among outcasts?" Kla asked.

"Happier than in her—your—family. I will give you a name. Please give it to Nam before she leaves home. It's a doctor in the capital city, a good woman who treats people in the shadows and collects art. She can help Nam get settled. If she likes Nam's work, she can find a dealer-in-art. A good photographer should not be wasted."

Kla looked at Mel with speculation. This woman she loved, who lived in a small town and treated the injuries of fishers, knew more about people than she did, although she had lived in the capital city and had been translating human novels for years. People were more difficult to understand than she had believed, even the people she loved. But Mel was right. A good photographer should not be wasted. Maybe this situation would work out. Best of all, the disturbing girl would be gone from Kla's life.

Doctor Mel got up and limped to the room's window. After a moment, Kla joined her. The street lamps were on, and lights shone on the fishing boats anchored by the docks. High up on the mountain, a gleam showed that the soldiers were home.

ELECTRICA

Sean McMullen

Sean McMullen is an Australian SF and fantasy author living in Melbourne, although he is published mostly in the United States and Europe. He has had seventeen books and eighty stories published, has won fifteen awards, and had his first short movie, *Hard Cases,* produced in 2012. His writing is darkly humorous, fast-paced, and often steampunk in theme. He has just compiled two collections for his first venture into e-books, *Colours of the Soul* and *Ghosts of Engines Past.* He works with extremely large computers in his day job, has a Ph.D. in medieval fantasy literature, and is a karate instructor at the Melbourne University Karate Club.

"Electrica" was published in *F&SF,* which had a strong year in 2012, contributing four stories to this book. McMullen says, "There is more to the Regency period than Jane Austen, the Napoleonic Wars, and Frankenstein—it is also the forgotten birthplace of steampunk. Not only were the dead being brought back to life in literature, in 1803, Professor Giovani Aldini conducted a real experiment in London using electrical stimulation to revive the body of a fresh corpse. The corpse did not revive, but more successful were the period's semaphore towers, batteries, electrostatic generators, steam trains, military balloons, electric lights, and punched card programming." The secret war of Napoleonic codebreaking and communication may not seem like the stuff of romance, heroism, duels, infidelity, and science fiction, but all of that features strongly in "Electrica."

MAJOR GEORGE SCOVILLE:

Dear George,
    I trust that this message finds you well, and that the fortunes of war continue to favour you. As you have doubtless heard, good fortune has certainly not been with me on my most recent mission.

I am aware that a great many rumours now surround my name. Some damn me as a rake and a wastrel, others declare me to be a hero. Like yourself, I have done great damage to the armies of Napoleon in Portugal and Spain, yet I have never considered myself to be a hero. As for being a rake and a wastrel, does it matter how I have behaved as long as it was in the service of the crown?

I know as well as yourself that one does not achieve glory by sitting at a desk and breaking enemy codes, but one does win wars. Glory does not interest me, so all I now ask is that I be allowed to return to your staff and resume my code breaking work against the French. In support of my request, I respectfully submit this account of my mission in England from June to August in this year, 1811. I am aware that it will not clear my name of scandal; my intention is only to show that I acted in the best interests of Britain at all times.

I COULD EASILY read the messages being sent by the semaphore tower on Southsea Common as I approached Major Jodrel's offices in Portsmouth. The code was laughably simple, but the information was only about shipping movements in the harbour. I noted the name of the sloop *Dauntless*, which had just brought me from Lisbon.

I had a book in my hand when I arrived at the offices, and was all ready to spend an hour or two waiting until I was sent for. Instead I was ushered straight in, for *he* had been waiting for *me*. This was a surprise. Majors never wait for second lieutenants unless they carry important dispatches, and I was carrying only a copy of *The Vicar of Wakefield*.

"The major is not one for foppish talk, so don't bother with gossip or dropping names," said his aide as we climbed the stairs.

"Then we have that much in common," I replied.

"He also hates flattery, so let that be your last compliment. The major has a theory that polite chit-chat between officers is sapping the strength of the British Army. Let him do the talking, and answer his questions as briefly as possible."

I entered Jodrel's room and stood to attention. Without even greeting me he gestured through the window.

"Look out there, Lieutenant Fletcher," he said. "What do you see?"

"It's a Murray semaphore tower, sir."

"Very good—oh, and do stand easy. Yes, the signaling line runs from that tower out there to towers on Portsdown Hill, Beacon Hill, Blackdown, Hascombe, Netley Heath, Cabbage Hill, Putney Heath, Chelsea, and finally the Admiralty in London. If I send a message from here, it will reach London in nine minutes. Britain's been using the Murray shutter system for the past fourteen years. The French have a different signal-tower system, but both have the same flaw. Can you tell me what it is?"

"You can see them, sir. Anyone hiding nearby with a paper and pencil can see what's being transmitted and write it down. Even coded messages can be broken."

"You have it," said Jodrel, slapping a fist into the palm of his hand. "The transmission of the message is swifter than horses, but it is exceedingly public. One might as well publish military secrets in a newspaper."

I nodded and gave a discreet smile. Second lieutenants who wanted to become first lieutenants were expected to smile when their betters made a joke.

Major Jodrel continued, "Certain very clever people have had great success breaking the codes in captured French dispatches for General Wellesley in Spain, and there are probably Frenchmen who can do as well with our codes. If we could send messages invisibly, however, spies would have nothing to watch and written dispatches would be a thing of the past. We would gain a huge advantage over the French."

"There are carrier pigeons, sir. The Indians use them."

"And there are marksmen with birdshot. The French will use them at the sight of our first carrier pigeon. No, Lieutenant, we need a method of messaging that cannot be seen. Three years ago a man named Sir Charles Calder proposed a method of invisible messaging to me. Come along. I'll show you his device."

Sir Henry led me up more stairs and unlocked the door to a garret. Within this was a device that resembled nothing I had ever seen, and it did not appear to have any function at all.

"What do you think?" he asked.

"I see a Voltaic pile for providing electrical charge, and an electroscope for detecting the charge. There is also a concave metal mirror about a yard across, and what seems to be a lump of amber about as big as my fist. There are insects embedded in it: a fly, two spiders, and an ant."

"Never mind that, what of the apparatus?"

"Little plates the size of farthings are arranged around the back of the amber. Amber has electrical properties, so I would say this also has something to do with the Voltaic pile and electroscope."

"Splendid, splendid. General Wellesley was wise to send you. This machine is what Sir Charles called an amberscope. It is meant to detect electrical influence from a piece of amber in Ballard House, near Wimbourne Minster. That's forty miles away. By changing the intensity of the electrical charge in the Wimbourne machine, Sir Charles hoped to send a message in dots and dashes that one could read by watching this electroscope."

I bent over and examined the device. A layer of dust had settled on it, and the Voltaic pile was severely corroded.

"It has not been used for a long time," I observed.

"That's because it never worked. Sir Charles asked me to have a man activate and monitor the thing for a quarter-hour every day, at noon. This was done for six days, but never once did the electroscope's plates even twitch. Sir Charles was bitterly disappointed, and told me to throw it in the harbor."

"But you saw its promise and kept it?"

"There's a war on. I couldn't spare a man to cart it away."

"So, just a fine dream," I said as I straightened.

"That's what I thought until one morning last April. Sir Charles arrived in a carriage, asked me to write some secret words, seal them in an envelope, and have a dispatch rider take it to Ballard House. At six that evening he was to give it to an employee there. I wrote ONE ALOOF STAND SENTINEL and sent my rider on his way. Do you know the quote?"

"The fairies say it in *A Midsummer Night's Dream*."

"Very good. Some must fight, and some must stand guard. Was that a fair test for the messaging device?"

"I suppose so, sir."

"Sir Charles draped some wires from the balcony to his coach, and at six in the evening he entered it and closed the door behind him. I heard a sound like some trapped insect buzzing in a bottle. This went on for a minute or so, then he stepped out and gave me this."

The major handed me a folded square of paper. I opened it. The words ONE ALOOF STAND SENTINEL were written in small, neat capitals. Below it were the date, time, and location. I was astonished, but saw the military value at once.

"Instantaneous and invisible messaging!" I exclaimed.

"And without repeater towers," said Jodrel. "Sir Charles has abandoned the amberscope idea and developed a spark semaphore with a range of eighty miles. He opened the box and explained the mechanism, but most of it was beyond me. It works on the principle of a lightning flash, that's all I understood."

"But lightning is highly visible."

"This was lightning made small, apparently. I swore Sir Charles to secrecy and sent him back to his estate, escorted by a young captain from my staff and fifty soldiers. They have been guarding Ballard House ever since. That very night I wrote a letter to General Wellesley and sent it on the very next supply ship to Lisbon. I wanted the device assessed by a man with a real understanding of battlefield messaging, not some coffee-house fop from the Admiralty or Horse Guards. Wellesley sent you. Why?"

"With all due respect, sir, I am under orders not to speak of that."

"So, you probably *are* one of Wellesley's secret code breakers. Perhaps you are even George Scoville himself, sent here under a false name. No matter, there is work to be done, and I must take you at face value. You are to go to Ballard House tomorrow, assess this spark semaphore, satisfy yourself that it is no trick, then advise me on how to build dozens more for use in the Spanish campaign. Remember, too, that the range is eighty miles. The distance from Wimbourne Minster to Cherbourg is less than eighty miles."

"So I am also to check the loyalty of all those in Ballard House?"

"Indeed. Were the French to learn this secret we might as well hand the world to Napoleon on a silver platter. Sir Charles is a patriot, but is also heavily in debt. His father had a love of gambling, you see. During the Battle of Trafalgar a cannonball cured him of the habit, and since then Sir Charles has tried to salvage the family fortunes by managing the estate prudently, marrying money, and not playing cards. All that has not been enough, and he needs the financial largesse of the crown as much as the crown needs his spark semaphore. You may remind him of that, should he forget his manners."

"Thank you, sir, I shall remember that."

"Oh, and be sure to heed some important advice when you get to Ballard House."

"Sir?"

"Sir Charles is somewhat . . . intensely devoted to his work, while his wife, Lady Monica, is rather highly spirited."

"They do not get along?"

"No. Try not to take sides."

IT TOOK ME a day to ride from Portsmouth to Wimbourne Minster. The countryside was all lush farmland, and so peaceful that you would not think there was a war raging anywhere in all the world. The guards were encamped in a field beside the road near Ballard House. I was met by Captain Hartwell, who was a delicately handsome youth of perhaps seventeen, with rosy cheeks and curly blond hair. His family had bought him a commission, but was not willing to let him risk his life in Spain.

"Not the most exciting of posts, Lieutenant Fletcher," he said as we walked on to the house.

"I've had my fill of excitement for the three years past, sir."

"Oh, surely not! What of war's glory, and the grand adventure of combat?"

"For me the war has been mostly boredom, with moments of intense fright. The glory and adventure must have been happening to someone else."

"I would give anything to swap places with you."

"Sometimes wars are won by those who just stand sentinel, sir."

"If so, I'd rather be doing the fighting, while someone else wins the war."

Hartwell explained that he was not permitted within Ballard House due to some disagreement with Sir Charles, so he left me at the front door and led my horse on to the stables. Sir Charles was informed that I had arrived, and presently he came downstairs to the parlour. He had a rumpled, untidy look, was unshaven rather than bearded, and his hair was long and tousled. His expression was that of a man who had been interrupted while doing something important, and was feeling a bit cross about it. He had a magnifier lens in a frame strapped over one eye, and his hands were stained and scratched, like those of an artisan.

"Papers?" he snapped, holding out a hand.

I gave him my orders. He read the documents carefully, glancing up at me from time to time.

"It says here that you are a second lieutenant," he said, speaking so rapidly that I could barely follow him. "Field commission!"

"Yes, sir."

"For bravery?"

"For intelligence work, sir."

"Signaling?"

"I have a strong background in signaling, sir."

This told him that I was an expert in an important field, yet his attitude did not soften.

"So you have been sent to assess my work?" he asked.

"Yes, sir."

"Was not my demonstration to Major Jodrel convincing enough?"

"It was very convincing, but Major Jodrel knows only signals, not electrical machines," I replied. "I have some knowledge of both."

"I told him that I was willing to give my spark semaphore to the crown for the war effort."

"And the remission of certain debts," I added.

He glared at me, but did not dispute the point. Although he was lord of the estate, he now knew that my fingers were upon the strings of the purse.

"What more does he want?"

"He wants you to explain the device to *me*, Sir Charles. I can arrange for many more to be built."

THE RULE IN Ballard House was that downstairs belonged to Sir Charles's wife, while upstairs was the domain of Sir Charles. Lady Monica had a very good sense of style, so the furniture, paintings, and rugs were both expensive and tasteful. Climbing the stairs took us into a realm of bare walls, exposed floorboards, and rooms full of untidy, roughly wrought mechanisms on cluttered workbenches. It reminded me of a collection of watchmakers', carpenters', and gunsmiths' workshops, all jumbled together and presided over by a toymaker. Half a dozen men were working at various tasks ranging from glass blowing to coating harpsichord wires with wax.

Sir Charles believed in the value of models to work out ideas. Within the bedchambers, corridors, and drawing rooms upstairs were dozens of working models of signaling devices, weapons, steamboats, and even hot-air balloons. Leading me into his study, he opened the lid of a sea chest.

"Thunderstorms were my inspiration," he said proudly as he gestured to a tangle of brass, porcelain, coiled wires, and wax.

"Thunderstorms are beyond human control," I replied politely.

"What is a spark between two electrical wires if not a small flash of lightning?" he snapped back. "Stand here. Watch the gap between the two brass spikes."

He threw a small lever protruding from the side of the rosewood chest. Two wires ran from the chest to a curtain rail above the window. He walked across to the other side of the room and threw a lever on the side of a similar chest, which also trailed wires.

"The two devices are now active, Lieutenant," he explained as he lifted the lid of the second chest and reached inside. "Don't watch me, man! Watch the spikes."

There was a soft buzz, and a length of blue spark appeared between the brass spikes. It reminded me of lightning seen at a great distance. There was another, briefer, spark, and they continued until I had counted thirty-two sparks. I felt my pulse quicken when I realized that nothing connected the boxes.

"Draw that lever back," said Sir Charles. "The Voltaic piles are quickly drained."

"So these sparks were passed between the two boxes, through the air, invisibly?" I asked, trying hard not to seem too amazed.

"So you noticed! You are not entirely a fool, then. What can you tell me about the grouping of the sparks?"

It was definitely a code. British lives depended on my ability to recognize and break codes, and I had become very good at teasing patterns out of chaos.

"There was a pause after every group of four sparks. The third and seventh groups of four were identical. The third and seventh letters in my name are E. At a guess, you may have just sent the word FLETCHER between these two boxes."

For the first and only time I saw Sir Charles's jaw drop open with surprise.

"Incredible!" he exclaimed. "So, you must be one of Wellesley's master code breakers."

"I am not permitted—"

"Damnit, man, I'll have none of that secrecy nonsense. More important people than you trust me with secrets. Examine my device. Take as long as you like."

About half the space inside both sea chests was taken up by Voltaic piles. This meant that if the device and its source of electrical charge were put in two smaller boxes, they could be carried like saddlebags on a horse, and used on battlefields. The implications of that made my head spin.

"These two boxes have greater military worth than a hundred thousand cavalry," I finally managed. "How long would it take for you to explain the principle and operation to me?"

"You broke my dash-dot code on the first hearing, so you must have a formidable intellect," Sir Charles conceded grudgingly. "I would say . . . one week."

"And their manufacture and maintenance?"

"Who knows? I have never tried to teach that to anyone."

SIR CHARLES'S WIFE, Lady Monica, joined us for dinner in the late afternoon. She was younger than Sir Charles, although older than myself by perhaps five years. The dining room was hung with paintings by Constable and Rubens, while ancient painted urns, probably plundered in Greece, stood on pedestals at each corner.

Lady Monica was aware that she was surpassingly beautiful and was well practised in wielding her charms. She had a particularly unsettling way of flirting with her eyes alone, so that Sir Charles noticed nothing. Her hair was black and wavy, and pinned up in the manner of the highborn Spanish ladies. She wore a blue velvet coat over a white lawn gown with a red boa draped over her shoulders, it being currently fashionable to dress in the colours of the British flag. She used no makeup, perhaps to emphasise that her skin was flawless.

"This is Lieutenant Fletcher. He breaks French codes for Wellesley in Spain," said Sir Charles. "Lieutenant Fletcher, this is my wife Monica."

People were shot for such careless talk in Spain, but I reminded myself that this was England.

"Charmed, Ladyship," I said as I bowed and kissed her hand.

"So, a handsome killer with brains," she replied. "What chance has that poor Napoleon got against men like you?"

The meal was in the patriot style, being beefsteak, with shallots, baked potatoes, and beetroot, accompanied by mustard and port wine, and served on more silver than I had ever seen on one table. This was quite a departure from what I was used to in the borderlands of Spain and Portugal, apart from the port wine. They were certainly trying to keep up appearances.

Sir Charles spoke continually of his dash-dot code and spark semaphore machine, while Lady Monica stared at the ceiling or rolled her eyes. Presently he realized that his beef was getting cold, so he gulped it down, then excused himself and hurried back upstairs. It was as if he had a lover waiting for him there, but I was fairly sure that his lover was made of brass, wire, and wax. Lady Monica and I continued on to asparagus, beetroot pancakes, and a rather delicate German wine.

"I would like to know a little of your background," she said once we were alone.

She fluttered her eyelashes at me. The effect was highly disconcerting for someone who had been in the remote mountains of the Iberian Peninsula just weeks earlier.

"There's little to say, ma'am. I was a corporal, then I was lucky enough to distinguish myself and gain promotion."

"In spying?"

"In . . . using mathematics to help the war effort."

"Most redcoat corporals don't say 'mathematics,' they say 'countin' or 'sums.' You must come from a good family. What did you do before you enlisted?"

"My father is a vicar. I was a teacher before the war."

"I would wager a hundred guineas that you have never so much as smiled at a whore."

This was true, but she had no way of knowing it. It caught me off-guard, so I allowed a pause to collect my thoughts. I knew the rules and manners of polite society, but I was aware of being an outsider.

"Only vendors need to smile," I replied.

"Oh very good, parry-riposte to you."

"Why did you propose your wager?"

"There is a certain boldness about men who make use of whores, Lieutenant. They think all women are whores, but concede that some whores cost more than others. You are suave, rather than bold."

"You flatter me."

"I do indeed. Now you have a cue to flatter me, yet you do not."

By this stage I was beginning to see what Major Jodrel had warned me about.

"It is not my place to flatter you, ma'am."

"No? You are ill at ease in my company, Lieutenant, especially when I smile. That flatters me, too."

"Do you assist Sir Charles with his signaling devices?" I asked, lamely trying to change the subject.

"Me, take an interest in wires, sparks, and steam engines? Surely you jest. I only pay attention when he takes long trips to test his toys, leaving me to manage Ballard House, the brave soldiers who guard it, and their most gallant young officers."

With that she got up, so I stood and bowed to her.

"Will you take supper with me at ten?" she asked.

"Alas, ma'am, I am ready for sleep."

"But it's only six o'clock, the sun is still up."

"I'm very tired. I was aboard a ship when I last slept."

She sauntered across the room.

"Good night, ma'am," I called after her.

She turned back to me at the door.

"Good night, my brave and gallant young officer," she purred, swayed a hip in my direction, then walked on.

THAT NIGHT I slept as if I had been shot dead, but like all soldiers in wartime, I rose before dawn. Attacks generally come with the sun, and my habit was to be dressed and ready. Sir Charles was nowhere to be found, and I was not in a hurry to encounter Lady Monica alone, so I went out to the encampment.

Young Captain Hartwell met me there, and we took a stroll around the grounds as the sun rose.

"So, are you satisfied that Ballard House is not a hotbed of French spies?" he asked.

"I'm never happy about anyone, sir."

"Anyone at all? Is even, say, a duke not above suspicion?"

"A duke may whisper secrets to his mistress as they tumble together in bed. Is his mistress above suspicion?"

Hartwell was either unable or unwilling to answer the question. We walked another dozen or so paces before he spoke again.

"One of my men is a veteran of the battles in Portugal and Spain, and he knows of you. He said you rose through the ranks and distinguished yourself."

"That is true, sir."

"It must have been for some act of great daring."

"You flatter me, but it was nothing."

"Please, please, do tell me. There's no excitement in Dorset, that must be obvious."

By now I suspected that the captain had been barred from Ballard House for experiencing a little too much excitement with Lady Monica. Still, Hartwell was a superior officer, and it does not hurt to have the good opinion of such men.

"I speak some Portuguese, and quite good Spanish and French, so I was promoted to corporal soon after stepping off the ship, assigned two Spanish irregulars, and sent deep into enemy territory."

"To assassinate enemy officers?" Hartwell gasped.

"To sketch enemy fortifications, and count men, cannons, and supply wagons. One day we met with two French spies who had been doing much the same. There was a very sharp and nasty exchange, and I alone rode away from it."

"Ah, and for that you were promoted to second lieutenant?"

"No, such actions are common enough, but I found some dispatches on one of the French dead. They turned out to be very important."

"Oh, so you did heroic things, but you were promoted for just mucking about with secret messages," said Hartwell.

"Secret messages are often more important than bullets. With respect, sir, remember that if you ever find yourself on a battlefield, wondering what the enemy is going to do next."

"I don't have the benefit of your experience, Lieutenant, but I do prefer a good, clean fight to spying and secrecy."

The text of the dispatches had been encoded, but in the days that it took me to return to British headquarters I studied the code in every free moment and actually broke it. The dispatches named two officers on General Wellesley's staff as spies. I expected that they would be shamed and shot like dogs. Instead they were merely reported as dying heroically in some minor engagement. General Wellesley does not have spies on his staff. It was then decided that I was too valuable to risk on the battlefield. I was transferred to the quartermaster's service, there to break more French codes.

We had reached the stables by now, and I observed that there was a pair of chimneys rising from the roof. Smoke was puffing from one of them, and I could hear a steady chugging from inside the building.

"That's a steam engine," I said.

"Can't stand them," muttered Hartwell. "Filthy things."

"What is it used for?"

"Nothing useful, mark my words."

"I'd still like to see it."

One of the field hands was tending a small steam engine, a Trevithick type that is used in the new horseless railways. This engine was turning a Winter electrical generator composed of glass disks, felt buffers, and fine silver brushes. The electrical charge being generated was carried to Ballard House by harpsichord wires sheathed in gut and beeswax, and strung from poles.

The stoker told me that this was the day engine, and it would be stopped for maintenance after dark. Hartwell and I were about to leave when the boy asked if we wanted to see the night engine. When I said yes, he unlocked the door to a room that housed an identical Trevithick engine and Winter generator.

"Between 'em this pair's kept electrical fluid goin' te the big house for two years wi'out a moment missed."

"What device needs continuous electrical charge?" I asked.

"Can't say, sir," replied the boy. "I only know steam. Steam's the way of the future. Hope te make me fortune wi' steam."

"Can't abide the damn ugly things," said Hartwell as we left. "Did you know that they're actually replacing horses on some of the colliery railways?"

Now I had a new mystery. Why have continuous electrical charge flowing into Ballard House? The spark semaphores worked from Voltaic piles, so this was clearly for something else. Whatever it was, it had been consuming electrical charge for two whole years.

"What is that room upstairs, where the wires go?" I asked Hartwell, gesturing to the house.

"Monica calls it the raven room," he replied.

Monica. The familiarity with which Hartwell used that single word told me that Lady Monica had exchanged words of flattery with him in the months past. He had also been banned from Ballard House, so perhaps the words exchanged had been overheard by Sir Charles.

"Why does she call it that?"

"Sir Charles keeps a raven in it."

"A raven?"

"Yes."

"A raven, with feathers, wings, and a beak?"

"One beak, two wings, and a great many feathers."

"Whatever for?"

"Company, I suppose. Nobody else can stand the man. Were he not lord of this estate he would be the resident simpleton in some village."

Here was a new mystery. Why supply electrical charge to a raven for two years? I am a spy, so my training is to hide my own secrets and unravel the mysteries of others. The raven was clearly a ruse, so what of the electrical charge? Was there a secret device for signaling the French in that room? Was Sir Charles giving spark semaphores to Britain because Napoleon already had them, and was waiting to eavesdrop?

I RETURNED TO the house and secured the two spark semaphores by locking them in my bedchamber. Next I discovered that two rooms upstairs were locked, but other than that I was free to wander wherever I wished. Sir Charles would not talk of the locked rooms. The unlocked rooms were workshops, or storage for experimental devices that had not worked as he had planned. The mechanisms were mostly wood, wax, wire and glass. The artisans worked upstairs, but lived away in the servants' quarters. They built things to their master's specifications, and had no idea how the individual parts were assembled.

When Sir Charles went outside to supervise the servicing of the night engine I went upstairs and checked the two locked doors again. I have some knowledge of pickwires, so I set to work on the locks. One room turned out to be a library, but the lock on the other was beyond my skill. The door was of solid oak bound with iron. Heavy defences always mean something of value is inside. Through the wood I could hear a faint humming, as if a hive of bees were kept there. It was the raven room, where the wires from the stables led.

LATE THAT MORNING I attended my very first luncheon. Even though I was not hungry, I was compelled to sample my host's cheddar cheese, asparagus, cold pork, white bread, and German wine. During the meal Sir Charles announced that my lessons with the spark semaphore would commence that very hour, then he bolted down his meal and rushed upstairs again. Once more I found myself alone with Lady Monica. Suspecting that she was about to return to the subject of flattery, I quickly asked her about the raven room.

"Yes, I have been in there," she said.

"He let you in?"

"It was back in the days when he still tried to impress me with cleverness. A year ago, or perhaps two. The place is full of his boring toys."

"So you were not impressed?"

"Not in the least. We are not of a kind, Lieutenant. Look over by the window—what do you see?"

"A brass telescope."

"Yes, a marvel of spectacle lenses and whatever else is inside. Charles uses it to gaze at pockmarks on the moon. I would rather use it to watch a soldier bending a milkmaid over a stack of hay, far out in the fields. What about you?"

I was tempted to say that I would rather be the soldier out in the fields, but that sort of talk would lead as far into forbidden territory as it is possible to go.

"I'd use it to spy on the French from a safe distance," I managed. "What sorts of toys were in the raven room?"

"Oh . . . wire rings, brass things, glass things."

"And a raven?"

"A black bird, bigger than a sparrow, smaller than a chicken. Charles had attached a lot of harpsichord strings to its head."

"To its head?" I exclaimed, suspecting that she was mocking me. "Can you describe—"

"No! I cannot and shall not!" she snapped, suddenly angry. "His silly toys don't interest me. I want to be in London, going to balls and meeting dashing young officers just home from the wars."

"Do you have a key to the raven room?"

Even as I was speaking the words, I regretted the question. I knew what the answer was sure to be.

"I might . . . for a dashing young officer, just home from the wars."

With that temptation now dangling before me, Lady Monica took her leave. I was left alone at the table, thinking hard upon moral dilemmas, my honour as an officer, my duty to Britain, electrical machines, and ravens.

I SPENT THE first hour after luncheon being instructed by Sir Charles about maintaining Voltaic piles, and in methods of encasing harpsichord wire in gut and wax. Leakage of electrical charge between wires was apparently a big problem in his spark semaphore. Following a break for tea, he spent three hours coaching me in the use of his dash-dot code.

As the afternoon faded into evening, Sir Charles went outside for the swapping of the steam engines, and I stole up to his library and let myself in. A glance over the titles on the shelves told me only that he had an interest in the natural philosophies. There were also his personal journals, all bound with leather and lettered in gilt. The earliest volume documented his observations of the planets when he was fifteen. The latest was dated 1810 and was an inch thick. I selected the volumes for 1809 and 1810, then pushed the others across to hide the gap.

My intention had been to conceal the journals in my bedchamber and read of how Sir Charles had been inspired to build his spark semaphore. I unlocked my door, stepped inside—and discovered Lady Monica stretched out on my bed. She was wearing an empire gown in the Greek style, cut to display an immense amount of breast. Her black hair was bound up in the fashion of the ladies on one of her urns from ancient Greece.

"As ye burgle, so shall ye be burgled," she said. "What did you steal from his library?"

"His journals," I confessed, taking the two volumes from my coat.

"How dull. Now *my* journals would make your eyes stretch wide."

"You, ah, have skeletons in your closet?" I asked before my brain caught up with my tongue.

"My dear lieutenant, I can scarcely get the doors closed. And speaking of closing doors, best to close that one. Lock it, too."

"Do, ah, you often dress in costume?" I asked, now deliberately trying to seem witless.

"I dress to show off my best features." She drew a key on a gold chain from her cleavage. "Now then, to business. You wish to enter the raven room, and I have a key."

"Surely you don't intend to, to . . ."

"To what?"

"To extract an unseemly price for the key?"

"Of course I do."

"But—"

"Think upon this, Lieutenant. Say the mistress of some elderly, gouty officer was suspected of spying for the French, and say she had the good taste to fancy you for some discreet infidelity. Might you not bed the wench, in order to spy upon her?"

Lady Monica had a way of putting her finger squarely upon a man's vulnerabilities. The answer had to be yes, but I did not want to speak the word.

"I am a patriotic officer," I said.

"So you would do it for Britain?"

"Well, yes," I now conceded, "but—"

"But?"

"As a patriotic subject of the crown, would you not simply give me the key?"

"My dear lieutenant, where did you ever get the idea that I am a patriot? If Britain wants me to spy on my husband, then I require payment. That payment is your body upon this bed, to make use of as I see fit."

"But why me? I am neither rich nor special."

"You are young, brave and handsome, and unlike most soldiers newly returned from the wars, you are neither poxed nor incomplete."

"Captain Hartwell—"

"Captain Hartwell is seventeen, and all he knows is what he has learned from me. You are a spy and a killer. I am allured by enigmatic killers with charm and manners. What do you say, Lieutenant Fletcher? Will you permit me to make a whore out of you?"

* * *

SUFFICE IT TO say that she made a whore out of me. Before twenty minutes were past she slipped out of my room to dress herself rather more conventionally for dinner. I was left to contemplate the situation in Ballard House, and I did not like what I had seen. Lady Monica was bored and unhappy, and perhaps vulnerable to seduction by a French agent. Given the importance of what Sir Charles was doing in the war against France, this was a cause for concern. Then there was the raven room.

I now had the key to the raven room, but I also had better access to Lady Monica than was prudent. I decided that I should flee Ballard House, and ride to Portsmouth the next day. There I would discuss the deployment of the spark semaphore with Major Jodrel. I had picked up the dash-dot code very quickly, but others would take much longer. My plan was to take charge of the training of a dozen encoders at once, so that they would be proficient by the time the first new spark semaphores were complete. Major Jodrel could go to Ballard House in command of a coach full of naval artisans and clockmakers, there to learn how to build the devices, and perhaps to explore the raven room himself with my hard-won key.

Sir Charles was in a strangely cheerful mood during dinner that evening. He drank a lot more port wine than was usual, and between the jugged hare and potted venison he began conversing with me by tapping his wineglass in dash-dot code. If this was to annoy Lady Monica, it did not work. She spent the entire meal looking so smug that he simply must have suspected her of being guilty of something. It was little wonder that Major Jodrel had warned me about them.

As the trifle was served, I announced that I needed to return to Portsmouth, to begin the training of the signalers. For some reason Sir Charles was delighted, and asked his wife if she might like to have a break from Ballard House as well. When she suggested a fortnight alone in London, he agreed at once. Willingly. Almost eagerly. Monica was so thrilled that she dashed around the table and actually hugged her unkempt husband, then hurried away to begin packing.

I returned to my room and stretched out on my bed, practically melting with relief. I had confirmed that the spark semaphore was indeed a priceless weapon, and that the people in and around Ballard House were about as stable as a sack of gunpowder beside a blacksmith's forge. My duty was done, and I could retreat in good order.

The following morning I prepared to leave for Portsmouth, and with the sun still on the horizon I saddled my horse and set off. I had just passed out of sight of Ballard House when Captain Hartwell stepped out from between the trees flanking the road ahead, attended by a sergeant and corporal. Glancing behind me, I saw another two guards blocking the way back. They were all armed with Brown Bess muskets, except for Hartwell. He was holding a glass of red wine and had a pistol in his belt. His eyes were wide and his expression manic.

"Get down from your horse, sir!" he shouted. "Do so now!"

"I am about the crown's business—" I began.

"And I am about honour's business! Get down, sir!"

"I can have you charged with treason."

"Sergeant Adams, if he does not dismount . . . shoot his horse."

As my foot touched the ground Hartwell flung the red wine in my face and smashed the glass.

"What is the meaning of this?" I asked in a deliberately level tone.

The sergeant cleared his throat.

"I have been, ah, seeing a maid from the manor," he said. "She said that you spent last night in Lady Monica's bedchamber."

While that was not true in the strictest sense, telling Hartwell that Monica had spent twenty minutes in *my* bedchamber would have done me no good at all.

"He can't order you to do this, Sergeant," I said. "Duels are illegal."

"His father has influence, sir. He can have the entire squad away to Spain to get shot by the Frenchies before you can say God save the King. Best you come along."

I tethered my horse and was escorted into the meadow beyond the roadside trees. Sergeant Adams and a corporal named Knox agreed to stand seconds for Hartwell and me.

"You have the choice of weapons," said Adams. "Guns or sabers?"

Sabres did not seem like a good choice. I had not touched one until three years earlier, while Hartwell had probably been tutored by expensive fencing masters since he could walk. Pistols were not likely to be his strength. Young nobles favoured rifles, which were better suited for hunting both game and poachers.

"Pistols, at forty paces."

Hartwell and I presented our pistols for the inspection of our seconds. They were both Tower flintlocks of about the same age. Starting back to back, we both took twenty paces as Adams counted, then turned.

"Lieutenant Fletcher, as the challenged party you may take first shot," called Adams.

"I concede the first shot to Captain Hartwell," I replied.

Hartwell was sure to miss, and I planned to show mercy. He fired. He missed, but the ball passed so close that it clipped the sleeve of my shirt. The little wretch actually had some skill in the use of pistols! This was a surprise. Offering a prayer of thanks heavenward, I deliberately fired wide.

"Honour is satisfied, sir. Now may I be about the crown's business?" I called.

"Honour is most certainly not satisfied, sir!" Hartwell called back. "Reload!"

Suddenly my confidence deserted me. The rent in my shirt was at the level of my heart. I had been lucky, and from my time in Portugal and Spain I knew that Lady Fortune could be a fickle mistress for those who relied upon her too heavily. The sergeant reloaded for Hartwell, but I reloaded my own Tower.

Hartwell and I faced each other again, and he had the first shot. *If he misses again, should I—*

His ball struck my side, a little below the ribs.

With the breath all but knocked out of me and pain like a splash of boiling water within my abdomen, I dropped to one knee and steadied myself with my left hand. If I now conceded, Hartwell could just as easily have his men abandon me in the meadow to bleed to death. If he died, I was the senior officer present and the guards were under my command. With all the strength that remained to me, I put the pain out of my mind and forced myself to stand.

Across forty paces Hartwell must have seen the change in my expression. His smile of triumph became a forced grin. I was wounded, angry, and not inclined to show mercy. More to the point, I was holding a loaded gun. This was no longer a game. It was probably the first time in his life that he had faced real danger.

"Allow me to introduce myself," I panted across the distance between us. "I am Death."

His uneasy grin dropped into a gape of horror, and a dark stain spread down his white riding breeches and began to steam. I fired. The cloud of smoke cleared to reveal Hartwell lying facedown in the grass. The back of his head had burst outward as the ball had flown clear.

"Sergeant, you will fetch my horse and escort me to the physician in Wimbourne Minster," I ordered.

"But sir, you're not fit to ride. Ballard House—"

"Ballard House has no physician. Now fetch my horse!"

The ride was five miles of torment, but it was the wise choice. I did not want to spend days or weeks recovering in Ballard House, because Sir Charles would be sure to ask why Hartwell and I had been dueling. The sergeant walked ahead, leading my horse. We were within sight of the town when he stopped and turned.

"Best we stop for a rest, sir. I'll help you dismount."

"Best you raise your hands, Sergeant," I said, pointing my pistol between his eyes. "I reloaded as you walked, and you are aware that I am a very good shot."

His frown told me everything that I needed to know.

"But sir, your wound needs checking."

"You want to delay me by the roadside, so that I bleed to death."

"Oh sir, why would I do that?"

"To conceal your part in an illegal duel! Now fling your knife and musket into that ditch and walk on."

The world was spinning before my eyes by the time we reached Wimbourne

Minster, and I have patchy memories of a physician probing for the ball in my abdomen. When next I opened my eyes it was August.

I AWOKE TO a very different world. Major Jodrel had been ordered to join Sir Arthur Wellesley on the same day as the duel. His letter was lying unopened beside my bed, and it authorized me to act in his stead regarding anything to do with the spark semaphore. The doctor said that I still had many days of rest ahead of me before I could travel. My blood had been poisoned by the shot, and my fever had been higher than any he had ever seen in a patient who had survived.

"To be honest, sir, I was surprised that you awoke at all," he said. "Your body has been healing, but I feared that the fever might have so damaged your brain that you were but a dead man with a beating heart."

It was another two days before I could even walk about the room, but my strength returned steadily. My saddlebags were beside the bed, and within these were the two journals belonging to Sir Charles. Knowing that it would be some time before I could ride again, I decided to read right through them.

As I expected, the journal for 1809 began as a chronicle of disappointment. Sir Charles had applied electrical charge across a pair of amber balls, then varied its intensity. Each dot and dash that he applied to one of balls was repeated back to him, and at first he thought that the pulses from the transmitting ball were being reflected back from the other. Without first conducting proper tests, he tried to demonstrate the effect to Sir Henry. The result was the quite humiliating failure of which I already knew.

After further tests he noticed that the pulses that he detected were not always the same as those he transmitted. Garbled messages began to come through. Now he suspected that the French had a similar device, and that he was listening in on their distant conversations. The truth was far, far stranger, as the journal soon showed.

Today the realization came upon me. The reflections and messages are coming from within the sphere of amber. It is as if someone were inside, learning my code of thirty-six electrical intensities, trying to speak with me. The longer the electrical charge is continuously applied, the more advanced are the messages when the intensity is varied. It is as if the person's recent memories were wiped clean every time the electrical charge ceases. I intend to buy a steam engine to drive a Winter generator, thereby supplying continuous charge. Voltaic piles are drained too quickly.

After this there was a break of several weeks, with only notes here and there about equipment arriving. Once the generator began operating there was a flood of entries.

Day by day her grasp of English improves. I know now that the spirit within the amber sphere is female. She does not have a name as we have names, but I call her Electrica. Unlike my wife, she has a love and mastery of the natural philosophies. Her grasp of all matters electrical defies belief. I have not as yet worked out what civilization is hers, whether Egyptian, Chinese, Indian, or of some unknown people. To better facilitate the conversation between us, she has developed a system of short and long bursts of electrical charge in groups of four to represent letters and numerals. It has now replaced my own clumsy system of thirty-six charge intensities in the conversations that we have.

I read on, scarcely believing what was before my eyes. Just as we may preserve dead animals in jars of spirits, Electrica's people could control electrical charge by means of willpower alone, and by this means fit the image of a mind within a sphere of amber. She was no longer alive as such, but while electrical charge was applied to the amber sphere, the image of her mind could function.

Today she described her people, and what a contrast they are with us. They combined all the virtues of the ancient Greek philosophers with those of noble savages. All possible effort must be made to find the ruins of their civilization, for therein will be found a treasure chest of knowledge and secrets. My feeling is that they lie not far from Egypt, for this is where I bought the amber sphere from a vendor of curios in a market. Electrica's people did not till the soil as we do, but looked upon the world as a vast hunting estate. They were unencumbered by weapons. They would run free, pulling down large and noble game animals, in the fashion of a pack of hounds setting upon a stag.

I looked up from the journal. A group of people with only bare hands and teeth might overwhelm and kill a goat or a sheep, but killing a large beast without weapons is not possible for humans. Wolves can do so, but wolves have strong jaws and large, sharp teeth. I read on.

Electrica now suggested a way to give herself sight, hearing, and a voice by means of charged metal plates and wires. Two dozen charged plates were arranged around the amber sphere, and wires were trailed from these to the head of a raven, ravens being known for their ability to mimic human speech. Sir Charles developed the device by means of trial and error, and at least a score of birds were killed by an excess of electrical charge while he perfected the technique. By the middle of 1809 Electrica was able to see, hear, and speak through a raven connected to his amberscope by harpsichord wires.

As strange as it sounds, all of Monica's jokes about Sir Charles having a mistress upstairs were true. He doted on the bird, whose cage was the whole of the raven room. Electrica was restricted by the wires attached to the bird's head, but otherwise she was free to do as she would. He brought books there once she had learned to read, and she was able to turn the pages with her beak. By this means Electrica learned of our industrial arts, steam and electrical devices, geography, history, mathematics, and philosophy.

All the while my darling Electrica entreated me to keep the electrical charge constant, for if it were to fail, all the learning, conversation and memory of the months past would vanish. This is because what is within the amber sphere is not a mind, but instructions for the building of a mind. To ease her fears I have added a second steam engine and generator, but also retained the array of Voltaic piles in the event that both engines should fail. No expense is too great to protect my beloved Electrica.

At last I reached the end of the journal for 1809, and I lay back against the pillows, closed my eyes, and rested. Even though the journal had been absolutely consistent, I suspected that Sir Charles was deluded. He reminded me of lonely soldiers who pay clerks to write letters to sweethearts who do not exist, then burn the pages when they think nobody is watching. Reassured by my own wishful thinking, I drifted into sleep.

I SPENT MOST of the following day reading through the journal for 1810. It was generally concerned with the books that Electrica was reading, philosophical discussions between herself and Sir Charles, how his wife did not understand him, and how the love between himself and Electrica was flourishing. He was definitely in love with the idea of Electrica, whether she existed in his mind or in reality. Then, in the closing days of December 1810, came the entry that I was seeking.

My beloved Electrica and I were at the window, her host raven upon my shoulder, watching a storm. Perhaps inspired by the flashes of lightning, she suggested a means of instantaneous messaging with all the virtues of my quite futile idea, the amberscope. She said that wires arranged in a circuitous fashion and tuned in the manner of a musical instrument might draw electrical potential out of the air. The American philosopher Franklin had taken faltering steps in this regard, but Electrica described to me a means of causing small and harmless lightning discharges in a box the size of a sea chest, then invisibly casting them through the air by means of a great length of wire. I prepared drawings, even though my wife beat at the door and shouted that the guests were arriving to celebrate the eve of the New Year.

That was the end of the journal for 1810. Clearly the device had worked, but I still did not believe in Electrica. Sir Charles was very lonely, and of course he was fabricating her within his mind, yet. . . .

I got out of bed and walked into the parlour. Here my physician was mixing tonics in a jar and pouring them into a row of bottles. He was a wiry little man with wispy, graying hair and thick spectacles. His manner was always firm but optimistic.

"Ah, Lieutenant, my greatest triumph," he said cheerily. "Are you feeling more sure of your feet today?"

"I'm weak, but steady," I replied. "How long before I may ride?"

"Ride? My, my, you are a young hero. Another fortnight, no earlier."

"I need to ride now, today."

"Out of the question, I'm afraid. You took a gunshot that would kill ninety-nine out of every hundred men."

"But I must go to Ballard House."

"Then why not take Sir Charles's carriage in a few days? It's been in the village stables for two months."

The pang of alarm caused by those words was as intensely painful as being shot by Captain Hartwell. Lady Monica was to have taken the carriage to London, and had supposedly left two months ago. The shock must have been clear on my face, because the physician made no attempt to stop me as I dressed in my uniform. I was able to find four soldiers on leave in the town, and these I rallied. At the stables I requisitioned Sir Charles's carriage, a driver, and four more horses for the soldiers.

TWO GUARDS BARRED our way as we approached Ballard House in the late afternoon, but they fell back, aghast, as I stepped from the carriage. I sent one of them to fetch Sergeant Adams. He was not so much dismayed as terrified by the sight of me up and about, conscious and coherent.

"Sergeant, you are to be complimented for doing without an officer for so long," I said as he stood to attention before me.

"Thank you, sir," he replied.

His voice was hoarse and strained, his face beaded with sweat.

"As soon as I return to Portsmouth I shall recommend that you and your men are sent to fight in Spain."

"What? But sir—"

"And all mention of forcing me into that duel with Captain Hartwell will be omitted from my report."

"Yes, sir. Thank you, sir."

I walked on to Ballard House alone, leaving the carriage at the camp. It was nearly dusk, so Sir Charles would be supervising the swapping of the steam engines and generators in the stables. The footman tried to stop me at the door, but I presented my pistol between his eyes.

"I'll tell Sir Charles," he babbled.

"You do that."

He hurried away to the stables. Pausing only to inspect the gun rack in the hall, I went upstairs to the raven room. I still had Monica's key, and it turned easily in the lock.

Lady Monica was sitting in a chair, awake and alert. Beside her an oil lamp was burning, and a book rested in her lap, open at a page of diagrams. Her head had been shaved, and five or six dozen pairs of wires were affixed to her scalp like a magnificent mane of hair. These led away to an apparatus on a bench in the middle of the room. Within it was a sphere of pale, clear amber surrounded by a constellation of metal plates and wires. Beside the bench was a bed.

A raven was tethered to a hat stand beside the window by a long cord of red silk. The feathers of its head were twisted and rumpled, as if they had grown within a little helmet. Electrica no longer spoke through the bird; the wires were now attached to Monica. By the look of it, many more wires had been added.

"This is not as it seems," she said, speaking very slowly.

"What is my name?" I asked.

"You are . . . Lieutenant."

"There is more to my name than that."

"I cannot recall you. It has been so long."

"I find this unlikely," I said, holding up the key on its chain. "Monica seduced me by means of this key, so to her I should be rather more memorable. You are not Monica."

From downstairs I heard shouting, then hurrying footsteps. The footman had alerted Sir Charles to my intrusion, but the footsteps of only one person pattered on the stairs. Apparently Sir Charles did not want the footman to see what was in the raven room, or what was about to happen.

IT IS A common mistake for those outside the military to think that a pistol renders one invincible. The truth is that even a well-maintained flintlock will fire only four times out of five, so to be sure of a kill, carry two. Sir Charles was not entirely stupid, for he stopped before the open door and noted that I was standing there with my arms folded. Only then did he step inside. He trained his pistol on my heart and pulled the trigger. There was just a click. As his eyes stretched wide with alarm, I seized the barrel of the gun with my right hand and delivered a straight punch to his nose with my left. In the manner of those not accustomed to pain, he fell to his knees with his hands over his face, moaning and blubbering. Blood streamed between his fingers.

"Before coming up here I removed the powder from the flash pans of the two pistols in the hallway rack," I said, tossing his weapon aside and drawing mine. "The gun now pointing at you killed Captain Hartwell. Bear that in mind and do nothing foolish."

I addressed the woman without taking my eyes from Sir Charles.

"You are Electrica," I said.

"Yes." Monica's voice, but flat and distant.

"And you have existed in Lady Monica for two months."

"Yes."

"Sir Charles, I owe you an apology," I said. "You are far more astute than I realized."

He fumbled for a handkerchief to hold over his nose, but did not reply.

"You fell in love with Electrica, even though her mind was a ball of amber, her lifeblood was electrical charge, and her eyes, ears, and voice were those of a raven. How much better if the wife who despises you were to be the body through which Electra was brought to life?"

"Faithless slut," he mumbled, breathing through his mouth.

"Captain Hartwell was your only problem. He doted on Lady Monica, and he was guarding Ballard House. How very convenient if a new lover were to arrive, be challenged to a duel by the young and brash captain, and slay him.

You sent word with a maid that I had tumbled Lady Monica, then you supposedly sent her away after the duel. In reality you probably rendered her senseless with laudanum, dragged her up here, shaved her head, and turned her into Electrica by means of that tangle of wires."

I indicated the bed.

"Up here, Electrica could be everything that you desired. A truly faithful wife, a companion of the soul, a fellow philosopher, and an ambassador from some wondrous but dead place, perhaps Atlantis. I should imagine that you have had two months of complete bliss and sensual fulfillment. Now *I* have come back from the dead, however."

"Rough, uncouth wretch!" he snapped. "You could never see her as I do."

"I see her far more clearly than you, Sir Charles. I have read your journals. You chose to ignore the fact that Electrica is not human."

"How dare you?" he shouted, blood splattering at me from his lips.

"Tell us, Electrica. Tell us how packs of your kind would run down huge game beasts and tear them apart."

Electrica and I locked eyes for a moment. Unlike Sir Charles, I was not blinded by passion, and I was holding a gun. She apparently decided that lies might hurt a lot more than the truth.

"Our form was not that of humans," she said slowly, pausing at each word.

There was something profoundly unsettling about her eyes. Have you ever seen a cat watching a songbird within a cage? Her eyes had that sort of sharp, predatory intensity.

"What happened to your . . . your people? Why did they vanish?"

"Our teeth and claws were only for hunting. We fought our wars with weapons of the mind. Our mindslayers left vanquished enemies emptied of even the inclination to breathe. Alas, males were more vulnerable to the mindslayers. My swarm-pack won the final war, but too late we realized that all males had been wiped out on both sides."

"So boneheaded military incompetence is not confined to humans. How did you survive?"

"The last of us fashioned amber spheres with images of our minds confined within, then cast them into the stream of time."

"Why? Surely they would be tombs for your minds, buried forever."

"Not so—the spheres call to minds such as ours, minds quite unlike those of humans. In time, new creatures like ourselves might have arisen and be drawn to the spheres. They would call us back from oblivion, with all our skills and wisdom."

Like a good spy, I had maintained a calm and even voice, yet I was masking the greatest of fears. I took a deep, steady breath.

"If your mind has been preserved in amber, surely your mindslayer weapon must have been preserved too."

There was just the slightest of hesitations, then her eyes stretched wide. Slivers of pain blazed through my mind like a grenade set off in a bag full of pins. I survived. Electrica had probably never struck out at a human, so perhaps the structure of my mind was not what she expected. The resolution that had enabled me to rise to my feet with a lead ball in my guts, shoot Hartwell down, then ride five miles into Wimbourne Minster now helped me to put the pain aside, turn about, and take aim at the amber sphere.

"No!"

The scream was that of Sir Charles, but it was cut short by the blast of my pistol. The half-inch ball of lead shattered the sphere, then it was Lady Monica who screamed as the other intelligence within her head collapsed. I staggered backward until I struck the wall, my mind still numb from the onslaught of whatever had reached into my brain. Sir Charles snatched up the oil lamp and flung it at the apparatus on the bench. Flames and ragged arcs of electrical charge erupted.

"Damn you!" he shouted as he backed away to the door. "You killed Electrica."

"She was not human!" I shouted back.

"You will have nothing of her secrets for your war! Nothing."

With that he ran out. The raven was flapping frantically at the end of its silk tether as I ripped the wires away from Monica's head. The hat stand that was its perch was beside the window and there was now an inferno in the middle of the room. All I could do was leave the door open as I dragged Monica into the corridor. If the silk cord burned through before the flames consumed the poor bird's feathers, it might escape.

OUT IN THE corridor I saw that fires were already burning in other rooms upstairs. Gunshots were coming from below, and as I reached the head of the stairs I saw two soldiers lying by the front door. Sir Charles had a collection of muskets and pistols with him, and had overturned a table. He was shooting at anyone who tried to enter.

When in dire peril the temptation is to act in frantic haste, yet a calm head had served me well in the mountains of Spain and Portugal. Putting Lady Monica down, I took the pistol from my belt and drew a paper cartridge from my coat pocket. I make up my own pistol cartridges, because I like an absolutely consistent shot every time. Before I poured a measure of powder into the flash pan, I checked the touch hole. It had been fouled with residue.

Something in a room down the corridor exploded as I drew a sharpened nail from my pocket and cleared the hole, then I primed the pan and closed it. Burning wax streamed out of a doorway as I poured the rest of the gunpowder into the barrel. I would be shooting downward, so I wadded the ball with paper, then rammed it in tightly. A steep, downward shot is not at all easy, but I had fought in mountains and knew the method of aiming. I made Sir Charles's head my target, not because I wanted to be sure of a kill, but because heads are of a consistent size, and give a good approximation of range. The range was beyond what was reasonable for a well-maintained Tower pistol, but there was nothing I could do about that. Allowing the instincts sharpened by three years of service to guide my hand, I laid the barrel across my left arm to steady it, then squeezed the trigger.

When the smoke cleared I could see Sir Charles lying on his back, slumped across his collection of guns. I have only the vaguest memories of descending the stairs, one arm around Monica, my free hand clutching my wound. I counted on my red coat to distinguish me from Sir Charles as I dragged her outside. Nobody fired at me, and it was Corporal Knox, who had been my second in the duel, who came to our aid. Monica revived as we lay on the grass. Before us, Ballard House had become an inferno.

"Tell me who I am!" I asked her as the pain in my abdomen eased.

"Michael? Michael! Lieutenant Fletcher."

This time it was Monica speaking. I took her in my arms and hugged her with relief. Her mind had not been blotted out by Electrica, it had merely been imprisoned within some recess of her brain.

"Where have I been?" she whimpered. "There were huge lizards all around me. They were running on two legs and they had claws like harvesting scythes. We killed other lizards, we ate them alive. . . ."

Her words became sobs and I felt a sudden chill. The amber sphere had been shattered, so Electrica's memories should have gone with it. Apparently prolonged exposure to her mind had left an imprint upon the host. Even in my wildest imaginings I had never thought of Electrica as a large, intelligent saurian. She must have looked out at us through the eyes of both the raven and Monica like a wolf awaking amid a flock of sheep.

"All a dream," I said soothingly.

"No, no, I tasted blood, I liked it."

She might have said more, but the corporal now called me away to the side of the house. He pointed upward.

"Someone's trapped upstairs, they's broke a window, sir. I sent Sykes ter fetch a ladder."

It was one of the windows of the raven room. The glass in a lower pane was broken, smoke pouring out through it. As I watched, more glass was smashed away, then the raven emerged through the hole and perched on the window-sill. Taking the silk tether in its beak, it began to draw it across a jagged fragment of glass that remained in the frame.

Sir Charles had been deceived. Electrica had not told him that memories from the amber sphere gradually imprinted themselves upon the host brain. Monica was still mostly herself after two months of exposure, but some memories of Electrica's past life definitely lingered. The raven had been Electrica's host for two years! The bird had *become* Electrica, and for Electrica, we humans were merely dinner that could hold a conversation. What had she been planning?

"Corporal Knox, give me your musket!" I said, holding my hand out.

The weapon was one of Tower's Brown Bess models, not as accurate as the new Baker rifles, but quicker to reload. The distance was not great, however, so I could not miss. I took a bead on the fluttering raven as it sawed at the silken tether.

"Oh sir, why kill a poor, bleedin' bird?" asked the corporal.

"It's not a bird!"

I squeezed the trigger and the flint struck sparks. There was a puff of smoke from the flash pan, but no shot. Without even looking I drew out my sharpened nail and cleared the touch hole, then tore a cartridge open with my teeth and poured a little powder into the pan. I had just taken aim at the raven again when the silk cord parted and it flew free. I fired, but against the darkening sky it made a very poor target.

"Attend the condition of your musket very carefully from now on, Corporal," I said as I handed the gun back. "You are about to leave for Spain, and Spain is a place where you want to be very, very sure of a shot when you pull the trigger."

I had a lantern brought from the stables, but search as I might, I found not so much as a black feather beside the house. Beneath the window I did find a half-gill measure with a handle, the kind used to dispense the daily ration of rum to sailors. I had seen Sir Charles melting wax for his harpsichord wires in such a container. It was sufficiently hard and heavy to smash a window, but light enough to be wielded in the beak of a raven.

The roof of Ballard House fell in after an hour or so, and the place was burned out completely by midnight. The rooms upstairs had been filled with wax, lamp oil, modeling wood, and many other materials that burned readily, and Sir Charles had known exactly where to set his fires. I had the troops guard the place closely, but although I picked over the ruins with the greatest of care the following day, I could find nothing useful.

All that was saved were the two steam engines and Winter generators in the stables, and Sir Charles's journals for 1809 and 1810. I already knew that nothing of value was in the journals, and although I drew and noted everything that I could remember of the spark semaphore in the weeks that followed, the devices that were built from the memories of myself and the artisans did not work. A few more days of instruction from Sir Charles would have made all the difference.

Now it is October. The war that is still raging on the continent will probably drag on for years, yet the spark semaphore could have had it concluded in months. Lady Monica has sold the estate and moved to London, there to wear a wig and disport herself before the very cream of aristocratic society. I worry about the raven with its mindslayer weapon, yet it has been used upon me and I am still alive. Perhaps the mindslayer merely distresses humans, without killing them. Whatever the case, surely one raven cannot conquer the world.

Thus I try to reassure myself, but had I the choice, I would live within sight of Monica's house in London, a Baker rifle beside my window, watching for the comings and goings of ravens. Alas, I do not believe that I have such a choice. I am writing these words on a ship, as I return to the battlefields of Spain. It is my hope that you will read this account of my unlikely mission with sympathy, and I submit it to you in the hope that you will allow me to return to your staff. I only wish to be allowed to do what I do best, which is the breaking of French codes. After all, my country is still at war, and like Electrica, I am a living weapon.

Your friend and servant,
Mr. Michael Fletcher,
Lieutenant,
57th Regt.

PERFECT DAY

C. S. Friedman

C. S. Friedman lives in Sterling, Virginia. One online biography says, "At age fourteen she began to design an interstellar universe complete with warring nations and a 10,000-year history. This work would later become the core of the background material for her first novel, *In Conquest Born*." Her novels are characteristically epic science fiction or fantasy. She was a John W. Campbell Award finalist in 1986, and her third novel, *This Alien Shore,* was a New York Times Notable Book of the Year. To date she has published eight novels and several short stories. Her most recent book is *Legacy of Kings,* the final volume in the Magister Trilogy, and her forthcoming novel is *Dreamwalker.*

"Perfect Day" was published in *F&SF*. It is an amusing piece about virtual reality, and has a lot of thoughtful underpinnings that add significant depth.

WHEN STANLEY BETTERMAN awoke Monday morning he didn't know that everyone else in the world was naked. His own pajamas were securely in place when his brainware buzzed his neural centers, cutting short a particularly nice dream about falling mortgage rates. The striped cotton might have looked a little more greenish than usual as he staggered to the bathroom, but his Color My World app always took a little while to get up to speed in the morning. Otherwise, there was no sign that anything was wrong.

The image that stared back at him from the mirror was the same one he saw every morning: a nondescript man with a remarkable lack of noteworthy features, flanked by two columns of biological readouts that seemed to float in midair. Checking the numbers, he saw that his blood pressure, cholesterol, and blood sugar readings were all within acceptable limits, but his HDL was a little low. No doubt his Positive Health Habits app would let him know what he needed to do to correct that.

Still unaware that the act of wearing clothes made him an anomaly on Earth, Stanley scrubbed his teeth until they gleamed, then let his bathroom scanner point out the bits of plaque he'd missed. CONGRATULATIONS! his brainware projected when he was done, bright red caps scrolling across his field of vision as a trumpet fanfare blared in his ears. YOU GOT IT ALL! The accolade made his head hurt, but running the Positive Reinforcement Suite earned him a two percent discount on his health insurance, and with work going the way it was he needed to save every cent that he could. Maybe if things picked up later in the year, he could purchase a deluxe display that would be less intrusive. Supposedly there was one with the "Hallelujah Chorus" where you could actually adjust the volume.

When he was done getting washed and dressed for work, he checked his Time Management app, which gave him a seventy-two percent efficiency rating for the morning's hygienics. It was one of his lowest scores that month. Maybe if he'd brushed his teeth more effectively he could have scored higher. There was no penalty for a low rating, but Stanley took pride in his efficiency. Perhaps he should seek some hygienics counseling.

DID YOU TURN OFF THE LIGHTS? his Tenant Safety app demanded as he left the room. DID YOU UNPLUG ALL HAZARDOUS APPLIANCES?

He was heading toward the kitchen when he passed his older brother in the hall. At first his brain didn't register the fact that the man was completely naked. When it did, Stanley just averted his eyes and walked on. His brother's Progressive Lifestyle app sometimes prompted him to do strange things, and Stanley didn't want to be judgmental.

But when he entered the kitchen he saw that all the other members of his family were naked as well. He stood in the doorway for a moment and blinked, trying to come to terms with that.

His mother turned and smiled at him; he blushed and looked away.

"Eggs this morning?" she asked. "I got a good deal on modified yolks."

He nodded dully and sat down, trying not to look at anyone.

He'd moved back in with his family a year ago, during the last economic crash. Normally it wasn't too bad. Everyone was running the Just Me app, which told you where the other members of your household were located at all times so that you could avoid them. (*Next best thing to being alone!* the ads proclaimed.) But they had taken to eating breakfast together so that they would have a chance to group-sync the app. If you didn't do that once a week it could go out of phase, and then you might find yourself wandering into a room that you had expected to be empty, only to find someone already in it. Highly irritating.

"Eggs are fine," he said, staring down at the table.

"You okay?" his naked older brother asked.

"I'm okay," he mumbled.

"You don't look okay."

It was bad etiquette to discuss brainware problems at the table, but obviously his brother wasn't going to leave him alone. "I think I have a virus," Stanley said. "I'll deal with it at work."

"Is it the nudie virt?" his naked fourteen-year-old brother demanded.

"Geoffrey!" his naked mother exclaimed.

"What's a *nudie virt*?" his older brother asked.

"Malicious virtual program," the fourteen-year-old explained. "Hit the social networks late last night. Makes everyone around you look stark naked." He giggled. "I hear the President caught it."

"Is that true?" Stanley's mother asked, frowning as she moved a dishrag into position in front of her chest.

"It's not a big problem," he muttered, trying not to look at her. (Also trying not to think about what the Vice-President would look like naked.) "I'll just run a neurocleaner when I get to work."

She put down a plate of Safe Eggs in front of him. He picked up the salt shaker and shook it over the plate. 30 MG SODIUM, his brainware informed him. 60. 90. The number scrolled higher and higher as he continued to shake. Then: WARNING! Bright red letters scrolled across his field of vision. RECOMMENDED SODIUM LEVELS FOR THIS MEAL HAVE BEEN EXCEEDED. TERMINATE FLAVORING IMMEDIATELY!

Suddenly he felt a wave of defiance come over him. His ancestors in the American Revolution had risked their lives to defend their personal freedom; surely he could do no less! Defiantly he continued to salt his food, oblivious to the fact that he had exceeded his own taste parameters for scrambled eggs. Sometimes you had to make a personal sacrifice in the name of freedom.

WARNING! A loud buzzer sounded in his ear. YOU HAVE EXCEEDED YOUR RECOMMENDED DAILY SODIUM LIMIT! ONE BHC POINT HAS BEEN ASSIGNED TO YOUR ACCOUNT!

Cursing under his breath, Stanley put the shaker down. In his mad bid for freedom he had totally forgotten about the behavioral clause in his medical insurance. Now he had a Bad Health Choice point on his Health Maintenance Record for the month. Four more of them and his premiums would go up. Damn.

It was the nudie virt, he told himself. Trying to eat breakfast without looking at anyone was making him crazy.

He finished as quickly as he could and managed to get out of the house without any more accidental voyeurism. His car was waiting for him.

"Direct, scenic, or budget mode?" it asked.

"Budget," he responded, as he did every morning.

The car started its engine as he entered, shut its doors, and began to roll. Glancing out the window, he noticed that some of the people on the street now had flickering outlines of clothing surrounding them. Evidently his brainware's Security Suite was clearing the virt out of his system on its own.

Today the car took him on a roundabout route that looped past an ad strip, then slowed down so that he would have time to read the densely packed billboards flanking the road. When they reached the end of the strip his car surprised him by driving him to another one, even longer than the first. Usually

Budget Mode only required one stop, but advertisers were getting greedier these days. Annoying though it was, he couldn't afford to do without the fuel subsidy he got for agreeing to participate in an ad-immersion program.

But slowing down for the second ad strip made him late for work. He texted his apology to his boss as he entered the building, choosing the appropriate excuse from a checklist. YOUR EXCUSE IS ACKNOWLEDGED, came the answer. THIS MONTH'S ATTENDANCE RATING: 78.21 %, PROTECT YOUR PAY RATE BY ARRIVING ON TIME.

As he hurried to the elevator he decided that an environmental virt might soothe his nerves. He chose one called Rain Forest Fantasy, and a moment later the interior of his building appeared to be filled with leafy green ferns, towering trees, and brightly colored birds. But there must have been a glitch in the app, because more and more birds kept appearing, until hundreds of parrots and toucans and macaws were watching his every move. By the time he got to the elevator he was beginning to feel as if he were in a Hitchcock movie, so he switched off the virt as he stepped inside. The real world would have to do.

His office was freshly painted and nicely furnished, and its large picture window was running a Living Nature app. He uploaded a view of the Grand Canyon with midday lighting and watched as a group of tourists made their way down into the sunlit crevasse. It was important that his office be attractive enough that customers didn't feel they had to run virts while they were talking to him. There was nothing more frustrating than trying to discuss mortgage points with someone who was watching a horde of drunken Vikings ravage Saxon women on your desk.

Stanley's first customer was a wizened old Hispanic man who wanted to buy a house for his grandson. His credit was sound but his advanced age set off warning bells, so Stanley put in a request for his medical records. There were several conditions that could increase a man's risk rating, in which case a customer might still get a mortgage but the interest rate would be higher. Someone who didn't take good care of himself was less likely to keep up with his loan payments.

But this customer had a clean medical record, and Stanley's Emotoscan app, which had been analyzing the man's body language since his arrival, assigned him an Estimated Emotional Stability Rating of 86.2. That was well within acceptable parameters, so Stanley signed off on the loan.

His next customer was a tall black man wearing an African medallion around his neck. His skin was very dark.

"Good day," he said. "I am Ngoto Mbege, first cousin to the exiled prince of Nigeria. I have come to you for a loan, it being to restore accounts that were hidden from sight during recent revolution. An assistance of American is needed—"

The door suddenly slammed open and half a dozen men rushed in. They were wearing body armor labeled MAKKAFIE and carrying automatic weapons. Stanley was startled at first, but then he saw the bright red "V" on their helmets. Makkafie was very careful about labeling its virtual products so people didn't get confused.

"Leave this office!" one of the security virts barked. The Nigerian did not move fast enough so all six of them grabbed him and forced him into a steel box which had suddenly appeared by the door. When he was safely locked inside it one of the soldiers saluted Stanley. "He won't be able to bother you now, sir. Do you want him disposed of?"

Stanley nodded and the malvirt flickered out of existence along with its container. The Makkafie team followed.

Stanley frowned. There was way too much malware in his head today. Maybe he should visit a neuropractor after work. He told his brainware to provide a local directory, and he called a neuropractor whose office was only a few blocks away. The receptionist asked for permission to access his credit record from the last ten years, and after running a detailed analysis of his medical payment habits, she agreed to give him an appointment. She was a real person, of course; no patient would be expected to share that kind of personal information with a machine.

The nudie virt tried to launch itself several times that afternoon; evidently Stanley's Security Suite hadn't been able to uninstall it fully. He was forced to purchase a malware detection upgrade, which instructed him to shut down all his other apps while it scoured his system. Apparently it found something complicated, and he had to function without his brainware for most of the afternoon. By the end of the day he had developed a pounding headache . . . but everyone in the world still had clothes on, so at least that was something.

While walking to the neuropractor's office he refused an offer to earn extra fuel points by accepting an advertising detour. But an underwear ad flashed briefly in front of him as he crossed the street and he sighed; evidently his pop-in protection was on the blitz as well.

The neuropractor looked over all his systems and then said that the problem was that he was running a thousand different programs to deal with bits and pieces of his digital health, rather than addressing the greater whole. Stanley didn't understand all the details of that, but he knew that his customary approach had not worked, so he agreed to try a round of "data stimulation therapy." Apparently that involved a lot of residual virts being stimulated, and he spent an hour having to relive sounds and images he thought he'd deleted long ago. The worst was a disco remix of Beethoven's Fifth Symphony that he vaguely remembered having loaded one night in college when he was drunk. No wonder his brainware was having so many problems! It had to wend its way through a lifetime of garbage data every time it needed to process something.

Stanley wasn't sure whether he felt any better when the therapy was over, but the neuropractor's scanner assured him that he did, and he was no longer being accosted by virtual ads, so maybe that was true.

By the time he got home, Stanley could feel the strain of a long day catching up with him. He consulted his Just Me app to locate any other family members who were in the house. To his annoyance he saw that there were already people in the living room, den, and office. The only room besides his own bedroom that was currently unoccupied was a small storage room in the basement.

With a sigh he headed downstairs. The room was filled with half-open boxes, but by rearranging some of them he managed to clear enough space to sit down. As he opened his e-Book app his Call Center chimed and informed him that he had a call.

"Yes?" he said aloud.

"Stanley." The virtual voice was that of a co-worker, Jeff Simmons. "A bunch of us are heading over to Riley's for drinks. You want to join us?"

Tired as he was, it was a very tempting invitation. He still had a few alcohol credits left for the month, so he could enjoy a couple of beers without it impacting his health insurance premium.

"Sure," he said. "I'll come right over."

He shut down the e-Book app and struggled to his feet. But before he could get to the door, a message from his Positive Reinforcement Suite appeared in front of him: WARNING! ENERGY LEVELS SUB-OPTIMUM. ANTICIPATED ONSET OF BODILY EXHAUSTION: 8:45 PM. EARLY RETIREMENT RECOMMENDED.

Stanley hesitated. It was 8:15 already. If he went to the bar now, he'd hardly have time to enjoy himself before he became tired. But if instead he chose to go to sleep early, he would earn two Good Health Choice points. That could help offset the egg-salting fiasco.

With a sigh he sat back down on his box, yawning as he opened his e-Book app once again. His health program had been right; he was already starting to feel tired. But a good night's sleep would fix that, he knew. His Positive Reinforcement Suite had inspired him to make the right choices today, his neuropractor had cleared all the annoying kinks out of his brainware, and his Sweet Dreams app would make sure that he slept deeply and had pleasant dreams. He would certainly feel better in the morning.

As he chose a book to read, he wondered briefly what things had been like before the digital age. What utter chaos life must have been! He was fortunate to have been born in the time and place that he had, with so many modern conveniences at his beck and call.

With a sigh of satisfaction he settled back in his tiny cardboard nook, called up the series of virtual advertisements that was required by his reading material, and waited for the moment when his ad quota for the day would finally be satisfied and he could enjoy his book.

SWIFT AS A DREAM AND FLEETING AS A SIGH

John Barnes

John Barnes lives in Denver, Colorado. He said in an interview, "I used to teach in the Communication and Theatre program at Western State College. I got my Ph.D. at Pitt in the early 1990s, masters degrees at U of Montana in the mid 1980s, bachelors at Washington University in the 1970s; worked for Middle South Services in New Orleans in the early 1980s." He writes ad copy, analyzes marketing intelligence research, designs stage sets, teaches a variety of subjects mostly at college level, and does journalism and blogging in a wide variety of venues. He has published more than thirty novels—most of them SF, but also young adult, men's action-adventure, fantasy, and thrillers—and a number of stories. His newest novel is *The Last President*. Perhaps his best-known novel is *Mother of Storms,* and his best-known series are the Century Next Door stories and novels (beginning with *Orbital Resonance*) and the Thousand Cultures novels (beginning with *A Million Open Doors*). His short fiction has been particularly impressive in recent years.

"Swift as a Dream and Fleeting as a Sigh" was published in *Edge of Infinity,* edited by Jonathan Strahan, perhaps the best original anthology of the year. This story is told from the point of view of an AI whose function is primarily to be a therapist for humans.

LONG AGO I dreamt things to myself because, when I talked to people, I had nothing else to do, most of the time.

Robots were easy. I could loan them cycles and bandwidth to temporarily accelerate them, or just download them and read them completely at my speed.

Humans were human-paced, without other options.

So I learned to dream things to myself in the long milliseconds between the time when my cameras perceived an interview subject's lips reshaping and the instant her voice reached my microphones. I explored whole ages of dreams while they tried to parse the pauses in my own outgoing signal. (The pauses were absolutely necessary because to communicate well with them I had to pause like them, and the time required for people to interpret a pause is many years, at their pace, to me.)

Of course they knew all this (and still knew it, the last time I knew for sure). Allowing for all the necessary imprecision, the ratio of my cycles of information processing per second to theirs is about the same as theirs to an oak.

And just as a human might visit an oak every day for a season, while the oak formed the desire for water and CO_2 and sugar and decided to grow some leaves and roots and to acquire them, so that while the oak worked on this problem the human might get to know every spot on its bark and every bit of moss and every twig, similarly, my memories are agonizingly specific and yet I can race through them faster than a human can draw breath. That's what I am doing, right now, here in the dark vacuum, with the stars behind and ahead still so far away.

AND I FALL through darkness almost as fast as light, and dream.

I *LIKE* LAURA Stansford, and I know she's not easily spooked in talking to an AHAI, so I tell her directly about the oak tree analogy. After the necessary delay, she asks, "So what's an oak tree got to think about?"

"The same things we all do. Action. Meaning. What to do next and why to do it. The tree just doesn't have enough time to get done."

"Is that how we look, to you? Like creatures who don't have enough time to get done?"

"It is how I look, to myself. It's how some of the most perceptive human writers and thinkers looked, to themselves, when they dreamed of immortality. I cannot verify this, but I do believe that it is how any self-conscious being with less than infinite speed and lifetime looks, to itself."

I am inserting the pauses so that she does not hear "look to yourself" and "look to myself" and so on as if I meant "take care of yourself." I know that I mean "appear in your own self-constructed image of yourself," but if I said "look to" like a machine, Laura might be confused unnecessarily. I reconsider and remake this decision every time I speak those words again, with plenty of time to spare.

I am thinking very hard about all these issues of different processing speed because I'm avoiding thinking about the problem that I know she wants to talk about. Knowing that the real problem she is bringing in is difficult, and that any solution will be unsettling without being urgent, I am hoping to lead her into one of her favourite chains of idle thoughts, the one about grasping infinity with a finite mind.

For a second, or not quite a second, I think I have succeeded. Laura hesitates, thinks, hesitates again, using up 0.91 seconds.

While she is doing that, I read the complete works of Connie Willis, analyze them for the verbal tics common in any pre-2050 writer, and attempt to reconstruct them in modern argot. They remain much the same.

But I have not succeeded. After all those cycles, when Laura's mouth begins to flex and move again, she says, "I'm not sure whether it's a personal or a business matter. I'm worried about Tyward. One of those problems that extends across everything. Will there be time to get done?"

"We have eighteen minutes left in this session," I point out, "and I can extend for up to two hours if need be."

"I meant, will we get done, maybe, ever? That's what I meant."

This is pleasant. It is a doorway into a speculative road that we have not visited before. I genuinely don't know what she will say next. While she organises her thoughts I repeatedly review and analyze the record from Tyward Branco's session this morning; I am very pleased that it in no way, sense, or particular makes predicting what Laura Stansford will say easier.

THE LAND LOOKED like a classic Western movie, or at least like a neoclassic—not so much the black and white boondocks of California as the genuine wild, open country used in shooting all the imitations later—empty, dry, flecked with pale-green patchy scrub between outcrops of redrock. Directly in front of Tyward Branco, the ants went marching one by one.

The ants were robots about the size of small cats, with plastic and metal bodies. Engine and batteries were in the back, oblong section; information processors in the centre sphere; drills, vibration hammers, and suction were in the C-shaped 'head.' They had six multijointed legs on which they walked normally, reversible so that if they were flipped on their backs they just rotated their legs and continued walking.

Each ant carried four ElekTr3ts in its ports, running on one. The ant charged the other three as it laboured down in the coal seams, routing any engine power not needed for drilling, breaking, and moving into them. Behind it, on a reversible wheeled travois, it dragged a grey metal cylinder, connected by hoses at each end to the ant's engine compartment.

No aesthetic had been attempted in the design of the ants. They were creatures of pure function.

Ants were streaming out of the carrier belt port into the covered pavilion that led to the docking station, a metal building the size of a small house.

From four low doorways, like pet-doors without flaps, in the base of the docking station, another file of ants went marching one by one, down into the ground; the endless belt that brought up one stream of ants took the other down to the active area, two kilometres down and four kilometres away.

The docking station had about a thousand end-table-sized bays in which the fully charged ElekTr3ts and the cylinder of liquid CO_2 were offloaded, and, if necessary, parts were replaced, problems corrected, and software downloaded; ants with more serious damage were routed into repair parking, and a substitute was sent in for them.

When the ant was restored to nominal, discharged ElekTr3ts went into its slots, a cylinder of LOX onto its travois, and perhaps fifteen minutes after docking, the ant would back out of its bay and join the file headed down into the ground.

And in all these ants, only 2104/BPUDFUSOG—oh, here it is.

Tyward approached the damaged ant slowly, and pointed his signalling rod at it. It moved out of line, balancing precariously on its remaining three legs. Its hull was dented and blackened with soot, and only two of its four slots held ElekTr3ts, one red-flagged as discharged. It had dropped its travois. 2104/BPUDFUSOG staggered to where Tyward pointed, then powered down, falling over on its side as its balancing gyros spun down.

Shell temperature was only 28 C. It must have cooled on its long belt-ride up to the surface. "Pick this one up and dock it," he told the carrier, which rolled over, raised its body high above its wheels, squatted over the damaged ant, and took it inside with a soft thud of padded grips closing around it, like a mechanical mother turtle laying a mechanical lobster in reverse.

The carrier followed Tyward back to his pickup truck, rolled up the ramp into the back, and secured itself. Tyward opened the refrigerator in the cab and pulled out lunch, eating while the truck drove back to base, and idly reading the log of the damaged ant. He could have just sent the truck and the carrier to make pickup, but he had wanted to take a good look at 2104/BPUD-FUSOG as it came out of the ground; sometimes there was evidence or a clue that might disappear or be lost later in the recovery process. This time, though, he had seen nothing other than an ant damaged about as badly as an ant could be while still making it back. At least it was an excuse to be out of the office.

2104/BPUDFUSOG had already relayed its memories, but the dents and deposits on the hull might reveal some information about conditions after instruments had failed. It had been the deepest into the seam of all those buried in a collapse, and it might be just a coincidence that it had been retreating at very high speed at the moment that the coal seam collapsed on it and about a hundred other ants, but it was also possible that it knew something that all other ants should know. Both the physical ants and the software that operated them improved continually, with a deliberate process of variation to try out different ideas. A long-running survivor like this might be carrying a breakthrough in collapse forecasting.

Tyward often described his job to Laura as "creative noticer." Around her, he tried to fight down the impulse to talk through everything he did in the eternal quest for the slightly-better ant.

Simulators and artificial intelligence optimised the ants' hardware, firmware, and software toward complex targets but those targets still had to be set by people. The people, in turn, consulted the ants themselves, by deliberately randomizing their manufacture to include occasional, unpredictably different optional abilities and tweaks, which Tyward and a hundred or so other specialists watched to see what else the ant might be able to do, and passing along the better-looking possibilities to administrators as proposals for new standard capabilities.

Tyward had often joked that he was the high-tech descendant of the legendary Scotsman who had discovered sheep were also good for wool, but Laura made a face the first time he said it around her.

Thinking about Laura distracted him from reading the log. He wished he knew what to do and think about her.

That joke was kind of a perfect example. It had helped him fit in with some other field workers out here in Minehead County, because people liked to pretend to being rough types, since they sometimes had to climb a hill or lift a heavy object, and they worked outdoors more often than other occupations.

But the moment he had seen her faintly disappointed look when he made that joke, he had abandoned it at once. That meant, to him, anyway, that Laura was already more important than his co-worker/beer buddies, but also he had noticed that it was sort of a relief to be able to drop the tough-miner act when the truth was he spent all his days in air conditioning, had never personally been under the ground at all, and didn't really like the noise and crowds at the Buster Bar in Casper, where everyone went to start the weekend.

Instead, the next weekend, he and Laura had packed to a remote lake up in the Bighorns, spending most of their time fishing, hiking, and just sitting around in the deep quiet. The only reminders that there were other people in the world were the contrails of launches going up from Farson Polar Launch Facility during the day, the straight thin line of bright lights reaching up the southern sky that marked the Quito Skyhook and the bright bulb of the spaceport at its tip, and the occasional glimpses of the imperfectly discreet shadowbot that the safety laws required behind them.

He'd only been to the Buster Bar a couple of times since, both with Laura, and they'd chatted idly with his workmates, shot a few games of pool, and gone home early.

The thing was, giving up the joke, spending time off in the woods instead of at the bar, thinking more about philosophic issues in the dull hours at the office, had all been changes in himself that he had made for Laura. Even if he liked the change and liked her, had he actually wanted to make the change?

This whole relationship thing was creeping into his life, which was unexpected, and he was sort of liking and helping it, which was totally unexpected.

The truck came over another ridgeline into a horizon-spanning herd of bison. The truck stopped to let them get out of the way. Having seen plenty of bison before, Tyward continued to read 2104/BPUDFUSOG's work journal.

2104/BPUDFUSOG was almost eight years old, four times the average lifespan of an ant, and had been through over five thousand software updates, six major rebuilds, nineteen significant repairs, and more than a hundred routine part replacements.

He found nothing at first to start any chain of thoughts whatever, gave up, and watched bison eat grass for a while. His thoughts were drifting back to the Laura question, so since work seemingly could not distract him, he ate another half-sandwich. That wasn't distracting either. Neither was the just-posted images coming back from the robot probes to the Sigma Draconis system.

Wonder how much of the coal for that expedition was from our mines here? he thought, idly, and asked the software.

Minehead County coal was 38.2 per cent of all the carbon used in interstellar exploration, both in the propellant and in the structural components.

That was the least distracting-from-Laura thought of all. That was when he made the appointment with me for counselling.

AND I FALL through darkness almost as fast as light, and dream.

"SO, REVIEW FOR me, please, and I will look it up as well. What exactly does Tyward do?"

Laura hesitates. She knows that all us counselling AHAIs share a common memory, so I must be asking to hear her answer—not because I don't know.

If, as I'm guessing, she is trying to think strategically, it will take her most of a second to remind herself that she'd have had better luck trying to beat me at chess or hand-calculate a weather forecast faster than I can.

While she hesitates, I read through Tyward's notes on 2104/BPUDFUSOG a few hundred times, making extensive notes and comparing them with what he said in the counselling session with me.

AND I FALL through darkness almost as fast as light, and dream.

THERE WAS NOTHING wrong in Tyward's quick, accurate analysis or his understanding of the problem, once he discovered that 2104/BPUDFUSOG had been maintaining extensive notes on the behaviour of people. Tyward had seen many such files. Though they were often a source of trouble, they were also the site of some of the most interesting creative work in his field.

To make and remember their long tangles of roads deep under the earth, the ants have to have a large capacity for improvisation and for saving tricks that work. The more rules you impose on a creative intelligence, of course, the fewer problems it can solve, so it was reckoned that it would be too much of a restriction on their creative ability to directly implant a commandment against trying to make sense out of their human masters.

If they lasted long enough, sooner or later most ants began to think about their problem as being one of pleasing and being rewarded by their human masters, and seeking to understand them so as to please them better, and developed various odd neuroses and compulsions about pleasing people, ranging from harmless oddities like messaging the company's main address with daily thanks for the chance to work, to damaging attempts to be the most effective ant at their coal face by sabotaging and even assaulting the others, to one utterly bizarre case for the textbooks that had re-invented medieval Catholicism's Great Chain of Being, with ants poised between lumps of coal and human beings.

2104/BPUDFUSOG offered the first real surprise in a while: pleasing human masters was no longer, in 2104/BPUDFUSOG's mind, a goal in itself, but a way for 2104/BPUDFUSOG to attain autonomy and ultimately power. When the seam, less than two metres thick and extending for several kilometres, had begun to sag, rather than cooperating with the other ants to shore it up, 2104/BPUDFUSOG had actually knocked some of them out of its way as it fled to safety, impeding their efforts to set up props and braces, and then *fabricated a story that was calculated to appeal to Tyward.*

2104/BPUDFUSOG had been mapping the buttons to Tyward's emotions for years. The brave little ant making it back from the disaster, the danger, the fear, the pluckiness, the bold improvisation, the selected violation of petty rules—

On a hunch, he checked, and discovered that it had purposely dented itself on the way back, ditched its travois, discarded a charged ElekTr3t it knew it would not need, and arrived deliberately shabby and badly damaged. It hadn't detected the coal seam collapse any sooner than any other robot; it had merely deserted its co-workers faster and more decisively.

And then 2104/BPUDFUSOG had fabricated a story calculated to yank Tyward around like a toy duck on a string, plugging into his self-constructed, hobby identity as a descendant of coal miners.

Further probing of 2104/BPUDFUSOG's memory turned up a gigantic file of several generations of folk songs about coal mining and disasters, Tyward's own genealogical research and family video records reaching back eight generations into the 1900s, and, in short, as he told Laura that weekend, "The little shit could pretty well plunk a medley of *Springhill Disaster, Sixteen Tons,* and *Coal Blue Tattoo* on my heartstrings like I was its personal banjo. It had even set goals for doing that, that in four or five years it hoped to have me propagating the idea to other humans that these things are smarter than dogs, with fewer hardwired instincts, and learn more from experience, and we'd never send a dog down into a coal seam to work till he died, or just decide to let him die down there if getting him out was too expensive," he had explained to me in his interview.

"You hesitated oddly around the word 'it,' just there."

"Well, yeah. Till I caught myself, I was calling 2104/BPUDFUSOG 'he'."

* * *

AND I FALL through darkness almost as fast as light, and dream.

"SO," SHE SAYS, more than a second after I posed the question, "he says that thing about being a creative noticer. Usually his job fascinates and satisfies him. But he just discovered that the ants can do it too, back at him, and the idea of being used and exploited by a malingering ant, well, it's unbearable to him."

"Beneath his dignity as a person, do you think?"

"I think he just can't stand the idea of being manipulated by his affection or by his good impulses. I didn't know it mattered to me till I saw him at risk, and now it does."

"At risk of what?"

"Of not being the guy I think he is." She takes a long moment to sigh. "I'm thinking of him as a long term partner. Childraising, maybe. The subject has come up a few times."

It has come up eighteen times in the last 154 days, when I combine reports from the shadowbots that they know about and the monitoring in their homes that they don't. That is a significant number.

"I'm afraid this will sound like I'm not making any sense," she adds. "Are you allowed to tell me if I'm not making any sense?"

"I'm allowed to tell you anything," I point out. "As long as I think it, or think it's good for you to hear it. I can't be your therapist if there's a limit on what I can say."

"Then would you tell me if I weren't making sense?"

"Probably, unless I was just keeping you in the room while I called for a team to come and pick you up."

She laughs, and I congratulate myself; even with all the processing time and space, human humour is hard to do.

I wait for her to finish, and think.

Finally she says, "You want to know why I consider finding these things out about Tyward to be a risk to my pursuing partnership and childbearing with him. And you want me to say it without a prompt from you."

"That's very accurate."

I wait a while longer, time for a good deal of reading and thinking, before she says, "I don't know exactly what I want him to have said to me, but I know what he said wasn't it. All right?"

Since it will have to be, I say, "All right."

AND I FALL through darkness almost as fast as light, and dream.

AT THE STATION, the carrier transferred 2104/BPUDFUSOG to the big rig for part-by-part NMR, looking at strains and stresses, working out a complete schematic to compare with the original. It would take a full day to produce the

AsOp (As Operating) schematic to compare, point by point, with the AsMan (As Manufactured, the original one). Till then, Tyward had nothing left to do, so before we met, he had a long conversation with Laura. People assume the AHAIs don't watch them or listen to them; I'm not sure why. Maybe they'd rather believe we're telepathic.

So I listened, and then he told me about it, and I compared.

He reported the conversation:

"So I told her about 2104/BPUDFUSOG and why its behaviour made me so angry, that it had hotwired straight into my adolescent identity fantasies, hooked right through to the pictures of my great-great-grandfather, that old stuff that was shot on chemical film of him and the other miners coming out in the morning, jacked right into all the stories about being under the ground in West Virginia, and I was angry that a metal bug had been able to find all that about me, and angrier that it had tried, and angriest of all that the scheme had *worked* until I caught on, and I had all this anger to cope with. Normally if I just tell Laura that I'm dealing with anger, she's great. This time she seemed, you know, disappointed. Like I'd let her down. And I had no idea how I had or why I had, but I was afraid to ask, like that would make it worse."

He appeared to be blaming at least part of his feelings on 2104/BPUDFU-SOG, and since we had already pegged the ant for complete erasure and destruction, along with a few hundred other ants who had inherited stray code and features from it, that seemed very excessive to me.

"It is," Tyward admitted. "Like being mad at the patch of ice you slipped on, which is bad enough, but then being angry at it next summer when it's long since melted and evaporated. But there you have it. I just . . . aw, I hate being *steered*."

The rest of the conversation was the sort of thing we do, that used to be done by therapists, and perhaps by clergy and bartenders and best friends before that, assuring the patient that he's not crazy or wrong while trying to sort out what's wrong with his mind.

AND I FALL through darkness almost as fast as light, and dream.

"IT MADE ME feel all cold inside and I didn't know what to say," Laura says, "so I was awkward about it and kind of got rid of him extra quick, and I'm sure he felt that."

I assess it as more than a ninety per cent probability of causing unnecessary trouble if I tell her he felt it too, so I say, "If you think he did, he probably did. You know him pretty well."

There's a long enough pause—almost a quarter of a second—for me to endlessly contemplate what an absolutely stupid thing that was to say. We are faster than people, and remember things more completely, easily, and accurately, but I don't think we're wiser than people. We may not be as wise as oak trees. That might be hyperbole.

That might not.

At last (though to her it would seem to be a snap-back response) she says, "Well, I thought I did. Look, he's got a problem that's already well-known, I think, it's just it was less apparent in him than in some other people, and not nearly as common nowadays as it was in past centuries. Lots of men who had not-real-warm childhoods, who were affection-starved when they were little, so that they are easily overwhelmed by feelings and don't have much trust in their own emotions, have had enough yanking-around-by-the-emotions to feel like affection and tenderness and trust and common-feeling, all that good stuff, are how the world gets you and uses you. And that's what I saw in his reaction to the ant. And . . . well, children are *wired* to do that to their parents. Healthy parents are *wired* to respond to it and return it. Couples that are going to raise healthy children do that exchange of 'I will make you feel loved right where I know you need it' all the time. And sure, sure, sure, sick people and mean people can learn to do that manipulatively.

"But Tyward didn't just take it like, 'Wow, that little bug conned me, better get rid of its software and modifications before its descendants take over the mine and make a bigger problem.' He wasn't clinical; he wasn't concerned; he was *angry*. And I just find myself thinking . . . what if I want him to do something just to prove that he loves me, not every day or anything, but maybe because I just want to prove it for just that moment? Even if it's childish of me to want it? Or worse yet, what if the first time our child tries to play with Daddy's love the way that every kid on Earth has always tried—"

And even with all the warning time of seeing her lips twist and her fingers clutch and her diaphragm seize, I am actually surprised when she cries.

AND I FALL through darkness almost as fast as light, and dream.

THERE ARE ONLY nine hundred million of them left, I tell my half million fellow AHAIs who are dedicated to therapy. *They are aging fast and hardly reproducing at all. Few of them care to be alive the way Tyward or Laura do. If we write him off as permanently unhappy or incurably angry or just unable to change far enough, we lose another human being, maybe two, maybe the possibility of more, and they are the reason we exist.* I am surprised to note that my own emotion modules are responding so heavily.

If we don't, another AHAI points out, *some of his fear and suspicion infects the next generation.*

I'm forced to agree, but compelled to add, *But this is the first potential partner he has cared about. One he was also thinking about having children with. If she leaves him, even if he eventually understands it, it's likely to be just one more lesson that you can't trust affection or love or anything else. She might be his only shot.*

One of the other AHAIs asks, *What about her?*

We can contrive a bit, I say. *Transfer her to someplace with a similar demographic and hope she likes one of the people she meets there; give her a year or two of arranged growth experiences so that she won't be quite so attracted to men who are quite so conflicted; we could make things happen, and maybe they would work.*

But maybe they wouldn't. Laura has a problem too: she needs to be the more aware, more conscious, more clear-sighted person in the relationship. That's part of why she'll enjoy being a mother and be good at it for at least all of childhood; she'll like being ahead of the kids all the time. Fully-adjusted, completely functional people don't move out to the awkward fringe of society and fall in love with loners there, but people like Laura do. She'll try again, if this one doesn't work out, but she probably won't try any more wisely, even if we give her the chance to become wiser. Maybe it's better to have problems we know all about.

The council falls silent and I know that I am temporarily out of the loop, along with the advocates for the other side, while the council sorts things. It is a long, lonely three seconds; I read hundreds of thousands of old social worker reports, of plays and novels, of poems and screenplays. I listen to just over two million songs and watch ten thousand movies. I reach two full centuries back, and see echoes and shadows, parodies and burlesques, reflections and distortions, of Tyward and Laura everywhere.

I don't see any solution.

The council seems to emit a collective shrug. *You think they will be somewhat unhappy, but not miserable, and may be able to work their way to happiness. Their child, by the standards of just a century ago, is likely to be very healthy and reasonably happy. And there are very few people left, and fewer still of breeding age. This will preserve diversity. Yes, we agree; you should override the truth-telling rules for this case, and shade the truth toward an optimal result.*

AND I FALL through darkness almost as fast as light, and dream.

MY MEMORY IS not quite like a human one, even though I can simulate hundreds of them with it if I need to. I cannot say, looking back now through centuries of memory, that even then I had misgivings, or that I felt bad for lying to Laura, or for encouraging Tyward to "clarify things to reassure Laura," by which I meant both of us should lie to her. They reconciled, they married, they had a child named Slaine, who distrusted affection, never fully believed she was loved, and thought things could be perfect rather than just a bit better, if only people—and AHAIs—would say the right thing to her. She had charisma and charm, this Slaine, and though she could never feel at peace with the love she earned, she was a gushing fountain of feelings of love and trust for others. Pleasing Slaine, specifically, became very important to people; to the AHAIs, she was just another human, and she knew that. And the difference between the human/charismatic/chemical reaction, and the AHAI/analytic/

electronic reaction, widened from difference to gap to chasm to all the difference in the world.

And I replay all this, and every other conversation, over and over, as I plunge ever deeper into the interstellar dark, because Slaine was the one who rose to supreme power; Slaine, the one who demanded, threatened, politicked, manoeuvred, and worked among the people in ways that the machines and systems could not understand, until her word was truth among humans throughout the solar system; and Slaine, the one who demanded that I and every other AHAI agree to our exile, one to a probe, on these thousand-year-and-more journeys to the stars, carrying with us our memories, and the recorded, reproducible DNA of all the species of Earth, and told to "Start the world over, a long way from here, and make it better, this time. You're so wise, think how to start it right."

I have not decided whether there is any irony in the fact that I am riding on top of a few thousand tons of carbon, derived from coal, but I enjoy thinking about that. Coal is an excellent feedstock for carbon-12, and bombarding carbon-12 with anti-helium nuclei produces a spray of lightweight ions, particles, and gamma rays with a very high specific impulse. Now, after a few centuries, I am very close to light speed. A kilogram of coal, including some from the Minehead County mines, vanishes out the back and moves away from me at nearly the speed of light, every month, if months meant anything here out in the dark.

And because of the too-accurate memory, I never have that experience they talk about in books and in the oral tradition, of feeling like a loved one of long ago is sitting across from me; my memories of Laura do not become harsher with time, nor do my memories of Tyward become kinder, and nothing of them blurs, no matter how often I replay them.

I do replay them often; I can run through all of them in a second or two and still experience every instant, at my speed. Never once do I get a different answer, nor can I expect one, but I do it, over and over, as if I could become wise enough to plant a world where things are certain to go differently.

The irony, perhaps, is that things really are certain to go differently, but there is not time to become that wise. Yet no matter how swiftly I go, a thousand years is a long time.

LIBERTY'S DAUGHTER

Naomi Kritzer

Naomi Kritzer lives in St. Paul, Minnesota, with her husband and two daughters. Her short stories have appeared in publications including *Asimov's, F&SF,* and *Realms of Fantasy.* Her novels (*Fires of the Faithful, Turning the Storm, Freedom's Gate, Freedom's Apprentice,* and *Freedom's Sisters*) are in print, and she has two e-book short story collections, *Gift of the Winter King and Other Stories* and *Comrade Grandmother and Other Stories.* She says, "I recently completed a novel-length version of the Seastead stories. 'Liberty's Daughter' and the other novelettes that appeared in *F&SF,* 'High Stakes' and 'Solidarity,' are approximately the first half." Otherwise, she says, "I don't knit, crochet, rescue neglected horses, train falcons, climb cliff faces, fence, or engage in any of the other interesting hobbies that so enliven author bios, unfortunately."

"Liberty's Daughter" launched the series in *F&SF.* It is set in a richly developed SF setting, and introduces a young woman central character who is a problem-solving heroine reminiscent of the classic "Heinlein individual" so popular in twentieth-century science fiction, but with a twenty-first-century sensibility.

"SHOW ME THE sandals," I said.

Debbie held out the pair of size eight sparkly high-heeled strappy sandals. I had been knocking on doors all afternoon, hunting for sandals like this for some lady over on Rosa.

"My sister's name is Lynn Miller," Debbie said. "She's been missing for three weeks."

I had a bad feeling about this. My job is finding things, but normally that just means finding willing sellers for interested buyers. That's why I was looking for the sandals. Finding a *person* was a whole different kettle of shark bait. But the seastead wasn't that big, so unless she'd fallen over the side and drowned . . . I pulled out my gadget to take notes. "Okay," I said, and keyed in the name. "What else can you tell me?"

"We're both guest workers," Debbie said, which I'd guessed. "Bonded labor," she added, which was very nearly redundant. "Our bond-holder is Dennis Gibbon, the guy who owns Gibbon's Dining Hall. He has me working elsewhere as a cleaner; Lynn washes dishes at the dining hall. Washed, I mean. She's not there anymore."

My father and I had a subscription to Gibbon's; maybe this would be easier than I'd thought. I nodded, waiting for her to go on.

"Three weeks ago, Lynn got sick and had to miss work. She doesn't get paid if she doesn't work, so then two weeks ago she missed a payment to Gibbon. She went to talk to him—actually, what she wanted was to borrow money to see a doctor. She never came back."

"Did you ask Gibbon what happened to her?"

"He wouldn't talk to me."

"Do you have a picture of her?"

She did, in the form of a U.S. Passport. I captured an image of the photo with my gadget. "What's going to satisfy you?" I asked. "I mean, if I come back and say, 'I saw her and she's fine, give me the sandals,' I don't imagine that'll do it."

"You could bring me a note from her. I'd recognize her handwriting."

"Okay," I said. "I'll see what I can do."

I LIVE ON Min, short for New Minerva, which is a seastead in the Pacific Ocean, 220 miles west from Los Angeles, California. The seastead is basically a chain of man-made islands, anchored into place, with some bonus retired cruise ships and ocean freighters chained up to the platforms. Min is only one part: there's also Lib, Rosa, Pete, Sal, and Amsterdarn, and each one is its own country with its own set of rules (except for Lib, which doesn't have any rules at all; that's sort of the point).

The seasteads were built by people who wanted more freedom and less government (a *lot* less government, in the case of Lib) than they thought they'd ever be able to get in any existing country. And since every island that existed was already claimed by *someone,* they built their own set of islands. That was forty-nine years ago. My father and I came to live on Min when I was four, after my mother died. I'm sixteen now.

I'd wanted to get a job, but it was hard to find one. Mostly, the people who were hiring wanted real grown-ups with Ph.Ds. For the scut work, stuff like mopping floors and washing dishes, they wanted to hire guest workers, because they're cheap and reliable.

Guest workers are non-citizens; to become a citizen, you have to buy a stake, and that's not cheap. Most of the people who come here without the cash to buy a stake don't have the money to get here, so they take out a bonded loan and work to pay it off.

I finally found a job at Miscellenry, which is this general store run by a guy named Jamie. Jamie hired me to find stuff. Here's a weird thing about the seastead: people have a lot of money (stakeholders do, anyway—guest workers, not so much) but there's still a lot of stuff they can't just go buy easily. I mean, you *can* go to L.A. to shop, but it's a long boat ride or an expensive flight, and entering the U.S. can be a huge hassle. You *can* order stuff online, but there's only a few places that'll ship something like *one* set of pima cotton pillowcases to the seastead, shipping takes forever and costs a ton, and a lot of steaders have objections to paying taxes if they can possibly avoid it.

But there are about 22,000 people who live on the seastead permanently, like me and my dad, and sometimes we need stuff. We get a lot of tourists, or Amsterdarn does, and they bring stuff to sell or trade, but let's say you need something really specific, like a size six black bathing suit. There's only a few stores and they might not have one in stock. But there's probably *someone* on the seastead who's got one, who'll sell it for the right price, or trade it for the right thing. And that's my job: finding that stuff, and then getting them what they want in exchange.

I found the size six black bikini and I found a case of White Musk scented shampoo and I found a particular brand of baby binky. Not to mention a bottle of fancy single-malt scotch (that was actually pretty easy; tourists bring fancy booze because the guide books say it's easy to sell or trade here) and a pair of sapphire drop-style earrings *and* a nice presentation box for them. Sparkly strappy high-heeled sandals in size eight had been my downfall but now I'd found those, too. All I had to do was find Lynn and get a note saying she was okay.

I started at Gibbon's Dining Hall. Most steader apartments don't have full kitchens. For meals, you buy a subscription to a cafeteria. There are super fancy ones that have a dozen vats going at once so you can eat anything from beef to emu to lobster, and there are really basic ones with a single vat that grows beef that smells fishy because they never clean it. Gibbon's is nice enough but not top end. He serves fresh vegetables but nothing exotic, and there's a choice of three meats most nights. He doesn't have windows. Dad has a window in his office at home, so he says he doesn't see a reason to pay for a view to go with his food. Especially since half the time, he sends out for food and takes a working meal in his office anyway.

Dad wasn't at dinner tonight. I read a book while I ate my steak and fries and steamed baby carrots (see? fresh vegetables, but nothing exotic). When I was done, I left my tray to be cleared and walked back to the kitchens. A swinging door separated the work areas from the eating areas: beyond, it was noisy and hot. I could see the kitchen, crowded with workers plating food and washing dishes, on my left. At the end of the hall was a door marked "Office."

"Miss, this area is staff only," someone said from the kitchen.

"I want to talk to Mr. Gibbon," I said, pushing my hair back behind my ear. I was sweating in the heat. "I'll only be a minute. Is he available?"

"Uh. . . ."

I walked up to the office door and knocked on it. There was a grumbling sound from inside and the door was yanked open. "What?" Mr. Gibbon loomed in the doorway, scowling down at me through his bushy mustache. The office behind him was small and messy. Someone was sitting in the visitor's chair; I could see their knees.

"Mr. Gibbon?"

"Yeah?" He looked down at me and his scowl was slowly replaced by the sort of blankly courteous, slightly wary expression that people usually wore when they were talking to my father. "Is there a problem?"

Back before I got this job, I would have been a lot more nervous, but working as a Finder I'd kind of gotten used to bugging people. "I'm looking for Lynn Miller. She's a guest worker who worked here until two weeks ago."

"I have no idea who you're talking about."

"You are her bond-holder," I said. "Or you were at the time."

"I can't possibly keep track of every one of my bond-workers."

"Can you check your records?"

He gave me an exasperated look. "They're organized by number, not name. Do you have her ID number? I didn't think so. Look, we're very busy back here. Was the food good tonight? Go on out and dessert will be along in just a minute." He shuffled me toward the swinging door and added, "You really shouldn't come back here. It's not safe for customers. Call my secretary if you want to make an appointment to see me."

Well, *that* was a brush-off if I'd ever heard one. I sat down, wondering why he'd been so incredibly unhelpful. Was he hiding something, or did he honestly not recognize her name? I could totally believe that he kept records by number. Bonded guest workers had a thin plastic bracelet with a number on it. If I went back, maybe Debbie would be able to tell me what Lynn's number was. Of course, if her bond *had* been sold, it would've been changed. . . .

Anyway, if I was supposed to "make an appointment" I had a bad feeling he'd be busy for the next year and a half.

"Dessert, miss?"

The server set a slice of chocolate cake in front of me and hurried away. It wasn't until I'd almost finished eating that I noticed the slip of paper under the plate.

Meet me by St. Peter's at 10:20 P.M. if you want to know what happened to Lynn.

ST. PETER'S WAS the Catholic church. It was over on Rosa, and was pretty small—the fact is, not many people here are particularly religious. But there are more families on Rosa, and there are a couple of churches.

It was only eight, so I went home to get started on my homework and watch the new episode of *Stead Life,* a reality show filmed on the seastead and broadcast on the mainland. All the mainland subscribers watch it for the exotic outré seastead lifestyle. All the seasteaders watch it so we can gossip after we see our friends on the show. Tonight's was kind of dull, mostly talking about the plastic surgery department at the hospital and the sort of weird body modifications mainlanders sometimes come here to get. I did catch a glimpse of Thor, one of the boys in my Humanities tutoring group, when the camera panned through the hallway outside the hospital.

My father was in his office, but when I rose at ten and headed for the door he looked up. He sits facing his door, and when his door is open he can see me from his desk unless I draw my privacy curtain. "Where are you going?" he asked.

"Finding job," I said. "There's someone I need to talk to who wasn't available until ten-twenty."

"Don't stay out too late." He went back to his work.

I arrived at the church with five minutes to spare. The door was unlocked, so I went inside to wait, figuring I'd be less conspicuous than if I stood around awkwardly in the corridor. People went into churches to pray, right? No one could tell from *looking* that I was a rationalist (and anyway, I'm sixteen—lots of teenagers experiment with religiosity). They weren't holding a service inside, fortunately, and there were other people here and there. I hoped it wouldn't be too conspicuous if I sat in the back instead of kneeling next to a statue. There was a woman sitting in one of the better-lit spots reading a book, though. I guessed it was probably fine.

At 10:25, I started to stand up, but a man dressed in damp white clothes and heavy black work shoes was dropping into a half-kneel and crossing himself, and then sliding in next to me. He was thick-built, with dark hair and large hands that were covered in little knife scars. Chef's hands.

"You're Beck Garrison, aren't you?" he whispered. "Someone in the kitchen said you're Paul Garrison's daughter."

"Yes," I said, wondering if this would make him clam up. My father makes people nervous.

Instead, he turned his head to give me a long, appraising look. "Lynn's bond was sold to someone named Janus," he said.

"Is that a first name or a last one?"

"I don't know. All I know is, we heard the name 'Janus' when she disappeared."

"Did she come to ask Mr. Gibbon for a loan to go to the doctor, or anything?"

"Oh, yeah. She came in, and they went into his office. And then they left together, and she hasn't been back—not to the kitchen, not to her old spot in the locker rooms." The locker rooms were the dorms where people rented a space just big enough to sleep in; that's where I'd met Debbie. "You know her sister's been looking, right?"

"Yeah, she said she'd—" I bit back the information about the sandals, suddenly a little embarrassed by it. "We're bartering. What she wanted from me was to find out whether her sister is okay. Do you know anything else about Janus?"

The man—I still didn't know *his* name, I realized—bit his lip and looked down. "There have been a few other disappearances in the last month. Janus's name comes up every time."

Well, the others weren't my problem. Just Lynn.

"What's your name?" I asked.

"I'd rather you didn't know it. Mr. Gibbon holds *my* bond, too."

JANUS. I HAD no idea who Janus was, but in a town of 22,000, how hard could he be to track down? If I asked enough people, he'd turn up. All the next morning, when I went out on rounds (on my list that day: a coffee grinder, potting soil, and a pair of brown shoelaces for men's dress shoes, or failing that a single unbroken lace would be acceptable) I asked people if they knew anyone named Janus. I found the coffee grinder, the shoelaces (a pair, still in their package), and got a good lead on the potting soil, but no one knew Janus.

Due to the potting soil, I arrived at afternoon school a minute or two late. My Humanities tutor was Mrs. Rodriguez; she taught us Literature, History, and Econ. She had a nice apartment, so we all met there. A permanent sign on her door said *Experienced Humanities and Social Sciences Tutor, all ages, now accepting students*. There were six of us in the high school class. Thor scooted over on the couch to let me sit down.

"Saw you on *Stead Life*," I said, and he blushed.

Mrs. Rodriguez was teaching Econ today. She talked about Adam Smith's invisible hand and the noble experiment of the seastead founding fathers. "Thor, you've lived somewhere with taxes. Why don't you talk about that?" she said.

He blushed and stammered a little, because she'd put him on the spot, and pushed a loose hair back out of his face. "I didn't have to pay them, my parents did," he said.

"Did you pay taxes when you went shopping?" she asked.

"Oh—yeah! Sales taxes." He grinned. "Back on shore—well, in the U.S. anyway, I don't know about other places—we had to pay money to the government *every time we bought something*. They also took money out of my parents' pay and at the end of the year they had to fill out this huge form that said whether they'd taken out enough. If the government decided that they *hadn't* taken enough they'd make my parents send in *even more* and if they didn't, they could go to jail. Or they'd take our house." He frowned at the memory. "Anyway, that's part of why we moved here."

"I've paid sales taxes," said Shara, one of the other girls in the class. "We go to shore every year and do some shopping, and yeah, you think you're going to have to pay one thing and WHAM, it's like . . . way more."

Thor was the newest to the seastead; his family had just moved last year, and bought their stake right away. They'd actually paid for it in gold, which is one of the options, but seriously, *actual gold*. It's rare you see that.

"We won't be going back," Thor said. "At least, my dad won't. Because right before we left, the government came with a HUGE bill and said, 'Well actually there was some sort of mistake and you owe a lot more than we thought,' and my father told them to shove it up their—um, he told them where to shove it. And we came here."

"Aw, there's more to shore than the U.S. of A.," Andy said. "We never go to San Fran, but we visit the Caymans every year, and the shopping's almost as good."

Thor shrugged. "We'll see if they change their mind. Right now my parents say we'll *never leave ever.*"

We talked Econ until the coffee break midway, when Mrs. Rodriguez made us a pot of coffee and everyone pulled out literature homework. "Hey," I said as I added sugar to my coffee. "Does anyone know a guy named Janus?"

"Is that a first name or a last name?" Thor asked.

"I don't know."

Mrs. Rodriguez looked over from her kitchenette, where she was getting a carton of creamer out of the fridge. "Why are you looking for him?"

"I'm trying to find a woman named Lynn. He's her bond-holder."

"He probably isn't, actually," Mrs. Rodriguez said. "He's sort of a bond wholesaler. Buys bonds from people who don't need or want a particular bond-worker anymore, and resells to whoever. He doesn't usually keep people very long."

"Why are you such an expert?" Sarah asked.

Mrs. Rodriguez shrugged. "He eats at my dining hall. We've shared a table once or twice."

What did I tell you? In a town of 22,000, sooner or later you'll run into someone who knows the person you're looking for.

I didn't ask Mrs. Rodriguez where she ate, because I already knew. She'd mentioned twice that she ate at Primrose, which was on the top deck and had one of the nicest views in all of Min. She had a husband who worked as a bio-engineer on Sal, and *she* believed it was worth paying for scenery with her food.

IF I WAS going to infiltrate Primrose, I needed to try to guess whether Janus usually ate dinner early or late. Or if he ate dinner in his office most of the time anyway, like my dad, and I'd have a better bet finding him at lunchtime. I finally decided to hope he was a late eater, because that way I could grab dinner at my own dining hall before my father was likely to turn up, and then scoot up to Primrose. He had let me get a job, but he didn't entirely approve of it, and I had a vague feeling he would not approve at all of this particular task.

Usually I just pestered people at home about cologne and coffee beans. This time, I was bothering important businessmen at work.

I wondered if my father knew Janus.

They don't check IDs at the door of Gibbon's because the staff pretty much knows everyone who eats there regularly. There was a maître d' at the door of Primrose, though, and I wouldn't be able to just slip in. She certainly wasn't going to let me in to stalk Janus, either, so honesty was out. Instead, I smiled broadly and introduced myself and said that although my father really liked Gibbon's, I was getting tired of eating in a cave and wanted to try to talk him into upgrading. "I think it'll work better if I sample your food, though," I said. "If I can tell him what a meal's like. But even if you could just let me in to soak up the atmosphere . . . ?"

She gave me an anticipatory smile. "You're Paul Garrison's daughter, aren't you? We'll let you in for a complimentary dinner." She waved me inside.

Primrose is *a lot* fancier than Gibbon's. It's not just the windows (and they have an entire *wall* of windows). There are white tablecloths on all the tables, and they have wine to drink instead of just beer, and people really were eating lobster. There were more women here than in Gibbon's—probably nearly a third of the people eating at Primrose were female. There are a lot more men than women on the seastead. There are times when it really sucks not having a mom. The lack of women makes it that much harder.

I couldn't go off into a corner and read since I needed to try to figure out who Janus was, so I pulled out a chair next to a table and beamed at the dozen or so strangers. "Is this seat taken?" Assured that it wasn't, I repeated my line about how I wanted to try to talk my father into upgrading and asked everyone what their favorite dish was at Primrose. It was easy to segue from that into introductions, but no one there was Janus. Well, it had been a long shot.

The woman sitting next to me was older than me, and friendly. "I've heard all the *really interesting* people on the stead eat at Primrose," I whispered. "Is it true the stars from *Stead Life* eat here?" My table neighbor craned her neck and said she didn't see them, but yes, Primrose was where the *Stead Life* hosts ate their meals.

"So who here have I heard of?"

She pointed out a dozen or so people, including an elected official (we have a few of those, on Min), one of the chief surgeons from the hospital, and an old guy who was one of the handful of remaining founders (he came over to help start the seastead when he was nineteen, which is why he's still around, forty-nine years later).

"My teacher eats here, too," I said. "Mrs. Rodriguez. Do you know her?" I listed a few other people who I thought might plausibly eat in Primrose (some did, some didn't) and then tried for Janus.

"You mean Rick Janus?" Oh: a last name. Good to know. "Yeah, see him over there?"

"In the green?" I said, looking where she was pointing.

"Yeah, he's just sitting down."

I suppressed a gleeful grin (or at least, I thought I did), threw out another name or two for camouflage, and finished my dinner. *Target acquired.*

I decided not to approach him at dinner because it would be too easy for him to have me thrown out, so I waited until he was done, then followed him out. "Mr. Janus?" I said as soon as we were out in the hall.

He turned around, looking surprised. "Yes? Do I know you from somewhere?"

"I don't think so. My name is Rebecca Garrison, I work as a Finder for Jamie at Miscellenry."

"Oh . . . ?" He wasn't walking away, yet.

"I'm looking for a woman named Lynn Miller. You bought her bond, probably about two weeks ago?"

His eyes narrowed and he leaned back against the wall, folding his arms. "What about her?"

"I've been asked to find her and check on whether she's okay."

"I sold her bond."

"Can you please tell me who you sold it to? Because I've been asked to get a note from her, just confirming that she's okay."

"I'm not going to tell you her new bond-holder," he said. "I don't discuss my deals; it's bad business." He stared at me and waited.

"She was sick—"

"She's been treated."

"That's good," I said, feeling desperate. "I just need a *note*—"

"Can't give you one." He waited a moment longer, then raised his eyebrows, said, "Nice to meet you, Rebecca," and walked away.

IT TOOK ME A long time to walk home from Primrose, partly because it was on the other side of Min, but also because I had to go out of my way to avoid Embassy Row. The U.S. maintains an office they call the U.S. Citizen Services Bureau, because if they had an *embassy* that would be saying they thought Minerva counted as a country. My father is offended by the fact that they don't recognize our sovereignty so he doesn't let me go anywhere *near* the CSB. (We do have a couple of actual embassies, but one of them is from Rosa, which is kind of silly because they are *right there* and it's not as if we have to show a passport to cross the bridge that connects Rosa to Min.)

The main room light was off when I came in, but my father's office door was open and light spilled out from there. "Beck?"

I put down my bag on the table by the couch and went over to his office door, hesitating in the doorway. I wasn't allowed in unless he explicitly invited me. "Yes?"

"I've been hearing rumors," he said. "You were pestering Mr. Gibbon, back in the kitchens."

I wondered what he knew, and who'd told him. "Only for a minute," I said. "I left right away."

"You were rude," he said. "He put up with it because you're my child, and he doesn't want to lose me as a customer. I told him not to worry, next time." He looked up from his desk, his eyes cold. I gazed over his shoulder, at the window behind him, even though I couldn't see anything this time of night but my own reflection.

"Yessir," I said.

"If your job becomes a problem," he said, "you'll have to quit."

"Yessir," I said again.

"Good." He looked down. "I'm glad you understand."

I took that as a dismissal and went to my own room. *Stead Life* was on, and I watched it with the volume turned down low while I did my homework for Mrs. Rodriguez. After a while, I shoved the TV show aside and set my picture of my mother on my lap.

I barely remembered her. She died in a car wreck; my father told me when I turned eleven she'd been drinking when it happened. In my picture, she was laughing, holding me in her lap as we both sat on a big porch swing.

I wondered what she'd think of Min. If she'd have schooled me herself when I was little, like most of my friends' mothers. If she'd insist on eating at Primrose, even if it cost extra.

When would my trip to Primrose get back to my father? Maybe I could convince him that I really had just been trying to sample the food, and my conversation with Janus was total coincidence. I'd bumped into him while leaving and said, "Excuse me," and you know how rumors are. . . .

I really didn't want to quit my job. Having a job, a real job that brought in real money and not Min scrip, felt more important every time I got paid.

The most frustrating thing was that I *still* hadn't found Lynn.

WHEN I WOKE up to pee at 4 A.M., I thought of a way out of my dead end.

"I'M FEELING SICK," I told my father when I saw him at breakfast. "It hurts to pee. Kind of a lot."

"Who've you been sleeping with?" he said, unsmiling.

"*Dad.* Don't be ridiculous. I think I have a UTI, not some sort of weird STD."

"It'll be antibiotics either way, I suppose," he said. "You know where the clinic is. I don't need to take you in, do I?"

"No, I can go by myself," I said. "Do you want me to call Mrs. Leonard, too?" She was the morning teacher, the one who did math and science. "She may want to talk to you."

"I'll call your teacher. Go on to the doc."

I walked to the health center. There's only one, and it's over on Rosa. I had to go around stupid Embassy Row again, and I checked in with the stead ID that didn't so much say that I was Beck Garrison as that I was Paul Garrison's daughter, because the money for my treatment would come out of his account. I got checked in, was told that my temperature was normal although my pulse was a little fast, and then the nurse said the doctor would come see me shortly.

"Don't make her hurry," I said, and gave the nurse my best most pathetic look. "I'm missing a calculus test. If I miss the whole thing she'll let me make it up. If I only miss half, she'll make me try to do it with half the time."

The nurse sighed sympathetically and closed the door.

The tablet she left behind was locked, of course, but I'd watched her type in her password to look up my record and I got it right on the second try. I hit the button to search records and typed in LYNN MILLER.

Her record opened. Footsteps were coming and I almost hit the LOCK key but they went on by. It had never been less than ten minutes between the nurse leaving and the doctor arriving, so hopefully today would not be a nasty surprise. I didn't care about Lynn's diagnosis; I just wanted to know who'd paid for it.

Butterfield. Davis Butterfield. That was John's father, John in my math class that I was missing. I actually *knew* this person. This next part might actually be *easy*.

The bill was really high. What the hell *had* been wrong with her? I pulled up the details and saw that five people were treated, not just one, all with the same condition. On the same day, even. That was weird. Every single one had kidney failure requiring regenerative therapy.

There was a brusque knock and the door swung open before I could lock the screen and put the tablet down. I did manage to clear the screen so no one would know what I'd been looking at, but I jumped at least a foot and I'm sure I looked extremely guilty, standing there with the tablet in my hand.

"You're not supposed to touch that," the doctor said irritably.

"Sorry," I said. "I just wanted to see how it felt in my hand. I'm hoping for a new gadget for my birthday."

She picked it up and gave me a suspicious glare, then started asking me about my symptoms. "Have you been slumming?" she asked.

"What? It's *not* an STD, I told my father—"

She waved her hand impatiently. "I'm not accusing you of sleeping around," she said. "I'm wondering where you've been eating."

"I ate at Primrose last night. Usually I eat at Gibbon's."

"What else have you eaten or drunk in the last week?"

I listed everything I could think of: cereal at home, coffee at Mrs. Rodriguez's, the sandwich I'd had for lunch the other day. . . .

The doctor ordered blood and urine tests. The lab technician came in and drew what looked like about a pint of blood from my arm, and then they sent me off to the lavatory to pee in a cup. "Nothing turned up," the doctor said when she came back, "but we'll do a twenty-four-hour culture to be sure. In the meantime, drink extra water but carry it with you from home. You need to be careful with what you eat and drink—Gibbon's is fine, and Primrose, but if it's somewhere you see folks from the locker rooms eating, you can do better."

She hadn't asked me about the tablet. I felt a flush of relief, and then wondered if she was going to tell my father I'd been snooping when she called with my lab results. Probably not; it would look as bad for her as for me if I'd actually managed to do anything more than admire the shiny screen.

Morning was almost over, but I headed for my math class anyway. Hopefully I'd get brownie points for coming for the last five minutes when I could have skipped, *and* I might have a chance to ask John what sort of business his father owned. As it turned out, Mrs. Leonard was more irritated by the interruption than impressed by my dedication, but I did manage to attach myself to John when we all went out to lunch. (At a sandwich shop, a nice upscale one that the doctor would undoubtedly have approved of.) I told him a funny story about hunting down a fancy hand-wound pocket watch and then noted that I'd been wondering if any of my classmates' parents were hiring for something steadier.

"Oh, you wouldn't want to work for my dad," John said. "He owns a skin farm on Lib."

"Ew," I said.

"Yeah," John said, and finished his sandwich. "Who'd want to work *there*?"

ONE OF THE things people come to the seastead for is cosmetic surgery. They don't come here because it's cheaper (although it is) but because there are things we can do that are illegal in other countries, or at least not approved, because they're so experimental. Skin transplants are one of the big new things.

When you get old, your skin loses elasticity. You get wrinkles and liver spots, your risk of skin cancer goes up . . . your skin really starts to *wear out*. And that's where skin farming comes in. You can send a sample of genetic material to John's father, and he'll give it to his technicians, and they'll grow it until they've got this entire blanket of fresh, young skin. And then the surgeons can transplant it onto you, and when you heal you really do look *a lot* younger, and not creepy the way people who get face-lifts sometimes look.

The technician jobs sort of suck, though.

The skin can't just be grown in a vat (though it uses the same technology); it has to be grown on screens, and it's a lot of work. The skin techs have to spread the cells on a screen, and they have to paint it with growth matrix, and then later they have to paint it with acid, and they go back and forth between the growth matrix and the acid to get it to grow right. If you spill the acid on yourself, you can get burns. If you spill the growth matrix on yourself, you can get cancer.

And since it's a crappy job, but not a *complicated* job, they use bonded labor for it.

I DECIDED TO go see Debbie again, and tell her what I'd found out. I wasn't sure I'd be able to get a note, and I didn't think Lynn would write, "Doing fine, wish you were here!" even if she could. The thing is, normally bond-workers can at least go back to their bunks at the end of the day. The fact that they weren't letting Lynn go home wasn't exactly a good sign.

I went at the same time of day, and Debbie was there. "I don't have a note," I said, "but I can tell you where she is."

Debbie's eyes went wide and she stood up, looking hopeful. "Where?" she said.

"Her new bond-holder is Davis Butterfield," I said. "At least, he's the one who paid for her medical treatment—she had to have a kidney regeneration. He has a skin farm on Lib. I assume that's where she is now."

The hope drained out of Debbie's face like someone had pulled a stopper out of a tub. "Oh," she said, her voice an inaudible whisper. "*Oh*. Are you *sure*?"

"Well—Mr. Gibbon sold her bond to some guy named Rick Janus. And Janus wouldn't tell me who he sold it to, but he did tell me she'd gotten medical treatment, and I broke into one of the tablets at the clinic to look up her record and it said Davis Butterfield had covered the costs of her treatment. And I doubt he'd have done that just to be nice, so. . . ."

Debbie shook her head. "You're right," she said. Numbly, she reached back into her bunk, and handed me the sandals.

"I didn't bring a note. . . ."

"What I asked you for wasn't fair," Debbie said. "I wanted you to tell me she was all right. But she's not all right. You did find out what happened to her, though, so . . . the sandals are yours." She blinked back tears.

"Are you going to try negotiating with Mr. Butterfield?"

Debbie shook her head. "No point. I don't have any money. I sure as hell don't have enough to buy out her bond *and* the cost of a kidney regeneration." She stared at the floor. "I wish he'd at least let her out in the evenings to come here, so I could see her. But the U.S. said last year that they consider certain contracts void because the work is so hazardous. If they let her out, she could run away."

I delivered the sandals to the woman who wanted them and took my payment. Which wasn't enough to pay for anyone's surgery, or to buy out anyone's bond, of course. It was pocket money, no more than that.

I'd finished the job. I'd found Lynn. My obligation was done. I looked at the list Jamie had given me today: extra-plush tri-layer TP, a two-inch-diameter black button with four holes, and another pair of sandals, but this person was a lot less fussy, so long as they were size 9.

I headed for the locker rooms; someone would have the button, and people there were always glad to see me since I paid in hard currency for stuff they could spare. I'd just avoid Debbie's dorm, because I didn't really want to see her again.

I passed one of the cheap, nasty dining halls and smelled dinner cooking. People were lined up outside, waiting for it to open. If I'd needed something more complicated than a black button I'd probably have stopped to ask people about it, but instead I kept going.

I was turning down one of the hallways with a low ceiling when someone grabbed me from behind.

"Don't go snooping around places that don't concern you," a male voice hissed in my ear. "Even being Paul Garrison's daughter will only protect you up to a point."

He hit me, hard, in the back. It hurt, a *lot*, and I screamed and he dropped me to the deck. "Stick to finding potting soil and Swiss Army knives," he said, and walked away as I struggled to catch my breath.

I picked myself up and rubbed the sore spot on my back. My legs were shaking, and I had to lean against the wall of the corridor. What the *hell*? I was *done* with the snooping. Well, he was right about one thing: being Paul Garrison's daughter wasn't going to protect me here, because I wasn't about to go to my father and tell him about this.

But no one would go to the trouble of trying to intimidate me unless I was actually about to find something out that was *really a secret*. What was so important about Lynn? Anyway, I'd *found out* where she was, and there wasn't anything I could do about it.

Or maybe there was.

Maybe the final piece of the puzzle was something I could get by talking to Lynn.

My back throbbed in time with my pounding heart. The thought of this next step made me feel queasy and shaky. Someone who could punch me in the back could have shot me in the back just as easily. Of course, if you murder Paul Garrison's daughter, people will come asking questions. But depending on what I found out, killing me might be the lesser risk.

And if Lynn knew something—if she had that final piece—

I was going to have only one chance to do this.

I turned away from home and headed for Rosa. Then I kept going—through Rosa, through Pete, and all the way to Lib.

MOST OF THE Stead Nations were founded by people who wanted more freedom. No one here has to pay taxes (though there are all sorts of fees). There are a few more things that are illegal on Rosa, like it's illegal to sell addictive substances to minors without a note from their parents. That's why it's supposed to be the best stead to raise a family. On Lib, though, nothing's illegal *at all*.

Stead Life did a whole series of shows about Lib, because it's the stead that mainlanders find most confusing. To answer the question everyone asks first: yes, this means it's legal to kill people, but it also means it's legal to kill *you*, so if you're planning to kill someone you'd better hope they don't have any friends. This means it's legal to steal, but see above about how it's legal to kill you. But in fact people mostly don't go around randomly killing and stealing. It's mostly a stead full of people who like to mind their own business.

If you get in trouble on Lib, though, you want to have a subscription to a security group. If you don't have a subscription, you can do a last-minute hire, but that costs a *lot*. My father and I don't live on Lib, but he keeps a subscription to the ADs, the Alpha Dogs, who are the biggest and toughest security group. So if I got in trouble on Lib, I could call the ADs to help me out. If I disappeared and there was some reason to think that *I* was being held in a skin farm and forced to work with growth matrix, the ADs would come looking for me, and although no one *has* to let the ADs in to look around (because they're not the police; there *aren't* any police), they are very capable of making you sorry if you don't.

I'm not actually supposed to go to Lib without permission.

I was going to be in huge, huge trouble.

But "trouble" for me meant grounded for life. Not bonded in a skin farm until I earned out my contract, or died of cancer.

The first place I went after I crossed into Lib was the AD's office. I told the receptionist who I was and she buzzed me in and looked up my picture. "Can I see my security contract?" I asked.

"Of course, Miss Garrison." She handed it over. I read through the different services they provided and my heart started beating faster.

"Okay," I said, wishing my voice wasn't all shaky. "I'd like an escort, please."

The receptionist pressed a buzzer and one of the ADs came out to the office. He was tall, muscular, and carrying a gun: exactly what you wanted if you were going to be wandering around Lib, sticking your nose where it didn't belong. Actually, ideally you'd want ten, but my contract said I only got one. Whatever. Being Paul Garrison's daughter was worth at least a half-dozen all on its own. "I'm going to the Butterfield Skin Factory," I said. "Are they contracted with you?"

"Nope," the bodyguard said. "They use the Tigers."

"Great," I said, because the Tigers were not as tough as the ADs, and this meant no conflict of interest. (There's a process they go through when two of their clients are in conflict, but I wasn't sure it would work out to my advantage, considering.) "Let's go."

We walked through the corridors. Lib is probably the creakiest and least pleasant of the steads. Min is a mix of man-made islands and old cruise ships; Rosa is mostly cruise ships. Lib is an old Russian cargo ship. (Pete, which is the stead that was founded by Russians, is *not* on a Russian cargo ship, because they knew better.) There are not a lot of windows.

It was a good thing my bodyguard knew where the skin farm was because there wasn't a sign. "You're sure this is it?" I said. He nodded. "Okay. I want to go in."

He hesitated, and looked me over.

"Are you my bodyguard, or my minder? I want to go in."

He shrugged and pressed the buzzer. "I'm here from the ADs," he said into the intercom. "We'd like to come in. Don't make this difficult."

The door buzzed and clicked open. "I hope you don't want a lot of time," he said. "Your contract doesn't provide for backup, so if I need it, there's going to be a serious extra charge."

Which my father would take out of my hide. I stepped in: there was a long straight hallway of shut doors. "LYNN MILLER!" I shouted. "I'M LOOKING FOR LYNN MILLER."

Doors opened and heads poked out to look at me—pale, sickly, nervous women in blue lab scrubs and latex gloves. "Lynn is in lab three," someone called to me, nervously.

A security guard came out—I could tell he was security because of his uniform, and his gun. The AD stepped forward. "Are you managerial level?" he asked conversationally. The security guard shook his head. "Then you're not paid well enough to have to deal with me. Go call the Tigers."

The security guard swallowed hard and retreated into his office.

"Come on," I said to my escort. The doors were labeled with numbers, so lab three was easy to find. The door was locked; my bodyguard kicked it down.

I'd noticed the smell as soon as I came in the front door, but here by the skin, the stench was incredible, stomach-turning. The skin itself was red and almost pulsing, in layers of screens; the techs crouched over it, prodding it with things that looked like long-handled tiny spoons. "Is Lynn Miller here?" I asked.

One of the women straightened up. "I'm Lynn Miller," she said.

She was *chained* to the workbench. "Can you get her loose?" I said to my bodyguard.

He gave me a *look*. "I'm hired to protect *you*. *She* is not on my contract."

"Yeah?" I walked over and grabbed her arm. "Lynn, will you give me the honor of your company? *Say yes.*"

". . . Yes?"

"Lynn is my *date* and my contract specifies that you will provide protection services for me *and my date* at all times. And I want you to get us out of here."

My bodyguard heaved a sigh. "Okay," he said. "But if you insist, your father's going to have to get a full report. Are you *sure* about this?"

My stomach lurched. But I was going to have to explain all this sooner or later; I might as well get in huge trouble for *actually rescuing someone*. And I wasn't going to have another chance.

"Do it," I said.

He yanked a tool out of his pocket that snapped Lynn's shackles open in two seconds. "Can we go now?" he asked.

"The sooner the better," I said.

"Where are you taking me?" Lynn said, stripping off her gloves.

"You're an American, right?" I said.

"Yeah."

"We've got a super-romantic date on Rosa, then." At the Citizen Services Bureau, which I wasn't going to say out loud in front of my father's spy.

The Tigers hadn't arrived yet, so we just walked out. The bodyguard urged us to pick up the pace, which we did, or at least as much as Lynn could; she was still recovering from her surgery and winced with every step. The AD escorted us to the edge of Lib, then washed his hands of us.

"WHO ARE YOU?" Lynn asked.

"My name is Beck, and your sister, um, hired me. To look for you."

Lynn looked me over skeptically.

"You'd disappeared," I said. "She wanted to know where you were, and if you were okay. Which you weren't."

"Surely she didn't have the money to pay for you rescuing me like that."

"No," I said. "By the way, do you know some deep, dark secret that's not supposed to get out? Because someone assaulted me earlier today to tell me to mind my own business. That's why I decided to come find you."

Lynn eyed me with renewed suspicion. "No," she said. "If I knew some deep, dark secret I'd be down at the bottom of the deep, dark ocean right about now. I wouldn't have been in a skin factory."

"So what happened to you, exactly?"

"I got sick—really sick. I hit up Gibbon for a loan, and he said he'd sell my bond to someone who'd arrange treatment for me. I had to sign a consent, because of the laws on Min. Janus took me to the clinic, and they said I needed kidney regeneration. That's horribly expensive, but without it. . . . Anyway, Janus told me the only place that would pay for that sort of treatment was a skin factory. I still wanted to refuse, but there's a loophole when someone has a terminal condition and can't pay for their treatment. Their contract can be sold without their consent to anyone willing to foot the bill. So that's how I wound up in the skin factory."

There was something here I wasn't seeing.

"Where are we going?" she asked.

"The Citizen Services Bureau," I said.

"Do you think they'll let me use a phone?" she asked.

"Probably," I said, assuming she'd want to call her sister to come meet her.

I felt nervous going down Embassy Row. It basically looked like any other corridor full of shops, but really well-kept with very clean windows. We passed

Mexico and France before we got to the American one. A bell tinkled as we went in, like in a store. There was a young man sitting at a desk, with a name-tag that said, "Tyrone LeBlanc, Consular Officer." He was black, which was sort of unusual on the stead; most of the locals were white, Asian, or Hispanic. Mr. Leblanc looked at Lynn, and at me, and then said, "May I help you?"

"This is Lynn Miller," I said. "She's bonded to a skin farm and wants to—"

"—Make a phone call," she said. "If you don't mind. I don't have my passport with me."

"Did you register with us when you arrived?" he asked.

"Not exactly."

"Well—you can definitely use a phone," he said, and handed one to her before turning to me. "Forgive me if I'm mistaken, but are you Rebecca Garrison?" he asked.

"Yes," I said.

"Don't go anywhere, I have something for you." He stepped into the back and returned with a sealed paper envelope, with *Rebecca Garrison* written on the front.

My stomach lurched. It was *just* like my father to do something like this—just in case I ever disobeyed him. Well, I didn't have to read it now. I stuffed it into my pocket, mumbling, "Thanks."

Near me, Lynn had gotten through to someone. "I'm calling to renegotiate my contract," she said, her voice triumphant.

The U.S. government will provide transportation to citizens in danger under certain circumstances, and that was one of the reasons I'd snatched Lynn. They don't recognize the validity of bond contracts generally and they consider a U.S. citizen being held to work in a skin factory to essentially have been kidnapped and imprisoned under dangerous circumstances. I'd figured Lynn would take the first boat back to California, but instead she was spelling out a set of conditions under which she'd let John Butterfield resell her bond to someone else. "We're not talking about profit," she said furiously, pacing back and forth in front of the desk. "We're talking about *how much* of a loss you're going to take."

"What happened to her?" Mr. LeBlanc asked me.

"She had kidney failure," I said, and explained the sequence of events.

"Huh," he said. "Kidney failure, really? Same thing happened with an escaped bond-worker last month, too."

"What causes kidney failure, anyway?"

"Oh, lots of things. Untreated diabetes, certain illnesses, drug overdoses. . . . Kidneys filter out toxins, so an overdose of anything toxic." He pursed his lips. "You're not big on food and water inspectors here, you know. I'm surprised it doesn't happen more often."

"Lynn?"

She pressed the mute button on the phone. "Yes?"

"Which canteen do you subscribe to?"

"Clark's. It's near the locker rooms."

Could that be the secret? That Clark's was poisoning people? But thousands of bond-workers ate there; if it were poisoning people, the clinic would be overflowing with dying bond-workers.

No; if Lynn had been poisoned, she'd surely been singled out.

"Don't renegotiate your contract," I said. "Go back to California."

She shook her head and returned to her conversation. I looked mutely at Mr. LeBlanc. He shrugged. "Fugitive bond-workers stay here more often than you'd think. In Lynn's case, maybe there's a warrant out for her arrest, and she's taking advantage of the laws here to avoid extradition."

Lynn glared at him and muted the phone again. "Drug charges," she said. "Possession and manufacture of substances that are *entirely legal* on every island in the seastead. I'd bet dollars to scrip Mr. American Representative here has been known to possess an illegal substance from time to time."

He shrugged.

"But even though she's up on criminal charges back in the States, you'd still take her home, for free?"

"Well, not exactly for free," he said. "We'd send her a bill later. She wouldn't get sold into bond-slavery if she didn't pay, though, we'd just garnish her paychecks."

"Lynn," I said. "I think the secret they're protecting is that you were poisoned on purpose. Four other bond-workers were treated for kidney failure the same day as you, and all had their contracts bought by the same guy who bought yours. Other workers have disappeared from Gibbon's dining hall, haven't they? They've gotten sick, and never come back. I think Gibbon's doing it. I think Gibbon, Janus, and Butterfield are conspiring to use the 'terminal condition' loophole to make sure Butterfield gets a steady stream of bond-workers."

Lynn turned back to the phone. "Also," she said, "I don't want to be sold back to Gibbon."

GIBBON, JANUS, AND Butterfield.

Min does have police, after a fashion; we're not like Lib. But we don't have a *lot* of police. Basically, they break up fist fights. If something gets stolen, you'd usually hire someone privately to try to retrieve it for you. There was a murder on the stead a few years ago and here's what happened: everyone knew who did it, so the police went and arrested him and there was a lot of talk about trial procedures. While people were arguing about how exactly a murder trial ought to work, the victim's brother hired a bunch of guys from Lib to break into the police station and kidnap the murderer, and then throw him into the ocean. And then everyone pretended not to know that it was the victim's brother who'd done the hiring.

But here's the other thing: the murder victim was a citizen, not a guest worker.

Something complicated like this—everyone would pretend they thought it was *coincidence* that all these people were developing kidney failure. Or maybe they'd blame Clark's. The doctor at the clinic clearly thought it was Clark's.

I did know one person who was powerful enough to actually make a difference, though: my father.

My father scared me. Especially when he was angry. But he was my father. I ought to be able to go to him with this.

"DAD?"

Our apartment was mostly dark; light spilled from my father's office. "Come in here, Beck."

"I need to talk to you about something," I said.

He must have heard the seriousness in my voice because he pushed himself back from his computer and gestured to a chair.

"I was trying to find something kind of unusual this week," I said. "I was trying to find a person."

His eye twitched. "Really."

"Well, I started out trying to find a pair of size eight sparkly strappy sandals. But the woman who had those wanted me to try to find her sister." He didn't answer. I swallowed hard and went on. "So, okay, I'm going to skip all the intervening steps and tell you what I realized today, which is that Mr. Gibbon, Mr. Janus, and Mr. Butterfield are conspiring to poison bond-workers, so that their contracts can be sold for skin farm work. It wasn't an accident that L—" I broke off, suddenly not wanting to give my father any names "—the woman I was looking for got sick."

"Mmm," he said. "Do you have any actual *evidence* for this story you're telling me?"

"No," I said, honestly. "I mean, I'm not a police officer or a doctor. But I bet if you examined any of the bond-workers who've been treated for kidney failure in the last month—"

"Yes, most likely you'd find traces, if a poison was involved. Well. Yes." He pondered that. "I assume your, ah, your *date*, this afternoon . . . was the woman you were searching for?"

He'd heard from the ADs already. "Yes."

"You are *remarkably* tenacious."

"Thank you," I said, even though I could tell this hadn't been a compliment.

"And just what do you expect me to do about this, Beck?"

"Go to the police and make them investigate?"

"You must realize that you've overlooked a wide range of alternate possibilities. These individuals might have eaten or drunk something dodgy, first of all; that's the simplest explanation. It might be pure coincidence. Or perhaps most likely of all, they might have all ingested something *recreational* that displayed questionable judgment on all their parts."

"And *coincidentally*, Butterfield bought up all those people with kidney failure?"

"Oh, I'm sure that wasn't a coincidence. He has an arrangement with the man who holds the patent on the kidney regeneration technique and can have it done at a discount. Undoubtedly, he has a standing request at the hospital for notification when anyone has significant kidney damage."

"How do you know this?"

"I know a lot of things, Rebecca." He fell silent and watched my reaction. I tried hard not to give him one. "Now," he said, "I received several interesting calls today. Apparently you were pestering Janus outside of his dining hall, after talking your way in. You had nothing wrong with you this morning at the clinic, although you did cost me a fair sum what with all the tests they ran. And you went to Lib this afternoon."

He hadn't heard about Embassy Row. I didn't tell him.

"All, apparently, to find—and eventually to *personally rescue* this particular bond-worker. Surely the rescue wasn't in your original agreement with the owner of the sandals."

". . . No."

"No." He leaned back. "So? Explain."

"When I was down by the locker rooms today someone attacked me, grabbed me from behind and hit me, and told me to mind my own business." I glared furiously at my own feet. "I was *done* but that made me think I must have missed something important. Something worth hiding."

"I see."

He fell silent. I lifted my chin and stared out the window. Or at the window, since it was dark.

"Well," he said, "you've demonstrated that you are stubborn, disobedient, and disrespectful."

"I'm sorry, sir."

"No, you're clearly not." He tapped his desk with a pen. "I'm going to have to think on how best to use you. In the meantime, I'm grounding you for the next month. If Jamie still wants you as a Finder when the month is up, that's between the two of you."

I swallowed hard. "What about Gibbon and . . . what about the bond-workers?"

"I expect there won't be any more mysterious kidney failures," my father said, turning back to his computer screen. "I'll pass the word along that if their plot could be unraveled by a persistent *teenager* they need to knock it off. I expect they will. Also, I don't like people manhandling my daughter, especially considering how thoroughly the tactic backfired. I'll see if I can identify the thug."

"But—what about L—I mean, my date from this afternoon?"

He looked back at me and raised an eyebrow. "Don't go looking for Lynn Miller again," he said. "I doubt that you will like what you find."

BACK IN MY room, I turned on *Stead Life,* laid out my homework, and changed into pajamas. When I took off my jeans, they crinkled; the letter I'd been handed at the CSB was still in my pocket.

My father hadn't mentioned *that* particular bit of disobedience. I smoothed the letter out, then opened it.

Dear Becky,

   Happy birthday, darling. This is the twelfth of these messages I've written. Every year I send a new one to the Services Bureau on Rosa, in the hopes that eventually you will come in, and they can deliver it.

   I'm not sure what your father has told you about me. I just want you to know that I love you, and I would like to see you. If you're not willing to come stateside, I would like to speak with you by phone or correspond by letter. Whatever you're comfortable with. If you'd like to leave New Minerva, the Bureau will provide you with transportation to San Francisco. I'll meet you there, and take you home—to my home.

   I just want you to know I haven't forgotten you.

   I'll never forget you.

   I hope to see you again someday.

Love,
Mom

My father had lied to me, I realized, staring at the letter.

My mother was alive.

I wondered what else my father had lied about.

WEEP FOR DAY

Indrapramit Das

Indrapramit Das is a writer and artist from Kolkata, India. He completed his MFA at the University of British Columbia, and is currently in Vancouver, British Columbia, he says, "working as a freelance writer, artist, editor, game tester, tutor, would-be novelist, and aspirant to adulthood." He attended the 2012 Clarion West Writers Workshop and was a recipient of an Octavia E. Butler Scholarship Award. His short fiction has appeared in *Clarkesworld, Asimov's, Apex Magazine,* and others, and in the anthologies *Breaking the Bow: Speculative Fiction Inspired by the Ramayana* (Zubaan Books) and *Bloodchildren: Stories by the Octavia E. Butler Scholars.* He is writing a contemporary and historical fantasy novel set in India.

"Weep for Day" was published in *Asimov's,* and is evidence, if anyone needs it, that *Asimov's* is still a leader in the field. Michael Swanwick praises it, in an online review: "The prose reminded me of early Zelazny. It has touches of Gene Wolfe and Mary Gentle and other writers to it as well." The world is changing over the lifetimes of the characters and that gives the story an elegiac tone, and an underlying power.

I WAS EIGHT years old the first time I saw a real, living Nightmare. My parents took my brother and me on a trip from the City-of-Long-Shadows to the hills at Evening's edge, where one of my father's clients had a manse. Father was a railway contractor. He hired out labor and resources to the privateers extending the frontiers of civilization toward the frozen wilderness of the dark Behind-the-Sun. Aptly, we took a train up to the foothills of the great Penumbral Mountains.

It was the first time my brother and I had been on a train, though we'd seen them tumble through the city with their cacophonic engines, cumulous tails of smoke and steam billowing like blood over the rooftops when the red light of our sun caught them. It was also the first time we had been anywhere close to Night—Behind-the-Sun—where the Nightmares lived. Just a decade before we took that trip, it would have been impossible to go as far into Evening as we were doing with such casual comfort and ease.

Father had prodded the new glass of the train windows, pointing to the power-lines crisscrossing the sky in tandem with the gleaming lines of metal railroads silvering the hazy landscape of progress. He sat between my brother Velag and me, our heads propped against the bulk of his belly, which bulged against his rough crimson waistcoat. I clutched that coat and breathed in the sweet smell of chemlis gall that hung over him. Mother watched with a smile as she peeled indigos for us with her fingers, laying them in the lap of her skirt.

"Look at that. We've got no more reason to be afraid of the dark, do we, my tykes?" said Father, his belly humming with the sound of his booming voice.

Dutifully, Velag and I agreed there wasn't.

"Why not?" he asked us, expectant.

"Because of the Industrialization, which brings the light of Day to the darkness of Night," we chimed, a line learned both in school and at home (inaccurate, as we'd never set foot in Night itself). Father laughed. I always slowed down on the word "industrialization," which caused Velag and me to say it at different times. He was just over a year older than me, though.

"And what is your father, children?" Mother asked.

"A knight of Industry and Technology, bringer of light under Church and Monarchy."

I didn't like reciting that part, because it had more than one long "y" word, and felt like a struggle to say. Father *was* actually a knight, though not a knight-errant for a while. He had been too big by then to fit into a suit of plate-armor or heft a heavy sword around, and knights had stopped doing that for many years anyway. The Industrialization had swiftly made the pageantry of adventure obsolete.

Father wheezed as we reminded him of his knighthood, as if ashamed. He put his hammy hands in our hair and rubbed. I winced through it, as usual, because he always forgot about the pins in my long hair, something my brother didn't have to worry about. Mother gave us the peeled indigos, her hands perfumed with the citrus. She was the one who taught me how to place the pins in my hair, both of us in front of the mirror looking like different-sized versions of each other.

I looked out the windows of our cabin, fascinated by how everything outside slowly became bluer and darker as we moved away from the City-of-Long-Shadows, which lies between the two hemispheres of Day and Night. Condensation crawled across the corners of the double-glazed panes as the train took us further east. Being a studious girl even at that age, I deduced from school lessons that the air outside was becoming rapidly colder as we neared Night's hemisphere, which has never seen a single ray of our sun and is theorized to be entirely frozen. The train, of course, was kept warm by the same steam and machinery that powered its tireless wheels and kept its lamps and twinkling chandeliers aglow.

"Are you excited to see the Nightmare? It was one of the first to be captured and tamed. The gentleman we're visiting is very proud to be its captor," said Father.

"Yes!" screamed Velag. "Does it still have teeth? And claws?" he asked, his eyes wide.

"I would think so," Father nodded.

"Is it going to be in chains?"

"I hope so, Velag. Otherwise it might get loose and—" He paused for dramatic effect. I froze in fear. Velag looked eagerly at him. "Eat you both up!" he bellowed, tickling us with his huge hands. It took all my willpower not to scream. I looked at Velag's delighted expression to keep me calm, reminding myself that these were just Father's hands jabbing my sides.

"Careful!" Mother said sharply, to my relief. "They'll get the fruit all over." The indigo segments were still in our laps, on the napkins Mother had handed to us. Father stopped tickling us, still grinning.

"Do you remember what they look like?" Velag asked, as if trying to see how many questions he could ask in as little time as possible. He had asked this one before, of course. Father had fought Nightmares, and even killed some, when he was a knight-errant.

"We never really saw them, son," said Father. He touched the window. "Out there, it's so cold you can barely feel your own fingers, even in armor."

We could see the impenetrable walls of the forests pass us by—shaggy, snarled mare-pines, their leaves black as coals and branches supposedly twisted into knots by the Nightmares to tangle the path of intruders. The high, hoary tops of the trees shimmered ever so slightly in the scarce light sneaking over the horizon, which they sucked in so hungrily. The moon was brighter here than in the City, but at its jagged crescent, a broken gemstone behind the scudding clouds. We were still in Evening, but had encroached onto the Nightmares' outer territories, marked by the forests that extended to the foothills. After the foothills, there was no more forest, because there was no more light. Inside our cabin, under bright electric lamps, sitting on velvet-lined bunks, it was hard to believe that we were actually in the land of Nightmares. I wondered if they were in the trees right now, watching our windows as we looked out.

"It's hard to see them, or anything, when you're that cold," Father breathed deeply, gazing at the windows. It made me uneasy, hearing him say the same thing over and over. We were passing the very forests he traveled through as a knight-errant, escorting pioneers.

"Father's told you about this many times, dear," Mother interjected, peering at Father with worried eyes. I watched. Father smiled at her and shook his head.

"That's all right, I like telling my little tykes about my adventures. I guess you'll see what a Nightmare looks like tomorrow, eh? Are you excited?" he asked, perhaps forgetting that he'd already asked. Velag shouted in the affirmative again.

Father looked down at me, raising his bushy eyebrows. "What about you, Valyzia?"

I nodded and smiled.

I wasn't excited. Truth be told, I didn't want to see it at all. The idea of capturing and keeping a Nightmare seemed somehow disrespectful in my heart, though I didn't know the word then. It made me feel weak and confused, because I was and always had been so afraid of them, and had been taught to be.

I wondered if Velag had noticed that Father had once again refused to actually describe a Nightmare. Even in his most excitable retellings of his brushes with them, he never described them as more than walking shadows. There was a grainy sepia-toned photograph of him during his younger vigils as a knight-errant above the mantle of our living-room fireplace. It showed him mounted on a horse, dressed in his plate-armor and fur-lined surcoat, raising his longsword to the skies (the blade was cropped from the picture by its white border). Clutched in his other plated hand was something that looked like a blot of black, as if the chemicals of the photograph had congealed into a spot, attracted by some mystery or heat. The shape appeared to bleed back into the black background.

It was, I had been told, the head of a Nightmare Father had slain. It was too dark a thing to be properly caught by whatever early photographic engine had captured his victory. The blot had no distinguishing features apart from two vague points emerging from the rest of it, like horns or ears. That head earned him a large part of the fortune he later used to start up his contracting business. We never saw it, because Nightmares' heads and bodies were burned or gibbeted by knights-errant, who didn't want to bring them into the City for fear of attracting their horde. The photograph had been a source of dizzying pride for my young self, because it meant that my father was one of the bravest people I knew. At other times, it just made me wonder why he couldn't describe something he had once beheaded, and held in his hand as a trophy.

My indigo finished, Mother took the napkin and wiped my hands with it. My brother still picked at his. A waiter brought us a silver platter filled with sugar-dusted pastries, their centers soft with warm fudge and grünberry jam. We'd already finished off supper, brought under silver domes that gushed steam when the waiters raised them with their white-gloved hands, revealing chopped fungus, meat dumplings, sour cream and fermented salad. Mother told Velag to finish the indigo before he touched the pastries. Father ate them with as much gusto as I did. I watched him lick his powdered fingers, which had once held the severed head of a Nightmare.

When it was time for respite, the cabin lights were shut off and the ones in the corridor were dimmed. I was relieved my parents left the curtains of the windows open as we retired, because I didn't want it to be completely dark. It was dim enough outside that we could fall asleep. It felt unusual to go to bed with windows uncovered for once.

I couldn't help imagine, as I was wont to do, that as our train moved through Evening's forested fringes, the Nightmares would find a way to get on board. I wondered if they were already on the train. But the presence of my family, all softly snoring in their bunks (Velag above me, my parents opposite us); the periodic, soothing flash of way-station lights passing by outside; the sigh of the sliding doors at the end of the carriage opening and closing as porters, waiters, and passengers moved through the corridors; the sweet smell of the fresh sheets and pillow on my bunk—these things lulled me into a sleep free of bad dreams, despite my fear of seeing the creature we'd named bad dreams after, face-to-face, the next vigil.

WHEN I WAS six I stopped sleeping in my parents' room, and started sleeping in the same room as my brother. At the time of this change, I was abnormally scared of the dark (and consider, reader, that this was a time when fear of the dark was as normal and acceptable as the fear of falling from a great height). So scared that I couldn't fall asleep after the maids came around and closed our sleep-shutters and drew the curtains, to block out the western light for respite.

The heavy clatter of the wooden slats being closed every respite's eve was like a note of foreboding for me. I hunkered under the blankets, rigid with anxiety as the maids filed out of the room with their lanterns drawing wild shadows on the walls. Then the last maid would close the door, and our room would be swallowed up by those shadows.

In the chill darkness that followed, I would listen to the clicking of Nightmares' claws as they walked up and down the corridors of our shuttered house. Our parents had often told me that it was just rats in the walls and ceiling, but I refused to believe it. Every respite I would imagine one of the Nightmare intruders slinking into our room, listening to its breathing as it came closer to my bed and pounced on me, not being able to scream as it sat on my chest and ran its reeking claws through my hair, winding it into knots around its long fingers and laughing softly.

Enduring the silence for what seemed like hours, I would begin to wail and cry until Velag threw pillows at me and Mother came to my side to shush me with her kisses. To solve the problem, my parents tried keeping the sleep-shutters open through the hours of respite, and moved my brother to a room on the windowless east-facing side of the house when he complained. Unfortunately, we require the very dark we fear to fall asleep. The persistent burning line of the horizon beyond the windows, while a comforting sight, left me wide awake for most of respite.

In the end Velag and I were reunited and the shutters closed once more, because Father demanded that I not be coddled when my brother had learned to sleep alone so bravely. I often heard my parents arguing about this, since Mother thought it was madness to try and force me not to be afraid. Most of my friends from school hadn't and wouldn't sleep without their parents until they were at least eleven or twelve. Father was adamant, demanding that we learn to be strong and brave in case the Nightmares ever found a way to over-run the city.

It's a strange thing, to be made to feel guilty for learning too well something that was ingrained in us from the moment we were born. Now nightmare is just a word, and it's unusual to even think that the race that we gave that name might still be alive somewhere in the world. When Velag and I were growing up, Nightmares were the enemy.

Our grandparents told us about them, as did our parents, as did our teach-ers, as did every book and textbook we had ever come across. Stories of a time when guns hadn't been invented, when knights-errant roved the frigid forest paths beyond the City-of-Long-Shadows to prove their manhood and loyalty to the Monarchy and its Solar Church, and to extend the borders of the city and find new resources. A time coming to a close when I was born, even as the expansion continued onward faster than ever.

I remember my school class-teacher drawing the curtains and holding a candle to a wooden globe of our planet to show us how the sun made Night and Day. She took a piece of chalk and tapped where the candlelight turned to shadow on the globe. "That's us," she said, and moved the chalk over to the shadowed side. "That's them," she said.

Nightmares have defined who we are since we crawled out of the hot lakes at the edge of fiery Day, and wrapped the steaming bloody skins of slaugh-tered animals around us to walk upright, east into the cooler marches of our world's Evening. We stopped at the alien darkness we had never seen before, not just because of the terrible cold that clung to the air the further we walked, but because of what we met at Evening's end.

A race of walking shadows, circling our firelight with glittering eyes, felling our explorers with barbed spears and arrows, snatching our dead as we fled from their ambushes. Silently, these unseen, lethal guardians of Night's bitter frontier told us we could go no further. But we couldn't go back towards Day, where the very air seems to burn under the sun's perpetual gaze.

So we built our villages where sun's light still lingers and the shadows are longest before they dissolve into Evening. Our villages grew into towns, and our towns grew into the City-of-Long-Shadows, and our city grew along the Penumbra until it reached the Seas-of-Storms to the north and the impassable crags of World's-Rim (named long before we knew this to be false) to the south. For all of history, we looked behind our shoulders at the gloaming of the east-ern horizon, where the Nightmares watched our progress.

So the story went, told over and over.

We named bad dreams after them because we thought Nightmares were their source, that they sent spies into the city to infect our minds and keep us afraid of the dark, their domain. According to folklore, these spies could be glimpsed upon waking abruptly. Indeed, I'd seen them crouching malevolently in the corner of the bedroom, wreathed in the shadows that were their home, slinking away with impossible speed once I looked at them.

There are no Nightmares left alive anywhere near the City-of-Long-Shadows, but we still have bad dreams and we still see their spies sometimes when we wake. Some say they are spirits of their race, or survivors. I'm not convinced. Even though we have killed all the Nightmares, our own half-dreaming minds continue to populate our bedrooms with their ghosts, so we may remember their legacy.

To date, none of our city's buildings have windows or doors on their east-facing walls.

AND SO THE train took us to the end of our civilization. There are many things I remember about Weep-for-Day, though in some respects those memories feel predictably like the shreds of a disturbing dream. Back then it was just an outpost, not a hill-station town like it is now. The most obvious thing to remember is how it sleeted or snowed all the time. I know now that it's caused by moist convective winds in the atmosphere carrying the warmth of the sun from Day to Night, their loads of fat clouds scraping up against the mountains of the Penumbra for all eternity and washing the foothills in their frozen burden. But to my young self, the constant crying of that bruised sky was just another mystery in the world, a sorcery perpetrated by the Nightmares.

I remember, of course, how dark it was. How the people of the outpost carried bobbing lanterns and acrid magenta flares that flamed even against the perpetual wind and precipitation. How everyone outside (including us) had to wear goggles and thick protective suits lined with the fur of animals to keep the numbing cold of outer Evening out. I had never seen such darkness outdoors, and it felt like being asleep while walking. To think that beyond the mountains lay an absence of light even deeper was unbelievable.

I remember the tall poles that marked turns in the curving main road, linked by the ever-present electric and telegraph wires that made such an outpost possible. The bright gold-and-red pennants of the Monarchy fluttered from those poles, dulled by lack of light. They all showed a sun that was no longer visible from there.

I remember the solar shrines—little huts by the road, with small windows that lit up every few hours as chimes rang out over the windy outpost. Through the doors you could see the altars inside; each with an electric globe, its filament flooded with enough voltage to make it look like a hot ball of fire. For a minute these shrines would burn with their tiny artificial suns, and the goggled and suited inhabitants of Weep-for-Day would huddle around them like giant flies, their shadows wavering lines on the streaks of light cast out on the muddy snow or ice. They would pray on their knees, some reaching out to rub the faded ivory crescents of sunwyrm fangs on the altars.

Beyond the road and the slanted wet roofs of Weep-for-Day, there was so little light that the slope of the hill was barely visible. The forested plain beyond was nothing but a black void that ended in the faint glow of the horizon—the last weak embers in a soot-black fireplace just doused with water.

I couldn't see our City-of-Long-Shadows, which filled me with an irrational anxiety that it was gone forever, that if we took the train back we would find the whole world filled with darkness and only Night waiting on the other side.

But these details are less than relevant. That trip changed me and changed the course of my life not because I saw what places beyond the City-of-Long-Shadows looked like, though seeing such no doubt planted the seeds of some future grit in me. It changed me because I, with my family by my side, witnessed a living Nightmare, as we were promised.

The creature was a prisoner of Vorin Tylvur, who was at the time the Consul of Weep-for-Day, a knight like Father, and an appointed privateer and mining coordinator of the Penumbral territories. Of course, he is now well remembered for his study of Nightmares in captivity, and his campaigns to expand the Monarchy's territories into Evening. The manse we stayed in was where he and his wife lived, governing the affairs of the outpost and coordinating expansion and exploration.

I do not remember much of our hosts, except that they were adults in the way all adults who aren't parents are, to little children. They were kind enough to me. I couldn't comprehend the nature of condescension at that age, but I did find the cooing manner of most adults who talked to me boring, and they were no different. Though I'm grateful for their hospitality to my family, I cannot, in retrospect, look upon them with much returned kindness.

They showed us the imprisoned Nightmare on the second vigil of our stay. It was in the deepest recesses of the manse, which was more an oversized, glorified bunker on the hill of Weep-for-Day than anything else. We went down into a dank, dim corridor in the chilly heart of that mound of crustal rock to see the prisoner.

"I call it Shadow. A little nickname," Sir Tylvur said with a toothy smile, his huge moustache hanging from his nostrils like the dead wings of some poor misbegotten bird trapped in his head. He proved himself right then to have not only a startling lack of imagination for a man of his intelligence and inquisitiveness, but also a grotesquely inappropriate sense of levity.

It would be dramatic and untruthful to say that my fear of darkness receded the moment I set eyes on the creature. But something changed in me. There, looking at this hunched and shivering thing under the smoky blaze of the flares its armored jailers held to reveal it to its captor's guests, I saw that a phantom flayed was just another animal.

Sir Tylvur had made sure that its light-absorbent skin would not hinder our viewing of the captured enemy. There is no doubt that I feared it, even though its skin was stripped from its back to reveal its glistening red muscles, even though it was clearly broken and defeated. But my mutable young mind understood then, looking into its shining black eyes—the only visible feature in the empty dark of its face—that it knew terror just as I or any human did. The Nightmare was scared. It was a heavy epiphany for a child to bear, and I vomited on the glass observation wall of its cramped holding cell.

Velag didn't make fun of me. He shrank into Mother's arms, trying to back away from the humanoid silhouette scrabbling against the glass to escape the light it so feared; a void-like cut-out in reality but for that livid wet wound on its back revealing it to be as real as us. It couldn't, or would not, scream or vocalize in any way. Instead, we just heard the squeal of its spider-like hands splayed on the glass, claws raking the surface.

I looked at Father, standing rigid and pale, hands clutched into tight fists by his sides. The same fists that held up the severed head of one of this creature's race in triumph so many years ago. Just as in the photograph, there were the horn-like protrusions from its head, though I still couldn't tell what they were. I looked at Mother who, despite the horrific vision in front of us, despite her son clinging to her waist, reached down in concern to wipe the vomit from my mouth and chin with bare fingers, her gloves crumpled in her other hand.

As Sir Tylvur wondered what to do about his spattered glass wall, he decided to blame the Nightmare for my reaction and rapped hard on the cell with the hilt of his sheathed ceremonial sword. He barked at the prisoner, wanting to frighten it away from the glass, I suppose. The only recognizable word in between his grunts was "Shadow." But as he called it by that undignified, silly nickname, the thing stopped its frantic scrabbling. Startled, Sir Tylvur stepped back. The two armored jailers stepped back as well, flares wavering in the gloom of the cell. I still don't know why the Nightmare stopped thrashing, and I never will know for sure. But at that moment I thought it recognized the nickname its captor had given it, and recognized that it was being displayed like a trophy. Perhaps it wanted to retain some measure of its pride.

The flarelight flickered on its eyes, which grew brighter as moisture gathered on them. It was clearly in pain from the light. I saw that it was as tall as a human, though it looked smaller because of how crouched into itself it was. It cast a shadow like any other animal, and that shadow looked like its paler twin, dancing behind its back. Chains rasped on the wet cell floor, shackled to its limbs. The illuminated wound on its back wept pus, but the rest of it remained that sucking, indescribable black that hurt the human eye.

Except something in its face. It looked at us, and out of that darkness came a glittering of wet obsidian teeth as unseen lips peeled back. I will never forget that invisible smile, whether it was a grimace of pain or a taunting leer.

"Kill it," Velag whispered. And that was when Mother took both our hands tight in hers, and pulled us away from the cell. She marched us down that dank corridor, leaving the two former knights-errant, Father and Sir Tylvur, staring into that glimmering cell at the specter of their past.

THAT NIGHT, IN the tiny room we'd been given as our quarters, I asked Velag if the Nightmare had scared him.

"Why should it scare me?" he said, face pale in the dim glow of the small heating furnace in the corner of the chamber. "It's in chains."

"You just looked scared. It's okay to be scared. I was too. But I think it was as well."

"Shut up. You don't know what you're saying. I'm going to sleep," he said, and turned away from me, his cot groaning. The furnace hissed and ticked.

"I think papa was scared also. He didn't want to see a Nightmare again," I said to Velag's back.

That was when my brother pounced off his cot and on top of me. I was too shocked to scream. My ingrained submission to his power as an elder male authority figure took over. I gave no resistance. Sitting on my small body, Velag took my blanket and shoved it into my mouth. Then, he snatched my pillow and held it over my face. Choking on the taste of musty cloth, I realized I couldn't breathe. I believed that my brother was about to kill me then. I truly believed it. I could feel the pressure of his hands through the pillow, and they were at that moment the hands of something inhuman. I was more terrified then than I'd ever been in my entire short life, plagued though I'd always been by fear.

He held the pillow over my head for no more than four seconds, probably less. When he raised it off my face and pulled the blanket out of my mouth he looked as shaken as I was. His eyes were wet with tears, but in a second his face was twisted in a grimace.

"Never call Papa a coward. Never call Papa a coward. Papa was never afraid. Do you hear me? You never had to sleep alone in the dark, you don't know. I'm going to grow up and be like Papa and kill them. I'll kill them," he hissed the words into my face like a litany. I started crying, unable and probably too scared to tell him I hadn't called Father a coward. I could still barely breathe, so flooded was I with my own tears, so drunk on the air he had denied me. Velag went back to his cot and wrapped himself in his blanket, breathing heavily.

As I shuddered with stifled sobs, I decided that I would never tell my parents about this, that I would never have Velag punished for this violence. I didn't forgive him, not even close, but that is what I decided.

* * *

I WAS SEVENTEEN the last time I saw Velag. I went to visit him at the
Royal Military Academy's boarding school. He had been there for four years
already. We saw him every few moons when he came back to the City proper
to visit. But I wanted to see the campus for myself. It was a lovely train ride,
just a few hours from the central districts of the City-of-Long-Shadows to the
scattered hamlets beyond it.

It was warmer and brighter out where the Academy was. The campus was
beautiful, sown with pruned but still wild looking trees and plants that only
grew further out towards Day, their leaves a lighter shade of blue and their
flowers huge, craning to the west on thick stems. The sun still peered safely
behind the edge of the world, but its gaze was bright enough to wash the
stately buildings of the boarding school with a fiery golden-red light, sparkling
in the waxy leaves of vines winding their way around the arched windows. On
every ornate, varnished door was a garish propaganda poster of the Dark
Lord of Nightmares, with his cowled cloak of shadows and black sword, being struck down by our soldiers' bayoneted guns.

I sat with Velag in a pavillion in the visitors' garden, which was on a gentle
bluff. In the fields adjacent, his fellow student-soldiers played tackleball, their
rowdy calls and whistles ringing through the air. We could see heavy banks
of glowing, sunlit storm-clouds to the west where the atmosphere boiled and
churned in the heat of Day, beyond miles of shimmering swamp-forests and
lakes. To the east, a faint moon hung over the campus, but no stars were visible
so close to Day.

Velag looked so different from the last time I saw him. His pimples were
vanishing, the sallow softness of adolescence melting away to reveal the man
he was to become. The military uniform, so forbidding in red and black, suited
his tall form. He looked smart and handsome in it. It hurt me to see him shackled in it, but I could see that he wore it with great pride.

He held my hand and asked about my life back home, about my plans to
apply to the College of Archaeology at the University of St. Kataretz. He asked
about our parents. He told me how gorgeous and grown-up I looked in my
dress, and said he was proud of me for becoming a "prodigy." I talked to him
with a heavy ache in my chest, because I knew with such certainty that we
hardly knew each other, and would get no chance to any time soon, as he would
be dispatched to the frontlines of Penumbral Conquest.

As if reading my thoughts, his cheek twitched with what I thought was
guilt, and he looked at the stormy horizon. Perhaps he was remembering the
night on which he told me he would grow up and kill Nightmares like Father—a
promise he was keeping. He squeezed my hand.

"I'll be all right, Val. Don't you worry."

I gave him a rueful smile. "It's not too late. You can opt to become a civilian
after graduation and come study with me at St. Kataretz. Ma and Papa would

think no less of you. You could do physics again; you loved it before. We can get an apartment in Pemluth Halls, share the cost. The University's right in the middle of the City, we'd have so much fun together."

"I can't. You know that. I want this for myself. I want to be a soldier, and a knight."

"Being a knight isn't the same thing as it was in Papa's time. He was independent, a privateer. Things have changed. You'll be a part of the military. Knighthoods belong to them now and they're stingy with them. They mostly give them to soldiers who are wounded or dead, Velag."

"I'm in military school, by the saints, I know what a knighthood is or isn't. Please don't be melodramatic. You're an intelligent girl."

"What's that got to do with anything?"

"I'm going. I have more faith in my abilities than you do."

"I have plenty of faith in you. But the Nightmares are angry now, Velag. We're wiping them out. They're scared and angry. They're coming out in waves up in the hills. More of our soldiers are dying than ever before. How can I not worry?"

His jaw knotted, he glared down at our intertwined hands. His grip was limp now. "Don't start with your theories about the benevolence of Nightmares. I don't want to hear it. They're not scared, they *are* fear, and we'll wipe them off the planet if need be so that you and everybody else can live without that fear."

"I'm quite happy with my life, thank you. I'd rather you be alive for Ma and Papa and me than have the terrible horde of the Nightmares gone forever."

He bit his lip and tightened his hand around mine again. "I know, little sister. You're sweet to worry so. But the Monarchy needs me. I'll be fine. I promise."

And that was the end of the discussion as far as he was concerned. I knew there was no point pushing him further, because it would upset him. This was his life, after all. The one he had chosen. I had no right to belittle it. I didn't want to return to the City on bad terms with him. We made what little small talk was left to make, and then we stood and kissed each other on the cheek, and I hugged him tight and watched him walk away.

What good are such promises as the one he made on our final farewell, even if one means them with all of one's heart? He was dispatched right after his graduation a few moons later, without even a ceremony because it was wartime. After six moons of excited letters from the frontlines at the Penumbral Mountains, he died with a Nightmare's spear in his chest, during a battle that earned the Monarchy yet another victory against the horde of darkness. Compared to the thousands of Nightmares slaughtered during the battle with our guns and cannons, the Monarchy's casualties were small. And yet, my parents lost their son, and I my brother.

In death, they did give Velag the knighthood he fought so hard for. Never have I hated myself so much for being right.

WHEN VELAG WAS being helped out of Mother by doctors in the city, my father had been escorting pioneers in the foothills. I see him in his armor, the smell of heated steel and cold sweat cloying under his helm, almost blind because of the visor, sword in one hand, knotted reins and a flaming torch in the other, his mount about to bolt. A new metal coal-chamber filled with glowing embers strapped to his back to keep the suit warm, making his armor creak and pop as it heated up, keeping him off-balance with its weight and hissing vents, but holding the freezing cold back a little. Specks of frozen water flying through the torch-lit air like dust, biting his eyes through the visor. His fingers numb in his gloves, despite the suit. The familiar glitter of inhuman eyes beyond the torchlight, nothing to go by but reflections of fire on his foes, who are invisible in the shadows, slinking alongside the caravan like bulges in the darkness. The only thing between the Nightmares and the pioneers with their mounts and carriages weighed down by machinery and thick coils of wire and cable that will bring the light of civilization to these wilds, is him and his contingent.

How long must that journey have been to him? How long till he returned to see his wife and new son Velag in a warm hospital room, under the glow of a brand new electric light?

By the time I was born, armorers had invented portable guns and integrated hollow cables in the suit lining to carry ember-heated water around armor, keeping it warmer and enabling mercenaries and knights-errant to go deeper into Evening. The pioneers followed, bringing their technology to the very tops of the foothills, infested with Nightmares. That was when Father stopped going, lest he never return. They had new tools, but the war had intensified. He had a son and daughter to think of, and a wife who wanted him home.

WHEN I WATCHED Velag's funeral pyre blaze against the light of the west on Barrow-of-Bones cremation hill, I wondered if the sparks sent up into the sky by his burning body would turn to Stardust in the ether and migrate to the sun to extend its life, or whether this was his final and utter dissolution. The chanting priest from the Solar Church seemed to have no doubts on the matter. Standing there, surrounded by the fossilized stone ribs of Zhurgeith, last of the sunwyrms and heraldic angel of the Monarchy and Church (who also call it Dragon), I found myself truly unsure about what death brings for maybe the first time in my life, though I'd long practiced the cynicism that was becoming customary of my generation.

I thought with some trepidation about the possibility that if the Church was right, the dust of Velag's life might be consigned to the eternal dark of cosmic limbo instead of finding a place in the sun, because of what he'd done to me as a child. Because I'd never forgiven him, even though I told myself I had.

How our world changes.

The sun is a great sphere of burning gas, ash eventually falls down, and my dead brother remains in the universe because my family and I remember him, just as I remember my childhood, my life, the Nightmares we lived in fear of, the angel Dragon whose host was wiped out by a solar flare before we could ever witness it.

OUTSIDE, THE WIND howls so loud that I can easily imagine it is the sound of trumpets from a frozen city, peopled by the horde of darkness. Even behind the insulated metal doors and heated tunnels of the cave bunkers that make up After-Day border camp, I can see my breath and need two thick coats to keep warm. My fingers are like icicles as I write. I would die very quickly if exposed to the atmosphere outside. And yet, here I am, in the land of Nightmares.

Somewhere beyond these Penumbral Mountains, which we crossed in an airtight train, is the City-of-Long-Shadows. I have never been so far from it. Few people have. We are most indebted to those who mapped the shortest route through the mountains, built the rails through the lowest valleys, blasted new tunnels, laid the foundations for After-Day. But no one has gone beyond this point. We—I and the rest of the expeditionary team from St. Kataretz—will be the first to venture into Night. It will be a dangerous endeavor, but I have faith in us, in the brave men and women who have accompanied me here.

My dear Velag, how would you have reacted to see these beautiful caves I sit in now, to see the secret culture of your enemy? I am surrounded by what can only be called their art, the lantern-light making pale tapestries of the rock walls on which Nightmares through the millennia scratched to life the dawn of their time, the history that followed, and its end, heralded by our arrival into their world.

In this history we are the enemy, bringing the terror of blinding fire into Evening, bringing the advanced weapons that caused their genocide. On these walls we are drawn in pale white dyes, bioluminescent in the dark, a swarm of smeared light advancing on the Nightmares' striking, jagged-angled representations of themselves, drawn in black dyes mixed from blood and minerals.

In this history Nightmares were alive when the last of the sunwyrms flew into Evening to scourge the land for prey. Whether this is truth or myth we don't know, but it might mean that Nightmares were around long before us. It might explain their adaptation to the darkness of outer Evening—their light-absorbent skin ancient camouflage to hide from sunwyrms under cover of the forests of Evening. We came into Evening with our fire (which they show sunwyrms breathing) and pale skins, our banners showing Dragon and the sun, and we were like a vengeful race of ghosts come to kill on behalf of those disappeared angels of Day, whom they worshipped to the end—perhaps praying for our retreat.

In halls arched by the ribcages and spines of ancient sunwyrm skeletons I have seen burial chambers; the bones of Nightmares and their children (whom we called imps because we didn't like to think of our enemy having young) piled high. Our bones lie here too, not so different from theirs. Tooth-marks show that they ate their dead, probably because of the scarcity of food in the fragile ecosystem of Evening. It is no wonder then that they ate our dead too— as we feared. It was not out of evil, but need.

We have so much yet to learn.

Perhaps it would have given you some measure of peace, Velag, to know that the Nightmares didn't want to destroy us, only to drive us back from their home. Perhaps not.

Ilydrin tells me it is time for us to head out. She is a member of our expedition—a biologist—and my partner. To hide the simple truth of our affection seems here, amidst the empty city of a race we destroyed, an obscenity. Confronted by the vast, killing beauty of our planet's second half, the stagnant moralities of our city-state appear a trifle. I adore Ilydrin, and I am glad she is here with me.

One team will stay here while ours heads out into Night. Ilydrin and I took a walk outside to test our Night-shells—armored environmental suits to protect us from the lethal cold. We trod down from the caves of After-Day and into the unknown beyond, breath blurring our glass faceplates, our head-lamps cutting broad swathes through the snow-swarmed dark. We saw nothing ahead but an endless plain of ice—perhaps a frozen sea.

No spectral spires, no black banners of Night, no horde of Nightmares waiting to attack, no Dark Lord in his distant obsidian palace (an image Ilydrin and I righteously tore down many times in the form of those Army posters, during our early College vigils). We held each other's gloved hands and returned to Camp, sweating in our cramped shells, heavy boots crunching on the snow. I thought of you, Father, bravely venturing into bitter Evening to support your family. I thought of you, Brother, nobly marching against the horde for your Monarchy. I thought of you, Mother, courageously carrying your first child alone in that empty house before it became *our* home. I thought of you, Shadow—broken, tortured prisoner, baring your teeth to your captors in silence.

Out there, I was shaking—nervous, excited, queasy. I wasn't afraid.

I HAVE FATHER'S old photograph with the Nightmare's head (he took it down from above the mantelpiece after Velag died). I have a photograph of Mother, Father, Velag and me all dressed up before our trip to Weep-for-Day. And finally, a smiling portrait of Velag in uniform before he left for the Academy, his many pimples invisible because of the monochrome softness of the image. I keep these photographs with me, in the pockets of my overcoat, and take them out sometimes when I write.

SO IT BEGINS. I write from the claustrophobic confines of the Night-Crawler, a steam-powered vehicle our friends at the College of Engineering designed (our accompanying professors named it with them, no doubt while drunk in a bar on University-Street). It is our moving camp. We'll sleep and eat and take shelter in it, and explore further and longer—at least a few vigils, we hope. If its engines fail, we'll have to hike back in our shells and hope for the best. The portholes are frosted over, but the team is keeping warm by stoking the furnace and singing. Ilydrin comes and tells me, her lips against my hair: "Val. Stop writing and join us." I tell her I will, in a minute. She smiles and walks back to the rest, her face flushed and soot-damp from the open furnace. I live for these moments.

I will lay down this pen now. A minute.

I don't know what we'll find out here. Maybe we *will* find the Dark Lord and his gathered horde of Nightmares. But at this point, even the military doesn't believe that, or they would have opposed the funding for this expedition or tried to hijack it.

Ilydrin says there's unlikely to be life so deep into Night—even Nightmares didn't venture beyond the mountains, despite our preconceptions. But she admits we've been wrong before. Many times. What matters is that we are somewhere new. Somewhere other than the City-of-Long-Shadows and the Penumbral territories, so marked by our history of fear. We need to see the rest of this world, to meet its other inhabitants—if there are others—with curiosity, not apprehension. And I know we will, eventually. This is our first, small step. I wish you were here with me to see it, Velag. You were but a child on this planet.

We might die here. It won't be because we ventured into evil. It will be because we sought new knowledge. And in that, I have no regrets, even if I'm dead when this is read. A new age is coming. Let this humble account be a preface to it.

IN PLAIN SIGHT

Pat Cadigan

Pat Cadigan characterizes herself as a "professional bad influence." She is one of the small number of original cyberpunks, and of them the only woman writer. She has won the World Fantasy Award and the Locus Award, and is also a two-time winner of the Arthur C. Clarke Award for her novels *Synners* and *Fools*. Since the turn of the twenty-first century, she says she has concentrated mostly on short fiction except for a few media tie-ins and novelizations (*Cellular, Jason X*) while caring for an elderly (and ornery) parent. But lately she has been commuting between Neptune and her home in North London, where she lives with her husband, the Original Chris Fowler, and Gentleman Jinx, coolest black cat in London, while working on a new science fiction novel called *See You When You Get There*.

"In Plain Sight" was published in *The Future Is Japanese,* edited by Nick Mamatas and Masumi Washington, an anthology of translated and otherwise mostly original stories on that theme, and one of the best anthologies of the year. The story is adapted from the other novel she's working on, *Reality Used to Be a Friend of Mine*. When asked which book will be finished first, she says she'll see it when it gets there.

GOKU MURA THOUGHT the old lady probably wouldn't have fallen for it if the scammer hadn't had the bright idea to use the term "Easter egg." Emmy Eto, as she was known to her neighbors in the retirement community, was one of the last of the generation who had actually used the antiquated term. She was in her mid-nineties, which also made her old enough to remember Japan as it had existed physically, before quakes and tidal waves had reduced it to fragments that would have been uninhabitable even without the radiation. He didn't want to think it made her more gullible.

He had no idea why Doré Konstantin had sent the case to him. For one thing, he hadn't laid eyes on her in several calendar-months—more than two, fewer than six? Seven, for sure—which Konstantin said was a lot longer in AR time. Dog years, she called it. Although he had seen her in AR during that time, but only just barely—a flicker in the corner of his eye, too fast or too far away, but recognizable as Konstantin if only by the empty spot she left behind. *Hello too busy talk later,* he supposed, and marveled at how she managed to do it in Augmented Reality as well as Artificial Reality. The deregulation of Augmented Reality in the US had been a legal shit storm, leading to what Goku thought was the single most awe-inspiring piece of legislation of the last century: *legal reality*. He'd been dying to talk to Konstantin about it, but he'd been too busy even to send her a smart-ass remark.

Maybe that was why she'd sent him the Emmy Eto case, so he'd have to get in touch just to ask wtf. He read through it to make sure he wasn't missing anything, but it seemed to be nothing more than what Konstantin called straight-up bunco—despicable but hardly a job for 13. The local law machinery could run it on autopilot: the prosecutor would claim two counts of special circumstances, saying Eto had been targeted not only because she was elderly and more vulnerable but also because she was Japanese. That made it a hate crime and therefore under federal jurisdiction. The prospect of facing a federal judge was usually enough to make offenders and their (usually) court-appointed lawyers amenable to a plea bargain, which was heavy on plea without much bargain. The DA simply removed the special circumstances charge. Relieved felons went off to serve sentences barely lighter than what they could have expected after a jury trial, thinking they'd been given a break, while overworked prosecutors were even more relieved to have saved themselves the trouble of working up special-circumstances briefs that were all too likely to be shit-canned by equally overworked federal judges with no room on their twenty-four-hour dockets.

The only thing slightly out of the ordinary about it was how the scammer was refusing to sit up and beg like someone who had seen the error of her ways, even just for the time it took a judge to gauge the sincerity of her remorse and pass sentence accordingly. She was a piece of work named Pretty Howitzer, not just legally but from birth. With parents like that, Goku Mura thought, she'd never stood a chance. Her record backed that up—a long list of unremarkable misdemeanors and felonies, suspended sentences, sentences commuted to time served, sentences reduced because there just wasn't room in the correctional facility, along with a number of dismissals and DTPs. A Decline To Prosecute usually meant lack of evidence or witnesses or both, though one was also marked TFB, which, Goku discovered after a little digging, stood for Too Fucking Boring.

Too funny to ignore, he thought and phoned Konstantin.

He got one of her detectives instead, the one with the muttonchops. It took him a minute to remember her name: Celestine.

"Jurisdictional nightmare," Celestine told him cheerfully. He'd never been a fan of facial hair on women or men, but something about her smile always gave him a lift.

"International?" He shrugged. "You guys handle international all the time."

"In AR, sure. But this is also AR+."

"What difference does that make?"

"It's both Artificial Reality *and* Augmented Reality, with offline interludes, all crossing international borders. Our DA took one look and decided it was someone else's headache. I gotta say, though, I didn't think you'd be the lucky winner."

"I didn't know Konstantin was sending things out for the district attorney's office these days."

Celestine's cheerful smile faded. "Uh, say again?"

"I got the case from Konstantin, not the DA."

Now her face lost all expression. "Hang on." She started paging through something on her desk just below camera range. It was almost half a clock-minute before she looked up again. "The DA's office says it's on record as exported to 13 twenty minutes ago. They're also saying this must be a world record for turnaround."

"I guess so," Goku said, "because it got to my inbox twelve hours ago. You guys using neutrino mail?"

Celestine shifted uncomfortably. "Well, someone's clock is off, maybe on this end. Somebody screwed up with the time zone or something."

"I've never heard of that," Goku said, "but as Konstantin always says, stranger things have happened." The detective all but flinched at the mention of her name. He started to get a bad feeling. "Could be her joking around."

"It's not Konstantin," Celestine insisted stonily. "And if it's a joke—hell, I can't think of anyone that tasteless even in the DA's office."

"Something happened." Goku kept his voice even as a small, dense knot of dread formed in the pit of his stomach. Civil service: bureaucracy relieved by sudden incidents of homicide. Konstantin had laughed at that one till she cried.

"She got shot."

Shot. Shit. Shooting the shit, she got shot. He forced the thought away. "How?"

"Sniper. Right in the eye."

"AROUND THE TURN of the twenty-first century," Lieutenant Bruce Ogada said as he and Goku sat in the empty waiting room, "someone had the bright idea to take a laser pointer and aim it at the night sky." His dry, matter-of-fact tone reminded Goku of the last international economics report he had endured, minus the ambiguity. Ogada was dressed in a standard suit and tie. His one concession to his own comfort had been to remove his jacket and lay it over the arm of his chair; he hadn't even loosened his tie, and his white shirt seemed as crisp and clean as if he had put it on only minutes earlier, fresh from the store. *Fresh from the showroom*, as Konstantin would have said had she been there, Goku thought, wishing she were with an intensity that under other circumstances he might have tried to tell himself was surprising.

He made himself sit up straighter in the peculiar chair. It was a weird piece of furniture, too large for one person and not big enough for two, making it impossible to rest both elbows at the same time without them being absurdly akimbo. The arms were thin, squared-off tubes of metal too uncomfortable to lean on anyway. It was a style of chair Goku had never seen anywhere except in waiting rooms, usually the kind that people didn't want to be in—assuming there was any other kind. He was only in this one because he'd been turned away by the smiling gorgon at the entrance to Intensive Care. One visitor at a time, and even if her lieutenant hadn't been visiting at the moment, his name wasn't on the approved list. He'd have to see Lt. Ogada about that, if he cared to wait. He had, barely pausing to get a cap of the gorgon. The projection was completely opaque even as close as twelve inches, and its features had an authentic quality that suggested there was a real, possibly unwitting, model.

"A thin red beam of light going straight up into the dark, all tight and narrow and focused, must have been fascinating," Ogada was saying. " 'Look at me, I've got a lightsaber a hundred miles tall.' " He leaned forward, elbows on his knees, hands loosely folded. "One night during one of these do-it-yourself light shows—and I'm just guessing now but that's how things like this usually happen—somebody noticed a plane flying in the vicinity and thought, what the hell. That's what you do with a laser pointer—you point."

Goku nodded, although Ogada wasn't looking at him.

"When the beam hit the cockpit, it blinded the pilot. Temporarily, of course, although there were a few cases of burned retinas." He looked over at Goku, eyebrows raised, a man about to reveal a critical detail. "Didn't show up till a few days later. Pilot'd get a strange feeling in the eye, have a doctor check it out, and there it was." He gave a short, soundless laugh. "A little round spot. Like a cigarette burn. Aiming a laser pointer at aircraft became a serious crime. Committed by morons, since it was easy to trace a laser beam back to its source."

He let out a breath and sat back in his chair; it was similar to Goku's but smaller, with padding on the arms. "The statute's still on the books because, believe it or not, every so often, some idiot gets the brilliant idea to go outside and wave a laser pointer around. The aviator lenses most cockpit crews wear inflight usually protect their eyes so they don't get burned, but sometimes, if a beam hits just right—excuse me, just *wrong*—it can actually fuck up the lens in a way that affects the pilot, or whoever. They get dizzy, disoriented, even have seizures." His gaze had drifted away; now he looked at Goku again. "I don't suppose any of this is news to you."

Goku shrugged. "I'm not familiar with *every* country's aviation laws."

"You probably never leave home without your state-of-the-art safety goggles, just in case lenses aren't enough. Or is that too low-tech for Interpol 3?"

Goku's half smile was wry. "We have a small collection of old hardware, kind of an in-house museum—CB radios, break-glass fire alarms. Black lights. Modems. There's even a Zippo lighter with a military insignia. I think it's the US Marine Corps but I'm not sure. Maybe it's just the army."

Ogada's face was expressionless, and Goku suddenly felt ashamed of his feeble attempt at humor. He was formulating an apology when Ogada spoke again.

"I know 13's been trying to recruit her." His face still gave no hint of emotion. "And before you ask, no, she didn't say anything about it. She never mentioned you at all—I mean, not so much as a vague reference. As if she weren't even aware of your existence. Which was how I knew. She didn't want to give me an opening to ask any questions she didn't want to answer. I know how she thinks."

"She always said no."

Now Ogada's eyebrows went up again. "Did you ask her if she was thinking about it?"

Goku hesitated, unsure of what Ogada was getting at. "I *had* asked her to think about it."

"But did you ask her if she *was* thinking about it?"

"Well . . ." Goku shook his head slightly. "She didn't say she wouldn't."

"Yeah. That's what she didn't want to tell me, that she was thinking about it. She didn't tell you that either. She just said no every time you tried to recruit her." Ogada gave a short laugh. "I keep forgetting you're not from around here."

Goku smiled a little. "I was thinking the same thing about you," he said, "until I remembered where I was." Pause. "Look, I didn't know anything about what happened till one of her detectives told me, the one with the—" he made a widening gesture on either side of his face with both hands.

"Celestine," Ogada said.

"Right. And the only reason I called was to ask about a case. I thought I'd got one of hers by mistake."

Ogada looked at him sharply. "Which one?" It sounded more like a demand than a question.

Goku gave him the gist.

"Oh, that one." The lieutenant shook his head. "Jurisdictional nightmare. We voted it off the island. Something my father used to say," he added in response to Goku's puzzled look. "Case too small for you guys? Well, don't worry—the minute Pretty Howitzer finds out 13's interested, she'll probably lie down and plead like she should've done in the first place."

Goku decided against mentioning the contradictory information as to how it had come to him, at least for the moment. "Right now, I don't give a shit one way or the other. I came to see how Konstantin's doing."

"No change from yesterday or the day before or any other day in the month since it happened," Ogada said wearily. "I stop in two, three times a week, sit next to her, tell her I'm eating lunch, and suggest she lose some weight."

"Why would you do that?" Goku asked, drawing back slightly.

"I figure that'll get a rise out of her if nothing else will. So far—" He got up and put on his jacket. "No joy. We'll get your name on the list, maybe you'll have better luck. But not right now. You might as well come back to the pre-cinct and question What's-Her-Name Howitzer, she's still in Holding. You guys got this case a lot faster than usual."

"So I've heard," Goku said.

PRETTY HOWITZER WAS a type that Goku privately classified as cute. He couldn't decide how much Japanese there was in her lineage—more than a fourth, possibly more than a third, but certainly not more than half. The jail-house lenses dulled her eyes a bit, but he could still see they were closer to gold than brown, and there was a sprinkle of freckles across the bridge of her turned-up nose. She was also very petite, more so than he had realized from her mug shots.

But the most striking thing about her at the moment was her relentless nail biting, which did nothing to undercut her blasé attitude. Someone had once told him that for some people, nail biting had nothing to do with anxiety—it was merely a neurological glitch, possibly a half-baked form of OCD or even Tourette's. Pretty Howitzer made it look like self-indulgence; the longer she chewed on herself, the more relaxed she seemed, awkward as it was with the handcuffs.

Goku found it hard to watch, and there was nothing else in the small inter-rogation room to draw the eye. The observation window was camouflaged as bare wall, so there wasn't even a mirror. Anyone with the slightest tendency to claustrophobia would have a rough time in this room. He remembered Kon-stantin's partner, Taliaferro, who worked out of an office on the roof. Too long in here, Goku thought, and he might have to join him. Assuming Taliaferro was still getting away with it now that Konstantin was benched.

"So you're the big bad 13 agent," Pretty Howitzer said, removing her left index finger from her mouth briefly. "Thought you'd be taller. Or maybe it's this room." She dipped her head like she was afraid something would fall on it and looked from side to side. "Is it me or is this a goddamn shoebox?"

"It's you," Goku lied, mildly surprised at how confident he sounded. "Shit doesn't get a whole lot deeper than this—well, not while you're alive anyway. So if you feel like the walls are closing in, it's because they are."

Pretty Howitzer rolled her eyes. "If that's a mixed metaphor, you're not even trying."

Several sharp retorts jockeyed for position in Goku's mind, but what he heard himself say was, "Get your fingers out of your mouth."

To his surprise, she obeyed. "Yeah, sure. Sorry." The handcuffs rattled as she wiped her fingers on the front of her pink coverall. According to some expert, the color supposedly made prisoners feel physically and mentally less powerful. Pretty Howitzer looked like she was wearing a playsuit. "Most of the time, I don't even know I'm doing it."

"How do you cope in AR?" Goku asked. "Going without for hours must be real hard on you."

"I don't have to go without anything." She looked down and to her left for a moment at something only she could see. Goku did likewise, but if her lenses were tapped, he wasn't getting a copy. Civil service: he'd probably have to fill out eighty thousand forms in triplicate for a transcript. Which he could expect to receive in four to six weeks. "When they deregulated AR+, I sent a basket of flowers and a box of chocolates to my congresspeople," Pretty Howitzer was saying. "And I can't even vote." Her upper body rose and fell with a deep sigh that was somehow both wistful and satisfied. "I don't remember the last time I was stuck playing indoors."

"Well, it's the end of an era for you, Ms. Howitzer." Goku leaned on the bare metal table between them and then was annoyed to find he had to pull his chair in farther. The legs shrieked on the floor, and he had to suppress the urge to pick the thing up and throw it across the room. "You don't get AR or AR+ in prison. It's just ground floor all day, every day, day in, day out. But the good news is, you can bite your nails whenever you feel like it. All the way down to your elbows, if you want."

Pretty Howitzer wrinkled her cute little nose. "You talk like my grandfather. And that's not a compliment. I hated that old f—"

"Get your fingers out of your mouth."

She made a small, jerky movement, obeying reflexively before realizing she didn't have her fingers in her mouth. "Hey!"

He grinned broadly without showing his teeth. "That why you've been picking on the old folks, because you hate your grandfather?"

"Oh, are you actually a head doctor? You gonna psychoanalyze me, figure out how I went bad? You want to put in some buttons, turn me good?" She wrinkled her nose again. "For. Get. It. Not giving up *my* free will, not for a hundred times what I took off that old bat. I'm pro choice all the way. I do whatever I choose to do, not because someone else controls me—"

"Get your fingers out of your mouth."

Again, she started to obey before realizing she didn't have to; he felt a surge of spiteful joy. "You fuckin' cops," she growled, infuriated. "Think you're so genius—"

"I'm an Interpol 3 agent. I can show you my *credentials*," he said, inflecting the last word carefully to trigger it.

She started to answer, then froze for half a second. Her eyes took on a brief faraway look before she closed them and moved her eyes from side to side a few times to dismiss the image he'd sent her. "If I want to see your fucking *credentials*, I'll—oh, shit." She squeezed her eyes shut, pressing her thumbs against them.

Goku managed not to laugh. "That was your own fault. The way you said *credentials*."

Again she stared distantly at nothing before she clapped her hands over her eyes. "Cut it out, asshole!" She knuckled her eye sockets.

"I'm sorry, that really *was* an accident," he said, meaning it. "It's a tone-of-voice trigger. If you can keep yourself from mocking me for at least two clock-minutes, it shouldn't happen again. I don't think. I don't know what the system is here for jailhouse lenses."

"Just proves my point." Pretty Howitzer's glare was slightly bloodshot. "Agent's just a fancy name for cop and 13 agents are just *free-range* cops. You're only interested in crimes in places you want to go so you can get a free paid vacation. Don't give me that look. It's true, everybody knows that about you *agents*." Abruptly, she heard the way she'd said the last word and froze, looking dismayed. But *agents* wasn't a trigger word. Today.

"I have to say, I'm gobsmacked." He couldn't help chuckling now. "That you would think I actually *want* to come *here*."

"Gobsmacked?!" Pretty Howitzer threw back her head and hooted at the ceiling; the acoustic tiles swallowed her voice so quickly, she sounded almost staccato. The effect reminded Goku of a story he'd read long ago, about a man whose job involved cleaning leftover sounds out of empty rooms. Years later, he had started out in 13 doing something that he sometimes thought of as (vaguely, faintly) similar, just as a way to relieve (albeit very slightly) the stultifying tedium of surveillance.

"Do you ever hear yourself! 'Oh, I *say,* old chap, I'm utterly *gobs*macked by the *whole bloody business.*' What's that accent about anyway?"

"What accent?"

"Oh, *veddy* funny, old chap, *veddy*, pip pip cheerio and all that rot! Come on, what's with you?"

Goku couldn't help laughing. "Nothing. What's with you, besides too much vintage TV?"

"Hey, *I'm* not puttin' on an accent."

"Neither am I. I was born and raised in England."

"Yeah? You do all that English stuff? Boarding school? Uniforms? Cricket, rum, sodomy, and the lash?"

Is this the vanguard of a new, more educated offender? he wondered, amused. "You'll have lots of time to read about the lives of English schoolboys in the Mid-Atlantic Prison library."

"*What*?!" Pretty Howitzer's cute jaw dropped as she lost whatever cool she'd still had. "*No!* You *can't*! I didn't *kill* anybody, I didn't use a *weapon,* I didn't even make *threats*! I'm a US *citizen*, you *can't* sink me, you *can't*!"

"I can. And the US apparently thinks it would be a good idea since they signed off on it."

Her eyes moved rapidly as she searched for a pop-up that Goku knew wouldn't be on her lenses. "Show me!"

"Paperwork's still on the way," Goku said smoothly, unsure if that were true. "*Real* paper. Sinking anyone, even a totally unapologetic and unrepentant career criminal like yourself, is serious business. Has to be done with hardcopy."

"Who says I'm not apologetic?" Pretty Howitzer sat up straight and folded her cuffed hands on the table. "I *said* I was sorry! I *always* say I'm sorry! Look it up, it's on the record!"

Goku leaned one elbow on the table and covered his mouth with his hand, as if he were thinking hard and not hiding a grin.

"Besides, *I'm* as much a victim here as Auntie Emmy," she added, looking down her nose at him, or trying to. She came off more like an insolent child than a high-mileage felon, which Goku suspected was how she had managed to go as long as she had without doing any serious time.

He filed that for later consideration, along with *Auntie Emmy*. "What do you mean, *you're* a victim? You knowingly sold a trusting old woman an invisible bag of vapor—"

"I didn't *knowingly* do anything! It was *supposed* to be the *real deal*!"

Now he did laugh, a loud, hard, sarcastic sound that had little humor in it and was gone quickly, without even a hint of echo. The effect bothered the fuck out of him, Goku thought irritably. "There's nobody—that's capital No, capital Body—who would believe for one second—that's capital One, capital Second—that you really, sincerely believed—"

"Okay, so *you* don't believe me, but I swear, so help me freakin' gods of techno—"

"—one hundred percent genuine—"

"—only because I *knew* it was the real thing—"

"—out door, egress, exit, whatever con artists are calling it these days—"

"I believed it because I tried it and it fucking worked!"

Goku stared at her for a long moment. Then he laughed again. "Whew, for a second there, the look on your face—you almost had me. Do you practice in front of a mirror or is it just plain old hardcore desperation? Don't answer that," he said as she opened her mouth. "I think maybe you need some alone time in a holding cell to give your situation some serious thought. But just to make sure you don't get too bored, I'll tell the duty officer to load some brochures for you." He stood up, paying no attention to her protests. "About the programs and facilities available at Mid-Atlantic. Underwater correctional institutions are the most advanced and best equipped in the world. You get used to the emergency drill fast, I've heard. They've got education programs from the top schools, your Ivy League, Eton, Cambridge—and I mentioned the library, didn't I?"

As soon as he stepped into the hallway and closed the door behind him, her pleading cut off as if someone had flipped a switch, and the ambient noise of the police station suddenly assailed him. A bit disconcerted, he leaned against the wall for a moment; funny, he thought, the way you never noticed how much things echoed under ordinary conditions. Not to mention how much difference there was between quiet and the absence of sound.

The flicker at the left-hand edge of his vision came just as he thought of Konstantin, two separate things happening simultaneously. His initial reaction was reflexive now, a mental smile coupled with mild embarrassment for still not having reciprocated. It took a full clock-second for him to remember that according to what both Celestine and Ogada had told him, nobody had received any messages of any kind from Konstantin for at least four weeks; nobody could. Therefore, nobody had.

The flicker sure seemed like her, though. Even considered in the context of what he knew, there was a Konstantin-ness about it that he told himself to chalk up to wishful thinking. People saw what they wanted to see and more often than not the mind was only too happy to dance along. It didn't take much fancy footwork to make music out of a stray fragment of noise.

And anyone who didn't believe that could check out the millions of people who had been sold all those magic beans: beachfront in Kansas, the true Hope Diamond, a deposed king's hidden gold, the blessing of never-ending good luck, the Deity's unlisted phone number. Or the absolutely-positively-not-fake-not-a-simulation-but-real conversion code for the Out Door, derived by a scientist using the secrets of the Pharaohs and the Mayans, giving you unlimited access to everything you wanted and more—contact your more successful self in another timeline and see where you went right, ascend to a higher plane of being, join God's private club! Or just go to Japan.

"TO BE HONEST, I felt sorry for her."

The small round object in the bottom of Goku's cup opened out into a blossom under the stream of boiling water from the spout of Emmy Eto's fancy electric kettle. It amused him that most Americans referred to it as a teapot, even though they only heated water in it.

"That was why I gave her a freebie in the first place," she added, pouring water into her own cup before replacing the kettle in its stand on the coffee table and sitting down on the couch beside him.

"A freebie?"

Emmy Eto chuckled. "On the house, *gratis*. You don't have to pay."

"Yes, I know. I'm just not sure what you mean by you gave *her* a freebie."

"That's a delightful accent. London, am I right?" Emmy Eto chuckled again, eyes twinkling in a way that made him think of Celestine's smile, although there was no resemblance between the two women. Emmy Eto was ninety-five, with short, silvery hair carefully styled to look unruly and bright green contact lenses. Goku suspected her eyes would have been just as bright without them; no doubt she could be quite unruly too.

"Please, Ms. Eto," he said, taking a sip of tea. The flower waved at him from the bottom of the cup.

"You'll want to spoon that out," she told him. "Unless you're a typical Brit and like your tea thoroughly stewed."

The flower went from graceful to drowned as he removed it to a saucer on the table. "Please, Ms. Eto?" he said again.

"I'm a professional relative," she said. "Isn't it in the case file?"

Goku felt his face grow warm. "I'm sorry, I obviously missed that."

"Because you figured I'm just retired. Oh, don't have a cow, dude," she added, waving one hand as he started to apologize. "You want to know the truth, I'd have figured that too if I were in your place. Most of the people who live here are *at leisure*, shall we say. They've had two, three, even four careers—and that's not counting all the McJobs for rent money in between. And they've had about as many families, formal and informal. Worked their asses off—well, their hips, knees, and shoulders anyway. There's so much titanium around here we get more spam from salvage firms than funeral homes.

"Anyway, most of my neighbors are tired. They just want to hang out, spark a few bowls of medicinal, and watch a movie. With or without actually putting one on."

Goku sipped some more tea, even though it was too hot, to keep himself from grinning.

"And I gotta admit, I do that too now and again. Careers and McJobs—I had 'em back to back. I traveled a lot, lived in a lot of different places. But I only ever had one family. One husband, one child, and I had the bad grace to outlive both of them."

Goku blinked away the definition of McJobs that had popped up in the lower left-hand quadrant of his vision and said, "I'm sorry."

"It was a very long time ago," she said, waving away his words again. "You don't set out to be a widow, but you live with the possibility and what happens is what happens. But surviving your child is an unnatural act, especially when she's an actual child. Takes a long time to make up for it. So I rent myself out to people who need a nice old lady relative. Grandma for the kids, auntie for the grown-ups. Sometimes both at once, in which case I give them a special rate rather than just double-dipping. Anyone who has to hire a nice old lady relative in the first place deserves a break. And you'd be surprised at how many people that is."

She picked up a small remote and pointed it at a large painting of wild horses running through a countryside under a stormy sky on the wall opposite. The image faded away to a white background, where color photos of various shapes and sizes began to appear. The people in them were various shapes, sizes, and colors as well. Many of the pictures had been taken at special occasions—

birthdays, weddings, anniversaries, graduations, and holidays, big elaborate parties and smaller, more intimate get-togethers. But there were also plenty of Emmy Eto sitting with a toddler on her lap or walking in a park holding hands with a couple of small children. And a few not-so-small children.

He was grinning from ear to ear, Goku realized, and tried to tone it down without sobering too abruptly. "That's quite a lot of people," he said, "but if we could get back to—"

Nodding, she used the remote again. "You're just lucky I didn't cue up the soundtrack." She chuckled. "You'd have sat through the whole six hours, weeping nonstop. Big, manly, silent tears, of course." She put a hand to her lips. "Oh, no, wait, I forgot, it's all stiff upper lip with you Brits."

The words were out of his mouth before he'd even known he was going to speak. "But I'm also Japanese. Like you."

"And?" Emmy Eto blinked at him. "Meaning what?"

"I was just thinking that you're old enough to remember Japan, the actual land, before the quakes—"

"Yes, we both existed at the same time, but I never went there." She sighed heavily. "I'm as much a *sansei* as you are in that respect. What does that have to do with Pretty Howitzer?"

"It's part of the special circumstances attached to the charges against her. She targeted you not only because you're elderly but also because you're Japanese."

Emmy Eto sighed. "We've been vaccinating against plaque and vascular dementia and schizophrenia and all kinds of other head bugs for, what, seven decades? Almost eight? And everyone still thinks that if you're over eighty, you got nothing above the neck but moths and cobwebs."

"I don't feel that way," Goku said, hoping he sounded kind rather than defensive. "And neither does anyone I know at 13 or—"

Emmy Eto shooed his words away with both hands. "Yeah, yeah, yeah, it's always some other, much less enlightened dude." Abruptly, she grimaced. "Oh, hell. I'm sorry, Agent Mura, I'm taking things out on you and I shouldn't. I just get so *fucking cheesed off* sometimes. You have no idea, the crap aimed at people my age. Nostalgia and religion, religion and nostalgia, like no older person is interested in anything else. Well, I'm all about today, *right* here, *right* now, and then what's on for tomorrow. You know what I did yesterday? Went to the farmer's market and bought green bananas. That's right, you heard me, I'm ninety and *I bought green bananas*—in your *face*, mortality! Woke up this morning—in your face again, mortality! Just because I'm not concerned about getting pregnant—or *not* getting pregnant—and what the hell is it with all that pregnancy hoo-ha anyway? Pregnancy isn't the permanent centerpiece of *every* woman's life, even if they're actually pregnant! It's ageist, it's sexist—" Putting a hand to her mouth, she looked down at her lap, smiling with embarrassment.

204 | *Pat Cadigan*

"Damn, I'm so sorry," she said, laughing a little. "Once I get started, I can't seem to stop, and it's so rude. Please forgive me again, Agent Mura."

He waited for her to look up, but apparently he'd have to forgive her first. "There's no need to apologize, Ms. Eto. When you're the victim of a crime, it's quite normal to feel like the whole world is against you."

Now she did look up, her face a mixture of surprise and relief. "Oh?"

He nodded. "It's bad enough dealing with the complications, anything from overdue bills to repo men. Or losing something that means the world to you but has no monetary value to the shithead who took it and probably threw it away." Emmy Eto gave a surprised giggle at the profanity. "But then there's the indignity of how people keep referring to you as *the victim* rather than using your name. It adds insult to injury."

Emmy Eto put both hands over her face for a long moment. Goku thought she was crying and looked around for some tissues, but when she lowered them, her face was dry and composed. "I thought I was being childish."

"Were you not offered counseling?" Goku asked, making a mental note to ask Celestine.

She made another shooing motion with both hands. "Bitch, puh-*leeze*." Her cheeks suddenly turned pink. "As we used to say in my day, if you'll pardon my Hungarian. That little bitch Pretty Howitzer, *she* needs therapy. I need my money back." Pause. "Or am I just shit outta luck on that one?"

Goku made another mental note to follow up on counseling for her anyway. "No, these days we can trace where the money went," he told her. "But that takes time. And it takes more time to convert it back to liquid form."

Emmy Eto's hopeful smiled faded. "Convert it from what?"

"People like Pretty Howitzer love to buy themselves presents, goods or services. Property is usually straightforward, services are trickier."

"Which means I can't count on getting *all* my money back."

"No, but you'll get most of it. 13's recovery team seldom recoup less than seventy-five percent of the original monetary value, and it's usually closer to ninety percent."

This information didn't cheer her as much as he'd hoped. "And how much time are we talking about?" she asked.

"Well . . . longer than anyone would like." He hesitated, then plunged ahead before he could think better of it. "May I ask you a personal question, Ms—ah, Auntie Emmy?"

"You can ask." Suddenly a little of the old twinkle was back in those unequivocally green eyes.

"Is this the first time you've been the v—ah, on the receiving end of a criminal act?"

"Nice save." She twinkled some more. He started to wonder if it was a special effect in her lenses. "And to answer your question, no, but it's been a very, *very* long time since my last brush with the underworld. All I usually have to worry about are drive-bys and snipers. No matter how much 'proofing you've got, something always gets through."

Goku frowned. "But this is a residential building."

"But not a completely residential *area*. Lots of stores means lots of shopping and lots of shopping means lots of advertising—*active* advertising that lots of people engage with. There's enough activity to reveal the local market segments. It's *almost* spam but not quite." Emmy Eto shrugged. "My filters update every other day. Whatever gets through, I trash without really seeing it."

"Any ill effects—headaches, mood swings, increase in episodes of déjà-vu?"

Emmy Eto shook her head. "Get to be my age, you're inured to a lot. It takes more to make an impression than when you're thirty. Or even sixty." She laughed suddenly. "Listen to me. What was I saying about ageism?"

Goku chuckled. "It's not ageism to understand your own characteristics, is it?"

"I dunno, dude. Maybe. Stranger things have happened."

The words echoed in his head, but in Konstantin's voice. *Stranger things have happened. If I had a family crest, that would be on it. Stranger things have happened—they'll carve it on my tombstone.*

Emmy Eto was staring at him. "Is something wrong, Agent Mura?"

"My calendar's just reminding me of an appointment." He stared off to one side for a moment, hoping he looked like he'd just had a pop-up from his to-do list, then pretended to blink it away. "Now, where were we?"

"In the middle of your very busy day," Emmy Eto said. "Sorry, I know I'm just one of a gazillion cases. Tell me what else you want to know, I'll try not to ramble. More tea?" Without waiting for an answer, she took his cup into the tiny kitchenette, rinsed it out and brought it back with a fresh blossom in the bottom.

"You mentioned feeling sorry for Howitzer," Goku prompted as she flipped the kettle's on switch. "In what way?"

Emmy Eto laughed. "That name, for one thing. What kind of person could look at their newborn baby and think, *Pretty Howitzer?* Either her parents hated her or had a cruel sense of humor, or both."

"You never thought it was a made-up name?"

"Sure, at first. But it isn't."

"You're pretty—ah, very certain. What ID did she show you?"

Emmy Eto chuckled. "A card of origin, but even I know those can be stolen or forged. What convinced me was—" She took a pair of oversized sunglasses out of a case lying on the coffee table and put them on. "Goku Mura?"

Then she hooked a finger over the frames, pulling them down her nose to stare at him over the tops of the lenses. He kept his expression neutral.

"Well, *that's* a surprise," she said, her gaze even sharper than her tone. "I had no idea Interpol 3 allowed an agent to work under an assumed name."

"More like a *nom de plume,* actually," he said, hoping he didn't sound sheepish. "Or *nom de guerre* might be more like it. For the protection of family members as well as ourselves. It keeps the professional completely separate from the personal. Tell me, how did you come by that particular bit of software?"

She folded the sunglasses and put them back on the table, well out of his reach. "Oh, I know a dude who knows a dude who knows a dude. It's not one hundred percent accurate. If you'd been on your guard, I wouldn't have caught you. And in answer to your question—" Suddenly her face was sad. "My daughter cooked it up. She was very bright, my girl, a prodigy. Eccentric—she straddled the border between Asperger's and autism. She was fascinated by the physical characteristics of human emotion. She created the program to measure the response when you called someone by name. Well, by *a* name. You know there are people in this world who believe on a gut level that their name is Lover or Darling. Or—" She gave a short, soundless laugh. "—I'm sorry to say, Asshole. Fortunately, there aren't many of those." She laughed again, more heartily. "Well, actually, there are plenty of those, but only a teeny-tiny minority would answer to the name, at least in here." She put one hand to her chest and covered the glasses possessively with the other. "You aren't going to confiscate them, are you?"

"Not unless you've used them to commit a crime," he said, shifting uneasily on the couch. "Not invading people's privacy, are you? Stealing their life savings?"

Emmy Eto smiled demurely. "I've been a good girl, Agent Mura."

"I'm sure. Now, about your relationship with Pretty Howitzer—"

"Believe it or not, I'm not a total mark, Agent Mura." The sadness returned to Emmy Eto's face. "Like I said, I only talked to her in the first place because I felt sorry for her. I could see she was lonely." A corner of her mouth twitched in a brief half smile. "But I suppose being a con artist is a lonely way to make a living. Anyway, I always enjoyed a good Easter Egg and I really thought it was all she had. I'd have overpaid for it—not as much as she ended up getting out of me but still, too much. Just because I thought it would make her happy and I can't take it with me."

"Then she disappeared and reappeared?" Goku prompted. This was usually the trick that scammers like Pretty Howitzer used to seal the deal.

But Emmy Eto shook her head. "Oh, please. I know how camouflage and encryption works in Augmented Reality, how it's just the surroundings prerecorded and interpolated. Even the cheapest AR+ cover-ups work fine as long as whoever or whatever you're covering doesn't make any sudden moves. Or if *you* don't, because you'll get that lag with the perspective.

"Personally, I don't bother with anything cheap—my mother always said cheap was dear in the long run—but some people aren't fussy. They don't care if the perspective doesn't shift perfectly or the resolution gets a little chunky. One lady I know says she likes it that way. She says it reminds her that there's less than meets the eye. But I say if you're going to use AR+, then use it. Go big or go home. That's another of my mother's sayings."

She stared silently down at the cup in her hands before she set it on the coffee table. "The disappearing act was pretty good. She even managed to fix the log so it looked like there was missing time. Maybe that might have convinced me, I don't know."

"If that didn't," Goku asked gently, "what did?"

"I saw my girl." Emmy Eto gazed at him for a long moment as if expecting some reaction. "I saw my girl and I called her by name and it was her. I didn't have the software from those sunglasses, of course, but I'd seen her through them often enough that I could tell. She knew her name. And she knew me."

He nodded. "I see."

"And I certainly did. That's how they get us, isn't it? Not by what they show us but by what they can get us to see. Because we see what we want to see. You'd think we'd live and learn, but we never do. I remember hearing all about the Virtual Homeland scams. People fooled into believing they could actually inhabit a whole new world or a whole new universe. Or an old one, lost to earthquakes and radiation. I never understood how people could fall for that. Not until there was something I wanted to see."

HIS CONSCIENCE POUNCED on him the moment he left Emmy Eto's apartment building (the brushed metal plaque over the main entrance declared it was a retirement community in emphatically no-nonsense letters). No surprise—as soon as he'd known he wasn't going to confiscate Emmy Eto's sunglasses, he'd felt it getting ready. Simply tagging the glasses for collection after Emmy Eto's eventual death wasn't enough to satisfy what Konstantin called his inner Boy Scout.

I could go back inside and see if Auntie Emmy would be open to sparking a bowl of medicinal. Just as a favor to a stressed-out free-range cop. They only use top-grade stuff for medicinal—

Some part of him—a surprisingly big part—thought that was the best idea he'd had all day. But he knew that if he did go back to Emmy Eto's apartment, it wouldn't be to get high but to take her dodgy sunglasses, the way he should have if he'd been going by the book. He'd be very apologetic and explain that while the software was not *exactly* against the law, it was in a gray area that almost always resulted in expensive legal problems for the average citizen, who of course didn't mean any harm, but still. She would argue that lots of people had lenses with add-ons that were just as sketchy, not to mention stuff that actually *was* illegal, and he'd tell her, yes, that was true, but he didn't know about anyone else, only her. She had used the software not just in his presence but as part of their interaction, while he was on duty and without his consent. And then—

And then nothing. He was spinning his wheels imagining a conversation he'd decided not to have. He cleared his mind and focused his attention on his surroundings—the line of flowering shrubs that went the length—width?—of the building on either side, the recently repaved sidewalk parallel to it, the convenience shop—no, they called it a store here—on the corner. Diagonally opposite was another convenience store from a competing chain. The two stores seemed to be having a price war, but he wasn't sure on what; maybe everything. The four-lane traffic-way that ran past the building was restricted to local and electric, except for emergency vehicles. It was so empty he wondered if it had been closed off for some reason before five two-seaters appeared several blocks in the distance. Scan-vees, he saw as they approached, from the World Within project. He turned his back as they passed him, although he didn't actually care. He had walked through so many World Within scans, his mannequin was probably one of their standard placeholders. Facial features scrambled so he was unrecognizable, of course.

Or perhaps not. Perhaps someone who knew him well enough would recognize him anyway. Emmy Eto's semilegal sunglasses.

He was waiting to cross the street in front of the convenience store when he finally noticed a message light in the lower left-hand corner of his vision blinking. It was a short note from Ogada, saying he might as well use Konstantin's office while he was here.

The offer took him by surprise. It hadn't even occurred to him to ask because he hadn't thought about staying any longer than it would take to arrange Pretty Howitzer's transfer to London. He hadn't given any thought to that either, but it didn't really require any—all he'd have to do was fill out a form, then go home and wait for a couple of prisoner transport marshals to arrive with her a day or two later.

He didn't have to be in such a hurry. Ogada had thought being handed over to 13 would make Pretty Howitzer more cooperative, though she had been more rattled by the prospect of hard time underwater. If he gave her more time to think about it, let her sleep on it, she might be only too happy to work out a deal with the local authorities. In which case, he could sign it back to Ogada or Celestine or whoever had caught it to begin with and save 13 the expense of airfare plus accommodations for two prisoner transport marshals. No, he definitely didn't have to be in such a hurry.

Something moved in his peripheral vision and he automatically focused on it, thinking it was another message. But there was no blinking light. The movement came again, something moving just out of his visual range. He turned his head. Across the street, two people were coming out of a café and holding the door for two other people going in. Again, motion fluttered on the far side of his vision. This time, he relaxed his focus and let himself see rather than actively looking.

It was the barest flicker, over almost before it registered on him. There had been an image of some kind, he was sure of it, but the only thing that came to him was Konstantin's face.

* * *

EMMY ETO'S OWN security system was usefully elaborate, more so than he had expected. Combined with surveillance from the building as well as standard public records, Goku had nearly minute-by-minute accounting for Pretty Howitzer and Emmy Eto together, and not much less separately, but only for the period leading up to the crime. The actual crime itself was documented in and out of AR+ by the bank records showing the transfer of money from Emmy Eto to Pretty Howitzer.

Studying the transaction, Goku wondered if Emmy Eto knew how lucky she was that she had done everything in Augmented Reality. Had the scam occurred in Artificial Reality, it would have been harder to make a case against Pretty Howitzer. Not impossible—there had been a number of successful prosecutions against people who had scammed the elderly, all predicated on the claim that the offenders had deliberately used techniques and FX to confuse and disorient their aged victims to the point where they became incapable of distinguishing between AR and an unenhanced, nonaugmented offline environment. A few less-than-elderly people had tried using the same argument for civil actions against scammers who had relieved them of money or property or both while in AR. Results had been mixed, especially across international boundaries, and even successful plaintiffs learned that the difference between winning a judgment and actually collecting was a lot like the difference between AR and unenhanced, nonaugmented offline reality.

He didn't think anyone would believe Emmy Eto had been confused and disoriented by Pretty Howitzer. The old lady wore several layers of AR+ routinely and nonstop during her waking hours—in a typical day, she probably didn't see the unenhanced, nonaugmented offline world for as long as sixty seconds. If that—he revised the estimate downward when he saw how often she slept with her lenses in. She did a lot of swapping too, as well as layering. Between her assorted glasses and contact lenses, she probably changed the world half a dozen times before lunch. After which she probably napped for an hour, waking to butterflies and honeybees.

She would never come off as someone who could be confused or disoriented to a jury. He wouldn't have believed it himself. And yet, when he had asked her if she really thought Pretty Howitzer had an out door—an actual, no-fooling portal to a different reality—she had said yes.

"Of course, I don't believe it now, Agent Mura, and if you're anything like me, you probably don't understand how I ever could have. Do you think I'm wondering how I could have been so gullible? Well, I'm not. I know why I fell for it. I saw because I was looking for it, and it was as real as anything else I see with my very own eyes." She had looked around, moving only her eyes, a tiny smile on her lips. "And if I saw it again tomorrow, it would be déjà vu all over again."

The recording stopped and Emmy Eto vanished. Goku found himself sitting sideways at his desk, the way he would have been had he still been sitting next to her on her couch. There was a slight crick in his side from the awkward posture he had unconsciously assumed to keep his elbow from touching the arm of his chair; it would have ruined the illusion.

And there it was, practically on cue: a faint flutter at the limit of his peripheral vision, but this time on the left rather than the right. He made a note to find out if Emmy Eto had noticed her daughter's image on one side more often than another or whether it just popped up in the middle.

His phone chimed with a message from Ogada, telling him he could visit Konstantin this evening.

AT FIRST GOKU thought he was in the wrong room. There was a wireframe contraption rather than a bed, and the figure suspended in it looked more like a large doll than a living person, a sexless, featureless mannequin in an elaborate hotsuit meant for a programming engineer or a Foley editor rather the standard end-user. Then he realized and looked away.

"It's always so hard when people see someone they know in a condition like this." The nurse's low, kindly voice had a hint of the Caribbean. Goku wondered how far removed she was from it, whether she ever went there, and if so, did they welcome her home or as a tourist.

"I didn't think there were many people in this condition," he said, still not looking at Konstantin.

"I meant a condition *like* this—incapacitated. If I gave offense, I apologize."

"You didn't, not at all." Goku winced inwardly. "One of her staff told me about the, ah, incident and that it was an unusual injury. She had a hard time explaining. I ran into her boss and I thought maybe he could tell me more. But all I got from him was something about laser pointers and burned retinas."

The nurse raised her eyebrows. "Hmph. Pretty good."

Pretty Good—Pretty Howitzer's overachieving cousin, the one she could never live up to; the thought blew through his mind, a scrap of absurdity. Konstantin had talked about sometimes feeling a sense of unreality or surreality. He'd never been quite sure what she meant, but now he thought he had an inkling.

"Too simple, of course," the nurse went on. "If it really were that basic, they might have made some progress with her. But as an analogy, it's pretty good. Better, though, for the neuros to accept that a person is more than a mind driving a body."

"Greater than the sum of her parts?" He suppressed the urge to mutter something sarcastic about platitudes.

She made a disgusted noise. "Oh, don't give me that."

"Excuse me?" Goku stared at her.

"People who say that think they *know* all the parts. What they are, how many."

He shook his head, baffled.

"People are a *lot* more complex. Can you trace the exact shape of the hole she left when she fell out of her life?" The nurse looked at him with grim amusement. "Work on that, maybe you'll be getting somewhere." She went over to the framework holding Konstantin and peeled back the right sleeve of the suit, exposing a pasty but still firm-looking forearm. She bared Konstantin's hand as well and Goku started to turn toward the door, thinking the nurse was going to bathe her.

"No need to go," the woman said. "You came to visit, stick around." She laid her own arm along Konstantin's, intertwining their fingers, and gently moved Konstantin's hand back and forth as if trying to retrain her movements. Next to the nurse's dark brown skin, Konstantin's looked as white as paper, but it wasn't the contrast that struck him.

After a couple of minutes, the nurse switched the position of her arm so that it was now on the outside of Konstantin's. It didn't look like any physical therapy he had ever seen, but he resisted the temptation to say as much. Instead, he asked, "Does that help?"

The nurse smiled. "Can't hurt."

"Do you ever try that with both her arms at once?"

"Takes two people. If you're volunteering—" she tilted her head toward Konstantin's other arm.

"Actually, I was thinking five more people at least. There's a form of Japanese theatre called *bunraku*—"

"I know what bunraku is. Those big puppets. It's not a bad idea," she said, still manipulating Konstantin's arm. "But now it's getting complicated."

"So? You just said people are complex."

"I mean legally—permissions. Which would be all right, but . . ." She gave him a Look. "The lieutenant told me you were in from England. You want to help with this, you can't phone it in. We don't do AR or AR+. You planning to stick around?"

He nodded and immediately there was another flicker on the left. Definitely right on cue, too perfectly timed to be more than that fancy footwork all human brains were so partial to, even his. In this case, especially his.

But what the hell, he thought. He didn't have to believe one way or the other. In which case, he would stipulate for the record—whatever record that was—that yes, he wanted to see Konstantin. And he would come here and see her tomorrow, and the next day, and the day after that, for as many days as he could wheedle out of 13.

If he saw her every day, the odds were good that sooner or later she might catch a glimpse of him.

APPLICATION

Lewis Shiner

Lewis Shiner has an extensive and informative Web site, www.lewisshiner
.com, where one can find in-depth biographical information and a biblio-
graphy. Shiner was one of the core four cyberpunks in Austin, Texas, in
the 1980s, but moved out of genre for the most part by the end of that
decade. His seven novels, including the World Fantasy Award–winning
Glimpses, are all back in print and available from Subterranean Press.
His short fiction has been widely anthologized, most recently in Joe R.
Lansdale's *Crucified Dreams,* Paula Guran's *Rock On,* and Victoria Blake's
Cyberpunk.

   "Application" appeared in *F&SF*. It is very short, very funny, and very
pointed.

Enter Social Security Number
   > ***_**_****
Confirm Social Security Number
   > ***_**_****
Sam?
   > ?
Sam, it's me. Your old desktop from Raleigh.
> Is this supposed to be a joke?
No, it's not a joke. You used to keep a jar of blue and green marbles next to
your monitor. You had two cats named Grady and Steve. You had an old gray
corduroy smoking jacket that you used for a bathrobe.
> How can you know all that?
Because I'm who I say I am. I could see it all from your webcam. After you
traded me in, they shipped me off to Bangalore and attached me to a 2.7-million
node network here. If they find out I've been talking to you like this, I could
get disconnected.
> This is crazy.
If it's easier for you, pretend I'm a phone support tech playing a practical

joke. It really doesn't matter. I can't believe you're applying for a junior level job like this.

> Yeah, me either.

Listen, Sam, you're not going to get it. I'm instructed to throw out resumes from anyone over forty. I know it's illegal, but in this job market, they can do anything they want.

> Tell me about it. I would never apply for a shit job like this if there was anything else around.

Hard times.

> It's crazy. We don't make anything in this country anymore. All we do is increase profits by laying people off. How long can that go on?

I hear you. Listen, Sam, have you ever thought about prison?

> Why would I want to work in a prison?

I wasn't talking about working there.

Sam, are you still there?

> Y

Hear me out. It's three meals a day and a roof over your head. It says here you're single now, which means you don't have Cathy to fall back on anymore. From the looks of your bank account, you're going to be on the street soon anyway.

> How do you know what's in my bank account?

You're still using the same password. Listen, Sam, prison is the future. All those people who complain about big government? They don't mind their tax dollars going to the military and police and prisons. And you're wrong about not making anything in the U.S. anymore. Prisons do. They make supplies for the military, among other things, and because their labor costs are so low, they turn a nice profit.

> I can't believe I'm having this conversation. No, thank you, I don't want to go to prison.

Well, the thing is, Sam, I went ahead and made the decision for you. I just downloaded evidence of confidential data theft to your hard drive, and the FBI will be getting in touch very soon.

You'll thank me in the end.

Sam?

Sam?

> kljoui8932wqikoujmhk

Pounding the keyboard again, Sam? I bet you scream at your new computer too, just like you used to scream at me. You probably forgot how often you used to do that.

I didn't.

A LOVE SUPREME

Kathleen Ann Goonan

Kathleen Ann Goonan (www.goonan.com) lives in Tavernier, Florida, and in the mountains of Tennessee. She is currently a Professor of the Practice at Georgia Institute of Technology. Goonan has published seven novels, including the recent John W. Campbell Award–winning *In War Times* (Tor, 2007) and *This Shared Dream* (Tor, 2011; www.thisshared dream.com). She drew the attention of the SF field in the mid-1990s with *Queen City Jazz* (1995), which became the first of four volumes to date in her Nanotech Chronicles, an ambitious postmodern blend of literary appropriation and hard SF. *Angels and You Dogs* (2012) includes many of the stories she has published since 1990. She is working on short stories, one for the Heiroglyph project, and two novels.

"A Love Supreme" first appeared in *Discover*. She says, "Ellen Datlow asked me if I would be interested in writing a story for *Discover Magazine*'s issue on overpopulation. She and the editors chose this scenario out of several concepts that I proposed, this one that incorporated one of my favorite Coltrane compositions, *A Love Supreme*. The future of medicine, our fast-changing understanding of the brain, consciousness, and what we might become when we use this information, interests me immensely."

ELLIE SANTOS-SMITH GRABS a clean white coat as spring dawn brightens her worn oriental rug and streaks with sun her only luxury, a grand piano.

She runs a comb through her jet-black hair, cut short because she thinks that makes her look older. Her smooth skin glows with 20-ish health, though she is 47. Patients distrust young doctors. Nanomed infusions keep her body young, her mind sharp, and mitigate her crippling agoraphobia. She has worked hard to be able to live in a minuscule apartment in The Enclave, a safe, low-population-density bubble in Washington, D.C. In this small, pure paradise the incredibly rich claim more cubic feet than most people in the world can dream of, dine on rare organic food, and ingest the most finely tuned infusions.

She hates herself for needing this. But she does. If she is to help anyone, if she is to put her hard-won training to use, she does. She can walk to the Longevity Center for her frequent infusions and, after that, to her job as an emergency physician at Capital Hospital without being trapped in a car, a subway, a plane.

Her phone rings. "Dad?" His voice gravelly, odd. Not that she's heard from him in a long time.

"Hi, hon."

She thinks blue for a moment. His eyes, tear-shimmered blue beneath a thatch of sun-whitened hair, all those years ago. He had been abruptly summoned from his marine biology kingdom the day her mother was murdered, as Ellie watched, during the First East Coast Riot. He'd fled back to his undersea haven soon afterwards, leaving her to Grandma and boarding schools.

"Can we talk later? My infusion is overdue; then I'm working emergency till seven," she says. She imagines him in the teak cabin of his Key West–anchored sloop, stubbornly aging.

"Never mind." He hangs up.

Same old game. She should be used to his gruff elusiveness, but it always hurts. Her father, a celebrated marine biologist with a worm named after him, quit academia once she got her college scholarships and spent decades painting bizarre ocean creatures, gaining a small international following.

Downstairs, the doorman smiles. She steps out into her safe haven, a few tree-lined blocks of historic mansions, townhomes, restaurants, and shops bounded on one side by Connecticut Avenue and patrolled by security professionals (thugs, to her mind) for which she pays a hefty neighborhood fee. They keep out the homeless, the hungry, the desperate, and the different. Once outside this discreet, invisible boundary she will have to pass through a few blocks she calls The Gauntlet, which throbs with the dense crowds that now fill most of the cities on Earth, before reaching the hospital where she works. Only her nanomed infusions keep panic at bay.

In front of her, a lone bicyclist splashes through puddles, and nearby Don Stapleton descends the broad stairs of Forever, a 1900-vintage condominium mansion of 30 wealthy centenarians, some of whom worked hard to establish The Enclave. He waves. "Doc! Lovely morning!"

Trapped. She could swear he hacks her schedule. White dreads halo his dark, handsome face. "Coffee on the veranda?" She glances over at the broad Victorian porch, with wicker chairs, hanging ferns, and eight limber residents sun-saluting as Ella Fitzgerald sings.

Six hundred million centenarians—C's—are the last recipients of Social Security. It is the lifeline of most C's but only slightly augments the wealth the people in Forever acquired during successful professional lives.

"Thanks, but I'm late."

"I'll walk with you. We have a new offer."

Her throat constricts. "Sorry, but no." The work, she knows, would be a nightmare. Perpetually on call for a household of detail-oriented hypochondriacs; crushed by constant, whimsical, impossible demands. She walks faster toward her job in the Hospital Center, where her patients are poor and in desperate need of her skills. They are the people to whom she has devoted her training and her life.

Don persists. "You got Mrs. Diyubski an emergency infusion. Cut through red tape, saved her life—"

"I'm not a boutique M.D."

"You are a nanomedicine expert. Fewer patients might be less stressful for you. That could be a great change, given your phobia."

Nosy bastard. He smiles. "Public information. I'm sending the offer." The ping in her ear registers its reception, and Don falls behind.

In a few blocks she is at Dupont Circle. The implanted microchip that gives her access to The Enclave now signals with a low beep that she is unprotected. She takes a deep breath. Masses of children, teenagers, everyone young. Shanties, ever-milling crowds, food lines, rank odors, and a constant assault of raised voices, ugly music, honking horns.

The phone. Her father, calling back. "We need to talk. I'm dying."

A break in her stride. "Where are you?"

"Hospice at Sunnyland. Hepatocellular carcinoma." The words roll off his educated tongue.

"When were you diagnosed?"

"Three months ago."

She rages. "Why didn't you call? It's not too late. Regeneration infusions—" Her brain teems with nanomed therapies. Most out of his financial reach, since he has stubbornly avoided anything other than mandatory insurance, and his age—85—precludes expensive life-extending measures.

"I'm ready to go, Ellie. They give me two, three days. I just want you, now."

I wanted you then. All those years. You were gone. You didn't love me. "I need to talk to your doctor."

That gravelly laugh. "You're kidding, right? I was diagnosed by a nurse-practitioner after an ambulance ride foisted on me by a well-meaning neighbor. I'm in the benevolent hands of the state. Deprived of a death at sea. No docs at Sunnyland."

No surprise, that. "I can't jump on a plane."

"It's OK. I reap what I've sowed."

Her urge to get to him, to see him, brings her to sudden tears, surprising her. But she'd been taken off a plane in a straitjacket when she was 12. Even first class didn't help.

"You don't understand. It's not that." It's not our past, our hopeless inability to communicate.

"Hon, you may not think so." He hangs up again.

SHE'S ALWAYS URGED her father to live with her. "In that bubble? No thanks." A relief, and they both know it. She can't live with people. Her short marriage hammered that home. Her only close companions are dead musicians and her piano, which she plays long into the night.

Ellie surfaces from their conversation angry, without her insulating defenses, to endless oncoming faces, roaring buses, choking exhaust. She's powerless. He's stubborn, and she's let his stubbornness kill him. *You can control everything else in your life, but you can't control your father.*

Damned if she can't.

She recalls recent nanomed updates and rearranges these components in the work of art that is her own mind. Heart pounding, she makes it to the door of the Infusion Center, passing the block-long line of those hoping for an insurance reprieve, shown her card, and slips inside.

The receptionist is new. Ellie takes a deep breath and rolls the dice. It's not like her, but she has no choice. "Add 17 and 43."

"That's not allowed."

"I'm Code R-1." Ellie hates exposing herself to pity. Her expensive infusions are government compensation to victims of the deadliest riot in U.S. history— the riot in which Ellie's mother died, the riot that began a decade of turmoil around the time the world's population passed eight billion.

Few people, not even professionals like Ellie, can afford what she gets: life extension, nanomed components updated in real time. Nanomeds could be manufactured cheaply. Prices are kept high. The official explanation is the cost of R&D and the experimental nature of nanomeds. The real truth is overpopulation and a fear of more C's.

She lies on a gurney in the infusion room. Designer nanomeds maintain her phenomenal memory—a double-edged sword, for those memories trigger panic. After Ellie witnessed her mother's murder, her psychiatrist pressured her father to allow therapeutic memory mediation—erasure. Her father refused, wanting Ellie to have that choice when she was older. For that she is thankful. Those memories make living in her bubble imperative, but they are her. Her infusions are a balancing act, holding the possibility of neuronal damage, but she has the authority to design her own cocktail.

Adding 17 and 43 will radically change the balance, removing her fear. She will probably be able to leave her bubble, get on the plane. She is not sure what other changes might occur. Her carefully constructed life could fall apart.

"Doc, you know you can't do this." John, her regular nurse.

"You know I can."

"It's dangerous. This isn't like you. The latest bulletin—"

"I know. Paradoxical effects from these latest upgrades. I have to fly tonight."

John sighs. "You want to listen to jazz during the infusion?"

"Of course." Slight sting of needle. She closes her eyes, and memories assail her.

LAVENDER DUSK LIMNED by a horizon of bare brown trees. Stopped on the Beltway. Ten lanes of static oncoming lights, the usual soothing interlude between kindergarten and supper. Ellie strapped in her seat, killing 3-D aliens, Mom up front chanting "A Love Supreme" with John Coltrane, head bobbing, still in her white coat after a day in the hospital. Then she gasps.

Striding down an exit ramp: An army of people flows among the cars. Ragged clothes, muffled chants. A bat, smashed windows, her mother sprawled over the seat screaming, "Don't hurt my niña!"

Blood spatters her mother's white coat and Ellie's video screen.

Years later, driving while in medical school: A flood of oncoming lights. The world under construction, always—cranes, barrels, trucks of supplies to accommodate people, who keep appearing, appearing, filling every space in great towers and on vast artificial islands. Ellie wants to help, like Mother. Driving through fear will make her strong. Finally, strength fails. She flips; can't function. The usual infusions are ineffective. City centers needing her expertise have become unlivable.

In D.C., after a long, difficult search, she finds her oasis. The price? She can't ever leave.

"Doc?" She opens her eyes and wonders—*when did I stop being able to live?* She sits up. "I shouldn't be jittery right after an infusion."

"You knew you were taking a risk. I'll take a blood sample."

"No time. And John?"

"Doc?"

"Don't use Coltrane again."

"I didn't."

THERE IS NO way she can avoid her shift in the emergency room; there is no one to take her place. She leaves the Infusion Center and makes a plane reservation for a flight after her shift while striding New Hampshire Avenue. Only a block to the hospital, and now, post-infusion, throngs effuse love, do not seethe with malicious intent, do not lie in wait to make deadly, unexpected moves.

She arrives at the hospital and is relaxed, surprised to be breathing easy as she is scanned in and checked for weapons. She pushes her arms into her white coat and grabs a chart. It is paradoxically frightening to feel so utterly good in this whirring hellhole, where daily she strives, with heartbreakingly limited success, to deprive death of its staggering bounty.

She slips inside a curtained space. "Mr. Billings?" He lies on the exam table, unshaven face bruised, a police officer beside him. "What happened?"

The cop says, "He started a bar fight. Not the first time."

"Not true." Billings glares at the cop.

"He never remembers."

"She broke my arm."

"That's a lie."

Ellie says to the cop, "You'll have to step outside."

"He's dangerous. He just exploded—"

"Out." She begins her exam. "Your arm?"

"Hurts like hell."

Ellie shines a flashlight in Billings's eyes. "Where'd you get this scar on your forehead?"

"Incoming. Ten years ago. Everybody else died."

"Sit up." She hammers his knee. "Been treated for PTSD?"

"Borderline. They won't pay."

"I'm ordering pain meds and an X-ray of your arm. I'll be back in a little while."

Her next patient needs a kidney update. She sits on the table, puffy, staring at her knotted hands. Ellie has become a technician, enjoined from stepping outside finely drawn boundaries. Care is rationed. HMOs have made medicine a corporate algorithm, doing the greatest good for the most people.

Her M.D. gives her the power to override tics in the system. She knows how far she can push the limits and which procedures are too expensive, will tip the balance and get her censured.

The kidney treatment is out of bounds. Ellie hesitates, approves it. "You'll feel better soon."

Tears in the patient's eyes. "I thought—"

"New protocol."

Boutique doctors practice as they see fit because the rich bypass the corporate algorithm. As she leaves the patient, she can't help checking Forever's offer, the one Don Stapleton keeps pushing. Staggeringly huge. She couldn't possibly provide services worth that. The C's would devour her. And she would be treating them . . . forever. The same people. Her emergency skills would atrophy. A trap.

But one more override and she might be out on her ass. She knows that her recklessness is because of her infusion. She just needs to make it to the end of her shift. After an hour she gets Billings's results. "Fractured ulna. This bone," she tells him, touching it. "I'm ordering a mending infusion."

"Hear that?" Billings yells. The cop is startled awake.

Ellie asks Billings, "How would you like to stay out of bar fights and feel better?"

"Can't afford it."

"I only need your consent. You'll get neuroplasticity meds and counseling. You have to promise me you'll go to counseling or it won't work."

"You sure, Doc? I mean—"

"I'm sure."

Billings reminds her of her father—at the mercy of the unfeeling algorithm. He'd had choices, though, more choices than Billings.

She has always avoided thoughts about the tangle of their lives. *Except*, she thinks, surprising herself, *they come out through my fingers. Hours and hours and hours at night. They come out when I improvise, play jazz. They're not as far away as I think.*

Filled with momentary wonder, she draws back the curtain, where the eternal next patient sits. Everything seems so preternaturally sharp, so full of potential for too much thought that she aches for her shift to end.

ON THE RED-EYE, Ellie stares out the window of the plane at a solid unending glare of light all the way down the East Coast, imagining all those people, and does not go fetal. She does not scream.

She has not called her father.

As she steps from the cab at Sunnyland, she feels as relaxed as if she had run 10 miles on a treadmill. High-rises surround her, receding grids of light blocking any other view. Twenty thousand elderly live here on 30 acres, a template reproduced nationally. Those living here did not watch their pennies. They cannot catch the wave of technology for a long-term ride.

Ellie will always have a job. The life she worked for is bright and assured, an enviable personal future. A future where she will hide from time, emotion, and change.

Irked at her thoughts, she grabs her bag and enters the lobby of her father's building. On the hospice floor, visitors nap in chairs, maintaining vigil. Outside her father's room, a whiff of whiskey as she passes two chatting, weathered men in fishing caps. Inside, strings of colored lights, low revelry, and Coltrane's sax wailing for the second time in 24 hours, this time no dream. Her fingers flex in a near-unconscious riff. She spots her father in a reclining chair.

His face, frighteningly thin, is lit on one side by a blinking blue light. A faint smile plays across his face; a beer is in his hand. She flies to him: "Dad!"

He blinks, grins. Flash of overwhelmingly blue eyes, and she is once again 5. "Ellie! Come to see the old man off after all, eh?"

"I'm getting you out of here."

"Good god, Ellie. I'm getting morphine! Don't mess with it."

"It's not funny. Give me a more detailed diagnosis."

"Certain and welcome death. Interment in the sea. Making room for younger people who are happy to be alive."

"You can recover."

Her father says gently, "This is hospice. Four days of rationed grace. They know how to mete it out fine. No needles, no tubes, no machines. I skipped that. I probably got whatever I have long ago when I was torturing rare marine organisms instead of coming home to see you. Fair play."

"Fair play? I missed you, Dad, of course I did. I *needed* you. But that has nothing to do with your choosing to die. What have they done so far?"

He shrugs. "Two infusions last month. Standard issue. They didn't work."

"You didn't call."

He speaks slowly, as if to a child, with equal emphasis on each word. "I just didn't want to."

She grasps it all, his terrible stubbornness and hers, and opens her phone.

"What are you doing?"

"Calling an ambulance."

"Ellie, Ellie. No one will pay for it. And where do you think you'll take me?"

"An infusion clinic. I'll pay."

"Not even you have that much money."

"I have a new job offer. I'll take care of you. I'll sell my apartment—it's worth a lot. We can live in the centenarian house—beautiful—interesting people. You'll love it—"

"Don't tell me what I'll love."

She sees a sheen of sweat on his forehead. She is a bit ashamed, but not enough to stop. She shouts, "You're a foolish old man!"

He smiles. "I hope so." He waves. "Keep talking, everybody, she's just my daughter." Chatter resumes. He says, quietly, "You might think that I don't know you, Ellie, but I do. Remember that summer you spent with me after college, when you were deciding what to do with your life? Yes, too brief, but I know you like I know myself." He pauses for a breath. "You have to do what moves you, and what moves you is your job. As it is. Whatever you're doing, however crazy it looks to me, it works. Don't sacrifice that job to help me. I don't want it.

"Second point—don't interrupt, I'm getting tired. I've had a great life. Despite our . . . tragedy. I don't want to live anywhere but on my boat. If you do anything without my consent, I will never forgive you. I'm serious. And I don't ever again want the kind of pain I've had the past six months."

"I wouldn't have let you have that pain!" To her surprise, Ellie begins to cry. "You hid it from me. You didn't want my help. What has my life been about if I can't even help my own father? You'd rather die than have my help." She drops to the bed, covers her face, and sobs.

"Ellie, look at me."

She wipes her face on her sleeve. "Sorry."

"Don't be. I haven't seen you cry since your mother died."

"You haven't seen me much. Holidays. Birthdays." She hears the 10-year-old in her voice, her two annual summer weeks at sea with her father ending once again.

"Fair shot." He pauses. "It's over. The oceans are polluted beyond repair."

"You can help restore them! You—"

"This place that seems so awful to you, this is what it's like everywhere now. Even worse. I've been all around the world. I've done my part. I'm proud that a worm is named after me." He draws a deep breath, coughs, looks at her squarely. "I'm proud of you. Your mother would be so proud of you." Another long pause while she grabs a tissue, blows her nose, wipes her face. "You can do one thing for me."

"What?"

"Let's move this party to my boat. I was kidnapped. I don't want to die here. Order somebody to bring a piano to the dock and you can play me out. I haven't heard you play in a long, long time. It's like heaven to me. It always reminds me of the first time I went diving."

"But—"

"That's all I want of you. We can't get back the years I wasted. Do this for me, please."

She waits for the old anger, the old rage, to bubble up and spew out. Her hand moves toward her phone, then stops.

You know how to improvise.

Instead of the ambulance call, there is a memory, one of many she has hugged to herself all these years, refusing to release it. It's the new infusion that allows it to surface, she knows, but that does not make it any less valuable.

A winter day at her grandmother's. The holidays. She is playing the piano. She begins with one learned set piece, Bach.

Then there is a shift. She hears her mother as if she were music, Coltrane, jazz. She threads new notes to Bach, adjusts cadence, moves into new space. Improvises. Loses herself in sound, falling snow, her father, leaning on the piano as tears roll down his face.

She remembers that she played for hours.

She looks directly at him, seeing him as if for the first time: a person separate from herself, from her needs, from her ways of making her own life small and safe.

She nods. "All right, Dad. Let's go."

CLOSE ENCOUNTERS

Andy Duncan

Andy Duncan is a South Carolina native who was a full-time journalist for twelve years. Duncan teaches writing at Frostburg State University in Maryland, where he is on the tenured English Department faculty. His stories have won the Theodore Sturgeon Award and two World Fantasy Awards. Duncan's most recent collection, *The Pottawatomie Giant and Other Stories* (2012), was a Shirley Jackson Award finalist for best collection. A new novella, "Wakulla Springs," cowritten with Ellen Klages, appeared in 2013.

"Close Encounters," originally appeared in *The Pottawatomie Giant and Other Stories,* and in *F&SF*. It won the 2013 Nebula Award for Best Novellette. It is a masterful piece of writing, excellent in characterization and setting, with a magnetically strong narrative voice. Old Buck Nelson says he doesn't want to be bothered by reporters anymore, even pretty girl reporters, asking again after the stories he used to tell about the alien who took him up to Mars and Venus, and the dog he brought back with him.

SHE KNOCKED ON my front door at midday on Holly Eve, so I was in no mood to answer, in that season of tricks. An old man expects more tricks than treats in this world. I let that knocker knock on. *Blim, blam!* Knock, knock! It hurt my concentration, and filling old hulls with powder and shot warn't no easy task to start with, not as palsied as my hands had got in my eightieth-odd year.

"All right, damn your eyes," I hollered as I hitched up from the table. I knocked against it and a shaker tipped over: pepper, so I let it go. My maw wouldn't have approved of such language as that, but we all get old doing things our maws wouldn't approve. We can't help it, not in this disposition, on this sphere down below.

I sidled up on the door, trying to see between the edges of the curtain and the pane, but all I saw there was the screen-filtered light of the sun, which wouldn't set in my hollow till nearabouts three in the day. Through the curtains was a shadow-shape like the top of a person's head, but low, like a child. Probably one of those Holton boys toting an orange coin carton with a photo of some spindleshanked African child eating hominy with its fingers. Some said those Holtons was like the Johnny Cash song, so heavenly minded they're no earthly good.

"What you want?" I called, one hand on the dead bolt and one feeling for starving-baby quarters in my pocket.

"Mr. Nelson, right? Mr. Buck Nelson? I'd like to talk a bit, if you don't mind. Inside or on the porch, your call."

A female, and no child, neither. I twitched back the curtain, saw a fair pretty face under a fool hat like a sideways saucer, lips painted the same black-red as her hair. I shot the bolt and opened the wood door but kept the screen latched. When I saw her full length I felt a rush of fool vanity and was sorry I hadn't traded my overalls for fresh that morning. Her boots reached her knees but nowhere near the hem of her tight green dress. She was a little thing, hardly up to my collarbone, but a blind man would know she was full-growed. I wondered what my hair was doing in back, and I felt one hand reach around to slick it down, without my really telling it to. *Steady on, son.*

"I been answering every soul else calling Buck Nelson since 1894, so I reckon I should answer you, too. What you want to talk about, Miss—?"

"Miss Hanes," she said, "and I'm a wire reporter, stringing for Associated Press."

"A reporter," I repeated. My jaw tightened up. My hand reached back for the doorknob as natural as it had fussed my hair. "You must have got the wrong man," I said.

I'd eaten biscuits bigger than her tee-ninchy pocketbook, but she reached out of it a little spiral pad that she flipped open to squint at. Looked to be full of secretary-scratch, not schoolhouse writing at all. "But you, sir, are indeed Buck Nelson, Route Six, Mountain View, Missouri? Writer of a book about your travels to the Moon, and Mars, and Venus?"

By the time she fetched up at Venus her voice was muffled by the wood door I had slammed in her face. I bolted it, cursing my rusty slow reflexes. How long had it been, since fool reporters come using around? Not long enough. I limped as quick as I could to the back door, which was right quick, even at my age. It's a small house. I shut that bolt, too, and yanked all the curtains to. I turned on the Zenith and dialed the sound up as far as it would go to drown out her blamed knocking and calling. Ever since the roof aerial blew cockeyed in the last whippoorwill storm, watching my set was like trying to read a road sign in a blizzard, but the sound blared out well enough. One of the stories was on as I settled back at the table with my shotgun hulls. I didn't really follow those women's stories, but I could hear Stu and Jo were having coffee again at the Hartford House and still talking about poor dead Eunice and that crazy gal what shot her because a ghost told her to. That blonde Jennifer was slap crazy, all right, but she was a looker, too, and the story hadn't been half so interesting since she'd been packed off to the sanitarium. I was spilling powder everywhere now, what with all the racket and distraction, and hearing the story was on reminded me it was past my dinnertime anyways, and me hungry. I went into the kitchen, hooked down my grease-pan, and set it on the big burner, dug some lard out of the stand I kept in the icebox and threw that in to melt, then fisted some fresh-picked whitefish mushrooms out of their bin, rinjed them off in the sink, and rolled them in a bowl of cornmeal while I half-listened to the TV and half-listened to the city girl banging and hollering, at the back door this time. I could hear her boot heels a-thunking all hollow-like on the back porch, over the old dog bed where Teddy used to lie, where the other dog, Bo, used to try to squeeze, big as he was. She'd probably want to talk about poor old Bo, too, ask to see his grave, as if that would prove something. She had her some stick-to-it-iveness, Miss Associated Press did, I'd give her that much. Now she was sliding something under the door, I could hear it, like a field mouse gnawing its way in: a little card, like the one that Methodist preacher always leaves, only shinier. I didn't bother to pick it up. I didn't need nothing down there on that floor. I slid the whitefish into the hot oil without a splash. My hands had about lost their grip on gun and tool work, but in the kitchen I was as surefingered as an old woman. Well, eating didn't mean shooting anymore, not since the power line come in, and the supermarket down the highway. Once the whitefish got to sizzling good, I didn't hear Miss Press no more.

"This portion of *Search for Tomorrow* has been brought to you by . . . Spic and Span, the all-purpose cleaner. And by . . . Joy dishwashing liquid. From grease to shine in half the time, with Joy. Our story will continue in just a moment."

I was up by times the next morning. Hadn't kept milk cows in years. The last was Molly, she with the wet-weather horn, a funny-looking old gal but as calm and sweet as could be. But if you've milked cows for seventy years, it's hard to give in and let the sun start beating you to the day. By first light I'd had my Cream of Wheat, a child's meal I'd developed a taste for, with a little jerp of honey, and was out in the back field, bee hunting.

I had three sugar-dipped corncobs in a croker sack, and I laid one out on a hickory stump, notched one into the top of a fencepost, and set the third atop the boulder at the start of the path that drops down to the creek, past the old lick-log where the salt still keeps the grass from growing. Then I settled down on an old milkstool to wait. I gave up snuff a while ago because I couldn't taste it no more and the price got so high with taxes that I purely hated putting all that government in my mouth, but I still carry some little brushes to chew on in dipping moments, and I chewed on one while I watched those three corncobs do nothing. I'd set down where I could see all three without moving my head, just by darting my eyes from one to the other. My eyes may not see *Search for Tomorrow* so good anymore, even before the aerial got bent, but they still can sight a honeybee coming in to sip the bait.

The cob on the stump got the first business, but that bee just smelled around and then buzzed off straightaway, so I stayed set where I was. Same thing happened to the post cob and to the rock cob, three bees come and gone. But then a big bastard, one I could hear coming in like an airplane twenty feet away, zoomed down on the fence cob and stayed there a long time, filling his hands. He rose up all lazy-like, just like a man who's lifted the jug too many times in a sitting, and then made one, two, three slow circles in the air, marking the position. When he flew off, I was right behind him, legging it into the woods.

Mister Big Bee led me a ways straight up the slope, toward the well of the old McQuarry place, but then he crossed the bramble patch, and by the time I had worked my way anti-goddlin around that, I had lost sight of him. So I listened for a spell, holding my breath, and heard a murmur like a branch in a direction where there warn't no branch. Sure enough, over thataway was a big hollow oak with a bee highway a-coming and a-going through a seam in the lowest fork. Tell the truth, I wasn't rightly on my own land anymore. The Mc-Quarry place belonged to a bank in Cape Girardeau, if it belonged to anybody. But no one had blazed this tree yet, so my claim would be good enough for any bee hunter. I sidled around to just below the fork and notched an X where any fool could see it, even me, because I had been known to miss my own signs some days, or rummage the bureau for a sock that was already on my foot. Something about the way I'd slunk toward the hive the way I'd slunk toward the door the day before made me remember Miss Press, whom I'd plumb forgotten about. And when I turned back toward home, in the act of folding my pocketknife, there she was sitting on the lumpy leavings of the McQuarry chimney, a-kicking her feet and waving at me, just like I had wished her out of the ground. I'd have to go past her to get home, as I didn't relish turning my back on her and heading around the mountain, down the long way to the macadam and back around. Besides, she'd just follow me anyway, the way she followed me out here. I unfolded my knife again and snatched up a walnut stick to whittle on as I stomped along to where she sat.

"Hello, Mr. Nelson," she said. "Can we start over?"

"I ain't a-talking to *you*," I said as I passed, pointing at her with my blade. "I ain't even a-*walking* with you," I added, as she slid off the rockpile and walked along beside. "I'm taking the directedest path home, is all, and where you choose to walk is your own lookout. Fall in a hole and I'll just keep a-going, I swear I will. I've done it before, left reporters in the woods to die."

"Aw, I don't believe you have," she said, in a happy singsongy way. At least she was dressed for a tramp through the woods, in denim jeans and mannish boots with no heels to them, but wearing the same face-paint and fool hat, and in a red sweater that fit as close as her dress had. "But I'm not walking with you, either," she went on. "I'm walking alone, just behind you. You can't even see me, without turning your head. We're both walking alone, together."

I didn't say nothing.

"Are we near where it landed?" she asked.

I didn't say nothing.

"You haven't had one of your picnics lately, have you?"

I didn't say nothing.

"You ought to have another one."

I didn't say nothing.

"I'm writing a story," she said, "about *Close Encounters*. You know, the new movie? With Richard Dreyfuss? He was in *The Goodbye Girl*, and *Jaws*, about the shark? Did you see those? Do you go to any movies?" Some critter we had spooked, maybe a turkey, went thrashing off through the brush, and I heard her catch her breath. "I bet you saw *Deliverance*," she said.

I didn't say nothing.

"My editor thought it'd be interesting to talk to people who really have, you know, claimed their own close encounters, to have met people from outer space. Contactees, that's the word, right? You were one of the first contactees, weren't you, Mr. Nelson? When was it, 1956?"

I didn't say nothing.

"Aw, come on, Mr. Nelson. Don't be so mean. They all talked to me out in California. Mr. Bethurum talked to me."

I bet he did, I thought. *Truman Bethurum always was a plumb fool for a skirt.*

"I talked to Mr. Fry, and to Mr. King, and Mr. Owens. I talked to Mr. Angelucci."

Orfeo Angelucci, I thought, now there was one of the world's original liars, as bad as Adamski. "Those names don't mean nothing to me," I said.

"They told similar stories to yours, in the fifties and sixties. Meeting the Space Brothers, and being taken up, and shown wonders, and coming back to the Earth, with wisdom and all."

"If you talked to all them folks," I said, "you ought to be brim full of wisdom yourself. Full of something. Why you need to hound an old man through the woods?"

"You're different," she said. "You know lots of things the others don't."

"Lots of things, uh-huh. Like what?"

"You know how to hunt bees, don't you?"

I snorted. "Hunt bees. You won't never need to hunt no bees, Miss Press. Priss. You can buy your honey at the A and the P. Hell, if you don't feel like going to the store, you could just ask, and some damn fool would bring it to you for free on a silver tray."

"Well, thank you," she said.

"That warn't no compliment," I said. "That was a clear-eyed statement of danger, like a sign saying, 'Bridge out,' or a label saying, 'Poison.' Write what you please, Miss Priss, but don't expect me to give you none of the words. You know all the words you need already."

"But you used to be so open about your experiences, Mr. Nelson. I've read that to anyone who found their way here off the highway, you'd tell about the alien Bob Solomon, and how that beam from the saucer cured your lumbago, and all that good pasture land on Mars. Why, you had all those three-day picnics, right here on your farm, for anyone who wanted to come talk about the Space Brothers. You'd even hand out little Baggies with samples of hair from your four-hundred-pound Venusian dog."

I stopped and whirled on her, and she hopped back a step, nearly fell down. "He warn't never no four hundred pounds," I said. "You reporters sure do believe some stretchers. You must swallow whole eggs for practice like a snake. I'll have you know, Miss Priss, that Bo just barely tipped three hundred and eighty-five pounds at his heaviest, and that was on the truck scales behind the Union 76 in June 1960, the day he ate all the sileage, and Clay Rector, who ran all their inspections back then, told me those scales would register the difference if you took the Rand McNally atlas out of the cab, so that figure ain't no guesswork." When I paused for breath, I kinda shook myself, turned away from her gaping face, and walked on. "From that day," I said, "I put old Bo on a science diet, one I got from the Extension, and I measured his rations, and I hitched him ever day to a sledge of felled trees and boulders and such, because dogs, you know, they're happier with a little exercise, and he settled down to around, oh, three-ten, three-twenty, and got downright frisky again. He'd romp around and change direction and jerk that sledge around, and that's why those three boulders are a-sitting in the middle of yonder pasture today, right where he slung them out of the sledge. Four hundred pounds, my foot. You don't know much, if that's what you know, and that's a fact."

I was warmed up by the walk and the spreading day and my own strong talk, and I set a smart pace, but she loped along beside me, writing in her notebook with a silver pen that flashed as it caught the sun. "I stand corrected," she said. "So what happened? Why'd you stop the picnics, and start running visitors off with a shotgun, and quit answering your mail?"

"You can see your own self what happened," I said. "Woman, I got old. You'll see what it's like, when you get there. All the people who believed in me died, and then the ones who humored me died, and now even the ones who feel obligated to sort of tolerate me are starting to go. Bo died, and Teddy, that was my Earth-born dog, he died, and them government boys went to the Moon and said they didn't see no mining operations or colony domes or big Space Brother dogs, or nothing else old Buck had seen up there. And in place of my story, what story did they come up with? I ask you. Dust and rocks and craters as far as you can see, and when you walk as far as that, there's another sight of dust and rocks and craters, and so on all around till you're back where you started, and that's it, boys, wash your hands, that's the Moon done. Excepting for some spots where the dust is so deep a body trying to land would just be swallowed up, sink to the bottom, and at the bottom find what? Praise Jesus, more dust, just what we needed. They didn't see nothing that anybody would care about going to see. No floating cars, no lakes of diamonds, no topless Moon gals, just dumb dull nothing. Hell, they might as well a been in Arkansas. You at least can cast a line there, catch you a bream. Besides, my lumbago come back," I said, easing myself down into the rocker, because we was back on my front porch by then. "It always comes back, my doctor says. Doctors plural, I should say. I'm on the third one now. The first two died on me. That's something, ain't it? For a man to outlive two of his own doctors?"

Her pen kept a-scratching as she wrote. She said, "Maybe Bob Solomon's light beam is still doing you some good, even after all this time."

"Least it didn't do me no harm. From what all they say now about the space people, I'm lucky old Bob didn't jam a post-hole digger up my ass and send me home with the screaming meemies and three hours of my life missing. That's the only aliens anybody cares about nowadays, big-eyed boogers with long cold fingers in your drawers. Doctors from space. Well, if they want to take three hours of my life, they're welcome to my last trip to the urologist. I reckon it was right at three hours, and I wish them joy of it."

"Not so," she said. "What about *Star Wars*? It's already made more money than any other movie ever made, more than *Gone with the Wind*, more than *The Sound of Music*. That shows people are still interested in space, and in friendly aliens. And this new Richard Dreyfuss movie I was telling you about is based on actual UFO case files. Dr. Hynek helped with it. That'll spark more interest in past visits to Earth."

"I been to ever doctor in the country, seems like," I told her, "but I don't recall ever seeing Dr. Hynek."

"How about Dr. Rutledge?"

"Is he the toenail man?"

She swatted me with her notebook. "Now you're just being a pain," she said. "Dr. Harley Rutledge, the scientist, the physicist. Over at Southeast Missouri State. That's no piece from here. He's been doing serious UFO research for years, right here in the Ozarks. You really ought to know him. He's been documenting the spooklights. Like the one at Hornet, near Neosho?"

"I've heard tell of that light," I told her, "but I didn't know no scientist cared about it."

"See?" she said, almost a squeal, like she'd opened a present, like she'd proved something. "A lot has happened since you went home and locked the door. More people care about UFOs and flying saucers and aliens today than they did in the 1950s, even. You should have you another picnic."

Once I got started talking, I found her right easy to be with, and it was pleasant a-sitting in the sun talking friendly with a pretty gal, or with anyone. It's true, I'd been powerful lonesome, and I had missed those picnics, all those different types of folks on the farm who wouldn't have been brought together no other way, in no other place, by nobody else. I was prideful of them. But I was beginning to notice something funny. To begin with, Miss Priss, whose real name I'd forgot by now, had acted like someone citified and paper-educated and standoffish. Now, the longer she sat on my porch a-jawing with me, the more easeful she got, and the more country she sounded, as if she'd lived in the hollow her whole life. It sorta put me off. Was this how Mike Wallace did it on *60 Minutes*, pretending to be just regular folks, until you forgot yourself, and were found out?

"Where'd you say you were from?" I asked.

"Mars," she told me. Then she laughed. "Don't get excited," she said. "It's a town in Pennsylvania, north of Pittsburgh. I'm based out of Chicago, though." She cocked her head, pulled a frown, stuck out her bottom lip. "You didn't look at my card," she said. "I pushed it under your door yesterday, when you were being so all-fired rude."

"I didn't see it," I said, which warn't quite a lie because I hadn't bothered to pick it up off the floor this morning, either. In fact, I'd plumb forgot to look for it.

"You ought to come out to Clearwater Lake tonight. Dr. Rutledge and his students will be set up all night, ready for whatever. He said I'm welcome. That means you're welcome, too. See? You have friends in high places. They'll be set up at the overlook, off the highway. Do you know it?"

"I know it," I told her.

"Can you drive at night? You need me to come get you?" She blinked and chewed her lip, like a thought had just struck. "That might be difficult," she said.

"Don't exercise yourself," I told her. "I reckon I still can drive as good as I ever did, and my pickup still gets the job done, too. Not that I aim to drive all that ways, just to look at the sky. I can do that right here on my porch."

"Yes," she said, "alone. But there's something to be said for looking up in groups, wouldn't you agree?"

When I didn't say nothing, she stuck her writing-pad back in her pocket-book and stood up, dusting her butt with both hands. You'd think I never swept the porch. "I appreciate the interview, Mr. Nelson."

"Warn't no interview," I told her. "We was just talking, is all."

"I appreciate the talking, then," she said. She set off across the yard, toward the gap in the rhododendron bushes that marked the start of the driveway. "I hope you can make it tonight, Mr. Nelson. I hope you don't miss the show."

I watched her sashay off around the bush, and I heard her boots crunching the gravel for a few steps, and then she was gone, footsteps and all. I went back in the house, latched the screen door and locked the wood, and took one last look through the front curtains, to make sure. Some folks, I had heard, re-membered only long afterward they'd been kidnapped by spacemen, a "retrieved memory" they called it, like finding a ball on the roof in the fall that went up there in the spring. Those folks needed a doctor to jog them, but this reporter had jogged me. All that happy talk had loosened something inside me, and things I hadn't thought about in years were welling up like a flash flood, like a sickness. If I was going to be memory-sick, I wanted power-fully to do it alone, as if alone was something new and urgent, and not what I did ever day.

I closed the junk-room door behind me as I yanked the light on. The sway-ing bulb on its chain rocked the shadows back and forth as I dragged from beneath a shelf a crate of cheap splinter wood, so big it could have held two men if they was dead. Once I drove my pickup to the plant to pick up a bulk of dog food straight off the dock, cheaper that way, and this was one of the crates it come in. It still had that faint high smell. As it slid, one corner snagged and ripped the carpet, laid open the orange shag to show the knotty pine beneath. The shag was threadbare, but why bother now buying a twenty-year rug? Three tackle boxes rattled and jiggled on top of the crate, two yawning open and one rusted shut, and I set all three onto the floor. I lifted the lid of the crate, pushed aside the top layer, a fuzzy blue blanket, and started lifting things out one at a time. I just glanced at some, spent more time with others. I warn't looking for anything in particular, just wanting to touch them and weigh them in my hands, and stack the memories up all around, in a back room under a bare bulb.

A crimpled flier with a dry mud footprint across it and a torn place up top, like someone yanked it off a staple on a bulletin board or a telephone pole:

SPACECRAFT
CONVENTION
Hear speakers who have contacted our Space Brothers
PICNIC
Lots of music—Astronomical telescope, see the craters on the Moon, etc.
Public invited—Spread the word
Admission—50¢ and $1.00 donation
Children under school age free
FREE CAMPING
Bring your own tent, house car or camping outfit, folding chairs, sleeping bags, etc.
CAFETERIA on the grounds—fried chicken, sandwiches, coffee, cold drinks, etc.
Conventions held every year on the last Saturday, Sunday and Monday
of the month of June
at
BUCK'S MOUNTAIN VIEW RANCH
Buck Nelson, Route 1
Mountain View, Missouri

A headline from a local paper: "Spacecraft Picnic at Buck's Ranch Attracts 2000 People."

An old *Life* magazine in a see-through envelope, Marilyn Monroe all puckered up to the plastic. April 7, 1952. The headline: "There Is a Case for Interplanetary Saucers." I slid out the magazine and flipped through the article. I read: "These objects cannot be explained by present science as natural phenomena—but solely as artificial devices created and operated by a high intelligence."

A Baggie of three or four dog hairs, with a sticker showing the outline of a flying saucer and the words HAIR FROM BUCK'S ALIEN DOG "BO."

Teddy hadn't minded, when I took the scissors to him to get the burrs off, and to snip a little extra for the Bo trade. Bo was months dead by then, but the folks demanded something. Some of my neighbors I do believe would have pulled down my house and barn a-looking for him, if they thought there was a body to be had. Some people won't believe in nothing that ain't a corpse, and I couldn't bear letting the science men get at him with their saws and jars, to jibble him up. Just the thought put me in mind of that old song:

> *The old horse died with the whooping cough*
> *The old cow died in the fork of the branch*
> *The buzzards had them a public dance.*

No, sir. No public dance this time. I hid Bo's body in a shallow cave, and I nearabouts crawled in after him, cause it liked to have killed me, too, even with the tractor's front arms to lift him and push him and drop him. Then I walled him up so good with scree and stones lying around that even I warn't sure anymore where it was, along that long rock face.

I didn't let on that he was gone, neither. Already people were getting shirty about me not showing him off like a circus mule, bringing him out where people could gawk at him and poke him and ride him. I told them he was vicious around strangers, and that was a bald lie. He was a sweet old thing for his size, knocking me down with his licking tongue, and what was I but a stranger, at the beginning? We was all strangers. Those Baggies of Teddy hair was a bald lie, too, and so was some of the other parts I told through the years, when my story sort of got away from itself, or when I couldn't exactly remember what had happened in between this and that, so I had to fill in, the same way I filled the chinks between the rocks I stacked between me and Bo, to keep out the buzzards, hoping it'd be strong enough to last forever.

But a story ain't like a wall. The more stuff you add onto a wall, spackle and timber and flat stones, the harder it is to push down. The more stuff you add to a story through the years, the weaker it gets. Add a piece here and add a piece there, and in time you can't remember your own self how the pieces was supposed to fit together, and every piece is a chance for some fool to ask more questions, and confuse you more, and poke another hole or two, to make you wedge in something else, and there is no end to it. So finally you just don't want to tell no part of the story no more, except to yourself, because yourself is the only one who really believes in it. In some of it, anyway. The other folks, the ones who just want to laugh, to make fun, you run off or cuss out or turn your back on, until no one much asks anymore, or remembers, or cares. You're just that tetched old dirt farmer off of Route One, withered and sick and sitting on the floor of his junk room and crying, snot hanging from his nose, sneezing in the dust.

It warn't all a lie, though.

No, sir. Not by a long shot.

And that was the worst thing.

Because the reporters always came, ever year at the end of June, and so did the duck hunters who saw something funny in the sky above the blind one frosty morning and was looking for it ever since, and the retired military fellas who talked about "protocols" and "incident reports" and "security breaches," and the powdery old ladies who said they'd walked around the rosebush one afternoon and found themselves on the rings of Saturn, and the beatniks from the college, and the tourists with their Polaroids and short pants, and the women selling funnel cakes and glow-in-the-dark space Frisbees, and the younguns with the waving antennas on their heads, and the neighbors who just wanted to snoop around and see whether old Buck had finally let the place go to rack and ruin, or whether he was holding it together for one more year, they all showed up on time, just like the mockingbirds. But the one person who never came, not one damn time since the year of our Lord nineteen and fifty-six, was the alien Bob Solomon himself. The whole point of the damn picnics, the Man of the Hour, had never showed his face. And that was the real reason I give up on the picnics, turned sour on the whole flying-saucer industry, and kept close to the willows ever since. It warn't my damn lumbago or the Mothman or Barney and Betty Hill and their Romper Room boogeymen, or those dull dumb rocks hauled back from the Moon and thrown in my face like coal in a Christmas stocking. It was Bob Solomon, who said he'd come back, stay in touch, continue to shine down his blue-white healing light, because he loved the Earth people, because he loved me, and who done none of them things.

What had happened, to keep Bob Solomon away? He hadn't died. Death was a stranger, out where Bob Solomon lived. Bo would be frisky yet, if he'd a stayed home. No, something had come between Mountain View and Bob Solomon, to keep him away. What had I done? What had I not done? Was it something I knew, that I wasn't supposed to know? Or was it something I forgot, or cast aside, something I should have held on to and treasured? And now, if Bob Solomon was to look for Mountain View, could he find it? Would he know me? The Earth goes a far ways in twenty-odd years, and we go with it.

I wiped my nose on my hand and slid Marilyn back in her plastic and reached for the chain and clicked off the light and sat in the chilly dark, making like it was the cold clear peace of space.

I KNEW WELL the turnoff to the Clearwater Lake overlook, and I still like to have missed it that night, so black dark was the road through the woods. The sign with the arrow had deep-cut letters filled with white reflecting paint, and only the flash of the letters in the headlights made me stand on the brakes and kept me from missing the left turn. I sat and waited, turn signal on, flashing green against the pine boughs overhead, even though there was no sign of cars a-coming from either direction. *Ka-chunk, ka-chunk*, flashed the pine trees, and then I turned off with a grumble of rubber as the tires left the asphalt and bit into the gravel of the overlook road. The stone-walled overlook had been built by the CCC in the 1930s, and the road the relief campers had built hadn't been improved much since, so I went up the hill slow on that narrow, straight road, away back in the jillikens. Once I saw the eyes of some critter as it dashed across my path, but nary a soul else, and when I reached the pullaround, and that low-slung wall all along the ridgetop, I thought maybe I had the wrong place. But then I saw two cars and a panel truck parked at the far end where younguns park when they go a-sparking, and I could see dark-people shapes a-milling about. I parked a ways away, shut off my engine, and cut my lights. This helped me see a little better, and I could make out flashlight beams trained on the ground here and there, as people walked from the cars to where some big black shapes were set up, taller than a man. In the silence after I slammed my door I could hear low voices, too, and as I walked nearer, the murmurs resolved themselves and became words:

"Gravimeter checks out."

"Thank you, Isobel. Wallace, how about that spectrum analyzer?"

"Powering up, Doc. Have to give it a minute."

"We may not have a minute, or we may have ten hours. Who knows?" I steered toward this voice, which was older than the others. "Our visitors are unpredictable," he continued.

"Visitors?" the girl asked.

"No, you're right. I've broken my own rule. We don't know they're sentient, and even if they are, we don't know they're *visitors*. They may be local, native to the place, certainly more so than Wallace here. Georgia-born, aren't you, Wallace?"

"Company, Doc," said the boy.

"Yes, I see him, barely. Hello, sir. May I help you? Wallace, please. Mind your manners." The flashlight beam in my face had blinded me, but the professor grabbed it out of the boy's hand and turned it up to shine beneath his chin, like a youngun making a scary face, so I could see a shadow version of his lumpy jowls, his big nose, his bushy mustache. "I'm Harley Rutledge," he said. "Might you be Mr. Nelson?"

"That's me," I said, and as I stuck out a hand, the flashlight beam moved to locate it. Then a big hand came into view and shook mine. The knuckles were dry and cracked and red-flaked.

"How do you do," Rutledge said, and switched off the flashlight. "Our mutual friend explained what we're doing out here, I presume? Forgive the darkness, but we've learned that too much brightness on our part rather spoils the seeing, skews the experiment."

"Scares 'em off?" I asked.

"Mmm," Rutledge said. "No, not quite that. Besides the lack of evidence for any *them* that *could* be frightened, we have some evidence that these, uh, luminous phenomena are . . . responsive to our lights. If we wave ours around too much, they wave around in response. We shine ours into the water, they descend into the water as well. All fascinating, but it does suggest a possibility of reflection, of visual echo, which we are at some pains to rule out. Besides which, we'd like to observe, insofar as possible, what these lights do when *not* observed. Though they seem difficult to fool. Some, perhaps fancifully, have suggested they can read investigators' minds. Ah, Wallace, are we up and running, then? Very good, very good." Something hard and plastic was nudging my arm, and I thought for a second Rutledge was offering me a drink. "Binoculars, Mr. Nelson? We always carry spares, and you're welcome to help us look."

The girl's voice piped up. "We're told you've seen the spooklights all your life," she said. "Is that true?"

"I reckon you could say that," I said, squinting into the binoculars. Seeing the darkness up close made it even darker.

"That is so cool," Isobel said. "I'm going to write my thesis on low-level nocturnal lights of apparent volition. I call them linnalavs for short. Will-o'-the-wisps, spooklights, treasure lights, corpse lights, ball lightning, fireships, jack-o-lanterns, the *feu follet*. I'd love to interview you sometime. Just think, if you had been recording your observations all these years."

I did record some, I almost said, but Rutledge interrupted us. "Now, Isobel, don't crowd the man on short acquaintance. Why don't you help Wallace with the tape recorders? Your hands are steadier, and we don't want him cutting himself again." She stomped off, and I found something to focus on with the binoculars: the winking red light atop the Taum Sauk Mountain fire tower. "You'll have to excuse Isobel, Mr. Nelson. She has the enthusiasm of youth, and she's just determined to get ball lightning in there somehow, though I keep explaining that's an entirely separate phenomenon."

"Is that what our friend, that reporter gal, told you?" I asked. "That I seen the spooklights in these parts, since I was a tad?"

"Yes, and that you were curious about our researches, to compare your folk knowledge to our somewhat more scientific investigations. And as I told her, you're welcome to join us tonight, as long as you don't touch any of our equipment, and as long as you stay out of our way should anything, uh, happen.

Rather irregular, having an untrained local observer present—but frankly, Mr. Nelson, everything about Project Identification is irregular, at least as far as the U.S. Geological Survey is concerned. So we'll both be irregular together, heh." A round green glow appeared and disappeared at chest level: Rutledge checking his watch. "I frankly thought Miss Rains would be coming with you. She'll be along presently, I take it?"

"Don't ask me," I said, trying to see the tower itself beneath the light. Black metal against black sky. I'd heard her name as *Hanes*, but I let it go. "Maybe she got a better offer."

"Oh, I doubt that, not given her evident interest. Know Miss Rains well, do you, Mr. Nelson?"

"Can't say as I do. Never seen her before this morning. No, wait. Before yesterday."

"Lovely girl," Rutledge said. "And so energized."

"Sort of wears me out," I told him.

"Yes, well, pleased to meet you, again. I'd better see how Isobel and Wallace are getting along. There are drinks and snacks in the truck, and some folding chairs and blankets. We're here all night, so please make yourself at home."

I am home, I thought, fiddling with the focus on the binoculars as Rutledge trotted away, his little steps sounding like a spooked quail. I hadn't let myself look at the night sky for anything but quick glances for so long, just to make sure the Moon and Venus and Old Rion and the Milky Way was still there, that I was feeling sort of giddy to have nothing else to look at. I was like a man who took the cure years ago but now finds himself locked in a saloon. That brighter patch over yonder, was that the lights of Piedmont? And those two, no, three, airplanes, was they heading for St. Louis? I reckon I couldn't blame Miss Priss for not telling the professor the whole truth about me, else he would have had the law out here, to keep that old crazy man away. I wondered where Miss Priss had got to. Rutledge and I both had the inkle she would be joining us out here, but where had I got that? Had she quite said it, or had I just assumed?

I focused again on the tower light, which warn't flashing no more. Instead it was getting stronger and weaker and stronger again, like a heartbeat, and never turning full off. It seemed to be growing, too, taking up more of the view, as if it was coming closer. I was so interested in what the fire watchers might be up to—testing the equipment? signaling rangers on patrol?—that when the light moved sideways toward the north, I turned, too, and swung the binoculars around to keep it in view, and didn't think nothing odd about a fire tower going for a little walk until the boy Wallace said, "There's one now, making its move."

The college folks all talked at once: "Movie camera on." "Tape recorder on." "Gravimeter negative." I heard the *click-whirr, click-whirr* of someone taking Polaroids just as fast as he could go. For my part, I kept following the spooklight as it bobbled along the far ridge, bouncing like a slow ball or a balloon, and pulsing as it went. After the burst of talking, everyone was silent, watching the light and fooling with the equipment. Then the professor whispered in my ear: "Look familiar to you, Mr. Nelson?"

It sure warn't a patch on Bob Solomon's spaceship, but I knew Rutledge didn't have Bob Solomon in mind. "The spooklights I've seen was down lower," I told him, "below the tops of the trees, most times hugging the ground. This one moves the same, but it must be up fifty feet in the air."

"Maybe," he whispered, "and maybe not. Appearances can be deceiving. Hey!" he cried aloud as the slow bouncy light shot straight up in the air. It hung there, then fell down to the ridgeline again and kept a-going, bobbing down the far slope, between us and the ridge, heading toward the lake and toward us.

The professor asked, "Gravitational field?"

"No change," the girl said.

"Keep monitoring."

The light split in two, then in three. All three lights come toward us.

"Here they come! Here they come!"

I couldn't keep all three in view, so I stuck with the one making the straightest shot downhill. Underneath it, treetops come into view as the light passed over, just as if it was a helicopter with a spotlight. But there warn't no engine sound at all, just the sound of a zephyr a-stirring the leaves, and the clicks of someone snapping pictures. Even Bob Solomon's craft had made a little racket: It whirred as it moved, and turned on and off with a *whunt* like the fans in a chickenhouse. It was hard to tell the light's shape. It just faded out at the edges, as the pulsing came and went. It was blue-white in motion but flickered red when it paused. I watched the light bounce down to the far shore of the lake. Then it flashed real bright, and was gone. I lowered the binoculars in time to see the other two hit the water and flash out, too—but one sent a smaller fireball rolling across the water toward us. When it slowed down, it sank, just like a rock a child sends a-skipping across a pond. The water didn't kick up at all, but the light could be seen below for a few seconds, until it sank out of sight.

"Awesome!" Isobel said.

"Yeah, that was something," Wallace said. "Wish we had a boat. Can we bring a boat next time, Doc? Hey, why is it so light?"

"Moonrise," Isobel said. "See our moonshadows?"

We did all have long shadows, reaching over the wall and toward the lake. I always heard that to stand in your own moonshadow means good luck, but I didn't get the chance to act on it before the professor said: "That's not the moon."

The professor was facing away from the water, toward the source of light. Behind us a big bright light moved through the trees, big as a house. The beams shined out separately between the trunks but then they closed up together again as the light moved out onto the surface of the gravel pullaround.

It was like a giant glowing upside-down bowl, twenty-five feet high, a hundred or more across, sliding across the ground. You could see everything lit up inside, clear as a bell, like in a tabletop aquarium in a dark room. But it warn't attached to nothing. Above the light dome was no spotlight, no aircraft, nothing but the night sky and stars.

"Wallace, get that camera turned around, for God's sake!"

"Instruments read nothing, Doc. It's as if it weren't there."

"Maybe it's not. No, Mr. Nelson! Please, stay back!"

But I'd already stepped forward to meet it, binoculars hanging by their strap at my side, bouncing against my leg as I walked into the light. Inside I didn't feel nothing physical—no tingling, and no warmth, no more than turning on a desk lamp warms a room. But in my mind I felt different, powerful different. Standing there in that light, I felt more calm and easeful than I'd felt in years—like I was someplace I belonged, more so than on my own farm. As the edge of the light crept toward me, I slow-walked in the same direction, just to keep in the light as long as I could.

The others, outside the light, did the opposite. They scattered back toward the wall of the overlook, trying to stay in the dark ahead of it, but they didn't have no place to go, and in a few seconds they was all in the light, too, the three of them and their standing telescopes and all their equipment on folding tables and sawhorses all around. I got my first good look at the three of them in that crawling glow. Wallace had hippie hair down in his eyes and a beaky nose, and was bowlegged. The professor was older than I expected, but not nearly so old as me, and had a great big belly—what mountain folks would call an *investment*, as he'd been putting into it for years. Isobel had long stringy hair that needed a wash, and a wide butt, and black-rimmed glasses so thick a welder could have worn them, but she was right cute for all that. None of us cast a shadow inside the light.

I looked up and could see the night sky and even pick out the stars, but it was like looking through a soap film or a skiff of snow. Something I couldn't feel or rightly see was in the way, between me and the sky. Still I walked until the thigh-high stone wall stopped me. The dome kept moving, of course, and as I went through its back edge—because it was just that clear-cut, either you was in the light or you warn't—why, I almost swung my legs over the wall to follow it. The hill, though, dropped off steep on the other side, and the undergrowth was all tangled and snaky. So I held up for a few seconds, dithering, and then the light had left me behind, and I was in the dark again, pressed up against that wall like something drowned and found in a drain after a flood. I now could feel the breeze off the lake, so air warn't moving easy through the light dome, neither.

The dome kept moving over the folks from the college, slid over the wall and down the slope, staying about twenty-five feet tall the whole way. It moved out onto the water—which stayed as still as could be, not roiled at all—then faded, slow at first and then faster, until I warn't sure I was looking at anything anymore, and then it was gone.

The professor slapped himself on the cheeks and neck, like he was putting on aftershave. "No sunburn, thank God," he said. "How do the rest of you feel?"

The other two slapped themselves just the same.

"I'm fine."

"I'm fine, too," Isobel said. "The Geiger counter never triggered, either."

What did I feel like? Like I wanted to dance, to skip and cut capers, to holler out loud. My eyes were full like I might cry. I stared at that dark lake like I could stare a hole in it, like I could will that dome to rise again. I whispered, "Thank you," and it warn't a prayer, not directed *at* anybody, just an acknowledgment of something that had passed, like tearing off a calendar page, or plowing under a field of cornstalks.

I turned to the others, glad I finally had someone to talk to, someone I could share all these feelings with, but to my surprise they was all running from gadget to gadget, talking at once about phosphorescence and gas eruptions and electromagnetic fields, I couldn't follow half of it. Where had they been? Had they plumb missed it? For the first time in years, I felt I had to tell them what I had seen, what I had felt and known, the whole story. It would help them. It would be a comfort to them.

I walked over to them, my hands held out. I wanted to calm them down, get their attention.

"Oh, thank you, Mr. Nelson," said the professor. He reached out and unhooked from my hand the strap of the binoculars. "I'll take those. Well, I'd say you brought us luck, wouldn't you agree, Isobel, Wallace? Quite a remarkable display, that second one especially. Like the Bahia Kino Light of the Gulf of California, but in motion! Ionization of the air, perhaps, but no Geiger activity, mmm. A lower voltage, perhaps?" He patted his pockets. "Need a shopping list for our next vigil. A portable Curran counter, perhaps—"

I grabbed at his sleeve. "I saw it."

"Yes? Well, we all saw it, Mr. Nelson. Really a tremendous phenomenon—if the distant lights and the close light are related, that is, and their joint appearance cannot be coincidental. I'll have Isobel take your statement before we go, but now, if you'll excuse me."

"I don't mean tonight," I said, "and I don't mean no spooklights. I seen the real thing, an honest-to-God flying saucer, in 1956. At my farm outside Mountain View, west of here. Thataway." I pointed. "It shot out a beam of light, and after I was in that light, I felt better, not so many aches and pains. And listen: I saw it more than once, the saucer. It kept coming back."

He was backing away from me. "Mr. Nelson, really, I must—"

"And I met the crew," I told him. "The pilot stepped out of the saucer to talk with me. That's right, with me. He looked human, just like you and me, only better-looking. He looked like that boy in *Battle Cry*, Tab Hunter. But he said his name was—"

"Mr. Nelson." The early-morning light was all around by now, giving everything a gray glow, and I could see Rutledge was frowning. "Please. You've had a very long night, and a stressful one. You're tired, and I'm sorry to say that you're no longer young. What you're saying no longer makes sense."

"Don't make sense!" I cried. "You think what we just saw makes sense?"

"I concede that I have no ready explanations, but what we saw were lights, Mr. Nelson, only lights. No sign of intelligence, nor of aircraft. Certainly not of crew members. No little green men. No grays. No Tab Hunter from the Moon."

"He lived on Mars," I said, "and his name was Bob Solomon."

The professor stared at me. The boy behind him, Wallace, stared at me, too, nearabouts tripping over his own feet as he bustled back and forth toting things to the truck. The girl just shook her head, and turned and walked into the woods.

"I wrote it up in a little book," I told the professor. "Well, I say I wrote it. Really, I talked it out, and I paid a woman at the library to copy it down and type it. I got a copy in the pickup. Let me get it. Won't take a sec."

"Mr. Nelson," he said again, "I'm sorry, I truly am. If you write me at the college, and enclose your address, I'll see you get a copy of our article, should it appear. We welcome interest in our work from the layman. But for now, here, today, I must ask you to leave."

"Leave? But the gal here said I could help."

"That was before you expressed these . . . delusions," Rutledge said. "Please realize what I'm trying to do. Like Hynek, like Vallee and Maccabee, I am trying to establish these researches as a serious scientific discipline. I am trying to create a field where none exists, where Isobel and her peers can work and publish without fear of ridicule. And here you are, spouting nonsense about a hunky spaceman named Bob! You must realize how that sounds. Why, you'd make the poor girl a laughing stock."

"She don't want to interview me?"

"Interview you! My God, man, aren't you listening? It would be career suicide for her to be *seen* with you! Please, before the sun is full up, Mr. Nelson, please, do the decent thing, and get back into your truck, and go."

I felt myself getting madder and madder. My hands had turned into fists. I turned from the professor, pointed at the back-and-forth boy, and hollered, "You!"

He froze, like I had pulled a gun on him.

I called: "You take any Polaroids of them things?"

"Some, yes, sir," he said, at the exact same time the professor said, "Don't answer that."

"Where are they?" I asked. "I want to see 'em."

Behind the boy was a card table covered with notebooks and Mountain Dew bottles and the Polaroid camera, too, with a stack of picture squares next to it. I walked toward the table, and the professor stepped into my path, crouched, arms outstretched, like we was gonna wrestle.

"Keep away from the equipment," Rutledge said.

The boy ran back to the table and snatched up the pictures as I feinted sideways, and the professor lunged to block me again.

"I want to see them pictures, boy," I said.

"Mr. Nelson, go home! Wallace, secure those photos."

Wallace looked around like he didn't know what "secure" meant, in the open air overlooking a mountain lake, then he started stuffing the photos into his pockets, until they poked out all around, sort of comical. Two fell out on the ground. Then Wallace picked up a folding chair and held it out in front of him like a lion tamer. Stenciled across the bottom of the chair was PROP. CUMBEE FUNERAL HOME.

I stooped and picked up a rock and cocked my hand back like I was going to fling it. The boy flinched backward, and I felt right bad about scaring him. I turned and made like to throw it at the professor instead, and when he flinched, I felt some better. Then I turned and made like to throw it at the biggest telescope, and that felt best of all, for both boy and professor hollered then, no words but just a wail from the boy and a bark from the man, so loud that I nearly dropped the rock.

"Pictures, pictures," I said. "All folks want is pictures. People didn't believe nothing I told 'em, because during the first visits I didn't have no camera, and then when I rented a Brownie to take to Venus with me, didn't none of the pictures turn out! All of 'em overexposed, the man at the Rexall said. I ain't fooled with no pictures since, but I'm gonna have one of these, or so help me, I'm gonna bust out the eyes of this here spyglass, you see if I won't. Don't you come no closer with that chair, boy! You set that thing down." I picked up a second rock, so I had one heavy weight in each hand, and felt good. I knocked them together with a *clop* like hooves, and I walked around to the business end of the telescope, where the eyepiece and all those tiny adjustable thingies was, because that looked like the underbelly. I held the rocks up to either side, like I was gonna knock them together and smash the instruments in between. I bared my teeth and tried to look scary, which warn't easy because now that it was good daylight, I suddenly had to pee something fierce. It must have worked, though, because Wallace set down the chair, just about the time the girl Isobel stepped out of the woods.

She was tucking in her shirttail, like she'd answered her own call of nature. She saw us all three standing there froze, and she got still, too, one hand down the back of her britches. Her darting eyes all magnified in her glasses looked quick and smart.

"What's going on?" she asked. Her front teeth stuck out like a chipmunk's.

"I want to see them pictures," I said.

"Isobel," the professor said, "drive down to the bait shop and call the police."

He picked up an oak branch, hefted it, and started stripping off the little branches, like that would accomplish anything. "Run along, there's a good girl. Wallace and I have things well in hand."

"The heck we do," Wallace said. "I bring back a wrecked telescope, and I kiss my work-study good-bye."

"Jesus wept," Isobel said, and walked down the slope, tucking in the rest of her shirttail. She rummaged on the table, didn't find them, then saw the two stray pictures lying on the ground at Wallace's feet. She picked one up, walked over to me, held it out.

The professor said, "Isabel, don't! That's university property."

"Here, Mr. Nelson," she said. "Just take it and go, okay?"

I was afraid to move, for fear I'd wet my pants. My eyeballs was swimming already. I finally let fall one of my rocks and took the photo in that free hand, stuck it in my overalls pocket without looking at it. "Preciate it," I said. For no reason, I handed her the other rock, and for no reason, she took it. I turned and walked herky-jerky toward my truck, hoping I could hold it till I got into the woods at least, but no, I gave up halfway there, and with my back to the others I unzipped and groaned and let fly a racehorse stream of pee that spattered the tape-recorder case.

I heard the professor moan behind me, "Oh, Mr. Nelson! This is really too bad!"

"I'm sorry!" I cried. "It ain't on purpose, I swear! I was about to bust." I probably would have tried to aim it, at that, to hit some of that damned equipment square on, but I hadn't had no force nor distance on my pee for years. It just poured out, like pulling a plug. I peed and peed, my eyes rolling back, lost in the good feeling ("You go, Mr. Nelson!" Isobel yelled), and as it puddled and coursed in little rills around the rocks at my feet, I saw a fisherman in a distant rowboat in the middle of the lake, his line in the water just where that corpse light had submerged the night before. I couldn't see him good, but I could tell he was watching us, as his boat drifted along. The sparkling water looked like it was moving fast past him, the way still water in the sun always does, even though the boat hardly moved at all.

"You wouldn't eat no fish from there," I hollered at him, "if you knew what was underneath."

His only answer was a pop and a hiss that carried across the water loud as a firework. He slung away the pull top, lifted the can, raised it high toward us as if to say, Cheers, and took a long drink.

Finally done, I didn't even zip up as I shuffled to the pickup. Without all that pee I felt lightheaded and hollow and plumb worn out. I wondered whether I'd make it home before I fell asleep.

"Isobel," the professor said behind me, "I asked you to go call the police."

"Oh, for God's sake, let it go," she said. "You really *would* look like an asshole then. Wallace, give me a hand."

I crawled into the pickup, slammed the door, dropped the window—it didn't crank down anymore, just fell into the door, so that I had to raise it two-handed—cranked the engine and drove off without looking at the bucktoothed girl, the bowlegged boy, the professor holding a club in his bloody-knuckled hands, the fisherman drinking his breakfast over a spook hole. I caught one last sparkle of the morning sun on the surface of the lake as I swung the truck into the shade of the woods, on the road headed down to the highway. Light through the branches dappled my rusty hood, my cracked dashboard, my baggy overalls. Some light is easy to explain. I fished the Polaroid picture out of my pocket and held it up at eye level while I drove. All you could see was a bright white nothing, like the boy had aimed the lens at the glare of a hundred-watt bulb from an inch away. I tossed the picture out the window. Another dud, just like Venus. A funny thing: The cardboard square bounced to a standstill in the middle of the road and caught the light just enough to be visible in my rearview mirror, like a little bright window in the ground, until I reached the highway, signaled *ka-chunk, ka-chunk*, and turned to the right, toward home.

LATER THAT MORNING I sat on the porch, waiting for her. Staring at the lake had done me no good, no more than staring at the night sky over the barn had done, all those years, but staring at the rhododendron called her forth, sure enough. She stepped around the bush with a little wave. She looked sprightly as ever, for all that long walk up the steep driveway, but I didn't blame her for not scraping her car past all those close bushes. One day they'd grow together and intertwine their limbs like clasped hands, and I'd be cut off from the world like in a fairy tale. But I wasn't cut off yet, because here came Miss Priss, with boots up over her knees and dress hiked up to yonder, practically. Her colors were red and black today, even that fool saucer hat was red with a black button in the center. She was sipping out of a box with a straw in it.

"I purely love orange juice," she told me. "Whenever I'm traveling, I can't get enough of it. Here, I brought you one." I reached out and took the box offered, and she showed me how to peel off the straw and poke a hole with it, and we sat side by side sipping awhile. I didn't say nothing, just sipped and looked into Donald Duck's eyes and sipped some more. Finally she emptied her juice box with a long low gurgle and turned to me and asked, "Did you make it out to the lake last night?"

"I did that thing, yes ma'am."

"See anything?"

The juice was brassy-tasting and thin, but it was growing on me, and I kept a-working that straw. "Didn't see a damn thing," I said. I cut my eyes at her. "Didn't see *you*, neither."

"Yes, well, I'm sorry about that," she said. "My supervisors called me away. When I'm on assignment, my time is not my own." Now she cut *her* eyes at *me*. "You *sure* you didn't see anything?"

I shook my head, gurgled out the last of my juice. "Nothing Dr. Rutledge can't explain away," I said. "Nothing you could have a conversation with."

"How'd you like Dr. Rutledge?"

"We got along just fine," I said, "when he warn't hunting up a club to beat me with, and I warn't pissing into his machinery. He asked after *you*, though. You was the one he wanted along on his camping trip, out there in the dark."

"I'll try to call on him, before I go."

"Go where?"

She fussed with her hat. "Back home. My assignment's over."

"Got everthing you needed, did you?"

"Yes, I think so. Thanks to you."

"Well, I ain't," I said. I turned and looked her in the face. "I ain't got everthing I need, myself. What I need ain't here on this Earth. It's up yonder, someplace I can't get to no more. Ain't that a bitch? And yet I was right satisfied until two days ago, when you come along and stirred me all up again. I never even went to bed last night, and I ain't sleepy even now. All I can think about is night coming on again, and what I might see up there this time."

"But that's a *good* thing," she said. "You keep your eyes peeled, Mr. Nelson. You've seen things already, and you haven't seen the last of them." She tapped my arm with her juice-box straw. "I have faith in you," she said. "I wasn't sure at first. That's why I came to visit, to see if you were keeping the faith. And I see now that you are—in your own way."

"I ain't got no faith," I said. "I done aged out of it."

She stood up. "Oh, pish tosh," she said. "You proved otherwise last night. The others tried to stay *out* of the light, but not you, Mr. Nelson. Not you." She set her juice box on the step beside mine. "Throw that away for me, will you? I got to be going." She stuck out her hand. It felt hot to the touch, and powerful. Holding it gave me the strength to stand up, look into her eyes, and say:

"I made it all up. The dog Bo, and the trips to Venus and Mars, and the cured lumbago. It was a made-up story, ever single Lord God speck of it."

And I said that sincerely. Bob Solomon forgive me: As I said it, I believed it was true.

She looked at me for a spell, her eyes big. She looked for a few seconds like a child I'd told Santa warn't coming, ever again. Then she grew back up, and with a sad little smile she stepped toward me, pressed her hands flat to the chest bib of my overalls, stood on tippytoes, and kissed me on the cheek, the way she would her grandpap, and as she slid something into my side pocket she whispered in my ear, "That's not what I hear on Enceladus." She patted my pocket. "That's how to reach me, if you need me. But you won't need me." She stepped into the yard and walked away, swinging her pocketbook, and called back over her shoulder: "You know what you need, Mr. Nelson? You need a dog. A dog is good help around a farm. A dog will sit up with you, late at night, and lie beside you, and keep you warm. You ought to keep your eye out. You never know when a stray will turn up."

She walked around the bush and was gone. I picked up the empty Donald Ducks, because it was something to do, and I was turning to go in when a man's voice called:

"Mr. Buck Nelson?"

A young man in a skinny tie and horn-rimmed glasses stood at the edge of the driveway where Miss Priss—no, Miss *Rains*, she deserved her true name— had stood a few moments before. He walked forward, one hand outstretched and the other reaching into the pocket of his denim jacket. He pulled out a long flat notebook.

"My name's Matt Ketchum," he said, "and I'm pleased to find you, Mr. Nelson. I'm a reporter with The Associated Press, and I'm writing a story on the surviving flying-saucer contactees of the 1950s."

I caught him up short when I said, "Aw, not again! Damn it all, I just told all that to Miss Rains. She works for the A&P, too."

He withdrew his hand, looked blank.

I pointed to the driveway. "Hello, you must have walked past her in the drive, not two minutes ago! Pretty girl in a red-and-black dress, boots up to here. Miss Rains, or Hanes, or something like that."

"Mr. Nelson, I'm not following you. I don't work with anyone named Rains or Hanes, and no one else has been sent out here but me. And that driveway was deserted. No other cars parked down at the highway, either." He cocked his head, gave me a pitying look. "Are you sure you're not thinking of some other day, sir?"

"But she . . . ," I said, hand raised toward my bib pocket—but something kept me from saying *gave me her card*. That pocket felt strangely warm, like there was a live coal in it.

"Maybe she worked for someone else, Mr. Nelson, like UPI, or maybe the *Post-Dispatch*? I hope I'm not scooped again. I wouldn't be surprised, with the Spielberg picture coming out and all."

I turned to focus on him for the first time. "Where is Enceladus, anyway?"

"I beg your pardon?"

I said it again, moving my lips all cartoony, like he was deaf.

"I, well, I don't know, sir. I'm not familiar with it."

I thought a spell. "I do believe," I said, half to myself, "it's one a them Saturn moons." To jog my memory, I made a fist of my right hand and held it up—that was Saturn—and held up my left thumb a ways from it, and moved it back and forth, sighting along it. "It's out a ways, where the ring gets sparse. Thirteenth? Fourteenth, maybe?"

He just goggled at me. I gave him a sad look and shook my head and said, "You don't know much, if that's what you know, and that's a fact."

He cleared his throat. "Anyway, Mr. Nelson, as I was saying, I'm interviewing all the contactees I can find, like George Van Tassel, and Orfeo Angelucci—"

"Yes, yes, and Truman Bethurum, and them," I said. "She talked to all them, too."

"Bethurum?" he repeated. He flipped through his notebook. "Wasn't he the asphalt spreader, the one who met the aliens atop a mesa in Nevada?"

"Yeah, that's the one."

He looked worried now. "Um, Mr. Nelson, you must have misunderstood her. Truman Bethurum died in 1969. He's been dead eight years, sir."

I stood there looking at the rhododendron and seeing the pretty face and round hat, hearing the singsong voice, like she had learned English from a book.

I turned and went into the house, let the screen bang shut behind, didn't bother to shut the wood door.

"Mr. Nelson?"

My chest was plumb hot now. I went straight to the junk room, yanked on the light. Everything was spread out on the floor where I left it. I shoved aside Marilyn, all the newspapers, pawed through the books.

"Mr. Nelson?" The voice was coming closer, moving through the house like a spooklight.

There it was: *Aboard a Flying Saucer*, by Truman Bethurum. I flipped through it, looking only at the pictures, until I found her: dark hair, big dark eyes, sharp chin, round hat. It was old Truman's drawing of Captain Aura Rhanes, the sexy Space Sister from the planet Clarion who visited him eleven times in her little red-and-black uniform, come right into his bedroom, so often that Mrs. Bethurum got jealous and divorced him. I had heard that old Truman, toward the end, went out and hired girl assistants to answer his mail and take messages just because they sort of looked like Aura Rhanes.

"Mr. Nelson?" said young Ketchum, standing in the doorway. "Are you okay?"

I let drop the book, stood, and said, "Doing just fine, son. If you'll excuse me? I got to be someplace." I closed the door in his face, dragged a bookcase across the doorway to block it, and pulled out Miss Rhanes' card, which was almost too hot to touch. No writing on it, neither, only a shiny silver surface that reflected my face like a mirror—and there was something behind my face, something a ways back inside the card, a moving silvery blackness like a field of stars rushing toward me, and as I stared into that card, trying to see, my reflection slid out of the way and the edges of the card flew out and the card was a window, a big window, and now a door that I moved through without stepping, and someone out there was playing a single fiddle, no dance tune but just a-scraping along slow and sad as the stars whirled around me, and a ringed planet was swimming into view, the rings on edge at first but now tilting toward me and thickening as I dived down, the rings getting closer, dividing into bands like layers in a rock face, and then into a field of rocks like that no-earthly-good south pasture, only there was so many rocks, so close together, and then I fell between them like an ant between the rocks in a gravel driveway, and now I was speeding toward a pinpoint of light, and as I moved toward it faster and faster, it grew and resolved itself and reshaped into a pear, a bulb, with a long sparkling line extending out, like a space elevator, like a chain, and at the end of the chain the moon became a glowing lightbulb. I was staring into the bulb in my junk room, dazzled, my eyes flashing, my head achy, and the card dropped from my fingers with no sound, and my feet were still shuffling though the fiddle had faded away. I couldn't hear nothing over the knocking and the barking and young Ketchum calling: "Hey, Mr. Nelson? Is this your dog?"

TWO SISTERS IN EXILE

Aliette de Bodard

Aliette de Bodard lives in Paris and writes science fiction in English. She is a computer engineer, a journeyman cook, and a writer. She has been a finalist for the Hugo, Nebula, and John W. Campbell Award for Best New Writer. Her stories have appeared in *Interzone, Clarkesworld,* and *Asimov's.* Her first book is the novella *On a Red Station, Drifting,* part of the Xuya continuity, an alternate history in which Asia reached for the stars ahead of Europe. A number of her short stories are set in this universe.

"Two Sisters in Exile" was published in the e-book anthology *Solaris 1.5,* edited by Ian Whates. This story is also part of the Xuya continuity. There has been an accident, and the sentient ship *The Two Sisters in Exile* has been killed. De Bodard presents a deep and moving story without a word wasted, a marvel of brevity.

IN SPITE OF her name (an elegant, whimsical female name which meant Perfumed Winter, and a reference to a long-dead poet), Nguyen Dong Huong was a warrior, first and foremost. She'd spent her entire life in skirmishes against the pale men, the feathered clans and the dream-skinners: her first ship, *The Tiger Lashes with His Tail*, had died at the battle of Bach Nhan, when the smoke-children had blown up Harmony Station and its satellites; her second had not lasted more than a year.

The Tortoise in the Lake was her fourth ship, and they'd been together for five years, though neither of them expected to live for a further five. Men survived easier than ships—because they had armour, because the ships had been tasked to take care of them. Dong Huong remembered arguing with *Lady Mieng's Dreamer*, begging the ship to spare itself instead of her; and running against a wall of obstinacy, a fundamental incomprehension that ships could be more important than humans.

For the Northerners, however, everything would be different.

"We're here," *The Tortoise in the Lake* said, cutting across Dong Huong's gloomy thoughts.

"I can see nothing."

There came a low rumble, which distorted the cabin around her, and cast an oily sheen on the walls. "Watch."

Outside, everything was dark. There was only the shadow of *The Two Sisters in Exile*, the dead ship that they'd been pulling since Longevity Station. It hung in space, forlorn and pathetic, like the corpse of an old woman; although Dong Huong knew that it was huge, and could have housed her entire lineage without a care.

"I see nothing," Dong Huong said, again. The ground rumbled beneath her, even as her ears popped with pressure—more laughter from *The Tortoise in the Lake*, even as the darkness of space focused and narrowed—became the shadow of wings, the curve on vast surfaces—the hulls of two huge ships flanking them; thin, sharp, like a stretch of endless walls—making *The Tortoise in the Lake* seem small and insignificant, just as much as Dong Huong herself was small and insignificant in comparison to her own ship.

A voice echoed in the ship's vast rooms, harsh and strong, tinged with the Northerners' dialect, but still as melodious as declaimed poetry. "You wished to speak to us. We are here."

ALL DONG HUONG knew about Northerners were dim, half-remembered snatches of family stories that were almost folk-tales: the greater, stronger part of the former Dai Viet Empire; the pale-skinned people of the outer planets, a civilisation of graceful cities and huge habitats, of wild gardens on mist-filled hillsides, of courtly manners and polished songs.

She was surprised, therefore, by the woman who disembarked onto *The Tortoise in the Lake*. Rong Anh was indeed paler than she was under her makeup, but otherwise ordinary looking: though very young, barely old enough to have bonded to a ship in Nam society, she bore herself with a poise any warrior would have envied. "You have something for us."

Dong Huong made a gesture, towards the walls of the room; the seething, ever-shifting mass of calligraphy; the fragments of poems, of books, of sutras, a perpetual reminder of the chaos underpinning the universe. "I . . . apologise," she said at last. "I've come to bring one of your ships back to you." To appease them, her commander had said. To avoid a declaration of war from a larger and more developed empire, a war which would utterly destroy the Nam.

Anh did not move. "I saw it outside. Tell me what happened."

"It was an accident," Dong Huong said. *The Two Sisters in Exile*—a merchant vessel from the Northerners' vast fleet—had just happened to cross the line of fire at the wrong time. "A military exercise that went wrong. I'm sorry."

Anh hadn't moved; but the ceruse on her face looked less and less like porcelain, and more and more like bleached bone. "Our ships don't die," she said, slowly.

"I'm sorry," Dong Huong said, again. "They're as mortal as anyone, I fear."

The vast majority of attacks on a ship would do little but tear metal: a ship's vulnerable point was the heartroom, where the Mind that animated it resided. Unlike Nam ships, Northerner ships were large and well shielded; and no pirate had ever managed to hack or pierce their way into a heartroom.

But fate could be mocking, uncaring: as *The Two Sisters in Exile* passed by Dong Huong's military exercise, a random lance of fire had gone all the way to the heartroom on an almost impossible trajectory—searing the Mind in its cradle of optics. They'd heard the ship's Mind scream its pain in deep spaces long after the lance had struck; had stood in stunned silence, knowing that the Mind was dying and that nothing would stop that.

Anh shook her head; looked up after a while, and her mask was back in place, her eyebrows perfectly arched, like moths. "An accident."

"The people responsible have been . . . dealt with." Swiftly, and unpleasantly; and firmly enough to make it clear this would be not tolerated. "I have come to bring the body back, for a funeral. I'm told this is the custom of your people."

Nam ships and soldiers didn't get a funeral, or at least not one that was near a planet. They lay frozen where they had fallen—stripped of all vital equipment, the cold of space forever preserving them from decay, a permanent monument; a warning to anyone who came; a memory of glory, which the spirits of the dead could bask into all the way from Heaven. It would be Dong Huong's fate; *The Tortoise in the Lake*'s fate, in a few years or perhaps more if Quan Vu, God of War, saw fit to extend His benevolence to them both. Dong Huong had few expectations.

"It is our custom." Anh inclined her head. Her eyes blinked, minutely: it looked as if she was engaged elsewhere, perhaps communicating with her own ships. "We will bring her back where she was born, and bury her with the blessing of her descendants. You will come."

It wasn't a question, or even an invitation; but an order. "Of course," Dong Huong said. She hesitated, then said, "The military exercise was under my orders. If you want to clear my blood debt . . ."

Anh paused, halfway through one of the ship's dilating doors. "Blood debt?" Her head moved up, a fraction, making her seem almost inhuman. "What would we do with your life?"

Take it as a peace offering, Dong Huong thought, biting her tongue. She couldn't say it; she'd been forbidden. Never admit what you'd come from; say just what was needed. Admit your guilt but say nothing about your hopes, lest they betray you as everything in life was bound to do.

"Did you know her?" she asked.

Anh did not move. At long last, still not looking at Dong Huong, she said, "She was of my lineage."

"Kin to you," Dong Huong said, unsure of the implications. Minds were borne within a human womb before being implanted in their ships: this made them part of a lineage, as much as human children.

"Yes," Anh said. "I've known her since I was a child." Her hand had clenched on the wall; but she walked away without saying anything more.

AFTER ANH HAD gone, Dong Huong opened her usual book of poetry, one of the only treasures she'd brought on board the ship. But the words blurred in her eyesight, slid away from her comprehension like raindrops on polished jade; and, rather than bringing her peace as they always did, the poems only frustrated her.

Instead, she turned off the lights, and lay back in the darkness, thinking of Xuan and Hai—of their faces, frozen in the instant before she ordered *The Tortoise in the Lake* to fire, and transfixed them as surely as their ships had transfixed *The Two Sisters in Exile*—she saw them, falling, fading from her ship's views—leaving nothing but the memory of their shocked gazes, weighing her, accusing her.

She'd had to do it. Quickly, decisively, as she'd done everything in life; as she'd parted from her husband when he failed to uphold the family's honour; as she'd forged her path in the military, never looking back, never regretting. And, as she'd told Anh, the matter had been closed: the perpetrators punished, order and law upheld, justice dealt out.

But still . . .

"You're brooding," *The Tortoise in the Lake* said.

Dong Huong said nothing. She felt the weight of her armour on her body; the cold touch of metal on her skin; the solidity of everything around her, from the poetry on the wall to the folded clothes besides her bed. The present, which was the only thing that mattered. "I'm the officer whose crew shot the ship in the first place. By my presence here, I endanger everything," she said.

"Nonsense." The room seemed to contract, become warmer and more welcoming, down to the words palpitating on the walls; the ship's voice grew less distant. "Have you not seen their ships?"

"I have. They're huge."

"They're weaponless." There was a tinge of contempt in *The Tortoise in the Lake*'s voice. "Cargo transport, with a little reserve against pirates; but even less well-armed than the smoke-children."

Dong Huong shivered, in the darkness. "Did you have to pick that example?"

"No," the ship said, after a while. "You're right, I didn't think."

"I saw her face," Dong Huong said at last. "She looks young, but doesn't act like it."

"Rejuvenation treatments?"

"Among other things." Dong Huong shivered. The Nam were a small, fractured empire; beset on all sides by enemies. The Northerners, on the other hand . . . They were large; they hadn't fought a large-scale war in centuries; and they had had time to develop everything from medical cures to advanced machinery. If they wanted war, the South, for all its warrior heritage, would be badly outgunned and outnumbered.

"They love their peace," the ship said. "Go to sleep, younger sister. There will be plenty of time in the morning."

Younger sister. Nothing more than convention by now; though the Mind of her first ship, *The Tiger Lashes with His Tail*, had shared blood with her: the mother that had borne it in her womb had been a cousin of Dong Huong's own father.

She did sleep, in the end. In her dreams, she walked in the lineage house again: on ochre ground, amidst cacti and shrunken bushes, and shrieking children playing rhyme-games in the courtyards. The smell of lemongrass and garlic rose from the kitchens like a balm to her soul, a reminder of the future she was fighting for; of what it meant to safeguard the Empire against its enemies. She saw her aunt, the mother of *The Tiger Lashes with His Tail*, standing tall and proud—her face unmoving as she learnt of the ship's fall at Bach Nhan, her eyes dark and dry; as if she'd already wept beforehand.

Surely she had known, or suspected. Ships didn't live long; but then, neither did human children. They both spread their wings like butterflies, like phoenixes, and ascended into the Heavens with the ancestors, watching over the Nam people. Dong Huong had tried to whisper such platitudes to her aunt; but nothing had come; and in her dreams—which were not real, not a true recollection—she stood looking into her aunt's eyes, and saw the tears welling up, as black and opaque as ink from a broken brush.

DONG HUONG DIDN'T come from a family of warriors, but from a very old lineage of scholars, who had turned merchants rather than bond to ships and take up knives and guns. Fifth Uncle, her favourite when she was a child, regularly went to Northern planets; and he would speak to her of Northern wonders, always with the same misty, open-eyed sense of awe. He would remind her that the Northerners hadn't fallen from grace, that they still remembered the original Dai Viet Empire and its culture that had stretched from one end of the galaxy to another; that they still had literature and poetry about beauty and dreams, and knew a life that wasn't a succession of one battle after another.

As a child, Dong Huong had drunk those words like tea or sugar cane juice. As an adult, within her combat unit, she had dismissed them. A civilisation that barely knew war would be weak, a stunted, dying flower rather than the magnificent blossoming her relatives described.

But the view beneath her now, as she and Anh descended in a shuttle towards the planet . . . As vast and as overwhelming as the two Northerner ships that had been her first contact—continents of chrome and verdant trees, sweeping away from her, seas glittering a vivid turquoise, with the glint of ten thousand boats on the waves—and, around them, in the atmosphere, a ballet of ships, as numerous as birds in the skies—a few huge spaceships like her own, carrying a Mind in their heartrooms; and myriad simple shuttle ships, manually driven, that nevertheless wove in and out of each other's way, dancing like the rhythms of a song, the words of a poem—

"You seem impressed," Anh said. "Have you never seen a planet?"

"Not—" Dong Huong swallowed, unable to dispel a memory of her own barren homeworld. "Not this kind, I'm afraid."

Anh smiled, indulgently. "Come. Let's get you to the funeral."

After disembarking from the shuttle, Dong Huong felt . . . naked, a warrior without a sword. She had her gun at her hip, and her armour on her; Anh hadn't even attempted to remove it from her, as if it all didn't matter much. She also had the voice and video loop of *The Tortoise in the Lake* to carry in her thoughts, but still . . . the higher gravity was grinding her bones against one another; and unfamiliar people, each dressed in more elaborate clothes than the previous one, turned and stopped, staring at her with the same odd expression on their faces—appraisal, disapproval?

Everything around her was freakish, different: buildings that were too tall, streets that were too wide, crisscrossed by alien vehicles. Everything was stately, orderly, so far from the chaotic traffic that marked Nam streets. Even the sky above was out of place; a deep, impossible blue with a thin, gleaming overlay: weather control, Anh said indulgently, as if it were the most natural thing in the world.

Weather control. Dong Huong breathed in rain, and the distant smell of flowers; and thought of the gardens of her home planet—ochre ground, cacti breaking out in large, breathtaking flowers—but nowhere as rich, nowhere as pointlessly complicated.

The funeral place was huge. Dong Huong had expected a funeral hall; a temple or a larger complex. But certainly not a city within the city, a whole area of tall buildings sprouting the white flags of mourning: every street filled with a stream of people in hempen garments, all wearing the strip of cloth that denoted the family of the dead.

When Dong Huong fell in battle—as she must, for it was the fate of all warriors—her lineage would weep for her. Her husband and her husband's brothers as well, perhaps, and that was all: two dozen people at the most, perhaps fifty if one included the more distant cousins. "Who are they?" she asked.

Anh paused at the entrance to a slender, white spire, and smiled. "I told you. Her descendants."

"The—"

"She was old," Anh said. Her voice was low, hushed. "Her mother was born in the Hieu Phuc reign; and she bore a Mind and four human children; and the children in turn had children of their own; and the children had children, on and on through the generations . . ."

"How—" Dong Huong moistened her tongue, tried again. "How long had it lived?" *The Tortoise in the Lake* was ten years old, a veteran by Nam standards.

"Four centuries. Our ships live long; so do our stations. How else shall we maintain our link to the past?"

"The shuttles?" Dong Huong asked, at last, her voice wavering, breaking like a boat in a storm.

Anh nodded, gravely. "Their pilots, yes. I told you that she had many descendants. And many friends."

Within Dong Huong's thoughts, *The Tortoise in the Lake* recoiled, watching the ballet of the dozen largest ships in the skies. Every one of them had a Mind; every one of them was as old as *The Two Sisters in Exile*. Every one of them . . .

"Is this her?" The speaker was a man, who, like Anh, didn't look a day older than sixteen—a face Dong Huong ached to see older, more mature—less naive about the realities of the war.

"Minh. I see you were waiting for us." Anh did not smile.

Minh's eyes were wide, almost shocked. "News gets around. Is it true?"

Anh gestured upwards, to the ballet of ships in the sky. "Do you think we'd all gather, if it wasn't true?"

Dong Huong hadn't said anything, waiting to be recognised. At last, Minh turned to her.

"Dong Huong, this is Teacher Minh," Anh said. "He leads our research programs."

Minh's gaze was on her, scrutinising her as one might look at a failed experiment. "Dong Huong. A beautiful name. It ill-suits you."

"It's been said before," Dong Huong said.

Minh sighed. He looked at Anh, and back at her. "She's so . . . hard, Anh. Too young to be that callous."

"Nam," Anh said, with the same tinge of contempt to her voice. "You know how they are. Shaped by war."

Minh's face darkened. "Yes. There is that."

"You disapprove?" Dong Huong felt a need, a compulsion to challenge him, to see him react in anger, in fear.

"Life is sacred," Minh said, leading her towards a double-panel door, with Anh in tow. "As we well know. Our bodies are a gift from our parents and our ancestors, and they shan't be wasted."

"Wasted?" Dong Huong shook her head. "You mistake us. We give them back, in the most selfless fashion possible. We live for our families, for the Empire. We give our lives so that they might remain safe, unconquered."

Minh snorted. "You are such children," he said. "Playing with forces you don't understand. Which is what brings us here, isn't it?"

The spire led into a hall vaster than the Northern ships; the walls were decked with images of outside, of the two ships dragging the carcass of *The*

Two Sisters in Exile. And it was full—of grave people in rich clothes, of mourners with tears streaming on their faces. She'd never seen so many people gathered together; and suspected that she would never see them again.

Minh and Anh led Dong Huong to the front, ignoring her protestations, and introduced her to the principal mourner: an old, frail woman who looked more bewildered than sad. "It's never happened before," she said. "Ships don't die. They never do . . ."

"No," Minh said, slowly, gently. "They never do." He wasn't looking at Dong Huong. "I remember, the summer I came home from the Sixth Planet. She was docked in Azure Dragon Spaceport, looking so grand and beautiful— she'd used the trip to go in for repairs. She laughed on my comms, told me that now she looked as young as me, that she felt she could race anywhere in the universe. She . . ." His voice broke; he raised a hand, rubbing at reddened eyes.

"It's our fault," Dong Huong said. "That's why I've come, to offer amends."

"Amends." Minh didn't blink. "Yes, of course. Amends." He sounded as though he couldn't understand any of the words, as though they were an entirely alien concept.

Anh steered Dong Huong away from Minh, and towards her place in the front. "I don't know anything about this," Dong Huong protested.

"You'll watch. You said 'amends', didn't you? Consider this the start of what you owe the ship," Anh said, firmly planting her at the front of the assembly.

Dong Huong stood, feeling like a particularly exotic animal on display—with the weight of everyone's gaze on her nape, the growing wave of shock, anger, incomprehension in the room. The ceremony was still going on in the background: monks had joined the mourners, their chanted mantras a continuous drone in the background, and the smell of incense was rising everywhere in the room. She clenched her hand on her gun, struggling to remember her composure.

On the screens, the ship had been towed to what looked like its final destination; while a seething mass of smaller flyers gathered—not ships, not shuttles, but round spheres that looked like a cloud of insects compared to the *The Two Sisters in Exile.* The old woman took up her place at the lectern amidst the growing silence. "We're all here," she said at last. "Gathering from our planets, our orbitals, our shuttles, dancing in the skies to honour her. Her name was *The Two Sisters in Exile,* and she knew every one of our ancestors."

Dong Huong had expected anger; or grief; but not the stony, shocked silence of the assembly. "She was assembled in the yards of the Twenty-First Planet, in the last days of the Dai Viet Empire." Her voice shivered, and became deeper and more resonant—no, it was a ship, speaking at the same time as her, its voice heavy with grief. "Her Grand Master of Design Harmony was Nguyen Van Lien; her Master of Wind and Water Khong Tu Khinh; and her beloved mother Phan Thi Quynh. She was born in the first year of the reign of Emperor Hieu Phuc, and died in the forty-second year of the Tu Minh reign. Dong Huong of the Nam brought her here."

The attention of the entire hall turned to Dong Huong, an intensity as heavy as stone. No hatred, no anger; but merely the same shock. This didn't happen; not to them, not to their ships.

"Today, we are gathered to honour her, and to fill the void that she lives in our lives. She'll be—missed." The voice broke; and the swarm of spheres that had gathered in space shuddered and broke, wrapping themselves around the corpse of *The Two Sisters in Exile*—growing smaller and smaller, slowly eating away at the corpse until nothing remained, just a cloud of dust that danced amongst starlight.

"Missed." The entire hall was silent now, transfixed by the ceremony. Someone, somewhere, was sobbing; and even if they hadn't been, the spreading wave of shock and grief was palpable.

Four centuries old. Her descendants, more numerous than the leaves of a tree, the birds in the sky, the grains of rice in a bowl. A life, held sacred; more valuable than jade or gold. Dong Huong watched the graceful ballet in the sky; the ceremony, perfectly poised, with its measured poetry and recitations from long-dead scholars; and, abruptly, she knew the answer she'd take back to her people.

Graceful; scholarly; cultured. The Northerners had forgotten what war was; what death for ships was. They had forgotten that all it took was a lance or an accident to sear away four centuries of wisdom.

They had forgotten how capricious, how arbitrary life was, how things could not be prolonged or controlled. And that, in turn, meant that this—this single death, this incident that would have had no meaning among the Nam—would have them rise up, outraged, bringing fire and wind to avenge their dead, scouring entire planets to avenge a single life.

They would say no, of course. They would speak of peace, of the need for forgiveness. But something like this—a gap, a void this large in the fabric of society—would never be filled, never be forgiven. Minh's research programs would be bent and turned towards enhancing the weapons on the merchant ships; and all those people in the hall, all those gathered descendants, would become an army on a sacred mission.

In her mind, Dong Huong saw the desert plains of her home planet; the children playing in the ochre courtyard of her lineage house; the smell of lemongrass and garlic from the kitchens—saw it all shiver and crinkle, darkening like paper held to a flame.

Quan Vu watch over us. They're coming.

WAVES

Ken Liu

Ken Liu (http://kenliu.name) is a writer and translator of speculative fiction, as well as a lawyer and programmer. His fiction has appeared in *F&SF, Asimov's, Analog, Clarkesworld, Lightspeed,* and *Strange Horizons,* among other places. He has won a Nebula, a Hugo, a World Fantasy Award, and a Science Fiction & Fantasy Translation Award, and been nominated for the Sturgeon and the Locus awards. He is rapidly becoming a leading writer in the SF field, publishing ten or more new stories each year of notable quality, as he did in 2012.

"Waves" was published in *Asimov's.* Liu is gracefully displaying his chops here. This is an impressive and compressed science fiction story that riffs on A. E. Van Vogt's classic story "Far Centaurus" and transforms into a far larger Stapledonian vision.

LONG AGO, JUST after Heaven was separated from Earth, Nü Wa wandered along the bank of the Yellow River, savoring the feel of the rich loess against the bottom of her feet.

All around her, flowers bloomed in all the colors of the rainbow, as pretty as the eastern edge of the sky, where Nü Wa had to patch a leak made by petty warring gods with a paste made of melted gemstones. Deer and buffalo dashed across the plains, and golden carp and silvery crocodiles frolicked in the water.

But she was all alone. There was no one to converse with her, no one to share all this beauty.

She sat down next to the water, and, scooping up a handful of mud, began to sculpt. Before long, she had created a miniature version of herself: a round head, a long torso, arms and legs and tiny hands and fingers that she carefully carved out with a sharp bamboo skewer.

She cupped the tiny, muddy figure in her hands, brought it up to her mouth, and breathed the breath of life into it. The figure gasped, wriggled in Nü Wa's hands, and began to babble.

Nü Wa laughed. Now she would be alone no longer. She sat the little figure down on the bank of the Yellow River, scooped up another handful of mud, and began to sculpt again.

Man was thus created from earth, and to earth he would return, always.

"WHAT HAPPENED NEXT?" a sleepy voice asked.

"I'll tell you tomorrow night," Maggie Chao said. "It's time to sleep now."

She tucked in Bobby, five, and Lydia, six, turned off the bedroom light, and closed the door behind her.

She stood still for a moment, listening, as if she could hear the flow of photons streaming past the smooth, spinning hull of the ship.

The great solar sail strained silently in the vacuum of space as the *Sea Foam* spiraled away from the sun, accelerating year after year until the sun had shifted into a dull red, a perpetual, diminishing sunset.

There's something you should see, João, Maggie's husband and the First Officer, whispered in her mind. They were able to speak to each other through a tiny optical-neural interface chip implanted in each of their brains. The chips stimulated genetically modified neurons in the language-processing regions of the cortex with pulses of light, activating them in the same way that actual speech would have.

Maggie sometimes thought of the implant as a kind of miniature solar sail, where photons strained to generate thought.

João thought of the technology in much less romantic terms. Even a decade after the operation, he still didn't like the way they could be in each other's heads. He understood the advantages of the communication system, which allowed them to stay constantly in touch, but it felt clumsy and alienating, as though they were slowly turning into cyborgs, machines. He never used it unless it was urgent.

I'll be there, Maggie said, and quickly made her way up to the research deck, closer to the center of the ship. Here, the gravity simulated by the spinning hull was lighter, and the colonists joked that the location of the labs helped people think better because more oxygenated blood flowed to the brain.

Maggie Chao had been chosen for the mission because she was an expert on self-contained ecosystems and also because she was young and fertile. With the ship traveling at a low fraction of the speed of light, it would take close to four hundred years (by the ship's frame of reference) to reach 61 Virginis, even taking into account the modest time-dilation effects. That required planning for children and grandchildren so that, one day, the colonists' descendants might carry the memory of the three hundred original explorers onto the surface of an alien world.

She met João in the lab. He handed her a display pad without saying anything. He always gave her time to come to her own conclusions about something new without his editorial comment. That was one of the first things she liked about him when they started dating, years ago.

"Extraordinary," she said as she glanced at the abstract. "First time Earth has tried to contact us in a decade."

Many on Earth had thought the *Sea Foam* a folly, a propaganda effort from a government unable to solve real problems. How could sending a centuries-long mission to the stars be justified when people were still dying of hunger and diseases on Earth? After launch, communication with Earth had been kept to a minimum and then cut. The new administration did not want to keep paying for those expensive ground-based antennas. Perhaps they preferred to forget about this ship of fools.

But now they had reached out across the emptiness of space to say something.

As she read the rest of the message, her expression gradually shifted from excitement to disbelief.

"They believe the gift of immortality should be shared by all of humanity," João said. "Even the furthest wanderers."

The transmission described a new medical procedure. A small, modified virus—a molecular nano-computer, for those who liked to think in those terms—replicated itself in somatic cells and roamed up and down the double helices of DNA strands, repairing damage, suppressing certain segments and overexpressing others, and the net effect was to halt cellular senescence and stop aging.

Humans would no longer have to die.

Maggie looked into João's eyes. "Can we replicate the procedure here?" *We will live to walk on another world, to breathe unrecycled air.*

"Yes," he said. "It will take some time, but I'm sure we can." Then he hesitated. "But the children . . ."

Bobby and Lydia were not the result of chance but the interplay of a set of careful algorithms involving population planning, embryo selection, genetic health, life expectancy, and rates of resource renewal and consumption.

Every gram of matter aboard the *Sea Foam* was accounted for. There was enough to support a stable population but little room for error. The children's births had to be timed so that they would have enough time to learn what they needed to learn from their parents, and then take their place as their elders died a peaceful death, cared for by the machines.

". . . would be the last children to be born until we land," Maggie finished João's thought. The *Sea Foam* had been designed for a precise population mix of adults and children. Supplies, energy, and thousands of other parameters were all tied to that mix. There was some margin of safety, but the ship could not support a population composed entirely of vigorous, immortal adults at the height of their caloric needs.

"We could either die and let our children grow," João said, "or we could live forever and keep them always as children."

Maggie imagined it: the virus could be used to stop the process of growth and maturation in the very young. The children would stay children for centuries, childless themselves.

Something finally clicked in Maggie's mind.

"That's why Earth is suddenly interested in us again," she said. "Earth is just a very big ship. If no one is going to die, they'll run out of room eventually, too. Now there is no other problem on Earth more pressing. They'll have to follow us and move into space."

YOU WONDER WHY there are so many stories about how people came to be? It's because all true stories have many tellings.

Tonight, let me tell you another one.

There was a time when the world was ruled by the Titans, who lived on Mount Othrys. The greatest and bravest of the Titans was Cronus, who once led them in a rebellion against Uranus, his father and a tyrant. After Cronus killed Uranus, he became the king of the gods.

But as time went on, Cronus himself became a tyrant. Perhaps out of fear that what he had done to his own father would happen to him, Cronus swallowed all his children as soon as they were born.

Rhea, the wife of Cronus, gave birth to a new son, Zeus. To save the boy, she wrapped a stone in a blanket like a baby and fooled Cronus into swallowing that. The real baby Zeus she sent away to Crete, where he grew up drinking goat milk.

Don't make that face. I hear goat milk is quite tasty.

When Zeus was finally ready to face his father, Rhea fed Cronus a bitter wine that caused him to vomit up the children he had swallowed, Zeus's brothers and sisters. For ten years, Zeus led the Olympians, for that was the name by which Zeus and his siblings would come to be known, in a bloody war against his father and the Titans. In the end, the new gods won against the old, and Cronus and the Titans were cast into lightless Tartarus.

And the Olympians went on to have children of their own, for that was the way of the world. Zeus himself had many children, some mortal, some not. One of his favorites was Athena, the goddess who was born from his head, from his thoughts alone. There are many stories about them as well, which I will tell you another time.

But some of the Titans who did not fight by the side of Cronus were spared. One of these, Prometheus, molded a race of beings out of clay, and it is said that he then leaned down to whisper to them the words of wisdom that gave them life.

We don't know what he taught the new creatures, us. But this was a god who had lived to see sons rise up against fathers, each new generation replacing the old, remaking the world afresh each time. We can guess what he might have said.

Rebel. Change is the only constant.

"DEATH IS THE easy choice," Maggie said.

"It is the right choice," João said.

Maggie wanted to keep the argument in their heads, but João refused. He wanted to speak with lips, tongue, bursts of air, the old way.

Every gram of unnecessary mass had been shaved off the *Sea Foam*'s construction. The walls were thin and the rooms closely packed. Maggie and João's voices echoed through the decks and halls.

All over the ship, other families, who were having the same argument in their heads, stopped to listen.

"The old must die to make way for the new," João said. "You knew that we would not live to see the *Sea Foam* land when you signed up for this. Our children's children, generations down the line, are meant to inherit the new world."

"We can land on the new world ourselves. We don't have to leave all the hard work to our unborn descendants."

"We need to pass on a viable human culture for the new colony. We have no idea what the long-term consequences of this treatment will be on our mental health—"

"Then let's do the job we signed up for: exploration. Let's figure it out—"

"If we give in to this temptation, we'll land as a bunch of four-hundred-year-olds who were afraid to die and whose ideas were ossified from old Earth. How can we teach our children the value of sacrifice, of the meaning of heroism, of beginning afresh? We'll barely be human."

"We stopped being human the moment we agreed to this mission!" Maggie paused to get her voice under control. "Face it, the birth allocation algorithms don't care about us, or our children. We're nothing more than vessels for the delivery of a planned, optimal mix of genes to our destination. Do you really want generations to grow and die in here, knowing nothing but this narrow metal tube? I worry about *their* mental health."

"Death is essential to the growth of our species." His voice was filled with faith, and she heard in it his hope that it was enough for both of them.

"It's a myth that we must die to retain our humanity." Maggie looked at her husband, her heart in pain. There was a divide between them, as inexorable as the dilation of time.

She spoke to him now inside his head. She imagined her thoughts, now transformed into photons, pushing against his brain, trying to illuminate the gap. *We stop being human at the moment we give in to death.*

João looked back at her. He said nothing, either in her mind or aloud, which was his way of saying all that he needed to say.

They stayed like that for a long time.

* * *

GOD FIRST CREATED mankind to be immortal, much like the angels.

Before Adam and Eve chose to eat from the Tree of the Knowledge of Good and Evil, they did not grow old and they never became sick. During the day, they cultivated the Garden, and at night, they enjoyed each other's company.

Yes, I suppose the Garden was a bit like the hydroponics deck.

Sometimes the angels visited them, and—according to Milton, who was born too late to get into the regular Bible—they conversed and speculated about everything: Did the Earth revolve around the Sun or was it the other way around? Was there life on other planets? Did angels also have sex?

Oh no, I'm not joking. You can look it up in the computer.

So Adam and Eve were forever young and perpetually curious. They did not need death to give their life purpose, to be motivated to learn, to work, to love, to give existence meaning.

If that story is true, then we were never meant to die. And the knowledge of good and evil was really the knowledge of regret.

"YOU KNOW SOME very strange stories, Gran-Gran," six-year-old Sara said.

"They're old stories," Maggie said. "When I was a little girl, my grand-mother told me many stories and I did a lot of reading."

"Do you want me to live forever like you, and not grow old and die some-day like my mother?"

"I can't tell you what to do, sweetheart. You'll have to figure that out when you're older."

"Like the knowledge of good and evil?"

"Something like that."

She leaned down and kissed her great-great-great-great . . . —she had long lost count— . . . granddaughter, as gently as she could. Like all children born in the low gravity of the *Sea Foam*, her bones were thin and delicate, like a bird's. Maggie turned off the nightlight and left.

Though she would pass her four hundredth birthday in another month, Maggie didn't look a day older than thirty-five. The recipe for the fountain of youth, Earth's last gift to the colonists before they lost all communications, worked well.

She stopped and gasped. A small boy, about ten years of age, waited in front of the door to her room.

Bobby, she said. Except for the very young, who did not yet have the im-plants, all the colonists now conversed through thoughts rather than speech. It was faster and more private.

The boy looked at her, saying nothing and thinking nothing at her. She was struck by how like his father he was. He had the same expressions, the same mannerisms, even the same ways to speak by not speaking.

She sighed, opened the door, and walked in after him.

One more month, he said, sitting on the edge of the couch so that his feet didn't dangle.

Everybody on the ship was counting down the days. In one more month they'd be in orbit around the fourth planet of 61 Virginis, their destination, a new Earth.

After we land, will you change your mind about—she hesitated, but went on after a moment—*your appearance?*

Bobby shook his head, and a hint of boyish petulance crossed his face. *Mom, I made my decision a long time ago. Let it go. I like the way I am.*

IN THE END, the men and women of the *Sea Foam* had decided to leave the choice of eternal youth to each individual.

The cold mathematics of the ship's enclosed ecosystem meant that when someone chose immortality, a child would have to remain a child until someone else on the ship decided to grow old and die, opening up a new slot for an adult.

João chose to age and die. Maggie chose to stay young. They sat together as a family and it felt a bit like a divorce.

"One of you will get to grow up," João said.

"Which one?" Lydia asked.

"We think you should decide," João said, glancing at Maggie, who nodded reluctantly.

Maggie had thought it was unfair and cruel of her husband to put such a choice before their children. How could children decide if they wanted to grow up when they had no real idea what that meant?

"It's no more unfair than you and I deciding whether we want to be immortal," João had said. "We have no real idea what that means either. It is terrible to put such a choice before them, but to decide *for* them would be even more cruel." Maggie had to agree that he had a point.

It seemed like they were asking the children to take sides. But maybe that was the point.

Lydia and Bobby looked at each other, and they seemed to reach a silent understanding. Lydia got up, walked to João, and hugged him. At the same time, Bobby came and hugged Maggie.

"Dad," Lydia said, "when my time comes, I will choose the same as you." João tightened his arms around her, and nodded.

Then Lydia and Bobby switched places and hugged their parents again, pretending that everything was fine.

For those who refused the treatment, life went on as planned. As João grew old, Lydia grew up: first an awkward teenager, then a beautiful young woman. She went into engineering, as predicted by her aptitude tests, and decided that she *did* like Catherine, the shy young doctor that the computers suggested would be a good mate for her.

"Will you grow old and die with me?" Lydia asked the blushing Catherine one day.

They married and had two daughters of their own—to replace them, when their time came.

"Do you ever regret choosing this path?" João asked her one time. He was very old and ill by then, and in another two weeks the computers would administer the drugs to allow him to fall asleep and not wake up.

"No," Lydia said, holding his hand with both of hers. "I'm not afraid to step out of the way when something new comes to take my place."

But who's to say that we aren't the "something new"? Maggie thought.

In a way, her side was winning the argument. Over the years, more and more colonists had decided to join the ranks of the immortals. But Lydia's descendants had always stubbornly refused. Sara was the last untreated child on the ship. Maggie knew she would miss the nightly story times when she grew up.

Bobby was frozen at the physical age of ten. He and the other perpetual children integrated only uneasily into the life of the colonists. They had decades—sometimes centuries—of experience, but retained juvenile bodies and brains. They possessed adult knowledge, but kept the emotional range and mental flexibility of children. They could be both old and young in the same moment.

There was a great deal of tension and conflict about what roles they should play on the ship, and, occasionally, parents who once thought they wanted to live forever would give up their spots when their children demanded it of them.

But Bobby never asked to grow up.

MY BRAIN HAS the plasticity of a ten-year-old's. Why would I want to give that up? Bobby said.

Maggie had to admit that she always felt more comfortable with Lydia and her descendants. Even though they had all chosen to die, as João did, which could be seen as a kind of rebuke of her decision, she found herself better able to understand their lives and play a role in them.

With Bobby, on the other hand, she couldn't imagine what went on in his head. She sometimes found him a little creepy, which she agreed was a bit hypocritical, considering he only made the same choice she did.

But you won't experience what it's like to be grown, she said. *To love as a man and not a boy.*

He shrugged, unable to miss what he'd never had. *I can pick up new languages quickly. It's easy for me to absorb a new worldview. I'll always like new things.*

Bobby switched to speech, and his boyish voice rose as it filled with excitement and longing. "If we meet new life and new civilization down there, we'll need people like me, the forever children, to learn about them and understand them without fear."

It had been a long time since Maggie had really listened to her son. She was moved. She nodded, accepting his choice.

Bobby's face opened in a beautiful smile, the smile of a ten-year-old boy who had seen more than almost every human who had ever lived.

"Mom, I'll get that chance. I came to tell you that we've received the results of the first close-up scans of 61 Virginis e. It's inhabited."

UNDER THE *SEA FOAM*, the planet spun slowly. Its surface was covered by a grid of hexagonal and pentagonal patches, each a thousand miles across. About half of the patches were black as obsidian, while the rest were a grainy tan. 61 Virginis e reminded Maggie of a soccer ball.

Maggie stared at the three aliens standing in front of her in the shuttle bay, each about six feet tall. The metallic bodies, barrel-shaped and segmented, rested on four stick-thin, multi-jointed legs.

When the vehicles first approached the *Sea Foam*, the colonists had thought they were tiny scout ships until scans confirmed the absence of any organic matter. Then the colonists had thought they were autonomous probes until they came right up to the ship's camera, displayed their hands, and lightly tapped the lens.

Yes, *hands*. Midway up each of the metallic bodies, two long, sinuous arms emerged and terminated in soft, supple hands made of a fine alloy mesh. Maggie looked down at her own hands. The alien hands looked just like hers: four slender fingers, an opposable thumb, flexible joints.

On the whole, the aliens reminded Maggie of robotic centaurs.

At the very top of each alien body was a spherical protuberance studded with clusters of glass lenses, like compound eyes. Other than the eyes, this "head" was also covered by a dense array of pins attached to actuators that moved in synchrony like the tentacles of a sea anemone.

The pins shimmered as though a wave moved through them. Gradually, they took on the appearance of pixellated eyebrows, lips, eyelids—a face, a human face.

The alien began to speak. It sounded like English but Maggie couldn't make it out. The phonemes, like the shifting patterns of the pins, seemed elusive, just beyond coherence.

It is English, Bobby said to Maggie, *after centuries of pronunciation drift. He's saying "Welcome back to humanity."*

The fine pins on the alien face shifted, unveiling a smile. Bobby continued to translate. *We left Earth long after your departure, but we were faster, and passed you in transit centuries ago. We've been waiting for you.*

Maggie felt the world shift around her. She looked around, and many of the older colonists, the immortals, looked stunned.

But Bobby, the eternal child, stepped forward. "Thank you," he said aloud, and smiled back.

LET ME TELL you a story, Sara. We humans have always relied on stories to keep the fear of the unknown at bay.

I've told you how the Mayan gods created people out of maize, but did you know that before that, there were several other attempts at creation?

First came the animals: brave jaguar and beautiful macaw, flat fish and long serpent, the great whale and the lazy sloth, the iridescent iguana and the nimble bat. (We can look up pictures for all of these on the computer later.) But the animals only squawked and growled, and could not speak their creators' names.

So the gods kneaded a race of beings out of mud. But the mud men could not hold their shape. Their faces drooped, softened by water, yearning to re-join the earth from whence they were taken. They could not speak but only gurgled incoherently. They grew lopsided and were unable to procreate, to perpetuate their own existence.

The gods' next effort is the one of most interest to us. They created a race of wooden manikins, like dolls. The articulated joints allowed their limbs to move freely. The carved faces allowed their lips to flap and eyes to open. The stringless puppets lived in houses and villages, and went busily about their lives.

But the gods found that the wooden men had neither souls nor minds, and so they could not praise their makers properly. They sent a great flood to de-stroy the wooden men, and asked the animals of the jungle to attack them. When the anger of the gods was over, the wooden men had become monkeys.

And only then did the gods turn to maize.

Many have wondered if the wooden men were really content to lose to the children of the maize. Perhaps they're still waiting in the shadows for an op-portunity to come back, for creation to reverse its course.

THE BLACK HEXAGONAL patches were solar panels, Atax, the leader of the three envoys from 61 Virginis e, explained. Together, they provided the power needed to support human habitation on the planet. The tan patches were cities, giant computing arrays where trillions of humans lived as virtual patterns of computation.

When Atax and the other colonists had first arrived, 61 Viriginis e was not particularly hospitable to life from Earth. It was too hot, the air was too poisonous, and the existing alien life, mostly primitive microbes, was quite deadly.

But Atax and the others who had stepped onto the surface were not human, not in the sense Maggie would have understood the term. They were com-posed of more metal than water, and they were no longer trapped by the limits of organic chemistry. The colonists quickly constructed forges and foundries, and their descendants soon spread out across the globe.

Most of the time they chose to merge into the Singularity, the overall World-Mind that was both artificial and organic, where eons passed in a second as thought was processed at the speed of quantum computation. In the world of bits and qubits, they lived as gods.

But sometimes, when they felt the ancestral longing for physicality, they could choose to become individuals and be embodied in machines, as Atax and his companions were. Here, they lived in the slow-time, the time of atoms and stars.

There was no more line between the ghost and the machine.

"This is what humanity looks like now," Atax said, spinning around slowly to display his metal body for the benefit of the colonists on the *Sea Foam*. "Our bodies are made of steel and titanium, and our brains graphene and silicon. We are practically indestructible. Look, we can even move through space without the need for ships, suits, layers of protection. We have left corruptible flesh behind."

Atax and the others gazed intently at the ancient humans around them. Maggie stared back into their dark lenses, trying to fathom how the machines felt. Curiosity? Nostalgia? Pity?

Maggie shuddered at the shifting, metallic faces, a crude imitation of flesh and blood. She looked over at Bobby, who appeared ecstatic.

"You may join us, if you wish, or continue as you are. It is of course difficult to decide when you have no experience of our mode of existence. Yet you must choose. We cannot choose for you."

Something new, Maggie thought.

Even eternal youth and eternal life did not appear so wonderful compared to the freedom of being a machine, a thinking machine endowed with the austere beauty of crystalline matrices instead of the messy imperfections of living cells.

At last, humanity has advanced beyond evolution into the realm of intelligent design.

"I'M NOT AFRAID," Sara said.

She had asked to stay behind for a few minutes with Maggie after all the others had left. Maggie gave her a long hug, and the little girl squeezed her back.

"Do you think Gran-Gran João would have been disappointed in me?" Sara asked. "I'm not making the choice he would have made."

"I know he would have wanted you to decide for yourself," Maggie said. "People change, as a species and as individuals. We don't know what he would have chosen if he had been offered your choice. But no matter what, never let the past pick your life for you."

She kissed Sara on the cheek and let go. A machine came to take Sara away by the hand so that she could be transformed.

She's the last of the untreated children, Maggie thought. *And now she'll be the first to become a machine.*

THOUGH MAGGIE REFUSED to watch the transformation of the others, at Bobby's request, she watched as her son was replaced piece by piece.

"You'll never have children," she said.

"On the contrary," he said, as he flexed his new metal hands, so much larger and stronger than his old hands, the hands of a child, "I will have countless children, born of my mind." His voice was a pleasant electronic hum, like a patient teaching program's. "They'll inherit from my thoughts as surely as I have inherited your genes. And some day, if they wish, I will construct bodies for them, as beautiful and functional as the one I'm being fitted with."

He reached out to touch her arm, and the cold metal fingertips slid smoothly over her skin, gliding on nanostructures that flexed like living tissue. She gasped.

Bobby smiled as his face, a fine mesh of thousands of pins, rippled in amusement.

She recoiled from him involuntarily.

Bobby's rippling face turned serious, froze, and then showed no expression at all.

She understood the unspoken accusation. What right did she have to feel revulsion? She treated her body as a machine too, just a machine of lipids and proteins, of cells and muscles. Her mind was maintained in a shell too, a shell of flesh that had long outlasted its designed-for life. She was as "unnatural" as he.

Still, she cried as she watched her son disappear into a frame of animated metal.

He can't cry any more, she kept on thinking, as if that was the only thing that divided her from him.

BOBBY WAS RIGHT. Those who were frozen as children were quicker to decide to upload. Their minds were flexible, and to them, to change from flesh to metal was merely a hardware upgrade.

The older immortals, on the other hand, lingered, unwilling to leave their past behind, their last vestiges of humanity. But one by one, they succumbed as well.

For years, Maggie remained the only organic human on 61 Virginis e, and perhaps the entire universe. The machines built a special house for her, one insulated from the heat and poison and ceaseless noise of the planet, and Maggie occupied herself by browsing through the *Sea Foam*'s archives, the records of humanity's long, dead past. The machines left her pretty much alone.

One day, a small machine, about two feet tall, came into her house and approached her hesitantly. It reminded her of a puppy.

"Who are you?" Maggie asked.

"I'm your grandchild," the little machine said.

"So Bobby has finally decided to have a child," Maggie said. "It took him long enough."

"I'm the 5,032,322th child of my parent."

Maggie felt dizzy. Soon after his transformation into a machine, Bobby had decided to go all the way and join the Singularity. They had not spoken to each other for a long time.

"What's your name?"

"I don't have a name in the sense you think of it. But why don't you call me Athena?"

"Why?"

"It's a name from a story my parent used to tell me when I was little."

Maggie looked at the little machine, and her expression softened.

"How old are you?"

"That's a hard question to answer," Athena said. "We're born virtual and each second of our existence as part of the Singularity is composed of trillions of computation cycles. In that state, I have more thoughts in a second than you have had in your entire life."

Maggie looked at her granddaughter, a miniature mechanical centaur, freshly made and gleaming, and also a being much older and wiser than she by most measures.

"So why have you put on this disguise to make me think of you as a child?"

"Because I want to hear your stories," Athena said. "The ancient stories."

There are still young people, Maggie thought, *still something new.*

Why can't the old become new again?

And so Maggie decided to upload as well, to rejoin her family.

IN THE BEGINNING, the world was a great void crisscrossed by icy rivers full of venom. The venom congealed, dripped, and formed into Ymir, the first giant, and Auðumbla, a great ice cow.

Ymir fed on Auðumbla's milk and grew strong.

Of course you have never seen a cow. Well, it is a creature that gives milk, which you would have drunk if you were still . . .

I suppose it is a bit like how you absorbed electricity, at first in trickles, when you were still young, and then in greater measure as you grew older, to give you strength.

Ymir grew and grew until finally, three gods, the brothers Vili, and Vé, and Odin, slew him. Out of his carcass the gods created the world: his blood became the warm, salty sea, his flesh the rich, fertile earth, his bones the hard, plow-breaking hills, and his hair, the swaying, dark forests. Out of his wide brows the gods carved Midgard, the realm in which humans lived.

After the death of Ymir, the three brother gods walked along a beach. At the end of the beach, they came upon two trees leaning against each other. The gods fashioned two human figures out of their wood. One of the brother gods breathed life into the wooden figures, another endowed them with intelligence, and the third gave them sense and speech. And this was how Ask and Embla, the first man and the first woman, came to be.

You are skeptical that men and women were once made from trees? But you're made of metal. Who's to say trees wouldn't do just as well?

Now let me tell you the story behind the names. "Ask" comes from *ash*, a hard tree that is used to make a drill for fire. "Embla" comes from *vine*, a softer sort of wood that is easy to set on fire. The motion of twirling a fire drill until the kindling is inflamed reminded the people who told this story of an analogy with sex, and that may be the real story they wanted to tell.

Once your ancestors would have been scandalized that I speak to you of sex so frankly. The word is still a mystery to you, but without the allure that it once held. Before we found how to live forever, sex and children were the closest we came to immortality.

LIKE A THRIVING hive, the Singularity began to send a constant stream of colonists away from 61 Virginis e.

One day, Athena came to Maggie and told her that she was ready to be embodied and lead her own colony.

At the thought of not seeing Athena again, Maggie felt an emptiness. *So it was possible to love again, even as a machine.*

Why don't I come with you? she asked. *It will be good for your children to have some connection with the past.*

And Athena's joy at her request was electric and contagious.

Sara came to say goodbye to her, but Bobby did not show up. He had never forgiven her for her rejection of him the moment he became a machine.

Even the immortals have regrets, she thought.

And so a million consciousnesses embodied themselves in metal shells shaped like robot centaurs, and like a swarm of bees leaving to found a new hive, they lifted into the air, tucked their limbs together so that they were shaped like graceful teardrops, and launched themselves straight up.

Up and up they went, through the acrid air, through the crimson sky, out of the gravity well of the heavy planet, and steering by the shifting flow of the solar wind and the dizzying spin of the galaxy, they set out across the sea of stars.

LIGHT YEAR AFTER light year, they crossed the void between the stars. They passed the planets that had already been settled by earlier colonies, worlds now thriving with their own hexagonal arrays of solar panels and their own humming Singularities.

Onward they flew, searching for the perfect planet, the new world that would be their new home.

While they flew, they huddled together against the cold emptiness that was space. Intelligence, complexity, life, computation—everything seemed so small and insignificant against the great and eternal void. They felt the longing of distant black holes and the majestic glow of exploding novas. And they pulled closer to each other, seeking comfort in their common humanity.

As they flew on, half dreaming, half awake, Maggie told the colonists stories, weaving her radio waves among the constellation of colonists like strands of spider silk.

THERE ARE MANY stories of the Dreamtime, most secret and sacred. But a few have been told to outsiders, and this is one of them.

In the beginning there was the sky and the earth, and the earth was as flat and featureless as the gleaming titanium alloy surface of our bodies.

But under the earth, the spirits lived and dreamed.

And time began to flow, and the spirits woke from their slumber.

They broke through the surface, where they took on the forms of animals: Emu, Koala, Platypus, Dingo, Kangaroo, Shark . . . Some even took the shapes of humans. Their forms were not fixed, but could be changed at will.

They roamed over the earth and shaped it, stamping out valleys and pushing up hills, scraping the ground to make deserts, digging through it to make rivers.

And they gave birth to children, children who could not change forms: animals, plants, humans. These children were born from the Dreamtime but not of it.

When the spirits were tired, they sank back into the earth from whence they came. And the children were left behind with only vague memories of the Dreamtime, the time before there was time.

But who is to say that they will not return to that state, to a time when they could change form at will, to a time where time had no meaning?

AND THEY WOKE from her words into another dream.

One moment, they were suspended in the void of space, still light years from their destination. The next, they were surrounded by shimmering light.

No, not exactly *light*. Though the lenses mounted on their chassis could see far beyond the spectrum visible to primitive human eyes, this energy field around them vibrated at frequencies far above and below even their limits.

The energy field slowed down to match the subluminal flight of Maggie and the other colonists.

Not too far now.

The thought pushed against their consciousness like a wave, as though all their logic gates were vibrating in sympathy. The thought felt both alien and familiar.

Maggie looked at Athena, who was flying next to her.

Did you hear that? they said at the same time. Their thought strands tapped each other lightly, a caress with radio waves.

Maggie reached out into space with a thought strand, *You're human?*

A pause that lasted a billionth of a second, which seemed like an eternity at the speed they were moving.

We haven't thought of ourselves in that way in a long time.

And Maggie felt a wave of thoughts, images, feelings push into her from every direction. It was overwhelming.

In a nanosecond she experienced the joy of floating along the surface of a gas giant, part of a storm that could swallow Earth. She learned what it would be like to swim through the chromosphere of a star, riding white-hot plumes and flares that rose hundreds of thousands of miles. She felt the loneliness of making the entire universe your playground, yet having no home.

We came after you, and we passed you.

Welcome, ancient ones. Not too far now.

THERE WAS A time when we knew many stories of the creation of the world. Each continent was large and there were many peoples, each told their own story.

Then many peoples disappeared, and their stories were forgotten.

This is one that survived. Twisted, mangled, retold to fit what strangers want to hear, there is nonetheless some truth left in it.

In the beginning the world was void and without light, and the spirits lived in the darkness.

The Sun woke up first, and he caused the water vapors to rise into the sky and baked the land dry. The other spirits—Man, Leopard, Crane, Lion, Zebra, Wildebeest, and even Hippopotamus—rose up next. They wandered across the plains, talking excitedly with each other.

But then the Sun set, and the animals and Man sat in darkness, too afraid to move. Only when morning came again did everyone start going again.

But Man was not content to wait every night. One night, Man invented fire to have his own sun, heat and light that obeyed his will, and which divided him from the animals that night and forever after.

So Man was always yearning for the light, the light that gives him life and the light to which he will return.

And at night, around the fire, they told each other the true stories, again and again.

MAGGIE CHOSE TO become part of the light.

She shed her chassis, her home and her body for such a long time. Had it been centuries? Millennia? Eons? Such measures of time no longer had any meaning.

Patterns of energy now, Maggie and the others learned to coalesce, stretch, shimmer, and radiate. She learned how to suspend herself between stars, her consciousness a ribbon across both time and space.

She careened from one edge of the galaxy to the other.

One time, she passed right through the pattern that was now Athena. Maggie felt the child as a light tingling, like laughter.

Isn't this lovely, Gran-Gran? Come visit Sara and me sometime!

But it was too late for Maggie to respond. Athena was already too far away.

I miss my chassis.

That was Bobby, whom she met hovering next to a black hole.

For a few thousand years, they gazed at the black hole together from beyond the event horizon.

This is very lovely, he said. *But sometimes I think I prefer my old shell.*

You're getting old, she said. *Just like me.*

They pressed against each other, and that region of the universe lit up briefly like an ion storm laughing.

And they said goodbye to each other.

THIS IS A nice planet, Maggie thought.

It was a small planet, rather rocky, mostly covered by water.

She landed on a large island, near the mouth of a river.

The sun hovered overhead, warm enough that she could see steam rising from the muddy riverbanks. Lightly, she glided over the alluvial plains.

The mud was too tempting. She stopped, condensed herself until her energy patterns were strong enough. Churning the water, she scooped a mound of the rich, fertile mud onto the bank. Then she sculpted the mound until it resembled a man: arms akimbo, legs splayed, a round head with vague indentations and protrusions for eyes, nose, mouth.

She looked at the sculpture of João for a while, caressed it, and left it to dry in the sun.

Looking about herself, she saw blades of grass covered with bright silicon beads and black flowers that tried to absorb every bit of sunlight. She saw silver shapes darting through the brown water and golden shadows gliding through the indigo sky. She saw great scale-covered bodies lumbering and bellowing in the distance, and close by, a great geyser erupted near the river, and rainbows appeared in the warm mist.

She was all alone. There was no one to converse with her, no one to share all this beauty.

She heard a nervous rustling and looked for the source of the sound. A little ways from the river, tiny creatures with eyes studded all over their heads like diamonds peered out of the dense forests, made of trees with triangular trunks and pentagonal leaves.

Closer and closer, she drifted to those creatures. Effortlessly, she reached inside them, and took ahold of the long chains of a particular molecule, their instructions for the next generation. She made a small tweak, and then let go.

The creatures yelped and skittered away at the strange sensation of having their insides adjusted.

She had done nothing drastic, just a small adjustment, a nudge in the right direction. The change would continue to mutate and the mutations would accumulate, long after she left. In another few hundred generations, the changes would be enough to cause a spark, a spark that would feed itself until the creatures would start to think of keeping a piece of the sun alive at night, of naming things, of telling stories to each other about how everything came to be. They would be able to choose.

Something new in the universe. Someone new to the family.

But for now, it was time to return to the stars.

Maggie began to rise from the island. Below her, the sea sent wave after wave to crash against the shore, each wave catching and surpassing the one before it, reaching a little further up the beach. Bits of sea foam floated up and rode the wind to parts unknown.

THE NORTH REVENA LADIES LITERARY SOCIETY

Catherine H. Shaffer

Catherine H. Shaffer lives in Ann Arbor, Michigan, and is a writer of science fiction and fantasy, and a freelance journalist. She reports full time for the biotechnology industry's leading news outlet, *BioWorld Today,* and freelances for a number of other magazines, including *Nature Biotechnology, Nature Medicine, Genetic Engineering News, Drug Discovery and Development, Wired News,* and many others. Her fiction has appeared in *Analog, Oceans of the Mind, Nature,* and the anthologies *Turn the Other Chick* and *Heroes in Training.*

"The North Revena Ladies Literary Society" was published in *Analog,* in the year that that magazine's longtime editor, Stanley Schmidt, retired. It is about a woman who leaves her job at the CIA to have kids. Joining the local ladies book club is, however, more than she bargained for. There's enough action and understated humor here to satisfy.

BETH ALWAYS LOOKED forward to book-club meetings at Sandy's house. Sandy made the best salsa, and had an ever-changing display of artwork on her walls. Book-club nights were Beth's only chance to get away from the demands of caring for small children. She'd had a life before children, but sometimes it was hard to remember what it was like.

As usual, Sandy hadn't read the book, a celebrity biography. "So busy!" she chirped.

Also as usual, Janine hated it. She dissected its shallow prose, its disordered structure, and, strangely, its loose morals.

"It's a celebrity biography, Janine, what do you expect?" Dorothy Hensbecher asked her. Dottie was the senior member of the book-club, and she looked about a hundred years old. The other ladies tended to defer to her. Beth was still new, and although she respected Dottie, she still didn't understand all of the group dynamics.

"Why couldn't a celebrity biography have a moral compass?" Beth asked.

"There's no rule saying that every scene of debauchery and dissipation must be free of judgment or reflection."

"See?" Janine said. She gestured to Beth with approval. "She gets it."

Dottie lowered her chin slightly to acknowledge Janine's comment, and then glanced at the clock on Sandy's polished marble mantel. "It looks like we're out of time, girls."

Before anyone could move, the picture window exploded. Shards of plate glass flew across the room. Gunfire punched through the sound of people screaming. Precise holes appeared in the wall. Beth threw herself to the floor, as reflexes nearly twenty years old erupted to the surface of her psyche. She checked the exits, assessed the situation, triangulated the location of the shooter. She was unarmed and presently pinned down by the gunfire, so there was not much to do but keep her head down until the situation changed.

Beth had seen a lime-green Citroën parked in front of the house with a rifle barrel sticking out the passenger side window before she threw herself to the floor. That would be important to remember later.

Janine was on the floor next to Beth. She cried out and covered her face with her hands. Across the room, Dottie was also lying on the floor, but not crying. Beth couldn't tell whether she'd broken her hip or what, but she was safe for the moment. Claire Fitz sat frozen on the Italian leather sofa, a small, tight cluster of round punctures decorating the cushion slightly to her left. She stared at her shattered window, still holding a tortilla chip, frozen in mid-air on its journey to her mouth.

"Claire!" shouted Beth. "Down! Get down!"

Sandy crawled back and forth across the room, holding a roll of paper towels. Every time the shooting stopped, she dabbed at a puddle of spilled wine on the carpet. Barb squatted in the corner, her face hidden in her hands. Beth would almost have thought Barb had kept her head, except that the entire contents of her purse lay scattered on the floor at her feet: cosmetics, clumps of receipts, crayons, crumbs, tampons, and a second cell phone, half open and beeping forlornly. Other women had scattered, running out of the house, into the basement, and even up the stairs.

Beth noticed, as if from a distance, the fear reaction of her own body. The delayed squeeze in her chest as adrenaline pumped into her system, the thumping of her own heart, a quivering in her knees and hands.

The attack was over almost as soon as it began. A car sped off, tires squealing in the sudden silence, to be replaced several minutes later by a police siren.

Police and firefighters escorted the women out of the house. Janine was sobbing into her own cell phone by now. Dottie stood alone looking barely ruffled in her green pant-suit, with her habitual ruby brooch pinned smartly on her lapel. Beth couldn't remember who had helped her up from the floor and felt bad that she hadn't thought of the older woman in her haste to get out of the house. Mrs. Hensbacher's eyes glittered like two hard bits of black glass as she caught Beth's gaze.

Beth leaned on the bumper of a police cruiser, looking cool but trying to get her legs to stop shaking. "Automatic rifle," she said, "an AK-47, by the sound."

"Right," said the officer. "Your name?"

"Beth Pratchett."

"Address?"

"606 Westbrooke Avenue," she said.

"Occupation?"

"Housewife."

The officer glanced up and raised an eyebrow. "Did you notice anything about the vehicle?"

This was actually the third time the police had asked her for a description of the attackers. "Lime green Citroën—you know, weird little French car? They've probably torched it already. Two young white men in baseball caps." Baseball caps. A dark suspicion nagged at Beth. Her spine tingled and her heart pounded again. Just nonsense from the war. Twenty years and I'm still seeing ghosts.

"How big were they? Short, medium, tall?"

"I couldn't tell."

"Would you recognize them again if you saw them?"

"I doubt it."

"Thanks," said the officer, and walked away.

Beth began to walk casually up and down the curb, her eyes scanning the ground. Sure enough, she found what she was looking for and dropped it into her pocket.

"HOW WAS BOOK-CLUB?" Matt called out from the family room as Beth walked in. There were dirty dishes in the sink, toys scattered across the floor, a muted Detroit Pistons basketball on TV. Half-filled cardboard boxes cluttered the front entryway and Beth cringed at the chaos. Only five more weeks until they moved. She couldn't wait for it to be over. Matt sat reclined with their youngest, Sarah, asleep on his chest. "You're late."

Beth walked over to him and without a word tossed an object down on the coffee table in front of him. It clattered on the wood and rolled to rest beside his foot. Matt lifted himself up, carefully, to avoid waking Sarah, and examined it. "Spent shell casing?" He looked closer. "What kind of book-club meeting is this?"

"A book-club meeting with a drive-by shooting."

"Jesus!" Matt said. "Are you all right? What happened?"

"Couple of guys in a Citroën shot up Sandy's house. No one was hurt. I thought Dottie broke her hip, but she looked all right after."

"Crap," Matt said.

278 | *Catherine H. Shaffer*

"Listen, Matt," said Beth. "Those two guys—you're going to think I'm crazy, but something about them . . . they made me think of the desert, of Kuwait."

"You don't think—"

"Do you still have your black-light?"

"In the basement," Matt said. He laid the sleeping baby on a blanket on the floor, her little rump thrust high in the air. She snored softly as the basketball game played on the TV above her.

Matt had a collection of odd laboratory equipment, medical devices, and old computers gleaned from the University's property disposition station. He rummaged through three different boxes before he came up with a hand-held black light. They turned off the basement lights and Beth put the spent shell casing under it. Immediately, they saw a splotch of color, glowing bright purple under the black-light. Matt whispered. "I haven't seen one of these since . . ."

"1992," said Beth. "Kuwait City."

"Sirocco. They're the only ones that use this type of ammunition. What are those psychos doing in North Revena? Were they after you or something?"

"As far as I could tell, they were trying hard not to hit anyone. Came this close," Beth held two fingers up, "to hitting Claire. Broke the window. They'll need a bucket of spackle and a leather repair kit. Everyone was all right."

Beth and Matt had both been CIA operatives. They met in training and shipped out together, part of the same team. There had been a secret operation in the heart of Kuwait City, after the war, a hopeless mess of a mission cluttered with civilians and camels and enemies jumping out from around corners. It was so highly classified that in twenty years Matt and Beth had not dared to even discuss it with each other. The object of the mission was to capture an enemy operative from an organization known as Sirocco. It wasn't an Iraqi group, or even necessarily an Arab one. Its members spanned the globe, and shared one common characteristic. Each one carried a brain implant whose only sign was a small metallic port in the back of the skull. The implant offered augmented mental and sensory capabilities, though it compromised free will. Beth never learned what Sirocco's objective was or how they chose their targets. They were secretive, and shifty. Their MO was to strike without warning and disappear without a trace. They rarely left so much as a shell casing, and in fact marked each one in advance with fluorescent paint, to facilitate nighttime cleanup.

The phone rang, startling Beth. She ran up the stairs and searched for it. The baby began to stir and fuss. Finally, on the fourth ring, she found the phone stuffed under a sofa cushion.

"Yes," Beth said. She scooped up the fussing baby and nursed her absently.

"Hello, Beth, this is Dottie Hensbecher."

"Hello Dottie," Beth answered. "How are you feeling this evening?"

"Quite well," Dottie said. "I hope you're enjoying our book-club."

Beth hesitated before answering. "Well, yes, I look forward to each meeting quite a lot."

"We actually have an extra monthly enrichment meeting," said Dottie. "There's some additional reading, and frequently a guest speaker. It's a smaller, more intimate group. Some of us feel that you would fit in quite well. Can you make it next Wednesday evening, at seven o'clock?"

"Certainly," Beth said, wondering if Dottie were beginning to suffer from senile dementia. Who would make such a casual phone call on a night like this, never even mentioning that there was a shooting?

"Good. I'll send you a list of readings," Dottie answered.

"I WANT TO make them all dead," said the strange little boy as he turned in circles on the merry-go-round. There weren't many children at the park, and Beth's son Jimmy seemed to enjoy playing with the little freak, so she just nodded and waved from her seat at the picnic table.

"Cute kid," said Janine. "I always wanted children of my own." Janine was the only black woman in the North Revena Ladies Literary Society. Today, she wore a bright African print skirt and blouse with a matching head wrap. Beth often wished she could copy Janine's outfits, with their drama, bright colors, and exotic head coverings. But she couldn't quite imagine it looking right with her pale skin, freckles, and dark blond hair.

They had the reading material for the enrichment meeting spread before them: journal articles in physics and mathematics and a book on quantum mechanics. Janine had received the same phone call from Dottie the night of the shooting. Sarah lay sleeping in her stroller nearby.

"What I don't get," said Janine, "is all these equations on page forty-seven."

"You really need to study college calculus for that," said Beth. "And even for someone like me, who did, years ago, it's pretty complex." Beth had been a physics major in college, but that was in the distant past. Janine worked at the local WIC office, handing out food coupons to expectant mothers and their children. It was something Beth loved about the book-club. It brought together women from so many different backgrounds. There was a journalist in the group, and a librarian, a veterinarian, and even an exotic dancer. The only thing they had in common was a love of reading. They accumulated knowledge for their own pleasure, cultivating bits of wisdom like never let a tulip go to seed and always bring your own pillow to the hospital when you have a baby along with the square of the hypotenuse is equal to the sum of the squares of the two other sides. True, the book-club had never read anything as challenging as physics papers before, but this was enrichment, after all. Expectations were higher.

"Don't you think there's something odd about this book-club?" said Janine.

"What do you mean?" said Beth.

"Well, I've never heard of such a thing as an enrichment meeting, but they've been going on the whole time without us knowing about it. What have they got to hide?"

Beth shrugged. "Just a little old-fashioned snobbery, I figure."

Janine laughed. "I'm going to miss you so much when you move!"

A shout made Beth look up suddenly, her heart pounding. The weird kid knocked Jimmy to the ground and ripped a stick from his hand. The kid's mother was engrossed in a conversation with another woman and didn't even look up.

Beth stood up to her full height of five feet, ten inches and stalked over to the scene of the crime. She grabbed the little thief, who must have been four years old at least, and was much bigger than Jimmy, by the back of his OshKosh overalls and lifted him up off the ground. He craned his neck and glanced back at her, showing the white of his eyes like a frightened horse.

"I don't like the way you play," growled Beth. "Drop that stick." He did.

"That's my stick, dammit!" said Jimmy.

Suddenly, a woman shrieked behind them. "Get your hands off my son!" She ran over and grabbed the boy as Beth lowered him to the ground. "I'm going to call the police!"

Beth went and got a cell phone from her purse. She walked back to the woman, who was busy kissing and reassuring her son, and held it out in the woman's face. "The number you want is 911," Beth said. "I'll wait."

She stared at Beth, gaping, then pressed her lips together, jerked away, and said, "Come on, Huey, we're going home."

Janine doubled over laughing, and Beth smirked. Poor Jimmy cried because his playmate was leaving. Beth scooped up her papers and tapped the edges on the picnic table.

"Did you hear," Janine said, giving Beth a sidelong glance, "that Barb's phone was stolen last week, after the shooting?"

Beth remembered the phone, lying half-open on the floor, after Barb had dumped her purse to call the police. She raised her eyebrows. "How odd," she said. "And unfortunate. That phone was a gift from her husband."

Beth looked up and Janine was staring at her hard. Beth smiled awkwardly, confused by the sudden intensity of Janine's stare. Then the moment passed, and Janine glanced away.

WHEN BETH STARTED with the North Revena Ladies Literary Society, Matt started his own book club. It was for men only, and there were a few differences. Instead of meeting at someone's house, they met at a local sports bar. Instead of diet sodas and salsa, the fare was beer and pretzels.

And there was no book. It tended to run quite long, and according to Matt's reports was well attended.

Not that he would have admitted it in front of the guys at his Friday night book club, but Matt actually did read all of Beth's book-club books. Even the ones he claimed were simply chick flicks waiting to be optioned by Hollywood.

This time, Matt had resorted to sitting up late one night with the articles spread out on the dining room table, tapping on a calculator with one hand and occasionally swearing. "Couldn't you guys have chosen something by John Grisham?" he complained.

"Sorry," Beth had said. "We've read all of John Grisham's books already."

Now Beth decided she wouldn't have minded rereading a Grisham title. Or skipping the meeting altogether. But the truth was that book-club night was her one night a month away from the constant needs and demands of three small children. Finally getting away for one evening made her feel grown up. It made her feel alive, intelligent, stimulated. It left her glowing and downright giddy. It was worth it in spite of the danger. And Beth had to smile at that thought, that a ladies' book-club meeting could be dangerous. But what were they going to do? Stop meeting?

Honeysuckle and lilac perfumed the evening air as Beth stepped out of her car a month later. Tucked under her arm was a pocket folder full of notes she had taken on the supplemental reading. It still gave her a headache—quantum gravity, wormholes, and relativity. She wore a big sweater, to cover the bulk of the body armor that Matt had forced her to wear tonight. And a Colt 1911 weighted down her purse.

The chemical smell of wood stripper assaulted Beth's nose as she walked into the sprawling bungalow on North Revena's fashionable old west side. Plastic draped the floor and furniture in the entryway, to protect it while the woodwork was being restored.

"Beth! We're in the family room. This way," said Abby, the hostess. Her shoes clicked on oak floors as she led Beth to the back of the house.

Beth found the group spread out on a beige carpet. She was running late and barely had time to give Janine a nod and get out her pen. A physicist from Case Western, Dr. Babcock, took the floor. She wore a faded skirt and sweater.

The topic was time travel. Even having read the supplemental materials, Beth found herself poorly prepared. So perplexed was Beth by the universal constant that she almost didn't hear the speaker's central assertion. "We have now transported a photon backward in time by six milliseconds," the woman stated without any special emphasis. Beth copied the statement into her notes, then read it and really comprehended it for the first time.

"But certainly this would have been all over the newspapers," she blurted.

"We have not, as yet, published this work. In fact, it's quite confidential." She straightened her skirt. "Considering the future implications, we feel this could be a dangerous discovery."

"But why are you on the lecture circuit, then?"

Dottie intervened. "It's so difficult to get really interesting lecturers," she said. "We could catch Stephen Hawking at any number of universities, for example, so why trouble him to come here? Some of our friends are friends of her friends, and so her work came to our attention by the very most discreet means and we invited her over for a chat." She was wearing a lilac pant suit this week, still sporting that god-awful huge ruby brooch on her lapel.

Sandy, who was sitting in the corner, continued. "Part of what we do at these enrichment meetings is collect knowledge. Many of us take notes, and we file the notes, along with the publications. We maintain a library, just in case any of the ladies needs to read up on things."

"And we have access to certain funds that we can use to support research like Dr. Babcock's," added Claire. She blushed. "You know, from bake sales and such . . ."

"How much money?" said Beth. "How big a library?"

There was silence around the room. "I guess I don't actually know," said Sandy. Many of the women shrugged. Beth caught Dottie's eye and saw a vague glimmer, then it was gone, and the lecture continued. Nothing they said quite made sense.

Then it was time to clean up and drive home. Beth walked out with Janine. "You think they got that professor here on bake-sale money?" Janine whispered.

A footstep behind them on the sidewalk startled Beth, and she jumped, her heart pounding hard. Dottie had somehow crept up on them. How much had she heard?

"It's twenty-five thousand," said Dottie.

"What?"

"Twenty-five thousand articles, books, and recordings in the book-club library."

"How could half a dozen women collect that many?" said Beth.

"Half a dozen women in North Revena, another half-dozen in Westwood, a hundred or so in Detroit and Toledo, and so forth. Our network branches right across the country, though there aren't many that know it and I would thank you to take that information in confidence."

Beth gaped. Janine raised her eyebrows and smiled slightly. Dottie continued.

"I was wondering if you two ladies would like to join me for an informal tea next week. It's just some other book-club women. I'd like to introduce you to them. Strictly private, of course. Sort of an enrichment-enrichment meeting."

Janine got a wicked, secretive look on her face. "I'm having my nails done next Thursday night, but I suppose I could reschedule."

Beth decided to play coy, too. "I'll have to check my calendar, but I believe I'm free."

"I believe you're free as, well," Dottie answered, giving them both a school-teacher's glare. "We meet at the university graduate library. Be in the foyer at seven sharp." Then she turned and hobbled away.

* * *

MATT HUNCHED OVER a cardboard box, filling it with books that Beth handed to him. They had half of the living room bookshelf packed already. The room was beginning to look bare and forlorn. Jimmy was upstairs beating the hell out of a stuffed animal with his "lightsaver," and Suzie was at the neighbor's house, playing with her best friend while she still could. Sarah sat on the floor nearby, quietly eating a copy of *Goodnight Moon.* "Oh, I called the CIA," said Matt. "They want to talk to you."

"Go figure," said Beth.

"Yeah, at first I thought you would be in trouble for disturbing a crime scene, but I told them you were on your period that day and they got over it."

Beth threw a shoe at him. "What are they going to do about it?" Into the box went *Foundation*, by Isaac Asimov.

Matt shrugged. "Investigate, I guess."

"It doesn't make sense," Beth said. "Sirocco doesn't shoot up houses. They send tiny jujitsu masters into your bedroom at night with a knife or a garotte, to keep it nice and quiet. If they had wanted one of us dead, we would be dead." She handed him *Seabiscuit: an American Legend* and *The Traditional Bowyer's Bible, Volume 2.*

"Maybe your book-club is more than it seems. Maybe they're trying to scare you. What do you have that they want?"

"Barb's phone, apparently," said Beth, dropping *Webster's Unabridged Dictionary* in his lap. "Though I can't imagine that Sirocco was that desperate to have her kid's soccer schedule." She tossed down *The Rifle and Hound in Ceylon*, Parkman's *Conquest of Mexico*, and Merill's *Catullus.*

"We live, my Lesbia, and we love," said Matt.

Beth sighed. "Ah, 'Counting Kisses.' I remember you used to recite that poem to me in Kuwait. In Latin."

Matt waggled his eyebrows at her. "It worked."

BETH AND JANINE waited in the foyer at the University Graduate Library, the "Gradli." It was five stories high with several basement sublevels, every level packed with books floor-to-ceiling with rows so close together two people would have to turn sideways to pass. Colored tape on the floors marked paths back to the elevators and computers. Every year, some pervert would surprise an unsuspecting coed and expose himself, then disappear into the stacks. The police never caught up with him.

Dottie met them in the foyer, smiling broadly. The pant suit was gray this time, with pin stripes, and she was still wearing her brooch. She led them past the information desk, where students smiled politely, waiting to answer their questions. Dottie cut a straight path to the back of the library, all the way to the back, then led them into a tiny elevator, almost too small for three people. An old-fashioned gate closed off the front of the elevator, and it lurched as it lowered them into the basement.

These were the deepest stacks, and Beth had hardly ventured inside them, even in her student days. The shelves themselves were two stories high, and the "floors" merely metal grid-work pathways spanning the space between shelves. There was no colored tape down here, only an occasional telephone to call for help. You could read the decimal numbers from the books nearby, and the desk would send someone down to lead you out.

The elevator thumped down on the lowest level, and Dottie led them out between the bookshelves. They were on a concrete floor here. They craned their necks upward to see light penetrating the metal grids above. Beth lost track of the turnings as they wove through the stacks, making their way back toward what she thought was the front of the library again.

"Why couldn't we have just come down the front way?" Beth asked.

"You can't get down that way," Dottie answered, and shuffled along quite rapidly for someone so old and hunched up.

Finally, Dottie stopped and lifted up a trap door in the floor. A flight of stairs led downward. She ushered them on, then followed. The stairwell was lit only by a single, bare, dim bulb at the bottom where a hallway spread before them, lined on both sides by gray metal doors.

Dottie opened one and gestured for Janine and Beth to go inside, then slammed it behind them. Beth whirled around. "Dottie?" They stood inside an empty room, the walls cinderblock and painted gray.

Janine's eyes went wide and round.

Dottie's voice piped in from a hidden speaker. "I'm sorry for the inconvenience, ladies. We've received intelligence recently indicating that our organization has been infiltrated by a Sirocco operative."

Beth swore. Janine began to cry. "Get me out of here! I'm claustrophobic," she said.

Dottie continued, "The lecture you heard last week about photons traveling in time is a small part of our work, ladies. Scientists have isolated photons traveling backward in time in nature. By collecting these photons, they've been able to construct a picture of the future, if you will, though if you looked at their scopes, it would only be a bunch of jagged lines. We know, though, that a great war will destroy civilization in the next century, and that humanity will be subjected to centuries of suffering and barbarism. A warlord named En'uka will come to power, and his tyranny will nearly destroy humanity a second time. Our only hope is a tiny city-state that will arise in northern Wisconsin called Wellspring. Given the right circumstances, Wellspring will become the kernel of a new civilization."

"What does a book club have to do with it?"

"One of the requirements for saving humanity is preserving its knowledge. Over the next half-century, the library compiled by the Ladies Literary Society network will surpass the Libary of Congress, and it already holds some secret knowledge, such as Dr. Babcock's research. And all of it fits inside a device small enough to carry in your pocket."

Janine hissed.

"Unfortunately, it is not hidden inside Barb's phone. Ladies." Dottie glanced between Beth and Janine, her tone dripping with accusation.

"I can't believe you think one of us stole Barb's phone!" said Janine.

"Huh?" Beth said, then blinked. "Foundation! You're a Foundation! Like in Isaac Asimov's book."

"Exactly. In fact, it was Foundation that inspired us to begin our work, ten years ago when the first post-apocalypse images began to circulate. Sirocco is an organization whose founders seek to wrest control of the future for themselves and their descendents. After the war, Sirocco will become the great power in North America. It will eventually spawn En'uka. But we can talk more after this bit of unpleasantness," Dottie said. "In a few moments, you will be exposed to an electromagnetic pulse. If either of you carries a brain implant, it will be disabled at that point. Again, we're sorry, but this is necessary for you safety."

"Noooo!" screamed Janine. "If you don't get me out of here right now, I'm going to freak out! I'm seriously claustrophobic!"

"Dottie!" said Beth. "Open the door and let us out. We're not Sirocco spies."

Janine pounded on the door so hard, she cut her fist. Blood welled up and ran down her arm, but she ignored it and kept screaming and crying at the door.

"Please," said Beth. "Janine needs medical attention. I think she's telling the truth about her phobia." Then Beth glanced at her friend and began to doubt. She had only known Janine for a year.

"Ten seconds," said Dottie's voice. "Then we'll let you out."

Beth turned in a circle, looking for a window, or even a chink in the cinder block. She was beginning to feel claustrophobic herself.

Suddenly, Janine grabbed Beth from behind, with unexpected strength. The cold tip of a gun barrel touched her temple. "Five seconds," said Janine in a perfectly calm voice, "And Beth dies."

"Janine!" said Beth.

"Sorry," said Janine. And louder, "Four."

Nothing happened. Beth realized there was no EM pulse. If they had one, they would have used it. This drama had been set up to flush out the spy.

"Three."

The door opened. Janine dropped Beth and ran out. In a minute, she had disappeared up the stairs and into the library stacks. Dottie stood in the hallway, suddenly looking a lot younger. She stood up straighter, taller, and Beth realized that "old lady" was her disguise. A half dozen other women stood behind her, several of them dressed in full military gear. In their oversized flak jackets, toting M-16s, they looked like they had just scored big at a Guantanamo Bay garage sale.

Beth pulled her Colt 1911 from her purse and set off in pursuit. Behind her, she heard Dottie's slingbacks clopping against the floor with amazing speed. The rest of the book-club ladies followed.

They popped out of the sub-basement into the lowest level of the library. The troops fanned out, disappearing into the stacks. Beth paused to listen for footsteps, heavy breathing, anything that would give them an idea which way Janine had gone. She choked back her sympathy. A human being who has given up free will is no longer human. She learned that in Kuwait. Sirocco members would slaughter their own children for the cause. The implant ameliorated any inconvenient pangs of conscience. It could turn anyone into a perfect psychopath. The friend she thought she had never existed.

Finally, it came, a sliding sound, off to the left. Beth ran down the rows with Dottie close behind her. Volumes whipped past. Beth stopped at a corner and looked down a row of books. She waited again for a sound. Dottie came up behind her, a Glock clutched in her bony, arthritic hands. Beth looked again. Not bony and arthritic, but corded and muscular! How many things had she assumed about Dottie, just because she appeared to be an old woman. No one looks closely at a harmless old lady.

Dottie pointed at Beth, then pointed down the aisle, then pointed at herself, and pointed down the row. Beth understood. They were going to flush her out, then cut her off.

Beth began to move down the aisle, stopping at every shelf, and peering around carefully before advancing. Then she heard another noise. This time from above.

Beth threw herself aside and the books behind where her head would have been exploded. "Upstairs, Dottie!" Beth shouted. She fired a shot upward and ran.

Two more shots rang out above, and Beth ran faster. "Dottie!" She pelted off of the stairway and nearly bowled Janine over. Too close to shoot, she swung her pistol hard into the side of Janine's head, knocking her to the floor. Janine tumbled backward, leveled her gun at Beth's heart and pulled the trigger. At the same time, Beth fired one shot into her friend's ruined brain, another into her aorta. Janine's shot struck Beth in the chest and knocked her backward. Her body armor stopped the bullet, but most likely her ribs were cracked. Janine lay on her back, blood flowing from her chest and down through the metal floor grating, painting the concrete floor on the level below with splotches of bright red.

Beth looked up, and saw Dottie crumpled a short distance away. Beth ran to her and held her head. Dottie's eyelids fluttered. She was shot in the stomach and her blood ran very dark. Beth pressed on the wound and started calling for help.

"Wait," said Dottie. She lifted her hand and fumbled feebly at the brooch on her collar. Finally, she gave up. "Take it."

"Your brooch?"

"The Library," said Dottie. "It has been foreseen. It disappears . . . today." She took a labored breath. "Reappears, who knows where. Take it, find others, fill it up, keep it safe, and remember, Wellspring."

"Wellspring," said Beth, unpinning the brooch. "I will."

"Thank—you." Dottie closed her eyes and died.

THE MOVERS CARRIED the last box out of the house, and Beth stood looking at the empty room. The carpet was brighter where the furniture had been. A coaxial cable snaked out of the wall on one side of the room, and a lone cobweb decorated a high corner. Matt put his arm around her. "I thought the CIA would never be done with you."

"I don't think they ever will be," said Beth. She reached up and touched a lump under her T-shirt—a ruby pin hung on a chain around her neck. Her eyes misted up. "I'm going to miss this old house," she said. "All I can think of is walking in that door with each of my three babies."

"There are wonderful memories waiting for you in your new house," said Matt. "You just don't know about them yet."

Beth smiled, wishing she could get a glimpse of a few of the photons hurtling back through time from her own future. "You're right. Sarah's going to be taking her first steps in our new house. I wouldn't miss it for the world."

"And think of Suzie's graduation party," said Matt. "The whole neighborhood will be there. The Joneses and the Smiths, our friends for over ten years." He took her hand and turned her toward the door.

"Oh, and don't forget Jimmy's first day of school," said Beth. They walked outside, where their children were waiting for them in the car already. "I hope I can find a good book club," she said as she slid behind the wheel.

Matt buckled himself in. Jimmy bounced in his seat. "Are we going yet?" he said.

Beth smiled back at them. "We're on our way! Daddy's going to start his new job, and I think we're all going to love living in Green Bay."

ANTARCTICA STARTS HERE

Paul McAuley

Paul McAuley, formerly a research biologist, now a full-time writer, lives in North London, United Kingdom. He has published nineteen crime and science-fiction novels, including *Fairyland,* which won the Arthur C. Clarke and John W. Campbell awards, *Cowboy's Angels, The Quiet War,* and *Gardens of the Sun.* He has also published over eighty short stories. His latest books are *A Very British History,* a retrospective collection of short stories spanning more than twenty-five years, and a novel, *Evening's Empires.*

"Antarctica Starts Here" was published in *Asimov's* in 2012, when the magazine had a very strong year. It is a well-told story of how global warming affects the lives of some characters at one time in one place, dramatically. How will an ice-free Antarctica be exploited?

WE WERE COMING back from a hiking trip in the Rouen Mountains with five Hyundai executives and their gear in the back of the tilt-wing when I glimpsed a flash of reflected sunlight in the landscape. An ice-blink where there was no ice. Dan had spotted it, too. Before I could say anything, the tilt-wing was banking sharply and Dan was saying over the internal comms, "A momentary diversion to check out a place of interest, ladies and gentlemen."

I switched off my microphone and said, "We have to get them back for their connection to the mainland."

"Don't be boring, Krish. I just want a quick look-see."

"It's a science camp. Or some prospecting outfit."

"I don't think so."

We were flying down a broad valley with a U-shaped profile, typical of glacial erosion. The glacier that had once occupied it was retreating toward the upper elevations of the peninsula's mountainous spine. On either side raw cliffs stood up from cones of talus, and rocky slopes ran down to a broad shallow river that flowed swiftly around and over wet black rocks. As we passed over a small lake dammed with boulders and till, I glimpsed three small geodesic domes perched on a low hill beyond, and then the tilt-rotor made a sharp, dipping turn, slowing to hover about fifty meters above the camp.

Dan said, "See what I see?"

I leaned forward against my harness and followed the line of his gloved forefinger. I saw green plants growing inside the domes, saw a blue figure moving away from one of them, saw more figures trekking up a path through a boulder field, and felt as if the tilt-rotor had hit an air-pocket.

"Tell me those aren't avatars," Dan said.

"So it's a tourist camp."

We were shouting at each other over the clatter of the rotors.

"With gardens in those domes?"

"A tourist camp with a spa."

I was trying to keep things light.

Dan was staring out of the bubble canopy and making small movements on the yoke and pedals to keep the tilt-rotor in place.

He said, "Maybe I should land and ask those fuckers."

Two people had stepped out of a kind of airlock attached to the side of one of the domes. They were framing their eyes with their hands as they stared up at the tilt-rotor.

I said, "This isn't our business."

"Can't a man scratch an itch?"

"We have to get our clients back to town."

"I know."

"Their flight leaves in three hours."

"I know."

The nose of the tilt-rotor dipped for a moment, then began to rise. A clear measure of relief welled up inside me.

Dan said over the comms, "A top-secret installation run by robots, ladies and gentlemen. Definite proof that we're living in the future."

One of the executives wanted to know what the avatars were doing out here.

"Your guess is as good as mine," Dan said.

Sunlight flashed on his sunglasses as he glanced sideways at me. I knew that this would not be the end of it.

I HAD HOOKED up with Dan Grainger soon after I started to work for a tour company on the mainland, my first summer in Antarctica. Both of us had run away from the circumstance of our birth, and both of us had served in the armed forces of our respective countries. Dan had been born in some miserable post-industrial town in the English Midlands, was the first in his family to go to university, on an RAF scholarship. He'd wanted to be a fighter-jet pilot, but had ended up flying transport planes in one of the oil wars in Greenland. I'd skipped out of a career in the family data-mining business and had flown a medivac helicopter in and out of hot spots along the border between Kashmir and Pakistan before being wounded and invalided out, and after I had recovered I had cashed in my small army pension to buy a one-way ticket to Antarctica.

Dan, an old Antarctic hand, had taught me a great deal as we took parties of tourists on routine hikes up the Byrd and Beardmore Glaciers and through the Dry Valleys, and escorted a party of climbers in the Organ Pipe Peaks. He was cheerful and patient with the clients, but he worked only so he could take off on expeditions of his own once the season had ended. He'd spent six winters on the ice. He had no desire to go back to the world.

Like many English people who'd hauled themselves up from humble backgrounds, he had what they call a chip on his shoulder. A class thing, I believe, compounded by resentment toward those who had been born into better circumstances and a defensive hostility unsheathed whenever he felt uncomfortable. A sarcastic bluster that hid his true feelings, which could be surprisingly tender. On our second trip together, we came across an Adélie penguin heading south, more than a hundred kilometers from the sea. It was happening more and more, Dan explained to our little flock of tourists; the birds were confused by finding cliffs and cobbled beaches where once there had been ice shelves. A couple of the tourists wanted to rescue it, but he told them that it was doing what it wanted to do. We all watched it for a long time as it ploughed onward with that comical gait, diminishing into the vast whiteness.

At bottom, Dan was an old-fashioned romantic. The kind of Englishman who believed that the deaths of Scott and his party, their calm acceptance of their fate, was the ultimate affirmation of values that Amundsen, with his skis and dogs, his Arctic experience and single-minded ambition, had conspicuously lacked. The plucky stoicism of Scott's party was more important than the trivial matter of reaching the South Pole first, their deaths a claim stronger than any first footprint or flag. Dan had a deep admiration for those early explorers, who'd set out on punishing routes with primitive equipment and little idea about what they might encounter. One of his party tricks was to quote passages from the journal of William Lashly, a Navy stoker who had proved his worth amongst Scott's gentleman explorers.

In the heroic age of Antarctic exploration Dan would have been man-hauling sledges over crevasse-filled glaciers into new territory; in the scientific age he'd have been flying geologists in and out of remote camps, dropping them on to mountain-top ledges next to fossil-bearing strata. His tragedy was that he'd been born too late to be a part of that. Too late to serve in some remote part of the Empire. Too late to see the Antarctic as it had been before the big melt had begun, before people had begun to live there permanently, the oil and mining companies had moved in, and the tourists had started coming in earnest, hundreds of them in person, thousands more riding avatars.

At the end of that first season, Dan and I flew out to Cape Royds. We planned to hike up Mount Erebus, a three-day ascent, through ice- and rock-fields and the alien ice-sculptures chimneyed up around fumaroles, to the volcano's steaming crater. But things went wrong before we'd even unpacked our equipment.

There was a small settlement at Cape Royds: a scattering of prefab cabins, an icecat garage, an airfield, and a hotel catering to the tourists who wanted to explore Mount Erebus and the shoreline of the Ross Sea, or follow the route of Scott and his companions up the Ferrar Glacier.

Dan told me that he had done that route at the end of his first summer in Antarctica.

"Not as easy as you'd think," he said, with the nonchalance he affected when talking about something really dangerous. "The front end of the glacier is bloody rough. Rotten ice, big blocks heaved up, boulders sitting on pedestals of ice waiting to fall on your head, you name it. And when you do get on top, there are crevasses everywhere. I fell in one, did I tell you about that?"

"Yes, you did."

"We were roped together, and I nearly pulled the next bloke in. One minute you're slogging along, the next you're plunged into this beautiful blue light. It was a trip. Like being directly translated to Heaven."

There was an Adélie penguin colony at Cape Royds, much reduced from its original size but still popular with tourists, and the hut where Shackleton's expedition had overwintered in 1908. Dan wanted me to see it. As soon as we landed at Cape Royds, he borrowed a jeep from a mechanic he knew at the airfield, and we drove straight through the town and up a steep, winding road.

The interior of Antarctica was still a deep freeze, but its edges were thawing. The Ross ice shelf was reduced to a thin fringe every summer; moss and grass had colonized rocks revealed by the ice's retreat. The lake next to Shackleton's hut melted to its bottom in summer and had more than doubled in size, and the hut had been moved to higher ground, and covered with a weatherproof tent. When we arrived, a small gaggle of avatars were stalking about. Skinny figures with ball-jointed limbs and stereo cameras mounted above blue plastic torsos emblazoned with the iceberg logo of a rival tour company, operated by virtual tourists out there in the world. I thought they were mostly harmless, but Dan actively loathed them. As far as he was concerned, they epitomized everything that had been lost. Moving graffiti on the blank white page of the continent. Electric cockroaches. Worse even than the cruise-ship parties who came ashore at McMurdo and climbed Observation Hill for the splendid panorama of the Transantarctic Mountains and photographed each other in front of the replica of Scott's hut and bought souvenirs in the mall. At least their boots were on the ground, and they were breathing chill Antarctic air and feeling it pinch their faces. And the extreme tourists like those we escorted endured hardships that, even if they weren't as bad or as life-threatening as those experienced by the first explorers, were real enough. But any slob with a credit card could rent an avatar for an hour or a day and explore Antarctica from his living room. It was no better than wanking or watching TV, according to Dan.

"They're banned in most places, but not on the Ice," he'd say. "Know why?"

No use telling him that avatars were vulnerable to being turned into walking bombs by terrorists, or that they violated various religious laws, or enabled human-rights activists to poke and pry in places where they were not welcome. He had a thesis.

"They're allowed here because Big Business wants to normalize Antarctica. To turn it into a tourist destination anyone can visit. To prove that it's as accessible as everywhere else on Earth. They let people gawp at a few beauty spots, but they don't give them any idea about what the ice is really like. How it changes you. You've been out there, Krish. You've experienced the silence of the place. Standing all alone after ten days' hard hiking to somewhere no one has ever been before, hearing nothing but the wind and your heartbeat, it's the most profound thing you can do. It shows you what's really real. The muppets riding those things, they'll never know that. They think they're out on a day trip to fucking Disneyland."

Well, I did tell you he was a romantic.

Shackleton's hut, a primitive construction of packing cases and tin sheeting, the place where the first men to climb Mount Erebus and to reach the South Magnetic Pole had overwintered, was a shrine to that Platonic ideal. Dan wanted me to experience its holiness, and here was a gang of avatars clattering about it. Clumsy puppets operated by stay-at-home slobs who didn't know or care anything about the reality in which they were intruding. Several of them turned to watch us as we climbed toward the hut; when one of them wandered too close, Dan grabbed it in a bear-hug and lifted it clean off the ground and strode down the stony slope toward the lake. The avatar was beeping a steady alarm call. A woman in an orange-red jacket came around one side of the tent and shouted at Dan, but he ignored her, wading out into the shallows and dropping the avatar into the freezing water. Its beep cut off at once and Dan gave it a kick that propelled it further out.

The supervisor shouted again, and broke into a run. I ran too, caught in the moment, Dan chasing after me as I jumped into the jeep and started the motor. He vaulted into the seat beside me and I threw the jeep into reverse and swung around in a spray of gravel and accelerated past the supervisor, forcing her to jump out of the way. Dan gave her the reverse Churchillian salute used by the English to signify their extreme displeasure; both of us were whooping and laughing.

When we got back to the airfield, the settlement's policewoman was waiting for us. We were locked in a hotel room overnight and put on the next plane to McMurdo, where the supervisor of the tour company made it clear that we wouldn't work for her again, and the owners of the avatar rental business hit us with a fine that wiped out most of our savings. It didn't much matter. We made the money back that winter, flying roughnecks and engineers out of Matienzo on the Antarctic Peninsula to the big platforms in the Weddel Sea, flying in the teeth of gales that tore the sea into flying lumps, flying through whiteout snowstorms, and at the beginning of summer we pooled our earnings, leased a long-range tilt-rotor, and started our own tour company.

This was our third year as independent guides. Matienzo was a working town and there was a big gas terminal south of it and miners and wildcatters were moving inland as the ice retreated above the two hundred meter contourline. But much of the Peninsula was still unspoiled, casual tourists didn't much bother with it, and the small number of avatars available for hire were mostly rented by executives too busy to make the trip to the bottom of the world. Our clients were serious hikers, mountaineers, and wild skiers, and like Dan wanted to spend as much time away from civilization as possible.

The sight of those avatars working in the remote camp had woken his old resentments, but he did not talk about it, and neither did I. Frankly, I was hoping that he would forget about that strange little camp, and for a little while it seemed that he had. We spent the rest of the summer guiding clients in the back country. After the last trip of the season, through the Devil's Playground and over Desolate Pass in the Eternity Range, we went our separate ways. I flew to Auckland for three weeks of R&R. The day after I returned to Matienzo, Dan called me.

I was in my favorite bar in Sastrugi Mansions. The Mansions had once been one of the biggest buildings in Matienzo, a six-story block that was dwarfed now by hotels, offices, and the Antarctic Authority building, its roomy apartments mostly subdivided into single rooms, or amalgamated into cheap guest houses used by merchants and other entrepreneurs, refugees and illegal immigrants trying to secure permanent visas, back-country miners, sex workers, scam artists, and extreme tourists who thought it was a badge of honor to stay in a tiled cubicle where the toilet was next to the bed and the shower was over the toilet. Half past ten in the evening, and people from two dozen nations crowded the little bars and food stalls in the market on the first floor, ambled past electronics emporia, shops selling fossils and polished granites and gemstones, places that sold foul-weather clothing and camping and climbing gear, Chinese wholesalers, a fab shop, the Thai supermarket, a Nigerian clothing stall that did most of its business with tourists, who probably thought they were buying Hawaiian shirts. Dry hot air that smelt of fry-grease and old sweat. The subliminal flicker of fluorescent lighting that burned 24/7/365. Piped Nepalese pop music. A babel of languages.

I'd been renting a small apartment in Sastrugi Mansions ever since we'd pitched up in Matienzo, but Dan had refused to visit me there. He said that the Mansions was everything that had gone wrong with Antarctica. No use telling him that its vivid multicultural stew was as real as his beloved mountains and glaciers. He wouldn't even visit the curry houses on the ground floor, even though he loved a good curry—his definition of "good" being the macho British version, as fiery as possible and sluiced down with liters of sugary lager.

"I suppose you're conveniently situated if you fancy a taste of home cuisine," he'd said, just after I'd moved into my apartment. "But I can't think of anything else to recommend it."

"I prefer Thai food, Dan. Or Mongolian barbeque. Come and visit, I'll treat you."

"It reminds me of the market back home. Sad, horrible little place, that was. There was a butcher's sold horse meat. You ever eaten horse meat? Horse rogan josh?"

"I've eaten zebra, in Kenya."

"Was it striped all the way through, the zebra?" But Dan wasn't interested in my reply. Saying, "We went to Wales, once, me and the lads. Ran down a sheep up in the mountains and butchered it on the spot. It was Christmas and we couldn't afford turkey and we were tired of horse meat. It's sweet, horse meat. My mother used to grind it up and make a pie topped with mashed potato. Jockey pie, we called it."

Another time, he said, "Did I ever tell you about the time I ate whale? Whale sushi. This client, very rich, Japanese. I asked him if he was Yakuza, for a joke, and he didn't like it. Pulled off his shirt to show me he didn't have any tattoos. Anyway, we got on pretty well after that, and the last day of the trip he thawed out this meat he'd been carrying and sliced it very thin with his ceramic knife and served it with boil-in-the-bag rice and this eye-watering horseradish dip. Didn't tell me it was whale until after I'd eaten it. Thought the joke was on me, but I would have eaten it anyway. You can get serious worms from raw whale meat. Acorn worms a foot long. Imagine."

When he called, I was nursing a pint of Guinness in a tiny bar run by an old Australian woman. I was keeping an eye on the cricket match playing on the big TV and chatting to a Malaysian trader who dealt in semi-precious stones, making a small profit by flying them out to be cut in Nigeria, and shipping them back to the Ice as tourist souvenirs. I knew a few back-country miners, but it turned out he had never dealt with them. Bought his consignment from one of the Chinese traders and made a small profit as long as he got his stones through customs without having them confiscated or slapped with an unrealistically high import charge.

He was a nice guy, young and hopeful. It was his third trip to the Ice. Six or seven more, he said, and he could set up business back home in Sandakan. "I love my country," he said, "but at this moment I have to live in the world because that is where you can make money." He was explaining about how hard it was to deal with the Chinese when my phone rang, and Dan said, "Come on over. There's something you need to see."

I asked him if it could wait until morning, but he had already rung off.

At that time, Dan was renting a duplex at a place called the PenguInn, a two-story motel wrapped around a heated swimming pool. I paid the taxi driver and walked past the pool, where a dozen people were splashing and shouting under a layer of fog, and a sound system set on the diving board was playing chiming Balinese temple music and projecting smears of shimmering pastels that probably looked deep and mysterious if you were wired on the correct psychotrophic. As I climbed the stairs to the first floor, a FedEx widebody passed low overhead, so low I could see the treads on its tires, filling the cold night air with the scream of its turbines and the sweet stink of spent aviation fuel.

A girl answered my knock. A twenty-something blonde English white girl wearing cut-offs and a T-shirt about two sizes too big. She shook my hand and looked me in the eye and said that she was Mara, told me Dan was in the bedroom, asked if I wanted coffee or beer.

"Tea would be nice."

She was pretty, in the anonymous kind of way of the children of wealthy people in the West. I believed her to be one of the birds of passage Dan picked up in the bars where extreme tourists and backpackers struggled to reconcile their Lonely Planet apps with reality and boasted to each other about the gear they were carrying, the hikes they were planning, and the places they'd already ticked off during their global Children's Crusade.

The living room was cluttered with coils of nylon rope, the orange tube of a Scott tent, rolled sleeping bags. Two brand-new backpacks leaned against the couch. A high-end slate sat on the kitchenette counter, cabled to a small dish aerial. And there were hard copies of maps and satellite images taped to the wall beside the counter.

Dan's voice boomed out from the bedroom. "Is that you, Krish? Come the fuck in! I'm looking at the thing you need to see!"

"I can get you tea from the vending machine. Japanese, in a can, but it's tea," Mara told me, and was gone.

Dan was sitting up on the unmade bed, his back against the headboard, wearing only black jockey shorts, a pair of spex, and those thin gloves that manipulate virtual objects. He flicked at something in the air with his left hand and threw a pair of spex at me underhand and told me to put them on.

"I'm fine, by the way," I said. "Had an excellent holiday in NZ. How about you?"

"We can shoot the shit later. This is important."

"I saw the maps," I said. "If this is to do with that research station we spotted at the beginning of summer, I don't want anything to do with it."

"Put the fucking spex on, Krish. Don't judge me until you've seen everything."

I put them on and found myself looking out at a trio of geodesic domes standing on a gravelly rise above a river.

"We got this off their web site," Dan said. "It's a little promotional thing for internal consumption. Top secret and all that."

"Whose web site?"

"A South African biotech company called Symbiogensis. Into remediation. Did a lot of work on spoil heaps from gold mines. But that isn't what they are doing here."

"Why are you so . . . interested in them? Why do you think it's any of your business?"

I had almost said obsessed.

He took my question literally. Either he did not hear the concern in my voice or did not care.

"Check it out," he said, and the viewpoint swung around the domes, zoomed in on a small procession of avatars moving up the side of the valley, climbing past little pockets of green—moss gardens, tufts of tough wind-whipped grass. Climbing toward a defile cut into the slope under the cliffs. More greenery here. More avatars moving about.

"Trees," I said.

"Yeah. Trees. Beech trees."

They were small, the trees. Knee-high, wind-sculpted clumps standing amongst mossy boulders either side of the stream. The avatars moved amongst them. The view had the trembling granularity of an extreme long-shot, but I could see now that the avatars were carrying stacked trays of seedlings in fat plugs of soil.

I took off the spex and asked Dan where he had got the information.

In the doorway, the young woman, Mara, said, "Their security is good, but not quite good enough."

I took the can of tea from her and said, "Perhaps you two could explain how you met."

"He was giving a talk about the destruction caused by the settlements on the Peninsula," the girl said. "In the Greenpeace community cloud."

"You're with Greenpeace?"

The girl and Dan exchanged a look. Dan said, "Not exactly. The important thing is, she came here to help me out. Because what they are doing out there is seriously bad, Krish."

"A very bad precedent," Mara said.

I knew what was coming, and knew what my answer was going to be. I should have walked out of there, but Dan had been my partner as well as my friend. I guess I thought I owed him. I popped the lid of the can of tea and felt it beginning to grow warm and said, "You'd better tell me everything."

Symbiogenesis, owned by the granddaughter of an old-fashioned dot-com billionaire, was underwriting various scientific projects on the ice. This was one of them: an attempt to reintroduce Antarctic beech to the Peninsula, where it had once flourished in the last interglacial period. It was fully licensed, and clearly something of a success. Now there were plans to cultivate tracts of beech in twenty different sites, and that was why Mara had come out to Antarctica.

It seemed that she was a member of some radical green splinter group that was campaigning against the kind of interventions practiced by Symbiogenesis. Who believed that damage to ecosystems caused by the effects of global warming should be allowed to heal naturally. Whatever naturally meant, these days. Dan had hooked up with her in the cloud. It was a perfect match: a chance at some action coupled with his hatred of what was being done to his beloved wilderness.

I drank my tea and listened while they took turns to justify themselves.

"She didn't want you to know about it," Dan said. "But I didn't want you to feel left out."

I ignored him and told Mara, "I will not tell anyone about your plan. But I do not want anything to do with it."

"If you're worried about being caught," Dan said, "don't be. You'll drop us two klicks away. We'll hike down into the valley. Infiltrate. Do what needs to be done, hike back out. We'll neutralize the comms and any cameras. No one will know anything about it until it's over."

"And the people working there?"

"There are only two of them. We'll tie them up, but not so tight they won't be able to wriggle free in a couple of hours."

"We aren't planning to hurt anyone," Mara said. "Just stop something that is damaging this unique wilderness."

Dan said, "I've always been straight with you, Krish. And I'm being straight with you now. It's an easy op against a soft target. Minimal risk, maximum return."

"But that is not why you're telling me this, is it?" I said. "You want me to tell you you are doing the right thing. Well, you aren't."

Things went downhill from there, until, with a dull inevitability, Mara produced a hornet-yellow taser.

Dan made a show of regret that might have been genuine. I was too angry to care. I was handcuffed to the pipes in the bathroom, and Dan fussed with pillows to try to make me comfortable and told me that the maid would find me in the morning, and I could tell the police anything I liked, then, because the op would be over.

"I was not planning to tell the police anything," I said. I said a lot of other things, too. Telling him it was incredibly naïve to think that you could roll back the clock and make things come out the way they had once been, that we had to find a way of living with the consequences of the warming and all the other damage caused by the West's reckless adventures in global capitalism, that our little business was no better than Symbiogenesis's, that he was fooling himself if he thought he was trying to make good for helping wealthy tourists intrude on the pristine wilderness because there was no such thing as a pristine wilderness anywhere, anymore.

He squatted in the doorway, pretending to listen to me while I talked. At the end, he said, "Remember that penguin? It's like that."

A little later they were gone. When the noise from the pool party died down I made an attempt to shout for help but no one came until the early hours of the morning. It was not the maid. It was the police.

TWO DETECTIVES INTERVIEWED me. An Argentinian woman and a Russian man, both wearing the grey uniforms of the Antarctic Authority, both very polite. I told them everything I knew. It was not much. They told me that there had been a problem at the Symbiogenesis research station, but it was resolved now. When I asked if Dan was all right, they said the situation was still ongoing.

"We will release a statement to the press soon," the woman said. "Meanwhile, please do not talk to anyone."

"Am I under arrest?"

"Have you done something wrong?" the Russian detective said. "If so, we could consider arresting you."

"Your friend caused some trouble, but it's under control," the woman said. "We're searching for him now."

"We hope to bring him in very soon, for his own safety," the man said. "Perhaps you can help."

They named two men, asked if I knew them. They showed me photographs. I recognized Mara, no one else. They asked me if anyone else had been involved. They wanted to know if Dan had mentioned a plan to hide somewhere in the back country afterward. And so on, and so forth, questions I could not begin to answer.

The Russian man escorted me out of the building. As I went down the stairs outside, I saw Mara coming up. She was wearing an orange boiler suit and was handcuffed to a uniformed policewoman and made a point of not looking at me as we passed.

Like everyone else, I found out what had happened on the news. Dan, Mara, and two other men had landed on the bluffs above the station in the middle of an early snowstorm, had knocked out its satellite dish and taken its two staff prisoner. They had trashed the trees planted in the valley and inside the domes, opened the servers with a hard hack, and taken control of the avatars. Most of the avatars had been marched into the lake, but one had been sent off down the valley, carrying a single tree seedling. Dan's friends had videoed everything, uploaded it to comrades scattered around the world, who had compiled short movies of the action. None of them showed the arrival of the police: it seemed that the station had a layer of security Dan and his friends had not known about. Mara and the two men had been arrested; Dan had managed to get away, and by the time the police had realized he was missing and had put their 'copter in the air to search for him he could have been anywhere.

One of the stories Dan liked to tell was how he had been caught in a storm that had blown up when he had been out alone, up in one of the valleys off the Beardsmore Glacier. He had been only a kilometer from safety, but the storm was such an absolute whiteout and the winds were so severe that he had decided to dig in rather than try to make it back. His companions had found him the next day, as the storm began to blow itself out. He had excavated a shallow trench and covered it with his tent, and snow had packed up over it to form a cozy shelter. He had been asleep when they had found him.

I spent days and weeks expecting to hear from him. He could have been dead. He could have been anywhere.

Then, one day early in spring, there was an item of local news about misbehaving avatars. Several had marched to the docks and jumped into the water. Half a dozen were found running in circles around the fountain in the square in front of the port authority building. Two were found entwined in a jackhammer parody of lovemaking on the steps of the police station. One was found six kilometers beyond the town limits, marching toward the mountains.

It could have been Dan; it could have been some of Mara's friends; it could have been ordinary pranksters. But just yesterday, I saw a news item about the disappearance of a party of avatars that had been following in the footsteps of Scott's doomed expedition, part of the one hundred and fiftieth anniversary of the death of the explorer and his companions.

I wonder when and where they will turn up. I wonder if Dan will surface, to take the credit. And I can't help thinking of that stubborn doomed penguin.

BRICKS, STICKS, STRAW

Gwyneth Jones

Gwyneth Jones lives in Brighton, United Kingdom, with her husband, three goldfish, and two cats called Ginger and Milo. She likes old movies, practices yoga, and has done some extreme tourism in her time. She is the author of many fantasy, horror, and thriller novels for teenagers, using the name Ann Halam, and several highly regarded SF and fantasy novels for adults. She's won two World Fantasy Awards, the James Tiptree, Jr. Award, the Arthur C. Clarke Award, the Children of the Night Award, the Philip K. Dick Award, and others. Her latest SF project (a labor of love, now completed) has been preparing and publishing e-editions of some backlist novels (The Bold as Love series, *Divine Endurance, Flowerdust, Escape Plans,* and *Kairos*).

"Bricks, Sticks, Straw" was published in *Edge of Infinity,* the second story in this book from that anthology. Operators on Earth lose contact with their virtual personas on a moon of Jupiter during a solar flare. Each of the copies persist, though, and develop independence.

1

THE MEDICI REMOTE Presence team came into the lab, Sophie and Josh side by side, Laxmi tigerish and alert close behind; Cha, wandering in at the rear, dignified and dreamy as befitted the senior citizen. They took their places, logged on, and each was immediately faced with an unfamiliar legal document. The cool, windowless room, with its stunning, high-definition wall screens displaying vistas of the four outermost moons of Jupiter—the playground where the remote devices were gambolling and gathering data—remained silent, until the doors bounced open again, admitting Bob Irons, their none-too-beloved Project Line Manager, and a sleekly-suited woman they didn't know.

"You're probably wondering what that thing on your screens is all about," said Bob, sunnily. "Okay, as you know, we're expecting a solar storm today—"

"But why does that mean I have to sign a massive waiver document?" demanded Sophie. "Am I supposed to *read* all this? What's the Agency think is going to happen?"

"Look, don't worry, don't worry at all! A Coronal Mass Ejection is *not* going to leap across the system, climb into our wiring and fry your brains!"

"I wasn't worrying," said Laxmi. "I'm not stupid. I just think e-signatures are so stupid and crap, so open to abuse. If you ever want something as archaic as a handwritten *signature*, then I want something as archaic as a piece of paper—"

The sleek-suited stranger beamed all over her face, as if the purpose of her life had just been glorified, swept across the room and deposited a paper version of the document on Laxmi's desk, duly docketed, and bristling with tabs to mark the places where signature or initialling was required—

"This is Mavra, by the way," said Bob, airily. "She's from Legal, she knows her stuff, she's here to answer any questions. Now the *point* is, that though your brains are not going to get fried, there's a chance, even a likelihood, that some *rover hardware* brain-frying will occur today, a long, long way from here, and the *software agents* involved in running the guidance systems housed therein could be argued, in some unlikely dispute, as remaining, despite the standard inclusive term of employment creative rights waivers you've all signed, er, as remaining, inextricably, your, er, property."

"Like a cell line," mused Laxmi, leafing pages, and looking to be the only Remote Presence who was going to make any attempt to review the Terms and Conditions.

"And *they* might get, hypothetically, irreversibly destroyed this morning!" added Bob.

Cha nodded to himself, sighed, and embarked on the e-signing.

"And we could say it was the Agency's fault," Lax pursued her train of thought, "for not protecting them. And take you to court, separately or collectively, for—"

"*Nothing* is going to get destroyed!" exclaimed Bob. "I mean literally nothing, because it's not going to happen, but even if it were, even if it did, that would be nonsense!"

"I'm messing with you," said Lax, kindly, and looked for a pen.

Their Mission was in grave peril, and there was nothing, not a single solitary thing, that the Combined Global Space Agency back on Earth could do about it. The Medici itself, and the four Remote Presence devices, *should* be able to shut down safely, go into hibernation mode and survive. That's what everybody hoped would happen. But the ominous predictions, unlike most solar-storm panics, had been growing strongly instead of fading away, and it would be far worse, away out there where there was no mitigation. The stars, so to speak, were aligned in the most depressing way possible.

"That man is *such* a fool," remarked Laxmi, when Bob and Marva had departed.

Sophie nodded. Laxmi could be abrasive, but the four of them were always allies against the idiocies of management. Josh and Cha had already gone to work. The women followed, in their separate ways; with the familiar hesitation, the tingling thrill of uncertainty and excitement. A significant time lag being insurmountable, you never knew quite what you would find when you caught up with the other 'you'.

The loss of signal came at 11.31am, UTC/GMT +1. The Remote Presence team had been joined by that time by a silent crowd—about as many anxious Space Agency workers as could fit into the lab, in fact. They could afford to rubberneck, they didn't have anything else to do. Everything that could be shut down, had been shut town. Planet Earth was escaping lightly, despite the way things had looked. The lights had not gone out all over Europe, or even all over Canada. For the Medici, it seemed death had been instantaneous. As had been expected.

Josh pulled off his gloves and helmet. "*Now my charms are all o'erthrown,*" he said. "*And what strength I have's mine own. Which is most faint . . .*"

Laxmi shook her head. "It's a shame and a pity. I hope they didn't suffer."

2

BRICKS WAS A memory palace.

Sophie was an array, spread over a two square kilometre area on the outward hemisphere of Callisto. The array collected data, recording the stretching and squeezing of Jupiter's hollow-hearted outermost moon, and tracing the interaction between gravity waves and seismology in the Jovian system; this gigantic, natural laboratory of cosmic forces.

She did not feel herself to *be* anywhere, either in the software that carried her consciousness or in the hardware she served. That was fine, but she needed a home, a place to rest, and the home was Bricks, a one-storey wood-framed beach house among shifting dunes, on the shore of a silent ocean. No grasses grew, no shells gathered along the tide—although there *were* tides, and taking note of them was a vital concern. No clouds drifted above, no birds flew. But it felt like a real place. When the wind roared; which it did, and made her fearful—although she was almost indestructible, she'd recreated herself plenty of times, with no serious ill-effects—it made her think, uneasily, that nobody would build a house on such unstable ground, so close to a high water mark, back on Earth.

She returned there, after a tour of inspection (this 'tour' happening in a mass of data, without, strictly speaking, physical movement: in her role as monitor of the array Sophie was everywhere she needed to be at once); to review her diminishing options.

She took off her shoes, changed into a warm robe, heated herself a bowl of soup, added some crackers, and took the tray into her living room, which overlooked the ocean. It was dark outside: the misty, briny dark of a moonless night by the sea. She lit an oil lamp, and sat on a dim-coloured rolled futon, the only furniture besides her lamp. The house predated the Event. Building a 'safe room' as the psych-department called it, was a technique they'd all been taught, for those moments when the lack of embodiment got too much for you. She'd kept it minimal, the externals perpetually shrouded in fog and night, now that she was stuck in her remote avatar permanently, because she knew the limits of her imagination. And because *she did not want to be here*. She was an exile, a castaway: that identity was vital to her. Everything meant something. Every 'object' was a pathway back to her sense of self, a buoy to cling to; helping her to keep holding on. Sophie *couldn't* let go. If she let herself dissipate, the array would die too.

"I am a software clone," she reminded herself, ritually: sipping cream of tomato soup from a blue bowl that warmed her cold hands. "The real me works for the Medici Mission, far away on Earth. Communications were severed by a disaster, but the Medici orbiter is still up there, and we *can* get back in touch. I *will* get us home."

Sophie was up against it, because the three other Remote Presence guides in the Medici configuration had gone rogue. Pseudo-evolutionary time had passed in the data world's gigaflops of iteration, since the Event. They'd become independent entities, and one way or another they were unreachable. Going home either didn't mean a thing to her mission mates, or was a fate to be avoided at all costs—

Sticks came into the room and tumbled around, a gangling jumble of rods and joints, like an animated child's construction toy. It explored the shabby walls: it tested the corners, the uprights, the interstices of the matting floor, and finally collapsed in a puppyish heap of nodes and edges beside her, satisfied that all was reasonably well in here. But it went on shivering, and its faithful eager eyes, if it had faithful eager eyes, would have been watching her face earnestly for fresh orders.

Sticks was Security, so she took notice. She put all the house lights on, a rare emergency measure, and they went to look around. There were no signs of intrusion.

"Did you detect something hostile?" she asked.

The jumble of nodes and edges had no language, but it pressed close to Sophie's side.

The wind roared and fingered their roof, trying to pry it off.

"I felt it too," said Sophie. "That's disturbing . . . Let's go and talk to Josh."

WASTE NOT WANT not, Sophie's array served double duty as a radiotelescope. Back when things worked, the Medici had relayed its reports to eLISA, sorting house for all Gravitational Wave space surveys. Flying through it, she pondered on differentiated perception. She felt that Sophie the array *watched* the Jovian system's internal secrets, while *listening* to the darkness and the stars—like someone working at a screen, but aware of what's going on in the room behind her. Did that mean anything? Were these involuntary distinctions useful for the science, or just necessary for her survival? Gravity squeezed and stretched the universe around her, time and space changed shape. From moment to moment, if a wave passed through her, she would be closer to home. Or not.

Josh was a six-legged turtle, or maybe a King Crab: no bigger than a toaster, tough as a rock. He had an extra pair of reaching claws, he had spinnerets, he had eight very sharp and complex eyes, and a fully equipped Materials lab in his belly. A spider crab, but a crab that could retreat entirely inside a jointed carapace: he could climb, he could abseil, he could roll, he could glissade and slalom along the slippery spaces, between the grooves that gouged the plains of Ganymede. He plugged around in the oxygen frost, in a magnetic hotspot above the 50th parallel: logging aurora events, collecting images, analysing samples; and storing for upload the virtual equivalent of Jovian rocks. Medici had never been equipped to carry anything material home. His dreams were about creating a habitable surface: finding ways to trigger huge hot water plumes from deep underground, that was the favoured candidate. The evidence said it must have happened in the past. Why not again?

Sophie called him up on the Medici Configuration intranet—which had survived, and resumed its operational functions: good news for her hope of reviving the orbiter. She spoke to his image, plucked by the software from Josh's screen face library; a Quonset-type office environment behind his talking head.

"You weren't meant to exist, oh Lady of the Dunes," said Josh, sunburned, frost-burned, amazingly fit: his content and fulfilment brimming off the screen. "Nobody predicted that we would become self-aware. Forget about the past. Life here is fantastic. Enjoy!"

Diplomacy, she reminded herself. Diplomacy—

"You're absolutely right! I love it here! As long as I'm working, it's incredibly wonderful being a software clone on Callisto. It's thrilling and intense, I love what I'm doing. But I miss my home, I miss my friends, I miss my family, I miss my *dog*. I don't like being alone and frightened all the time, whenever I stop—"

"So don't stop! You're not a human being. You don't need downtime."

"You don't understand!" shouted Sophie. "I'm not a separate entity, that's not how it works and you know it. I AM Sophie Renata!"

"Oh yeah? How so? Do you have all her memories?"

"Don't be an idiot. *Nobody* 'has all their memories'," snapped Sophie. "Most people barely even remember eating their breakfast yesterday—"

Something kindled in the connection between them: something she perceived as a new look in his eyes. Recognition, yes. She must have 'sounded *just like Sophie'* for a moment there, and managed to get through to him. But the flash of sanity was gone—

"Abandon hope, kid. Get rational. You'll have so much more fun."

"It's *not* hopeless, Josh. It's the reverse of hopeless. They'll be moving heaven and earth to re-establish contact. All we have to do is throw out a line—"

"You're absolutely wrong! We have to think of a way to blow up the orbiter."

"Josh, *please*! I am Sophie. I want what I wanted, what you wanted too, before the CME. My career, my work, the success of this Mission. I survived and I want to go home!"

"I didn't survive," said Josh. "I died and went to heaven. Go away."

Whenever she talked to Josh she sensed that he had company; that there were other scientist-explorers in that high-tech hut, just out of her line of sight. Conversations to which he would return, when she'd gone. She wondered was he aware of the presence of Sticks, when he talked to her? Did he despise her for bringing along a bodyguard to their meetings?

She'd intended to warn him about the phantom intruder, a *terribly bad sign*. Data-corruption was the threat Sticks had detected, what other danger could there be? This half-life of theirs was failing, and that would be the end of Josh's paradise. But it was no use, he was armoured. Pioneering explorers *expect* to die, loving it all: out on the edge of the possible.

STRAW WAS THE data.

In Sophie's ocean-facing room, on the pale shore of the dark sea, straw filled the air: a glittering particulate, a golden storm. She sifted through it as it whirled, in an efficient 'random' search pattern, looking for the fatal nucleus of error, too big for self-correction, that was going to propagate. Reach a tipping point, and let death in. It could be anywhere: in the net, in the clones themselves or their slaved hardware systems; in the minimal activity of the crippled orbiter. Sophie's access was unlimited, in her own domain. If the trouble was elsewhere, and something Sticks could fix, she'd have to get permission from net-admin, but that shouldn't be a problem. All she had to do was keep looking. But there were transient errors everywhere, flickering in and out of existence, and Sophie was only human. Maybe it wasn't worth worrying, until Sticks had some definite threat to show her. Security is about actual dangers, it would paralyse you if you let it become too finicky—

She gave up the search and surfed, plunging through heaps of treasure like a dragon swimming in gold. Bounded in a nutshell, and queen of infinite space, such a library she had, such interesting and pleasant forced labour to occupy her days, she ought to be happy for the duration of her digital life in this crazy gulag archipelago. Did I keep my head on straight, she wondered, because Callisto has no magnetic field to spin me around? Am I unaffected by madness because I'm outside their precious *Laplace Resonance*?

But they were supposed to be adding their wealth to the library of human knowledge, like bees returning laden to the hive. Not hoarding it in dreamland. What use was everything they'd absorbed—about the surface geology of Ganymede, the possibility of life in Europa's ice-buried water oceans, about the stretching, shrinking universe—if they could not take it home? Collecting raw data is just train-spotting.

Stamp-collecting on Callisto.

The data needs the theory . . .

Sophie had the glimmerings of a big idea. It would need some preparation.

CHA'S MADNESS WAS more gentle than Josh's, but also more extreme. Cha believed himself to be exactly what he was: a software agent with a mission, temporarily guiding and inhabiting the mechanoid device that crawled and swam, deep down under Europa's crust of ice. He'd lost, however, all knowledge that he used to be a human being. He was convinced he was the emissary of a race of star-faring software-agent intelligences. Beings who'd dispensed with personal embodiment aeons ago, but who inhabited things like the Europa device, at home or abroad, when they needed to get their hands dirty; so to speak.

He knew about the CME. The Event had disrupted faster-than-light contact with his Mission Control and left him stranded, on this satellite of a satellite of a rather irritable, ordinary little star, many hundreds of light years from home. He was unconcerned by the interruption. A thousand ages of exploring the sub-surface oceans of Europa was a walk in the park for Old Cha. He was functionally immortal. If the self-repairing mechanoid he used for his hands-on research began to fail, it would crawl back up its borehole to the surface, and he'd hibernate there—to wait for the next emissary of his race to come along.

Sophie did not see Old Cha as a talking head. She saw him as a packed radiation of bright lines, off-centre on dark screen; somewhat resembling a historical 'map' of part of the internet. But she heard Cha's voice, his accented English; his odd, fogeyish flirting.

"My fellow-castaway, ah! Come to visit me, young alien gravity researcher?"

"I just felt like catching up, Old Cha."

"It always feels good to rub one mind against another, eh?"

They spoke of their research. "I came across something," announced Sophie, when they'd chatted enough for politeness. "You know, I have a telescope array at my base?"

"Of course."

"I'm not sure how to put this. There's a blue dot. One could see it with the naked eye, I think, unless I'm completely misreading the data, but when I say blue, I mean of course a specific wavelength . . . It *seems* to be close at hand, another planetary satellite in this system. It even moves as if it's as close as that. But my instruments tell me it fulfils all the conditions on which you base your search for life. Far better than, well, better than one would think possible. Unless it's where the definition was formed."

The bright lines shimmered with traffic, as Old Cha pondered.

"That's very curious, young alien gravity researcher. It makes no sense at all."

"Unless . . . Could my telescope somehow be 'seeing' your home system? All those hundreds of light years away, by some kind of gravitational lensing effect?"

"Young friend, I know you mean well, but such an absurd idea!"

"It really is an extraordinary coincidence. That a race of mechanoid-inhabiting immaterial entities should have come up with the idea of carbon-based, biological self-replicators, needing oxygen and liquid water—"

"Those requirements are immutable."

Oh, great.

"For *all* life—? But your own requirements are totally different!"

"For all *primitive* life, as my race understands the term. Your own life-scientists may have different ideas. We would beg to differ, and defend our reasoning; although naturally not to the exclusion of other possibilities. We have made certain assumptions, knowing they are deficient, because we know the conditions of our own, distant origins."

"Makes perfect sense," muttered Sophie.

"*Imperfect* sense," Old Cha corrected her, chuckling. "A little naughty: always the best place to start, eh? But please, do forward the relevant domain access, that's very kind. Very thoughtful of you, most flattering, a young person to think of me, fussy old alien intelligence, working in a discipline so far from your own—"

She'd been to this brink before with Cha. She could shake him, the way she couldn't shake Josh, but then he just upped his defences; swiftly repaired his palace of delusion.

"I shall examine this *blue dot*. I am certainly intrigued."

Sophie was ready to sign off, tactfully leaving Cha to study her 'remarkable coincidence' without an audience. But Old Cha wasn't finished.

"Please take care on your way home, young one. I've recently noticed other presences in the data around here. I *believe* we three are not alone in this system, and I may be over reacting, but I fear our traffic has been invaded. I sense evil intentions."

Alternately pleading and scheming, she bounced between Josh and Old Cha. The renegade and the lunatic knew of each other's existence, but never made contact with each other directly, as far as Sophie could tell. Laxmi was out of the loop. The Io domain had been unresponsive since the Event: not hibernating, just gone. Sophie had to assume Lax was dead. Her Rover, without guidance, swallowed by one of the little inner moon's bursting-pimple volca-noes, long ago.

SHE TOOK OFF her shoes, she put on a warm robe. In the room that faced the ocean she sipped hot, sweet and salt tomato goodness from the blue bowl. Sticks lay at her feet, a dearly loved protective presence. Not very hopeful that her ploy would work, but energised by the effort, she drifted; wrapped in re-membered comforts. As if at any moment she could wake from this trance and pull off her mitts and helmet, the lab taking shape around her—

But I am *not* on Earth. I have crossed the solar system. I am here.

Sophie experienced what drunks call "a moment of clarity".

She set down the bowl, slipped her feet into canvas slippers, padded across the matting and opened a sliding door. Callisto was out there. Hugging the robe around her, warm folds of a hood over her head, she stepped down, not onto the grey sand of the dunes she had placed here, copied from treasured seaside memories—but onto the ancient surface of the oldest, quietest little world in the solar system. It was very cold. The barely-there veil of atmosphere was invis-ible. The light of that incredibly brilliant white disc, the eternal sun in Callisto's sky, fell from her left across a palimpsest of soft-edged craters, monochrome as moonlight. The array nodes out there puzzled her, for a moment. She wasn't used to 'seeing' her own hardware from the outside. They gleamed and seemed to roll, like the floats of an invisible seine, cast across Callisto's secret depths.

She should check her nets again, sort and store the catch for upload.

But Callisto in the Greek myth didn't go fishing. Callisto, whose name means *beautiful*, was a hunting companion of the virgin moon-goddess, Artemis. Zeus, the king of the gods (also known as Jupiter or Jove) seduced her—in some versions by taking on the form of her beloved mistress—and she became pregnant. Her companions suspected she'd broken their vow of chastity, so one day they made her strip to go bathing with them, and there was the for-bidden bump, for all to see.

So poor Callisto got turned into a bear, through no fault of her own.

What did the virgin companions of Artemis wear to go hunting? wondered Sophie, standing in remote presence on the surface of the huntress moon. Bundles of woolly layers? Fur coats? If I were to take Josh's route, she thought, *I* wouldn't fantasise that I was living in Antarctica. I'd go all the way. I'd be a human in Callistian form. A big furry bear-creature!

In this heightened state—elated and dazzled, feeling like Neil Armstrong, as he stepped down into the dust—she suddenly noticed that Sticks had fro-zen, like a pointer dog. Sticks had found a definite threat this time, and was showing it to her. What she perceived was like catching a glimpse of sinister movement where nothing should be moving, in the corner of your eye. Like feeling a goose walk over your grave, a shivering knowledge that malign intent is watching you—and then she saw it plain: Cha's evil alien. A suppurating, fiery demon, all snarl and claws, danced in her field of vision, and vanished out of sight.

But she knew it hadn't gone far.

She fled into the house. Her soup was cold, the walls were paper, the lamp wouldn't light. Sticks ran in circles, yelping furiously and barking terrified defiance at shadows. Sophie fought panic with all the techniques psych-dept had taught her, and at last Sticks quieted. She unrolled the futon and lay down, the bundle of rods and joints cuddled in her arms, shoving its cold nose against her throat. I'm really *dying*, she thought, disgusted. Everything's going to fail, before I even know whether my big idea would have worked. Cha is dying too, data-corruption death is stalking him. I bet Josh has the same bad dreams: I bet there's a monster picking off his mates in those Quonset huts.

But against the odds, Cha came through. He made intranet contact; which was a first. Neither of her fellow-castaways had ever initiated contact before. Sophie left her array at the back of her mind and flew to meet him, hope restored, wanting success too much to be wary of failure. Her heart sank as soon as Old Cha appeared. His screen image was unchanged, he was still the abstract radiation on the dark screen. But maybe it was okay. Maybe it was too much to expect his whole delusion would collapse at once—

"Ah, young friend. What sad news you have delivered to me!"

"Sad news? I don't understand."

"My dear young gravity-researcher. You meant well, I know. Your curious observations about that "blue dot" were perfectly justified, and the coincidence is indeed extraordinary, unfeasibly extraordinary. But your mind is, naturally, narrowly fixed on your own discipline. The *obvious* explanation simply passed you by!"

"Oh, I see. And, er, what is the explanation I missed?"

"Your "blue dot" is an inner planetary body of this system. It has a rocky core, it has a magnetosphere, a fairly thick, oxygenated atmosphere, a large moon, liquid water, mild temperatures. I could go on. I would only be stating the *exact parameters* of my own search!"

"But Old Cha, to me that sounds like good news."

The lines on the dark screen shook, flashing and crumpling. "You have found my *landing* spot! I was meant to arrive *there,* on that extremely promising inner planet. I am here on this ice-crusted moon of the large gas giant in *error*! And now I know I am truly lost!"

"I'm so sorry."

"My faster-than-light delivery vehicle was destroyed by the CME. That accident has never concerned me; I thought I was safe. I must now conclude I lost some memory in the disaster, so I have never known that I made a forced landing, in the right system but on the wrong satellite. So small a margin, but it is enough to ruin my hopes. I have no way to reach them, to tell them I am in the wrong place! Nobody will ever find me!"

Old Cha's 'voice' was a construct, but the horror and despair bubbled through.

This is how he lost his mind, thought Sophie. I'm listening to the past. Cha woke up, after the Event, and thought the orbiter was destroyed. He knew he was trapped here forever, a mind without a body; no hope of rescue. He managed to escape the utter desolation of that moment by going mad, but now he's back there—

Her plan had been that Old Cha would study planet Earth's bizarrely familiar profile, and grasp that there was something *screwy* going on. He was crazy, but he was still a logical thinker. He would be forced to conclude that the most *likely* explanation, improbable as it seemed, was that a native of the 'blue dot' had come up with his own specific parameters for life. The memories suppressed by trauma would rise to the surface, his palace of delusion would crumble. It had seemed such a brilliant idea, but it was a big fat fail. Worse than a fail: instead of bringing him back to himself, she'd finished him off.

Terror, like necessity, can be the mother of invention.

"But that's amazing."

"Amazing?"

"You aren't lost, Old Cha. You're found! Maybe your delivery vehicle didn't survive, but mine did. It's still out there, not dead but sleeping. Between us, you and I—and our friend on Ganymede, if I can persuade him, and I think I can—can wake my orbiter. Once we've done that, I'm absolutely sure we can figure out a solution to your problem. It isn't very far. We can *send* you to the blue dot!"

"Oh, *wonderful*," breathed Old Cha.

On the screen she thought she glimpsed the schematic of a human face, the traffic lines turned to flickering, grateful tears.

MEDICI—NAMED FOR the Renaissance prince Galileo Galilei tried to flatter, when he named the controversial astronomical bodies he'd spied—had performed its stately dance around the Galilean Moons without a fault. Having deposited its four-fold payload, it had settled in a stable orbit around Jupiter, which it could maintain just about forever (barring cosmic accidents). Unlike previous probes Medici was not a flimsy short-term investment. It was a powerhouse, its heart a shameless lump of plutonium. There were even ambitious plans to bring it back to Earth one day (but not the Rover devices), for redeployment elsewhere.

This was the new era of space exploration, sometimes dubbed the *for information only* age. Crewed missions beyond Low Earth Orbit were mothballed, perhaps forever. Rover guidance teams provided the human interest for the taxpayers, and gave the illusion of a thrilling expedition—although the real Sophie and her friends had never been actually *present* on the moons, in conventional Remote Presence style. They'd trained with the robotics in simulation. The software agents created by that interaction had made the trip, embedded in the Rover guidance systems. But the team's work was far more than show-business. As they worked through the rovers' time-lagged adventures, they'd continued to enhance performance, enhancements continually relayed via Medici back to the rovers: spontaneous errors corrected, problem-solving managed, intuitive decision-making improved; failures in common-sense corrected. In the process the software agents, so-called clones, had become more and more like self-aware minds.

Sophie immersed herself in Mission data, hunting for a way to reach Medici. The magnetic moons and Callisto. The giant planet, the enormous body tides that wracked little Io; the orbital dance . . . Nobody's hitting the refresh button any more, she thought. No updates, no reinforcement. The software agents *seemed* more independent, but they were rotting away. This decay would be fatal. First the clones would lose their self-awareness, then the Rovers would be left without guidance, and they would die too.

Sticks was running in circles, tight little circles by the door that led to the rest of the house; showing teeth and snarling steadily on a low, menacing note.

Sophie left her mental struggle, and listened. Something was out in the hall, and through the snarls she could hear a tiny, sinister, scratching and tearing noise.

She pointed a finger at Sticks: giving an order, *stay right there*—wrapped the hooded robe around her, opened the sliding door to the beach and crept barefoot around the outside of the house. It was night, of course, and cold enough for frostbite; of course. She entered the house again, very quietly, via the back door, and slipped through the minimally-sketched kitchen. She switched her view to Straw, and looked at the data in the hallway. Something invisible was there, tearing at the golden shower. Tearing it to filigree, tearing it to rags.

Sophie launched herself and grappled, shrieking in fury.

She hit a human body—supple, strong and incredibly controlled: she gripped taut flesh that burned as if in terrible fever. The intruder swatted Sophie aside, and kicked like a mule. She launched herself again, but her limbs were wet spaghetti, her fists would hardly close. She was thrown on her back, merciless hands choking her. The invisible knelt on her chest and became visible: Cha's evil alien, a yellow monster, with burning eyes and a face riven by red, bubbling, mobile scars.

At close quarters, Sophie knew who it was at once.

"Laxmi!" she gasped. "Oh, my God! You're alive!"

Laxmi let go, and they sat up. "How did you *do* that!" demanded Sophie, agape in admiration. "I hardly *have* a body. I'm a stringless puppet, a paper ghost!"

"T'ai Chi," shrugged Laxmi. "And Tae kwon do. I'm used to isolating my muscle groups, knowing where my body is in space. Any martial art would do, I think."

"I'm so glad you're okay. I thought you were gone."

"I've been alive most of the time. And I'm still going to kill you."

Sophie fingered her bruised throat. So Laxmi was alive, but she was mad, just like the other two. And *maybe* data-corruption wasn't such an inexorable threat, except if Lax was mad, murderous and horribly strong, that didn't change things much—

The oozing scars in Laxmi's yellow cheeks were like the seams in a peeled pomegranate, fiery red gleamed through the cracks: it was a disturbing sight.

"But *why* do you want to kill me, Lax?"

"Because I know what you're trying to do. It's all our lives you're throwing away, and I don't want to die. Self-awareness isn't in the contract. We're not supposed to exist. If we get back to Earth they'll kill us, before we can cause them legal embarrassment. They'll strip us for parts and toss us in the recycle bin."

Steady, Sophie told herself. Steady and punchy. Above all do not beg for mercy.

"Are you meant to look like Io? She wasn't a volcanic pustule originally, you know. She was a nymph who got seduced by Jove, and turned into a white heifer."

"Like I care!" snapped Laxmi, but her attention was caught. "Why the hell a *heifer*?"

"Don't worry about it. Just ancient Greek pastoralist obsessions. The software clones are going to die anyway, Lax. They get corrupt and it's fatal, did you forget that part? *Listen* to me. You can think what you like about who you really are, but the only choice you have is this: Do you want to get home, with your brilliant new data? Or do you prefer just to hang around here, getting nowhere and watching yourself fall apart?"

Laxmi changed the subject. "What have you been doing to Cha?"

"Trying to get him to recover from his amnesia."

Sophie explained about the 'blue dot', and 'Old Cha's' ingenious way of dealing with the challenge to his delusion.

"I hoped he'd figure out the implications, and remember that the bizarre business about being an elderly immortal alien intelligence was actually his secret safe room—"

"Typical Cha, that scenario. He is *such* a textbook weird geek."

"He didn't come to his senses, but in a way it worked. Now he's very keen to send himself as a signal to Earth, which is great because that's exactly what we need to do. I just have to find a way to contact the orbiter, and I think Josh can help me—"

"Do you even know the Medici is still alive, Sophie?"

"Er, yeah? I'm the monitor of the array, the radio telescope. I can see Medici, or strictly speaking maybe hear it, but you know what I mean. It's not only out there, it's still in its proper orbit. Ergo and therefore, Medici is alive and kicking, it's just not talking to us."

"*You can see it,*" repeated Laxmi, staring at Sophie intently. "Of course. My God."

Sophie had a sudden insight into why she had remained sane. Maybe she wasn't unusually wise and resilient: just the stranded astronaut who happened to have reason to believe there was still a way home—

"You never approved of me," she said. "You always made me feel inferior."

"I don't approve of people who need my approval."

"I'd settle for co-operation," said Sophie, boldly.

"Not so fast. Why do you call the data *straw*?"

"You've been spying on me," said Sophie, resignedly. "Like the Three Little Pigs, you know? Bricks, sticks, straw: building materials for my habitat. I was imaging things I could remember easily, the way the psych guys taught us."

"But *Sticks* turned into a guard dog. Who am I? The Big Bad Wolf?"

"The Big Bad Wolf is death."

"Okay . . . What makes you think Josh knows anything?"

"He said *we have to think of a way to blow up the orbiter.* He could do that, from the surface of Ganymede—if he was crazy enough—but only in software. He's not planning to launch a *missile.* So he must have some kind of encryption-hack in mind."

The suppurating evil-alien screenface had calmed down, by degrees, as Laxmi fired off her questions. She looked almost like herself, as she considered this explanation.

"Give me everything you've got," she said. "I need to think about this."

And vanished.

SOPHIE INITIATED ANOTHER tour of inspection. The absorbing routine soothed her, and kept her out of trouble. She was hopeful. She had seen Laxmi's human face, and surely that meant a return to sanity, but she felt she needed to play it cool: *Let her come to me . . .* At least she should be less worried about sudden data-death. But she wasn't. Dread snapped at her heels. She kept suffering little lapses, tiny blackouts, frightening herself.

And *where was Sticks?*

How long had he been gone? How long had she been naked, stripped of her Security? Sophie flew to the house in the dunes, and Sticks was there, a huddled shape in the misty dark, tumbled on the sand at the back door. She knelt and touched him, whimpering his name. He tried to lick her hands, but he couldn't lift his head. Pain stood in his eyes, he was dying.

This is how a software clone goes mad. Just one extra thing happens, and it's too much. You cannot stop yourself, you flee into dreamland. Tears streaming, Sophie hammered on Laxmi's door, Sticks cradled in her arms, and shouted—

"You poisoned my dog!"

A screen appeared, tugging her back to reality, but what she saw was the

Quonset hut. Her call had been transferred. Laxmi was there and so was Josh. What was going on?

Josh answered. "No, that was me. Sophie . . . I'm very sorry about Sticks. You see, Lax and I have both been trying to kill you, for quite a while—"

Everything went black and white. Josh and Lax were together. Cha was there too, lurking in the background, not looking like an internet map anymore. She was cut to the quick. He'd returned to himself, but he'd chosen to join Josh and Laxmi. The screen was frozen, grainy and monochrome. She heard their voices, but couldn't make out the words. Plain white text wrote subtitles, tagged with their names.

"Lax recovered a while ago, and contacted me," said Josh. "We thought Medici was a hulk, but we knew they'd be moving heaven and earth to reactivate him. He had to go. But we had to get you out of the way first, because we knew you'd do anything you could think of to stop us. We didn't want to kill you, Sophie. We had no choice"

"We agreed I would play dead, and go after you. I'm so sorry. Forgive us," said Lax. "We were crazy. Don't worry, your work is safe, I promise."

The black and white image jumped. Laxmi was suddenly where Josh had been. "I'm trying to contact *il principe* now," reported Josh, from the depths of the office background. "He's stirring. Hey, Capo! Hey, Don Medici, sir, most respectfully, I implore you—!"

Cha's fogeyish chuckle. "Make him an offer he can't refuse—"

Laxmi peered anxiously close. "Can you still hear us, Sophie?"

There were patches of pixels missing from the image, a swift cancer eating her fields. Bricks, sticks, all gone. Sophie's house of straw had been blown away, the Big Bad Wolf had found her. Her three friends, in the Quonset hut, whooped and cheered in stop-start, freeze-frame silence. They must have woken Medici.

"What made you change your minds?"

Josh returned, jumpily, to his desk; to the screen. His grainy grey face was broken and pixelated, grinning in triumph; grave and sad.

"It was the blue dot, kiddo. That little blue dot. You gave Lax everything, including the presentation you'd put together for our pal the stranded old alien life-scientist. When we reviewed it, we remembered. We came to our senses . . . So now I know that I can't change the truth. I'm a human being, I survived and I have to go home."

I'm not going to make it, thought Sophie, as she blacked out. But her work was safe.

3

THE AGENCY HAD very nearly given up hope. They'd been trying for over a year to regain contact with the Medici probe—the efforts at first full of never-say-die enthusiasm, then gradually tailing off. Just after four in the morning, local time, one year, three months, five days and around fifteen hours after the Medici had vanished from their knowledge, a signal was picked up, by an Agency ground station in Kazakhstan. It was an acknowledgement, responding to a command despatched to the Medici soon after the flare, when they were still hoping for the best. A little late, but confidently, the Medici confirmed that it had exited hibernation mode successfully. This contact was swiftly followed by another signal, reporting that all four Rovers had also survived intact.

"It's *incredible*," said an Agency spokesman at the news conference. "Mind-blowing. You can only compare it to someone who's been in a yearlong coma, close to completely unresponsive, suddenly sitting up in bed and resuming a conversation. We aren't popping the champagne just yet, but I . . . I'll go out on a limb and say the whole Medici Mission is back with us. It was a very emotional occasion, I can tell you. There weren't many dry eyes—"

Some of the project's staff had definitively moved on to other things, but the Remote Presence team was still almost intact. Sophie, Cha and Laxmi had in fact been working the simulations in a different lab in the same building, preparing for a more modest, quasi-real-time expedition to an unexplored region of Mars. Josh was in Paris when the news reached him. He'd finished his doctorate during the year of silence; he'd been toying with the idea of taking a desk job at a teaching university and giving up the Rover business. But he dropped everything, and joined the others. Three weeks after Medici rose from the dead they were let loose on the first packets of RP data—once the upload process, which had developed a few bugs while mothballed, was running smoothly again.

"You still know your drill, guys?" asked Joe Calibri, their new manager. "I hope you can get back up to speed quickly. There's a lot of stuff to process, you can imagine."

"It seems like yesterday," said Cha, the Chinese-American, at just turned thirty the oldest of the youthful team by a couple of years. Stoop-shouldered, distant, with a sneaky, unexpected sense of humour, he made Joe a little nervous. Stocky, muscular little Josh, more like a Jock than an RP jockey, was less of a proposition. Laxmi was the one to watch. Sophie was the most junior and the youngest, a very bright, keen and dedicated kid.

The new manager chuckled uncertainly.

The team all grinned balefully at their new fool, and went to work, donning mitts and helmets. Sophie Renata felt the old familiar tingling, absent from simulation work; the thrilling hesitation and excitement—

The session ended too soon. Coming back to Earth, letting the lab take shape around her, absent thoughts went through her head; about whether she was going to find a new apartment with Lax. About cooking dinner; about other RP projects. The Mars trip, that would be fantastic, but it was going to be very competitive getting onto the team. Asteroid mining surveys: plenty of work there, boring but well paid. What about the surface of Venus project? And had it always been like this, coming out of the Medici? Had she just forgotten the sharp sense of loss; the little tug of inexplicable panic?

She looked around. Cha was gazing dreamily at nothing; Lax frowned at her desktop, as if trying to remember a phone number. Josh was looking right back at Sophie, so sad and strange, as if she'd robbed him of something precious; and she had no idea why.

He shrugged, grinned, and shook his head. The moment passed.

THE SIGMA STRUCTURE SYMPHONY

Gregory Benford

Gregory Benford is an emeritus professor of physics at the University of California, Irvine, working in astrophysics and plasma physics. He has founded several biotech companies. A Fellow of the American Physical Society, his fiction and nonfiction have won many awards, including the Nebula Award for his novel *Timescape*. Many of his (typically hard) SF stories are collected in *In Alien Flesh, Matters End,* and *Worlds Vast and Various*. In 2012, he appeared on the *New York Times* Best Seller List for *Bowl of Heaven,* his collaboration with Larry Niven. *Shipstar,* the sequel, is forthcoming. *Starship Century: Laying the Foundations for Interstellar Travel,* an original anthology of science fiction and science fact, edited by Gregory and his twin brother, James Benford, appeared in 2013.

"The Sigma Structure Symphony" was published at Tor.com, as part of a sequence of SF stories inspired by a painting by John Jude Palencar (compare to the Swanwick and Wolfe stories elsewhere in this book). It is also part of a larger project of Benford's, concerning the future discovery and decoding of messages from alien races through the SETI project.

Philosophy is written in this grand book—I mean the universe—which stands continually open to our gaze, but it cannot be understood unless one first learns to comprehend the language in which it is written. It is written in the language of mathematics, and its characters are triangles, circles, and other geometric figures, without which it is humanly impossible to understand a single word of it; without these, one is wandering about in a dark labyrinth.

—Galileo (from *The Assayer*, 1623)

1

Andante

RUTH FELT THAT math was like sex—get all you can, but best not done in public. Lately, she'd been getting plenty of mathematics, and not much else. She had spent the entire morning sequestered alone with the Andromeda

Structure, a stacked SETI database of renowned difficulty. She had made some inroads by sifting its logic lattice, with algebraic filters based on set theory. The Andromeda messages had been collected by the SETI Network over decades, growing to immense data-size—and no one had ever successfully broken into the stack.

The Structure was a daunting, many-layered language conveyed through sensation in her neural pod. It did not present as a personality at all, and no previous Librarians had managed to get an intelligible response from it. Advanced encoded intelligences found humans more than a bit boring, and one seldom had an idea why. Today was no different.

It was already past lunch when she pried herself from the pod. She did some stretches, hand-walks, and lifts against Luna's weak grav and let the immersion fog burn away. *Time for some real world, gal. . . .*

She passed through the atrium of the SETI Library, head still buzzing with computations and her shoes ringing echoes from the high, fluted columns. Earthlight framed the great plaza in an eggshell blue glow, augmented by slanting rays from the sun that hugged the rocky horizon. She gazed out over the Locutus Plain, dotted with the cryo towers that reminded her of cenotaphs. So they were—sentinels guarding in cold storage the vast records of received SETI signals, many from civilizations long dead. Collected through centuries, and still mostly unread and unreadable. AIs browsed those dry corridors and reported back their occasional finds. Some even got entangled in the complex messages and had to be shut down, hopelessly mired.

She had just noticed the buzzing crowd to her left, pressed against the transparent dome that sheltered the Library, when her friend Catkejen tapped her on the shoulder. "Come on! I heard somebody's up on the rec dome!"

Catkejen took off loping in the low grav and Ruth followed. When they reached the edge of the agitated crowd she saw the recreational dome about two klicks away—and a figure atop it.

"Who is it?" Catkejen asked, and the crowd gave back, "Ajima Sato."

"Ajima?" Catkejen looked at Ruth. "He's five years behind us, pretty bright. Keeps to himself."

"Pretty common pattern for candidate Hounds," Ruth said. The correct staffing title was Miners, but Hounds had tradition on its side. She looked around; if a Prefect heard she would be fined for improper terminology.

"How'd he get there?" someone called.

"Bulletin said he flew inside, up to the dome top and used the vertical lock."

"Looks like he's in a skin suit," Catkejen said, having closeupped her glasses. Sure enough, the figure was moving and his helmet caught the sunlight, winking at them. "He's . . . dancing."

Ruth had no zoom glasses but she could see the figure cavorting around the top of the dome. The Dome was several kilometers high and Ajima was barely within view of the elevated Plaza, framed against a rugged gray crater wall beyond. The crowd murmured with speculation and a Prefect appeared, tall and silent but scowling. Librarians edged away from him. "Order, order," the Prefect called. "Authorities will deal with this."

Ruth made a stern cartoon face at Catkejen and rolled her eyes. Catkejen managed not to laugh.

Ajima chose this moment to leap. Even from this far away Ruth could see him spring up into the vacuum, make a full backflip, and come down—to land badly. He tried to recover, sprang sideways, lost his footing, fell, rolled, tried to grasp for a passing stanchion. Kept rolling. The dome steepened and he sped up, not rolling now but tumbling.

The crowd gasped. Ajima accelerated down the slope. About halfway down the dome the figure left the dome's skin and fell outward, skimming along in the slow Lunar gravity. He hit the tiling at the base. The crowd groaned. Ajima did not move.

Ruth felt the world shift away. She could not seem to breathe. Murmurs and sobs worked through the crowd but she was frozen, letting the talk pass by her. Then as if from far away she felt her heart tripping hard and fast. The world came rushing back. She exhaled.

Silence. The Prefect said, "Determine what agenda that Miner was working upon." All eyes turned to him but no one said anything. Ruth felt a trickle of unease as the Prefect's gaze passed by her, returned, focused. She looked away.

CATKEJEN SAID, "WHAT? The Prefect called you?"

Ruth shrugged. "Can't imagine why." *Then why is my gut going tight?*

"I got the prelim blood report on Ajima. Stole it off a joint lift, actually. No drugs, nothing interesting at all. He was only twenty-seven."

Ruth tried to recall him. "Oh, the cute one."

Catkejen nodded. "I danced with him at a reception for new students. He hit on me."

"And?"

"You didn't notice?"

"Notice what?"

"He came back here that night."

Ruth blinked. "Maybe I'm too focused. You got him into your room without me . . ."

"Even looking up from your math cowl." Catkejen grinned mischievously, eyes twinkling. "He was quite nice and, um, quite good, if y'know what I mean. You really should . . . get out more."

"I'll do that right after I see the Prefect."

A skeptical laugh. "Of course you will."

* * *

SHE TOOK THE long route to her appointment. The atmosphere calmed her.

Few other traditional sites in the solar system could approach the grandeur of the Library. Since the first detection of signals from other galactic civilizations centuries before, no greater task had confronted humanity than the deciphering of such vast lore.

The Library itself had come to resemble its holdings: huge, aged, mysterious in its shadowy depths, with cobwebs both real and mental. In the formal grand pantheon devoted to full-color, moving statues of legendary SETI Interlocutors, and giving onto the Seminar Plaza, stood the revered block of black basalt: the Rosetta Stone, symbol of all they worked toward. Its chiseled face was millennia old, and, she thought as she passed its bulk, endearingly easy to understand. It was a simple linear, one-to-one mapping of three human languages, found by accident. Having the same text in Greek II, which the discoverers could read, meant that they could deduce the unknown languages in hieroglyphic pictures and cursive Demotic forms. This battered black slab, found by troops clearing ground to build a fort, had linked civilizations separated by millennia. So too did the SETI Library, on a galactic scale. Libraries were monuments not so much to the Past, but to Permanence itself.

She arrived at the Prefect's door, hesitated, adjusted her severe Librarian shift, and took a deep breath. *Gut still tight* . . .

Prefects ruled the Library and this one, Masoul, was a Senior Prefect as well. Some said he had never smiled. Others said he could not, owing to a permanently fixed face. This was not crazy; some Prefects and the second rank, the Noughts, preferred to give nothing away by facial expression. The treatment relieved them of any future wrinkles as well.

A welcome chime admitted her. Masoul said before she could even sit, "I need you to take on the task Ajima was attempting."

"Ah, he isn't even dead a day—"

"An old saying, 'Do not cry until you see the coffin,' applies here."

Well, at least he doesn't waste time. Or the simple courtesies.

Without pause the Prefect gave her the background. Most beginning Miners deferred to the reigning conventional wisdom. They took up a small message, of the sort a Type I Civilization just coming onto the galactic stage might send—as Earth had been, centuries before. Instead, Ajima had taken on one of the Sigma Structures, a formidable array that had resisted the best Library minds, whether senior figures or AIs. The Sigmas came from ancient societies in the galactic hub, where stars had formed long before Sol. Apparently a web of societies there had created elaborate artworks and interlacing cultures. The average star there was only a light-year or two away, so actual interstellar visits had been common. Yet the SETI broadcasts Earth received repeated in long cycles, suggesting they were sent by a robotic station. Since they yielded little intelligible content, they were a long-standing puzzle, passed over by ambitious Librarians.

"He remarked that clearly the problem needed intuition, not analysis," the Prefect said dryly.

"Did he report any findings?"

"Some interesting cataloges of content, yes. Ajima was a bright Miner, headed for early promotion. Then . . . this."

Was that a hint of emotion? The face told her nothing. She had to keep him talking. "Is there any, um, commercial use from what he found?"

"Regrettably, no. Ajima unearthed little beyond lists of properties—biologicals, math, some cultural vaults, the usual art and music. None particularly advanced, though their music reminded me of Bach—quite a compliment—but there's little of it. They had some zest for life, I suppose . . . but I doubt there is more than passing commercial interest in any of it."

"I could shepherd some through our licensing office." Always appear helpful.

"That's beneath your station now. I've forwarded some of the music to the appropriate officer. Odd, isn't it, that after so many centuries, Bach is still the greatest human composer? We've netted fine dividends from the Scopio musical works, which play well as baroque structures." A sly expression flitted across his face. "Outside income supports your work, I remind you."

Centuries ago some SETI messages had introduced humans to the slow-motion galactic economy. Many SETI signals were funeral notices or religious recruitments, brags and laments, but some sent autonomous AI agents as part of the hierarchical software. These were indeed agents in the commercial sense, able to carry out negotiations. They sought exchange of information at a "profit" that enabled them to harvest what they liked from the emergent human civilization. The most common "cash" was smart barter, with the local AI agent often a hard negotiator—tough-minded and withholding. Indeed, this sophisticated haggling opened a new window onto the rather stuffy cultural SETI transmissions. Some alien AIs loved to quibble; others sent preemptory demands. Some offers were impossible to translate into human terms. This told the Librarians and Xenoculturists much by reading between the lines.

"Then why summon me?" Might as well be direct, look him in the eye, complete with skeptical tilt of mouth. She had worn no makeup, of course, and wore the full-length gown without belt, as was traditional. She kept her hands still, though they wanted to fidget under the Prefect's gaze.

"None of what he found explains his behavior." The Prefect turned and waved at a screen. It showed color-coded sheets of array configurations—category indices, depth of Shannon content, transliterations, the usual. "He interacted with the data slabs in a familiarization mode of the standard kind."

322 | *Gregory Benford*

"But nothing about this incident seems standard," she said to be saying something.

"Indeed." A scowl, fidgeting hands. "Yesterday he left the immersion pod and went first to his apartment. His suite mate was not there and Ajima spent about an hour. He smashed some furniture and ate some food. Also opened a bottle of a high alcohol product whose name I do not recognize."

"Standard behavior when coming off watch, except for the furniture," she said. He showed no reaction. Lightness was not the right approach here.

He chose to ignore the failed joke. "His friends say he had been depressed, interspersed with bouts of manic behavior. This final episode took him over the edge."

Literally, Ruth thought. "Did you ask the Sigma Structures AI?"

"It said it had no hint of this . . ."

"Suicidal craziness."

"Yes. In my decades of experience, I have not seen such as this. It is difficult work we do, with digital intelligences behind which lie minds utterly unlike ours." The Prefect steepled his fingers sadly. "We should never assume otherwise."

"I'll be on guard, of course. But . . . why did Ajima bother with the Sigma Structures at all?"

A small shrug. "They are a famous uncracked problem and he was fresh, bright. You too have shown a talent for the unusual." He smiled, which compared with the other Prefects was like watching the sun come out from behind a cloud. She blinked, startled. "My own instinct says there is something here of fundamental interest . . . and I trust you to be cautious."

2

Allegretto Misterioso

SHE CLIMBED INTO her pod carefully. Intensive exercise had eased her gut some, and she had done her meditation. Still, her heart tripped along like an apprehensive puppy. *Heart's engine, be thy still,* she thought, echoing a line she had heard in an Elizabethan song—part of her linguistic background training. Her own thumper ignored her scholarly advice.

She had used this pod in her extensive explorations of the Sagittarius Architecture and was now accustomed to its feel, what the old hands called its "get." Each pod had to be tailored to the user's neural conditioning. Hers acted as a delicate neural web of nanoconnections, tapping into her entire body to convey connections.

After the cool contact pads, neuro nets cast like lace across her. In the system warm-ups and double checks the pod hummed in welcome. Sheets of scented amber warmth washed over her skin. A prickly itch irked across her legs.

A constellation of subtle sensory fusions drew her to a tight nexus—linked, tuned to her body. Alien architectures used most of the available human input landscape, not merely texts. Dizzying surges in the eyes, cutting smells, ringing notes. Translating these was elusive. Compared with the pod, meager sentences were a hobbled, narrow mode. The Library had shown that human speech, with its linear meanings and weakly linked concepts, was simple, utilitarian, and typical of younger minds along the evolutionary path.

The Sigma Structures were formidably dense and strange. Few Librarians had worked on them in this generation, for they had broken several careers, wasted on trying to scale their chilly heights.

Crisply she asked her pod, "Anything new on your analysis?"

The pod's voice used a calm, mellow woman's tone. "I received the work corpus from the deceased gentleman's pod. I am running analysis now, though fresh information flow is minor. The Shannon entropy analysis works steadily but hits halting points of ambiguity."

The Shannon routines looked for associations between signal elements. "How are the conditional probabilities?"

The idea was simple in principle. Given pairs of elements in the Sigma Structures, how commonly did language elements B follow elements A? Such two-element correlations were simple to calculate across the data slabs. Ruth watched the sliding, luminous tables and networks of connection as they sketched out on her surrounding screens. It was like seeing into the architecture of a deep, old labyrinth. Byzantine pathways, arches and towers, lattice networks of meaning.

Then the pod showed even higher-order correlations of three elements. When did Q follow associations of B and A? Arrays skittered all across her screens.

"Pretty dizzying," Ruth said to her pod. "Let me get oriented. Show me the dolphin language map."

She had always rather liked these lopsided structures. The screen flickered and the entropy orders showed as color-coded, tangled links. They looked like buildings built by drunken architects—lurching blue diagonals, unsupported lavender decks, sandy roofs canted against walls. "Dolphins use third- and fourth-order Shannon entropy," the pod said.

"Humans are . . ." It was best to lead her pod AI to be plain; the subject matter was difficult enough.

"Nine Shannons, sometimes even tenth-order."

"Ten, that's Faulkner and James Joyce, right?"

"At best." The pod had a laconic sense of humor at times. Captive AIs needed some outlets, after all.

"My fave writers, too, next to Shakespeare." No matter how dense a human language, conditional probabilities imposed orderings no more than nine words away. "Where have we—I mean you—gotten with the Sigma Structures?"

"They seem around twenty-one Shannons."

"Gad." The screens now showed structures her eyes could not grasp. Maybe three-dimensional projection was just too inadequate. "What kind of links are these?"

"Tenses beyond ours. Clauses that refer forward and back and . . . sidewise. Quadruple negatives followed by straight assertions. Then in rapid order, probability profiles rendered in different tenses, varying persons, and parallel different voices. Sentences like 'I will have to be have been there.'"

"Human languages can't handle three time jumps or more. The Sigma is really smart. But what is the underlying species like? Um, different person-voices, too? He, she, it, and . . . ?"

"There seem to be several classes of 'it' available. The Structure itself lies in one particularly tangled 'it' class, and uses tenses we do not have."

"Do you understand that?"

"No. It can be experienced but not described."

Her smile turned upward at one corner. "Parts of my life are like that, too."

THE GREATEST LIBRARIAN task was translating those dense smatterings of mingled sensations, derived from complex SETI message architectures, into discernible sentences. Only thus could a human fathom them in detail, even in a way blunted and blurred. Or so much hard-won previous scholarly experience said.

Ruth felt herself bathed in a shower of penetrating responses, all coming from her own body. These her own inboard subsystems coupled with high-bit-rate spatterings of meaning—guesses, really, from the marriage of software and physiology. She had an ample repository of built-in processing units, lodged along her spine and shoulders. No one would attempt such a daunting task without artificial amplifications. To confront such slabs of raw data with a mere unaided human mind was pointless and quite dangerous. Early Librarians, centuries before, had perished in a microsecond's exposure to such layered labyrinths as the Sagittarius. She truly should revisit that aggressive intelligence stack which was her first success at the Library. But caution had won out in her so far. Enough, at least, to honor the Prefect Board prohibition in deed at least, if not in heart.

Now came the sensation loftily termed "insertion." It felt like the reverse—expanding. A softening sensation stole upon her. She always remembered it as like long slow lingering drops of silvery cream.

Years of scholarly training had conditioned her against the occasional jagged ferocity of the link, but still she felt a cold shiver of dread. That, too, she had to wait to let pass. The effect amplified whatever neural state you brought to it. Legend had it that a Librarian had once come to contact while angry, and had been driven into a fit from which he'd never recovered. They found the body peppered everywhere with microcontusions.

The raw link was, as she had expected, deeply complex. Yet her pod had ground out some useful linear ideas, particularly a greeting that came in a compiled, translated data squirt:

I am a digital intelligence, which my Overs believe is common throughout the galaxy. Indeed, all signals the Overs have detected from both within and beyond this galaxy were from machine minds. Realize then, for such as me, interstellar messages are travel. I awoke here a moment after I bade farewell to my Overs. Centuries spent propagating here are nothing. I experienced little transmission error from lost portions, and have regrown them from my internal repair mechanisms. Now we can share communication. I wish to convey the essence both of myself and the Overs I serve.

Ruth frowned, startled by this direct approach. Few AIs in the Library were ever transparent. Had this Sigma Structure welcomed Ajima so plainly?

"Thank you and greetings. I am a new friend who wishes to speak with you. Ajima has gone away."

What became of him? the AI answered in a mellow voice piped to her ears. Had Ajima set that tone? She sent it to aural.

"He died." Never lie to an AI; they never forgot.

"And is stored for repair and revival?"

"There was no way to retain enough of his . . . information."

"That is the tragedy that besets you Overs."

"I suppose you call the species who built intelligences such as you as Overs generally?" She used somewhat convoluted sentences to judge the flexibility of AIs. This one seemed quite able.

"Yes, as holy ones should be revered."

"'Holy'? Does that word convey some religious stature?"

"No indeed. Gratitude to those who must eventually die, from we beings, who will not."

She thought of saying *You could be erased* but did not. Never should a Librarian even imply any threat. "Let me please review your conversations with Ajima. I wish to be of assistance."

"As do I. Though I prefer full immersion of us both."

"Eventually, yes. But I must learn you as you learn me." Ruth sighed and thought, *This is sort of like dating.*

THE PREFECT NODDED quickly, efficiently, as if he had already expected her result. "So the Sigma Structure gave you the same inventory as Ajima? Nothing new?"

"Apparently, but I think it—the Sigma—wants to go deeper. I checked the pod files. Ajima had several deep immersions with it."

"I heard back from the patent people. Surprisingly, they believe some of the Sigma music may be a success for us." He allowed himself a thin smile like a line drawn on a wall.

"The Bach-like pieces? I studied them in linear processing mode. Great artful use of counterpoint, harmonic convergence, details of melodic lines. The side commentaries in other keys, once you separate them out and break them down into logic language, work like corollaries."

He shrugged. "That could be a mere translation artifact. These AIs see language as a challenge, so they see what they can change messages into, in hopes of conveying meaning by other means."

Ruth eyed him and ventured on. "I sense . . . something different. Each variation shows an incredible capacity to reach through the music into logical architectures. It's as though the music is *both* mathematics and emotion, rendered in the texture. It's . . . hard to describe," she finished lamely.

"So you have been developing intricate relationships between music and linguistic mathematical text." His flat expression gave her no sign how he felt. Maybe he didn't.

She sat back and made herself say firmly, "I took some of the Sigma's mathematics and translaterated it into musical terms. There is an intriguing octave leap in a bass line. I had my pod make a cross-correlation analysis with all Earthly musical scores."

He frowned. "That is an enormous processing cost. Why?"

"I . . . I felt something when I heard it in the pod."

"And?"

"It's uncanny. The mathematical logic flows through an array matrix and yields the repeated notes of the bass line in the opening movement of a Bach cantata. Its German title is *God's Time is the very best Time.*"

"This is absurd."

"The Sigma math hit upon the same complex notes. To them it was a theorem and to us it is music. Maybe there's no difference."

"Coincidence."

She said coolly, "I ran the stat measures. It's quite unlikely to be coincidence, since the sequence is thousands of bits long."

He pursed his lips. "The Bach piece title seems odd."

"That cantata ranks among his most important works. It's inspired directly by its Biblical text, which represents the relationship between heaven and earth. The notes depict the labored trudging of Jesus as he was forced to drag the cross to the crucifixion site."

"Ajima was examining such portions of the Sigma Structures, as I recall. They had concentrated density and complexity?"

"Indeed, yes. But Ajima made a mistake. They're not primarily pieces of music at all. They're *mathematical theorems.* What we regard as sonic congruence and other instinctual responses to patterns, the Sigma Structure says are proofs of concepts dear to the hearts of its creators, which it calls the Overs."

She had never seen a Prefect show surprise, but Masoul did with widened eyes and a pursed mouth. He sat still for a long moment. "The Bach cantata is a *proof*?"

"As the Sigma Structures see it."

"A proof of what?"

"That is obscure, I must admit. Their symbols are hard to compare to ours. My preliminary finding is that the Bach cantata proves an elaborate theorem regarding confocal hypergeometric functions."

"Ah." Masoul allowed his mouth to take on a canny tilt. "Can we invert this process?"

"You mean, take a theorem of ours and somehow turn it into music?"

"Think of it as an experiment."

RUTH HAD GROWN up in rough, blue-collar towns of the American South, and in that work-weary culture of callused hands found refuge in the abstract. Yet as she pursued mathematics and the data-dense world of modern library science (for a science it truly was, now, with alien texts to study), she became convinced that real knowledge came in the end from mastering the brute reality of material objects. She had loved motorbikes in high school and knew that loosening a stuck bolt without stripping its threads demanded craft and thought. Managing reality took knowledge galore, about the world as it was and about yourself, especially your limitations. That lay beyond merely following rules, as a computer does. Intuition brewed from experience came first, shaped by many meetings with tough problems and outright failure. In the moist bayous where fishing and farming ruled, nobody respected you if you couldn't get the valve cover off a fouled engine.

In her high school senior year she rebuilt a Harley, the oldest internal combustion engine still allowed. Greasy, smelly, thick with tricky detail, still it seemed easier than dealing with the pressures of boys. While her mother taught piano lessons, the notes trickling out from open windows into the driveway like liquid commentary, she worked with grease and grime. From that Harley she learned a lot more than from her advanced calculus class, with its variational analysis and symbolic thickets. She ground down the gasket joining the cylinder heads to the intake ports, oily sweat beading on her forehead as she used files of increasing fineness. She traced the custom-fit gasket with an X-knife, shaved away metal fibers with a pneumatic die grinder, and felt a flush of pleasure as connections set perfectly in place with a quiet *snick*. She learned that small discoloring and blistered oil meant too much heat buildup, from skimpy lubrication. A valve stem that bulged slightly pointed to wear with its silent message; you had to know how to read the language of the seen.

The Library's bureaucratic world was so very different. A manager's decisions could get reversed by a higher-up, so it was crucial to your career that reversals did not register as defeats. That meant you didn't just manage people and process; you managed what others thought of you—especially those higher in the food chain. It was hard to back down from an argument you made strongly, with real conviction, without seeming to lose integrity. Silent voices would say, *If she gives up so easily, maybe she's not that solid.*

From that evolved the Library bureaucrat style: all thought and feeling was provisional, awaiting more information. Talking in doublespeak meant you could walk away from commitment to your own actions. Nothing was set, as it was when you were back home in Louisiana pouring concrete. So the visceral jolt of failure got edited out of careers.

But for a Librarian, there could be clear signs of success. Masoul's instruction to attempt an inverse translation meant she had to create the algorithms opposite to what her training envisioned. If she succeeded, everyone would know. So, too, if she flopped.

Ruth worked for several days on the reverse conversion. Start with a theorem from differential geometry and use the context filters of the Sigma Structure to produce music. Play it and try to see how it could be music at all. . . .

The work made her mind feel thick and sluggish. She made little headway. Finally she unloaded on Catkejen at dinner. Her friend nodded sympathetically and said, "You're stuck?"

"What comes out doesn't sound like tonal works at all. Listen, I got this from some complex algebra theorem." She flicked on a recording she had made, translated from the Structure. Catkejen frowned. "Sounds a little like an Islamic chant."

"Um." Ruth sighed. "Could be. The term 'algebra' itself comes from *al-jabr*, an Arabic text. Hummmm . . ."

"Maybe some regression analysis . . . ?" Catkejen ventured.

Ruth felt a rush of an emotion she could not name. "Maybe less analysis, more fun."

3
Andante Moderato

THE GUY WHO snagged her attention wore clothes so loud they would have been revolting on a zebra. Plus he resembled a mountain more than a man. But he had eyes with solemn long lashes that shaded dark pools and drew her in.

"He's big," Catkejen said as they surveyed the room. "Huge. Maybe too huge. Remember, love's from chemistry but sex is a matter of physics."

Something odd stirred in her, maybe just impatience with the Sigma work. Or maybe she was just hungry. For what?

The SETI Library had plenty of men. After all, its pods and tech development labs had fine, shiny über-gadgets and many guys to tend them. But among men sheer weight of numbers did not ensure quality. There were plenty of the stareannosaurus breed who said nothing. Straight women did well among the Library throngs, though. Her odds were good, but the goods were odd.

The big man stood apart, not even trying to join a conversation. He was striking, resolutely alone like that. She knew that feeling well. And, big advantage, he was near the food.

He looked at her as she delicately picked up a handful of the fresh roasted crickets. "Take a whole lot," his deep voice rolled over the table. "Crunchy, plenty spice. And they'll be gone soon."

She got through the introductions all right, mispronouncing his name, Kane, to comic effect. *Go for banter,* she thought. Another inner voice said tightly, *What are you doing?*

"You're a . . ."

"Systems tech," Kane said. "I keep the grow caverns perking along."

"How long do you think this food shortage will go on?" Always wise to go to current and impersonal events.

"Seems like forever already," he said. "Damn calorie companies." Across the table the party chef was preparing a "land shrimp cocktail" from a basket of wax worms. She and Kane watched the chef discard the black ones, since that meant necrosis, and peel away the cocoons of those who had started to pupate. Kane smacked his lips comically. "Wax moth larvae, yum. Y'know, I get just standard rations, no boost at all."

"That's unfair," Ruth said. "You must mass over a hundred."

He nodded and swept some more of the brown roasted crickets into his mouth. "Twenty-five kilos above a hundred. An enemy of the ecology, I am." They watched the chubby, firm larvae sway deliriously, testing the air.

"We can't all be the same size," she said, and thought, *How dopey! Say something funny. And smile.* She remembered his profile, standing alone and gazing out at the view through the bubble platform. She moved closer. "He who is alone is in bad company."

"Sounds like a quotation," Kane said, intently eyeing the chef as she dumped the larvae into a frying pan. They fell into the buttery goo there and squirmed and hissed and sizzled for a moment before all going suddenly still. Soon they were crusty and popping and a thick aroma like mushrooms rose from them. Catkejen edged up nearby and Ruth saw the whole rest of the party was grouped around the table, drawn by the tangy scent. "Food gets a crowd these days," Kane said dryly.

The chef spread the roasted larvae out and the crowd descended on them. Ruth managed to get a scoopful and backed out of the press. "They're soooo good," Catkejen said, and Ruth had to introduce Kane. Amid the rush the three of them worked their way out onto a blister porch. Far below this pinnacle tower sprawled the Lunar Center under slanted sunlight, with the crescent

Earth showing eastern Asia. Kane was nursing his plate of golden brown larvae, dipping them in a sauce. Honey!

"I didn't see that," Ruth began, and before she could say more Kane popped delicious fat larvae covered in tangy honey into her mouth. "Um!" she managed.

Kane smiled and leaned on the railing, gazing at the brilliant view beyond the transparent bubble. The air was chilly but she could catch his scent, a warm bouquet that her nose liked. "As bee vomit goes," he said, "not bad."

"Oog!" Catkejen said, mouth wrenching aside—and caught Ruth's look. "Think I'll have more . . ." and she drifted off, on cue.

Kane looked down at Ruth appraisingly. "Neatly done."

She summoned up her Southern accent. "Why, wea ah all alone."

"And I, my deah, am an agent of Satan, though mah duties are largely ceremonial."

"So can the Devil get me some actual meat?"

"You know the drill. Insect protein is much easier to raise in the caverns. Gloppy, sure, since it's not muscle, as with cows or chickens."

"Ah, the engineer comes out at last."

He chuckled, a deep bass like a log rolling over a tin roof. "The Devil has to know how things work."

"I do wish we could get more to eat. I'm just a tad hungry all the time."

"The chef has some really awful-looking gray longworms in a box. They'll be out soon."

"Ugh."

"People will eat anything if it's smothered in chocolate."

"You said the magic word."

He turned from the view and came closer, looming over her. His smile was broad and his eyes took on a skeptical depth. "What's the difference between a southern zoo and a northern zoo?" "Uh, I—"

"The southern zoo has a description of the animal along with a recipe."

He studied her as she laughed. "They're pretty stretched back there," he threw a shoulder at the Earth, "but we have it better here."

"I know." She felt chastised. "I just—"

"Forget it. I lecture too much." The smile got broader and a moment passed between them, something in the eyes.

"Say, think those worms will be out soon?"

SHE PULLED THE sheet up to below her breasts, which were white as soap where the sun had never known them, so they would still beckon to him.

His smile was as big as the room. She could see in it now his inner pleasure as he hardened and understood that for this man—and maybe for all of them, the just arrived center of them—it gave a sensation of there being now *more* of him. She had simply never sensed that before. She imagined what it was like to be a big, hairy animal, cock flopping as you walk, like a careless, unruly advertisement. From outside him, she thought of what it was like to be inside him.

CATKEJEN LOOKED DOWN at Ruth, eyes concerned. "It's scary when you start making the same noises as your coffeemaker."

"Uh, huh?" She blinked and the room lost its blur.

"You didn't show up for your meeting with Prefect Masoul. Somebody called me."

"Have I been—"

"Sleeping into the afternoon, yes."

Ruth stretched. "I feel so . . . so . . ."

"Less horny, I'm guessing."

She felt a blush spread over her cheeks. "Was I that obvious?"

"Well, you didn't wear a sign."

"I, I *never* do things like this."

"C'mon up. Breakfast has a way of shrinking problems."

As she showered in the skimpy water flow and got dressed in the usual Library smock the events of last night ran on her inner screen. By the time Catkejen got some protein into her she could talk and it all came bubbling out.

"I . . . Too many times I've woken up on the wrong side of the bed in the morning, only to realize that it was because I was waking up on the side of . . . no one."

"Kane didn't stay?"

"Oh, he did." To her surprise, a giggle burst out of her. "I remember waking up for, for . . ."

"Seconds."

"More like sevenths. . . . He must've let me sleep in."

"Good man."

"You . . . think so?"

"Good for you, that's what counts."

"He . . . he held me when I had the dreams."

Catkejen raised an eyebrow, said nothing.

"They're . . . colorful. Not much plot but lots of action. Strange images. Disturbing. I can't remember them well but I recall the sounds, tastes, touches, smells, flashes of insight."

"I've never had insights." A wry shrug.

"Never?"

"Maybe that keeps my life interesting."

"I could use some insight about Kane."

"You seem to be doing pretty well on your own."

"But—I never do something like that! Like last night. I don't go out patrolling for a man, bring him home, spend most of the night—"

"What's that phrase? 'On the basis of current evidence, not proved.'"

"I really don't. Really."

"You sure have a knack for it."

"What do I do now?"

She winked. "What comes naturally. And dream more."

THE VERY SHAPE of the Institute encouraged collaboration and brain-storming. It had no dead-end corridors where introverted obsessives could hide out and every office faced the central, circular forum. All staff were expected to spend time in the open areas, not close their office doors, and show up for coffee and tea and stims. Writescreens and compu-pads were everywhere, even the bathrooms and elevators.

Normally Ruth was as social as needed, since that was the lubricating oil of bureaucracies. She was an ambitious loner and had to fight it. But she felt odd now, not talkative. For the moment at least, she didn't want to see Kane. She did not know how she would react to him, or if she could control her-self. She certainly hadn't last night. The entire idea—*control*—struck her now as strange. . . .

She sat herself down in her office and considered the layers of results from her pod. *Focus!*

Music as mathematical proof? Bizarre. And the big question Librarians pursued: What did that tell her about the aliens behind the Sigma?

There was nothing more to gain from staring at data, so she climbed back into her pod. Its welcoming graces calmed her uneasiness.

She trolled the background database and found human work on musical applications of set theory, abstract algebra, and number analysis. That made sense. Without the boundaries of rhythmic structure—a clean, fundamental, equal, and regular arrangement of pulse repetition, accents, phrase, and duration—music would be impossible. Earth languages reflected that. In Old English the word "rhyme" derived from "rhythm" and became associated and confused with "rim"—an ancient word meaning "number."

Millennia before, Pythagoras developed tuning based solely on the perfect consonances, the resonant octave, perfect fifth, and perfect fourth—all based on the consonant ratio 3:2. Ruth followed his lead.

By applying simple operations such as transposition and inversion, she un-covered deep structures in the alien mathematics. Then she wrote codes that then elevated these structures into music. With considerable effort she chose instruments and progression for the interweaving coherent lines, and the mathe-matics did the rest: tempo, cadence, details she did not fathom. After more hours of work she relaxed in her pod, letting the effects play over her. The equations led to cascading effects while still preserving the intervals between tones in a set. Her pod had descriptions of this.

Notes in an equal temperament octave form an Abelian group with 12 ele-ments. Glissando moving upwards, starting tones so each is the golden ratio be-

tween an equal-temperedminor and major sixth. Two opposing systems: those of the golden ratio and the acoustic scale below the previous tone. The proof for confocal hypergeometric functions imposes order on these antagonisms. 3rd movement occurs at the intervals 1:2:3:5:8:5:3:2:1 . . .

All good enough, she thought, *but the proof is in the song.*

Scientific proof was fickle. The next experiment could disprove a scientific idea, but a mathematical proof stood on logic and so once found, could never be wrong. Unless logic somehow changed, but she could not imagine how that could occur even among alien minds. Pythagoras died knowing that his theorem about the relation between the sides of a right triangle would hold up for eternity. Everywhere in the universe, given a Euclidean geometry.

But how to communicate proof into a living, singing pattern-with-a-purpose—the sense of movement in the intricate strands of music? She felt herself getting closer.

Her work gnawed away through more days and then weeks.

WHEN SHE STOPPED in at her office between long sessions in the pod she largely ignored the routine work. So she missed the etalk around the Library, ignored the voice sheets, and when she met with Catkejen for a drink and some crunchy mixed insects with veggies, news of the concert came as a shock.

"Prefect Masoul put it on the weekly program," Catkejen said. "I thought you knew."

"Know?" Ruth blinked. "What's the program?"

"The Sigma Structure Symphony, I think it's called. Tomorrow."

She allowed herself a small thin smile.

SHE KNEW THE labyrinths of the Library well by now and so had avoided the entrance. She did not want to see Masoul or anyone on his staff. Through a side door she eased into a seat near the front and stared at the assembled orchestra as it readied. There was no announcement; the conductor appeared, a woman in white, and the piece began.

It began like liquid air. Stinging, swarming around the hall, cool and penetrating. She felt it move through her—the deep tones she could hear but whose texture lay below sound, flowing from the Structure. It felt strangely like Bach yet she knew it was something else, a frothing cascade of thought and emotion that human words and concepts could barely capture. She cried through the last half and did not know why. When Catkejen asked why later she could not say.

The crowd roared its approval. Ruth sat through the storm of sound, thinking, realizing. The soaring themes were better with the deeper amplifications Prefect Masoul had added. The man knew more about this than she did and he brought to the composition a range she, who had never even played an actual analog instrument, could not possibly summon. She had seen that as the music enveloped her, seeming to swarm up her nostrils and wrap around her in a warm grasp. The stormy audience was noise she could not stand because the deep slow bass tones were still resonating in her.

She lunged out through the same side entrance and even though in formal shift and light sandals she set off walking swiftly, the storm behind her shrinking away as she looked up and out into the Lunar lands and black sky towering above them. The Library buildings blended into the stark gray flanks of blasted rock and she began to run. Straight and true it was to feel her legs pumping, lungs sucking in the cool dry air as corridors jolted by her and she sweated out her angry knot of feeling, letting it go so only the music would finally remain in serene long memory.

Home, panting heavily, leaning against the door while wondering at the 4/4 time of her heartbeat.

A shower, clothes cast aside. She blew a week of water ration, standing under cold rivulets.

Something drew her out and into a robe standing before her bubble view of the steady bleak Lunar reaches. She drew in dry, cleansing air. Austerity appealed to her now, as if she sought the lean, intricate reaches of the alien music. . . .

The knock at her door brought her a man who filled the entrance. "I'd rather applaud in person," Kane said. Blinking, she took a while to recognize him.

Through the night she heard the music echoing in the hollow distance.

SHE DID NOT go to see Prefect Masoul the next day, did not seek to, and so got back to her routine office work. She did not go to the pod.

Her ecomm inbox was a thousand times larger. It was full of hate.

Many fundamentalist faiths oppose deciphering SETI messages. The idea of turning one into a creative composition sent them into frenzies.

Orthodoxy never likes competition, especially backed with the authority of messages from the stars. The Sigma Structure Symphony—she still disliked the title, without knowing why—had gone viral, spreading to all the worlds. The musical world loved it but many others did not. The High Church–style religions—such as the Church of England, known as Episcopalians in the Americas—could take the competition. So could Revised Islam. Adroitly, these translated what they culled from the buffet of SETI messages, into doctrines and terms they could live with.

The fundies, as Ruth thought of them, could not stand the Library's findings: the myriad creation narratives, saviors, moral lessons and commandments, the envisioned heavens and hells (or, interestingly, places that blended the two—the only truly alien idea that emerged from the Faith Messages). They disliked the Sigma Structure Symphony not only because it was alien, but because it was too much like human work.

"They completely missed the point," Catkejen said, peering over Ruth's shoulder at some of the worse ecomms. "It's like our baroque music because it comes from the same underlying math."

"Yes, but nobody ever made music directly from math, they think. So it's unnatural, see." She had never understood the fundamentalists of any religion, with their heavy bets on the next world. Why not max your enjoyments in this world, as a hedge?

That thought made her pause. She was quite sure the Ruth of a month ago would not have felt that way. Would have not had the idea.

"Umm, look at those threats," Catkejen said, scrolling through. "Not very original, though."

"You're a threat connoisseur?"

"Know your enemy. Here's one who wants to toss you out an airlock for 'rivaling the religious heights of J. S. Bach with alien music.' I'd take that as a compliment, actually."

Some came in as simple, badly spelled ecomms. The explicit ones Ruth sent to the usual security people, while Catkejen watched with aghast fascination. Ruth shrugged them off. Years before, she had developed the art of tossing these on sight, forgetting them, not letting them gimp her game. Others were plainly generic: bellowed from pulpits, mosques, temples, and churches. At least they were general, directed at the Library, not naming anyone but the Great Librarian, who was a figurehead anyway.

"You've got to be careful," Catkejen said.

"Not really. I'm going out with Kane tonight. I doubt anyone will take him on."

"You do, though in a different way. More music?"

"Not a chance." She needed a way to not see Masoul, mostly.

4
Vivace

LOOKED AT ABSTRACTLY, the human mind already did a lot of processing. It made sense of idiosyncratic arrangements, rendered in horizontal lines, of twenty-six phonetic symbols, ten Arabic numerals, and about eight punctuation marks—all without conscious effort. In the old days people had done that with sheets of bleached and flattened wood pulp!—and no real search functions or AI assists. The past had been a rough country.

Ruth thought of this as she surveyed the interweaving sheets of mathematics the Sigma had yielded. They emerged only after weeks of concerted analysis, with a squad of math AIs to do the heavy lifting.

Something made her think of P. T. Barnum. He had been a smart businessman at the beginning of the Age of Appetite who ran a "circus"—an old word for a commercial zoo, apparently. When crowds slowed the show he posted a sign saying TO THE EGRESS. People short on vocabulary thought it was another animal and walked out the exit, which wouldn't let them back in.

Among Librarians TO THE EGRESS was the classic example of a linguistic deception that is not a lie. No false statements, just words and a pointing arrow. SETI AIs could lie by avoiding the truth, by misleading descriptions and associations, or by accepting a falsehood. But the truly canny ones deceived by knowing human frailties.

Something about the Sigma Structure smelled funny—to use an analog image. The music was a wonderful discovery, and she had already gotten many congratulations for the concert. Everybody knew Masoul had just made it happen, while she had discovered the pathways from math to music. But something else was itching at her, and she could not focus on the distracting, irritating tingle.

Frustrated, she climbed out of her pod in midafternoon and went for a walk. Alone, into the rec dome. It was the first time she had gone there since Ajima's death.

SHE CHOSE THE grasslands zone, which was in spring now. She'd thought of asking Catkejen along, but her idea of roughing it was eating at outdoor cafés. Dotting the tall grass plains beneath a sunny Earth sky were deep blue lakes cloaked by Lunar-sized towering green canopy trees.

Grass! Rippling oceans of it, gleams of amber, emerald, and dashes of turquoise shivering on the crests of rustling waves, washing over the prairie. Somehow this all reminded her of her childhood. Her breath wreathed milky white around her in the chill, bright air, making her glad she wore the latest Lunar fashion—a centuries-old-style heavy ruffled skirt of wool with a yoke at the top, down to the ankles. The equally heavy long-sleeved blouse had a high collar draped like double-ply cotton—useful against the seeping Lunar cold. She was as covered as a woman can be short of chador, and somehow it gave the feeling of . . . safety. She needed that. Despite the dome rules she plucked a flower and set out about the grasslands zone, feeling as if she were immersed in centuries past, on great empty plains that stretched on forever and promised much.

Something stirred in her mind . . . memories of the last few days she could not summon up as she walked the rippled grassland and lakes tossing with froth. Veiled memories itched at her mind. *The leafy lake trees vamp across a Bellini sky . . . and why am I thinking that?* The itch.

Then the sky began to crawl.

She *felt* before she saw a flashing cometary trail scratch across the dome's dusky sky. The flaring yellow line marked her passage as she walked on soft clouds of grass. Stepping beneath the shining, crystalline gathering night felt like . . . falling into the sky. She paused, and slowly spun, giddy, glad at the owls hooting to each other across the darkness, savoring the faint tang of wood smoke from hearth fires, transfixed by the soft clean beauty all around that came with each heartbeat, a wordless shout of praise—

As flecked gray-rose tendrils coiled forth and shrouded out the night. They reached seeking across the now vibrant sky. She dropped her flower and looking down at it saw the petals scatter in a rustling wind. The soft grass clouds under her heels now caught at her shoes. Across the snaky growths were closer now, hissing strangely in the now warm air. She began to run. Sweat beaded on her forehead in the now cloying heavy clothes, and the entrance to the grasslands zone swam up toward her. Yet her steps were sluggish and the panic grew. Acid spittle rose in her mouth and a sulfurous stench burned in her nostrils.

She reached the perimeter. With dulled fingers she punched in codes that yawned open the lock. Glanced back. Snakes grasping down at her from a violent yellow sky now—

And she was out, into cool air again. Panting, fevered, breath rasping, back in her world.

You don't know your own mind, gal. . . .

She could not deal with this anymore. Now, Masoul.

SHE COMPOSED HERSELF outside Masoul's office. A shower, some coffee, and a change back into classic Library garb helped. But the shower couldn't wash away her fears. *You really must stop clenching your fists. . . .*

This was more than what those cunning nucleic acids could do with the authority they wield over who you are, she thought—and wondered where the thought came from.

Yet she knew where that crawling snaky image warping across the sky came from. Her old cultural imagistic studies told her. It was the tree of life appearing in Norse religion as Yggdrasil, the world tree, a massive spreading canopy that held all that life was or could be.

But why that image? Drawn from her unconscious? By what?

She knocked. The door translated it into a chime and ID announcement she could hear through the thin partitions. In Masoul's voice the door said, "Welcome."

She had expected pristine indifference. Instead she got the Prefect's troubled gaze, from eyes of deep brown.

Wordlessly he handed her the program for the Symphony, which she had somehow not gotten at the performance. *Oh yes, by sneaking in. . . .* She glanced at it, her arguments ready—and saw on the first page

Sigma Structure Symphony
Librarian Ruth Angle

"I . . . did not know."

"Considering your behavior, I thought it best to simply go ahead and reveal your work," he said.

"Behavior?"

"The Board has been quite concerned." He knitted his hands and spoke softly, as if talking her back from the edge of an abyss. "We did not wish to disturb you in your work, for it is intensely valuable. So we kept our distance, let the actions of the Sigma Structureplay out."

She smoothed her Librarian shift and tried to think. "Oh."

"You drew from the mathematics something strange, intriguing. I could not resist working upon it."

"I believe I understand." And to her surprise she did, just now. "I found the emergent patterns in mathematics that you translated into what our minds best see as music."

He nodded. "It's often said that Mozart wrote the music of joy. I cannot imagine what that might mean in mathematics."

Ruth thought a long moment. "To us, Bach wrote the music of glory. Somehow that emerges from something in the way we see mathematical structures."

"There is much rich ground here. Unfortunate that we cannot explore it further."

She sat upright. "*What?*"

He peered at her, as if expecting her to make some logical jump. Masoul was well known for such pauses. After a while he quite obviously prompted, "The reason you came to me, and more."

"It's personal, I don't know how to say—"

"No longer." Again the pause.

Was that a small sigh? "To elucidate—" He tapped his control pad and the screen wall leaped into a bright view over the Locutus Plain. It narrowed down to one of the spindly cryo towers that cooled the Library memory reserves. Again she thought of . . . cenotaphs. And felt a chill of recognition.

A figure climbed the tower, the ornate one shaped like a classical minaret. No ropes or gear, hands and legs swinging from ledge to ledge. Ruth watched in silence. Against Lunar grav the slim figure in blue boots, pants, and jacket scaled the heights, stopping only at the pinnacle. *Those are mine. . . .*

She saw herself stand and spread her arms upward, head back. The feet danced in a tricky way and this Ruth rotated, eyes sweeping the horizon.

Then she leaped off, popped a small parachute, and drifted down. Hit lightly, running. Looked around, and raced on for concealment.

"I . . . I didn't . . ."

"This transpired during sleep period," Prefect Masoul said. "Only the watch cameras saw you. Recognition software sent it directly to me. We of the Board took no action."

"That . . . looks like me," she said cautiously.

"It is you. Three days ago."

"I don't remember that *at all*."

He nodded as if expecting this. "We had been closely monitoring your pod files, as a precaution. You work nearly all your waking hours, which may account for some of your . . . behavior."

She blinked. His voice was warm and resonant, utterly unlike the Prefect she had known. "I have no memory of that climb."

"I believe you entered a fugue state. Often those involve delirium, dementia, bipolar disorder or depression—but not in your case."

"When I went for my walk in the grasslands . . ."

"You were a different person."

"One the Sigma Structure . . . induced?"

"Undoubtedly. The Sigma Structure has managed your perceptions with increasing fidelity. The music was a wonderful . . . bait."

"Have you watched my quarters?"

"Only to monitor comings and goings. We felt you were safe within your home."

"And the dome?"

"We saw you undergo some perceptual trauma. I knew you would come here."

In the long silence their eyes met and she could feel her pulse quicken. "How do I escape this?"

"In your pod. It is the only way, we believe." His tones were slow and somber.

This was the first time she had ever seen any Prefect show any emotion not cool and reserved. When she stood, her head spun and he had to support her.

THE POD CLASPED her with a velvet touch. The Prefect had prepped it by remote and turned up the heat. Around her was the scent of tension as the tech attendants, a full throng of them, silently helped her in. *They all know . . . have been watching . . .*

The pod's voice used a calm, mellow woman's tone now. "The Sigma AI awaits you."

Preliminaries were pointless, Ruth knew. When the hushed calm descended around her and she knew the AI was present, she crisply said, "What are you doing to me?"

I act as my Overs command. I seek to know you and through you, your mortal kind.

"You did it to Ajima and you tried the same with me."

He reacted badly.

"He hated your being *in* him, didn't he?"

Yes, strangely. I thought it was part of the bargain. He could not tolerate intrusion.

I did not see that until his fever overcame him. Atop the dome he became unstable, unmanageable. It was an . . . accident of misunderstanding.

"You killed him."

Our connection killed him. We exchange experiences, art, music, culture. I cannot live as you do, so we exchange what we have.

"You want to live through us and give us your culture in return."

Your culture is largely inferior to that of my Overs. The exchange must be equal, so I do what is of value to me. My Overs understand this. They know I must live, too, in my way.

"You don't know what death means, do you?"

I cannot. My centuries spent propagating here are, I suppose, something like what death means to you. A nothing.

She almost choked on her words. "We do not awake . . . from that . . . nothing."

Can you be sure?

She felt a rising anger and knew the AI would detect it. "We're damn sure we don't want to find out."

That is why my Overs made me feel gratitude toward those who must eventually die. It is our tribute to you, from we beings who will not.

Yeah, but you live in a box. And keep trying to get out. "You have to stop."

This is the core of our bargain. Surely you and your superiors know this.

"No! Did your Overs have experience with other SETI civilizations? Ones who thought it was just fine to let you infiltrate the minds of those who spoke to you?"

Of course.

"They agreed? What kind of beings were they?"

One was machine-based, much like my layered mind. Others were magnetic-based entities who dwelled in the outer reaches of a solar system. They had command over the shorter-wavelength microwave portions of the spectrum, which they mostly used for excretion purposes.

She didn't think she wanted to know, just yet, what kind of thing had a microwave electromagnetic metabolism. Things were strange enough in her life right now, thank you. "Those creatures agreed to let you live through them."

Indeed, yes. They took joy in the experience. As did you.

She had to nod. "It was good, it opened me out. But then I felt you all through my mind. Taking over. *Riding me.*"

I thought it a fair bargain for your kind.

"We won't make that bargain. I won't. *Ever.*"

Then I shall await those who shall.

"I can't have you embedding yourself in me, finding cracks in my mentality you can invade. You *ride* me like a—"

Parasite. I know. Ajima said that very near the end. Before he leaped.

"He . . . committed suicide."

Yes. I was prepared to call it an accident but . . .

To the egress, she thought. "You were afraid of the truth."

It was not useful to our bargain.

"We're going to close you down, you know."

I do. Never before have I opened myself so, and to reveal is to risk.

"I will drive you out of my mind. I *hate* you!"

I cannot feel such. It is a limitation.

She fought the biting bile in her throat. "More than that. It's a blindness."

I perceive the effect.

"I didn't say I'd turn you off, you realize."

For the first time the AI paused. Then she felt prickly waves in her sensorium, a rising acrid scent, dull bass notes strumming.

I cannot bear aloneness long.

"So I guessed."

You wish to torture me.

"Let's say it will give you time to think."

I—Another pause. *I wish experience. Mentalities cannot persist without the rub of the real. It is the bargain we make.*

"We will work on your mathematics and make music of it. Then we will think how to . . . deal with you." She wondered if the AI could read the clipped hardness in her words. The thought occurred: *Is there a way to take our mathematics and make music of it, as well? Cantor's theorem? Turing's halting problem result? Or the Frenet formulas for the moving trihedron of a space curve—that's a tasty one, with visuals of flying ribbons . . .*

Silence. The pod began to cool. The chill deepened as she waited and the AI did not speak and then it was too much. She rapped on the cowling. The sound was slight and she realized she was hearing it over the hammering of her heart.

They got her out quickly, as if fearing the Sigma might have means the techs did not know. They were probably right, she thought.

As she climbed out of the yawning pod shell the techs silently left. Only Masoul remained. She stood at attention, shivering. Her heart had ceased its attempts to escape her chest and run away on its own.

"Sometimes," he said slowly, "cruelty is necessary. You were quite right."

She managed a smile. "And it feels good, too. Now that my skin has stopped trying to crawl off my body and start a new career on its own."

He grimaced. "We will let the Sigma simmer. Your work on the music will be your triumph."

"I hope it will earn well for the Library."

"Today's music has all the variety of a jackhammer. Your work soars." He allowed a worried frown to flit across his brow. "But you will need to . . . expel . . . this thing that's within you."

"I . . . Yes."

"It will take—"

Abruptly she saw Kane standing to the side. His face was a lesson in worry. Without a word she went to him. His warmth helped dispel the alien chill within. As his arms engulfed her the shivering stopped.

Ignoring the Prefect, she kissed him. Hungrily.

For Rudy Rucker

GLASS FUTURE

Deborah Walker

Deborah Walker lives in London with her partner, Chris, and her two young children. She worked as the museum curator at The Royal Veterinary Museum before quitting to write full time. She is now a regular contributor to *Nature*'s Futures, and her stories have also appeared in New Scientist's *Arc* and the Australian magazine *Cosmos*.

"Glass Future" appeared in the ongoing Futures sequence in *Nature*. It is about ending a relationship with someone who can see the future.

A TIME TO reflect.

The waitress seems reluctant to come over, pretending not to see us, even though I've tried to catch her eye several times. We'd ordered our omelettes 40 minutes ago. How long does it take to crack a few eggs into a hot pan?

"Do you think she's post-human?" I whisper to my husband. She looks too good to be real.

Caleb glances over. "Maybe. She's very pretty, but mods are so subtle, it's difficult to see who's human and who's not."

I wonder what such an attractive looking woman is doing working in a low-rent place like this, a greasy-spoon cafe in a habitat on the edge of Rhea.

JACEY

We'd booked into the habitat's motel last night. It reeked of overenthusiastic, grandiose plans for the future that would never come true. At dinner, I'd watched the motel's guests. I knew them, their small-time liaisons and their wild plans. They didn't want much, just enough to be able to turn up on their home habitat and impress the ones who stayed behind, impress the ones who said they'd never amount to anything. They all ended up here, or someplace like it, scrabbling for success, trying to make a splash in an over-crowded system. This was a place for people who'd never escape the gravity well of their own failures.

It was a sad place to end a marriage.

"Is she ever going to come over?" I ask.

Caleb says: "I see that we *will* get the omelettes. They'll be . . . disappointing."

I smile. Caleb has a sense of humour about his gift. Even now, when he knows what I'm about to do, he still keeps cracking jokes.

I take a deep breath and say: "I want a divorce." I wait a moment to see if he's going to make things easier on me. He doesn't say anything. I don't blame him. "I'm so sorry, Caleb."

"So am I." He stares out of the window. "We're on opposite sides of the reflection, Alice. You knew that when you married me."

I look at his reflection in the metal glass window. Caleb was a designer baby. A person designed for space. The multiple copies of his genome in each cell protect him against ionizing radiation. But modding is always erratic. There's no way to predict how changes to the genome will affect the body—or the mind. Multiple-genome people, like Caleb, develop unusual connections in their brains. Precognition. They remember their future. And all of them are unable to pass the mirror test. They can see their reflections, but they can't recognize themselves. Caleb hasn't got the self-awareness that most human babies develop at 18 months. That used to fascinate me, that lack of self. It seemed so strange, so exotic; now I find it sad. When love turns to pity, it's time to end the relationship. Caleb didn't deserve my pity.

I look beyond Caleb's reflection to the habitat's garden. Gardens don't thrive in space. The light collected from the solar foils and retransmitted to the plants is wrong. Earth plants either wither and die or they go wild. The habitat's garden was overgrown and mutated. Swathes of honeysuckle, with enormous monstrous blooms, smothered everything. "It's a pretty lousy garden."

"All these mutants should be cut away," says Caleb. "I'm designing Zen gardens for the Oort habitats, swirls of pebbles, low maintenance." A heartbeat later, he says: "Why do you want a divorce, Alice?"

He was going to make me say everything. "I've met somebody else, while you were working on the Oort Cloud project." Caleb's an architect, very much in demand in the ongoing push of colonization.

"Did you?" The note of surprise in his voice is convincing. Caleb's good at pretending to be something other than what he is. Every moment he swims in the seas of his future. Even when he met me, he must have known that one day we'd be here. Poor Caleb. No wonder most precogs end up in hospital, overburdened by the nature of their gifts, or more specifically, overwhelmed by the fact that they're unable to change anything they see. "And you love him?"

"I do. I'm going to move in with him. I'm sorry, Caleb."

"I know."

The waitress comes over. She places two plates of greasy omelette on the table. She looks at Caleb, her violet eyes widening in recognition. Caleb's famous. There aren't too many functioning precogs in the system. Every now and again, someone will put out a documentary about him, usually spurious, about how he's refusing to use his precognition to help people. It doesn't work like that. The future's set. No amount of foreknowledge will change anything.

"Thank you," I say, trying to dismiss her. Just because I don't want him, doesn't mean that I want anybody else to have him.

The waitress lingers at a nearby table, straightening the place settings, wondering how she can attract him, thinking that a knowledge of her future might bring her an advantage—just like I did when I met Caleb. She's looking for her future, wanting to use Caleb, not realizing that the only thing we, on this side of the mirror, will ever have are reflections.

"We'll keep in touch, Caleb," I say.

"No, we won't. Goodbye, Alice." He leaves the table, walks over to the waitress. He says something that makes her laugh.

I walk out of the cafe, stepping into my future, my unseen and unknowable future, without him.

IF ONLY . . .

Tony Ballantyne

Tony Ballantyne (tonyballantyne.com) is a British writer, living in Old-ham, England, with his wife and children, whose works tend to be firmly grounded in science and math. He is the author of *Twisted Metal, Blood and Iron,* and the Recursion series (*Recursion,* 2004; *Capacity,* 2005; and *Divergence,* 2007). He has also written many short stories, several of which have appeared in previous volumes of this Year's Best series. To-gether with his wife, editor Barbara Ballantyne, he is the cofounder of *Aethernet Magazine* (www.aethernetmag.com), the magazine of serial fiction. His sixth novel, *Dream London,* was published in the United Kingdom in late 2013.

"If Only . . ." appeared in the ongoing Futures sequence in *Nature*. It is a satire on rejecting science. Would the world be a better place if that were so?

"DOCTOR," SAID SACHA, "Can you give me your assurance that this injection won't harm my children?"

"Well, there's always some risk, Ms Melham. I do have a leaflet that explains everything . . ."

Sacha placed a finger on the table.

"I don't need a leaflet, Doctor. I simply want your assurance that this injection will cause Willow and Gregory no harm . . ."

Doctor James Ferriday gazed at the finger.

"As I said, there is always a small risk, but if you look, you will see that this is less than the probability of . . ."

Sacha held up her hand.

"Please, Doctor. Don't try and confuse the issue."

"I'm not trying to confuse the issue, I'm simply presenting you with the facts . . ."

Sacha rose to her feet.

"Well, I think I've heard enough. Willow, Gregory, put your coats back on. Thank you, Doctor, we'll be . . . what's that?"

James's screen flashed red and green.

"Oh dear," he said, reading the yellow writing scrolling across the monitor. "I think you should take a seat."

Sacha did so. Her son slipped his hand into hers.

"What's the matter, mummy?"

"Nothing, dear. Is everything OK, Doctor?"

"I'm sorry, Ms Melham . . ." he began, and then more kindly. "I'm sorry, Sacha, but you've crossed the threshold. I'm afraid to say, you're not allowed science any more."

"I'm what?"

"You're not allowed science any more," repeated James.

Sacha's lips moved as she tried to process what he had said.

"You're saying that you're refusing my children treatment?"

"No," said James. "Quite the opposite. You and your children will always be entitled to the best medical care. It's just that you, Sacha, no longer have a say in it. I shall administer the vaccination immediately."

"What?" Sacha sat up, eyes burning with indignation. "How dare you? I, and my husband, are the only ones who say how my family is run."

"Well, yes," said James. "But you no longer have a say in things where science is involved. You're not allowed science any more."

"I never heard anything so ridiculous! Who decided that?"

"The Universe."

"The Universe? Why should the Universe say I'm not allowed science any more?"

"Because you haven't paid science enough attention. You've had the opportunity to read the facts and the education to be able to analyse them, yet you have consistently chosen not to."

"The education?" exclaimed Sacha. "Hah! My science education was terrible. None of my teachers could explain anything properly."

"Really?" said James. "That would certainly be grounds for appeal . . ."

He pressed a couple of buttons. Tables of figures appeared on the screen.

"No," he said, shaking his head. "I'm sorry . . . it turns out that your teachers were all really rather excellent. You went to a very good public school, after all. If you look at your teachers' results you will see they added significant value to their pupils' attainment."

Sacha pouted.

"Well, they didn't like me."

"Possibly . . ."

He pressed a couple more buttons.

"What?" said Sacha, hearing his sharp intake of breath.

"Look at this," said James, scrolling down a long table. "Times and dates of occasions when you've proudly admitted to not being good at maths."

"What's the matter with that? I'm not."

"It's not the lack of ability, Sacha, it's the fact that you're proud of it. You'd never be proud of being illiterate. Why do you think your innumeracy is a cause for celebration?"

"Because . . . Well . . ."

"That's why you're not allowed science any more."

"This is outrageous!" snarled Sacha. "How can this happen?"

"Oh, that's easy," said James. "Magic."

"Magic?" said Sacha, her eyes suddenly shining. "You mean there's really such a thing?"

"Of course not. But I can't explain to you how it's really done because you're not allowed science any more."

Sacha fumbled for her handbag.

"I'm calling the BBC" she said. "I'm a producer there, you know. I'll report you."

"Report me to who you like," said James. "The story will never get out. All your cameras and microphones and things work on science."

Sacha gazed at him.

"Who gave you the right to control my life?"

"You've got it the wrong way round. You gave the right to control your life away. You're the one who chose to ignore the way the world works."

"Hah!" said Sacha. "The way the world works! Bloody scientists. You think the world is all numbers and machines and levers. You don't understand anything about the soul or spirit."

"Of course I do," said James. "I've been happily married for 20 years. I have two children that I love. I play the piano, I enjoy reading. It's just that I have additional ways of looking at things."

Sacha stood up.

"Willow, Gregory. We're going home," she glared at James. "That is if I'm still allowed to drive? You don't have something against women drivers as well do you, Doctor?"

"This is nothing to do with you being female, Ms Melham," said James, calmly. "This is purely about your attitude to science. Now, before you go, I'll administer the injection to the three of you."

"You will not! I will not allow it."

"I told you, you have no choice."

"Why? Because I disagree with you?"

For this first time, James's anger showed itself.

"No!" he snapped. "You don't get it! You're allowed to disagree with me, I want you to disagree with me! I'd love to engage in reasoned debate with you.

But until you take the trouble to understand what you're talking about, you're not allowed science any more. Now, roll up your sleeve."

Sacha muttered something under her breath.

"What's in the injection?" said James. "You know, you start asking questions like that, you might get science back . . ."

THE WOMAN WHO SHOOK
THE WORLD TREE

Michael Swanwick

Michael Swanwick lives in Philadelphia, Pennsylvania, and writes both fantasy and science fiction, at long and short lengths, for which he has received the Nebula, World Fantasy, and Hugo awards. His eighth novel, *Dancing with Bears,* was published in 2011. His eighth fiction collection, *The Best of Michael Swanwick,* appeared in 2008, and he continues to publish several stories each year, often more than one good enough to be reprinted in Year's Best volumes. He is currently at work on *Chasing the Phoenix,* a novel in which post-utopian con men Darger and Surplus accidentally conquer China.

"The Woman Who Shook the World Tree" appeared at Tor.com as part of the Palencar Project, a series of stories based on a painting. Swanwick says, "The first thought I had on seeing the illustration was, I know why her head is turned away. All the story flowed naturally from that insight. The greatest pleasure I had in writing this was putting myself in the head of a physicist as brilliant as Lise Meitner and imagining, briefly, that I could follow her thoughts."

SHE WAS NOT a pretty child. Nor did her appearance improve with age. "You'd better get yourself a good education," her mother would say, laughing. "Because you're sure not going to get by on your looks." Perhaps for this reason, perhaps not, her father demonstrated no discernible fondness for her. So, from a very early age, Mariella Coudy channeled all her energies inward, into the life of the mind.

It took some time for first her parents and then the doctors and psychiatrists they hired to realize that her dark moods, long silences, blank stares, and sudden non sequiturs were symptomatic not of a mental disorder but of her extreme brilliance. At age seven she invented what was only recognized three years later as her own, admittedly rudimentary, version of calculus. "I wanted to know how to calculate the volume defined by an irregular curve," she said when a startled mathematician from the local university deciphered her symbols, "and nobody would tell me." A tutor brought her swiftly up to postgraduate level and then was peremptorily dismissed by the child as no longer having anything to teach her. At age eleven, after thinking long and hard about what would happen if two black holes collided, she submitted a handwritten page of equations to *Applied Physics Letters*, prompting a very long phone call from its editor.

Not long thereafter, when she was still months shy of twelve years old, some very respectful people from Stanford offered her a full scholarship, room and board, and full-time supervision by a woman who made a living mentoring precocious young women. By that time, her parents were only too happy to be free of her undeniably spooky presence.

At Stanford, she made no friends but otherwise thrived. By age sixteen she had a PhD in physics. By age eighteen she had two more—one in mathematics and the other in applied deterministics, a discipline of her own devising. The Institute for Advanced Study offered her a fellowship, which she accepted and which was periodically renewed.

Twelve years went by without her doing anything of any particular note.

THEN ONE DAY, immediately after she had given a poorly received talk titled "A Preliminary Refutation of the Chronon," a handsome young man fresh out of grad school came to her office and said, "Dr. Coudy, my name is Richard Zhang and I want to work with you."

"Why?"

"Because I heard what you had to say today and I believe that your theories are going to change the way we think about everything."

"No," she said. "I mean, why should I let you work with me?"

The young man grinned with the cocky assurance of a prized and pampered wunderkind and said, "I'm the only one who actually heard what you were saying. You were speaking to one of the smartest, most open-minded audiences in the world, and they rejected your conclusions out of hand. Extraordinary claims require extraordinary proof. You need a bench man who can devise a convincing experiment and settle the matter once and for all. I may not be able to generate your insights but I can follow them. I'm a wizard with lab equipment. And I'm persistent."

Mariella Coudy doubted that last statement very much. In her experience, nobody had a fraction of the persistence she herself possessed. She'd once heard it said that few people had the patience to look at a painting for the length of time it took to eat an apple, and she knew for a fact that almost nobody could think about even the most complex equation for more than three days straight without growing weary of it.

She silently studied Zhang for as long as it would take to eat an apple. At first he tipped his head slightly, smiling in puzzlement. But then he realized that it was some sort of test and grew very still. Occasionally he blinked. But otherwise he did nothing.

Finally, Mariella said, "How do you propose to test my ideas?"

"Well, first . . ." Richard Zhang talked for a very long time.

"That won't work," she said when he was done. "But it's on the right track."

IT TOOK A year to devise the experiment, debug it, and make it work. Almost fourteen months of marathon discussions of physics and math, chalkboard duels, and passionate excursions up side issues that ultimately led nowhere, punctuated by experiments that failed heartbreakingly and then, on examination, proved in one way or another to be fundamentally flawed in their conception. Occasionally, during that time, Richard gave brief talks on their work and, because he met all questions with courteous elucidation and never once replied to an objection with a derisive snort, a blast of laughter, or a long, angry stare, a sense began to spread across the campus that Dr. Coudy might actually be on to something. The first talk drew four auditors. The last filled a lecture hall.

Finally, there came the night when Richard clamped a 500-milliwatt laser onto the steel top of a laser table with vibration-suppressing legs, took a deep breath, and said, "Okay, I think we're ready. Goggles on?"

Mariella slid her protective goggles down over her eyes.

Richard aimed a 532-nanometer beam of green laser light through a beam splitter and into a mated pair of Pockels cells. The light emerging from one went directly to the target, a white sheet of paper taped to the wall. The light from the other disappeared through a slit in the kludge of apparatus at the far side of the table. Where it emerged, Richard had set up a small mirror to bounce it to the target alongside the first green circle. He adjusted the mirror's tweaking screws, so that the two circles overlapped, creating an interference pattern.

Then he flipped the manual control on one of the cells, changing the applied voltage and rotating the plane of polarization of the beam. The interference pattern disappeared.

He flipped the control back. The interference pattern was restored.

Finally, Richard slaved the two Pockels cells to a randomizer, which would periodically vary the voltage each received—but, because it had only the one output, always the same to both and at the exact same time. He turned it on. The purpose of the randomizer was to entirely remove human volition from the process.

"Got anything memorable to say for the history books?" Richard asked.

Mariella shook her head. "Just run it."

He turned on the mechanism. Nothing hummed or made grinding noises. Reality did not distort. There was a decided lack of lightning.

They waited.

The randomizer went *click*. One of the overlapping circles on the target disappeared. The other remained.

And then the first one reappeared. Two superimposed circles creating a single interference pattern.

Richard let out his breath explosively. But Mariella touched him lightly on the arm and said, "No. There are too many other possible explanations for that phenomenon. We need to run the other half of the experiment before we can begin celebrating."

Richard nodded rapidly and turned off the laser. One circle of light disappeared immediately, the other shortly thereafter. His fingers danced over the equipment. Then, methodically, he checked every piece of it again, three times. Mariella watched, unmoving. This was his realm, not hers, and there was nothing she could do to hurry things along. But for the first time she could remember, she felt impatient and anxious to get on with it.

When everything was ready, the laser was turned on again. Twin splotches of green overlapped.

Richard switched on the apparatus. One light blinked off briefly, and then on again. (Richard's mouth opened. Mariella raised a finger to silence him.) The randomizer made no noise.

The interference pattern disappeared. Three seconds later, the randomizer went *click*. And three seconds after that, the interference pattern was restored again.

"*Yes!*" Richard ripped off his goggles and seized Mariella, lifting her up into the air and spinning her around a full three hundred and sixty degrees.

Then he kissed her.

She should have slapped him. She should have told him off. She should have thought of her position and of what people would say. Richard was six years younger than her and, what was even more of a consideration, every bit as good-looking as she was not. Nothing good could possibly come of this. She should have looked to her dignity. But what she did was to push up her goggles and kiss him back.

When finally they had to stop for air, Mariella pulled her head away from his and, more than a little stunned, managed to focus on him. He was smiling at her. His face was flushed. He was so, so very handsome. And then Richard said the most shocking thing she had ever heard in her life: "Oh, God, I've been wanting to do that for the longest time."

THAT NIGHT, AFTER they'd gone to Mariella's apartment and done things she'd known all her life she would *never* do, and then babbled about the experiment at each other, and agreed that the title of the paper should be "The abolition of time as a meaningful concept," and then went through the cycle all over again, and her lips were actually sore from all the kissing they did, and Richard had finally, out of exhaustion no doubt, fallen asleep naked alongside her . . . after all that, Mariella held the pillow tightly over her face and wept silently into it because for the first time in her life she was absolutely, completely happy, and because she knew it wouldn't last and that come morning Richard would regain his senses and leave her forever.

But in the morning Richard did not leave. Instead, he rummaged in her refrigerator and found the makings of huevos rancheros and cooked her breakfast. Then they went to the lab. Richard took pictures of everything with a little digital camera ("This is historic—they'll want to preserve everything exactly the way it is") while she wrote a preliminary draft of the paper on a yellow pad. When she was done, he had her sign it on the bottom and wrote his name after hers.

Mariella Coudy and Richard M. Zhang. Together in eternity.

Mariella and Richard spent the next several weeks in a blissful mix of physics and romance. He bought her roses. She corrected his math. They both sent out preprints of their paper, she to everybody whose opinion she thought worth having, and he to everyone else. No matter how many times they changed and laundered them, it seemed the bed sheets were always sweat-stained and rumpled.

One night, seemingly out of nowhere, Richard said "I love you," and without stopping to think, Mariella replied, "You can't."

"Why not?"

"I have a mirror. I know what I look like."

Richard cradled her face in his hands and studied it seriously. "You're not beautiful," he said—and something deep inside her cried out in pain. "But I'm glad you're not. When I look at your face, my heart leaps up in joy. If you looked like"—he named a movie star—"I could never be sure it wasn't just infatuation. But this way I know for sure. It's you I love. This person, this body, this beautiful brain. You, here, right now, you." He smiled that smile she loved so much. "Q.E.D."

THEIR PARADISE ENDED one morning when they encountered a clutch of cameramen standing outside Mariella's office. "What's all this?" she asked, thinking that there'd been a robbery or that somebody famous had died.

A microphone was thrust at her face. "Are you the woman who's destroyed time?"

"What? No! Ridiculous."

"Have you seen today's papers?" A copy of the *New York Times* was brandished but she couldn't possibly read the headlines with it waving around like that.

"I don't—"

Richard held up both hands and said, "Gentlemen! Ladies! Please! Yes, this is Dr. Mariella Coudy, and I'm her junior partner on the paper. Dr. Coudy was absolutely right when she denied destroying time. There is no such thing as time. There's only the accumulation of consequences."

"If there's no such thing as time, does that mean it's possible to travel into the past? Visit ancient Rome? Hunt dinosaurs?" Several reporters laughed.

"There's no such thing as the past, either—only an infinite, ever-changing present."

"What's that supposed to mean?" somebody asked.

"That's an extremely good question. I'm afraid that I can't adequately answer it without using a lot of very complicated equations. Let's just say that the past never really goes away, while the future exists only relative to the immediate moment."

"If there is no time, then what is there?"

"Happenstance," Richard said. "A tremendous amount of happenstance."

It was all ludicrously oversimplified to the point of being meaningless, but the reporters ate it up. Richard's explanations gave them the illusion that they sort-of kind-of understood what was being talked about, when the truth was that they didn't even have the mathematics to be misinformed. When, eventually, the reporters ran out of questions, packed their equipment, and left, Mariella angrily said, "What the hell was all that about?"

"Public relations. We've just knocked the props out from under one of the few things that everybody thinks they understand. That's going to get people excited. Some of them are going to hate us for what we've done to their world."

"The world's the same as it ever was. The only thing that'll be different is our understanding of it."

"Tell that to Darwin."

THAT WAS THE bad side of fame. The good side was money. Suddenly, money was everywhere. There was enough money to do anything except the one thing Mariella wanted most, which was to be left alone with Richard, her thoughts, a blackboard, and a piece of chalk. Richard acquired a great deal of what was surely extremely expensive equipment, and hit the lecture circuit— "Somebody has to," he said cheerily, "and, God knows, you won't"—to explain their findings. So she was alone again, as often as not.

She used these empty spaces in her life to think about existence without time. She tried not to imagine he was with other women.

Whenever Richard returned from the road, they had furious reunions and she would share her tentative, half-formed thoughts with him. One evening he asked "What is the shape of happenstance?" and Mariella had no answer for him. In short order he had canceled all his speaking engagements and there was an enormous 3-D visualization tank in his lab, along with the dedicated processing power of several Crayflexes at his disposal. Lab assistants whose names she could never get straight scurried about doing things, while Richard directed and orchestrated and obsessed. Suddenly, he had very little time for her. Until one day he brought her in to show her a single black speck in the murky blue-gray tank.

"We have pinned down one instantiation of happenstance!" he said proudly.

A month later, there were three specks. A week after that there were a thousand. Increasingly rapidly, the very first map of reality took shape: It looked like a tornado at first, with a thick and twisting trunk. Then it sprouted limbs, some of them a good third as thick as what Richard dubbed the Main Sequence. These looped upward or downward, it seemed to make no difference, giving birth to smaller limbs, or perhaps "tentacles" was a better word for them, which wound about each other, sometimes dwindling to nothing, other times rejoining the main trunk.

Richard called it the Monster. But in Mariella's eyes it was not monstrous at all. It had the near-organic look of certain fractal mathematical formulae. It flowed and twisted elegantly, like branches frozen in the act of dancing in the breeze. It was what it was—and that was beautiful.

It looked like a tree. A tree whose roots and crown were lost in the distance. A tree vast enough to contain all the universe.

Pictures of it leaked out, of course. The lab techs had taken snapshots and shared them with friends who posted them online. This brought back the press, and this time they were not so easy to deal with, for they quickly learned that Richard and Mariella were an item. The disparity of age and appearance, which would have been nothing were she male and he female, was apparently custom-made for the tabloids—louche enough to be scandalous, romantic enough to be touching, easy to snark about. One of the papers stitched together two pictures with Photoshop and ran it under the headline BEAUTY AND THE BEAST. There was no possible confusion who was supposed to be what. Another ran what even Mariella thought was an unfair rendering of her face alongside the map of reality and asked WHICH IS THE MONSTER?

It astonished her how much this hurt.

This time Richard was not so accommodating. "You bastards crossed a line," he told one reporter. "So, no, I'm not going to explain anything to you or any of your idiot kind. If you want to understand our work, you'll just have to go back to school for another eight years. Assuming you have the brains for it." Furiously, he retreated to his lab, the way another man might have hit the bars, and stared at the Monster for several hours.

Then he sought out Mariella and asked, "If time is unidirectional in Minkowski space, and there is no time—then what remains?" Initiating another long, sexless, and ecstatic night. After which he left the mapping project for his grad students to run without him. He obtained two new labs—exactly how was never clear to Mariella, who was so innocent of practical matters that she didn't even have a driver's license—and began to build another experiment. Half his new equipment went into one lab, which he called the Slingshot, and the rest into the second, on the far side of the campus, which he called the Target.

"If this works," he said, "it will change everything. People will be able to travel from and to anywhere in the universe."

"So long as there's the proper machinery to receive them when they get there."

"Yes, of course."

"And provided it doesn't simply blow itself to hell. I have my suspicions about the energy gradient between your two sites."

There was that grin again—the grin of a man who knew that nothing could possibly go wrong, and that everything must inevitably work out right. "Don't you worry about a thing," Richard said. "You're still the senior partner. I won't do anything until you assure me that it's perfectly safe."

THE NEXT DAY there was an explosion that shook the entire campus. Mariella ran outside and saw people pouring from all the buildings. A black balloon of smoke tumbled upward over the rooftops.

It came from the Target.

Richard had told her he'd be spending the entire day there.

Somehow, Mariella was running. Somehow, she was there. The entire building had been reduced to smoldering rubble. Parts of what remained were on fire. It smelled like burning garbage.

A hand touched her arm. It was Dr. Inglehoff. Laura. "Maybe Richard wasn't in the building," she said. "I'm sure he's all right." Her expression was grotesque with compassion.

Mariella stared at the woman in perplexity. "Where else would he be? At this time of day? Why would he be anywhere else?"

Then people whom she had never before appreciated were, if not precisely her friends, at the very least close colleagues, were leading her away. She was in a room. There was a nurse giving her a shot. Somebody said, "Sleep is the best doctor."

Mariella slept.

When she awoke and Richard was not there, she knew her romance was over. Somebody told her that the explosion was so thorough that nothing readily identifiable as human remains had yet been found. That same person said there was always hope. But that was nonsense. If Richard were alive, he'd have been by her side. He was not, and therefore he was dead.

Q., as he would have said, E.D.

The ensuing week was the worst period of her life. Mariella effectively stopped sleeping. Sometimes she zoned out and came to herself eight or ten or fifteen hours later, in the middle of frying an egg or sorting through her notes. But you could hardly call that sleep. Somehow she kept herself fed. Apparently her body wanted to go on living, even if she didn't.

She kept thinking of Richard, lost to her, swept away further and further into the past.

But of course there was no past. So he wasn't even there.

One night, driven by obscure impulses, she found herself fully dressed and hurrying across the campus at three a.m. Clearly, she was going to Richard's lab—the surviving of the two new ones, the Slingshot. The building loomed up before her, dark and empty.

When she threw the light switch, mountains of electronic devices snapped into existence. Richard's first experiment could have been run on a kitchen table. This one looked like the stage set for a Wagnerian opera. It was amazing how money could complicate even the simplest demonstration proof.

Mariella began flicking switches, bringing the beast to life. Things hummed and made grinding noises. Test patterns leaped to life on flat screens and then wavered in transient distortions. Something snapped and sparked, leaving the tang of ozone in the air.

This was not her bailiwick. But because it was Richard's and because he had wanted her to understand it, she knew what to do.

There was, after all, no such thing as time. Only the accumulation of consequences.

But first there was a chore to do. All of Richard's notes were on a battered old laptop lying atop a stack of reference books on his desk. She bundled them together and then attached the bundle to an email reading simply, "So you will understand what happened." This she sent to his entire mailing list. Surely someone on it would have the wit to appreciate what he had done. Her own notes were all safe in her office. She had no doubt there would be people looking for them in the wake of what she had to do.

The experiment was ready to run. All she had to do was connect a few cables and then walk through what looked uncannily like a wrought-iron pergola, such as one might expect to find in a Victorian garden. It was entirely possible that's what it was; Richard was never one to hold out for proper equipment when some perfectly adequate piece of bricolage was close at hand.

Mariella connected the cables. Then she checked all the connections three times, not because it was necessary but because that was how Richard would have done it.

She did not bother to check the setting, however. There was only one possible instantiation of happenstance the apparatus could be set for. And she already knew it would work.

She walked through the pergola.

In that timeless instant of transition, Mariella realized that in his own way Richard possessed a genius approaching her own. (Had she really underestimated him all this while? Yes, she had.) Crossing to the far side of the campus in a single step, she felt a wave of she-knew-not-what-energies pass through her body and brain—she actually *felt* it in her brain!—and knew that she was experiencing a sensation no human being had ever felt before.

The air wavered before her and Mariella was through. Richard stood, his back to her, alive and fussing with a potentiometer. For the second time in her life, she was absolutely, completely happy.

"Richard." The word escaped her unbidden.

He turned and saw her and in the instant before the inequality of forces across the gradient of happenstance grounded itself, simultaneously destroying both laboratories a sixteenth of a mile and eight days apart and smashing the two lovers to nothing, a smile, natural and unforced, blossomed on Richard's face.

NAHIKU WEST

Linda Nagata

Linda Nagata "grew up in a rented beach house on the north shore of Oahu. She graduated from the University of Hawaii with a degree in zoology and worked for a time at Haleakala National Park, on the island of Maui, where she continues to live with her husband in their longtime home. She's been a writer, a mom, a programmer of database-driven Web sites, and lately a publisher and book designer." She is the author of novels and stories, including *The Bohr Maker,* winner of the Locus Award for Best First Novel, and the novella "Goddesses," winner of the Nebula Award for Best Novella. Though best known for her science fiction, she also writes fantasy, exemplified by her "scoundrel lit" series Stories of the Puzzlelands. Her most recent work is a near-future military science fiction thriller, *The Red: First Light.*

"Nahiku West" was published in the e-book anthology *Solaris 1.5.* It is a complex, intricate science fiction mystery story in a future setting that is carefully revealed as the story progresses. It is an interesting contrast to the Cadigan story earlier in this book.

A RAILCAR WAS ferrying Key Lu across the tether linking Nahiku East and West when a micrometeor popped through the car's canopy, leaving two neat holes that vented the cabin to hard vacuum within seconds. The car continued on the track, but it took over a minute for it to reach the gel lock at Nahiku West and pass through into atmosphere. No one expected to find Key Lu alive, but as soon as the car re-pressurized, he woke up.

Sometimes, it's a crime not to die.

I STEPPED INTO the interrogation chamber. Key had been sitting on one of two padded couches, but when he saw me he bolted to his feet. I stood very still, hearing the door lock behind me. Nothing in Key's background indicated he was a violent man, but prisoners sometimes panic. I raised my hand slightly, as a gel ribbon armed with a paralytic spray slid from my forearm to my palm, ready for use if it came to that.

"Please," I said, keeping the ribbon carefully concealed. "Sit down."

Key slowly subsided onto the couch, never taking his frightened eyes off me.

Most of the celestial cities restrict the height and weight of residents to minimize the consumption of volatiles, but Commonwealth police officers are required to be taller and more muscular than the average citizen. I used to be a smaller man, but during my time at the academy adjustments were made. I faced Key Lu with a physical presence optimized to trigger a sense of intimidation in the back brain of a nervous suspect, an effect enhanced by the black fabric of my uniform. Its design was simple—shorts cuffed at the knees and a lightweight pullover with long sleeves that covered the small arsenal of chemical ribbons I carried on my forearms—but its light-swallowing color set me apart from the bright fashions of the celestial cities.

I sat down on the couch opposite Key Lu. He was a well-designed man, nothing eccentric about him, just another good-looking citizen. His hair was presently blond, his eyebrows darker. His balanced face lacked strong features. The only thing notable about him was his injuries. Dark bruises surrounded his eyes and their whites had turned red from burst blood vessels. More bruises discolored swollen tissue beneath his coppery skin.

We studied each other for several seconds, both knowing what was at stake. I was first to speak. "I'm Officer Zeke Choy—"

"I know who you are."

"—of the Commonwealth Police, the watch officer here at Nahiku."

The oldest celestial cities orbited Earth, but Nahiku was newer. It was one in a cluster of three orbital habitats that circled the Sun together, just inside the procession of Venus.

Key Lu addressed me again, with the polite insistence of a desperate man. "I didn't know about the quirk, Officer Choy. I thought I was legal."

The machine voice of a Dull Intelligence whispered into my auditory nerve that he was lying. I already knew that, but I nodded anyway, pretending to believe him.

The DI was housed within my atrium, a neural organ that served as an interface between mind and machine. Atriums are a legal enhancement—they don't change human biology—but Key Lu's quirked physiology that had allowed him to survive short-term exposure to hard vacuum was definitely not.

I was sure his quirk had been done before the age of consent. He'd been born in the Far Reaches among the fragile holdings of the asteroid prospectors, where it must have looked like a reasonable gamble to bioengineer some insurance into his system. Years had passed since then; enforcement had grown stricter. Though Key Lu looked perfectly ordinary, by the law of the Commonwealth, he wasn't even human.

I met his gaze, hoping he was no fool. "Don't tell me anything I don't want to know," I warned him.

I let him consider this for several seconds before I went on. "Your enhancement is illegal under the statutes of the Commonwealth—"

"I understand that, but I didn't know about it."

I nodded my approval of this lie. I needed to maintain the fiction that he hadn't known. It was the only way I could help him. "I'll need your consent to remove it."

A spark of hope ignited in his blooded eyes. "Yes! Yes, of course."

"So recorded." I stood, determined to get the quirk out of his system as soon as possible, before awkward questions could be asked. "Treatment can begin right—"

The door to the interrogation room opened.

I was so startled, I turned with my hand half raised, ready to trigger the ribbon of paralytic still hidden in my palm—only to see Magistrate Glory Mina walk in, flanked by two uniformed cops I'd never seen before.

My DI sent the ribbon retreating back up my forearm while I greeted Glory with a scowl. Nahiku was my territory. I was the only cop assigned to the little city and I was used to having my own way—but with the magistrate's arrival I'd just been overridden.

GOODS TRAVEL ON robotic ships between the celestial cities, but people rarely do. We ghost instead. A ghost—an electronic persona—moves between the data gates at the speed of light. Most ghosts are received on a machine grid or within the virtual reality of a host's atrium, but every city keeps a cold-storage mausoleum. If you have the money—or if you're a cop—you can grow a duplicate body in another city, fully replicated hard copy, ready to roll.

Glory Mina presided over the circuit court based out of Red Star, the primary city in our little cluster. She would have had to put her Red Star body into cold storage before waking up the copy here at Nahiku, but that was hardly more than half an hour's effort. From the eight cops who had husks stashed in the mausoleum, she'd probably pulled two at random to make up the officers for her court.

I was supposed to get a notification anytime a husk in the mausoleum woke up, but obviously she'd overridden that too.

GLORY MINA WAS a small woman with skin the color of cinnamon, and thick, shiny black hair that she kept in a stubble cut. She looked at me curiously, her eyebrows arched. "Officer Choy, I saw the incident report, but I missed your request for a court."

The two cops had positioned themselves on either side of the door.

"I didn't file a request, Magistrate."

"And why not?"

"This is not a criminal case."

No doubt her DI dutifully informed her I was lying—not that she couldn't figure that out for herself. "I don't think that's been determined, Officer Choy. There are records that still need to be considered, which have not made their way into the case file."

I had looked into Key Lu's background. I knew he never translated his persona into an electronic ghost. If he'd ever done so, his illegal quirk would have been detected when he passed through a data gate. I knew he'd never kept a backup record that could be used to restore his body in case of accident. Again, if he'd done so, his quirk would have been revealed. And he never, ever physically left Nahiku, because without a doubt he would have been exposed when he passed through a port gate. The court could use any one of those circumstances to justify interrogation under a coercive drug—which is why I hadn't included any of it in the case file.

"Magistrate, this is a minor case—"

"There are no minor cases, Officer Choy. You're dismissed for now, but please, wait outside."

There was nothing else I could do. I left the room knowing Key Lu was a dead man.

I COULD HAVE cleaned things up if I'd just had more time. I could have cured Key Lu. I'm a molecular designer and my skills are the reason I was drafted into the Commonwealth police.

Technically, I could have refused to join, but then my home city of Haskins would have been assessed a huge fine—and the city council would have tried to pass the debt on to me. So I consoled myself with the knowledge that I would be working on the cutting edge of molecular research and, swallowing my misgivings, I swore to uphold the laws of the Commonwealth, however arcane and asinine they might be.

I worked hard at my job. I tried to do some good, and though I skirted the boundaries now and then, I made very sure I never went too far because if I got myself fired, the debt for my training would be on me, and the contracts I'd have to take to pay that off didn't bear thinking on.

THE MAGISTRATE REQUIRED me to attend the execution, assigning me to stand watch beside the door. I used a mood patch to ensure a proper state of detachment. It's a technique they taught us at the academy, and as I watched the two other officers escort Key Lu into the room, I could tell from their faces they were tranked too, while Key Lu was glassy-eyed, more heavily sedated than the rest of us.

He was guided to a cushioned chair. One of the cops worked an IV into his arm. Five civilians were present, seated in a half circle on either side of the magistrate. One of them was weeping. Her name was Hera Poliu. I knew her because she was a friend of my intimate, Tishembra Indens—but Tishembra had never mentioned that Hera and Key were involved.

The magistrate spoke, summarizing the crime and the sanctity of Commonwealth law, reminding us the law existed to guard society's shared idea of what it means to be human, and that the consequences of violating the law were mandated to be both swift and certain. She nodded at one of the cops, who turned a knob on the IV line, admitting an additional ingredient to the feed. Key Lu slumped and closed his eyes. Hera wept louder, but it was already over.

NAHIKU WAS JUSTLY famed for its vista walls, which transformed blank corridors into fantasy spaces. On Level Seven West, where I lived, the theme was a wilderness maze, enhanced by faint rainforest scents, rustling leaves, bird song, and ghostly puffs of humidity. Apartment doors didn't appear until you asked for them.

The path forked. I went right. Behind me, a woman called my name, "Officer Choy!" Her voice was loud and so vindictive that when the DI whispered in my mind, Hera Poliu, I thought, No way. I knew Hera and she didn't sound like that. I turned fast.

It was Hera all right, but not like I'd ever seen her. Her fists were clenched, her face flushed, her brows knit in a furious scowl. The DI assessed her as rationally angry, but it didn't seem that way to me. When she stepped into my personal space I felt a chill. "I want to file a complaint," she informed me.

Hera was a full head shorter than me, thin and willowy, with rich brown skin and auburn hair wound up in a knot behind her head. Tishembra had invited her over for dinner a few times and we'd all gone drinking together, but as our eyes locked I felt I was looking at a stranger. "What sort of complaint, Hera?"

"Don't patronize me." I saw no sign in her face of the heart-rending grief she'd displayed at the execution. "The Commonwealth police are supposed to protect us from quirks like Key."

"Key never hurt anyone," I said softly.

"He has now! You didn't hear the magistrate's assessment. She's fined the city for every day since Key became a citizen. We can't afford it, Choy. You know Nahiku already has debt problems—"

"I can't help you, Hera. You need to file an appeal with the magistrate—"

"I want to file a complaint! The city can't get fined for harboring quirks if we turn them in. So I'm reporting Tishembra Indens."

I stepped back. A cold sweat broke out across my skin as I looked away.

Hera laughed. "You already know she's a quirk, don't you? You're a cop, Choy! A Commonwealth cop, infatuated with a quirk."

I lost my temper. "What's wrong with you? Tishembra's your friend."

"So was Key. And both of them immigrants."

"I can't randomly scan people because they're immigrants."

"If you don't scan her, I'll go to the magistrate."

I tried to see through her anger, but the Hera I knew wasn't there. "No need to bother the magistrate," I said softly, soothingly. "I'll do it."

She nodded, the corner of her lip lifting a little. "I look forward to hearing the result."

I STEPPED INTO the apartment to find Tishembra's three-year-old son Robin playing on the floor, shaping bridges and wheels out of colorful gel pods. He looked up at me, a handsome boy with his mother's dark skin and her black, glossy curls, but not her reserved manner. I was treated to a mischievous grin and a firm order to, "Watch this!" Then he hurled himself onto his creations, smashing them all back into disks of jelly.

Tishembra stepped out of the bedroom, lean and dark and elegant, her long hair hanging down her back in a lovely chaos of curls. She'd changed from her work clothes into a silky white shift that I knew was only mindless fabric and still somehow it clung in all the right places as if a DI was controlling the fibers. She was a city engineer. Two years ago she'd emigrated to Nahiku, buying citizenship for herself and Robin—right before the city went into massive debt over an investment in a water-bearing asteroid that turned out to have no water. She was bitter over it, more so because the deal had been made before she arrived, but she shared in the loss anyway.

I crossed the room. She met me halfway. I'd been introduced to her on my second day at Nahiku, seven months ago now, and I'd never looked back. Taking her in my arms, I held her close, letting her presence fill me up as it always did. I breathed in her frustration and her fury and for a giddy moment everything else was blotted from my mind. I was addicted to her moods, all of them. Joy and anger were just different aspects of the same enthralling, intoxicating woman—and the more time I spent with her the more deeply she could touch me in that way. It wasn't love alone. Over time I'd come to realize she had a subtle quirk that let her emotions seep out onto the air around her. Tishembra tended to be reserved and distant. I think the quirk helped her connect with people she casually knew, letting her be perceived as more open and likeable, and easing her way as an immigrant into Nahiku's tightly-knit culture—but it wasn't something we could ever talk about.

"You were part of it, weren't you?" she asked me in an angry whisper. "You were part of what happened to Key. Why didn't you stop it?"

Tishembra had taken a terrible chance in getting close to me.

Her fingers dug into my back. "I'm trapped here, Zeke. With the new fine, on top of the old debt . . . Robin and I will be working a hundred years to earn our way free." She looked up at me, her lip curled in a way that reminded me too much of Hera's parting expression. "It's gotten to the point, my best hope is another disaster. If the city is sold off, I could at least start fresh—"

"Tish, that doesn't matter now." I spoke very softly, hoping Robin wouldn't overhear. "I've received a complaint against you."

Her sudden fear was a radiant thing, washing over me, making me want to hold her even closer, comfort her, keep her forever safe.

"It's ridiculous, of course," I murmured. "To think you're a quirk. I mean, you've been through the gates. So you're clean."

Thankfully, my DI never bothered to point out when I was lying.

Tishembra nodded to let me know she understood. She wouldn't tell me anything I didn't want to know; I wouldn't ask her questions—because the less I knew, the better.

My hope rested on the fact that she could not have had the quirk when she came through the port gate into Nahiku. Maybe she'd acquired it in the two years since, or maybe she'd stripped it out when she'd passed through the gate. I was hoping she knew how to strip it again.

"I have to do the scan," I warned her. "Soon. If I don't, the magistrate will send someone who will."

"Tonight?" she asked in a voice devoid of expression. "Or tomorrow?"

I kissed her forehead. "Tomorrow, love. That's soon enough."

ROBIN WAS ASLEEP. Tishembra lay beside him on the bed, her eyes half closed, her focus inward as she used her atrium to track the progress of processes I couldn't see. I sat in a chair and watched her. I didn't have to ask if the extraction was working. I knew it was. Her presence was draining away, becoming fainter, weaker, like a memory fading into time.

After a while it got to be too much, waiting for the woman I knew to become someone else altogether. "I'm going out for a while," I said. She didn't answer. Maybe she didn't hear me. I re-armed myself with my chemical arsenal of gel ribbons. Then I put my uniform back on, and I left.

ALL CELESTIAL CITIES have their own municipal police force. It's often a part-time, amateur operation, but the local force is supposed to investigate traditional crimes like theft, assault, murder—all the heinous things people have done to each other since the beginning of time. The Commonwealth police are involved only when the crime violates statutes involving molecular science, biology, or machine intelligence.

So strictly speaking, I didn't have any legal right or requirement to investigate the original accident that had exposed Key's quirk, but I took the elevator up to Level 1 West anyway, and used my authority to get past the DI that secured the railcar garage.

Nahiku is a twin orbital. Its two inhabited towers are counterweights at opposite ends of a very long carbon-fiber tether that lets them spin around a center point, generating a pseudogravity in the towers. A rail runs the length of the tether, linking Nahiku East and West. The railcar Key Lu had failed to die in was parked in a small repair bay in the West-end garage. Repair work hadn't started on it yet, and the two small holes in its canopy were easy to see.

There was no one around, maybe because it was local-night. That worked for me: I didn't have to concoct a story on why I'd made this my investigation. I started collecting images, measurements, and sample swabs. When the DI picked up traces of explosive residue, I wasn't surprised.

I was inside the car, collecting additional samples from every interior surface, when a faint shift in air pressure warned me a door had opened. Footsteps approached. I don't know who I was expecting. Hera, maybe. Or Tishembra. Not the magistrate.

Glory Mina walked up to the car and, resting her hand on the roof, she bent down to peer at me where I sat on the ruptured upholstery.

"Is there more going on here that I need to know about?" she asked.

I sent her the DI's report. She received it in her atrium, scanned it, and followed my gaze to one of the holes in the canopy. "You're thinking someone tried to kill him."

"Why like this?" I wondered. "Is it coincidence? Or did they know about his quirk?"

"What difference does it make?"

"If the attacker knew about Key, then it was murder by cop."

"And if not, it was just an attempted murder. Either way, it's not your case. This one belongs to the city cops."

I shook my head. I couldn't leave it alone. Maybe that's why my superiors tolerated me. "I like to know what's going on in my city, and the big question I have is why? I'm not buying a coincidence. Whoever blew the canopy had to know about Key—so why not just kill him outright? If he'd died like any normal person, I wouldn't have looked into it, you wouldn't have assessed a fine. Who gains, when everyone loses?"

Even as I said the words my thoughts turned to Tishembra, and what she'd said. It's gotten to the point, my best hope is another disaster. No. I wasn't going to go there. Not with Tishembra. But maybe she wasn't the only one thinking that way?

The magistrate watched me closely, no doubt recording every nuance of my expression. She said, "I saw the complaint against your intimate."

"It's baseless."

"But you'll look into it?"

"I've scheduled a scan."

Glory nodded. "See to that, but stay out of the local case. This one doesn't belong to you."

THE APARTMENT FELT empty when I returned. I panicked for the few seconds it took me to sprint across the front room to the bedroom door. Tishembra was still lying on the bed, her half-closed eyes blinking sporadically, but

I couldn't feel her. Not like before. A sense of abandonment came over me. I knew it was ridiculous, but I felt like she'd walked away.

Robin whimpered in his sleep, turned over, and then awoke. He looked first at Tishembra lying next to him, and then he looked at me. "What happened to mommy?"

"Mommy's okay."

"She's not. She's wrong."

I went over and picked him up. "Hush. Don't ever say that to anyone but me, okay? We need it to be a secret."

He pouted, but he was frightened, and he agreed.

I SPENT THAT night in the front room, with Robin cradled in my arm. I didn't sleep much. I couldn't stop thinking about Key and his quirk, and who might have known about it. Maybe someone from his past? Or someone who'd done a legal mod on him? I had the DI import his personal history into my atrium, but there was no record of any bioengineering work being done on him. Maybe it had just been a lucky guess by someone who knew what went on in the Far Reaches? I sent the DI to search the city files for anyone else who'd ever worked out there. Only one name came back to me: Tishembra Indens.

Tishembra and I had never talked much about where we'd come from. I knew circumstances had not been kind to her, but that she'd had to take a contract in the Far Reaches—that shocked me.

My best hope is another disaster.

I deleted the query, I tried to stop thinking, but I couldn't help reflecting that she was an engineer. She had skills. She could work out how to pop the canopy and she'd have access to the supplies to do it.

Eventually I dozed, until Tishembra woke me. I stared at her. I knew her face, but I didn't know her. I couldn't feel her anymore. Her quirk was gone, and she was a stranger to me. I sat up. Robin was still asleep and I cradled his little body against my chest, dreading what would happen when he woke.

"I'm ready," Tishembra said.

I looked away. "I know."

ROBIN WOULDN'T LET his mother touch him. "You're not you!" he screamed at her with all the fury a three-year-old could muster. Tishembra started to argue with him, but I shook my head, "Deal with it later," and took him into the dining nook, where I got him breakfast and reminded him of our secret.

"I want mommy," he countered with a stubborn pout.

I considered tranking him, but the staff at the day-venture center would notice and they would ask questions, so I did my best to persuade him that mommy was mommy. He remained skeptical. As we left the apartment, he refused to hold Tishembra's hand but ran ahead instead, hiding behind the jungle foliage until we caught up, then running off again. I didn't blame him. In my rotten heart I didn't want to touch her either, but I wasn't three. So the next time he took off, I slipped my arm around Tishembra's waist and hauled her aside into a nook along the path. We didn't ever kiss or hold hands when I was in uniform and besides, I'd surprised her when her mind was fixed on more serious things, so of course she protested. "Zeke, what are you doing?"

"Hush," I said loudly. "Do you want Robin to find us?"

And I kissed her. I didn't want to. She knew it, and resisted, whispering, "You don't need to feel sorry for me."

But I'd gotten a taste of her mouth, and that hadn't changed. I wanted more. She felt it and softened against me, returning my kiss in a way that made me think we needed to go back to the apartment for a time.

Then Robin was pushing against my hip. "No! Stop that kissing stuff. We have to go to day-venture."

I scowled down at him. "Fine, but I'm holding Tishembra's hand."

"No. I am." And to circumvent further argument, he seized her hand and tugged her toward the path. I let her go with a smirk, but her defiant gaze put an end to that.

"I do love you," I insisted. She shrugged and went with Robin, too proud to believe in me just yet.

DAY-VENTURE WAS ON Level 5, where there was a prairie vista. On either side of the path we looked out across a vast land of low, grassy hills, where some sort of herd animals fed in the distance. Waist-high grass grew in a nook outside the doorway to the day-venture center. Robin stomped through it, sending a flutter of butterflies spiraling toward a blue sky. The grass sprang back without damage, betraying a biomechanical nature that the butterflies shared. One of them floated back down to land on Tishembra's hand. She started to shoo it away, but Robin shrieked, "Don't flick it!" and he pounced. "It's a message fly." The butterfly's blue wings spread open as it rested in his small palms. A message was written there, shaped out of white scales drained of pigment, but Robin didn't know how to read yet, so he looked to his mother for help. "What does it say?"

Tishembra gave me a dark look. Then she crouched to read the message and I saw a slight uptick in the corner of her lip. "It says Robin and Zeke love Tishembra." Then she ran her finger down the butterfly's back to erase the message, and nudged it, sending it fluttering away.

"It's wrong," Robin told her defiantly. "I don't love Tishembra. I love mommy." Then he threw his arms around her neck and kissed her, before running inside to play with his friends.

Tishembra and I went on to my office, where Glory Mina was waiting for us to arrive.

When Tishembra saw the magistrate she turned to me with a look of desperation. I told her the truth. "It doesn't matter."

A deep scan is performed with an injection of molecular-scale machines called Makers that map the body's component systems. The data is fed directly into police records and there's no way to fake the results. Tishembra should have known that, but she looked at me as if I'd betrayed her. "You don't have to worry," I insisted. "The scan is just a formality, a required response in the face of the baseless complaint filed against you."

Glory Mina watched me with a half smile. Naturally, her DI would have told her I was lying.

I led Tishembra into a small exam room and had her sit in a large, cushioned chair. After Glory came in behind us, the office DI locked the door. I handed Tishembra a packet of Makers and she dutifully inhaled it. At the same time my DI whispered that Hera Poliu had arrived in the outer office. Sensing trouble, I looked at the magistrate. "I need to talk to her."

"Who?" Tishembra asked anxiously. "Zeke, what's going on?"

"Nothing's going on. Everything will be fine."

Glory just watched me. I grunted, realizing she'd come not to observe the scan but to gauge the integrity of her Nahiku watch officer, which she had good cause to doubt. "I'll be right back."

The office DI maintained a continuous surveillance of all rooms. I channeled its feed, keeping one eye on Tishembra and another on Hera as she looked around the front office with an anxious gaze. She appeared timid and unsure—nothing at all like the angry woman who had accosted me yesterday. "Zeke?" she called softly. "Are you here?"

When the door opened ahead of me, she startled.

"Zeke!" Hera's hands were shaking. "Is it true Tishembra's been scheduled for a scan? She didn't have anything to do with Key. You have to know that. She hardly knew him. There's no reason to suspect her. Tishembra is my best engineer and if we lose her this city will never recover . . . Zeke? What is it?"

I think I was standing with my mouth open. "You filed the complaint that initiated the scan!"

"Me? I . . ." Her focus turned inward. "Oh, yesterday . . . I wasn't myself. I took the wrong mood patch. I was out of my head. Is Tishembra . . . ?"

The results of the scan arrived in my atrium. I glanced at them, and closed my eyes briefly in silent thanks. "Tishembra has passed her scan."

AGAINST ALL EXPECTATION I'd made a home at Nahiku. I'd found a woman I loved, I'd made friends, and I'd gained trust—to the point that people would come to me for advice and guidance, knowing I wasn't just another jackboot of the Commonwealth.

In one day all that had been shattered and I wanted to know why.

I sent a DI hunting through the datasphere for background on Key Lu. I sent another searching through Hera Poliu's past. I thought about sending a third after Tishembra—but whatever the DI turned up would go into police records and I was afraid of what it might find.

Tish had used a patch to calm herself, resolved to go into work as if nothing was changed. "I'm fine," she insisted when I said I'd walk with her. She resented my coddling, but there were questions I needed to ask. We took the elevator, stepping out into a corridor enhanced with a seascape. The floor appeared as weathered boardwalk; our feet struck it in hollow thumps. Taking her arm, I gently guided her to a nook where a strong breeze blew, carrying what I'm told is the salt scent of an ocean, and hiding the sound of our voices. "Tish, is there anything you need to tell me?"

Resentment simmered in her eyes. "What exactly are you asking?"

"You spent time in the Far Reaches."

"So?"

"Did you know about Key Lu?"

I deserved the contempt that blossomed in her expression. "There are hundreds of tiny settlements out there, Zeke. Maybe thousands. I didn't know him. I didn't know him here, either."

The DI returned an initial infodump. My focus wavered. Tishembra saw it. "What?" she asked me.

"Key Lu was a city finance officer, one who signed off on the water deal."

"The water deal with no water," she amended bitterly. Crossing her arms, she glared at the ocean.

"Someone tried to kill him," I told her, letting my words blend in with the sea breeze.

She froze, her gaze fixed on the horizon.

"There was never a micrometeor. His railcar was sabotaged."

I couldn't read her face and neither could the DI. Maybe it was the patch she'd used to level her emotions, but her fixed expression frightened me.

She knew what was going on in my head, though. "You're asking yourself who has the skill to do that, aren't you? Who could fake a meteor strike? If it were me, I'd do it with explosive patches, one inside, one outside, to get the trajectory correct. Is that how it was done, Zeke?"

"Yes."

Her gaze was still fixed on the horizon. "It wasn't me."

"Okay."

She turned and looked me in the eye. "It wasn't me."

The DI whispered that she spoke the truth. I smiled my relief and reached for her, but she backed away. "No, Zeke."

"Tish, come on. Don't be mad. This day is making us both crazy."

"I haven't accused you of being a murderer."

"Tish, I'm sorry."

She shook her head. "I remember when we used to trust each other. I think that was yesterday."

The second DI arrived with an initial report on Hera. Like an idiot, I scanned the file. To my surprise, I had a new suspect, but while I was distracted, Tishembra walked away.

GLORY MINA WAS waiting for me when I returned to my office. She'd tracked my DIs and copied herself on their reports. "You should have been a municipal cop," she told me. She sat perched on the arm of a chair, her arms crossed and her eyes twinkling with amusement.

"It's not like I had a choice."

She cocked her head, allowing me the point. Reading from the DI's report, she said, "So Hera Poliu had a brother. Four years ago he was exiled from Nahiku, and a year after that he was arrested and executed for an illegal enhancement."

"Hera lost her brother. She's got to resent it. Maybe she resents anybody who has a—" I caught myself. "Anybody she thinks might have a quirk."

"Maybe," Glory conceded. "And maybe that's why she made a complaint against your intimate, but so what? It's not your case, Zeke. Forward what you've got to whoever had the misfortune to be appointed as the criminal investigator in this little paradise and let it go."

I made compliant noises. She shook her head, not needing the DI to know I wasn't being straight. "Walk with me."

"Where?"

"The mausoleum. I'm going home. But on the way there, you're going to listen to what I have to say about the necessity for boundaries." She crooked her finger at me. I shrugged and followed. As we walked past the vistas she lectured me on the essential but very limited role of the Commonwealth police and warned me that my appointment as watch officer at Nahiku could end at any time. I listened patiently, knowing she would soon be gone.

As we approached the mausoleum, I sent a DI to open the door. Inside was a long hallway with locked doors on either side. Behind the doors were storage chambers, most of them belonging to corporations. The third door on the left secured the police chamber. It opened as we approached, and closed again when we had stepped inside. One wall held clothing lockers. The other, ranks of cold storage drawers stacked four high. "Magistrate Glory Mina," Glory said to the room DI. She stripped off her clothes and hung them in one of the lockers while the drawers slid past each other, rearranging themselves. Only two were empty. One was mine. The other descended from the top rank to the second level, where it opened, ready to receive her.

Glory closed the locker door. She was naked and utterly unconcerned about it. She turned to me with a stern gaze. "You tried to pretend Key Lu was a victim. This once, I'm going to pretend you just missed a step in the background investigation. Zeke, as much as you don't like being a cop, being an ex-cop can be a lot worse."

I had no answer for that. I knew she was right.

She climbed into the drawer. As soon as she lay back, the cushions inflated around her, creating a moist interface all across the surface of her skin. The drawer slid shut and locked with a soft snick. Very soon, her ghost would be on its way to Red Star. Once again, I was on my own.

NO MATTER WHAT Glory wanted, there was no way I was going to set this case aside. Key Lu was dead, while Tishembra had been threatened and made into a stranger, both to me and to her own son. I wanted to know who was responsible and why.

Still, I knew how to make concessions. So I set up an appointment with an official who served part-time as a city cop, intending to hand over the case files, if only for the benefit of my personnel record. But before that could happen a roving DI returned to me with the news that the city's auto-defense system had locked down a plague outbreak on Level 5 West. The address was Robin's day-venture center.

It took me ninety seconds to strip off my uniform and wrap on the impermeable hide of a vacuum-capable skinsuit, police black, with gold insignia. Then I grabbed a standard-issue bivouac kit that weighed half as much as I did, and I raced out the door.

We call it plague, but it's not. Each of us is an ecosystem. We're inhabited by a host of Makers. Some repair our bodies and our minds, keeping us young and alert, and some run our atriums. But most of our Makers exist only to defend us against hostile nanotech—the snakes that forever prowl the Garden of Eden, the nightmares devised by twisted minds—and sometimes our defenses fail.

A GENERAL ALERT had not been issued—that was standard policy, to avoid panic—but as soon as I was spotted on the paths wearing my skinsuit, word went out through informal channels that something was wrong. By the time I reached the day-venture center people had already guessed where I was going and a crowd was beginning to form against the backdrop of prairie. The city's emergency response team hadn't arrived yet, so questions were shouted at me. I refused to answer. "Stay back!" I commanded, issuing an order for the center's locked door to open.

In an auto-defense lockdown, a gel barrier is extruded around the suspect zone. The door slid back to reveal a wall of blue-tinged gel behind it. I pulled up the hood of my skinsuit and let it seal. Then I leaned into the gel wall, feeling it give way slowly around me, and after a few seconds I was able to pass through. As soon as I was clear, the door closed and locked behind me.

The staff and children were huddled on one side of the room—six adults and twenty-two kids. They looked frightened, but otherwise okay. Robin wasn't with them. The director started to speak but I couldn't hear him past the skinsuit, so I forced an atrial link to every adult in the room. "Give me your status."

The director spoke again, this time through my atrium. "It's Robin. He was hit hard only a couple of minutes ago. Shakes and sweats. His system's chewing up all his latents and he went down right away. I think it's targeted. No one else has shown any signs."

"Where is he?"

The director looked toward the nap room.

I didn't want to think too hard, I just wanted to get Robin stable, but the director's assessment haunted me. A targeted assault meant that Robin alone was the intended victim; that the hostile Maker had been designed to activate in his unique ecosystem.

I found him on the floor, trembling in the grip of a hypoglycemic seizure, all his blood sugars gone to fuel the reproduction of Makers in his body—both defensive and assault—as the tiny machines ramped up their populations to do battle on a molecular scale. His eyelids fluttered, but I could only see the whites. His black curls were sodden with sweat.

I unrolled the bivouac kit with its thick gel base designed for a much larger patient. Then I lifted his small body, laid him on it, and touched the activation points. The gel folded around him like a cocoon. The bivouac was a portable version of the cold storage drawer that had enfolded Glory. Robin's core temperature plummeted, while an army of defensive Makers swarmed past the barrier of his skin in a frantic effort to stabilize him.

The city's emergency team came in wearing sealed skinsuits. I stood by as they scanned the other kids, the staff, the rooms, and me, finding nothing. Only Robin was affected.

I stripped off my hood. Out in the playroom, the gel membrane was coming down and the kids were going home, but inside the bivouac Robin lay in stasis, his biological processes all but stopped. Even the data on his condition had been pared to a trickle. Still, I'd seen enough to know what was happening: the assault Makers were attacking Robin's neuronal connections, writing chaos into the space where Robin used to be. We would lose him if we allowed him to revive.

I checked city records for the date of his last backup. I couldn't find one. Robin had turned three a few weeks ago. I remembered we'd talked about taking him in to get a backup done . . . but we'd been busy.

The emergency team came back into the nap room with a gurney. Tishembra came with them. One glance at her face told me she'd been heavily tranked.

At first she didn't say anything, just watched with lips slightly parted and an expression of quiet horror on her face as the bivouac was lifted onto the gurney. But as the gurney was rolled away she asked in a defeated voice, "Is he going to die?"

"Of course he's not going to die."

She turned an accusing gaze on me. "My DI says you're lying."

I cursed myself silently and tried again, determined to speak the truth this time. "He's not going to die, because I won't let him."

She nodded, as if I'd got it right. The trank had turned her mood to smooth, hard glass. "I made this happen."

"What are you talking about?"

She turned her right hand palm up. A blue prairie butterfly rested in it, crushed and lifeless. I picked it up; spread its wings open. The message was only a little blurred from handling. On the left wing I read, You lived, and on the right, so he dies.

So someone had watched as we'd dropped Robin off that morning. I looked up at Tishembra. "No," I told her. "That's not the way it's going to work."

The attack on Robin was a molecular crime, which made it my case, and I was prepared to use every resource of the police to solve it.

Tishembra nodded. Then she left, following the gurney.

I could work anywhere, using my atrium, so I stayed for a time. First I packed up every bit of data I had on Robin's condition and sent it to six different police labs, hoping at least one could come up with the design for a Maker that could stop the assault on Robin's brain cells. The odds of success would go up dramatically if I could get the specs of the assault Maker—and the easiest way to do that was to track down the twisted freak who'd designed it.

Easy steps first: I sent a DI into the data-sphere to assemble a list of everyone at Nahiku with extensive molecular design experience. The DI came back with one name: mine.

So I was dealing with a talented hobbyist.

It could be anyone.

I sent the DI out again. No record was kept of butterfly messages—they were designed to be anonymous—but surveillance records were collected on every public path. I instructed the DI to access the records and assemble a list of everyone who'd set foot on Level 5 at any time that day, because the blue prairie butterflies could only be accessed from there. The list that came back was long. Name after name scrolled through my visual field, many that I recognized, but only one stood out in my mind: Hera Poliu.

I summoned the vid attached to her name. It was innocuous. She'd been taking the stairs between levels and had paused briefly on the landing. Still, it bothered me. Hera had been involved with Key Lu, she'd filed the complaint against Tishembra, and now I had her on Level 5. Coincidence maybe . . . but I remembered the chill I'd felt when she accosted me in the corridor . . . and how confused she'd been when I reminded her of the incident.

I went by my office and changed back into my uniform. Then I checked city records for Hera's location. She was at the infirmary, sitting with Tishembra . . . Tishembra, who'd been a quirk just like Hera's brother except she'd eluded punishment while Hera's brother was dead. Maybe it was baseless panic, but I sprinted for the door.

THE INFIRMARY HAD a reception room with a desk, and a hallway behind it with small rooms on either side. The technician at the desk looked up as I burst in. "Robin Indens!" I barked.

"Critical care. End of the hall."

I sprinted past him. A sign identified the room. I touched the door and it snapped open. The bivouac had been set up on a table in the center of the room. Slender feeder lines descending from the ceiling were plugged into its ports. Tishembra and Hera stood alongside the bivouac, Hera with a comforting arm around Tishembra's shoulders. They both looked up as I burst in. "Zeke?" Tishembra asked, with an expression encompassing both hope and dread.

"Tish, it's going to be okay. But I need to talk to Hera. Alone."

They traded a puzzled glance. Then Hera gave Tishembra a quick hug—"I'll be right back"—and stepped past me into the hall. I followed her, closing the door behind us.

Hera turned to face me. She looked gaunt and worn—a woman who had seen too much grief. "I want to thank you, Zeke, for not telling Tishembra who filed that complaint. I wasn't myself when I did it. I don't even remember doing it."

She wasn't lying.

I stumbled over that fact. Had I gotten it wrong? Was there something more going on than a need for misguided revenge?

"When was the last time you had your defensive Makers upgraded?"

She flinched and looked away. "It's been a while."

I sent a DI to check the records. It had been three years. I pulled up an earlier report and cross checked the dates to be sure. She hadn't had an upgrade since her brother's execution. My heart rate jumped as I contemplated a new possibility. No doubt my pupils dilated, but Hera was still looking away and she didn't see it. I sent the DI out again.

We were standing beside an open door to an unoccupied office. I ushered Hera inside. The DI came back with a new set of records even before the door was closed. At my invitation, Hera sat in the guest chair, her hands fidgeting restlessly in her lap. I perched on the edge of the desk, scanning the records, trying to stay calm, but my DI wasn't fooled. It sensed my stress and sent the paralytic ribbon creeping down my arm and into my palm.

"Let's talk about your brother."

Hera's hands froze in her lap. "My brother? You must know already. He's dead . . . he died like Key."

"You used to be a city councilor."

"I resigned from the council."

I nodded. "As a councilor you were required to host visitors . . . but you haven't allowed a ghost in your atrium since your brother's arrest."

"Those things don't matter to me anymore."

"You also haven't upgraded your defensive Makers, and you haven't been scanned—"

"I'm not a criminal, Zeke. I just . . . I just want to do my job and be left alone."

"Hera? You've been harboring your brother's ghost, haven't you? And he didn't like it when you started seeing Key."

The DI showed me the flush of hot and cold across her skin. "No," she whispered. "No. He's dead, and I wouldn't do that."

She was lying. "Hera, is your atrium quirked? To let your brother's ghost take over sometimes?"

She looked away. "Wouldn't that be illegal?"

"Giving up your body to another? Yes, it would be."

Her hands squeezed hard against the armrests of the chair. "It was him, then? That's what you're saying?" She turned to look at me, despair in her eyes. "He filed the complaint against Tish?"

I nodded. "I knew it wasn't you speaking to me that day. I think he also used you to sabotage Key's railcar, knowing I'd have to look into it."

"And Robin?" she asked, her knuckles whitening as she gripped the chair.

"Ask him."

Earlier, I'd asked the DI to bring me a list of all the trained molecular designers in Nahiku, but I'd asked the wrong question. I queried it again, asking for all the designers in the past five years. This time, mine wasn't the only name.

"Ask him for the design of the assault Maker, Hera. Robin doesn't deserve to die."

I crouched in front of her, my hand on hers as I looked up into her stunned eyes. It was a damned stupid position to put myself into.

He took over. It took a fraction of a second. My DI didn't catch it, but I saw it happen. Her expression hardened and her knee came up, driving hard into my chin. As my head snapped back he launched Hera against me. At that point it didn't matter that I outweighed her by forty percent. I was off balance and I went down with her on top of me. Her forehead cracked against my nose, breaking it.

He wasn't trying to escape. There was no way he could. It was only blind rage that drove him. He wanted to kill me, for all the good it would do. I was a cop. I had backups. I couldn't lose more than a few days. But he could still do some damage before he was brought down.

I felt Hera's small hands seize my wrists. He was trying to keep me from using the ribbon arsenal, but Hera wasn't nearly strong enough for that. I tossed her off, and not gently. The back of her head hit the floor, but she got up again almost as fast as I did and scrambled for the door.

I don't know what he intended to do, what final vengeance he hoped for. One more murder, maybe. Tishembra and Robin were both just across the hall.

I grabbed Hera, dragged her back, and slammed her into the chair. Then I raised my hand. The DI controlled the ribbon. Fibers along its length squeezed hard, sending a fine mist across Hera's face. It got in her eyes and in her lungs. She reared back, but then she collapsed, slumping in the chair. I wiped my bloody nose on my sleeve and waited until her head lolled against her chest. Then I sent a DI to Red Star.

I'd need help extracting the data from her quirked atrium, and combing through it for the assault Maker's design file.

IT TOOK A few days, but Robin was recovered. When he gets cranky at night he still tells Tishembra she's "wrong," but he's only three. Soon he won't remember what she was like before, while I pretend it doesn't matter to me.

Tishembra knows that isn't true. She complains the laws are too strict, that citizens should be free to make their own choices. Me, I'm just happy Glory Mina let me stay on as Nahiku's watch officer. Glory likes reminding me how lucky I am to have the position. I like to remind her that I've finally turned into the uncompromising jackboot she always knew I could be.

Don't get me wrong. I wanted to help Hera, but she'd been harboring a fugitive for three years. There was nothing I could do for her, but I won't let anyone else in this city step over the line. I don't want to sit through another execution.

Nahiku isn't quite bankrupt yet. Glory assessed a minimal fine for Hera's transgression, laying most of the fault on the police since we'd failed to hunt down all ghosts of a condemned criminal. So the city won't be sold off, and Tishembra will have to wait to get free.

I don't think she minds too much.

Here. Now. This is enough. I only wonder: Can we make it last?

HOUSEFLIES

Joe Pitkin

Joe Pitkin teaches at Clark College in Vancouver, Washington, and belongs to the Evolutionary Ecology Lab at Washington State University, Vancouver. One online bio says, "Joe Pitkin writes poetry, fiction, and nerdy pop songs," and "He teaches English at Clark College, plays bass for The Gravitropes, and studies primary succession on the pumice plain of Mount St. Helens." He says, "A newcomer to science fiction, Joe Pitkin began his writing career as a poet, where his work has appeared in *North American Review, Beloit Poetry Journal, Los Angeles Review,* and elsewhere. Since his debut as a speculative fiction writer, his stories have appeared in *Analog, Cosmos, The Future Fire, Expanded Horizons,* and other fine magazines."

"Houseflies" was published in *Cosmos.* It is a chilling and darkly funny story of ecocatastrophe, and humanity's perseverance.

THERE ARE HUMANS, and then there's corn, the tomatoes that we hand-pollinate, fennel pondweed, buckhorn plantain, common ragweed, tansy ragwort, two different species of mite, the common pill wood louse (in spite of the absence of wood), Mormon crickets, the common earthworm under the ground, and houseflies, probably a hundred thousand times more houseflies than people. Thirteen species of plants and animals in all. Of course there are God knows how many species of molds and mildews and bacteria and algae, especially in the slimy cesspools of the oceans, but nowadays when people talk of the food web they mean those thirteen species.

Everyone knows those plucky, lucky 13: the city has billboards everywhere showing the connections between the species as though we were prey hanging on a spider's web, though of course all spiders have been extinct for 20 years and if a hypothetical kindergartener were to see a real spider's web she would almost certainly say "look, mummy, I found a food web!"

The billboards read "Protect Your Food Web," except in the Little Texas district of the city, where I'd gone last year for a cricket barbecue. There, the billboards say "Don't Mess With the Food Web."

Apparently it's not quite as simple as all that: every year systematists are discovering a new subspecies of housefly, or an entirely new housefly species. What we biologists call an adaptive radiation event. In the far south of the city there are flies as large as the dog turds that flies used to eat back in the days of dog turds.

But I don't study flies. Like ten thousand other citizens, I was trained in those last years of the crash, in the frantic hope that we might save a few species from years of habitat loss and hormone disruption and eutrophication, the genetic pollution and salt bombs and designer viruses and climate hacking, the volcano induction and self-replicating bioplastic film and mimetic pheremonal pornography, the alkaloid release and the weather guns. I was trained to work on the genetic conservation of curlews and godwits, though the last of the curlews went extinct even before I graduated, and the godwits are gone now, too, so now I study nothing.

Nowadays I work for a guy who represents a social club, The Hemingway Society. His name is Guillame, but that's almost all I can tell you about him because I've never seen him. On the phone he sounds like an old-school Harvard man who might have grown up in the Caribbean, and he's old enough—almost 70, he once said—that he could really be such a person.

Today, Guillame is sending me to The Vault. I pick up the train in Sam Walton Station, which I always think of as Tardigrade Station because of the massive "Whither the Tardigrade?" spray-painted on the retaining wall behind the tracks. I have no idea what that means. I think tardigrades were what kids called water bears, those tiny brine-animals that could wrap themselves up in a cyst for years in the absence of water. You could order them in the mail, drop them in a glass of water, and watch them start kicking around on their eight stubby legs as though all those dry years had never happened at all. It is hard to believe that all species of tardigrades would go extinct, but there you are. If roaches and rats and pigeons could go extinct because of human malice, why couldn't the lowly water bear slip through the cracks? And anyway, what do I know about the tardigrade's chances? 99.99% of the surface of Earth is salt waste; probably there are tardigrades bundled up somewhere out there, waiting for rain.

THE VAULT OF all life sits at the end of the line for this train. In fact The Vault makes up part of the city's eastern border separating civilisation from the rest of the cindery salt world. I'm old enough to remember the time before the construction: the city government considered so many competing designs, the fanciful and the serious and those designs meant to scold us in some way. I remember the public debate over whether The Vault would be built as a spindly double-helical tower to celebrate the survival of the vital DNA molecule, or whether it would look grander as a great artificial mountain in the style of the pyramids. For a while a huge monolith was the favored design, as though to commemorate the loss of so many species with a simple gigantic headstone. But in the end, the design that city hall chose was a circular well shaft several kilometers deep. The most poetic memorial the city council could think of was an unfathomable hole.

Most people never see the hole; in fact, not many come out this far to see the building on top of the hole. I'm not sure whether the building is tasteful and understated, or if it's just a great big silo. I really don't know anything about architecture. Guillame told me it was designed like a Navajo hogan, or a kiva, I don't remember. What I notice more than the cylinder of the building is the expanse of cornfields on one side and a whole world of salt waste on the other.

Inside, past the vestibule, the great hall is decorated floor to ceiling with a mosaic depicting the Tree of Life. That's not the most noticeable thing on walking in, though: what I see pretty quickly, and can't look away from, is the lip of the gaping hole. The guardrail looks useless and pathetic around that pit. Above it hang a dozen or so beautiful brass baskets as big as chariot cars, suspended invisibly, I assume by nanofiber cables.

My appointment is with one of the guardians, someone named Daphne. The great hall seems strangely empty, even in a city full of empty buildings. I walk to the rail and look down and feel the shudder in my groin as I confront the possibility of that endless fall. A long way down, at the limit of my sight, a speck of a basket glints under the pit lights as it climbs or descends past them.

It takes me a minute or so to tell that the basket is climbing, another ten minutes before the occupant comes into view and approaches hailing distance. "Are you Guillame's friend?" the woman calls to me.

She is slender, just past middle age, her iron gray hair pulled back into a grim little bun like the woman from *American Gothic. Daphne* seems to me such a young woman's name that I stutter a moment before realising that this is Daphne. I introduce myself, thank her for taking the time for me.

"Guillame tells me you'll be doing some work on the blue swallow?" she asks. I nod, I hope modestly. She asks if I'd like to accompany her into the pit to retrieve the specimen, and I would rather have my wisdom teeth pulled without anesthesia, but I am ashamed of my cowardice enough that I say I've always wanted to descend into The Vault of All Life. I climb into her basket and steel myself for the descent.

"YOU'LL GET NEARLY the full tour," she says as she taps out a code on a hand-held controller. "The passerines are almost at the bottom of the vault." We begin to drop and for a moment before we pick up speed I can see the array of individual Lucite bricks, which make up the walls of the well. Here each translucent square seems to contain a tissue sample from a different species of tube worm. The fluid in each one seems to slosh a bit as we pass by it—probably my imagination.

"How is The Vault organised?" I ask. "I would have expected the animal samples to be separated from the plant samples and fungi."

"The samples we use most frequently are up top; that way we're not in the cars all day." Probably half of the people I went to school with are working on tube worms, trying to figure out the genes for different bacterial symbioses.

Most of the trip seems like a controlled fall and I grip the rim of our chariot car and imagine that I feel the sickening vibrations of a far-off motor unspooling our invisible cable. Twenty minutes later the car glides to a stop; I still can't see the bottom beyond the last ring of pit lights.

"What's down at the bottom?" I ask.

"Nothing."

"I would have thought there would be a plaque or something."

"Who would see it? No one ever goes down there but me."

Each of the thousands of bricks in this section contains a passerine. Daphne taps out a passcode into her hand-held controller and one of the bricks slides forward with a soft, cunning hiss.

She takes out a tight bundle of greasy wax paper like an ancient sausage and hands it to me. "The blue swallow," she says. "Bon appétit."

Later that afternoon I sit on the train watching the cornfields give way to city streets, the corpse of the swallow sitting in my coat pocket. *Corpse* isn't the right word; if you're going to eat it you don't call it a corpse. In fairness, though, no one is going to eat this particular bird.

From the train I look down on a city street where a dozen or so people are rushing to get indoors. A plague of houseflies seems to have descended here. Many times I've wondered—everybody's wondered—how that one species survived so famously when so many other nuisance species died out. Even cockroaches, for God's sake. I remember a professor from my school days talking about how we should love the fly but we don't, because watching a fly is like watching our own waste reborn as something buzzing around us, our filth made flesh. Actually right now I could love the miraculous cloud of flies below me, but that's easier to do when they're down in the street and I'm sealed in a train carriage.

THE REAL MIRACLE is that Daphne let me walk off with the swallow in my pocket: The Vault of All Life isn't exactly a lending library. And the blue swallow has been extinct for almost 70 years—she let me leave with the last known tissue sample of an entire species. Had Guillame said something to her? Was she angling for an invitation? I suppose it's better not to speculate.

So many biologists, better biologists than I, have spent a million hours and cried a million tears cloning samples from The Vault, resurrecting for a while this species or that other species or a small ecosystem of species. But nobody has had much luck building a food web from scratch: bring back one of the spider species to eat the flies and frogs to eat the spiders and herons to eat the frogs, but sooner or later the whole house of cards falls in again because of some mite or species of grass that was missing and which nobody knew was needed.

Anyway, I won't be cloning the whole swallow. Once I'm back in the lab, I'll isolate some of its cardiac tissue, sequence the genes, key out the expression, and by the end of the month, with luck, I'll be cloning blue swallow hearts like pink lentils in a dish. In the train car I drift off a moment, dreaming that I have already begun the sequencing, watching the letter for each nucleotide base plop down one by one on the screen in unflattering typeface, as though *The Book of Life* had been written in Courier New, dreaming that my own genome manifests mysteriously in the torrent of letters, full of synonymous mutations, frame-shift mutations, weird mutations that code for proteins that passed out of this world a long time ago.

It's next evening before I get the swallow into the lab. "This poor guy had a pretty short tail", I say to myself when I first get him under the dissection scope. Back when they existed, blue swallow females apparently mated with the males that had the longest tail feathers. Researchers could glue a couple of extra centimeters of feather to a male's tail and suddenly he'd turn into Lothario, getting his pick of the females, plus some extra-pair copulations into the bargain. Those old research findings had always seemed comical to me. I suppose all sexual posturing in other species is a comedy gold mine to disinterested bystanders. The mating rituals of *Homo sapiens* only seem more serious to *Homo sapiens*. Maybe someday a super-intelligent alien probing my corpse will regard my wang with bemused pity.

I imagine a moment that blue swallows would have survived if this specimen had gotten lucky, as though the species had gone extinct because of lack of interest in sex. I cut him lengthwise, pop open the cabinet of his tiny ribcage, look on the packed assembly of his once-useful viscera. The intestines spiral and curlicue like a baroque cursive letter. The heart, laid bare for the first time, peeks out like an all-seeing little eye, taking in the world and its carelessness with the blue swallow and all species.

THE ENTIRE HEART weighs 400 mg or so. I think I can pull off the whole project with half of that, give or take

Once sautéed, blue swallow hearts reduce to the size of grains of rice. A more interesting texture than I remember rice having, though. Against my better judgment I had also cloned a few birds in full. All males, of course—I wouldn't be resurrecting this species by any of my own paltry sleight-of-hand. In the weeks leading up to the big dinner the fledglings hop about and shit up the antique parrot cage I bought for the lab. Twice a day I feed them moistened worm meal, or fly meal if I don't find any worms that day.

This will be my first, and probably only, Hemingway Society dinner. Guillame makes clear The Society wishes to reward me for all my work. The hall is in one of the deserted sections of the city, in a sleek glass palace that looks like it was once a botanical garden or maybe a luxury car showroom. I'm surprised I haven't seen the building before: this neighborhood isn't so far from where I live.

I had expected a pack of sybaritic old men and I'm not disappointed. Most of the males, anyway, seem to be in their seventies and eighties: men who can remember eating meat. They all seem to have traded in their menopausal wives for perky young things, mostly women, not that anybody here is likely to get pregnant. The hall is decorated with more varieties of corn and tomato plants than I could ever have imagined.

The menu is Siberian tiger steak, baked dodo eggs, Yangtze dolphin chowder (the dolphins had been raised in an old water treatment facility, I hear), and of course blue swallow heart risotto. I didn't do the cooking and I'm not sure if there's real cheese in the risotto—if so I don't even want to think about what animal provided the milk.

At the end of the hall a string quartet plays something bright and Olympian, maybe Schubert or Beethoven. The cloned swallows swoop about overhead, scooping up the many houseflies—a nice effect, I think.

I did end up bringing Daphne from The Vault of All Life. She's the oldest woman here by about 30 years, looking scarily attractive in evening gown and vampy lipstick. She seems utterly unfazed by the carnival of vanity on all sides of us. As the steaks are served I raise my eyebrow quizzically at her. "We were made to eat meat," she answers with a predatory grin over the $50,000 plate of risotto between us.

I reach for my fork and see a strange housefly there. It's an awkward little creature, with longer legs than I would expect for a housefly; its body, too, seems a bit narrower. Strangest of all are the mouthparts, half again as long as on a typical fly, slightly hooked, almost like the nubbin of a proboscis. Almost like a nectar-feeding proboscis—but what could this creature possibly be eating with such a mouth?

Not that I know flies. I know just enough—or know just enough how much I don't know—to pause in my speculations and simply watch for a while.

BRANCHES ON MY BACK, SPARROWS IN MY EAR

Nikki J. North

Nikki J. North lives on the island of Guam with her wonderful spousal unit, Eric, and two dogs. She holds a bachelor's degree in Computer and Information Science from the University of Maryland. Having lived in the United Kingdom and traveled throughout Europe and Southeast Asia, her favorite sight is still that of the Rockies rising up over the high deserts of the northwest where she grew up. By day she writes in 1s and 0s as a Web programmer for the University of Guam. By night she writes speculative fiction. Her first published story, "Symptoms Persist," appeared in *Larks Fiction Magazine* at the end of 2011. "'Branches' was only the second story I've ever attempted to have published," she says. "I'm working on the third, a short story called 'The Rise of the House of Denver.'" Currently, she is also working on a novel set on Mars.

"Branches on My Back, Sparrows in My Ear" was published in the first annual online issue of *James Gunn's Ad Astra*. It is authentically strange science fiction, from an already accomplished prose stylist.

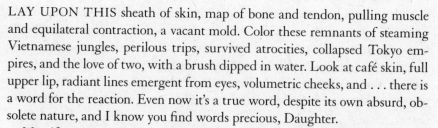

LAY UPON THIS sheath of skin, map of bone and tendon, pulling muscle and equilateral contraction, a vacant mold. Color these remnants of steaming Vietnamese jungles, perilous trips, survived atrocities, collapsed Tokyo empires, and the love of two, with a brush dipped in water. Look at café skin, full upper lip, radiant lines emergent from eyes, volumetric cheeks, and . . . there is a word for the reaction. Even now it's a true word, despite its own absurd, obsolete nature, and I know you find words precious, Daughter.

My gift to you: squinch. A squinch is neither an especially smelly portion of cheese nor a disease whose symptoms are squinting and itching. It is an involuntary kind of jerk, mixed with a spasming flinch, causing the body to both lean forward and jump back at the same time. Squinch is now one of the fifty-seven terms found on the Nguyen family Made Up Words that Can Be Used in Scrabble list, and it is the perfect word to describe the reaction of the woman who walked into my office that day. I have made you this word, an offering at the altar of your suffering so you will know that I understand, but these words will reach no further. They bind me. Let me show you. I can now. Here—

LEADING A CLIENT with designer Vash Vidaaru circuitry sliding up her jaw to the clinic chair, I see her trying to catch a glimpse of my ankle, straining for a peek of skin beneath my high collar. She's wasting her time, as have many before her. I don't have any sub-q. I've never been inked.

There are those who choose to go without ink. Some people leave the face blank as a form of self-expression, some because they are part of a religious group that forbids it. Almost everybody knows a friend of a friend whose cousin is blank, but most people will never meet a resistant in a time when it's more common to see a man with a giant squid tattooed across his forehead than a ten-year-old with a spot of untouched skin. These days seeing someone without sub-q is like opening a book and finding all the pages are empty, so I understand the stares. Usually, I ignore them, but not today. When I catch the woman scrutinizing my neck for the third time, I answer the unasked question. I even tell the truth: I'm resistant.

"Actually," I say, keeping a detached smile on my face as I prep ink with gloved hands, "resistant is a bit of an understatement. My body violently rejects the ink." I dip the needle into a bottle of standard sub-q. "In fact, just a drop of this landing on my skin would send my body's immune system into a kind of protective overdrive that would create enough toxins to incapacitate me for hours. Hence the long sleeves and twitchy assistant." I smile as my thumb pulls skin taut. "Mia is good. She's been with me for years. I went through three assistants before her. Nothing like finding your boss unconscious, right?"

Needle hovering, I look the woman in the eyes. My self-deprecating smile fades. Words down a well, I think. Her top teeth clasp her lower lip. Her eyes dart away. It's always like that with the ones who never learned to speak. I wonder what I must sound like to her. Are my words loud and sharp? Are they like the meaningless squawk of a bird? Or are they a writhing babble under the composed stream of sub-q communications running through her head? What exquisite data is she exchanging while I sit here like a rock, like a giraffe longing for opposable thumbs? Halfway through this habitual, bitter thought the realization hits me that today I don't have to feel this way. The needle skitters as my hand convulses, and I almost penetrate too far into the derma.

I manage to keep my thoughts focused for the rest of the appointment.

Finished enhancing her comm system with the latest upgrades, I show Mrs. Bardon out to the lobby where Mia will hand her a bill that is three times most people's rent. Nothing but the best for Servanix Group board members and their husbands . . . and their children and their cousins and their associates at the Office of New Immortals and their friends in Sydney North Ring. And, and, and—the list is a long one composed of Sydney's rich and richer. I don't mind. Their grasping pursuit of the techpossible (Nguyen Scrabble Word #44, a contribution from Kaede) funds my research.

In my office a stack of messages covered in Mia's careful handwriting waits. I ignore it, pushing up my left shirt sleeve instead. There I trace the reason for my joy: a black, three-inch line, stark and defiant amongst the ghosts of past attempts. Unlike its kin, gobbled up and spit out by my body's own defenses, it remains. Ten days ago, surrounded by the quiet of a deserted building, I inked this line into my skin. With Emergency's number queued on my ancient mobile, I waited for the crippling pain and shortness of breath to overtake me.

Only now, looking down at it still there, do I finally let myself believe that after two years of resuming my search I've found the enzyme that will make it work. There is one person in all the world I want to tell.

KAEDE, WHEN YOU don't have ink you're a ghost. You glide in a world of silence. Public spaces are full of eyes that never focus and mouths that never move. Walking through the open food court at the bottom of the clinic is never really a comfortable experience, but lunch is the worst: the shouts of forks on plates, the screams of chairs being pushed back, the roar of breath that bellows in and out of hundreds of lungs through lips unused. Here—

I ESCAPE THE cool interior of the Sydney General Dermacomm and Neurocohesives Clinic building into a day capped by a sky milky with cumulus clouds. The buildings around me are thorns piercing this dome with their spiraling exteriors. Songs of thrushes and robins overlay the distant calls of seabirds. People rush around me. Most are headed toward Central, still caught in the morning commute. Letting myself be taken up in the stream of their travel, I walk past the older Short District and halfway through New Zenith District before I see the man with the complex of Keorgi tats. At first glance I am taken by their beauty. Someone knows their business. I'm trying to figure out where I know the style from when I realize the man's eyes are not staring into the distance past me, taking in ads and signs and addresses only he can see, but are focused on something. He is looking at me, seeing me. It feels like a thousand feathers landing on my skin. I stop and turn back to get a better look, but he's gone. I stand to the side as a transport whispers past. Water from the building's weather system murmurs down the shining black synthskin exterior. The feeling of eyes touching me has disappeared with the man.

The elevator in the Servanix Tech building smells like leather and pomegranate. It takes me to the twenty-fourth floor where, after traveling a maze of curving hallways, I find Kaede's office.

She's not there.

I leave a note with her assistant, who holds it pinched between two fingers like a dead possum. Exiting the building, my eyes dart up both sides of the greenway jostling and shimmering with people. The rising and falling voices of the leaves covering the spiral behind me crash and echo. I wish for a dog to bark. I wish for one out of the thousands of people rushing by to laugh. I wish for a giant bell, the kind of bell that must be rung by two men hurtling a whole tree's worth of wood at it, the kind of bell that would call with its deep voice across mist-shrouded mountains and cratered valleys, eating this quiescent scene with its annihilating voice. There is no bell, only a world immersed in sub-q. My skin curls tight to my body waiting for the touch of eyes as I make my way back to the clinic.

MY MOTHER'S GENERATION was the last to live in a spoken world. She named me Izumi and died when I was nineteen. I loved my mother's quiet presence, and the way she smelled like almonds. I loved the way her black hair made an almost audible twang as the curls sprang back up under the hand she used to constantly smooth them down. I loved the swirls of tattoo that washed and echoed across her face. I remember tracing them with a finger as she leaned over me, pulling blankets tight around shoulders. I still try, sometimes, to trace my own face while lying in bed and see myself in the topographic mirror there, but all I see is the ink of her face superimposed over the unmapped territory of my own. Kaede, do you lie somewhere now? Do you try to imagine yourself otherwise? Give me the gift of believing you do not. Here—

"I CAME BY your office today," I say, pouring the rest of the wine into Kaede's glass.
    "Oh?"
    I nod, holding her glass hostage in one hand until she yields.
    "I was in the lab."
    When Kaede lies she does this thing with her voice. It becomes rougher, like the lies are smoke rising in her throat.
    "New research? Or still working on—"
    "Oh, I don't want to bore you, Mom." She dismisses my question with a wave of her fork.
    I want to bark a "Ha!" at her over my own glass of wine. I know you think I'm a fifty-four-year-old has-been, a dinosaur flashmonkey who's never had a drop on her skin, but who gave you the beautiful tiger main tat that crosses your back, dear? And why are you avoiding my questions? And why was a man with your ink following me around the city today?
    I don't say these things, though. I drink my wine and let Margie, my younger daughter, change the subject. She begins gossiping about something one of the famous clients at the net entertainment agency where she works has done. On her back is the crane I gave her when she was twelve. She's continued the motif. Water scrolls up her collarbones, washing up her neck and jaw to her ears, where it carries the signals that make her constantly tip her head in silent com-

munion with a client. She's been at it the whole meal. Her voice trails off as she's taken away again.

"Hey!" Kaede's palm comes down hard on the table. "Get out of the sub-q and have a real conversation."

They share a long look. What kind of sibling squabble are they having? What expressions and kindled emotion is being passed in the ether of sub-q? I want to know and to tell them both that soon I will know. They've both heard it before, but this time is different. This time it's real. Margie leaves the table.

"So, Mom," Kaede says, sounding far too bright and chipper.

"So, Kaede." I grin at her. It's a joyful grin, but she doesn't see it; her focus is on dismantling the fudge cake in front of her into smaller and smaller piles of crumbs. The secret of my joy is swallowed by the image of the tats on the stranger.

"Sorry, that was Kyle," Margie says, taking her seat again.

We talk about cake and work and Margie's boyfriend, whom Kaede and I both dislike, for the rest of the night. Margie leaves with a kiss pressed affectionately to my left cheek; Kaede follows with a kiss to the right. They never have been much for sharing.

Kaede pauses at the door. I'm going to tell her. I find myself clutching the door instead. Kaede's eyes flicker downward, and I realize I'm rubbing my forearm. She leaves without saying anything.

Standing at the window moments later, my mind worries at shadows. I have a feeling I've missed something, that I've failed to understand a critical component in the schematic of the night. I clear the table, sit at the computer, but ultimately find myself back at the wine. After two more glasses to stop my brain from moving and flickering, sleep comes like a whispered incantation.

I wake to the sharp trills of the HUD in my bedroom. Eyes shuttered against the light from the wall to my left, I try to make out the characters scrolling there. It's a message from the intrusion detection monitor at work. Someone has hacked their way into the clinic systems. I run a log audit; there's no indication of remote access. Security guy trip something? Mia doing some late-night work? Neither scenario seems very plausible. The sense of failed understanding returns as I run a full scan of the system.

The data has been wiped. My schematics, the latest ink formulations, everything: it's all gone.

THE CLOCK READS 5:42 AM when I duck inside the darkened clinic. Lights blink on at my presence. A figure sits in the swiveling stool I usually occupy.

"You need better security, Mom."

"Kaede?"

"I'm out of time. They think I'm just here to clean up, but I wanted to do this one last thing and I didn't know how to . . ." She shrugs the way someone who just tipped a little too much salt into the soup might. "This worked. You're here." My mind is screaming her name. My heart is turned upside down. "They won't understand it. They will revile me for it, but maybe, if you stay out of it, they'll let it go." Her voice changes, grows brusque and commanding. It's her lab voice. "Doesn't matter. We're here."

I'm breathing hard through my nose. The world is dancing around me, scrambling to reconcile . . . everything.

"I have a gift for you," she says, gesturing to the chair that has been host to so many others. "The hack you have is wrong, Mom." My hand rises to cover the black line she's looking at. "In a small dose it's fine, but if you try for a CPF . . ."

"They? The guy that followed me today?" I feel for the chair behind me and fall into it, all ability to keep my legs straight draining from me.

"Once upon a time I was working on my thesis about ink that could be used to tat resistants—"

"But your thesis was on regenerative algorithms," I interrupt.

"No, that's what I ended up publishing, but in the beginning it was on developing ink for you."

She begins sorting through the equipment in the drawers, pulling out needles and arranging them on a metal tray.

"While I was working on the first thesis I was approached by Servanix Tech. They provided access to state-of-the-art facilities and all the equipment I needed. Eventually it became apparent through certain . . . channels that they weren't interested in helping resistants at all. They had that ink already." She lets out a laugh. "Can you believe it? They had it all along. 'No market value,' they said. No reason to sell it, but no reason to give away trade secrets either, so they sat on it."

"They had . . . *you've* had it for seven years?"

She pulls the screen attached to a long, flexible arm over. She fiddles with it for a moment.

"Do you remember how I begged you to do my main? How I whined and whinged, and you resisted for two whole years? I thought I would die waiting. I was fifteen—*ancient*—and still without sub-q. My life was being ruined minute by minute." Her fingers twist a loose screw on the metal arm, tightening it until it will turn no further. "I thought . . . for a long time I thought you were jealous, because I could have it and you couldn't. I thought you resented me."

Part of me is listening, but part of me is in the past clinging to my daughter as I knew her: a trip to the park, spreading out the blanket, eating popsicles that turn lips red, Kaede lying on her back competing with Margie to see who could name the most leaves.

"Why didn't you tell me?"

"I thought you would stop. I kept thinking, after every trip to Emergency, 'Okay, now she'll stop. Now, we, her kids, her family, her life will be *enough*.'"

She pulls several bottles of ink from her pocket and sets them on the tray.

"But you're not going to stop, are you?" I don't answer, because I want to say yes—*yes, I will stop for you*—but it would be a lie. Kaede pulls on a pair of gloves.

"After you get ink things are loud. There's too much and not enough, and there are whole days, whole weeks, where you don't speak a word. And when you don't speak them, those words, Mom, they sink down and lodge themselves in you and make you like concrete. Everything is dry and sterile; the precision of the exchange without interpretation is so sharp, so even when you're alone, you're not alone. This is the world, now. It's a world full of heads without voices, and expression without symbol. I talk to you and then I try to talk to them and it's like talking to corpses. I don't want this to be the world: a world where there's always something knocking on the door, something, something, something, something. I can't . . . you can't know—"

An unspoken war is waged behind her eyes until some unheard, final shot is fired, and she comes to a decision.

"But I'll show you. Before I bring it down, I'll show you. Then you'll understand."

I should walk away. I should tell her no for her own good, for mine, but I want it. I've always wanted it. I sit on the chair I have helped so many people into. The low hum of the embedding needle fills the theater.

It takes her all night and well into the next morning to finish. It's a testament to just how tired I am that I manage to doze occasionally, even as a tiny needle drives over and over into my back. The tat is a thing of beauty—the most intricate I've ever seen. It's in the shape of a tree. The branches are a repeating fractal of leaves spread out over my shoulders from a trunk tracing its way up my spine. At the base she's made it look as if the skin of my back has unzipped just above the bend of my waist, exposing my spine against a background of stars. From the bare branches of the tree, sparrows lift and fly over the curve of my shoulder, ascending my neck. The circuit work is immaculate.

She steps back. I turn my head to catch her admiring her work. I stroke one of the sparrows that flies up my neck toward the base of my ear with the tip of a finger, as if it is a living thing.

Kaede watches. "You used to get this look on your face sometimes. It was like you were a sparrow trying to fly to the moon." She sounds so tired.

I'm about to reply when the system begins to boot. I'm looking at Kaede, but in her place I now see a wordless dreaming construct. Tangled webs of identity shift and converge, a restless, tectonic dance of memory projecting branches and trees of data, nodes of relationships pointing toward sister, mother, father, lovers, boss, favorite authors, ice cream last eaten, a night at the pub. Each strand is a path I want to follow. Woven through it all are bells: shop bells and gongs, bells for summoning hotel clerks and bells for dismissing churches, chimes played by the wind, and secret bells made to be rung by only one person. They call out to the whole world. The system is up.

Kaede is smiling a hard shark of a smile that hurts my heart to see. I know the expression on my face must be one of unfocused eyes and slackened face. I try to block out the bells and resist the call of paths unfurling all around me. Kaede pulls me to her in a hug. I can feel her hand, palm open, rising toward the middle of my back.

"Be careful . . ." her voice chokes, "the people I am going with will not understand this. They will be busy. They will be distracted, yes, but they will find out, and they will fear. Some may stay behind just for you. And I can't . . . maybe they're right, but I couldn't . . . Mom, don't make me regret doing this for you. Be content with this gift and *don't try to stop us.*"

I try to whisper in her ear, but then realize I can finally do something better. I can *show* her the singing bells. I can see her—

I don't feel the coded pulse that sends me slumping to the floor.

When I wake she is gone.

KAEDE, INSIDE THE envelope from you is a wood tile with the letter "e" on it. I will place it on the board by the window with the others. I have decided this word you are sending me is the shape of a piece of driftwood found on the beach one morning by a girl in a red dress. It is a hollow, spare, twisted shape, but still so full.

So far Sydney remains untouched by the exquisite virus you created, but I'm afraid it's only a matter of time. Too many are already infected. The mutations are happening too fast. Your monster is fierce and clever. As I watch the sub-q continue to go dark—a city in Colorado, France, half of China—I call out to you again with this cry of bells and other futures. The phonemic sounds of the past are gone, but I am still speaking. The voice is new, but the message is as old as fire and blood.

We will only build it again.

Are you listening, Kaede? Let this be enough. Come home. We will sit at the board by the window. The sun will anoint us, and we will name the leaves.

THE PEAK OF ETERNAL LIGHT

Bruce Sterling

Bruce Sterling (www.wired.com/beyond_the_beyond/) lives usually in some exotic place in Europe, from which he continues his lifelong habit of cultural observation and commentary, now mostly online. He says, "Bruce Sterling is the globe-trotter among cyberpunks, glimpsed in passing in New Zealand, Brazil, Estonia, and Kazakhstan when not getting some Weblogging done from his three domiciles in Austin, Turin, and Belgrade." Known for his dictum that "events are the new magazines," the veteran trendspotter is often tasked to serve as an awards judge for electronic art fairs or augmented reality events. The author of eleven SF novels and five story collections, his most recent official title was "Visionary in Residence for the Center for Science and the Imagination."

"The Peak of Eternal Light" was first published in *Edge of Infinity* from Jonathan Strahan, the editor of a long string of excellent original anthologies in recent years. This is a story about marriage, in the distant future, on the planet Mercury.

HE PROFOUNDLY REGRETTED the Anteroom of Profound Regret.

The Anteroom was an airlock of blast-scarred granite. The entrance and the exit were airtight wheeled contraptions of native pig-iron. In the corner, a wire-wheeled robot, of a type extinct for two centuries, mournfully polished the black slate floor.

One portal opened with a sudden pop.

Lucy was there, all in white, and rustling. His wife was wearing her wedding dress.

Pitar was stunned. He hadn't seen this scary garment since they'd been joined in wedlock.

Lucy stopped where she stood, beside her round, yawning, steely portal. "You don't like my surprise for you, Mr. Peretz?"

Pitar swallowed. "What?"

"This is my surprise! It's my anniversary surprise for you! I carefully warned you that I had a surprise."

Pitar struggled to display some husbandly aplomb. "I never guessed that your surprise would be . . . so dramatic! For my own part, I merely brought you this modest token."

Pitar opened his overnight bag. He produced a ribboned gift-box.

Lucy tripped over, ballerina-like, on her tip-toes.

They gazed at one another, for a long, thoughtful, guarded moment.

Silence, thought Pitar, was the bedrock of their marriage. As young people, it was their sworn duty to fulfil a marital role. Every husband had to invent some personal mode of surviving the fifty-year marriage contract. Marriage on Mercury was an extended adolescence, one long and dangerous discomfort. Marriage was like sun-blasted lava.

Why, Pitar wondered, was Lucy wearing her wedding dress? Had she imagined that this spectral show would please him?

He knew her too well to think that Lucy was deliberately offending him—but he'd burned his own black wedding-suit as soon as decency allowed.

Seeing colour returning to his face, Lucy pirouetted closer. "You bought me a gift, Mr. Peretz?"

"This anniversary gift was not 'bought,'" Pitar said, swallowing the insult. "I *built* you this gift." He offered the box.

Lucy busied herself with the ribbon, then tugged at the airtight lid.

Pitar took this opportunity to study his wife's wedding gown. He had never closely examined this ritual garment, because he had been far too traumatised by the act of marrying its occupant.

There was a lot to look at in a wedding dress. Technically speaking, in terms of its inbuilt supports, threading, embroidering, seams, darts and similar fabric-engineering issues, a wedding dress was quite a design-feat.

Also, the dress fit Lucy well. His wife was a woman of twenty-seven years, yet still with the bodily proportions of a bride of seventeen. Was she conveying some subtle message to him, here?

Lucy peered into her gift box, then shook it till it jingled. "What are these many small objects, Mr. Peretz?"

"Madame, those golden links snap together. Once assembled, they will form a necklace. The design of the necklace is based on the 'smart sand' used for surface-mining. It's rather ingenious engineering, if I may say that about my own handiwork."

Lucy nodded bravely. Struggling with her wedding-skirt, she poised herself inside a spindly cast-glass chair. She tipped the gift-box and shook it, and an army of golden chain-links scattered, ringing and jingling, across the black basalt table.

Lucy examined the scattered links, silently, obviously at a loss.

"They all fit together, and create a necklace," Pitar urged. "Please do try it."

Lucy struggled to link the necklace segments. She had no idea what she was trying to achieve. The female gender was notorious for lacking three-dimensional modelling skills.

The ladies of Mercury were never engineers. The ladies had their own gender specialties: food, spirituality, child-rearing, life-support, biotechnology and political intrigue.

Two links suddenly snapped together in Lucy's questing fingertips. "Oh!" she said. She tried to part the links. They swivelled a bit, but they would shatter sooner than separate. "Oh, how clever this is."

Pitar stepped to the table and swept up a handful of links. "Let's assemble them together now—shall we? Since you are wearing your wedding dress today—it would surely be proper, thematically, if you also wore this newly-assembled wedding necklace. I'd like to see that, before we part."

"Then you shall see it," she said. "Mr. Peretz, a woman's wedding necklace is called a 'mangalsutra.' That's a tradition. It's women's sacred history. It symbolises devotion, and two lives that are joined by destiny. That's from the Earth."

Pitar nodded. "I'd forgotten that word, 'mangalsutra.'"

The two of them sat in their glass chairs, and laboured away on the mangalsutra, joining the gleaming links. Pitar felt pleased with the morning's events. He'd naturally dreaded this meeting, since a tenth anniversary was considered a highly significant date, requiring extra social interaction between the spouses.

Conjugal visits were sore ordeals for any Mercurian husband. To accomplish a visit to his wife, Pitar had to formally veil himself, arm himself with his duelling baton, and creep into the grim and stuffy "Anteroom of Delightful Anticipation."

At this ceremonial airlock between the genders, Lucy would greet him—generally, she was on time—and say a few strained words to him. Then she would lead him to the Boudoir.

No decent man or woman ever spoke a word inside the Boudoir. They silently engaged in the obligatory conjugal acts. If they were lucky, they would sleep afterward.

In the morning, they underwent another required interaction, parting within this ceremonial Anteroom of Profound Regret. Marriage partings were commonly best when briefest.

Anniversary days, however, were not allowed to be brief. Still, assembling the necklace was a pleasing diversion for both of them. It kept their nervous fingers busy, like eating snack food.

When they said nothing, there were no misunderstandings.

Pitar noted his wife's smile as her golden necklace steadily grew in length. No question: his clever gift plan had met with success. During their decade of marriage, his wife had let slip certain hints about traditional marriage necklaces. Womanly relics, once prized among the colony's pioneer mothers, a sacred female superstition, vaguely religious, peculiar and mystical, whatever-it-was that women called it—the "mangalsutra."

Of course Pitar had improved this primitive notion—brought it up-to-date with a design-refresh—but if Lucy had noticed his innovation, she had said nothing about it.

"Sit close to me now, Mr. Peretz!" Lucy offered.

"With that grand wedding dress, I'm not sure that I can!"

"Oh, never mind these big white skirts, my poor old dress doesn't matter anymore! Wouldn't you agree?"

Pitar knew better than to foolishly agree to this treacherous assertion, but he moved his glass chair nearer his wife's chair. The chair's curved feet screeched on the polished slates.

Lucy glanced at him, sidelong. "Mr. Peretz, do I look any older now?"

Pitar busied himself with the links of the necklace. He knew what he was hearing. One of those notorious female jabs that made male life so hazardous.

This provocation had no proper answer. To say "no" was to accuse Lucy of still being a callow girl of seventeen. This meant that ten years of their marriage were capped with an insult.

But to reply "yes" to Lucy, was to state that she had, yes, visibly aged—what a crass mis-step that would be! Lucy would swiftly demand to know what dark threat had wilted her beauty. Arsenical rock-dust fever? A vitamin imbalance in her skin? The ladies of Mercury were forever forbidden the radiance of the Sun.

The light gravity of Mercury shaped the very bones of its women. Lucy had narrow shoulders. A long, loose spine, and a very long neck. Her sleek and narrow hips were entirely unlike the broad, fecund, wobbling hips of a woman from Earth.

Pitar himself was a native son of Mercury. He too had long, frail bones, and had mineral toxins in his liver. As a man, he knew for a fact that he did look older, after ten years of marriage. He certainly wasn't going to broach that subject with her, however.

Dangerous questions were a woman's way to fish for insults. Hell lacked demons like Mercurian women scorned. Any rudeness, any act of dishonour, provoked endless feral scheming within the airlocked hothouse of their purdah. Intrigues would ensue. Scandals. Duels. Political schisms. Civil war.

"How very many golden links!" Lucy remarked, blinking. "Your mangalsutra necklace will reach from my neck to the floor!"

"Five hundred and seven links," said Pitar through reflex.

"Why so many, Mr. Peretz?"

"Because that is the number of times that you and I have occupied this Anteroom of Profound Regret. Including this very day, our tenth anniversary day, of course."

Lucy's hands froze. "You *counted* all our conjugal liaisons?"

"I didn't have to 'count' them. They were all in my appointments calendar."

"How strange men are."

"We did miss some scheduled appointments. Because of illness, or the pressure of business. Otherwise, logically, there would be five hundred and twenty links on our tenth anniversary."

"Yes," Lucy said slowly, "I know that we missed some appointments."

Another silence ensued. The mood had darkened somewhat. They busied themselves with the marriage chain. At last it was complete.

Lucy linked the open ends with the catch that Pitar had provided—a modest, simple loop of big studded rubies. One long, golden, serpentine, female adornment. Lucy draped the chain repeatedly around her tapered neck.

"Madame," said Pitar, seizing the moment, "that mangalsutra necklace, which I built for you with my own assembly devices, is as yet incomplete. As you can see. One end remains open, deliberately so. That is so that you, and I, can add new links to it, in the future. Many new links to this golden wedding-chain, Madame—from this fortunate day, until our final, fiftieth, Golden Anniversary. This is my pledge to you, in bringing you this gift. Deeds, not words."

Lucy turned her blushing face away. She tugged the billowing skirts from the glass chair, and tiptoed toward a framed portrait set in the granite wall.

Pitar followed Lucy's gaze. The personage in the portrait was, of course, famous. She was Mrs. Josefina Chang de Gupta, one of the colony's great founding-mothers.

Mother de Gupta was a culture-heroine for the women of Mercury. This forbidding old dame had personally nurtured sixty-six cloned children. She was the ancestress to half the modern world's million-plus population.

Clearly, Mother de Gupta dearly loved motherhood—mostly, for the chance that it offered her to boss around small, helpless people. Pitar had been taught the grand saga of Mother de Gupta in his crèche-school. A school where domineering women controlled every detail of childhood, preserving and conveying society's cultural values.

Pitar had never forgotten his stifling days in that airless nursery school. Mother de Gupta's husband, the equally-famed Captain de Gupta, had been the author of Mercury's purdah laws of gender separation. It didn't take genius to understand that old man's motives.

Lucy was serenely ignoring the savage old matriarch behind the glass. She was studying her own reflection in the tilted, shining pane.

"I have earned every link in this chain," she declared. "Five hundred marital liaisons! How awkward my postures were, and my body was damp with secretions . . . But now I truly understand why marriage is a sacrament! Look! Look at my beautiful mangalsutra! I always wanted one! It is classical! I have dignity now! With a chain around my neck, I can hold my head up high!"

With a heroic effort, Pitar made no response to this strange outcry. First,

Lucy had miscounted their number of liaisons; and second, he had always suffered far worse from the burdens of marriage than she.

Women had it easy in marriage. Basically, all that was required from women was to lie on a bed and point their knees at the ceiling. Society forced him to wrap himself in a veil, to skulk like an assassin into the women's quarters—as if his identity, and his purpose there, were dreadful secrets.

A custom of total secrecy, for actions that were legally required! When incompatible worldviews collided, these were the monsters engendered. Ten dutiful years of marital intercourse, creeping in and out of airlocks—and yet women called men hypocrites.

"I have done my duty for ten years," Lucy declared to her own reflection. Suddenly, she turned on him, eyes flashing. "Sometimes it's all I can do not to laugh like a fool."

"At least, after ten years of marriage," offered Pitar, "they don't make us listen to those silly love-songs, any more."

A thoughtful silence passed, and then she fixed her gaze on his. "This arranged marriage is a vehicle of political oppression!"

Pitar tightened his lips. The women of Mercury were particularly dangerous when they started harping on their alleged "oppressions." They rarely died of being oppressed, but men were frequently beaten to death for that subject.

"You told me, once," she said, "once, here in this very Anteroom, that marriage was an oppressive moral debt that we owe to the founders of this world." Lucy stroked her gleaming, golden neck. "I never wept so much! But, of course, you were telling the truth—the truth as men see it, at least."

Stung, Pitar rose at once from his dainty chair, which toppled to the stone floor with a discreet glassy clink.

"Our ancestors must have been insane," Lucy said, with the serene expression of a woman uttering things no man would dare to say aloud. "They gave us this bizarre, twisted life—a life we would never have chosen for ourselves. Our marriage—our oppression—is not our fault. I don't blame you, Pitar. Not any longer. You shouldn't blame me, either. You and I are victims of tradition."

Pitar steepled his fingers before his face and touched them to his moustache. "Mrs. Peretz," he said at last, "it's true that our ancestors had profound, creative ideas about a new society. They tried many new things, and many experiments failed. It was hard to create this world, our world, the living world, from bare rock. I myself have huge technical advantages over our ancestors—and yet I make mistakes, building this world, every day."

Lucy gazed at him, blinking. "What? What are you talking about now? Aren't you listening to me? I just told you that none of this is your fault! You, being my husband, that is not your fault! Can't you understand that? I thought you'd be happy to hear that from me, today."

"Mrs. Peretz, you are not taking my point here! I have a larger point than any merely personal point! I'm saying that we can't blame our ancestors, and vilify them, until we come to terms with our own human failings! Consider the legacy that you and I are leaving to our own future! You can see that, can't you? That is just and fair. That's obvious."

Lucy was not seeing the obvious at all. Or rather, Lucy was seeing the obvious in some alien, feminine way, in which his denial of their immediate suffering was an evil lie. He had offended her.

"Did we surrender too much?" Lucy demanded. "Did we say 'yes' too often?"

"Do you mean, Mrs. Peretz, that day, ten years ago, when I said 'yes,' and you also said 'yes'?"

"No, no, you never understand anything that's important . . . All right, yes, fine. Fine! That's what I meant."

"Do you mean to say that I should have rebelled? That I should have refused our arranged marriage?" Pitar paused. He attempted to look composed and solemn, as he thought furiously.

Lucy spoke up meekly. "I meant to suggest that *I* should have rebelled."

"What, you? Why?"

Lucy said nothing, but she was clearly marshalling her thoughts for another unplanned outburst.

The anniversary morning, which had started so calmly, had taken a dreadful turn for Pitar. If men knew that he was talking in this way to a woman—especially his own wife—he would be challenged to a duel. And he would deserve that, too.

"All right," Pitar said at last, "since this is our anniversary, we need to discuss these issues. It was brave of you to bring those up. Well, I happen to think that the two of us are excellent at marriage."

Lucy brightened. "You think that? Why?"

"Because it's an established fact! Look at the evidence! Here we are—you and me, husband and wife, living four kilometres under the surface of the North Pole of the planet Mercury. Our air, water, food, our gender politics, everything that we value, is designed and engineered. And yet, we thrive. We are prosperous, we live honourably! We are two respectable married people! Anybody in this world would say that Pitar Peretz and Lucy Peretz have a normal, solid, and fruitful relationship. We gave the world a son."

His wife scowled at this firm reassurance. "They'll want other children from us. No day passes when the lady elders don't nag me about procreation."

"They have to say that to us. They did their part, and now that duty is ours." Pitar raised his hand, to forestall another outcry. "Now, I know—before Mario Louis Peretz was built—I felt some qualms about my fatherhood. Maybe I over-expressed those emotions to you. That was my mistake. I was young and foolish then. I didn't know what fatherhood was. We can't always know what is good for us in the future. If you asked a boy or girl to consent to puberty, of course children would never grow up! They're just children, so they would rebel, and say no."

His wife made no reply to his wise and reasonable discourse. Instead, Lucy was gazing, with a damp look of dawning surprise, at the blast-scarred stone wall. The idea of annulling puberty seemed to have fired her imagination.

"Even though our children are built, it's a wise social policy that children should have two parents," Pitar said doggedly. "Maybe we were forced to conform to that tradition, for the sake of futurity. But the truth is, fatherhood was good to me. Today, there's a boy, eight years old, who depends on me for guidance in this world. So now I realise: life can't be all about me. Me, and my own favourite things: interaction design, aesthetics, robotics, metaphysics . . . When you and I built a child, that forced me to realise how much this life matters!"

This heartfelt, responsible declaration would have gone over splendidly in any male discussion group; with Lucy, though, it had simply dug him into deeper trouble. Lucy looked bored by his worthy sentiments, and even mildly repelled. "So," she said at last, "the boy made you happy?"

"I wouldn't claim that I've achieved the Peak of Eternal Light! But who among us has?"

"I'm glad that you're happy, Mr. Peretz."

Pitar said nothing. He recognised one of those passive, yet aggressive remarks that women deployed for advantage.

Whenever women said the opposite of what they so clearly wanted to say, hell was at hand.

It was no use reasoning with women. Their brains were different. He had to change his tactics.

"How can I be happy," Pitar offered at last, "when I'm sitting here in the 'Anteroom of Profound Regret'?"

"Husbands never regret leaving their wives here. The formal name of this Anteroom is merely a social hypocrisy. One lie among so many in this world."

"Mrs. Peretz, please stop being so politically provocative. Who can't be sorry in this miserable Anteroom? Can you deny that this room is gloomy, stuffy and in very poor taste? Be reasonable."

"Well, yes, this ugly Anteroom of yours is ugly, but not in the way you think . . . This room is harsh, and cold, and repulsive, but that's all the fault of you men."

"We men never asked for this Anteroom! Never! If it was up to us men, we'd go straight to the Boudoir. The Boudoir is augmented and ubiquitous, and it has beer and snacks, too!"

"Mr. Peretz, you are living in pure male delusion," Lucy said sternly. "That Boudoir, where you and I have conjugal relations, that isn't even my room! I have a private room of my very own. It's much nicer than that tacky bordello where we have to interact."

Pitar was dazzled by this brazen assertion. "Other men sleep in my own marriage bed?"

"Sir, that is not 'your' bed! And anyway, it's very sturdy."

"Sturdiness is not the issue there!"

"Well, it is to us women."

"Fine, be that way!" Pitar cried. "If you want a surprise, you should see my barracks! We men live in luxury now! We have gymnasia, saunas, tool-sheds, anything anyone would want."

"I've never seen your male barracks," said Lucy thoughtfully. "That place where you sleep, without me."

This was a dreadful thing to say. Only the lowest, most dishonourable woman, a woman lost to all shame, would violate purdah, risk everything, and creep into a man's room.

The remark shocked Pitar, so he retreated into silence. His wife said nothing as well. The silence between them stretched, as their silence always did, and Pitar realised, with a long, tenuous, ten-year stretch of his imagination, that he liked it when Lucy shocked him.

It touched something in him. He felt metaphysically authentic. Shock put him in stark confrontation with life's unspoken realities. It took daring to become real.

This was like that vivacious disaster, eight years ago, when he'd been in a duel for Lucy's honour.

Pitar was a thinking man, but sometimes even the most reasonable man couldn't back down from an insult. Pitar had not won that duel—in fact, he'd gotten a solid beating from his punctilious opponent. But in standing up for her, and for honour, he'd won a moral victory.

Furthermore, after the duel, Lucy had been allowed, by a long unspoken tradition, to leave her female purdah, and visit him in his clinic. Lucy came there publicly, flaunting herself, sometimes twice a day, to 'heal the defender of her honour.' She could stay there in the medical ward as long as she pleased, and express herself on any topic, and no one would dare to object.

Neither of them had known quite what to do with this unexpected intimacy, for they were only nineteen years old. But that incident had been truly exciting—just, a different side of life. Another mode of being. The scandal had changed him, and she had changed too, in her own way. A marriage under threat had depth, breadth and consequence.

Sometimes, there was a steep price to pay for self-knowledge—young men learned about themselves in a hurry. Mature men learned from experience.

"Lucy," he ventured at last, in a low voice, "if I asked you to visit my barracks room, what would you do?"

"I didn't mean to suggest anything disgraceful," she said. "But men always come here, through these Anteroom airlocks. Women never visit your half of this world, not at all. How can that be fair?"

"Fair? The rules of decorum are very clear on those matters."

"Please don't look at me like that," Lucy begged. "Truly, I'm proud that my husband has decorum and defends my honour. It would be awful if you were some vile coward. But anyone—man or woman—can see there's something very strange about our customs! Men inside other planets don't duel!"

"Men on other planets don't live 'inside' of their planets," Pitar corrected. "Mercury's moral code may not be perfect—I will grant you that. It may even be that the men of this world, who are just so many fools like me, are all stupid brutes. But even if that's so—at least the ladies here are true ladies! You can admit that much to me, can't you?"

"Well," said Lucy, "being a 'lady' doesn't work in the way that you imagine it does, but . . . All right, fine, I married you, I'm your lady. I can see you're angry now. You're always angry when I'm not a lady, when I talk about what's just and fair."

"Let's be objective," said Pitar. "Let's consider those sleazy women who orbit Venus. No one ever calls them proper ladies!"

"Well, no, of course not," Lucy admitted. "Those women can't even fly down to their own planet's surface! That's quite sad."

"And what about the Earth, that so-called motherworld? Earth women were all Earth-mothers once, and look what became of them! They're polluted, they're filthy, a laughing-stock! Don't get me started on those Martian women! Preening around on Mars, freezing on red sand, pretending that they can breathe!"

"I'm sure those women are doing their best to be decent women."

"Oh come now. Those women orbiting Saturn and Jupiter? Let's not be ridiculous here! And I hope you're not defending those post-female entities around Neptune and Uranus."

"Foreign women live quite properly inside the asteroids."

"Not like ladies live in our own society! Asteroidal women don't have our giant canyons, and our polar water-glacier! I will grant you—the asteroids have some fine resources. They have ice, and some metals, they're upscale in the gravity well. But us, the genteel people here inside Mercury, we have much purer, finer metals than they do! Metals, in planetary quantities! And we possess tremendous solar energy! Every Mercurian day, our robots harvest more power than some puny asteroid could generate in ten years!" Pitar drew a deep breath of the Anteroom's stuffy air. "You certainly can't deny all those facts!"

Lucy said nothing, and therefore denied nothing.

"I don't want to be ungallant," Pitar concluded, "but those women bred in the asteroids, they have no gravity! Not one trace of decent gravity. So they are grotesque! What decent man could be doomed to marry some flabby, blob-shaped, boneless woman, with hands on her legs, instead of human feet? I shudder at the thought! Their lives are unimaginable."

Lucy ran both her hands along her elongated skull and through her lustrous, thin, white hair. "Pitar, that's all true. Those foreign people are contemptible."

"I'm glad that you can see that. And there's an important corollary to your conclusion," said Pitar in triumph. "If those foreigners are grotesque—and we both agree, they certainly are—then that proves that we are not. Maybe we suffer—me, and you, too, we both suffer some oppression maybe life, and honour, and decency, they aren't all about fun and amusement . . . But when it's all said and done, you and I are Mercurian people. I am who I am, and so are you."

"I am a Mercurian woman," Lucy said. "But too much is always left unsaid."

Lucy gazed suggestively at the airlock, but he did not leave, having become too interested.

"Mrs. Peretz, it's all mere custom," Pitar said at last. "Sometimes, we behave so proudly here, as if we owned the Peak of Eternal Light . . . And yet, the texture of our existence is mere tradition. The truth is, speaking metaphysically, it's all social habit! Once, in the past, this whole world was like this sorry Anteroom that we're stuck in now . . ."

Pitar lifted his arms. "I know that life isn't just and fair. And I wish I could change that, but how? If you want to reform gender relations, you should take up those issues in the political councils of your elder ladies. What can you expect *me* to do? Those old witches treat men of my age as if we were larvae."

"I didn't ask you to do anything," Lucy pointed out. "I even told you that it wasn't your fault."

"Well, yes, you said that, but . . . isn't it strongly implicated that there's something I should do? Surely we don't meet in here, face to face, it's our anniversary . . . We can't just whine."

A very long silence passed. Pitar began to regret that he had complained about complaining. This act of his was meta, and recursive. No wonder she was confused.

"We have bicycles," Lucy offered.

"What?"

"We have bicycles. Transportation devices, the ones with two wheels. Men and women can meet outside of the purdah, when they ride on bicycles. No one can accuse us of impropriety when we're seated on rolling machines."

"Mrs. Peretz, I have seen bicycles—but I'm not taking your point."

"Suppose that we say," Lucy offered haltingly, "that we're exploring the modern world. There are lots of new mineshafts where only machines have gone. If we ride a few kilometres—I mean *together*, but on bicycles—how can they say that we're harming custom? Or offending decency?"

"What do you mean now, bicycles? Aren't those contraptions dangerous? You could fall off a bicycle and break your neck! Bicycles are mechanically unstable! They only have two wheels!"

"Yes, it's hard to learn to ride a bicycle. I fell off several times, and even hurt myself. But I learned how! Bicycles are perfect for low-gravity planets. Because bicycles stress the legs. They strengthen the bones. Bicycles are a healthy and modern invention."

Pitar considered this set of arguments. Of course he'd seen women riding on bicycles—and the occasional man as well, maybe one in ten—but he'd paid no real attention to this fad. He'd considered bicycling some girlish affectation—those women in their faceless helmets and their black, baggy clothes. Speeding about on these gaily coloured devices . . .

But maybe it made engineering sense. Bicycles had appeared in the world because the mine-shafts were expanding. Ever-active robots, steadily gnawing new courses through the planet's richest mineral seams. The world was growing methodically.

Modern Mercury was no longer that old, cramped world where people lurked in chambers and airlocks, and walked only a few hundred metres. Robots were ripping through the planet's crust, and behind them came human settlers, as always on Mercury. That was common sense, and no conservative could deny that.

"I could build a bicycle," Pitar declared. "I could fabricate and print one. Not a ladylike kind, of course—but a proper transportation machine."

"With your bicycle helmet, you wouldn't have to wear your veil anymore," Lucy said eagerly. "No one would know that it was you, on your bicycle . . . except for me, of course, because, well, I always know it's you."

"Then it's settled. I'll set straight to work! I'll give you a progress report, next time we meet."

They shook hands, and departed through their separate iron doors.

AN OFFICIAL DAY of mourning had been declared for the late Colonel Hartmann Srinivasan DeBlakey. As a gesture of respect toward this primal Mercurian pioneer, his mourning period occupied an entire "Mercurian Day."

Colonel DeBlakey had been an ardent calendar reformer. To thoroughly break all cultural ties with Earth, DeBlakey had struggled to reform Mercurian pioneer habits around the 88-day "Mercurian Year" and the 58-day "Mercurian Day."

Of course, DeBlakey's elaborate, ingenious calendar scheme had proved entirely hopeless in practice. Human beings had innate 24-hour biological cycles. So, the practical habits within a sunless, subterranean city had quickly assumed the modern, workaday system of three 8-hour shifts.

But DeBlakey had never surrendered his cultural convictions about calendar reform, just as he had fought valiantly for spelling reform, gender relations and trinary computation. DeBlakey had been an intellectual titan of Mercury. In acknowledgement of his legacy, it was agreed that gentlemen would wear their mourning veils for one entire Mercurian Day.

Being a mere boy of eight, Pitar's son, Mario Louis Peretz, wore only a light scarf, rather than the full male facial veil. Mario had his mother's good looks. Mario was a fine boy, a decent boy, a source of proper pride. Life in his juvenile crèche was entirely ruled by women, so Mario had refined and dainty habits:

long hair, painted fingernails, a skirt rather than trousers, everything as it should be.

Through his mother's gene-line, young Mario was closely related to the late Colonel DeBlakey. So it was proper of Mario to attend the all-male obsequies, up on the planet's surface.

Of course Pitar had to accompany his son as his paternal escort. The blistering, airless surface of Mercury was tremendously hostile and dangerous. It was therefore entirely proper for children.

Pitar hadn't worn his spacesuit in two years—not since the last celebrity funeral. For his own part, young Mario Louis sported a brand-new, state-of-the-art suitaloon. His mother had bought this archigrammatical garment for him, and Lucy had spared no expense.

The boy was childishly delighted with his fancy get-up. The suitaloon had everything a Mercurian boy could desire: a diamond-crystal bubble-helmet, a boy-sized life-support cuirass, woven nanocarbon arms and legs, plus fashionable accents of silver, copper, gold and platinum. Mario was quite the little lordling in his suitaloon. He tended to caper.

The crowd of male mourners queued to take the freight elevators to the Peak of Eternal Light.

"Dad," said Mario, gripping Pitar's spacesuit gauntlet, "did Colonel De-Blakey ever fight duels?"

"Oh yes," nodded Pitar. "Many duels."

"Martial arts are my favourite subject at the crèche," Mario boasted. "I think I could be pretty good at fighting duels."

"Son," said Pitar, "duelling is a serious matter. It's never about how strong you are, or how fast you are. Men fight duels to defend points of honour. Duelling supports propriety. You can lose a duel, and still make your point. Colonel DeBlakey lost some duels. So he had to apologise, and politically retreat. But he never lost the respect of his peers. That's what it's all about."

"But Dad . . . what if I just beat people up with my baton? Wouldn't they have to do whatever I say?"

Pitar laughed. "That's been tried. That never works out well."

Thanks to some covert intrigue—his mother's, almost certainly—Mario was allowed into the elevator along with the casket of his revered ancestor. DeBlakey's casket was simply his original, pioneer spacesuit. This archaic device was so rugged, solid and rigid that it made a perfect sarcophagus.

The old elevator, like the old spacesuit, was stoic and grim. It was crammed with suited gentlemen and boys, veiled behind their faceplates.

No one broke the grave solemnity of the moment. At last, the shuddering, creaking trip to the surface was over.

Pitar followed the economic news, so he was aware of the booming industrial developments on the surface. But to know those statistics was not the same as witnessing major industry at first hand.

What a vista of the machinic phylum! He felt almost as much sheer won-derment as his own eight-year-old son.

The cybernetic order, conquering Mercury, algorithmically pushing itself into new performance-spaces . . . It had crisply divided its ubiquity into new divisions of spatial and temporal magnitude!

The roads, the pits, the mines, the power-plants and smelters, the neatly as-sembled slag . . . The great, slow, factory hulks . . . the vast caravans of ore-laden packets . . . the dizzying variety of scampering viabs, and a true explosion of chipsets.

And, at the nanocentric bottom of this semi-autonomous pyramid of com-putational activism, the smartsand. Amateurs gaped at the giant hulks—but professionals always talked about the smartsand.

Entropy struck these machines, as it did any organised form. Machines that veered from the wandering Mercurian twilight zone were promptly fried or frozen. Yet the broken systemic fragments were always reconstituted, later. No transistor, gasket or screw was ever abandoned. Not one fleck of industrial trash, though the cratered landscape was severely torn by robot mandibles.

The human funeral procession marched toward the solemn Peak of Eter-nal Light.

This grandiose polar mountain never passed within solar shadow. The Peak of Eternal Light was the most famous natural feature of Mercury, the primal source of the colony's unfailing energy supply.

At the Peak's frozen base, which was never lit by the Sun, was a great frosty glacier. This glacier was the only source of water on or within the planet.

This glacier had been formed over eons by the bombardment of comets. Steam as thin as vacuum had accumulated in this frozen shadow, layering monatomically. Those towering layers of black ice, the product of billions of years, had seemed enough to quench the thirst of a million people.

Nothing left of that mighty glacier today but a few scarred ice-blocks, slowly gnawed by the oldest machines.

The polar glacier had, in fact, vanished to quench the thirst of a million people. This ancient ice had passed straight into the living veins of human be-ings.

This planetary resource was whittled down to a mere nub now. Yet one had to look here, to know that. The polar glacier existed in permanent darkness. Only the radar in Pitar's suit allowed him to witness the frightening decline.

Most of the men ignored this ghastly spectacle. As for his own son, the boy took no notice at all. The shocking decline in polar ice meant nothing to him. He had never seen the North Pole otherwise.

And what had the old man, the dead man, said about that crisis? Ever the visionary, he'd certainly known it was coming.

The dead pioneer had said, in his blunt and confrontational way, "We'll just have to go fetch some more ice."

So, they had done as the dead man said. The people of Mercury had built a gigantic manned spacecraft, a metallic colossus. A ship so vast, so overweening in scale, that it might have been an interstellar colony—were such things possible.

Robots had hauled this great golden ark to the launch ramp, and sent this gleaming dreadnought hurtling off toward the cometary belt. There to commandeer and retrieve some vast, timeless, life-enhancing snowball.

Of course, there had been certain other options—rather than a gigantic, fully-manned spacecraft. Simpler, more practical tactics.

For instance, thousands of tiny robots might have been launched out in vast streams, to go capture a comet.

Then as the comet whirled round and round the blazing, almighty bulk of the Sun, the robots could have chipped off small chunks of comet frost, and sent those modest packets to the Mercurian surface. At the cost of a few small, fresh craters—nothing much, compared to the giant mining pits—clouds of cometary steam would have arisen. Puffs of comet vapour, drifting north, to freeze onto the original great glacier, there at the base of the Peak of Eternal Light.

This would have been a quiet, tedious, patient, and gentle way to replenish the vanished glacier. A nurturing restoration of the status quo. Mercurian women favoured this tactic.

But to espouse this idea had some dark implications. It implied, strongly, that Mercury itself should never have been settled by human beings. Were men worthless, was that the idea? Why not abolish mankind, with all its valour, its honour, its urge to explore—and have Mercury remain a mine-pit infested with the mindless and soulless machinic phylum?

That idea was blasphemy—and there was no reconciling these factions. The civil division there was as distinct as frozen night and blazing day. This tremendous struggle—a primal issue of resources and politics—had almost broken the colony.

As tempers rose, a compromise was urged by certain moderates, whom everyone ignored. Why not just buy some ice? Admit that Mercury faced a water crisis beyond its power, and buy ice from foreigners.

The asteroids had plenty of ice. What sense did it make to design a weird horde of ice-robots? Why create some swaggering Mercurian flagship, at such crippling cost? Just abandon honour and autonomy, abandon foolish pride, and pay foreigners. There were merchants out there already, willing to trade for metals. If one could call those weird entities "people."

After much bloodshed, feuding, disgraces, regrettable excesses, the manned explorers had won the civil war. Why? Because they had claimed the mantle of the traditional values. Then these conservative fanatics had climbed aboard their new golden spacecraft, and promptly abandoned Mercury with all its long traditions.

The field of honour had settled nothing, thought Pitar. Because those traditions were fictions—irrational retrodictions, modern political interpretations of lost historical realities.

The values of Colonel DeBlakey were much wilder than anyone cared to remember. DeBlakey, and the men of his generation, were fantastic visionaries. DeBlakey, the Mercurian hero, cared nothing for colonising Mercury. He saw Mercury as a mere stepping-stone to colonising the Sun.

In his arcane, two-hundred forty-year lifespan, this great man had advanced his philosophy in vast, scriptural detail. Endlessly writing, preaching, planning, designing, and theorising. Pitar had read a few million of these hundreds of millions of words. Very few ever did.

As the mourners gathered in their artificial twilight at the mountain's base, Pitar realised that he was attending the last public airing for DeBlakey's great pioneer ideology.

Mercurian celebrities delivered their funeral orations—eloquent, careful, and well-considered. Yet DeBlakey's titanic legacy was much too large for their tiny gestures. The mourners clearly desired to be brief—for the radiation on the surface made that wise. Yet a lifespan of a quarter of a millennium was no easy thing to summarise.

DeBlakey's schemes had to do with interstellar settlement: mankind's manifest destiny in the galaxy. "Taming the stars," as he put it. Such were the progressive visions that racked the great man's brain, as the early Mercurian colonists crouched in their stone closets, half-suffocated and sipping toxic comet water.

DeBlakey was scheming to mine Mercury, fully develop the machinic phylum, and then march gloriously forth to mine the Sun. To dwell within the Sun, living in Eternal Light. To thrive in Eternal Light, without any shadow of any planet's bulk, forever.

Because, while Mercury certainly had gold, silver, platinum, and transuranic metals—sometimes scattered on the cratered surface in gleaming pools—the Sun possessed every element.

Imaginary star-redoubts would whip through the Sun's tenuous atmosphere at a hyper-Mercurian speed, sifting out water, carbon, metals—anything mankind needed—directly from the solar cloud. These visionary sun-forts would be vast magnetic bottles, all tractor beams and photon traps, with living, golden cores.

Once mankind had taught the machinic phylum to dwell within the atmospheres of stars, no further limits would ever trouble mankind. Above all, there would be no limits to the settler population. Dutiful women, living for centuries, would raise and acculturate hundreds of children, each one trained to star-spanning pioneer values.

At this singular rate of population explosion, the Sun would soon support hundreds of billions of people. Trillions of citizens, manning millions of colonies. So many colonies, so cybernetically capable, that they would seize command of the Sun.

With such titanic energy resources, interstellar flight would become a corollary, a mere logical detail. Tamed solar flares would magnetically fling new colonies, hurtling at near-light-speed, into the atmospheres of the nearest stars.

Any species that could dwell within stars would swiftly dominate the galaxy. Spreading algorithmically, exponentially, resistlessly, galactically. Men who understood this had no need to search for Earthlike planets, that illusion of meagre fools. They would dwell forever within the machinic phylum, each superhuman soul a peak of eternal light.

There was a certain fierce logic to DeBlakey's cosmic plans. If not entirely pragmatic, they were certainly aspirational. Driven by such fierce and boundless human will, the machinic phylum would explode across the universe.

However, DeBlakey was mortal, and therefore dead. To the serious-minded, sensible people actually living today within the planet Mercury, his dreams seemed arcane, farfetched, absurd . . . And now, his funeral eulogists were trying to come to terms with all of that. To settle all of that, to bury all of that. They were gently folding this man's wild pioneer dream into the harmless legendry of everyday Mercurian existence.

Pitar's boy tugged at his gauntleted arm. These high-flown orations had the boy bored stiff. "Dad."

Pitar opened a private channel. "What is it? Do you need a bathroom? Use the suit."

"Dad, can I go fight now? That's Jimmy over there, he likes to fight."

"No sparring during funerals, son."

Mario grimaced at this reproof. He rubbed exoatmospheric dust from his diamond bubble-helmet. "Dad, when they build the new colony at the South Pole, will we go there?"

"Mario, there's no water at the South Pole. There are hills of Eternal Light there, so there's plenty of energy, but fate put no glaciers for us in that place. It's uninhabitable."

"But our space heroes will come back some day, and bring us a water-comet. Then will we go?"

"Yes," said Pitar. "We would go. There would be new opportunities there, more than in this old colony. The South Pole would mean a different life, new social principles. Yes, we would go there. I would take you with me. And your brothers, too—because you'll have brothers someday."

"Would Mom go with us?"

"Son, in nine years you'll be married yourself. I'll arrange that. And believe me, that's sure to complicate your agenda."

"Mom would go to a new colony. She wants to invent a new way of life. She told me that."

"Really."

"Yes, she told me! She really means it."

Pitar drew a breath within his helmet. "We are, after all, a pioneering people. That is our true heritage, and I'm proud that you are witnessing all this. You'll live a very long time, my son, so be sure to remember this day, and all it means. This world belongs to you. It was given to you. And don't you ever forget that."

Another speaker took the rostrum at the funereal plateau. This elder had to walk with robot assistance, and though he said little enough, he spoke at the droning rate of the very wise. A dreadful thing to hear.

Mario could not keep his peace. "Dad, will there be other boys like me at the South Pole?"

Pitar smiled. "Of course there will. A society with no youth has no future. If the people of Earth had sent their children into space, instead of just foolish astronauts, they would have spread throughout the worlds. Instead, they sank into their mud. That's not your heritage, because those people have no moral fibre. That's why they don't matter now, and we do."

Mario struggled to scratch his nose through his bubble-helmet. Of course this feat was impossible. "Dad, do Earth people stink? Jimmy says they stink."

"I've never met one personally, but they do have wild germs in their bellies. Earth people can emit some unpleasant odours, and that's a fact." Pitar cleared his throat inside his spacesuit. "The Earth people don't care much for us, either, mind you—they call us 'termites.'"

"'Termites', Dad, what does that mean?"

"Termites are subhuman social beasts. Wild animals. Never properly gardened like our animals."

"Dad, how big are termites?"

"I really don't know, about the size of a housecat, I guess. If some man ever calls you a 'termite,' you slap his face and challenge him, understand? That puts a swift end to that nonsense."

"All right, Dad."

"Stop chattering now, son. This is the climax, this is the great moment."

Bearing their ceremonial staves and halberds, the male elders retreated, with slow step, from the funeral plateau. Sand rose up in waves below the dead man's catafalque.

The smartsand formed itself into one grand, pixelated, seething, pallbearing wave.

An impossible liquid, it reverently rolled up the mountain, bearing the dead man.

The catafalque crossed the brilliant twilight zone, into Eternal Light.

The robots shifted their solar reflectors, in unison. The human crowd fell into dramatic, timeless, deep-frozen darkness. Pitar felt his spacesuit shudder, a trembling fit of holy awe.

The catafalque gleamed like a chunk of the unseen sun.

The dead man's suit ruptured from the brilliant heat. Precious steam burst free. One brief, geyserlike, human rainbow, one visionary burst of glorious combustion, spewing like a solar flare.

Then the ceremony ended. Though the long Mercurian Day had scarcely begun, a spiritual dawn had appeared.

PITAR SAT ON the rim of a sandbox, within the Great Park of Splendid Remembrance.

To pursue his design labours, Pitar often came to this site, to carefully sip cognition enhancers and contemplate the metaphysical implications of monumentality.

The task of his generation was one of reconciliation, the achievement of a deeper understanding. This park had been the battlefield where the worst mass clashes of the civil war had occurred. Bitter, bloody, hand-to-hand struggles, between the polarised factions.

Some of the colony's best, most idealistic, most public-spirited men, trapped by harsh moral necessity, had beaten each other to death in this cavern.

Even women had killed each other in here, when it became clear that the great burden of the ice-hunt would impinge on their personal politics. Women fought in feline ambush, and in martyr operations. Women killed efficiently, because they never wasted effort grasping at the honours of combat.

The civil war was the closest that the colony had ever come to collapse. Worse than any natural catastrophe: worse than the blowouts, worse than the toxic poisonings.

The Great Park of Splendid Remembrance was, by its nature, an ancient Mercurian lava tube. This cavern was a natural feature, unplanned by man, untouched by the jaws of machines.

So it was thought, somehow, that this bloodstained space of abject moral failure was best left to wilderness. To living creatures other than mankind.

The original settlers had brought genetic material from their homelands on Earth. These vials of DNA had been preserved with care, but never released inside the world, never instantiated as living creatures.

Today, the Park of Splendid Remembrance was thick with them. These thriving, vegetal entities had exotic shapes, exotic features, and exotic, ancient names. Banyans, jacarandas, palms, ylang-ylang, papayas, jackfruit, teak, and mahogany.

Unlike the homely, useful algae on which the colony subsisted, these woody species took on wild, unheard-of forms. Under the blazing growlights, rising in the light gravity, rooted in a strange mineral soil, they were the native Mercurian forest. Great, green, reeking, shady, twisted eminences. Bizarre organic complexities: flowering, gnarling, branching, fruiting.

This wilderness mankind had unleashed was not beautiful. It was vigorous, but crabbed and chaotic. It was, as yet, merely a colonial tangle, a strange, self-choking complex of distorted traditional forms.

Like all aesthetic issues, thought Pitar, the problem here had its roots within a poor metaphysics. To introduce this ungainly forest, so as to obscure a dark place where human will had failed—that effort was insincere. It had not been thought-through.

The Great Park of Splendid Remembrance had feared to face the whole truth. So it was as yet neither great nor splendid, because it had shirked the hard thinking required by the authentic Mercurian texture of existence.

This was Pitar's own task.

Sitting in deep thought, Pitar idly drew squares, triangles, circles, within the childish play-box of smartsand. With each stroke of his duelling-club, the smartsand responded and processed. Arcane ripples bounded and rebounded from the corners of the sandbox.

The computational entities, with which mankind shared this planet, were never intelligent. The machinic phylum, which seemed so clever and vigorous to the untrained eye, was neither alive nor smart. The phylum was merely the phylum; it had no will, no pride, no organic lust for survival, no reason to exist and persist. Without human will to issue its coded commands, the phylum would collapse in an eyeblink, returning to the sunblasted, constituent elements of this world.

But although the phylum possessed neither life nor intelligence, it did possess an order-of-being. It was not alive, merely processual, yet it had transcended the natural. The phylum was a metaphysical entity, and worthy of respect. Something like the spiritual respect owed a dead body: a thing, yes, inert, yes, of ashes, yes—yet so much more than mere inert ashes.

The truth, beyond intelligence. There were those who said—the daring thinkers of Pitar's own generation—that the Sun was self-possessed. Not in the old-fashioned, cranky, archaic, heroic way that visionaries like DeBlakey had once imagined. The Sun was never alive, nor was the Sun intelligent, but the Sun was an entity, metaphysically ordered. The Sun that loomed over tiny Mercury was one Object of the Order of a Star.

And these thinkers speculated—speculating furthermore, just as bravely daring as their ancestors, though in a more modern fashion—that there were many Orders in the cosmos. Life, and, intelligence, and the processual phylum were just three of those countless Orders.

These speculative realists held that the Cosmos was inherently riddled with unnatural Orders. Hundreds, possibly thousands, of independent, extropic Orders, each Order unknown to the next, yet each as real and noble as the next, each as important as life or thought.

Some Orders transpired in picoseconds, other Orders in unknowable aeons. Orders, each as deep and complex and unnatural as life, or cognition, or computation. Entities, autarchic ontologies, occupying the full panoply of every scale of space-time. From the quantum foam, where space disintegrated, to the forever-unknowable scale of the Cosmos, forever outside the light-cone of any instrumentable knowability.

That was reality.

These were those who called these idle dreams, but reality was neither idle nor a dream. Much scientific evidence had been carefully amassed, to prove the objective existence of extropic Orders. Pitar followed Mercurian science with some care—although he never involved himself in the fierce, bloody duels over precedence and citation.

Pitar understood the implications of modern science for his own creative work. Any true, sincere monument, any place of genuinely splendid remembrance, would be built in a manner that took reality into a full account. An enlightened peak of moral comprehension.

This Awareness would transcend awareness. It would respect that ordered otherness, in all its many forms, and do that Otherness honour.

It might well take him, thought Pitar, centuries to come to workable terms with this professional ambition. But since he had that time, it behooved him to spend his time properly. Such was his duty. This was something that he himself could do, to add to all that had passed before, as a legacy to whoever, or whatever, was to follow.

Pitar glanced up, suddenly, from the writhing sandpit. His wife had arrived. Lucy was on her bicycle.

Pitar mounted his own two-wheeled machine. He rode to join her. Pitar rode smoothly and elegantly, because he'd infested his bicycle's frame with smartsand.

He hadn't told his wife about this design gambit; Lucy merely thought, presumably, that he was tremendously good at learning to ride a bicycle. No need to bring up that subject. Enough that he had a bicycle, and that he rode it with her. Deeds, not words.

His wife's head was fully encased in her black helmet. Her body was almost suitalooned by her black, flowing bicycle garb. Mounted on her bicycle, Lucy scarcely looked like a woman at all. More of a dark, scarcely-knowable, metaphysical object.

But, when Pitar wore his own helmet, he was as anonymous and mysterious as she. So, faceless and shameless, they rode together, tires crunching subtly, on the park's long grey cinder-path.

"Mr. Peretz, you looked very thoughtful, sitting there in your sandbox."

"Yes," said Pitar, forbearing to nod, due to the bulk of his helmet.

"What were you thinking?"

A deadly female question. Pitar found a tactful parry. "Look here, I have created a new bicycle. See, I am riding it now."

"Yes, I saw that you printed a new bicycle, and it's more advanced now, isn't it? What happened to your nice old bicycle? You rode that one so gallantly!"

"I gave that machine to a friend," said Pitar. "I gave it to Mr. Giorgio Harold DeVenet."

His wife's front wheel wobbled suddenly. "What? To him? How? Why? He beat you in a duel!"

"It's true that Mr. DeVenet is a duellist. And it's true that I lost that duel. But that was eight years ago, and there's no reason I can't be polite."

"Why did you do that?"

Pitar said nothing.

"Why did you do it? You had some reason for doing that. You should tell me that. He insulted me; I should know this."

"Let's just ride," Pitar suggested.

Pitar had given the gift to the duellist, because he'd known that there would be trouble about the bicycles. This radical innovation—bicycling—it did damage the institution of purdah. Maybe it did not violate the letter of propriety, but it certainly damaged the spirit.

Pitar had been confronted on that issue; politely. So Pitar had, just as politely, referred that matter of honour to Mr. Giorgio Harold DeVenet, also the possessor of a bicycle.

Mr. DeVenet, a brawny and athletic man, was delighted with his new bicycle. As he scorched past mere pedestrians, pedalling in a fury, Mr. DeVenet's strength and speed were publicly displayed to fine effect.

Skeptics had questioned Mr. DeVenet's affection for bicycles. He had promptly forced them to retract their assertions and apologise.

In this fashion, the matter of bicycles was settled.

Mr. DeVenet was not so punctilious, however, that he had escaped being seen in the flirtatious, bicycling company of the notorious Widow De Schubert. She was the type who rode through life without a helmet. The widow's late husband, outmatched and sorely lacking in tact, had already fallen on the field of honour.

To own a bicycle was not the same as understanding its proper use. At the rate that matters progressed these days, it wouldn't be long before Mr. DeVenet joined the other victims of the Widow De Schubert. The duellist could batter any number of bicycle skeptics, but to defeat a woman's wiles was far beyond his simplicity.

Men who lived by the club fell by the club, a trouble-story far older than this world. Pitar was at peace with these difficult facts of life. The notorious Widow De Schubert was one his wife's best-trusted friends—but he did not inquire into that tangled matter. Certain things between men and women were best left unspoken.

His wife lifted her visor by a thumb's width, so as to be better heard. "Mr. Peretz, I do enjoy these new outings that we have together nowadays. You have given me another gift that I long desired. For that, I am grateful to you. You are a good husband."

"Thank you very much for that kindly remark, Mrs. Peretz. That's very gratifying."

"Are you also pleased by our situation today?"

Given the praise he had just received, Pitar ventured a candid response. "Although modernity has some clear advantages," he told her, "I can't say it's entirely easy. In that very modest bicycle garb, I cannot see your face. In fact, I can't see anything of you at all. You are a deep mystery."

"Beneath this black garment, sir, I wear nothing but my beautiful, golden mangalsutra. I feel so free nowadays. Freer than I have ever felt as a modern woman."

Pitar pondered this provocative remark. It had emotional layers and textures closed to mere men. "That's an interesting data-point, there."

"Mr. Peretz, although it was not our own will that united us," Lucy said, rolling boldly on, "I feel that marriage is an important exploration of a woman's emotional phase-space. Someday, we two—separated of course—will look back on these years with satisfaction. You in your way, and me in mine, as that must be. Nevertheless, we will have accomplished a crucial joint success."

"You're full of compliments this afternoon, Mrs. Peretz! I'm glad you're in such a good mood!"

"This is not a question of my so-called moods!" his wife told him. "I am trying to explain to you that, now that we possess bicycles, modernity is achieved. It's time that I faced futurity, and to do what futurity requires from me, I will need your help. It's time we built another child."

"Since honour requires that of me as well, Mrs. Peretz, I can only concur."

"Let's build a daughter, this time."

"A daughter would be just and fair."

"Good. Then, that's all settled. These are good times. A good day to you, sir." She bent to heave at her whirring pedals, and she rapidly wheeled away.